# twilight

## THE GRAPHIC NOVEL  VOLUME 2

**STEPHENIE MEYER**

ART AND ADAPTATION BY YOUNG KIM

Yen Press

Twilight: The Graphic Novel
Volume 2

Art and Adaptation: Young Kim
Inking Assistant: Ashley Marie Witter
Background Assistant: Haya C.

Text copyright © 2005 by Stephenie Meyer
Illustrations © 2011 Hachette Book Group, Inc.

Yen Press
Hachette Book Group
237 Park Avenue, New York, NY 10017

Visit our websites at www.HachetteBookGroup.com and
www.YenPress.com

Yen Press is an imprint of Hachette Book Group, Inc.
The Yen Press name and logo are trademarks of Hachette Book Group, Inc.

First Hardcover Edition: October 2011

ISBN: 978-0-316-13319-7

10 9 8 7 6 5 4 3 2 1

RRD-C

Printed in the United States of America

twilight

THE GRAPHIC NOVEL ❦ VOLUME 2

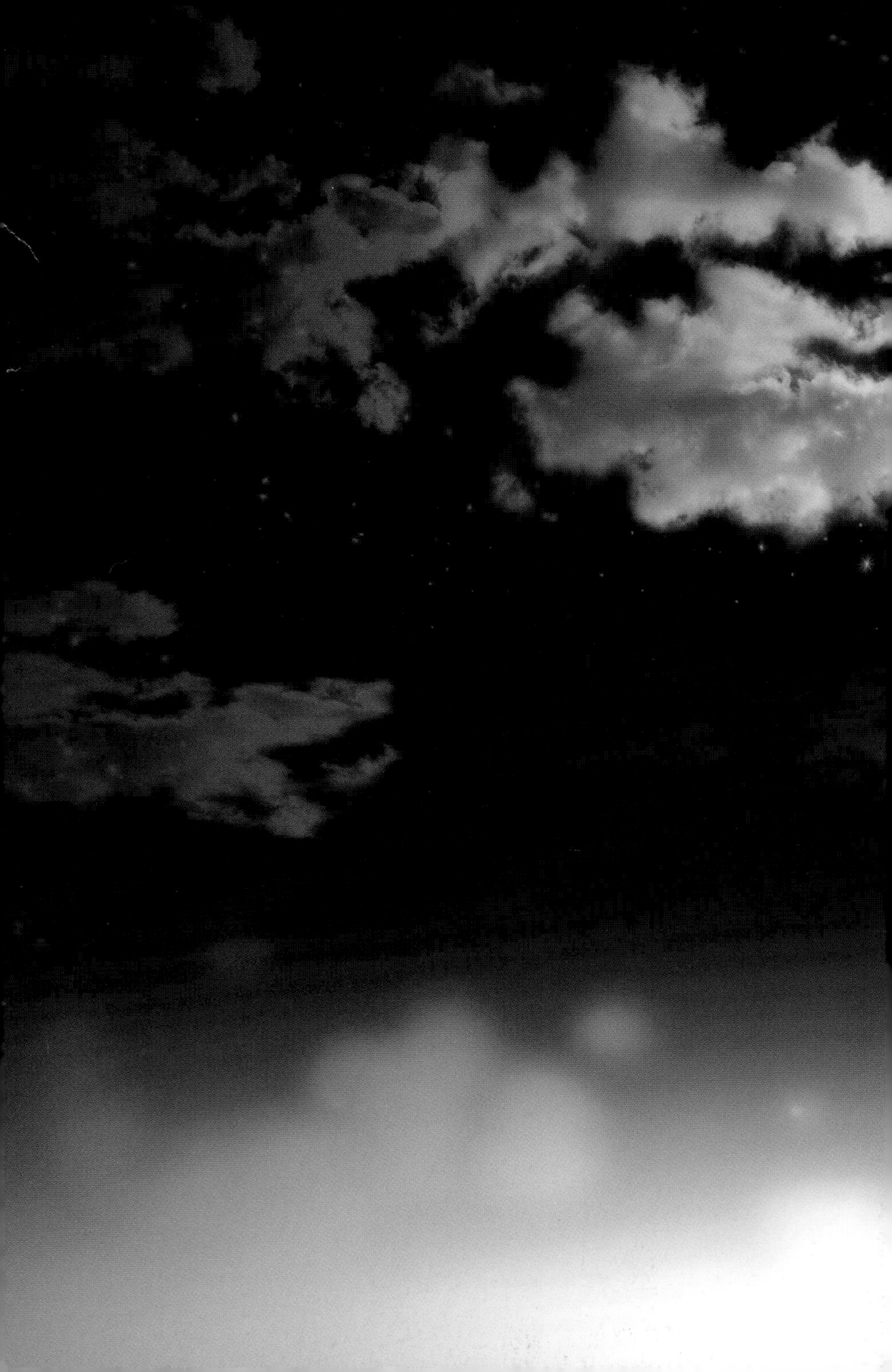

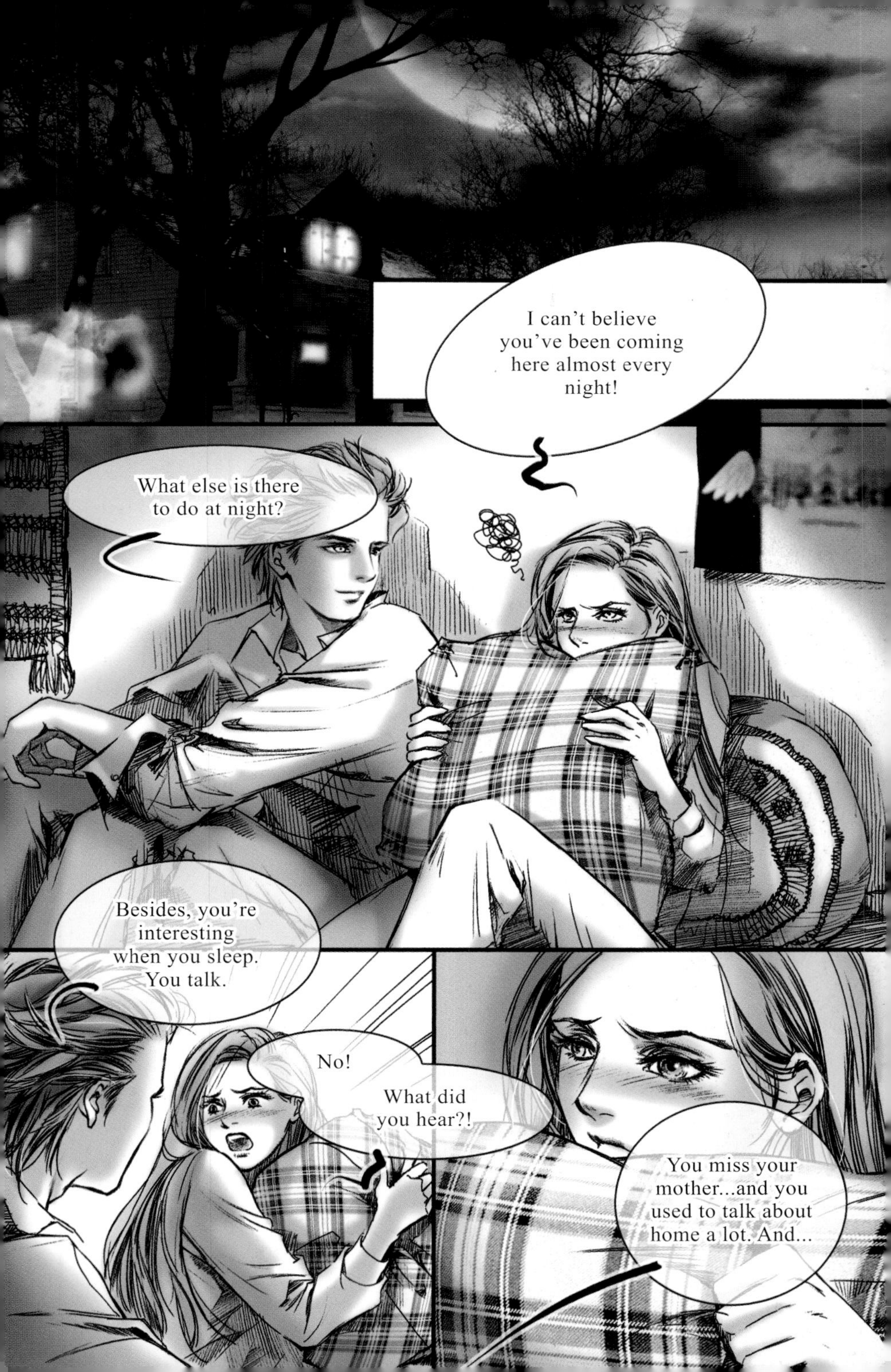
I can't believe you've been coming here almost every night!
What else is there to do at night?
Besides, you're interesting when you sleep. You talk.
No!
What did you hear?!
You miss your mother...and you used to talk about home a lot. And...

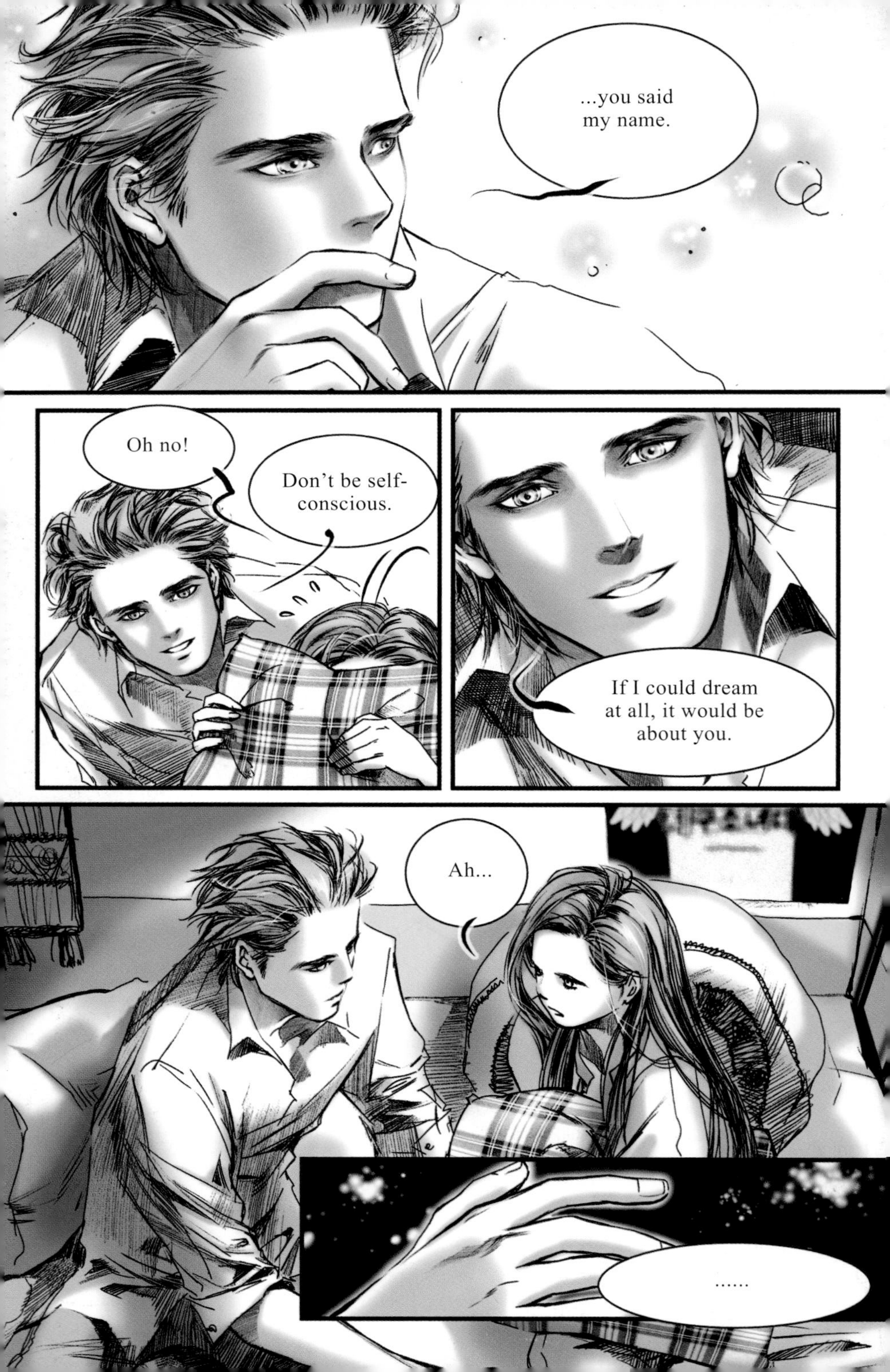
...you said my name.
Oh no!
Don't be self-conscious.
If I could dream at all, it would be about you.
Ah...
......

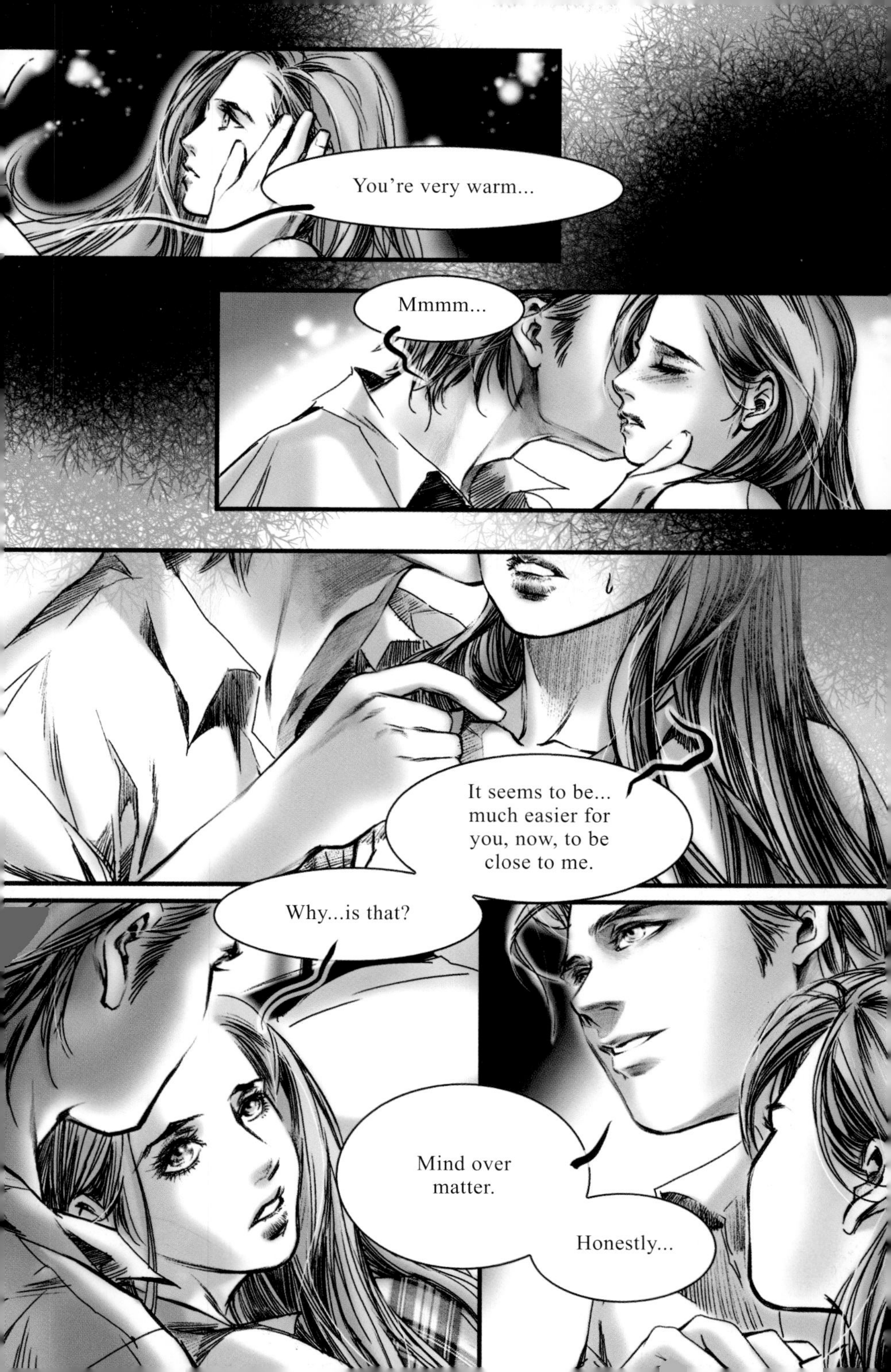
You're very warm...
Mmmm...
It seems to be... much easier for you, now, to be close to me.
Why...is that?
Mind over matter.
Honestly...

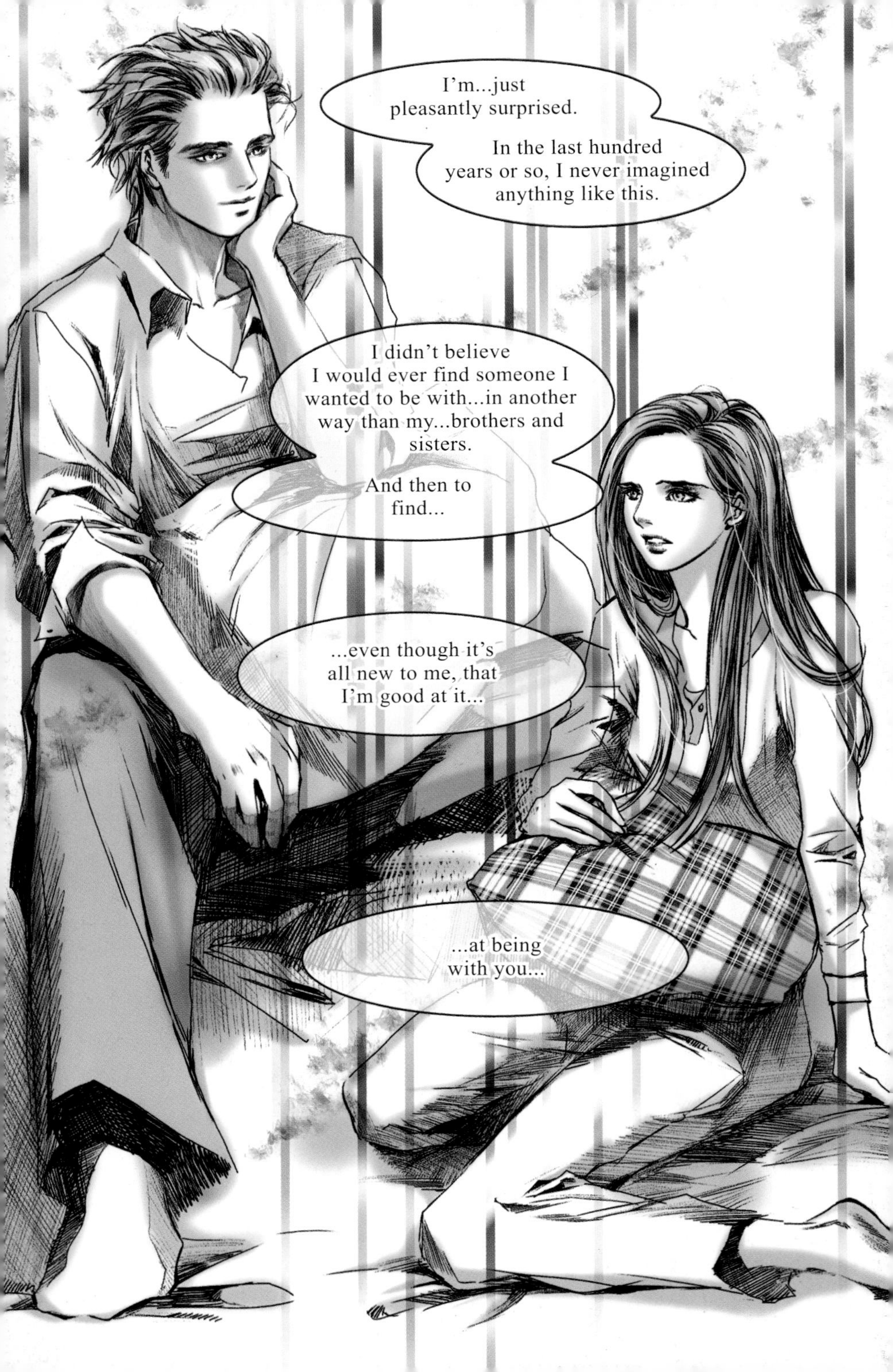
I'm...just pleasantly surprised.
In the last hundred years or so, I never imagined anything like this.
I didn't believe I would ever find someone I wanted to be with...in another way than my...brothers and sisters.
And then to find...
...even though it's all new to me, that I'm good at it...
...at being with you...

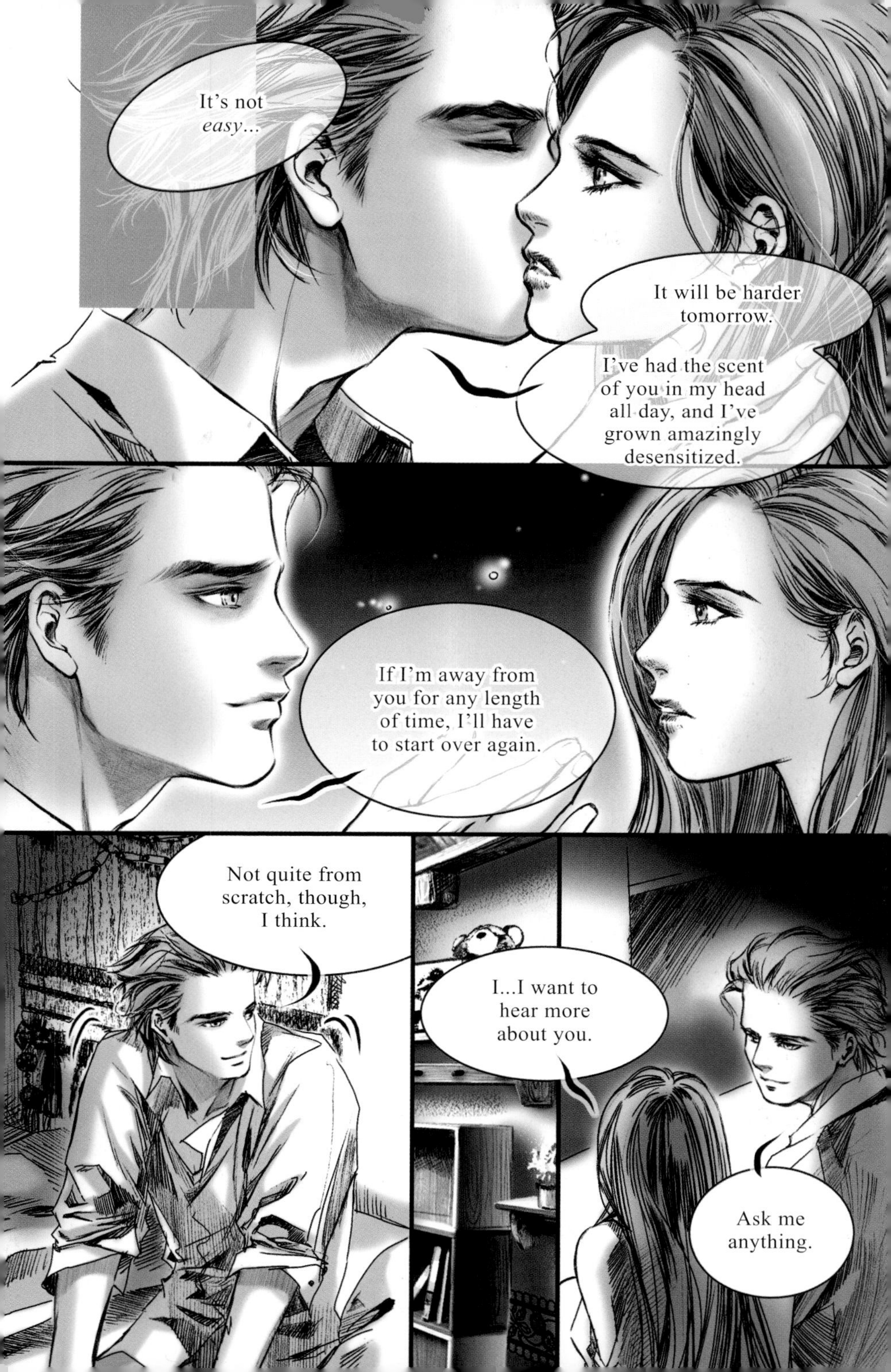
It's not *easy*...
It will be harder tomorrow.
I've had the scent of you in my head all day, and I've grown amazingly desensitized.
If I'm away from you for any length of time, I'll have to start over again.
Not quite from scratch, though, I think.
I...I want to hear more about you.
Ask me anything.

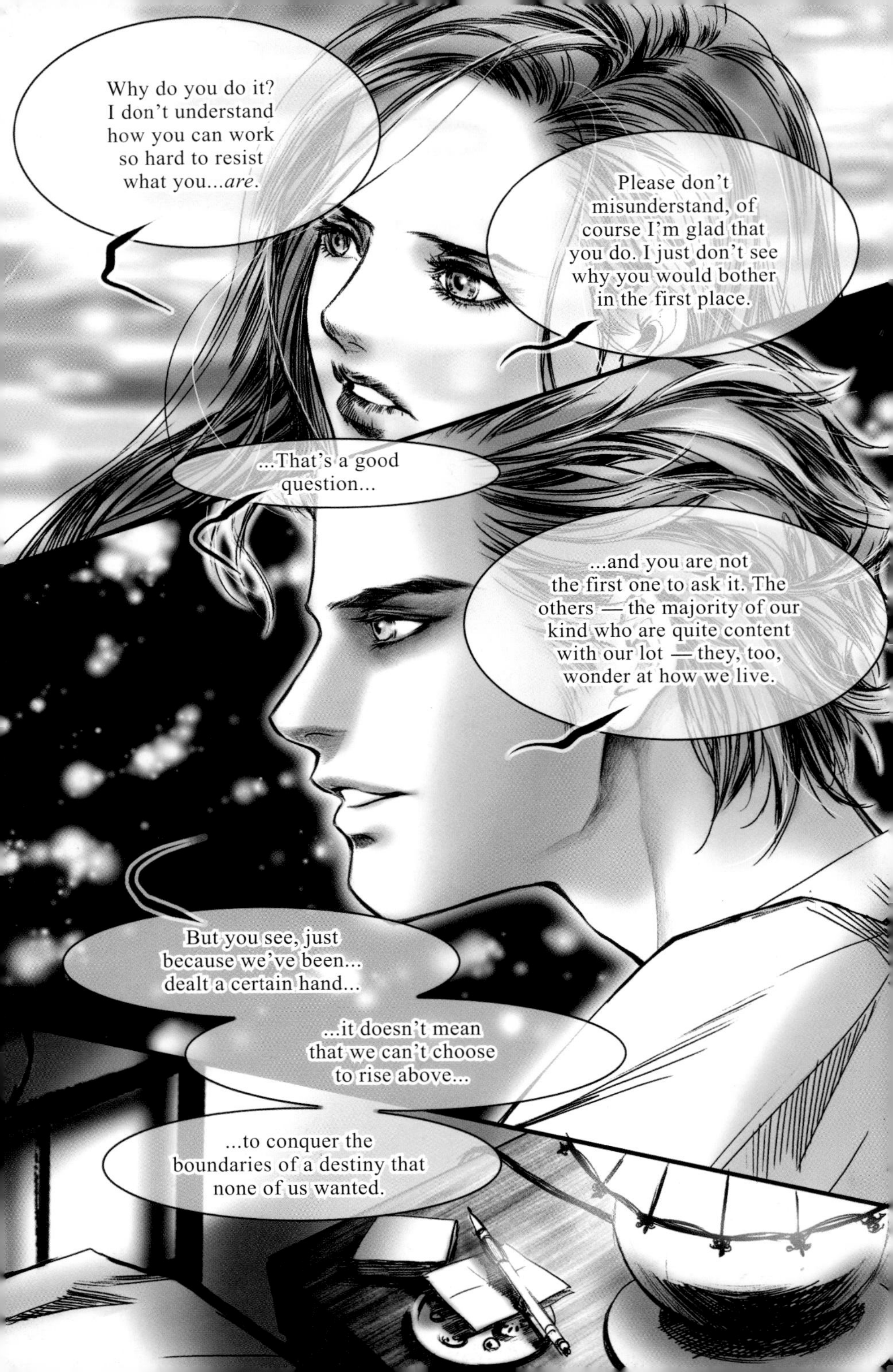
Why do you do it? I don't understand how you can work so hard to resist what you...*are*.
Please don't misunderstand, of course I'm glad that you do. I just don't see why you would bother in the first place.
...That's a good question...
...and you are not the first one to ask it. The others — the majority of our kind who are quite content with our lot — they, too, wonder at how we live.
But you see, just because we've been... dealt a certain hand...
...it doesn't mean that we can't choose to rise above...
...to conquer the boundaries of a destiny that none of us wanted.

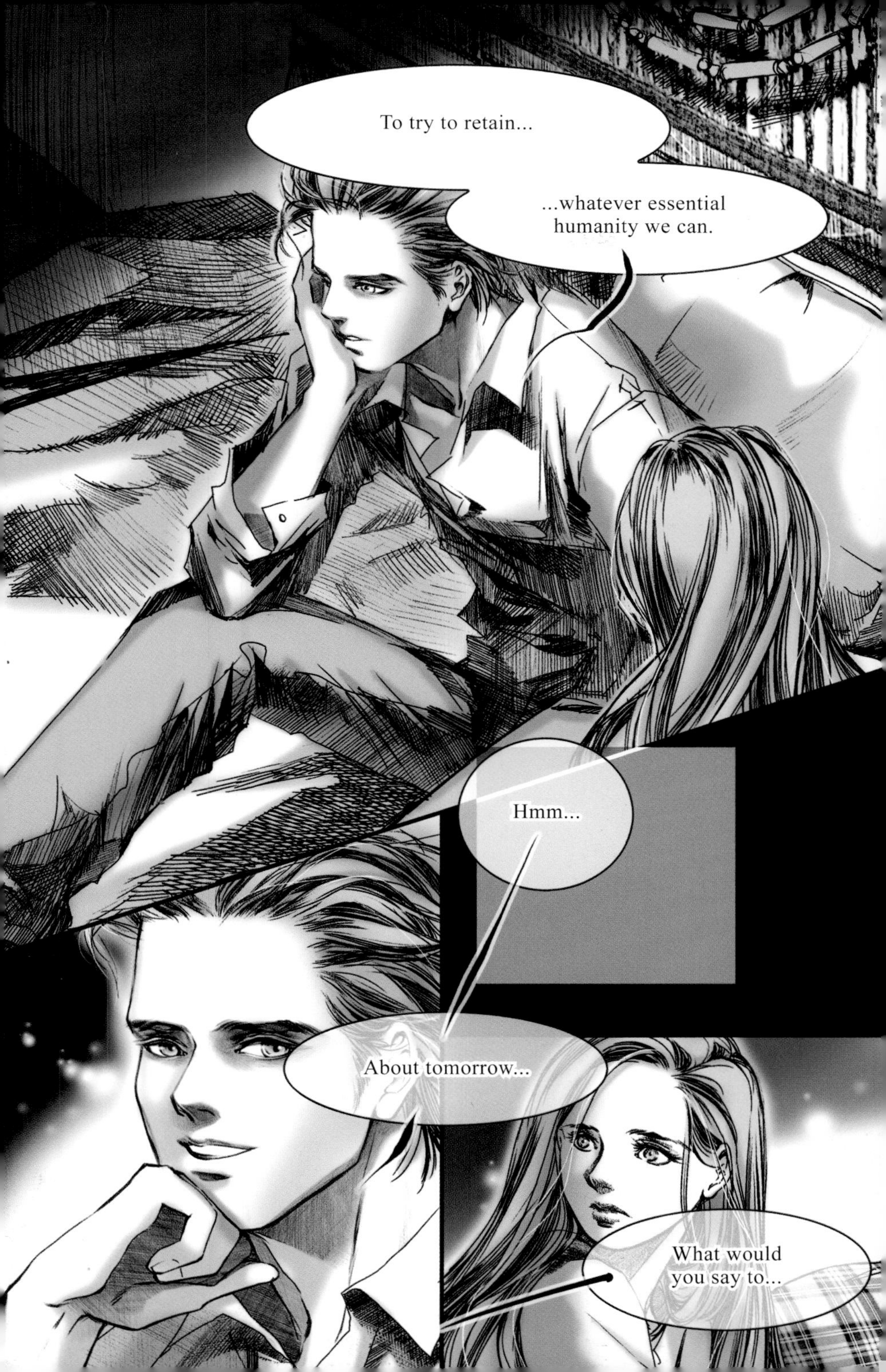
To try to retain...
...whatever essential humanity we can.
Hmm...
About tomorrow...
What would you say to...

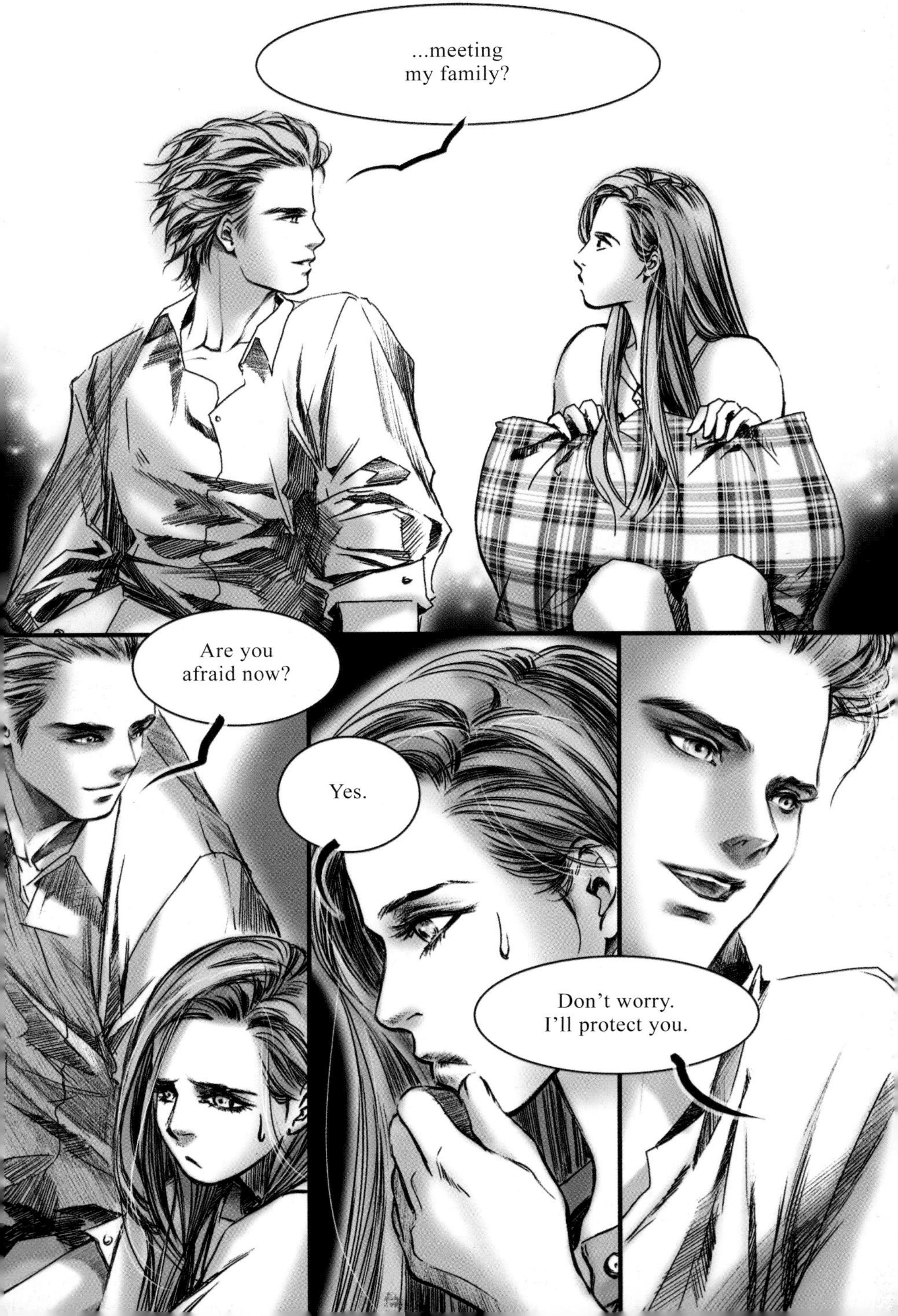
...meeting
my family?
Are you
afraid now?
Yes.
Don't worry.
I'll protect you.

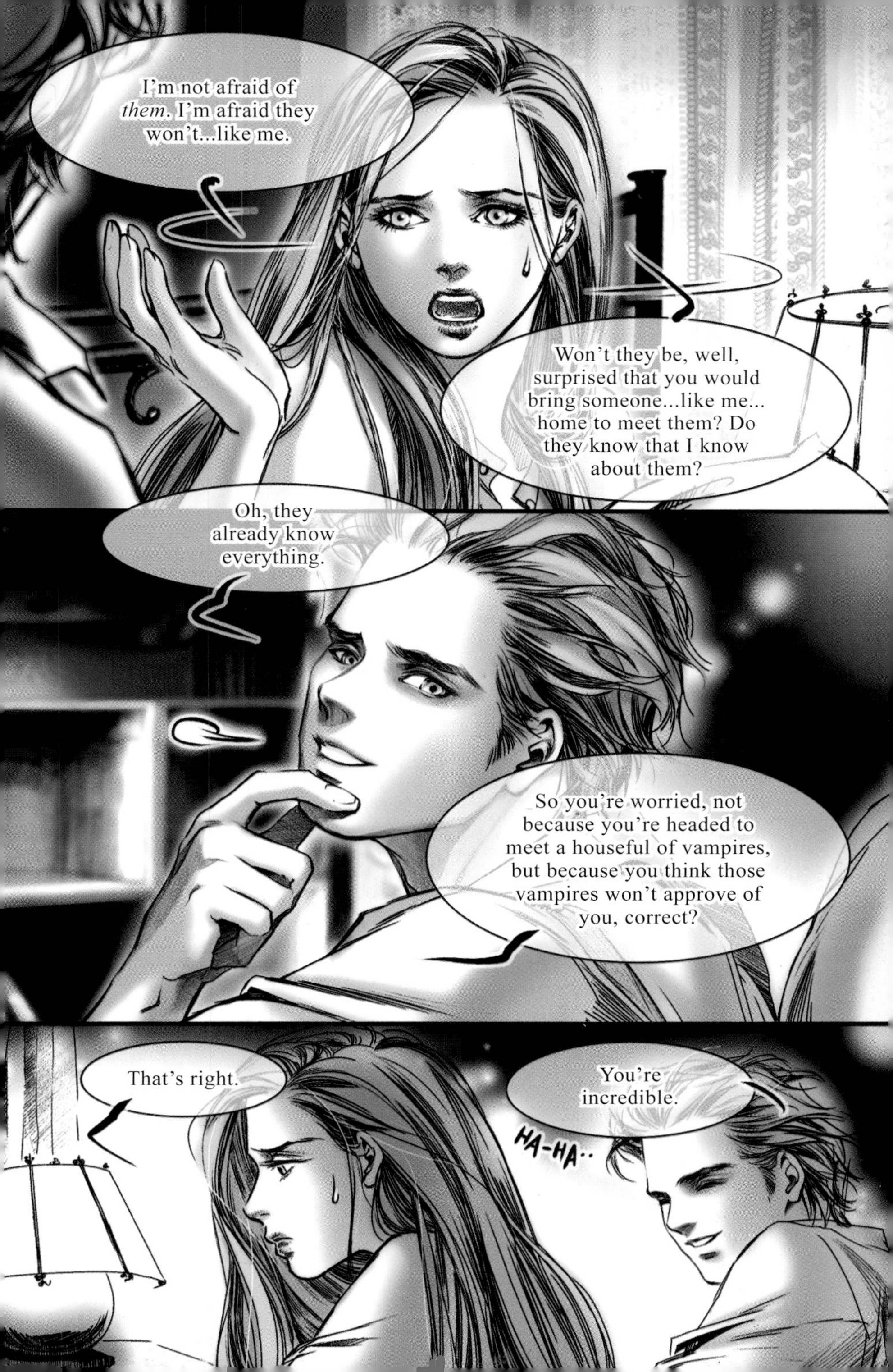
I'm not afraid of *them*. I'm afraid they won't...like me.
Won't they be, well, surprised that you would bring someone...like me... home to meet them? Do they know that I know about them?
Oh, they already know everything.
So you're worried, not because you're headed to meet a houseful of vampires, but because you think those vampires won't approve of you, correct?
That's right.
HA-HA..
You're incredible.

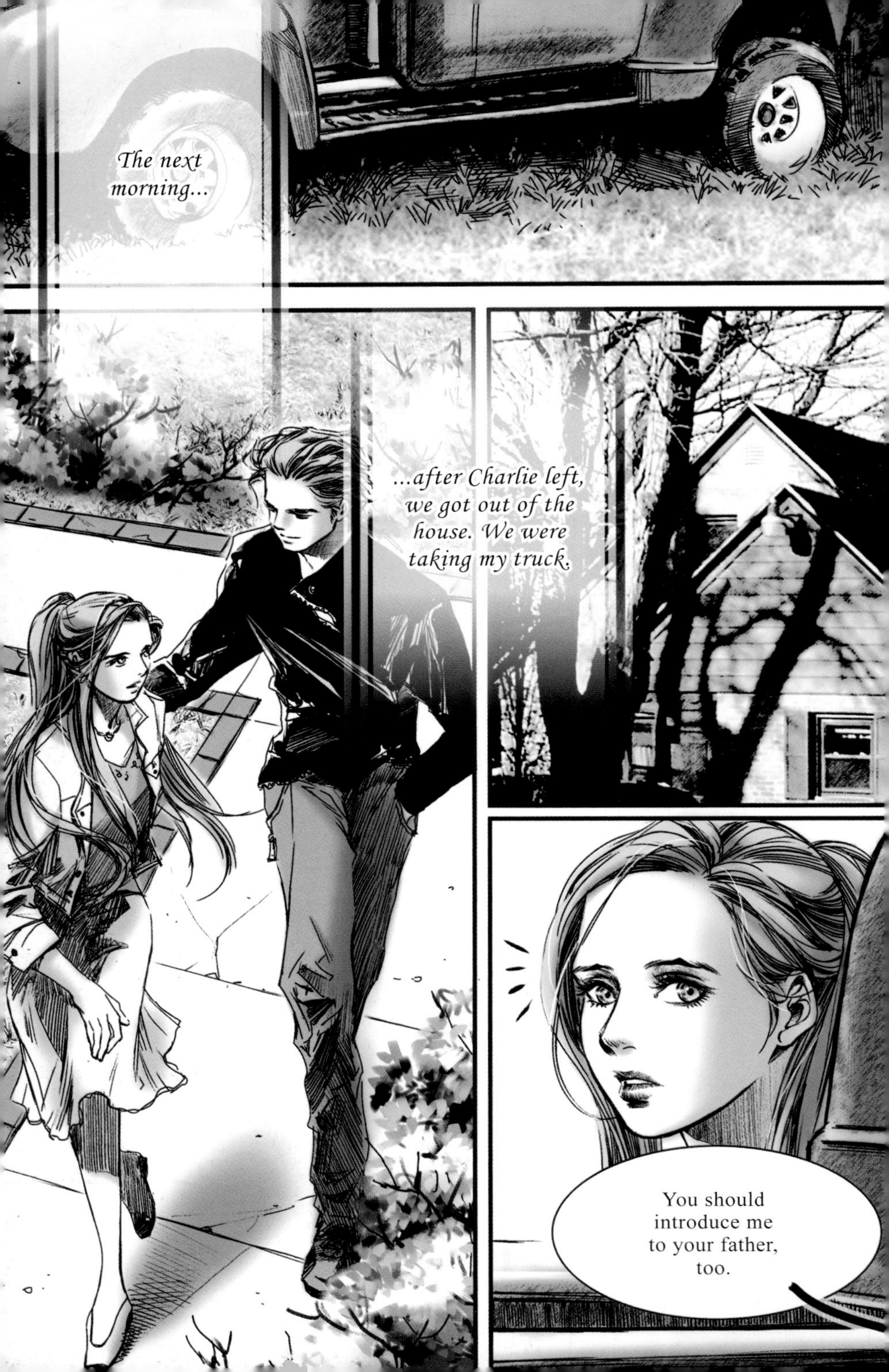
The next morning...
...after Charlie left, we got out of the house. We were taking my truck.
You should introduce me to your father, too.

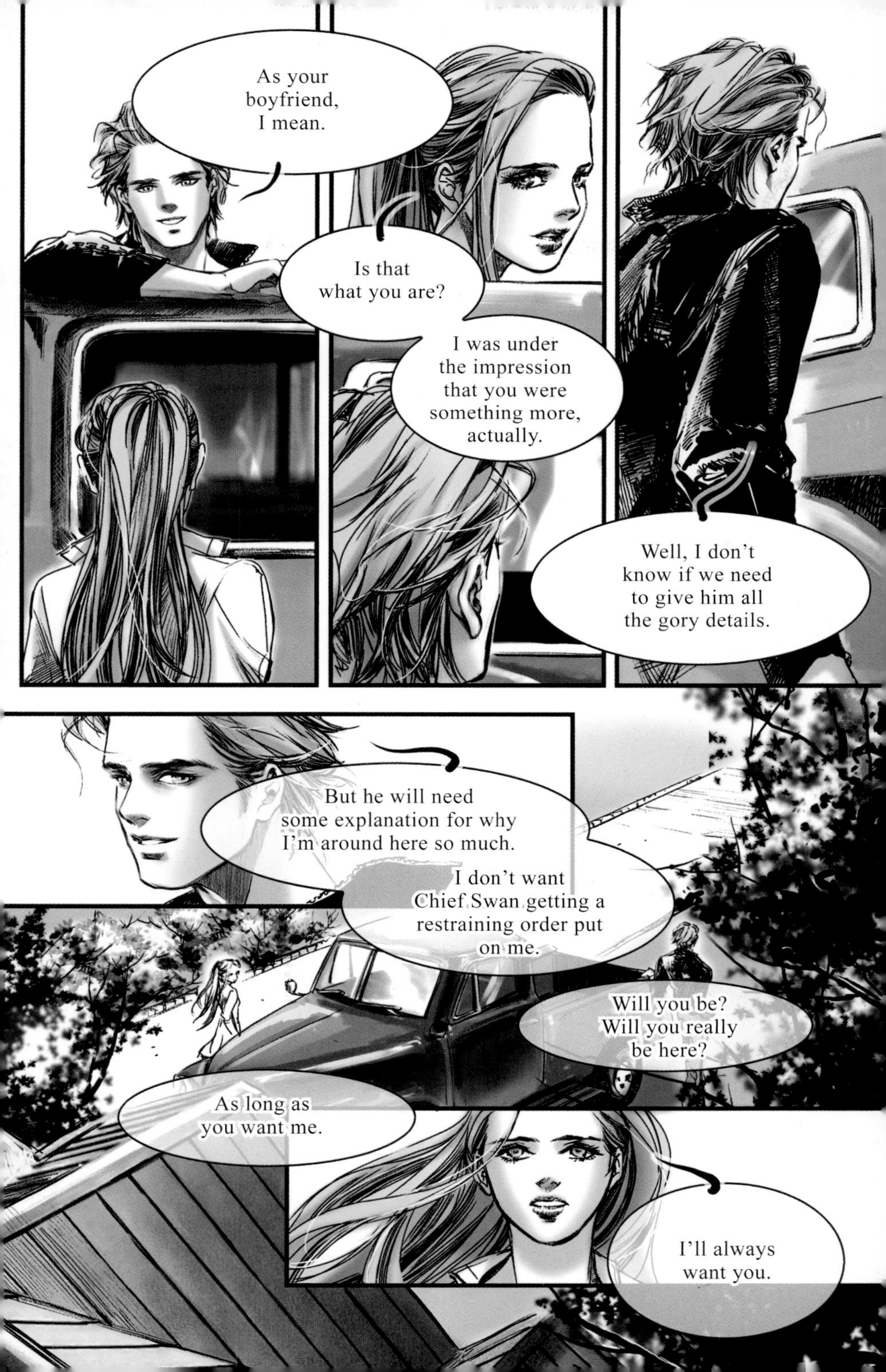
As your boyfriend, I mean.
Is that what you are?
I was under the impression that you were something more, actually.
Well, I don't know if we need to give him all the gory details.
But he will need some explanation for why I'm around here so much.
I don't want Chief Swan getting a restraining order put on me.
Will you be? Will you really be here?
As long as you want me.
I'll always want you.

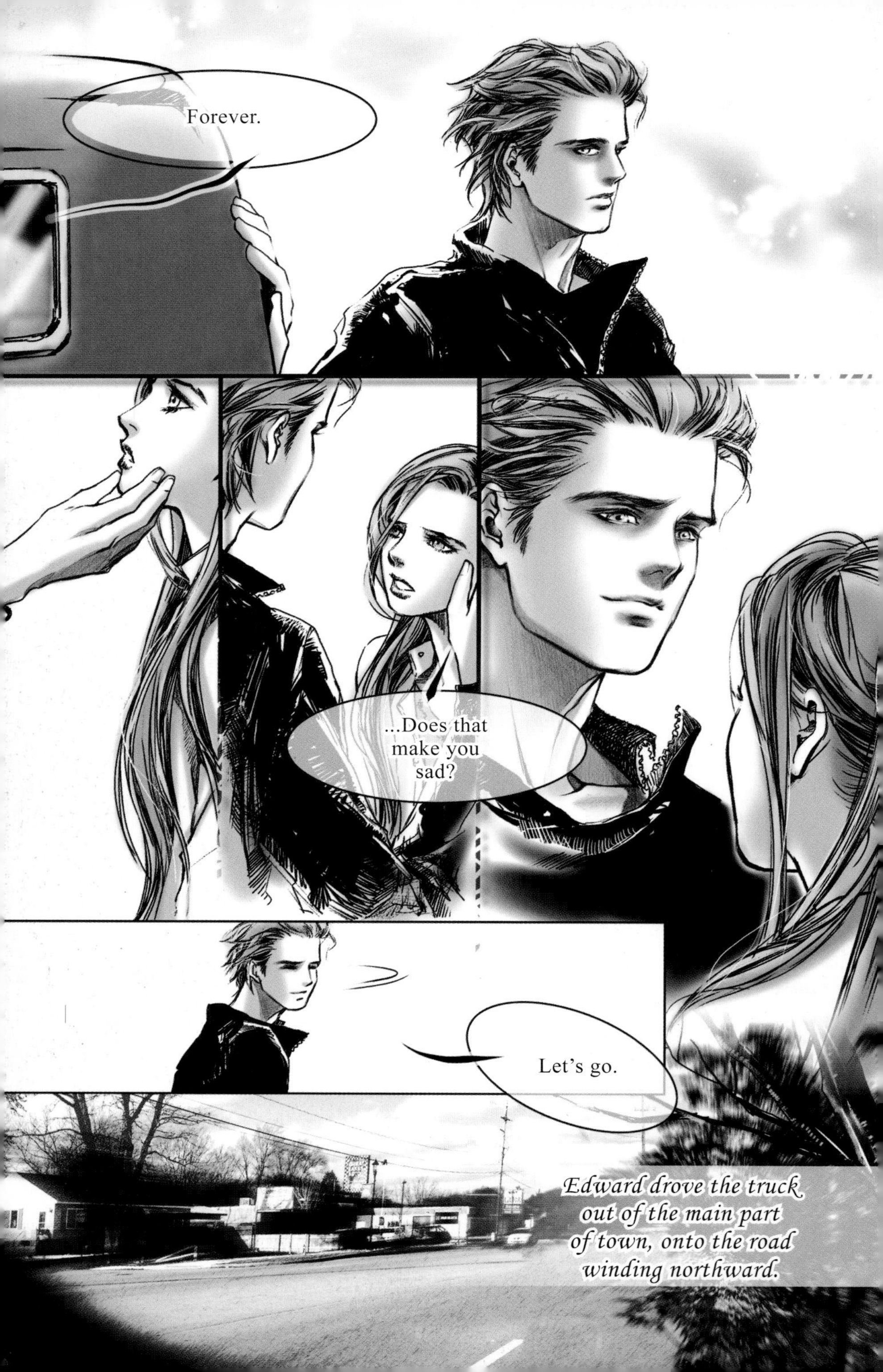
Forever.
...Does that make you sad?
Let's go.
*Edward drove the truck out of the main part of town, onto the road winding northward.*

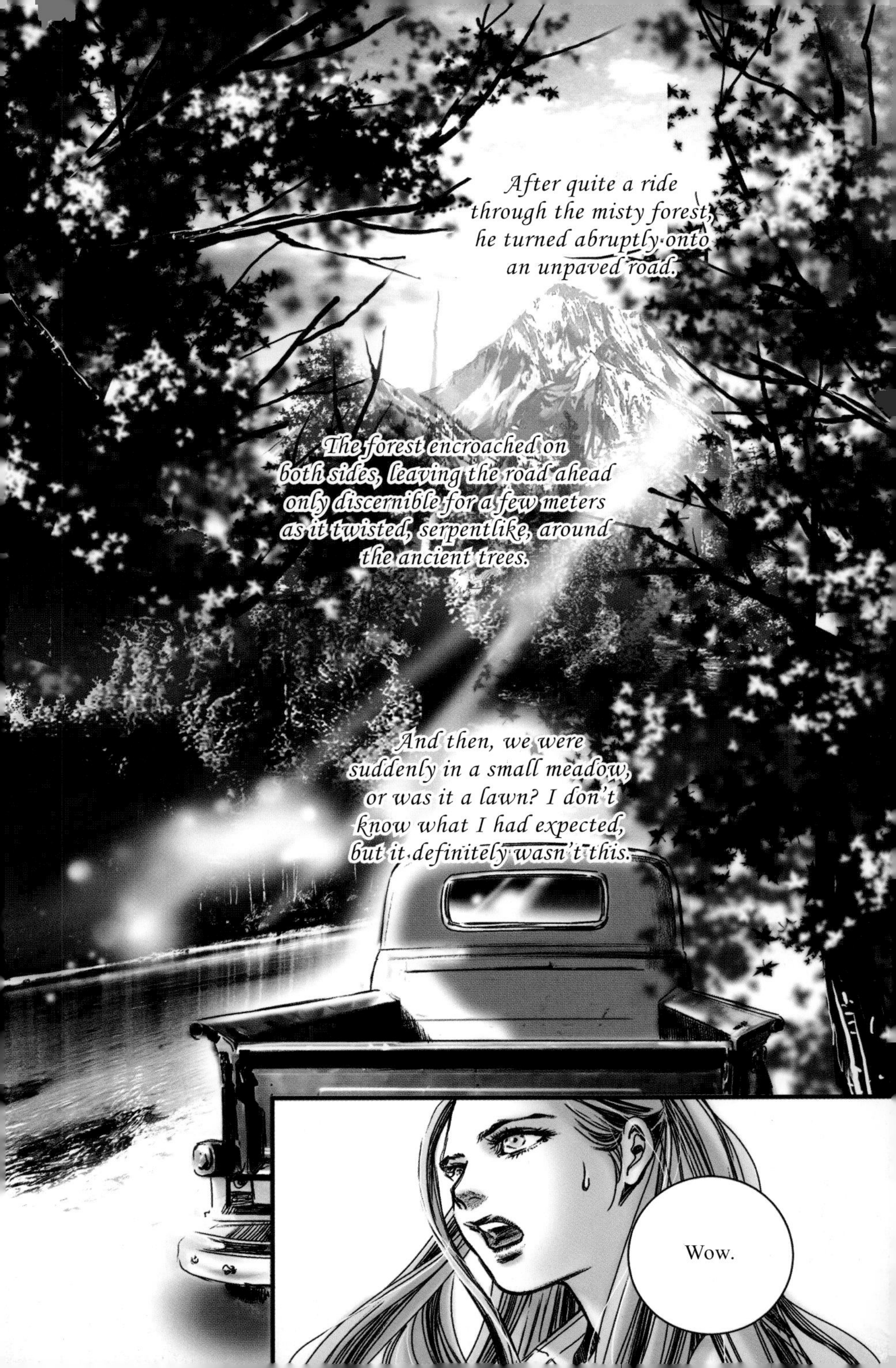
After quite a ride through the misty forest, he turned abruptly onto an unpaved road.
The forest encroached on both sides, leaving the road ahead only discernible for a few meters as it twisted, serpentlike, around the ancient trees.
And then, we were suddenly in a small meadow, or was it a lawn? I don't know what I had expected, but it definitely wasn't this.
Wow.

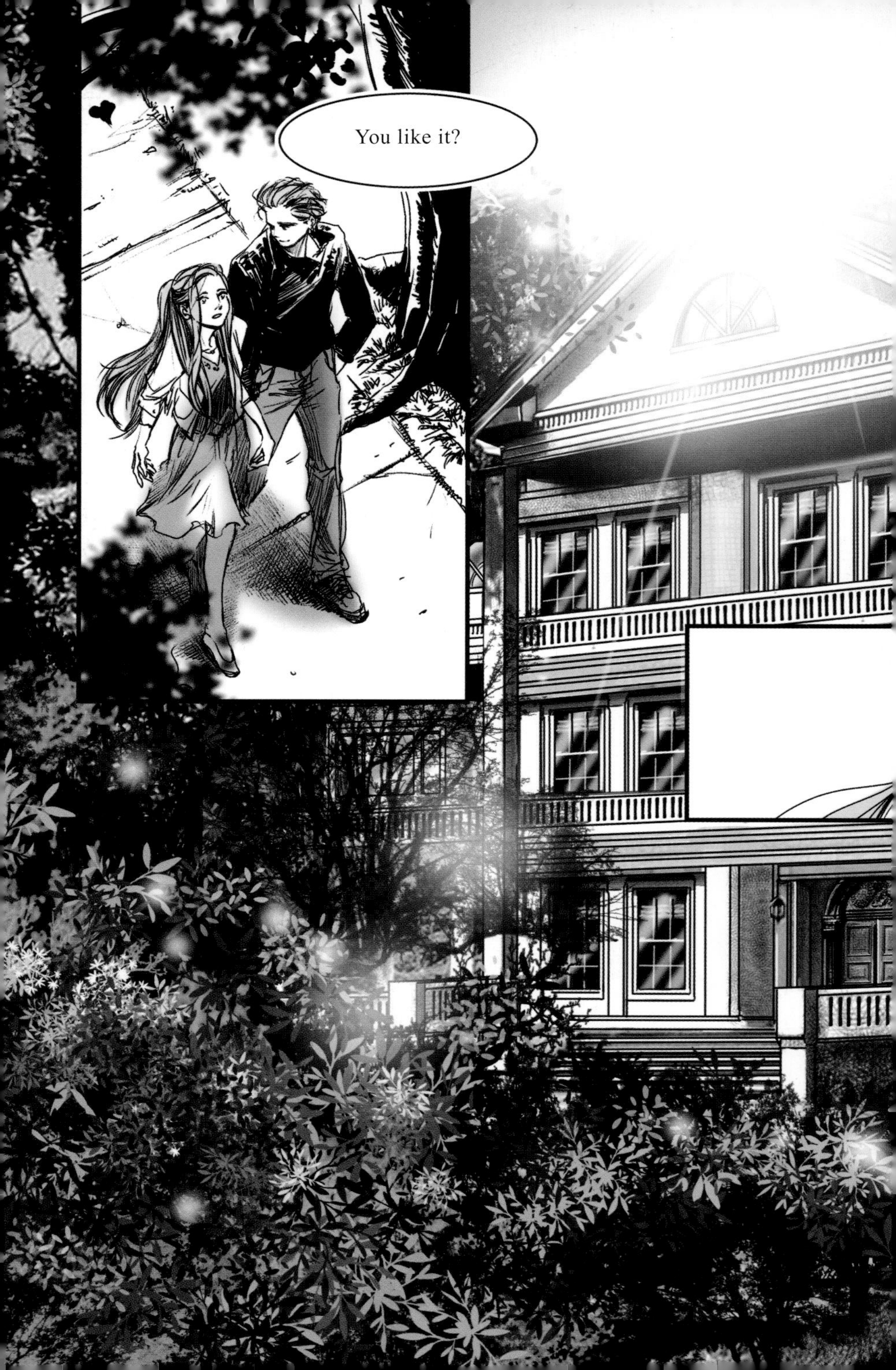
You like it?

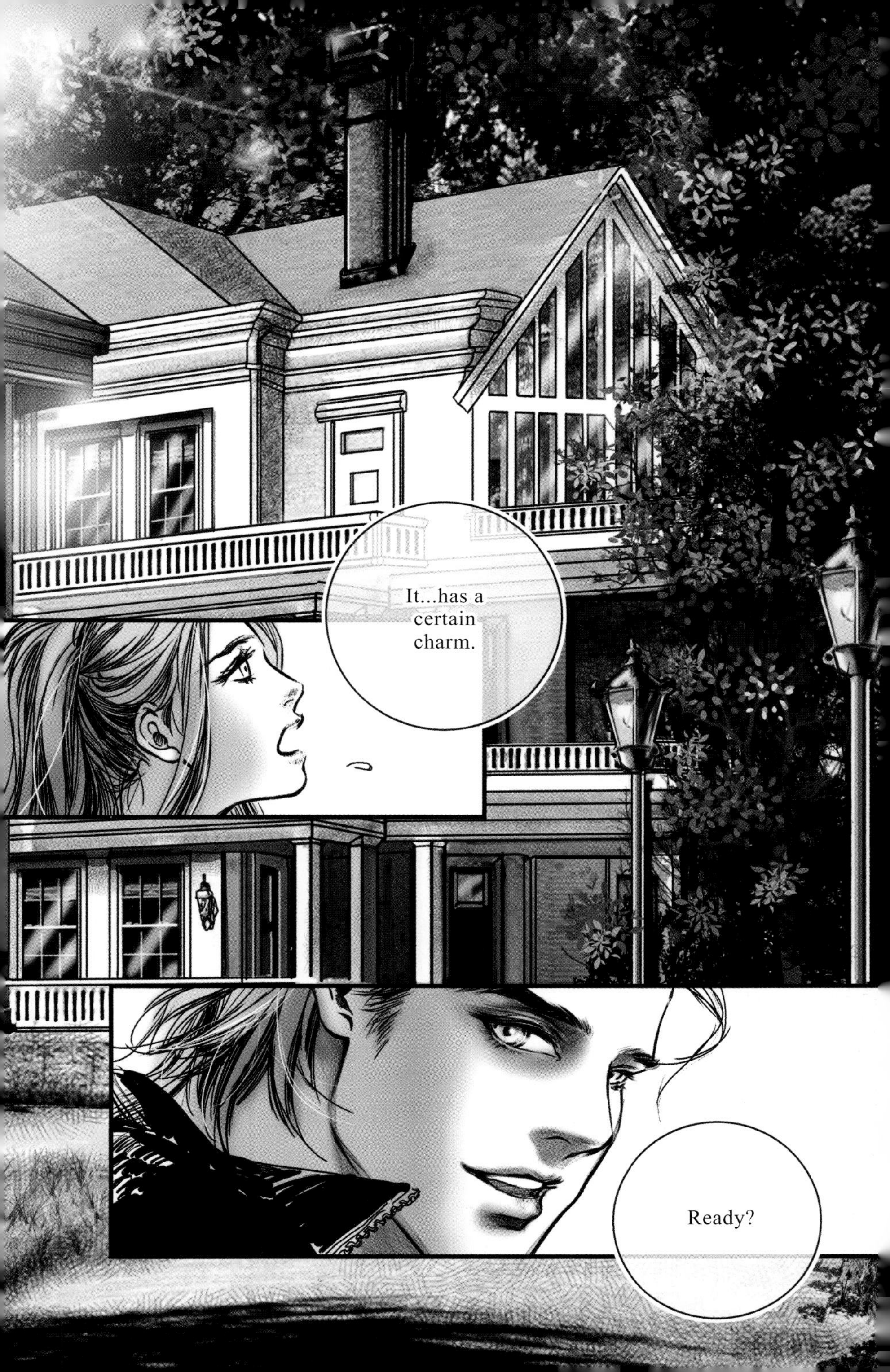
It...has a certain charm.
Ready?

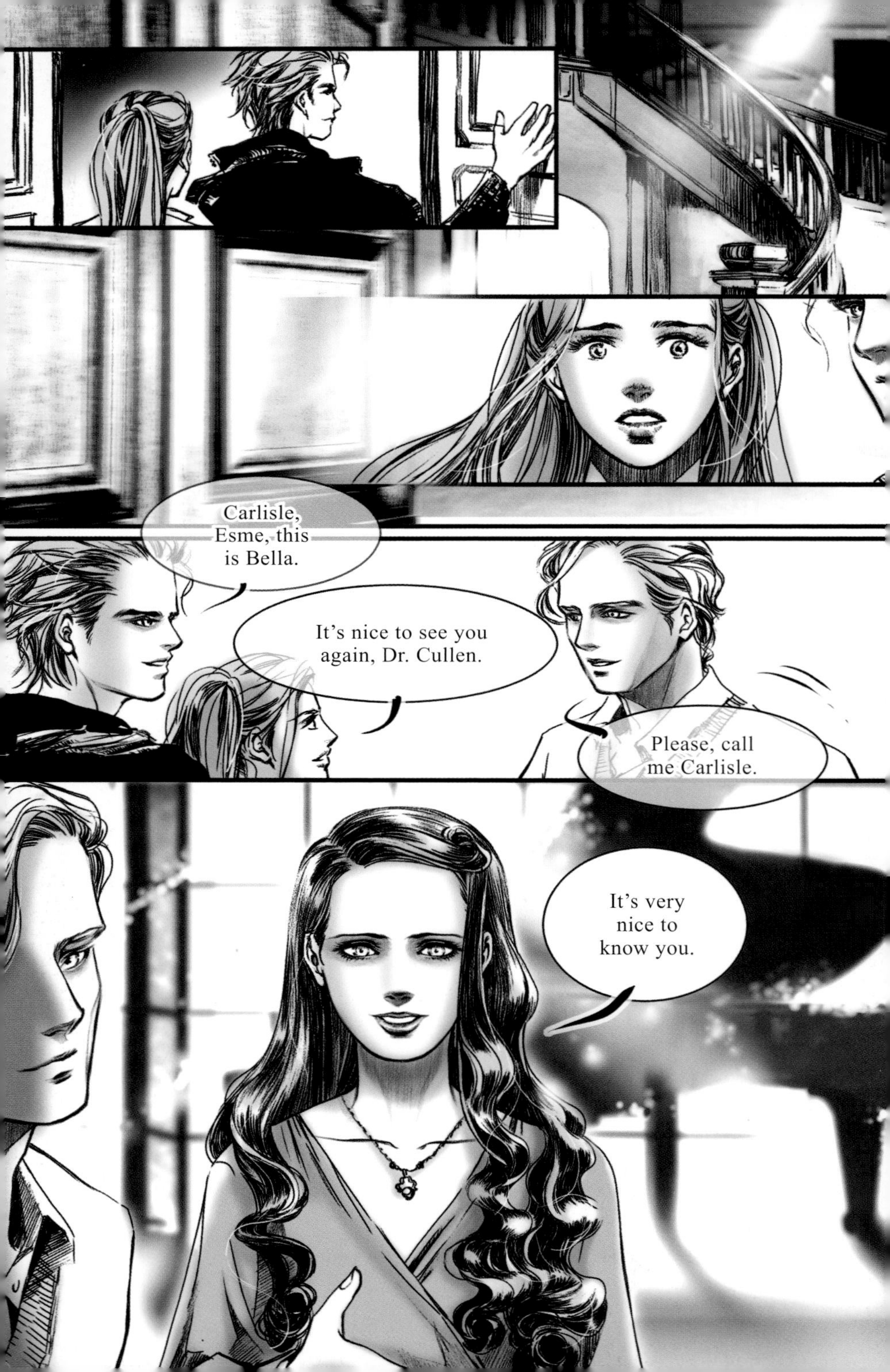
Carlisle, Esme, this is Bella.
It's nice to see you again, Dr. Cullen.
Please, call me Carlisle.
It's very nice to know you.

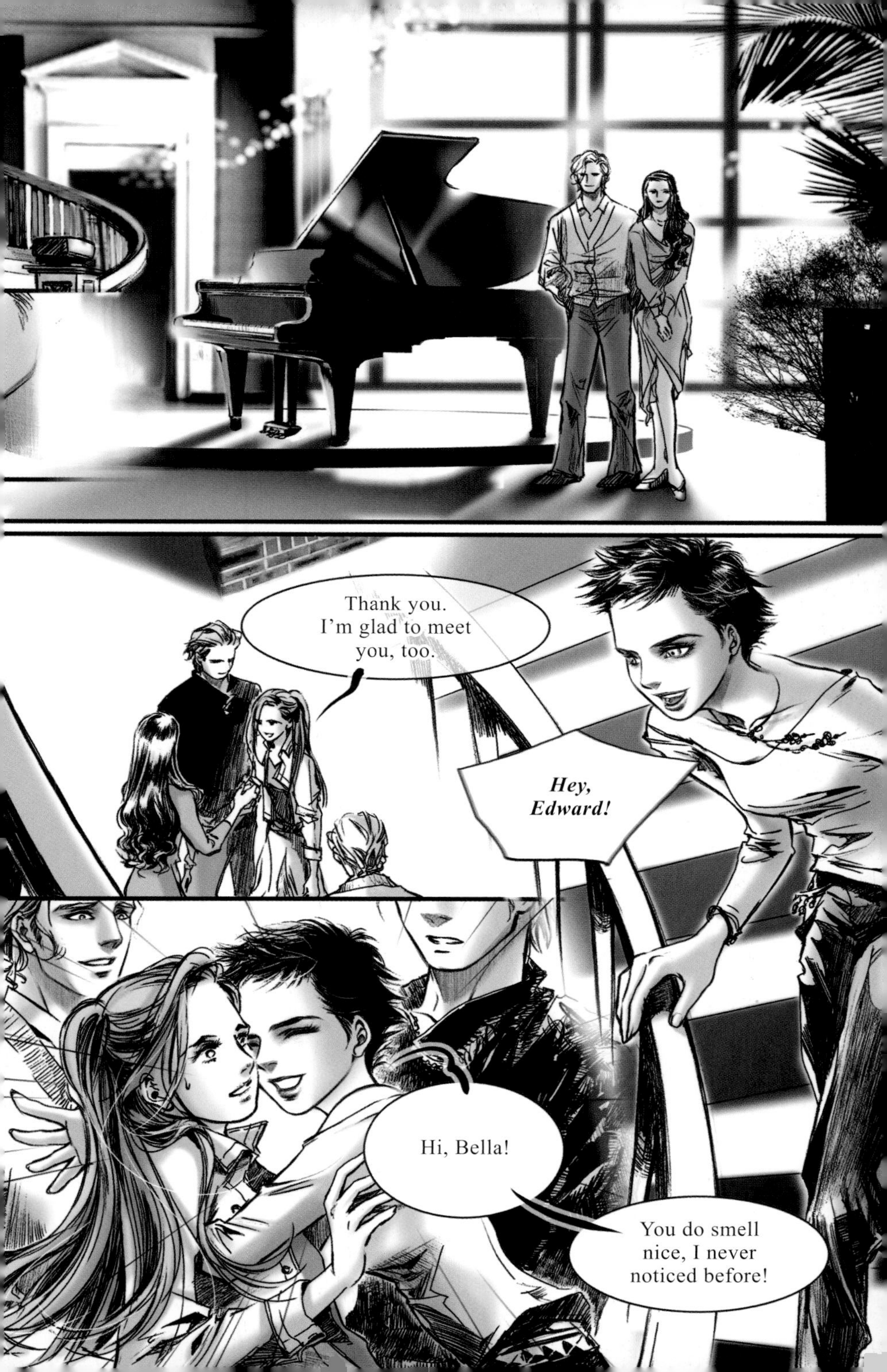
Thank you. I'm glad to meet you, too.
Hey, Edward!
Hi, Bella!
You do smell nice, I never noticed before!

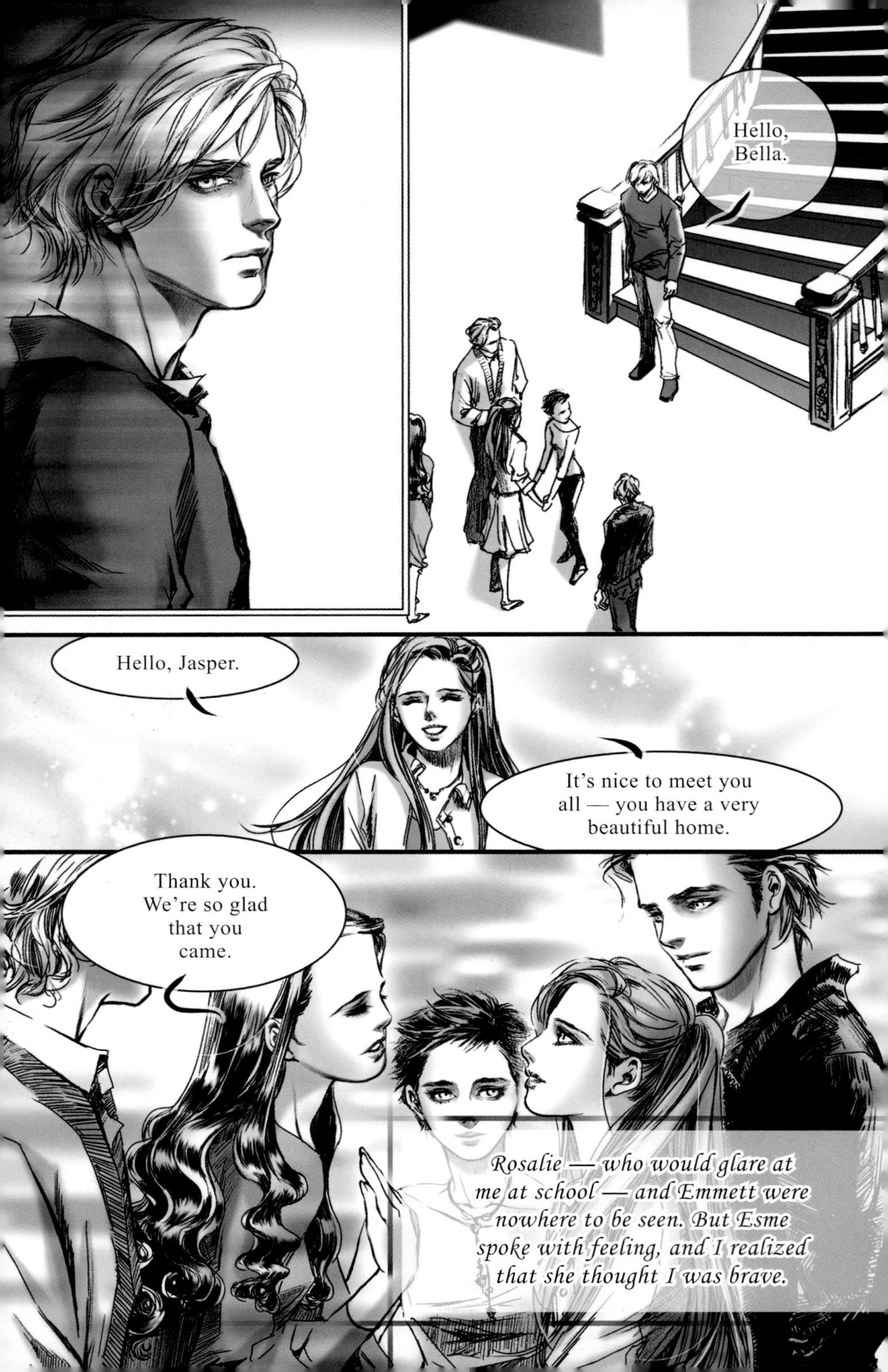
Hello, Bella.
Hello, Jasper.
It's nice to meet you all — you have a very beautiful home.
Thank you. We're so glad that you came.
*Rosalie — who would glare at me at school — and Emmett were nowhere to be seen. But Esme spoke with feeling, and I realized that she thought I was brave.*

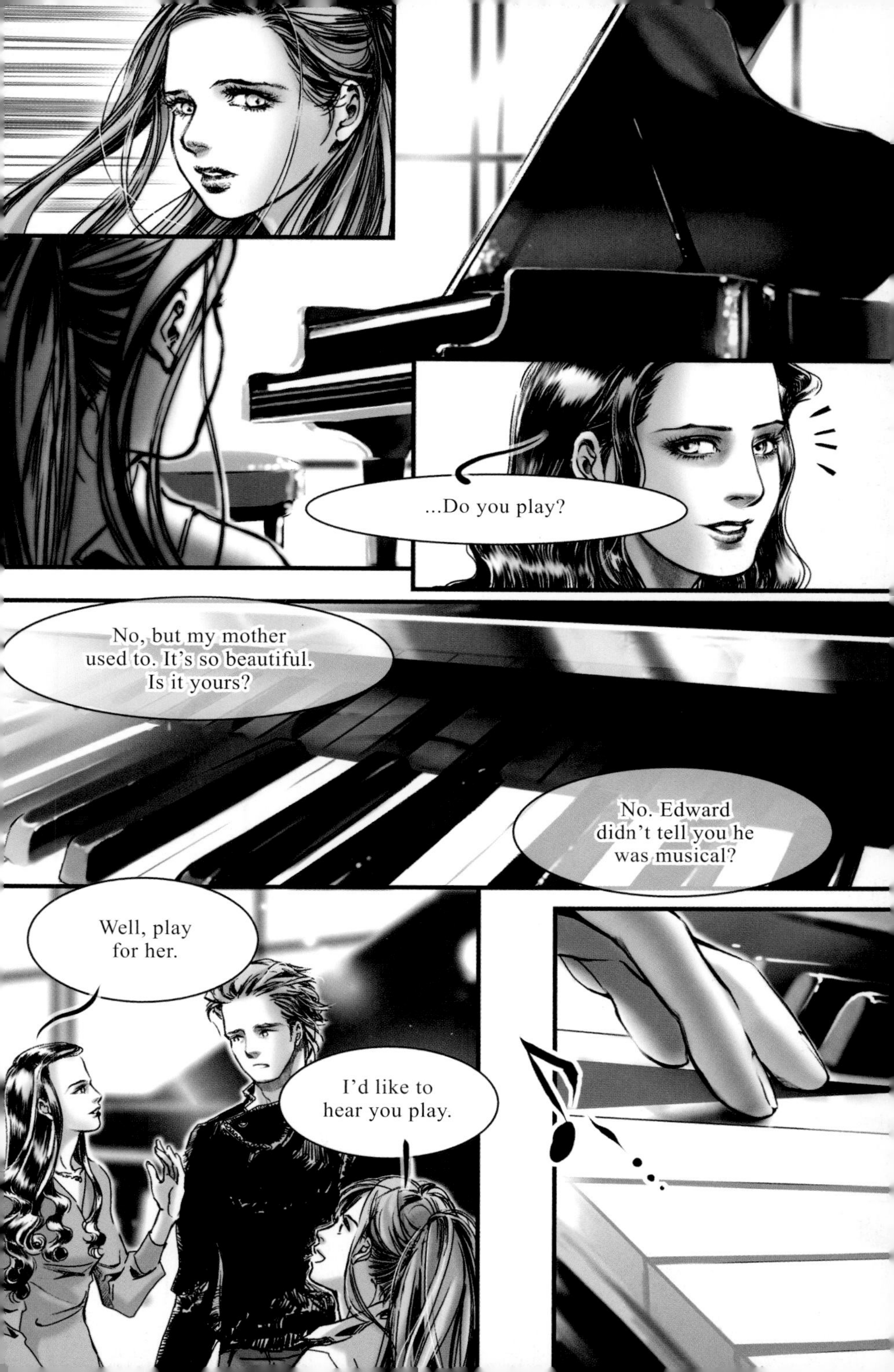
...Do you play?
No, but my mother used to. It's so beautiful. Is it yours?
No. Edward didn't tell you he was musical?
Well, play for her.
I'd like to hear you play.

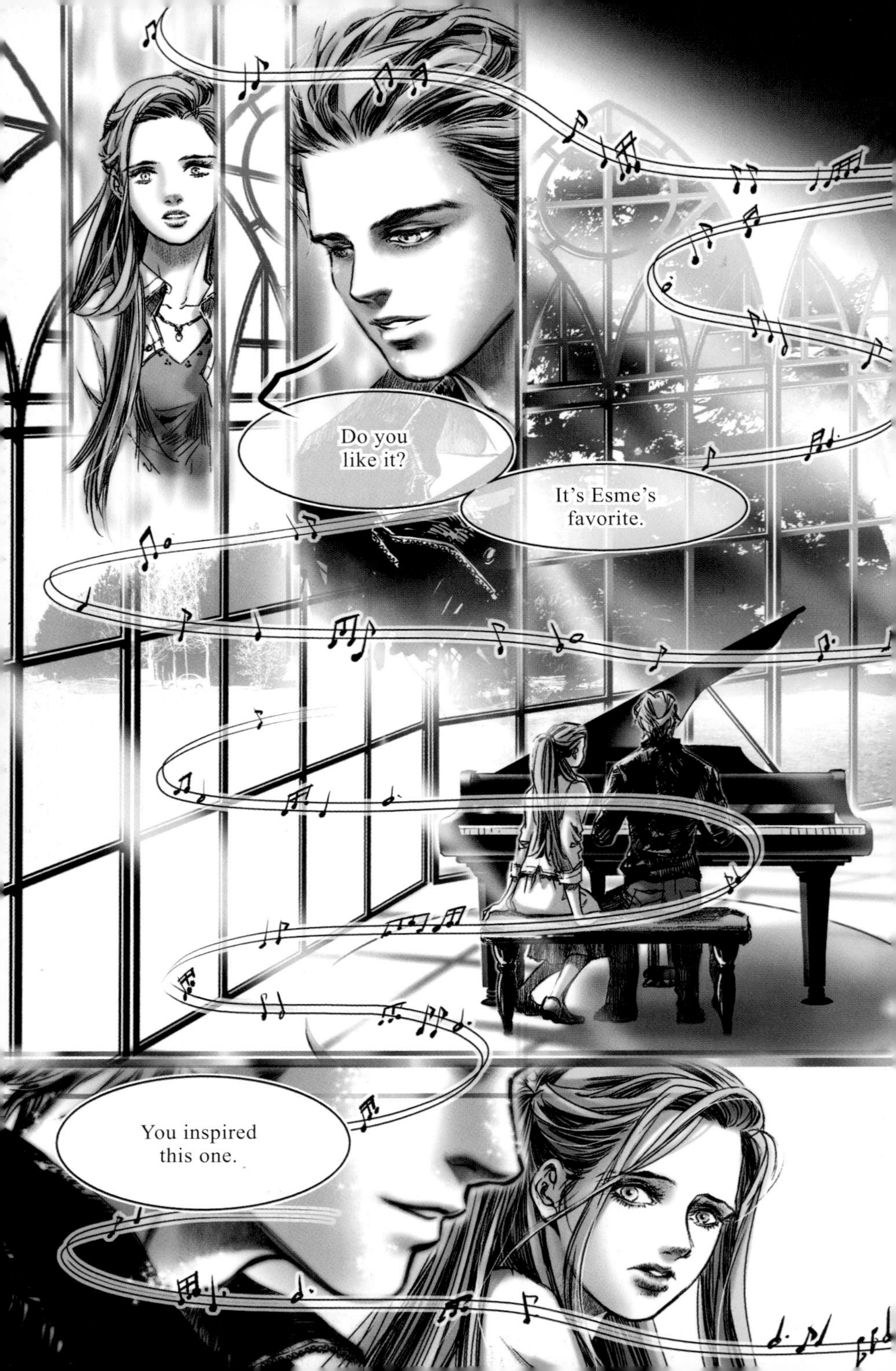
Do you like it?
It's Esme's favorite.
You inspired this one.

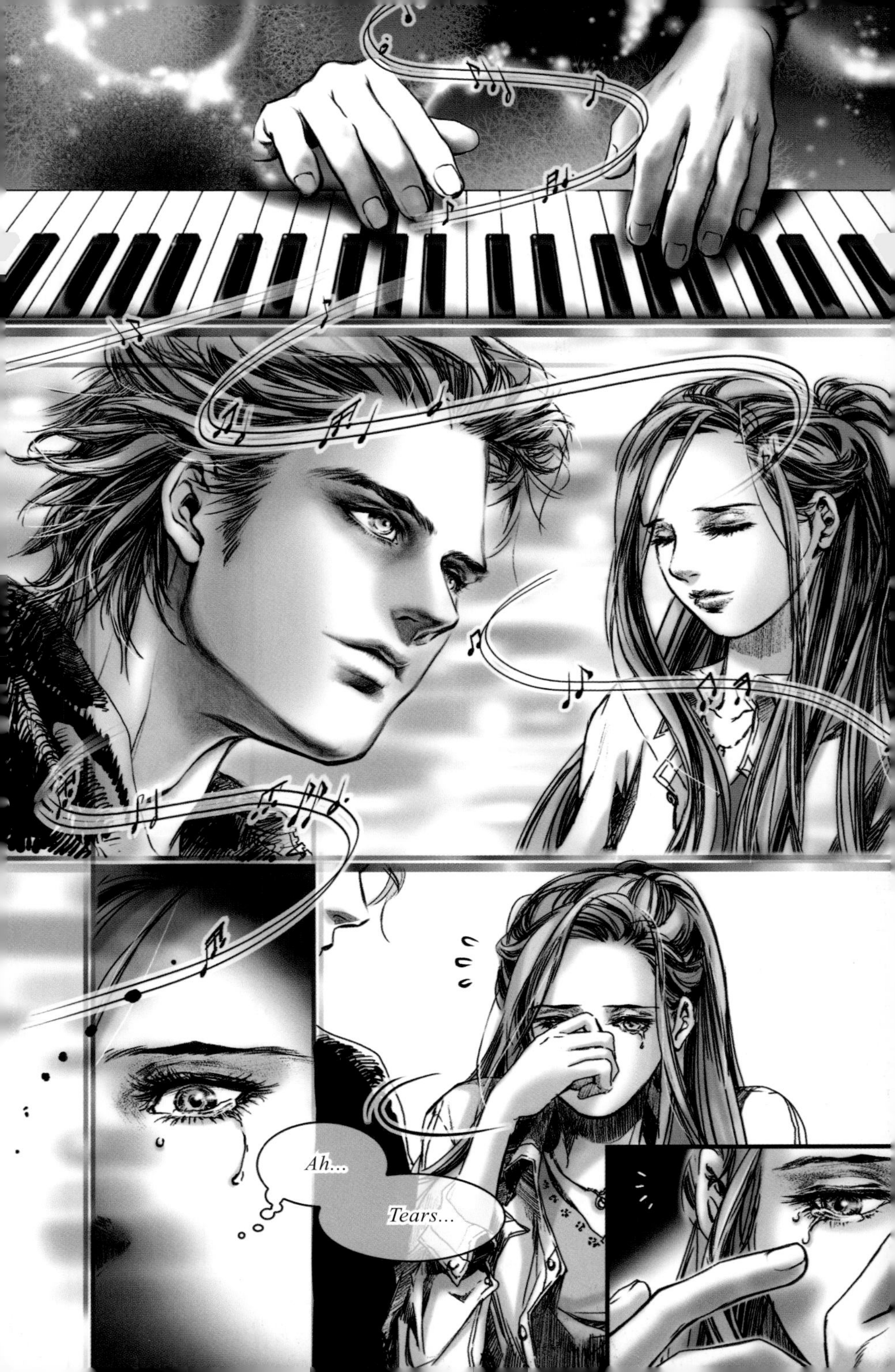
Ah...
Tears...

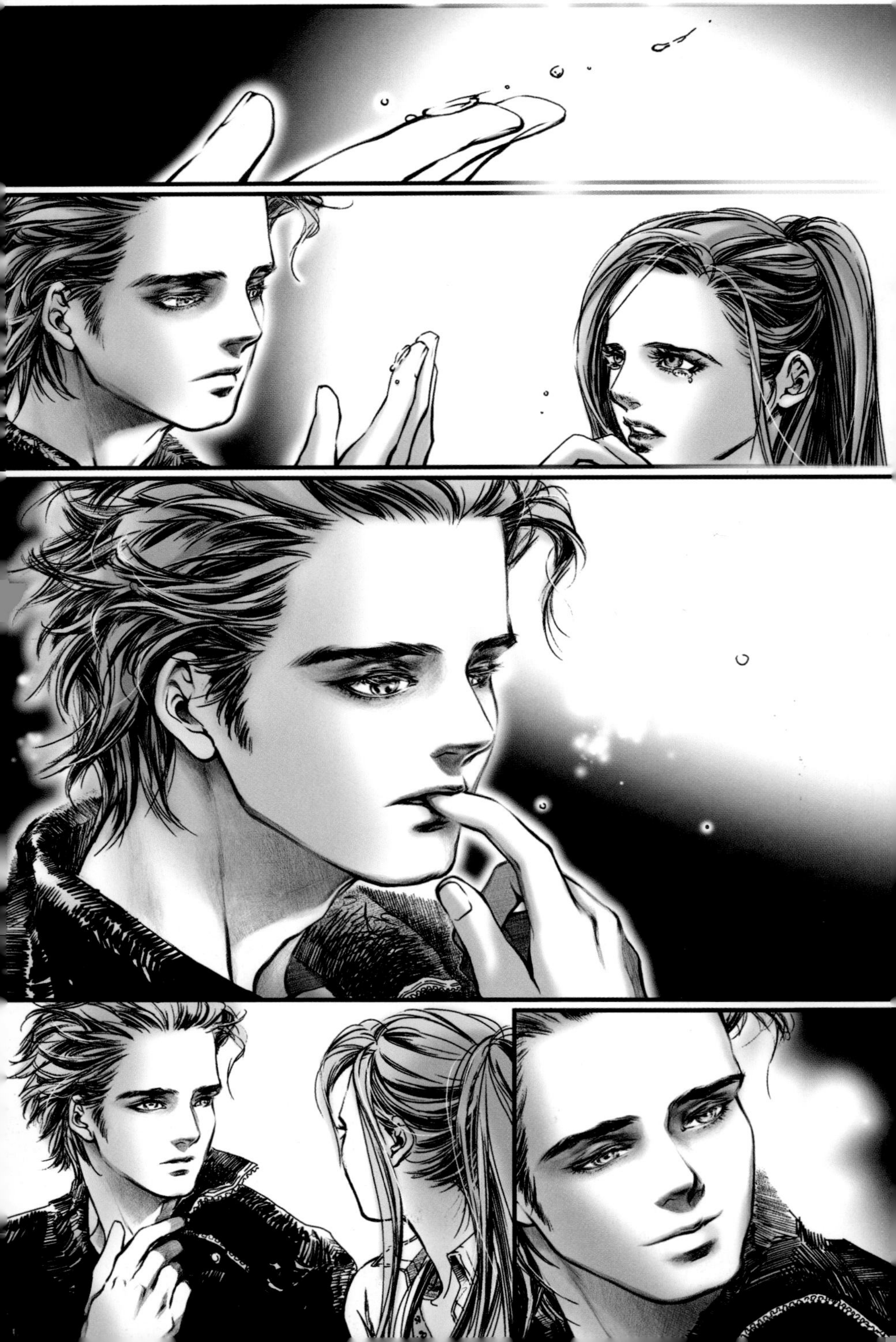

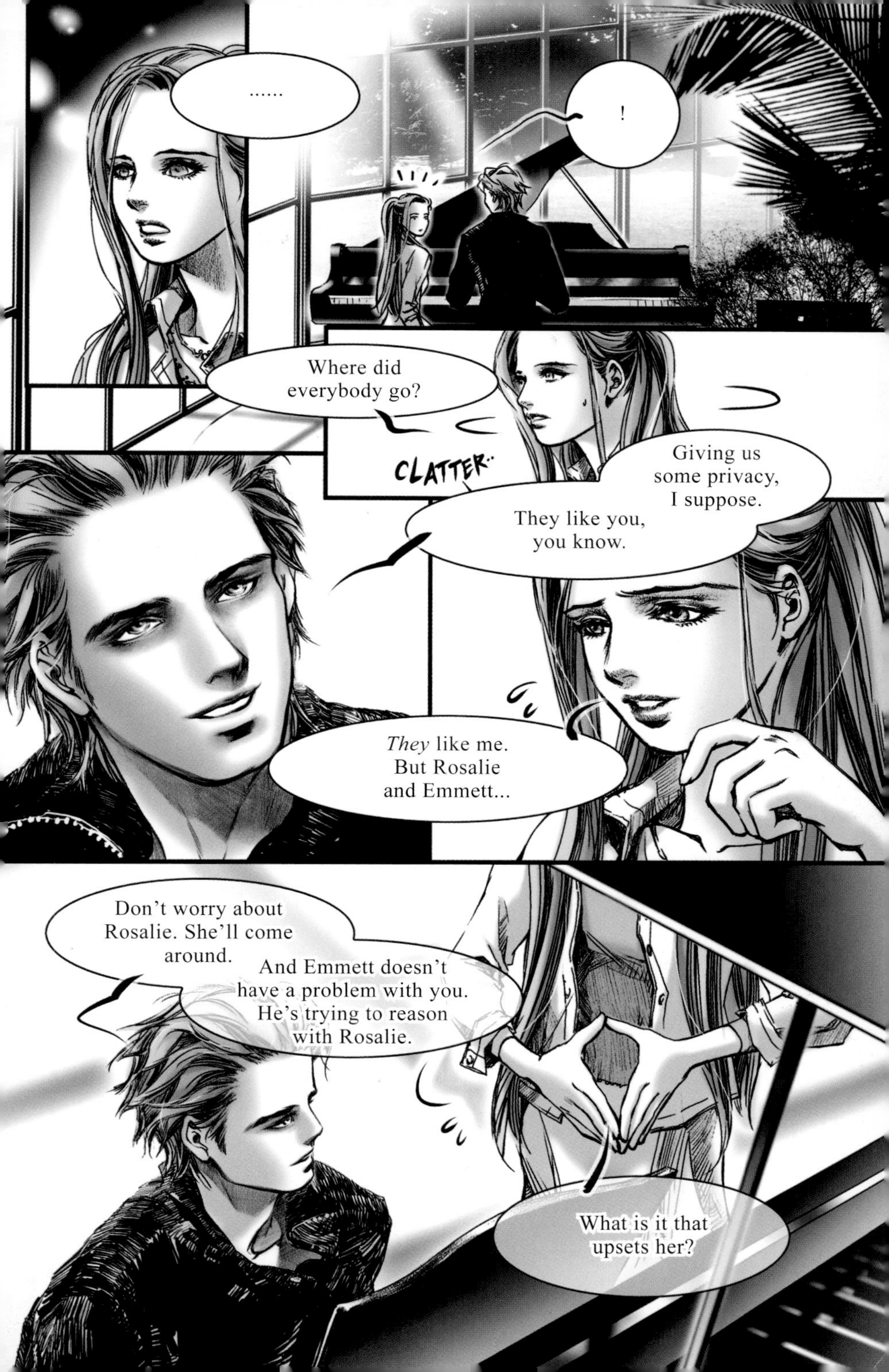
......
!
Where did everybody go?
CLATTER..
Giving us some privacy, I suppose.
They like you, you know.
*They* like me. But Rosalie and Emmett...
Don't worry about Rosalie. She'll come around.
And Emmett doesn't have a problem with you. He's trying to reason with Rosalie.
What is it that upsets her?

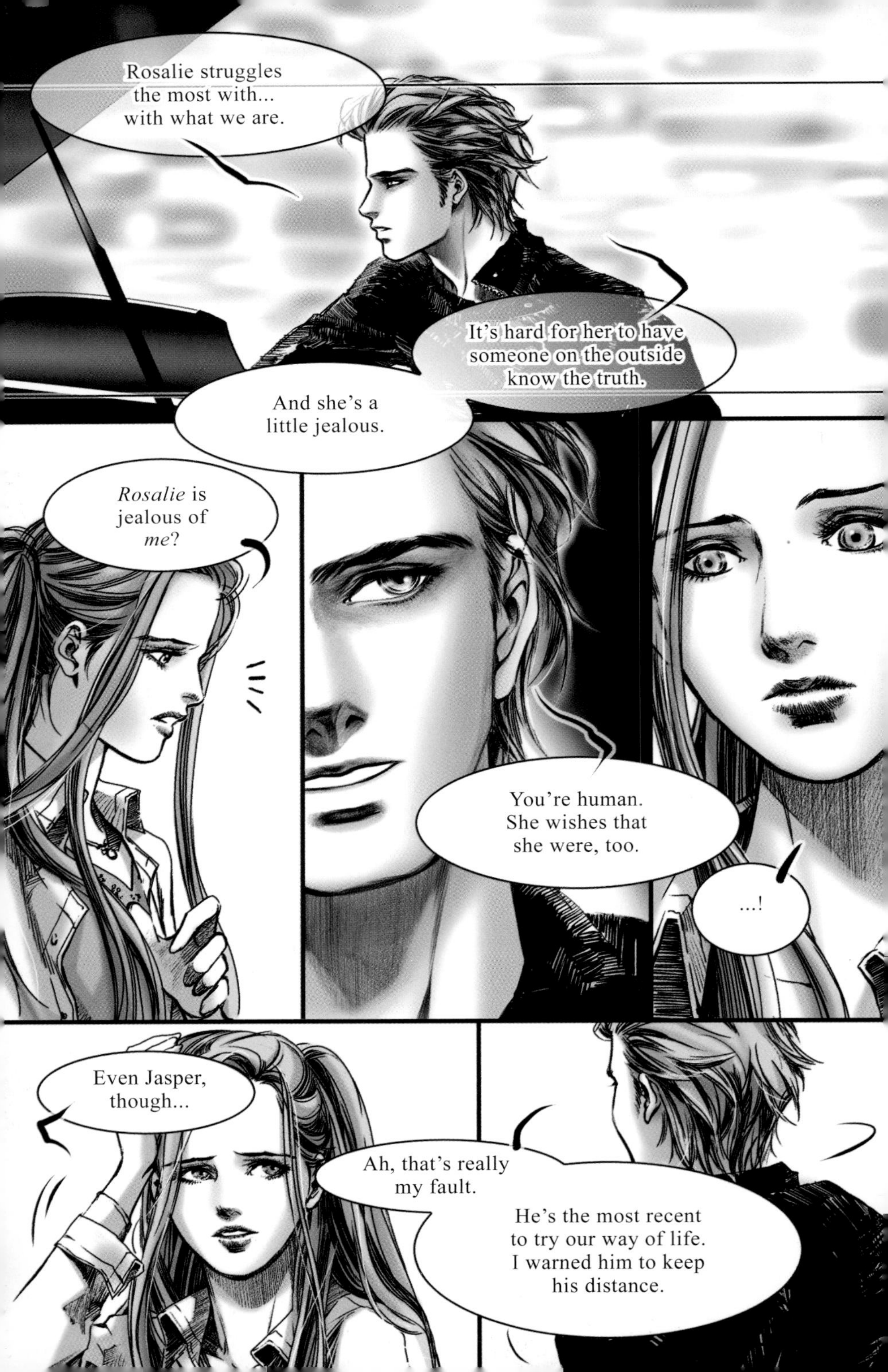
Rosalie struggles the most with... with what we are.
It's hard for her to have someone on the outside know the truth.
And she's a little jealous.
*Rosalie* is jealous of *me*?
You're human. She wishes that she were, too.
...!
Even Jasper, though...
Ah, that's really my fault.
He's the most recent to try our way of life. I warned him to keep his distance.

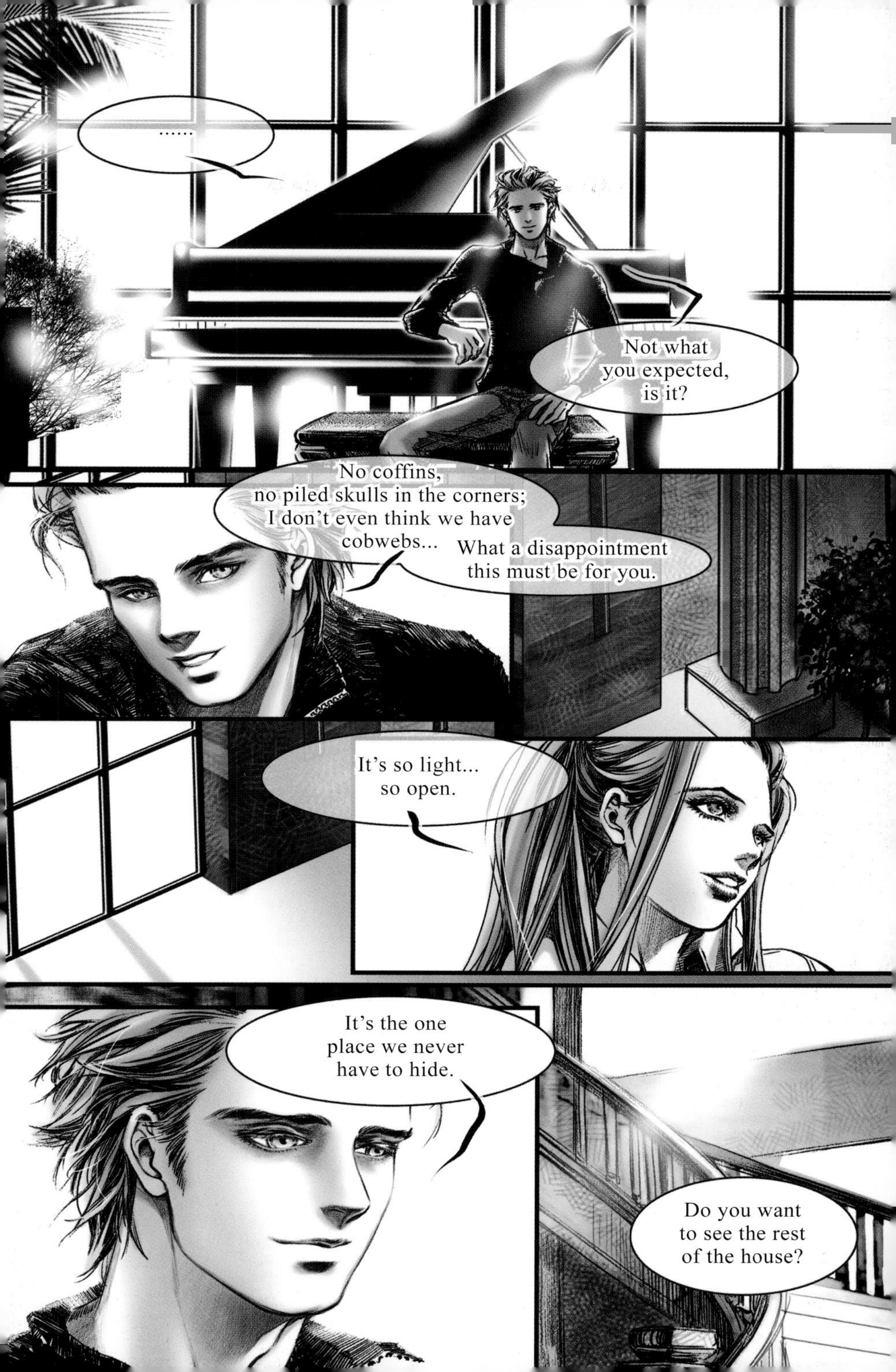
......
Not what you expected, is it?
No coffins, no piled skulls in the corners; I don't even think we have cobwebs...
What a disappointment this must be for you.
It's so light... so open.
It's the one place we never have to hide.
Do you want to see the rest of the house?

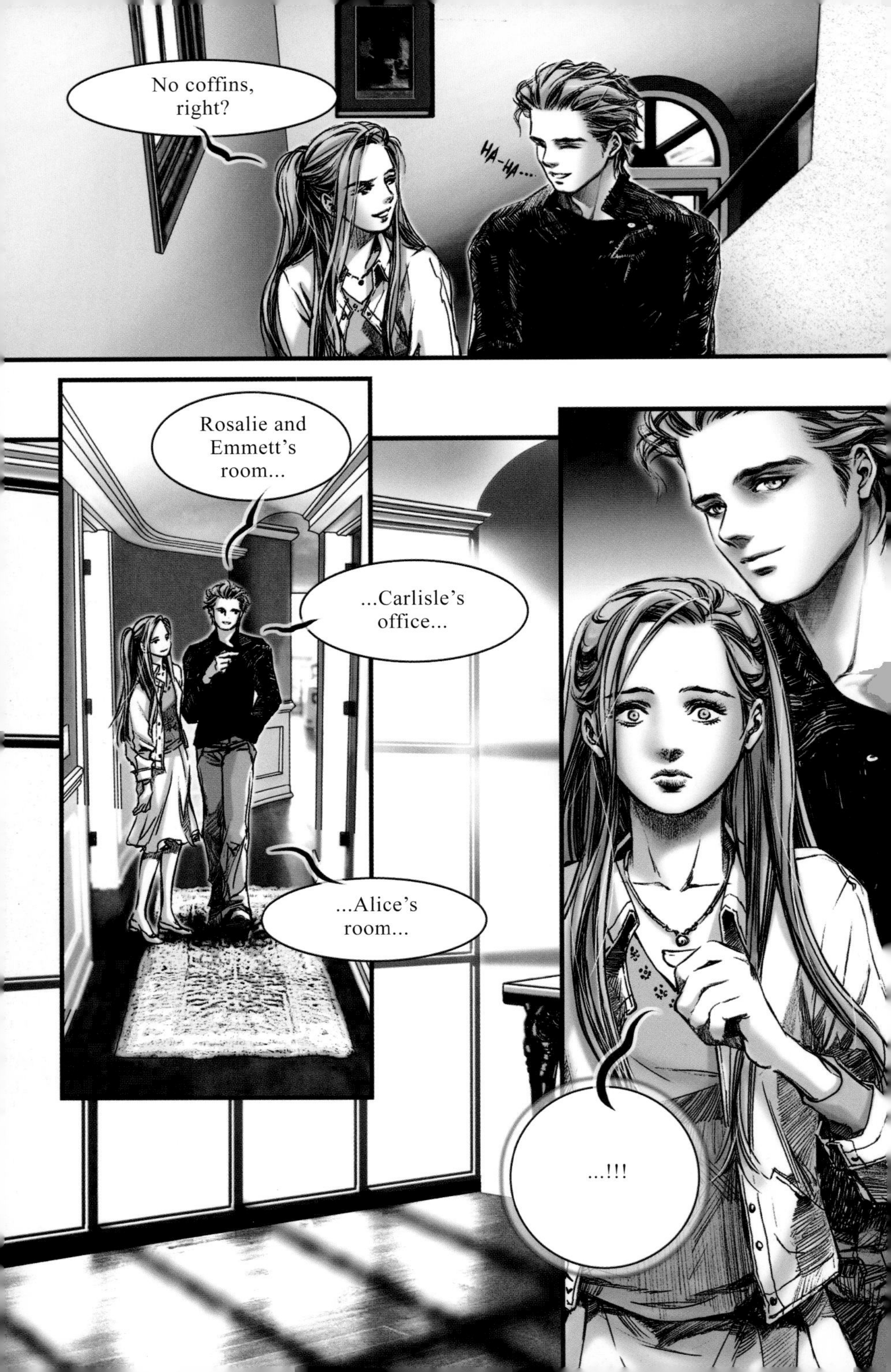
No coffins, right?
HA-HA...
Rosalie and Emmett's room...
...Carlisle's office...
...Alice's room...
...!!!

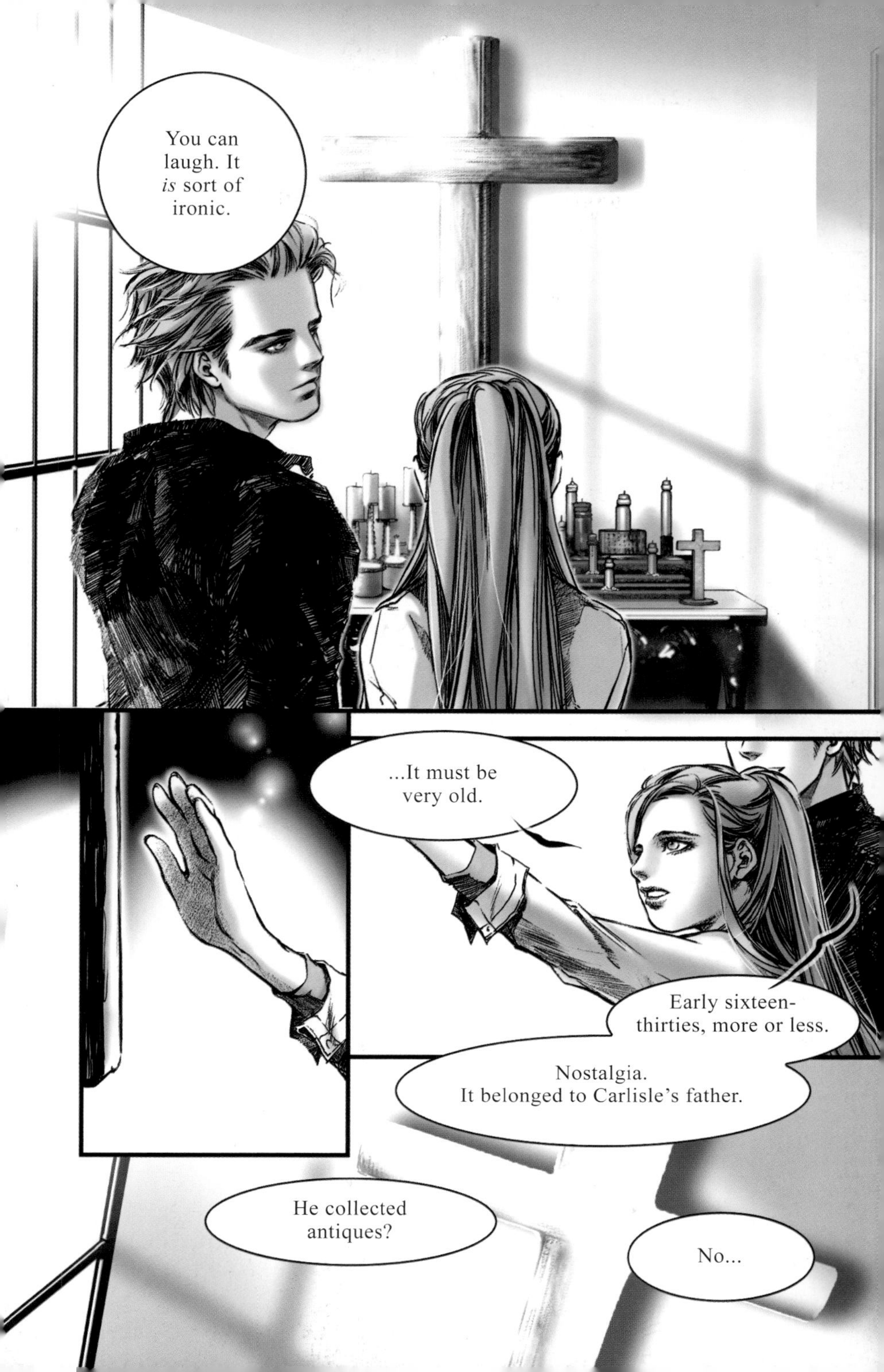
You can laugh. It *is* sort of ironic.
...It must be very old.
Early sixteen-thirties, more or less.
Nostalgia. It belonged to Carlisle's father.
He collected antiques?
No...

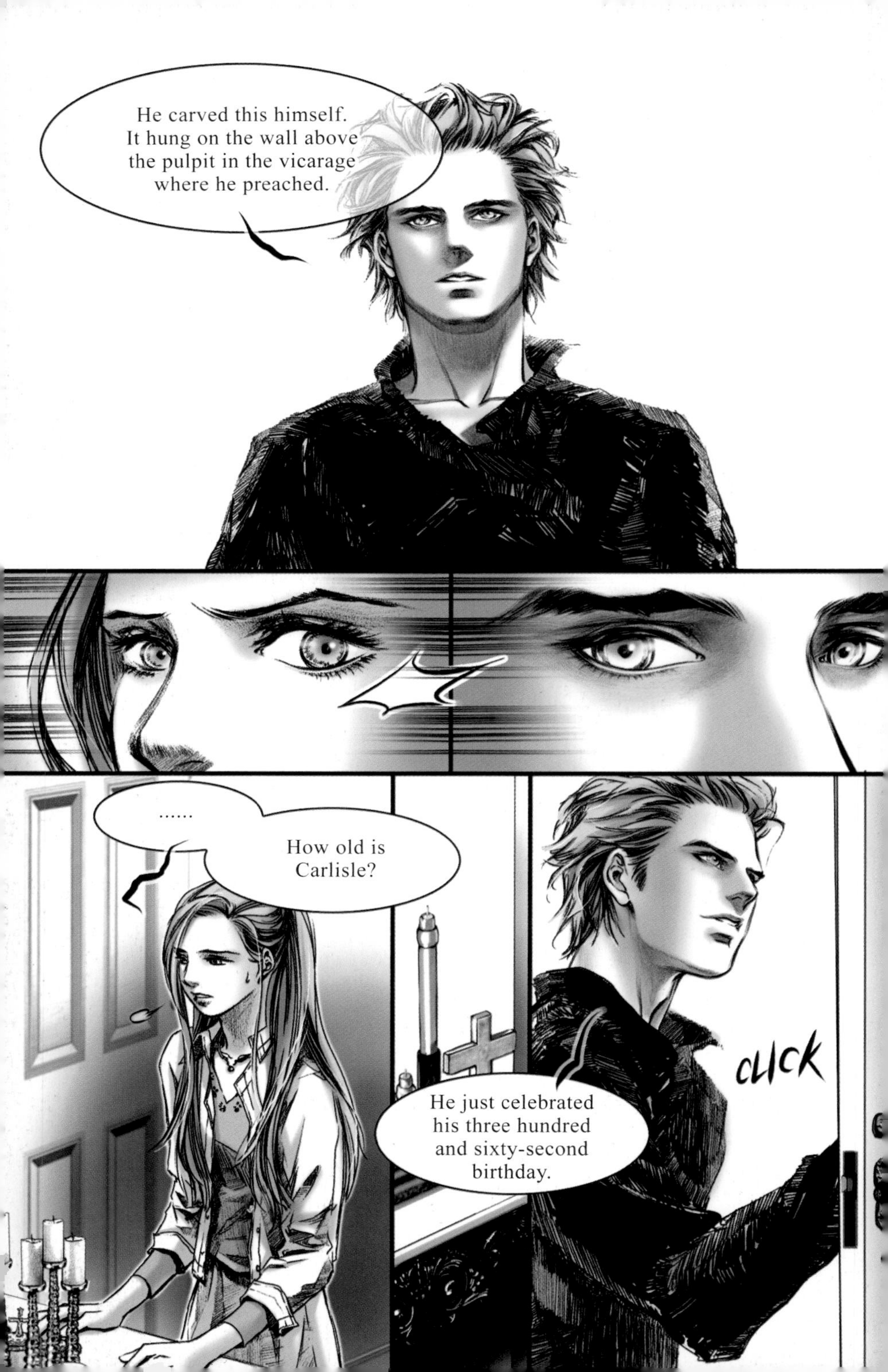
He carved this himself. It hung on the wall above the pulpit in the vicarage where he preached.
......
How old is Carlisle?
CLICK
He just celebrated his three hundred and sixty-second birthday.

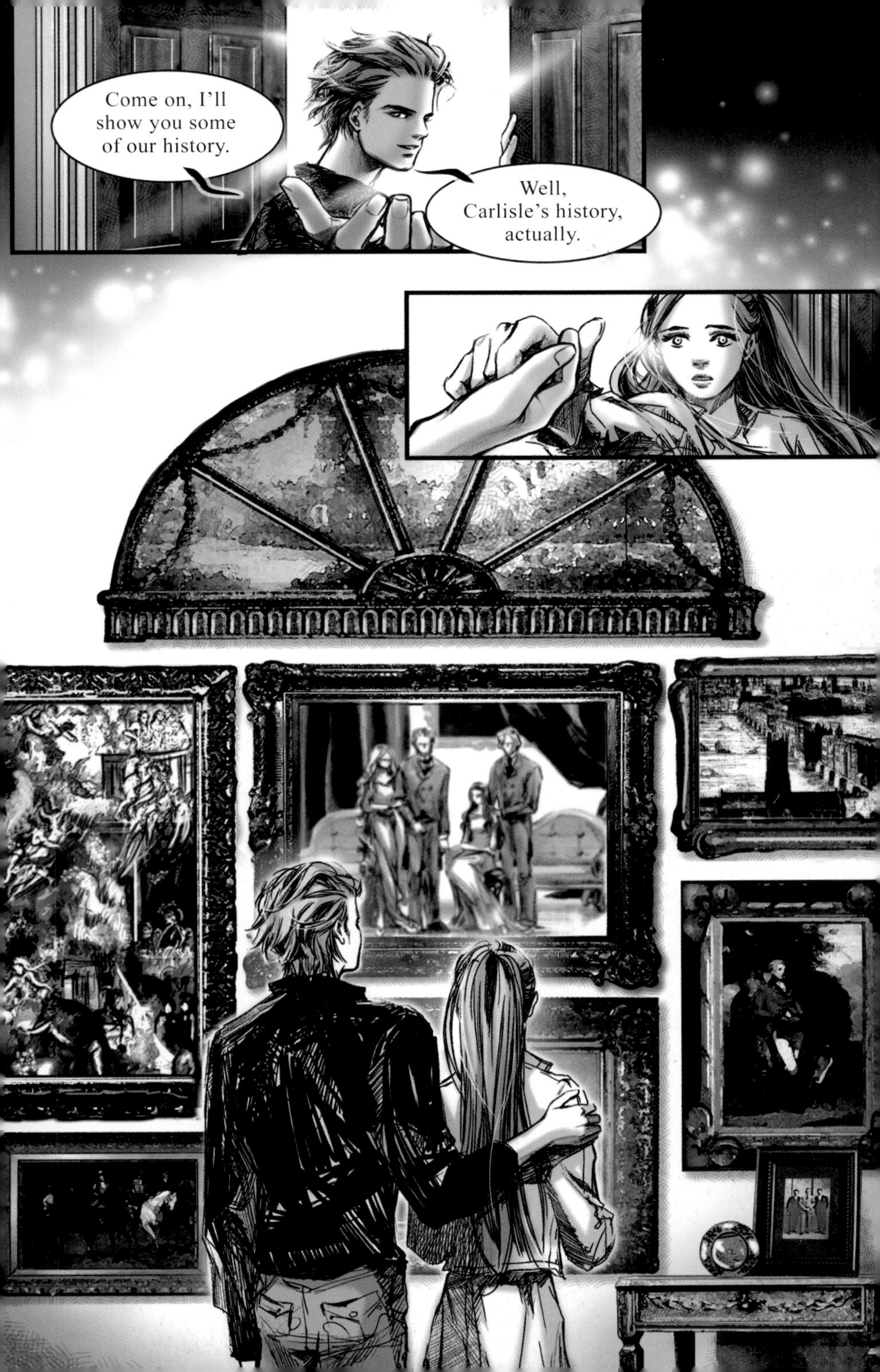
Come on, I'll show you some of our history.
Well, Carlisle's history, actually.

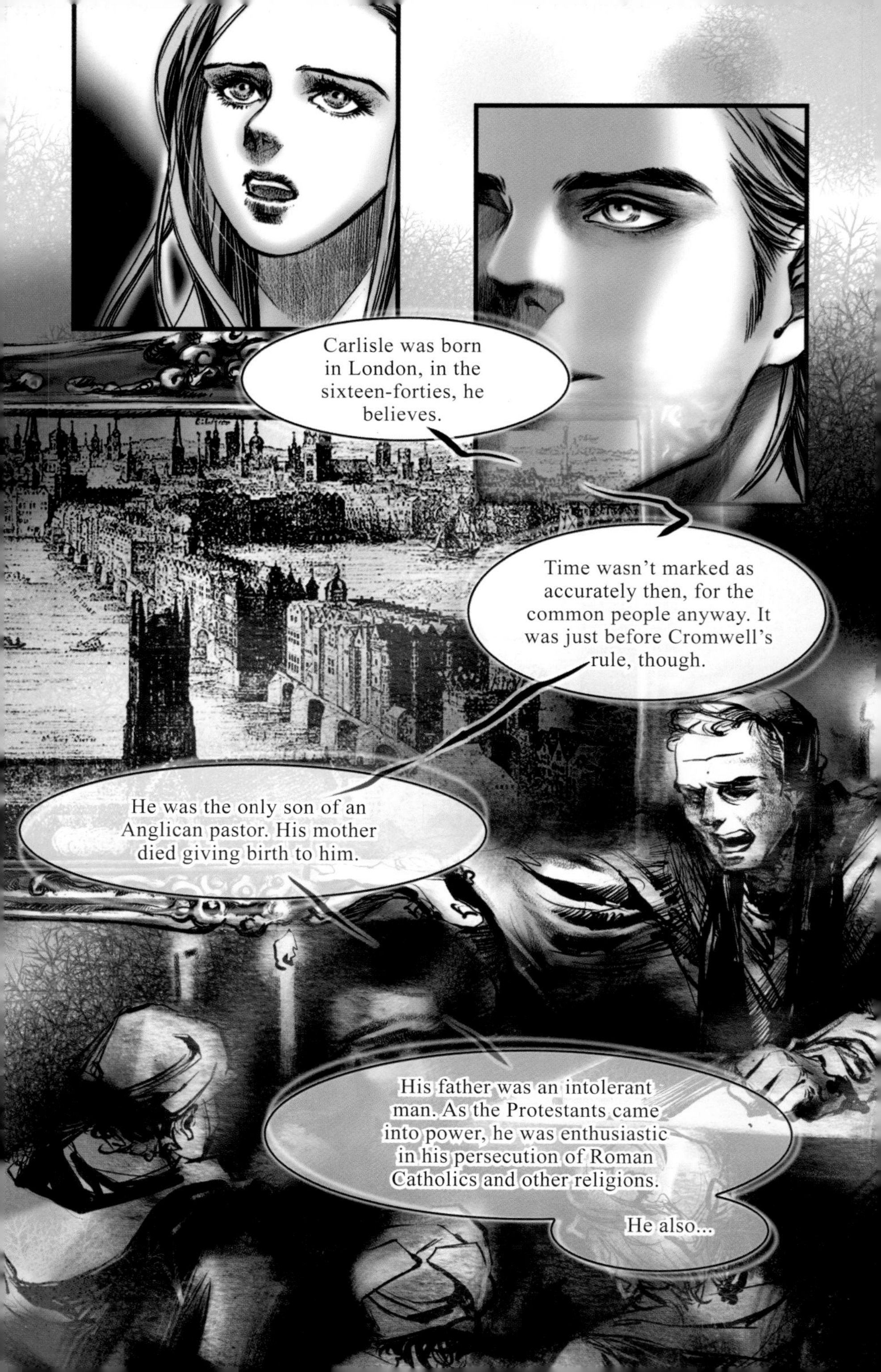
Carlisle was born in London, in the sixteen-forties, he believes.
Time wasn't marked as accurately then, for the common people anyway. It was just before Cromwell's rule, though.
He was the only son of an Anglican pastor. His mother died giving birth to him.
His father was an intolerant man. As the Protestants came into power, he was enthusiastic in his persecution of Roman Catholics and other religions.
He also...

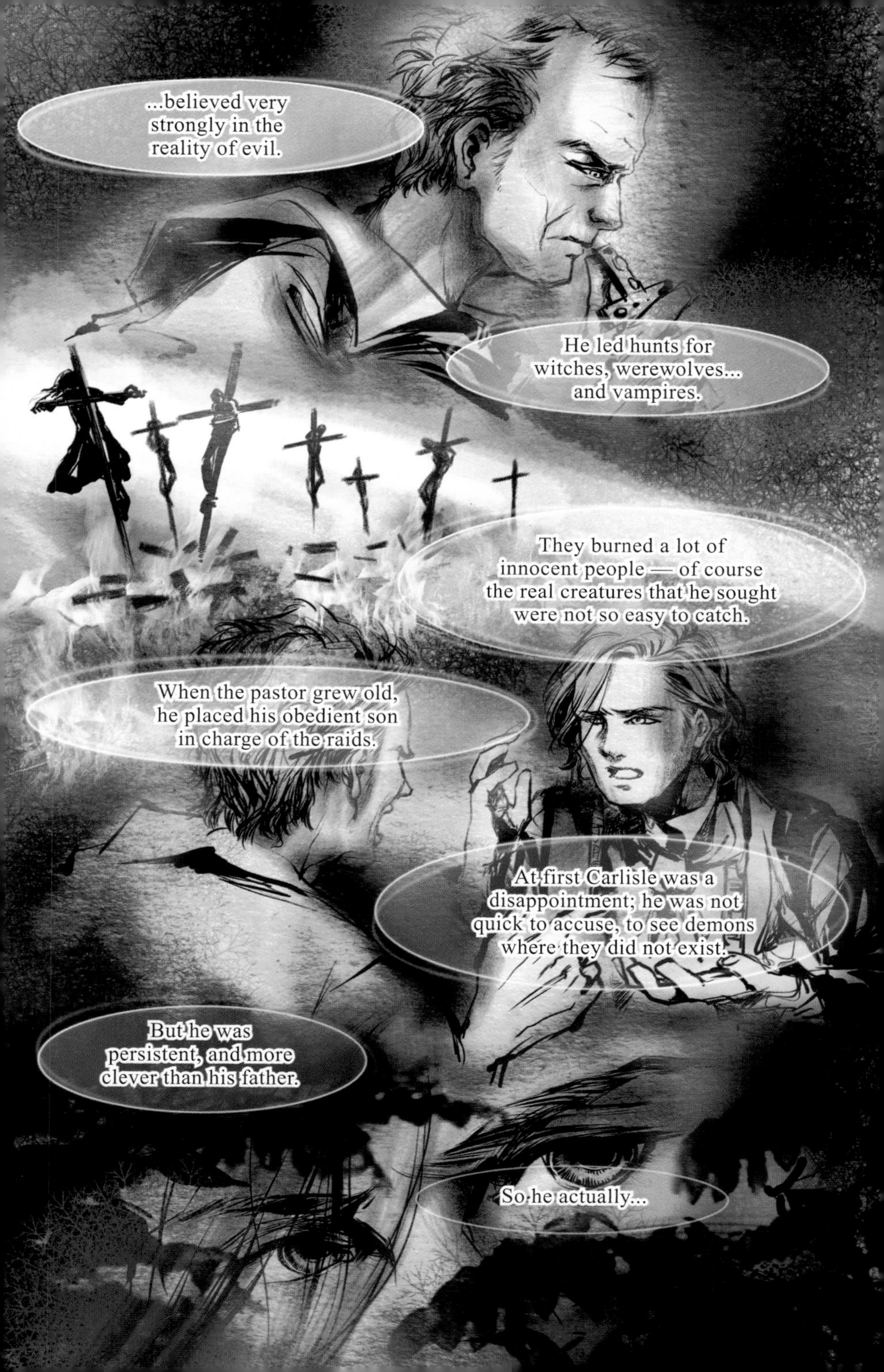
...believed very strongly in the reality of evil.
He led hunts for witches, werewolves... and vampires.
They burned a lot of innocent people — of course the real creatures that he sought were not so easy to catch.
When the pastor grew old, he placed his obedient son in charge of the raids.
At first Carlisle was a disappointment; he was not quick to accuse, to see demons where they did not exist.
But he was persistent, and more clever than his father.
So he actually...

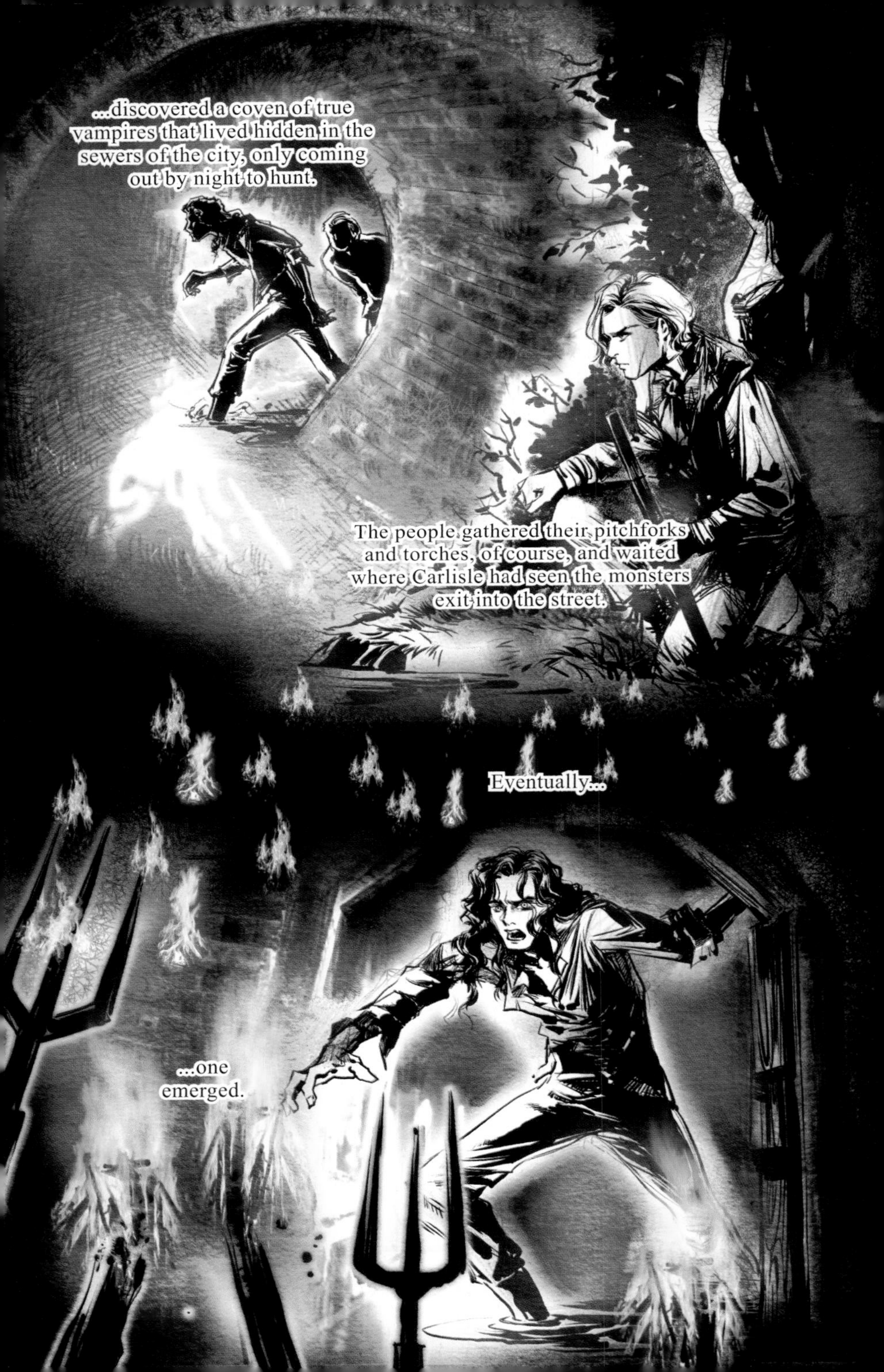
...discovered a coven of true vampires that lived hidden in the sewers of the city, only coming out by night to hunt.
The people gathered their pitchforks and torches, of course, and waited where Carlisle had seen the monsters exit into the street.
Eventually...
...one emerged.

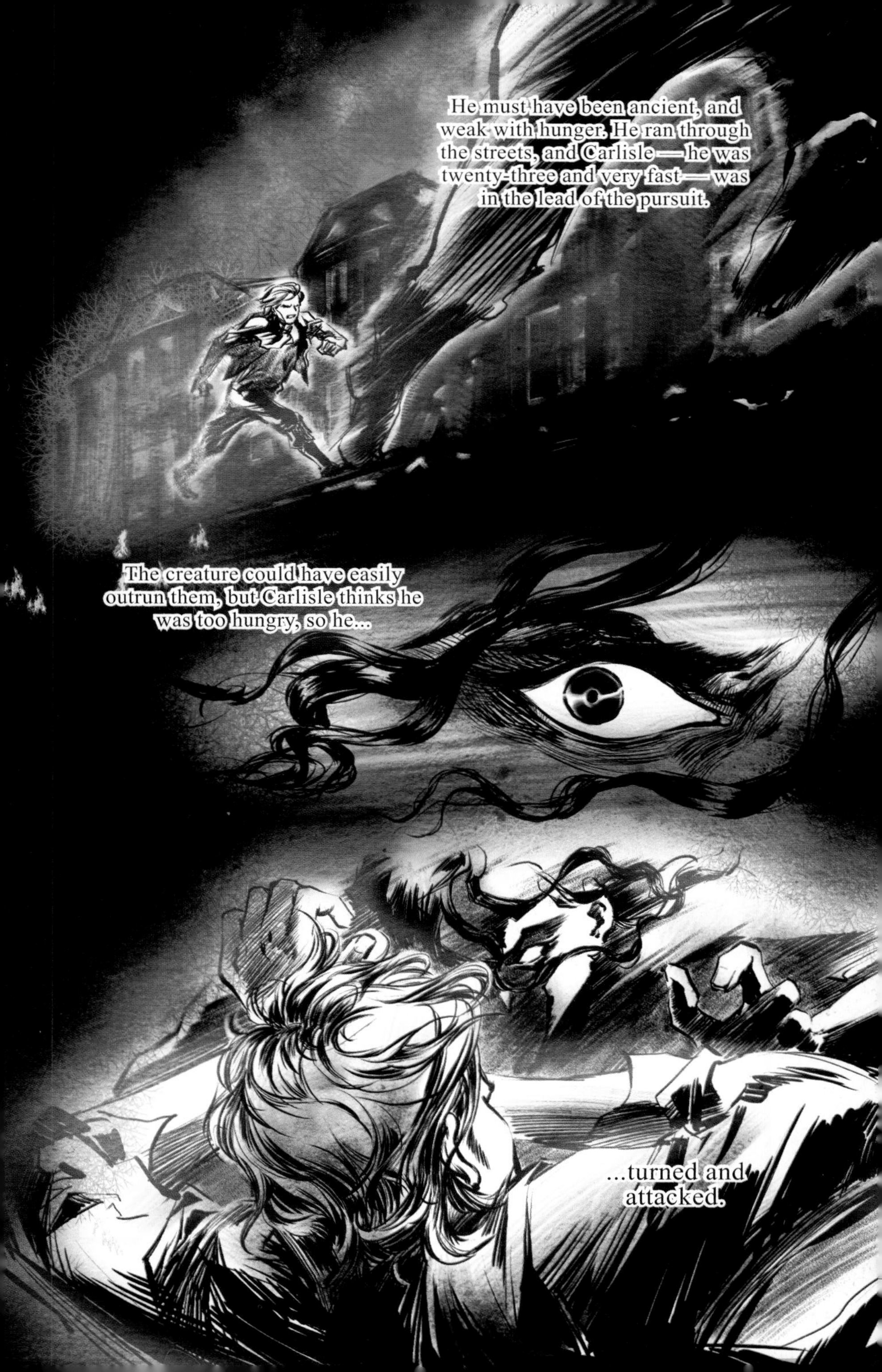
He must have been ancient, and weak with hunger. He ran through the streets, and Carlisle — he was twenty-three and very fast — was in the lead of the pursuit.
The creature could have easily outrun them, but Carlisle thinks he was too hungry, so he...
...turned and attacked.

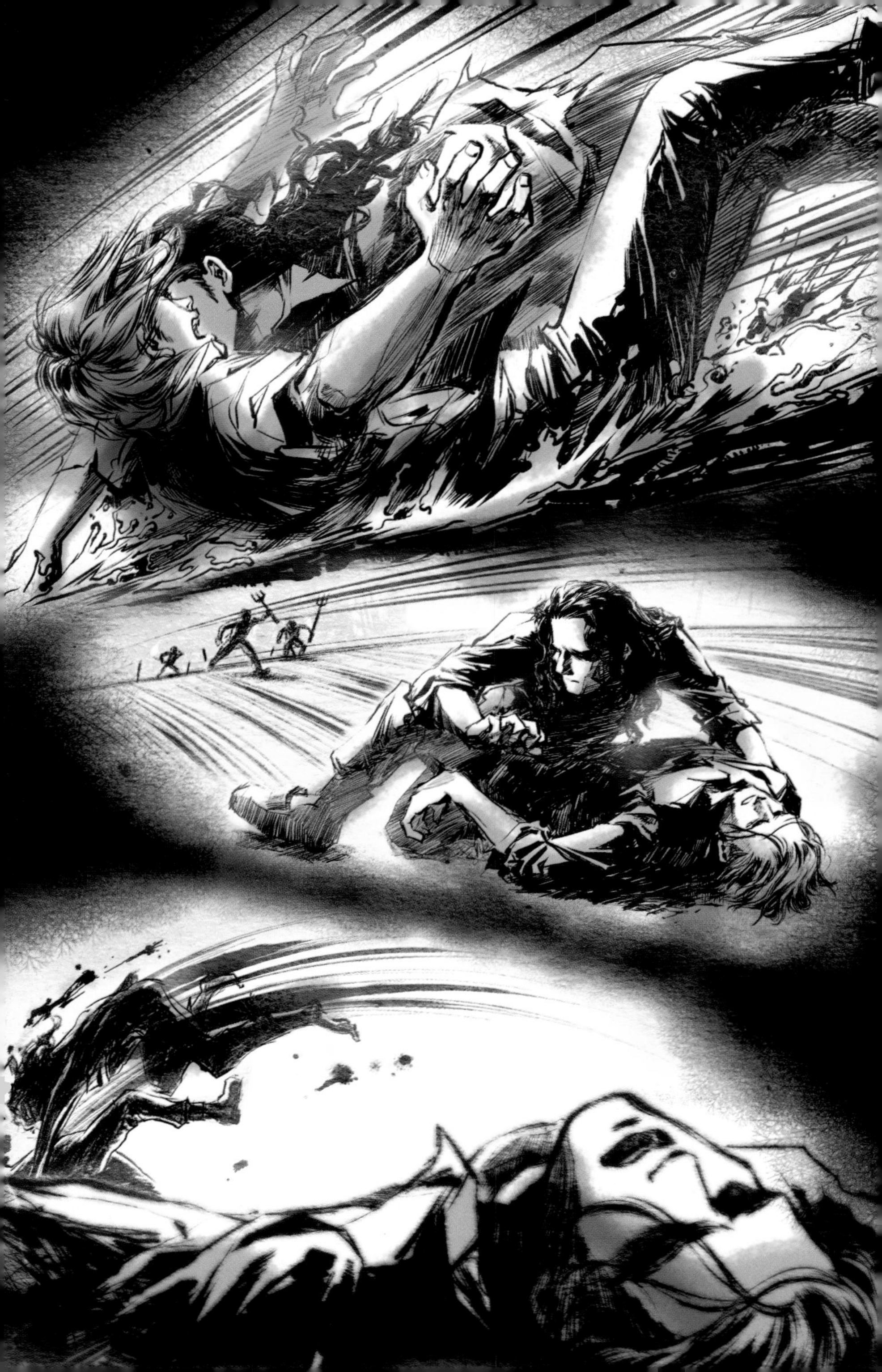

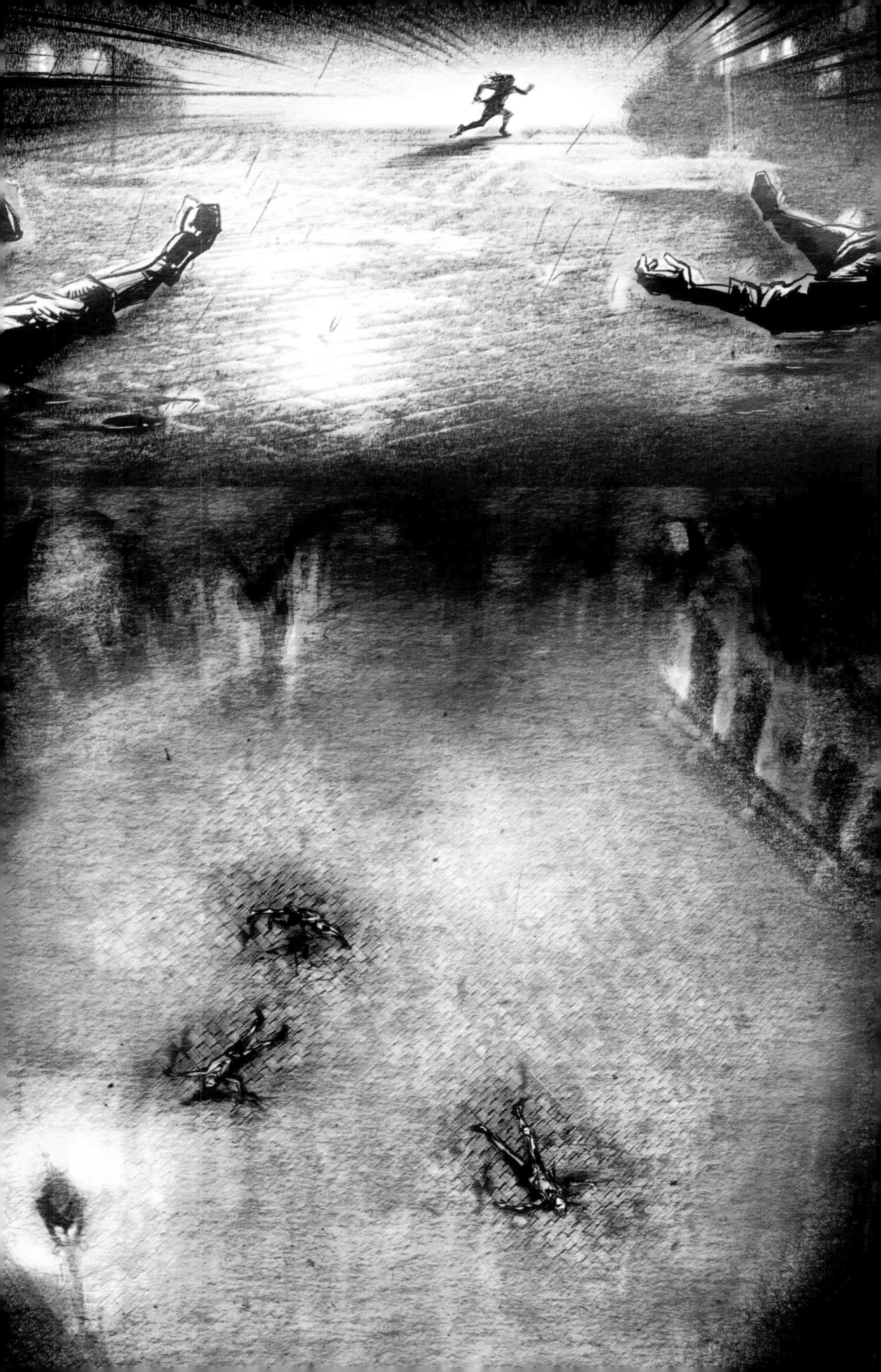

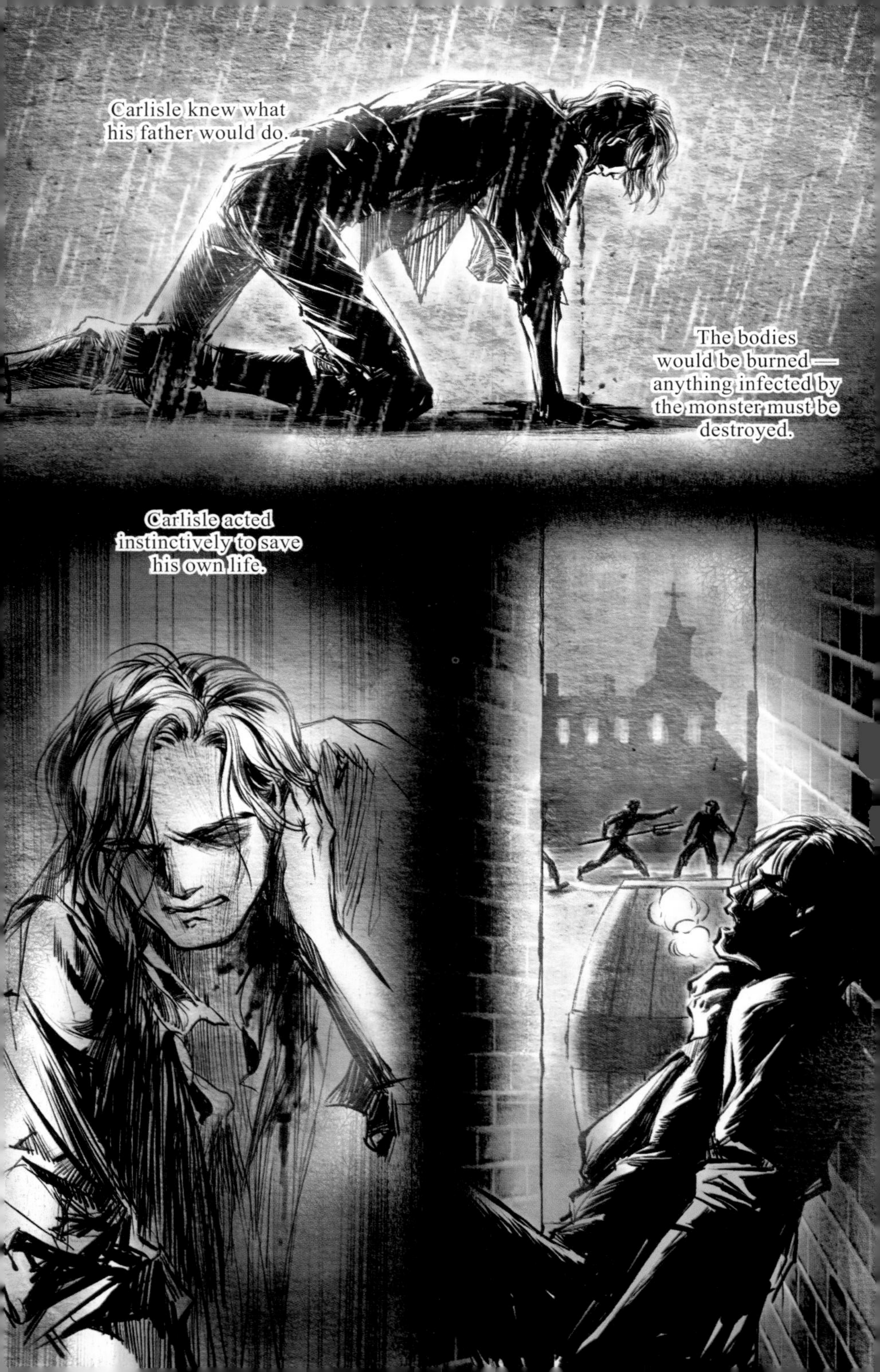
Carlisle knew what his father would do.
The bodies would be burned — anything infected by the monster must be destroyed.
Carlisle acted instinctively to save his own life.

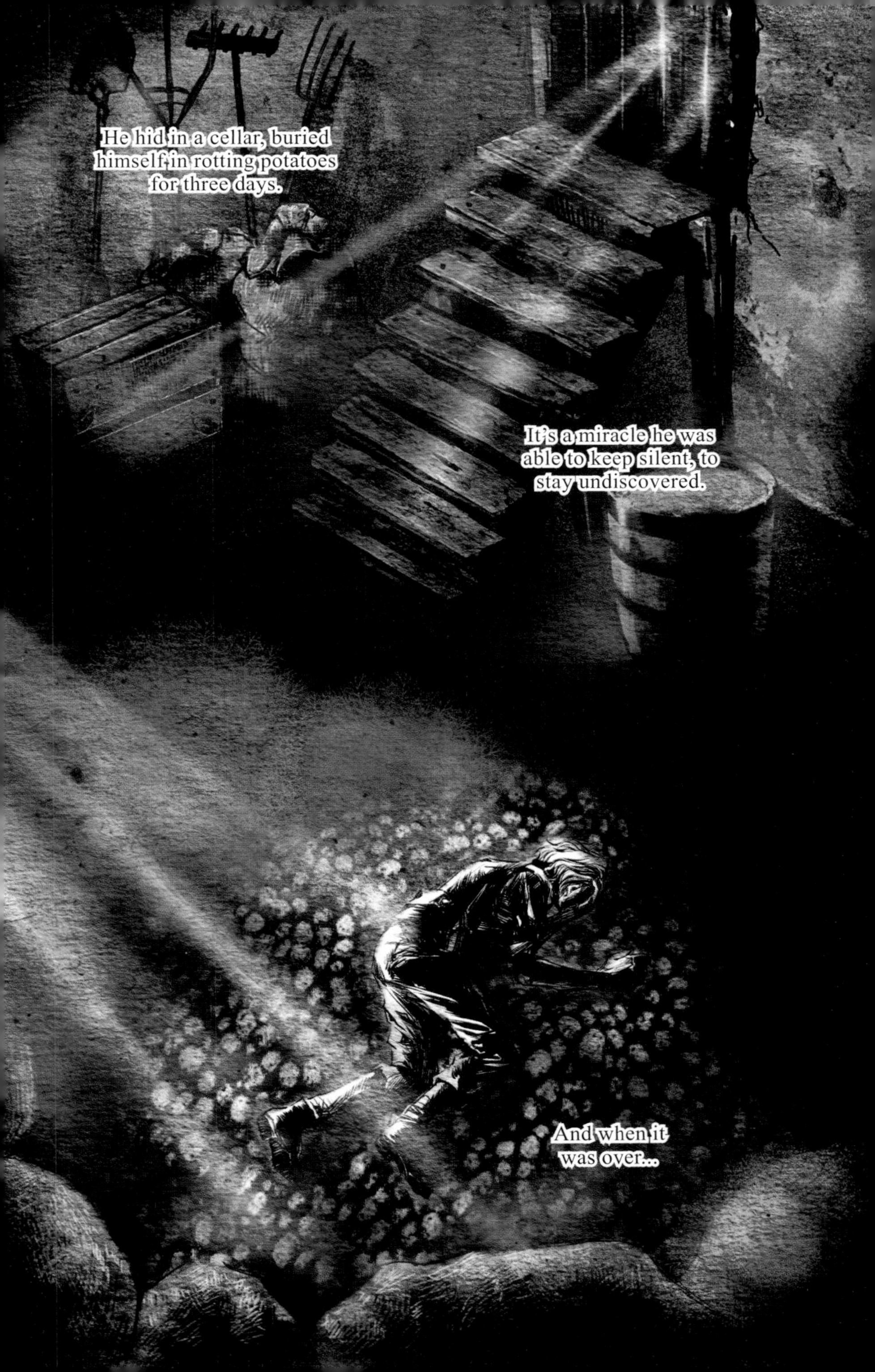
He hid in a cellar, buried himself in rotting potatoes for three days.
It's a miracle he was able to keep silent, to stay undiscovered.
And when it was over...

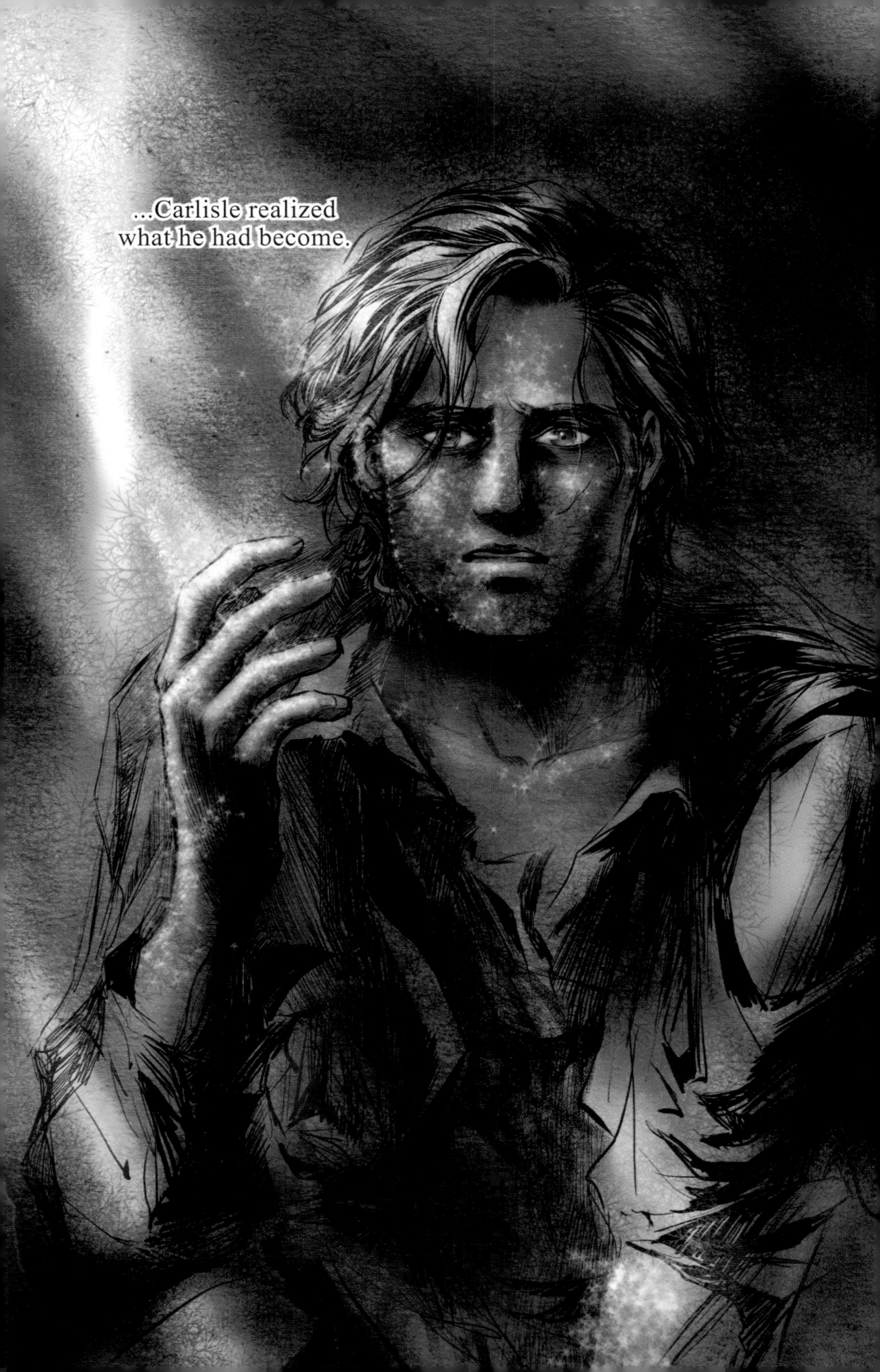
...Carlisle realized
what he had become.

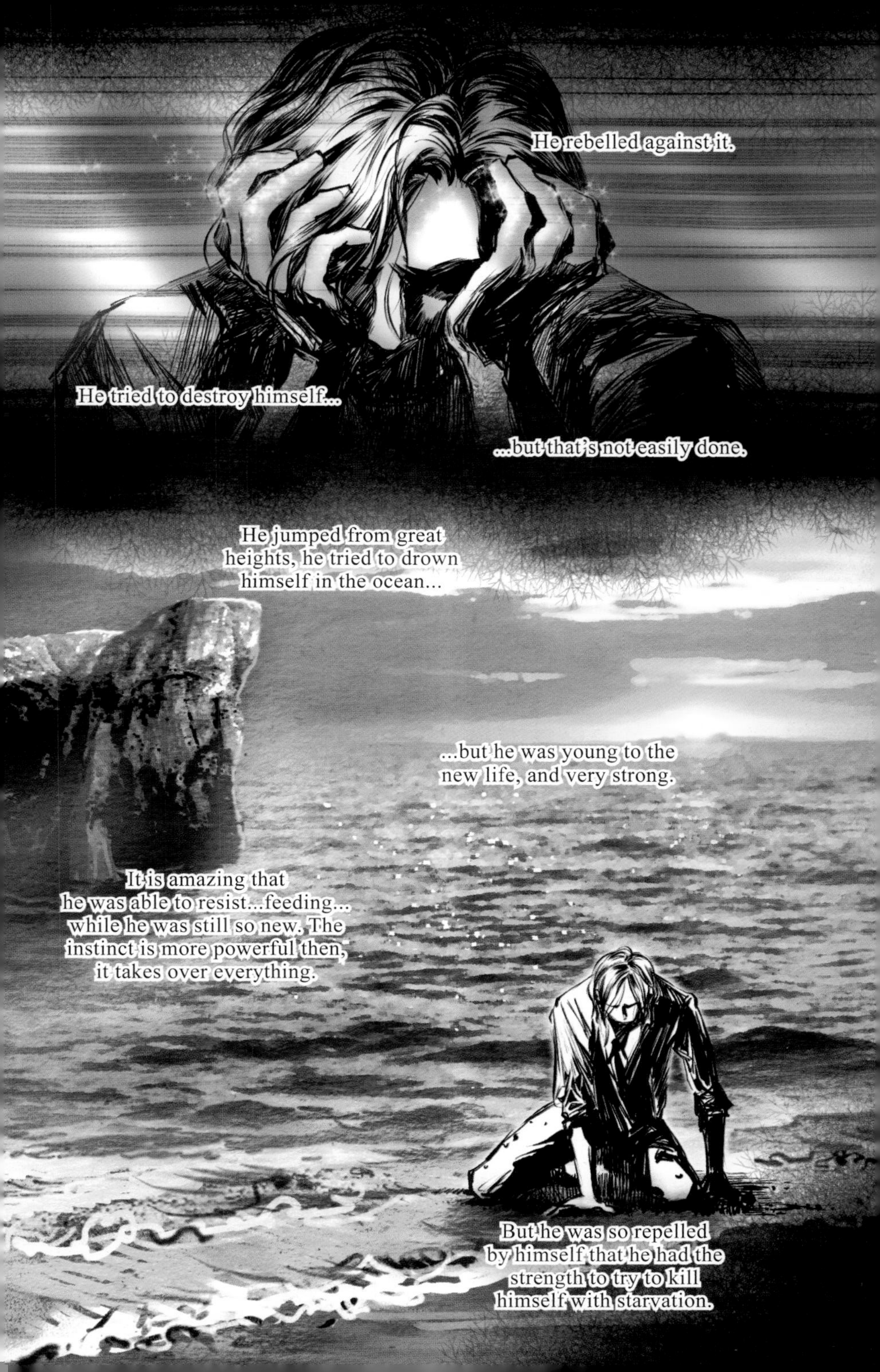
He rebelled against it.
He tried to destroy himself...
...but that's not easily done.
He jumped from great heights, he tried to drown himself in the ocean...
...but he was young to the new life, and very strong.
It is amazing that he was able to resist...feeding... while he was still so new. The instinct is more powerful then, it takes over everything.
But he was so repelled by himself that he had the strength to try to kill himself with starvation.

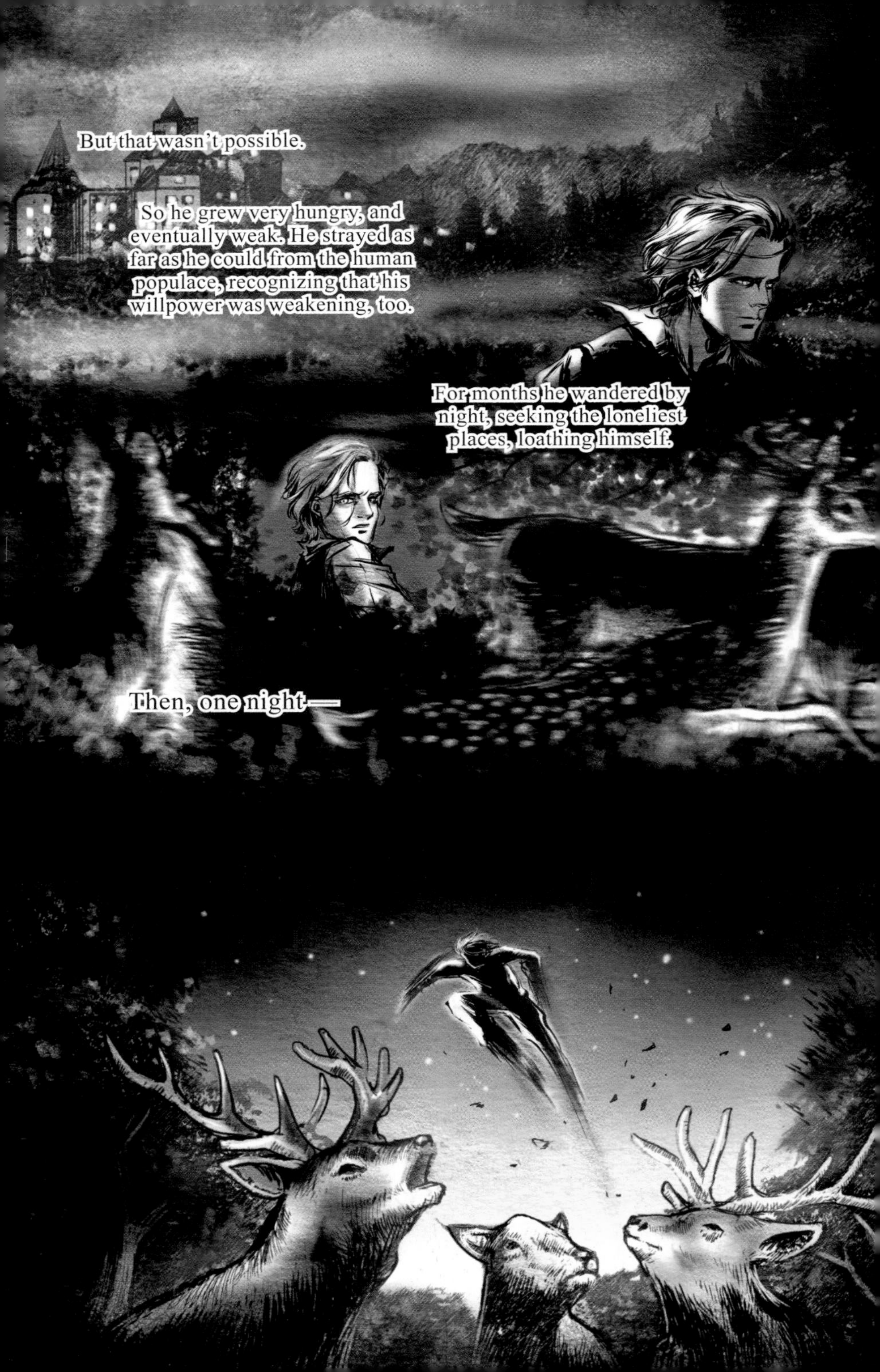
But that wasn't possible.
So he grew very hungry, and eventually weak. He strayed as far as he could from the human populace, recognizing that his willpower was weakening, too.
For months he wandered by night, seeking the loneliest places, loathing himself.
Then, one night—

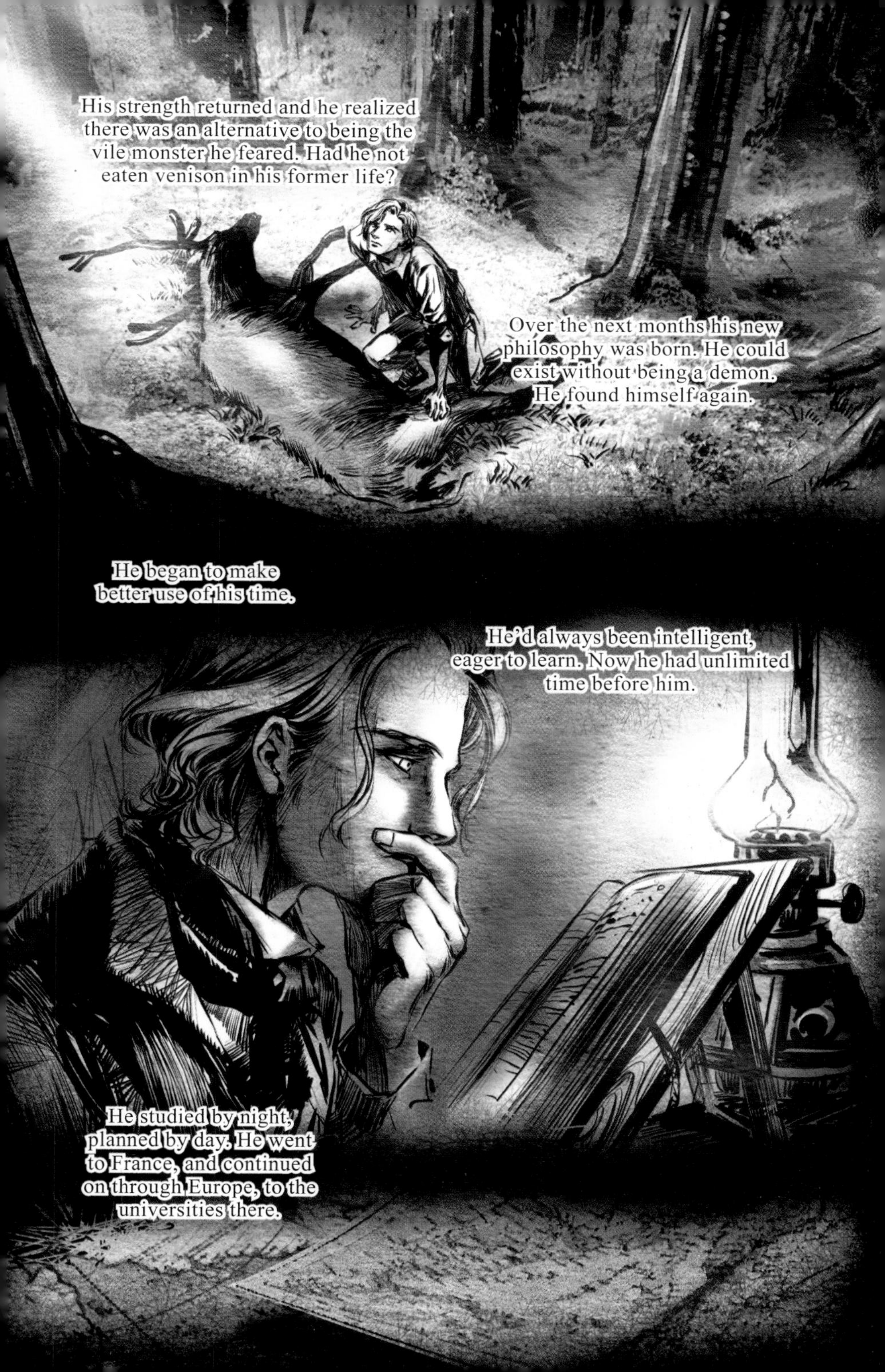
His strength returned and he realized there was an alternative to being the vile monster he feared. Had he not eaten venison in his former life?
Over the next months his new philosophy was born. He could exist without being a demon. He found himself again.
He began to make better use of his time.
He'd always been intelligent, eager to learn. Now he had unlimited time before him.
He studied by night, planned by day. He went to France, and continued on through Europe, to the universities there.

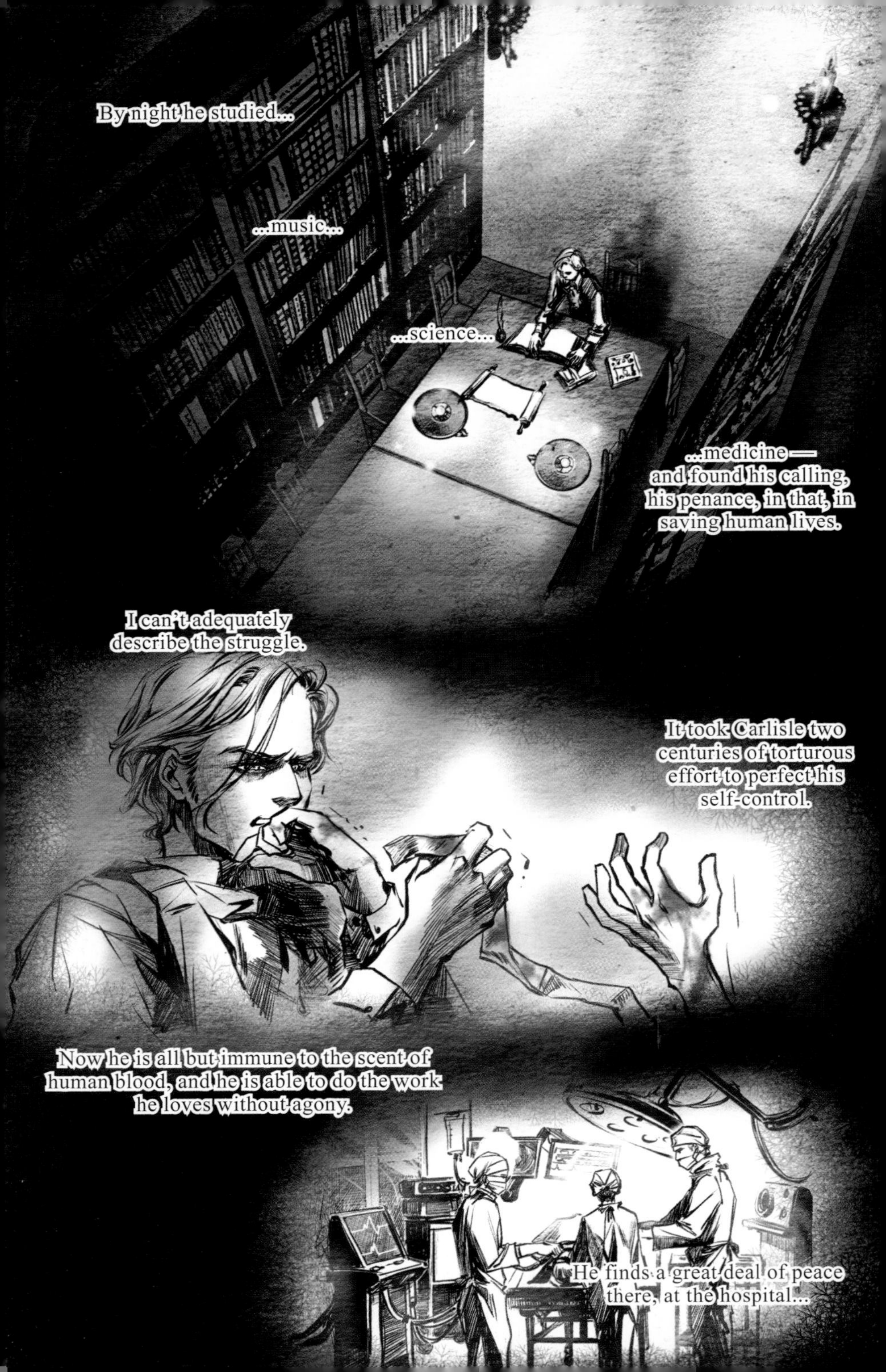
By night he studied...
...music...
...science...
...medicine — and found his calling, his penance, in that, in saving human lives.
I can't adequately describe the struggle.
It took Carlisle two centuries of torturous effort to perfect his self-control.
Now he is all but immune to the scent of human blood, and he is able to do the work he loves without agony.
He finds a great deal of peace there, at the hospital...

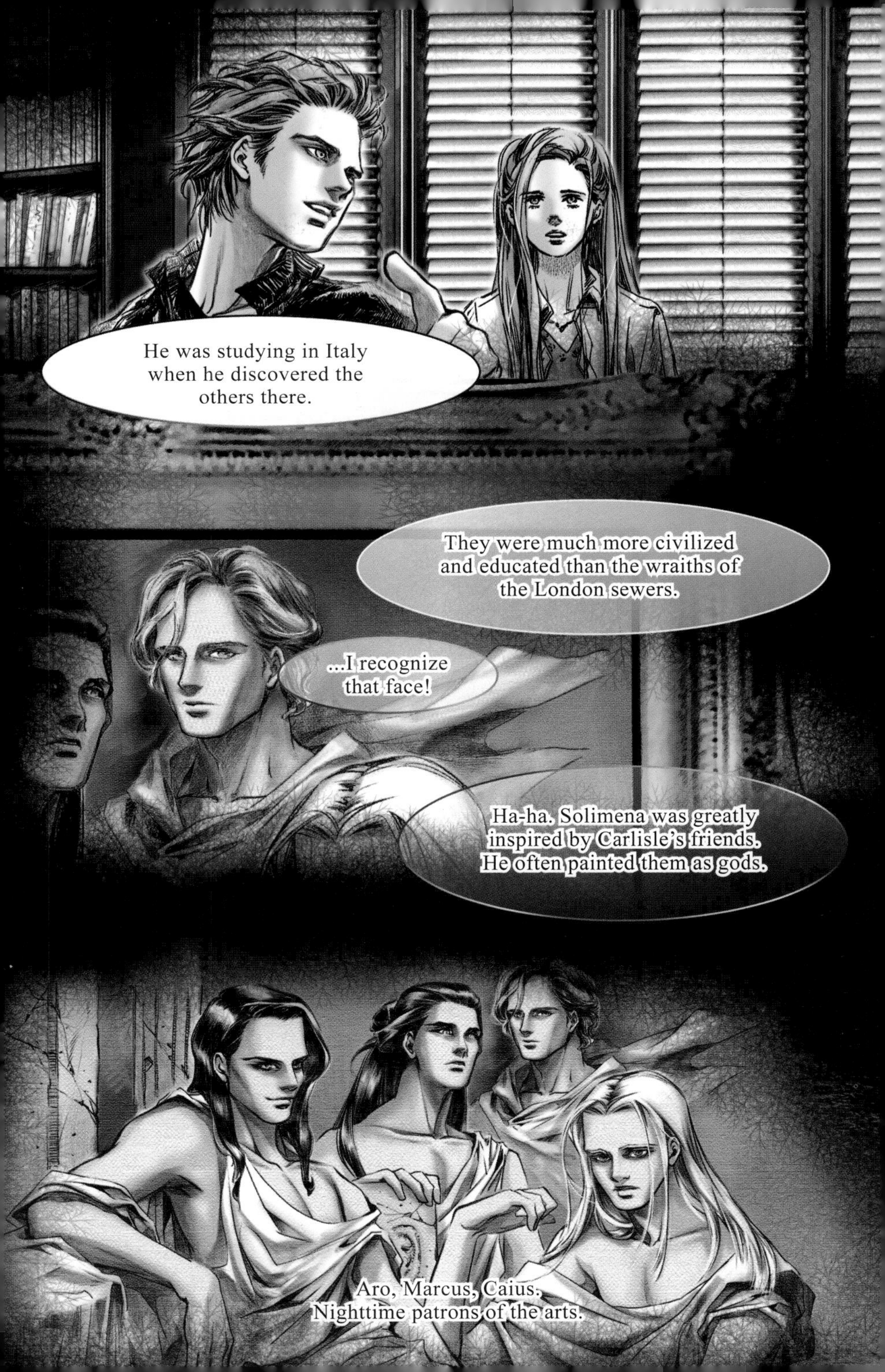
He was studying in Italy when he discovered the others there.
They were much more civilized and educated than the wraiths of the London sewers.
...I recognize that face!
Ha-ha. Solimena was greatly inspired by Carlisle's friends. He often painted them as gods.
Aro, Marcus, Caius. Nighttime patrons of the arts.

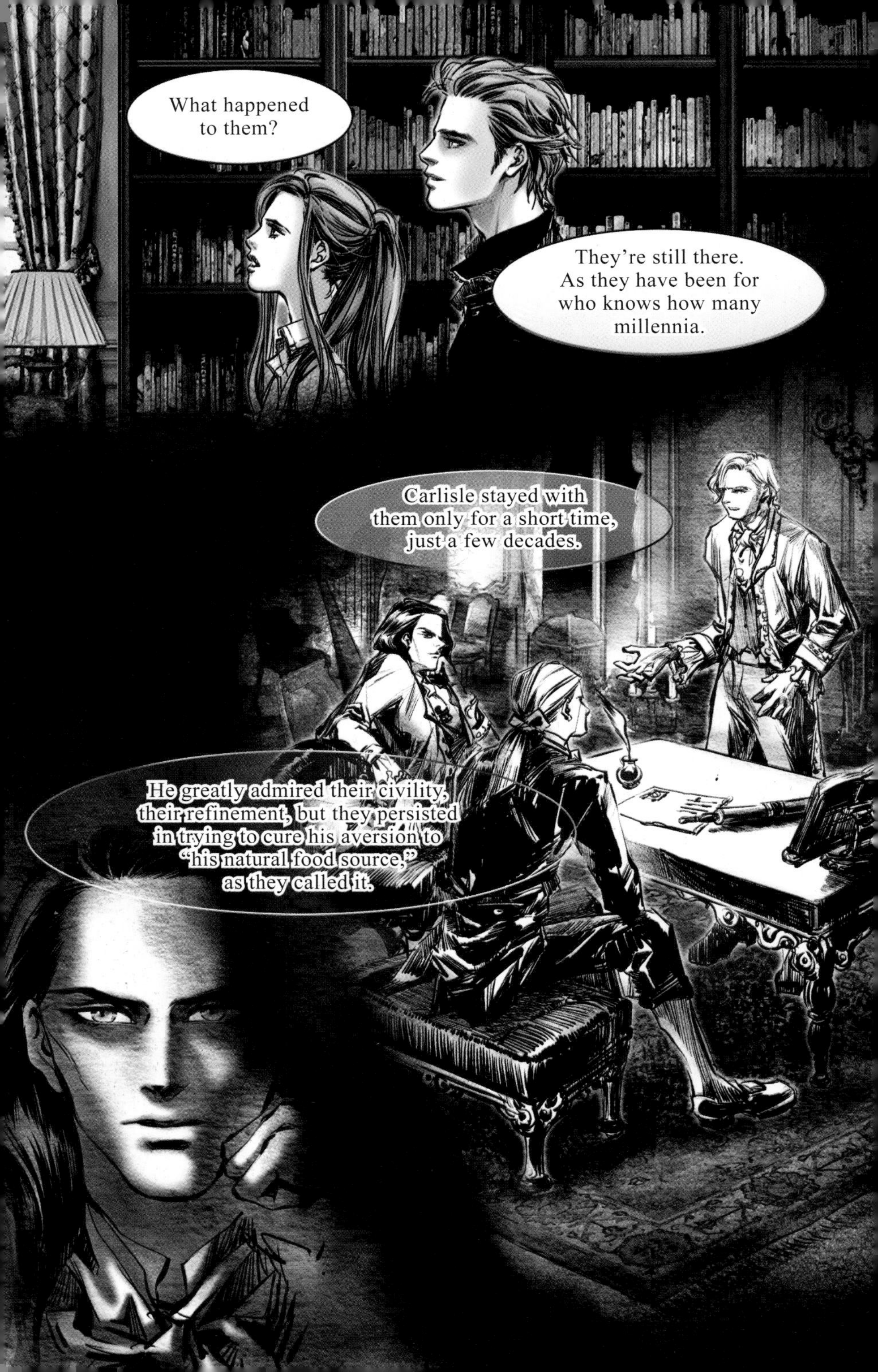
What happened to them?
They're still there. As they have been for who knows how many millennia.
Carlisle stayed with them only for a short time, just a few decades.
He greatly admired their civility, their refinement, but they persisted in trying to cure his aversion to "his natural food source," as they called it.

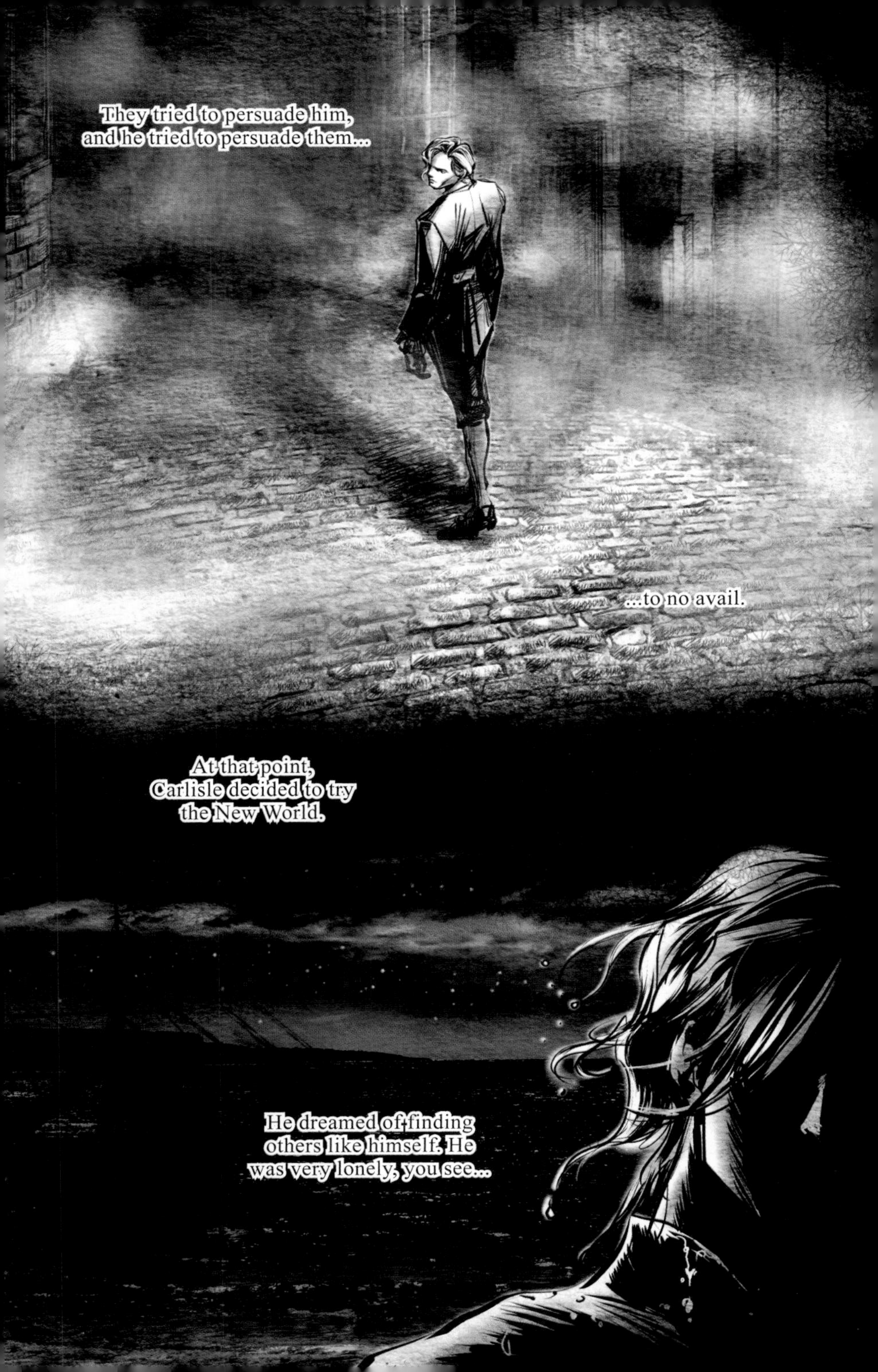
They tried to persuade him, and he tried to persuade them...
...to no avail.
At that point, Carlisle decided to try the New World.
He dreamed of finding others like himself. He was very lonely, you see...

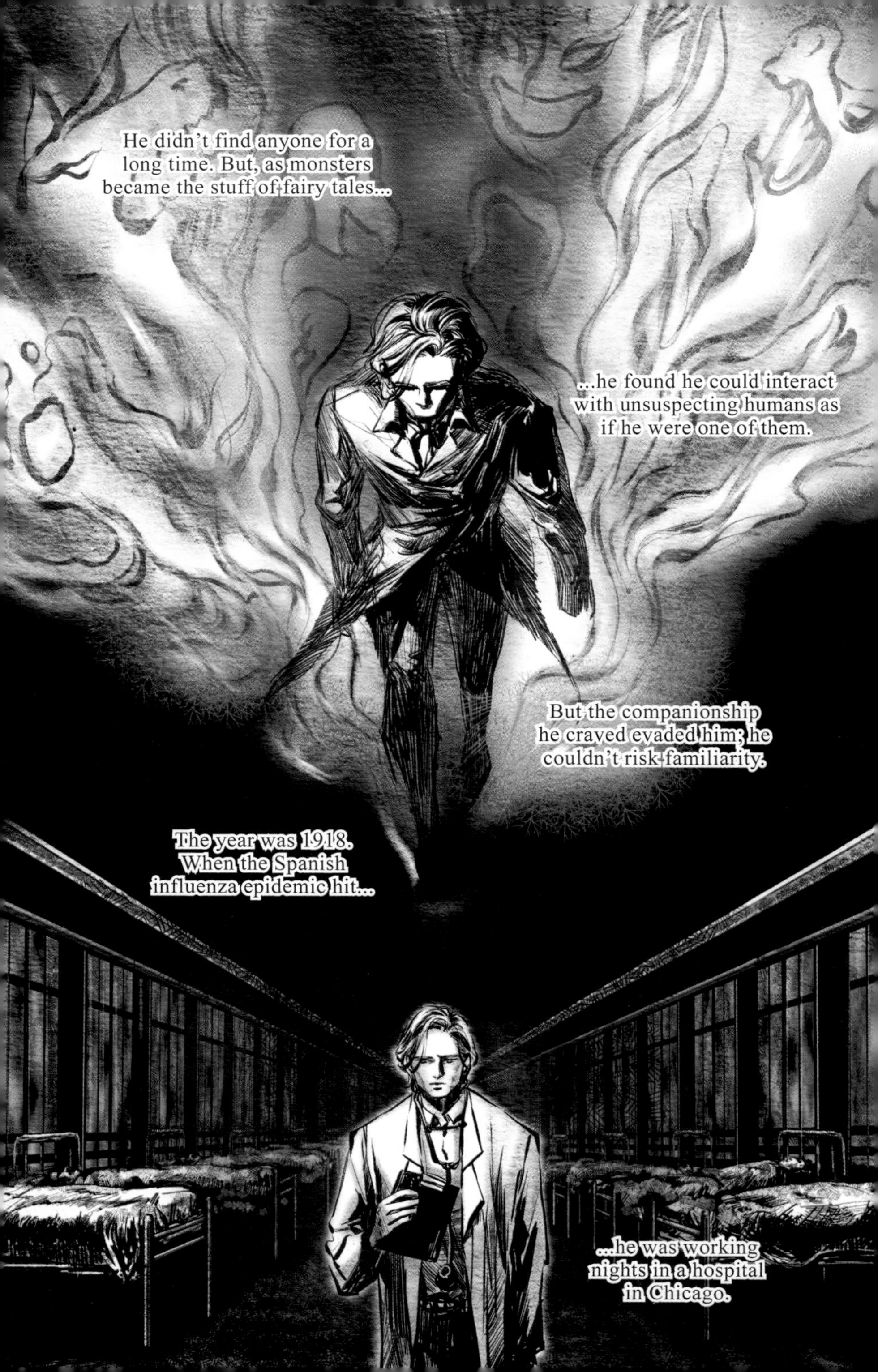
He didn't find anyone for a long time. But, as monsters became the stuff of fairy tales...
...he found he could interact with unsuspecting humans as if he were one of them.
But the companionship he craved evaded him; he couldn't risk familiarity.
The year was 1918. When the Spanish influenza epidemic hit...
...he was working nights in a hospital in Chicago.

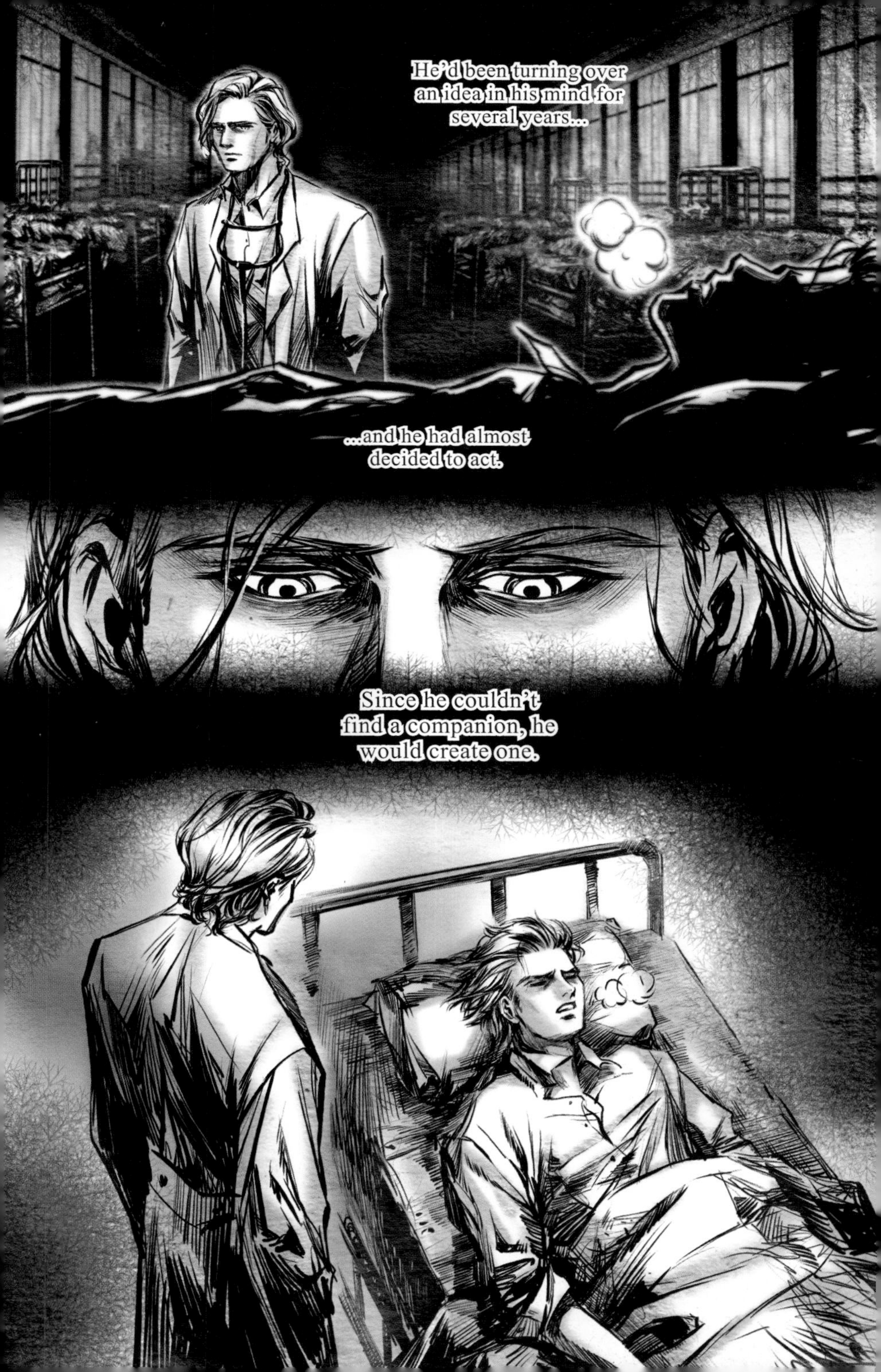
He'd been turning over an idea in his mind for several years...
...and he had almost decided to act.
Since he couldn't find a companion, he would create one.

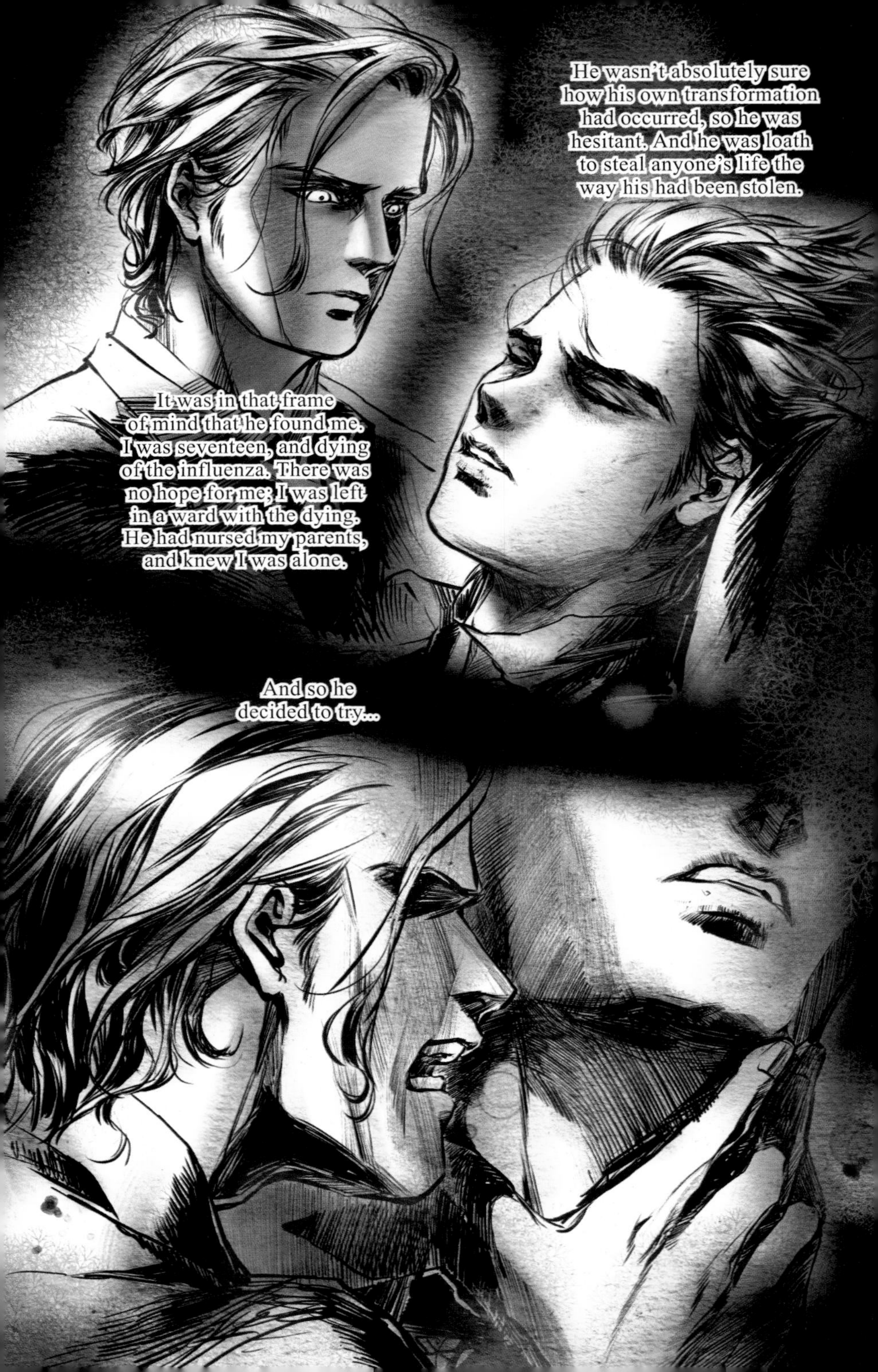
He wasn't absolutely sure how his own transformation had occurred, so he was hesitant. And he was loath to steal anyone's life the way his had been stolen.
It was in that frame of mind that he found me. I was seventeen, and dying of the influenza. There was no hope for me; I was left in a ward with the dying. He had nursed my parents, and knew I was alone.
And so he decided to try...

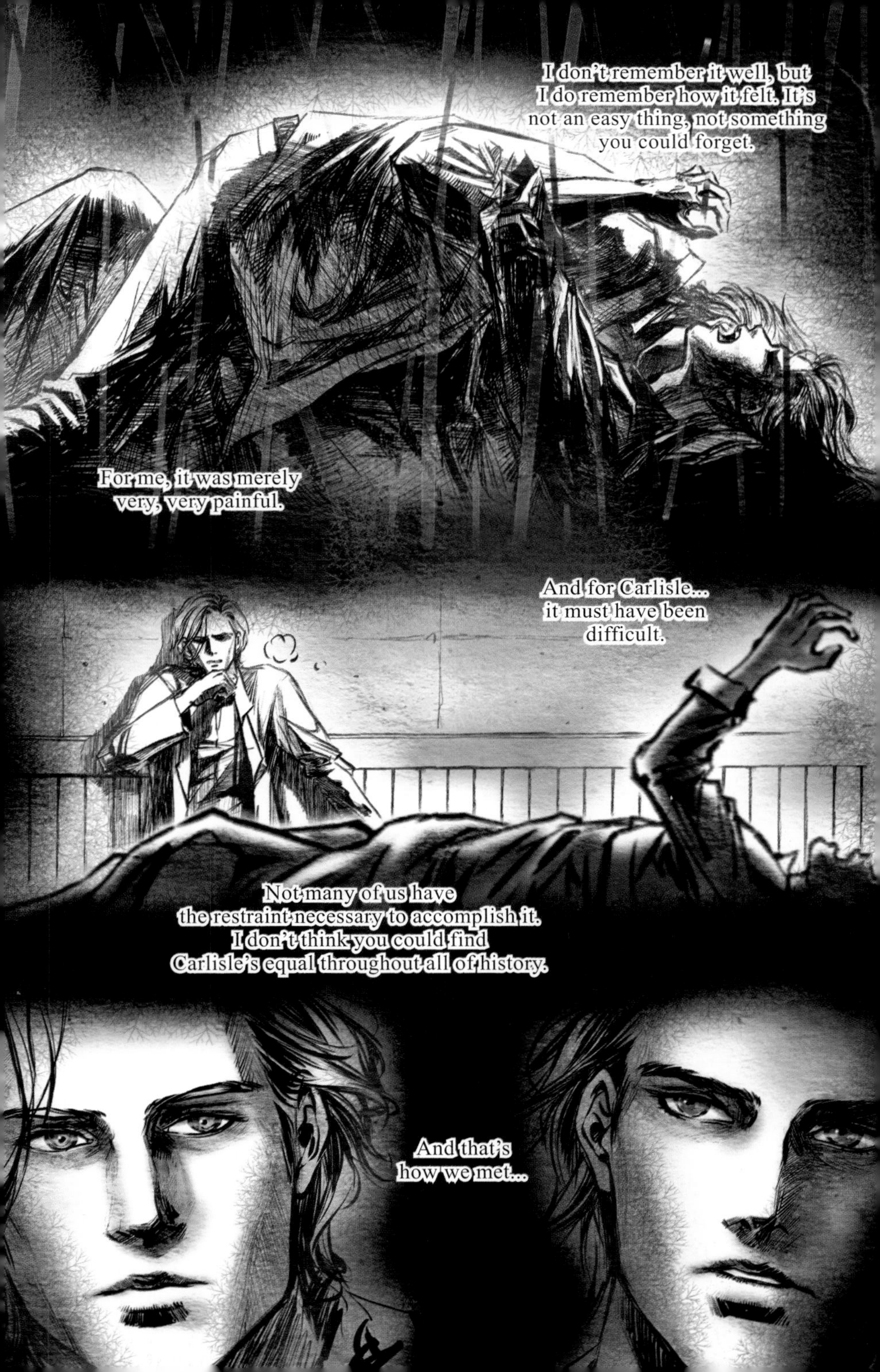
I don't remember it well, but I do remember how it felt. It's not an easy thing, not something you could forget.
For me, it was merely very, very painful.
And for Carlisle... it must have been difficult.
Not many of us have the restraint necessary to accomplish it. I don't think you could find Carlisle's equal throughout all of history.
And that's how we met...

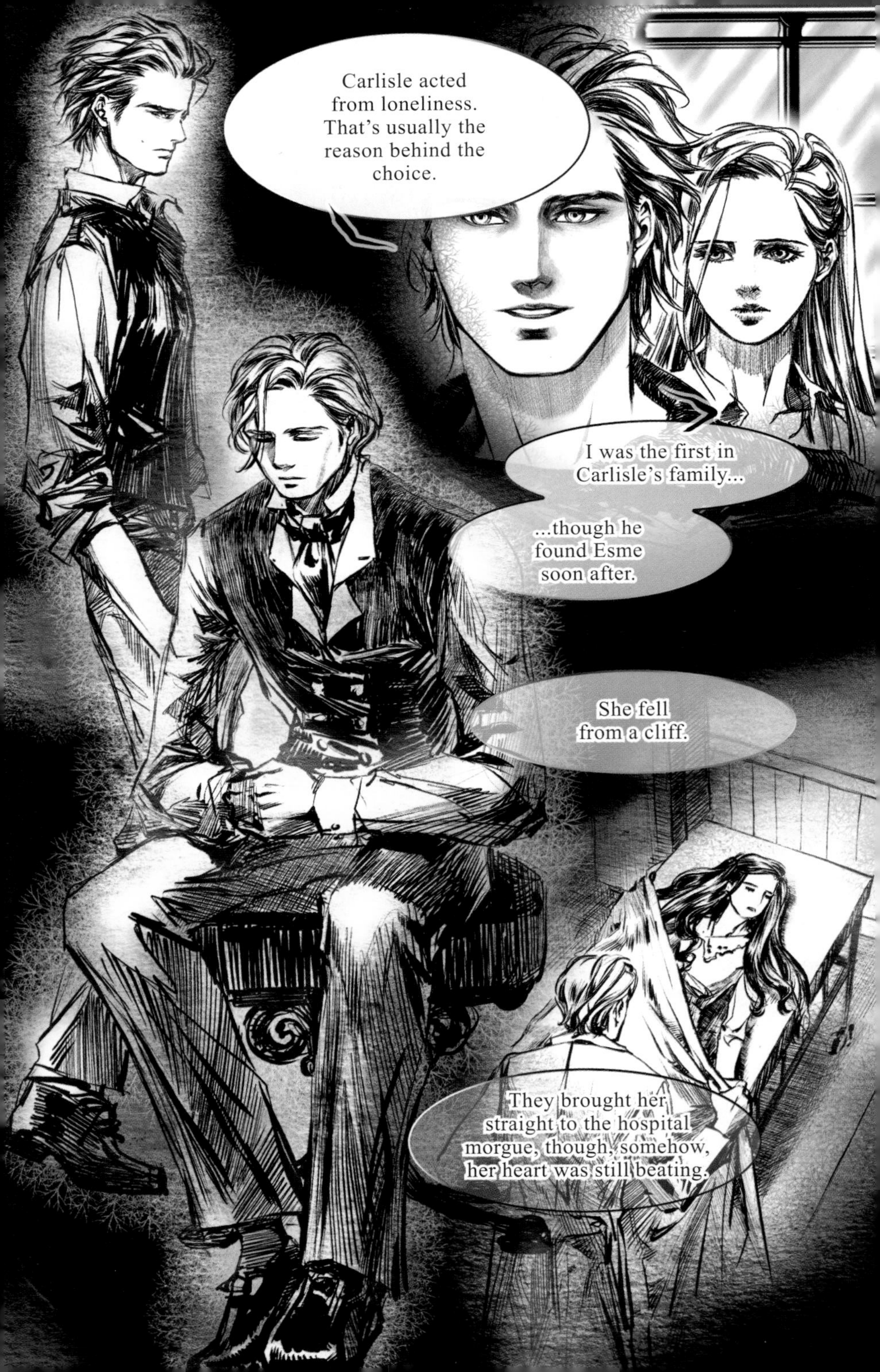
Carlisle acted from loneliness. That's usually the reason behind the choice.
I was the first in Carlisle's family...
...though he found Esme soon after.
She fell from a cliff.
They brought her straight to the hospital morgue, though, somehow, her heart was still beating.

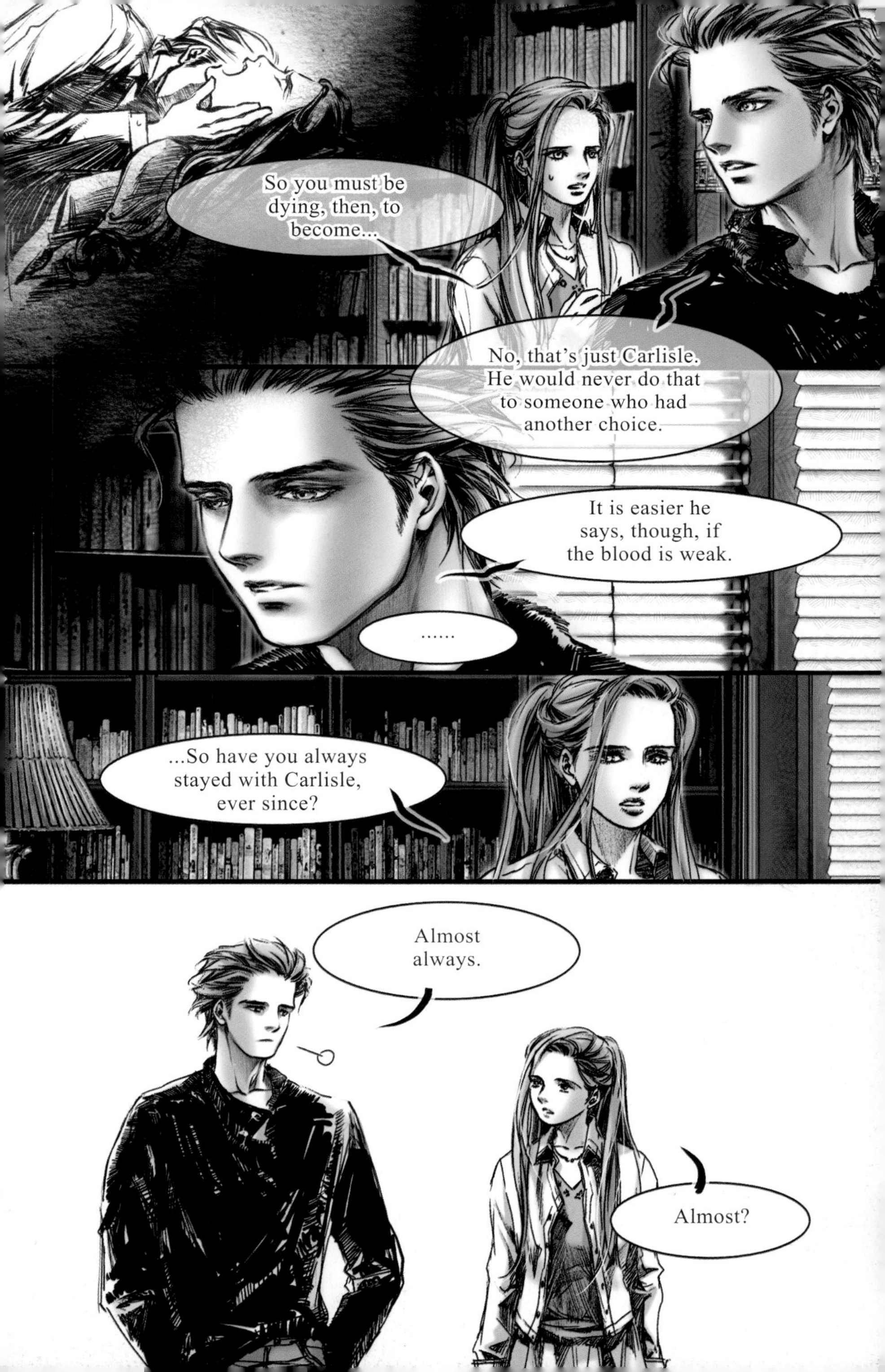

So you must be dying, then, to become...
No, that's just Carlisle. He would never do that to someone who had another choice.
It is easier he says, though, if the blood is weak.
......
...So have you always stayed with Carlisle, ever since?
Almost always.
Almost?

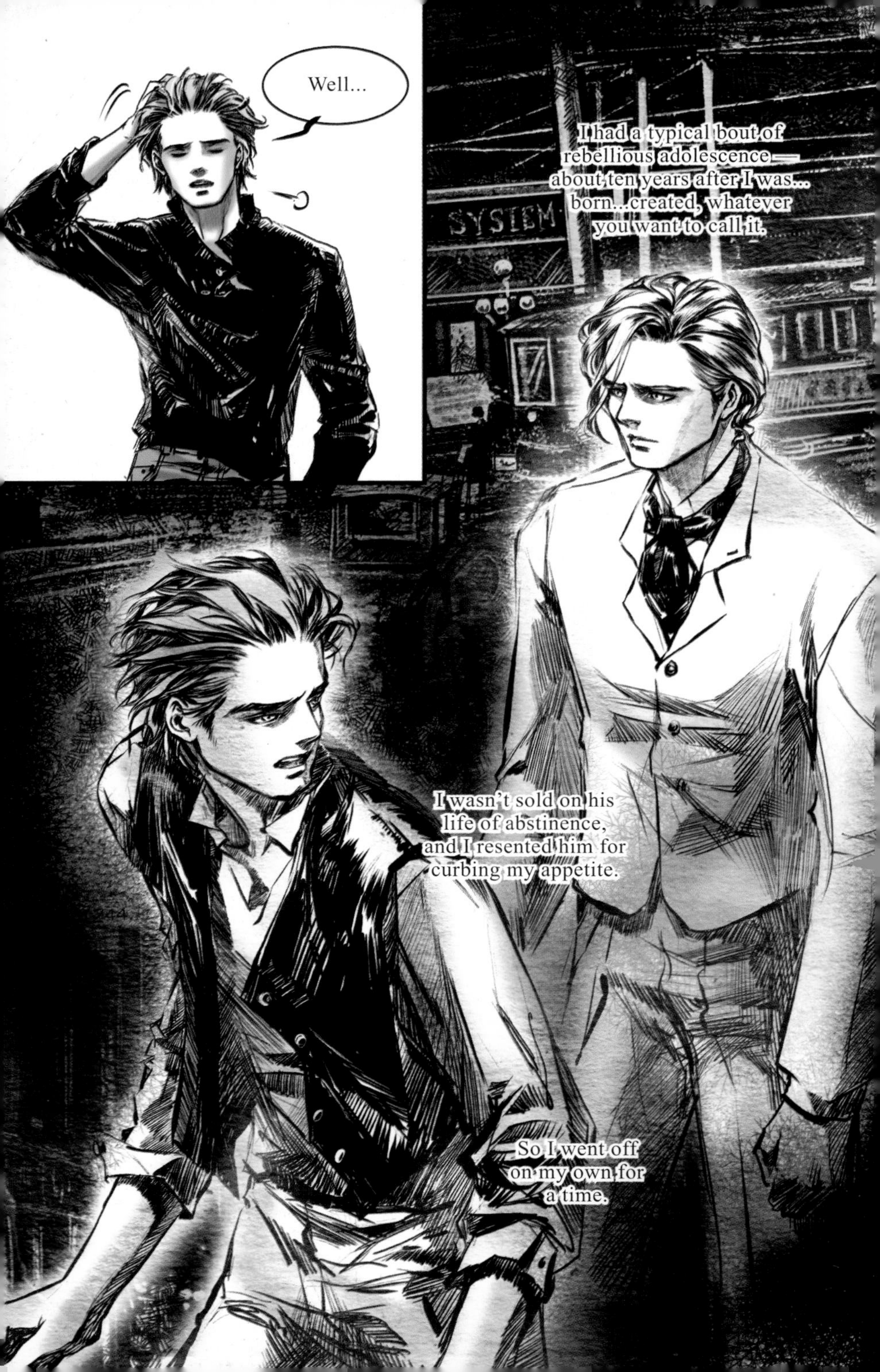
Well...
I had a typical bout of rebellious adolescence — about ten years after I was... born...created, whatever you want to call it.
SYSTEM
I wasn't sold on his life of abstinence, and I resented him for curbing my appetite.
So I went off on my own for a time.

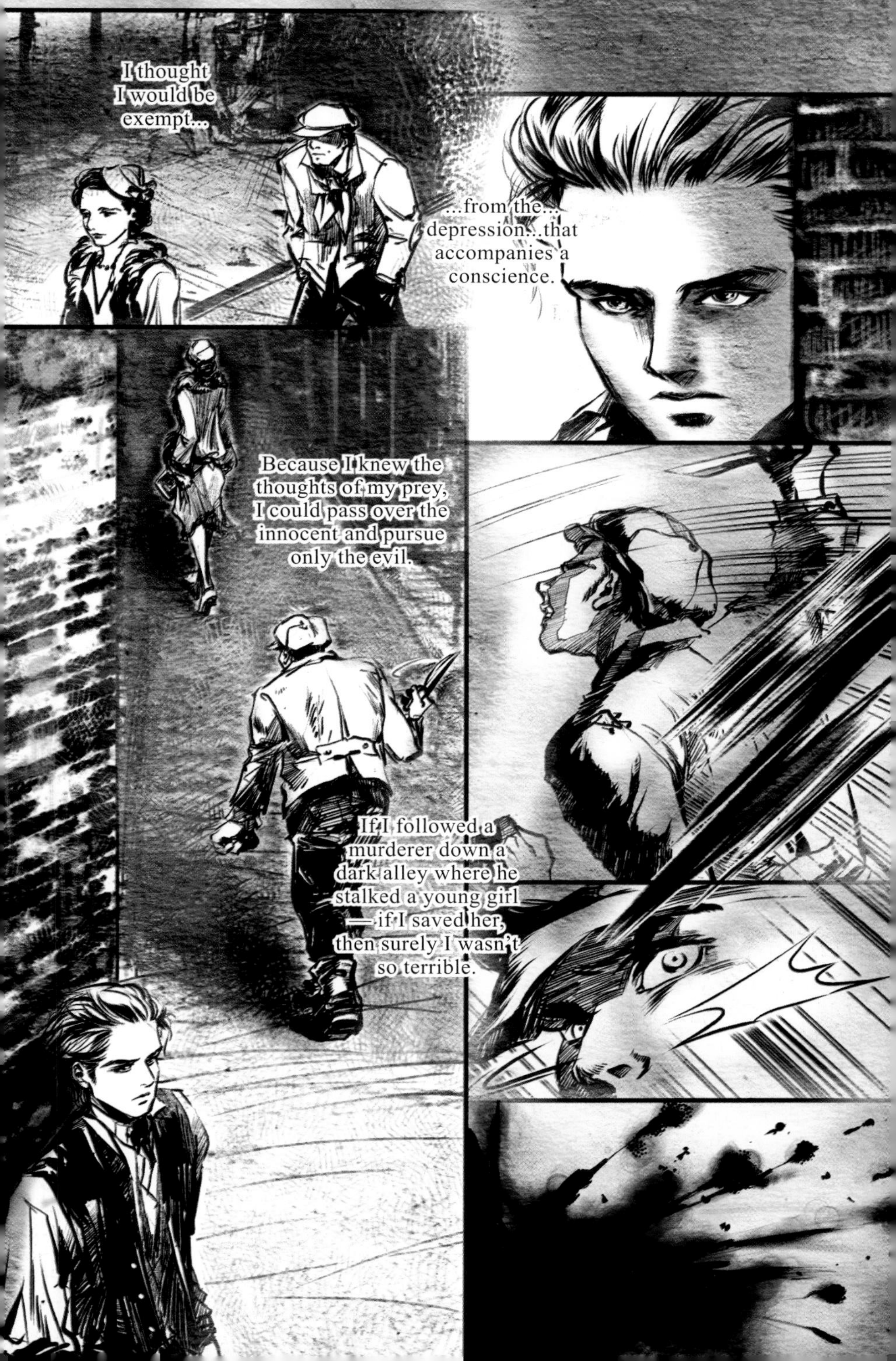

I thought I would be exempt...
...from the... depression...that accompanies a conscience.
Because I knew the thoughts of my prey, I could pass over the innocent and pursue only the evil.
If I followed a murderer down a dark alley where he stalked a young girl —if I saved her, then surely I wasn't so terrible.

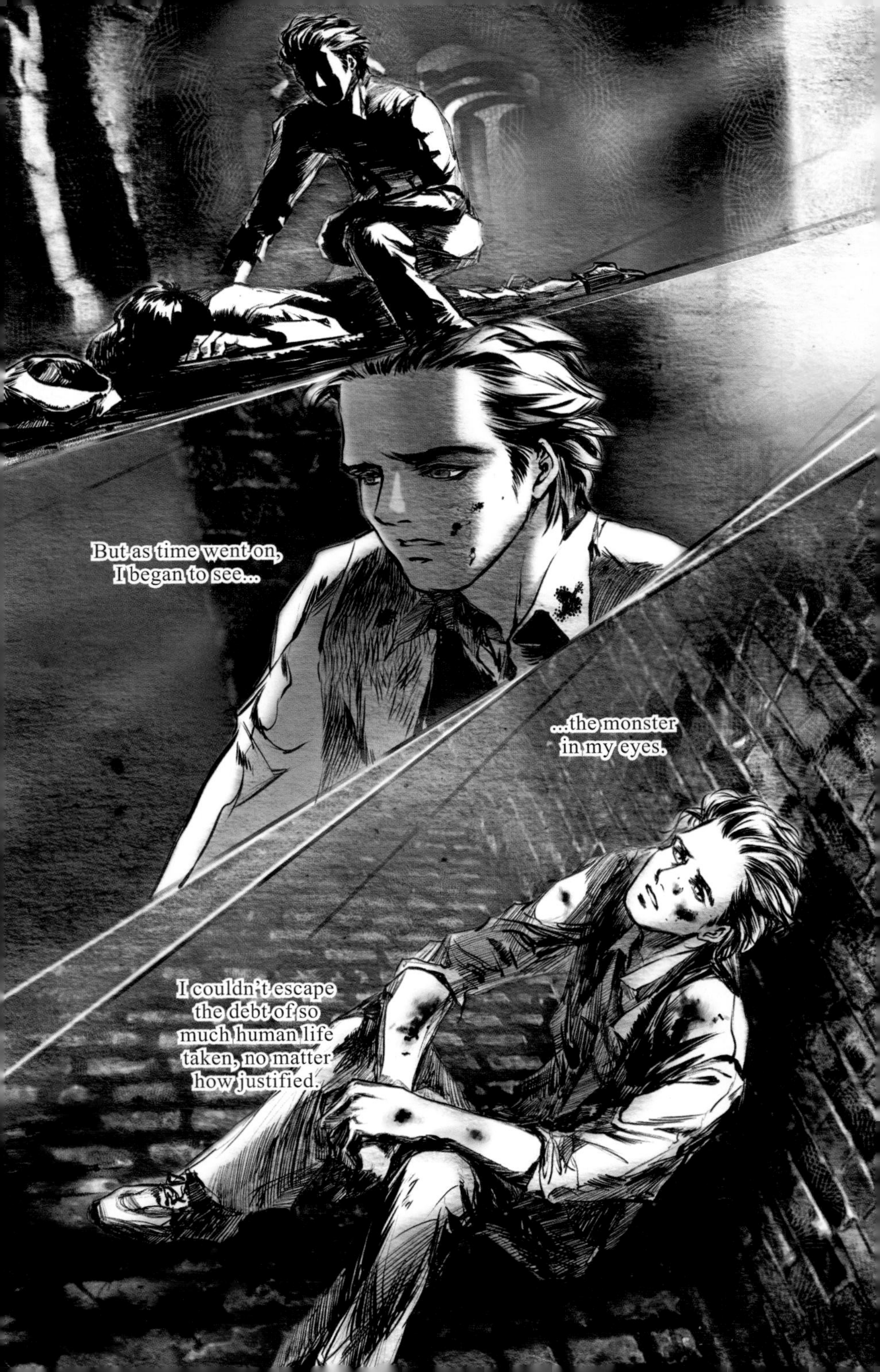
But as time went on, I began to see...
...the monster in my eyes.
I couldn't escape the debt of so much human life taken, no matter how justified.

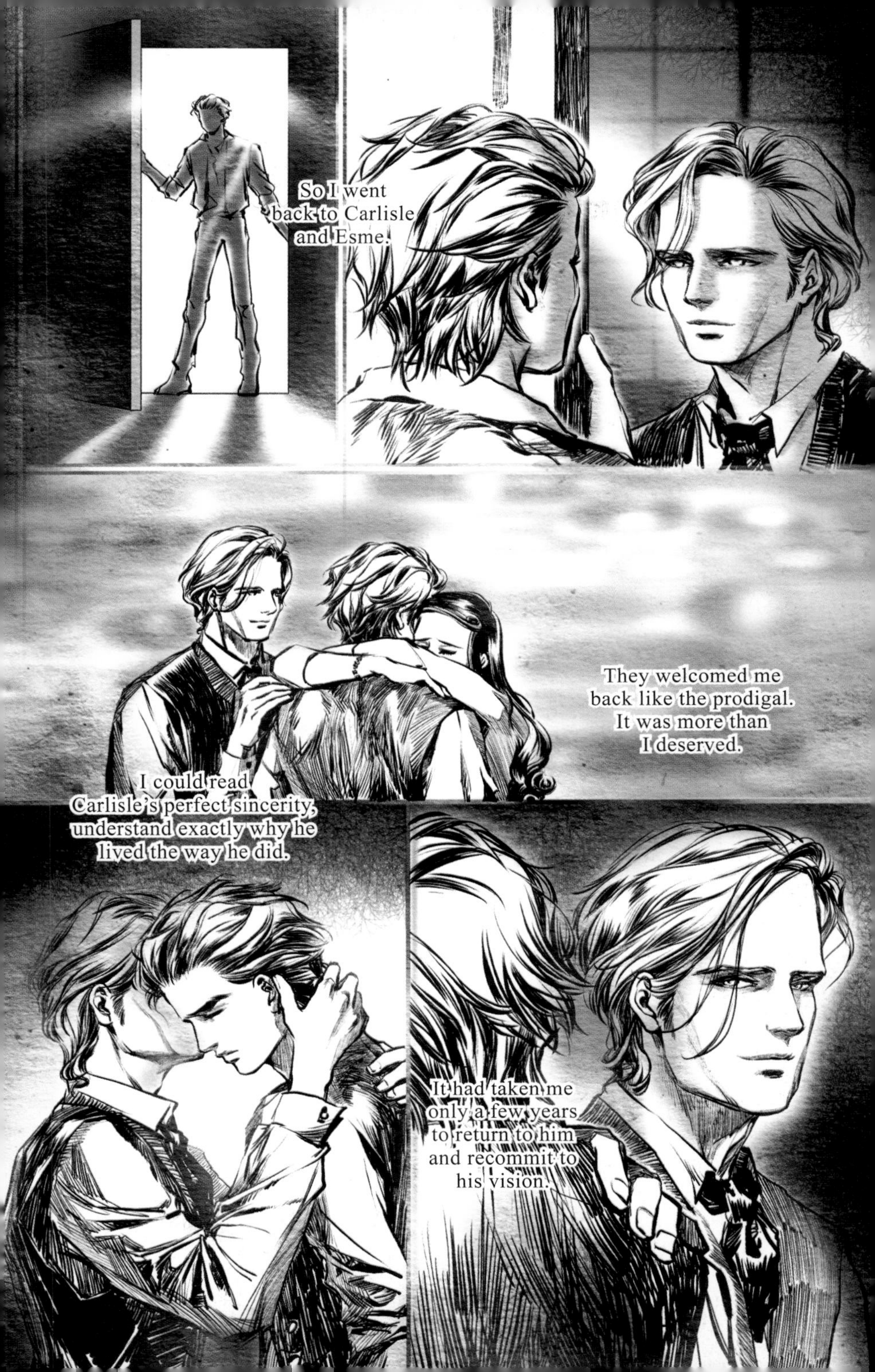
So I went back to Carlisle and Esme.
They welcomed me back like the prodigal. It was more than I deserved.
I could read Carlisle's perfect sincerity, understand exactly why he lived the way he did.
It had taken me only a few years to return to him and recommit to his vision.

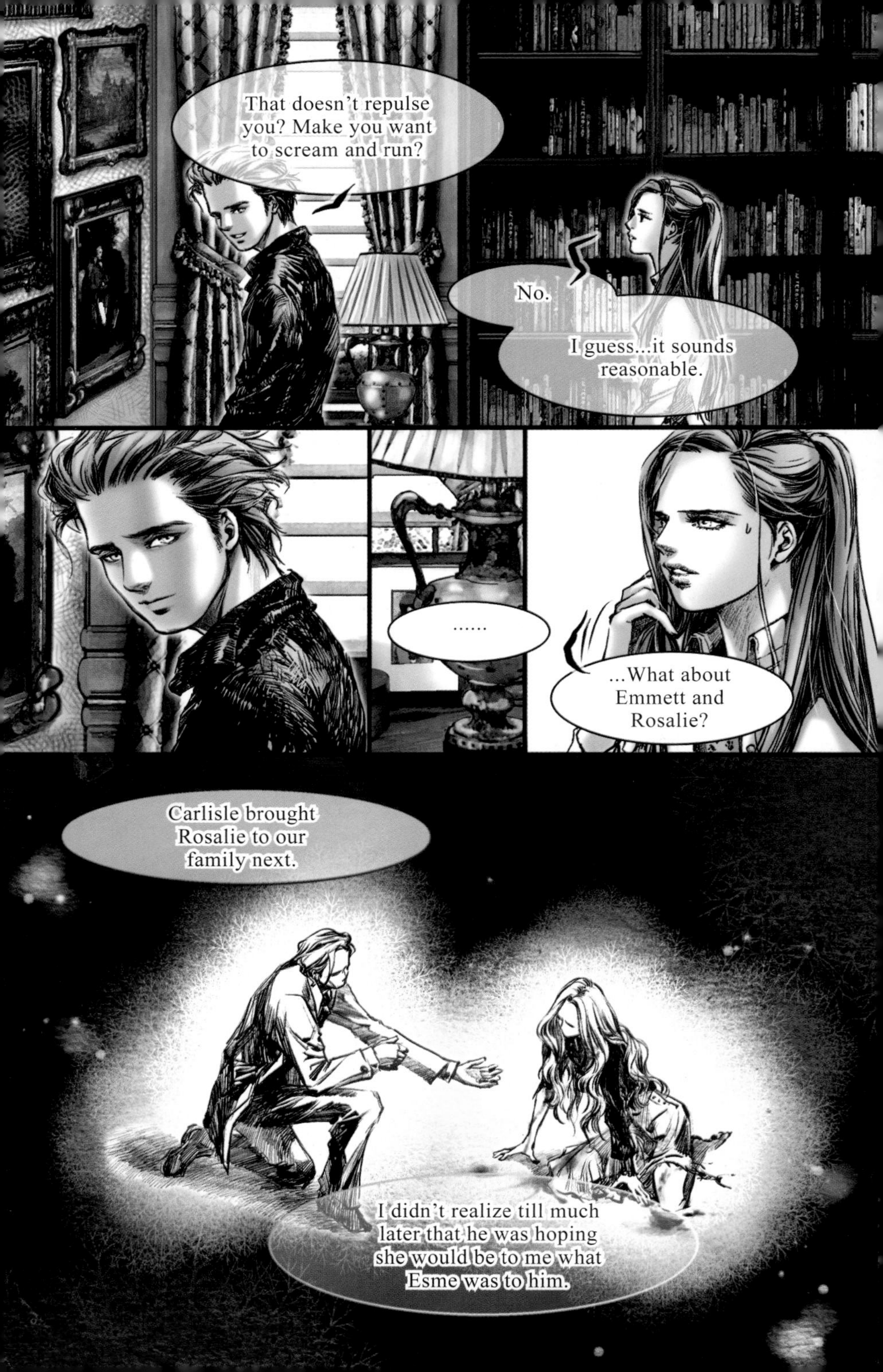

That doesn't repulse you? Make you want to scream and run?
No.
I guess...it sounds reasonable.
......
...What about Emmett and Rosalie?
Carlisle brought Rosalie to our family next.
I didn't realize till much later that he was hoping she would be to me what Esme was to him.

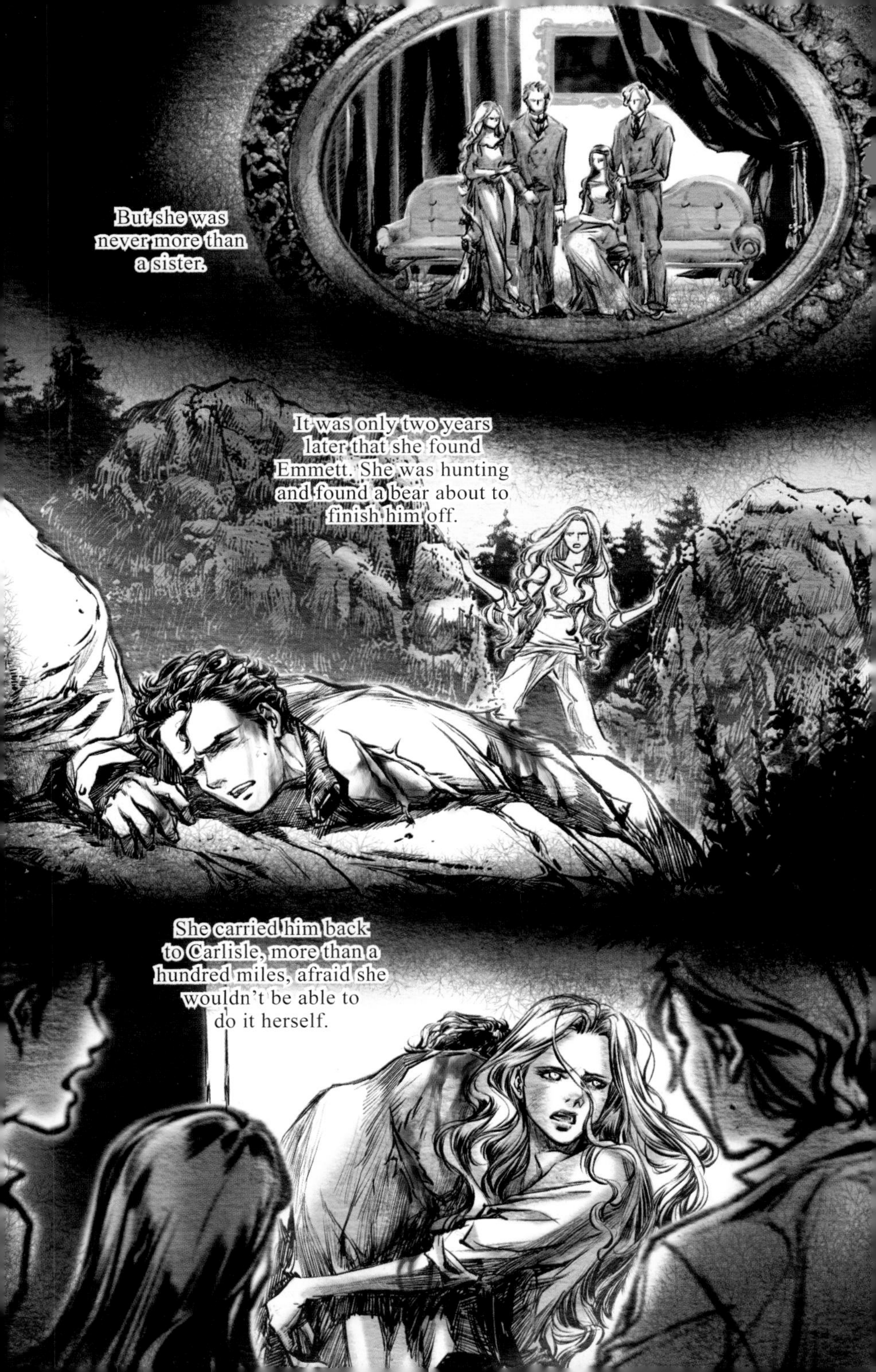
But she was never more than a sister.
It was only two years later that she found Emmett. She was hunting and found a bear about to finish him off.
She carried him back to Carlisle, more than a hundred miles, afraid she wouldn't be able to do it herself.

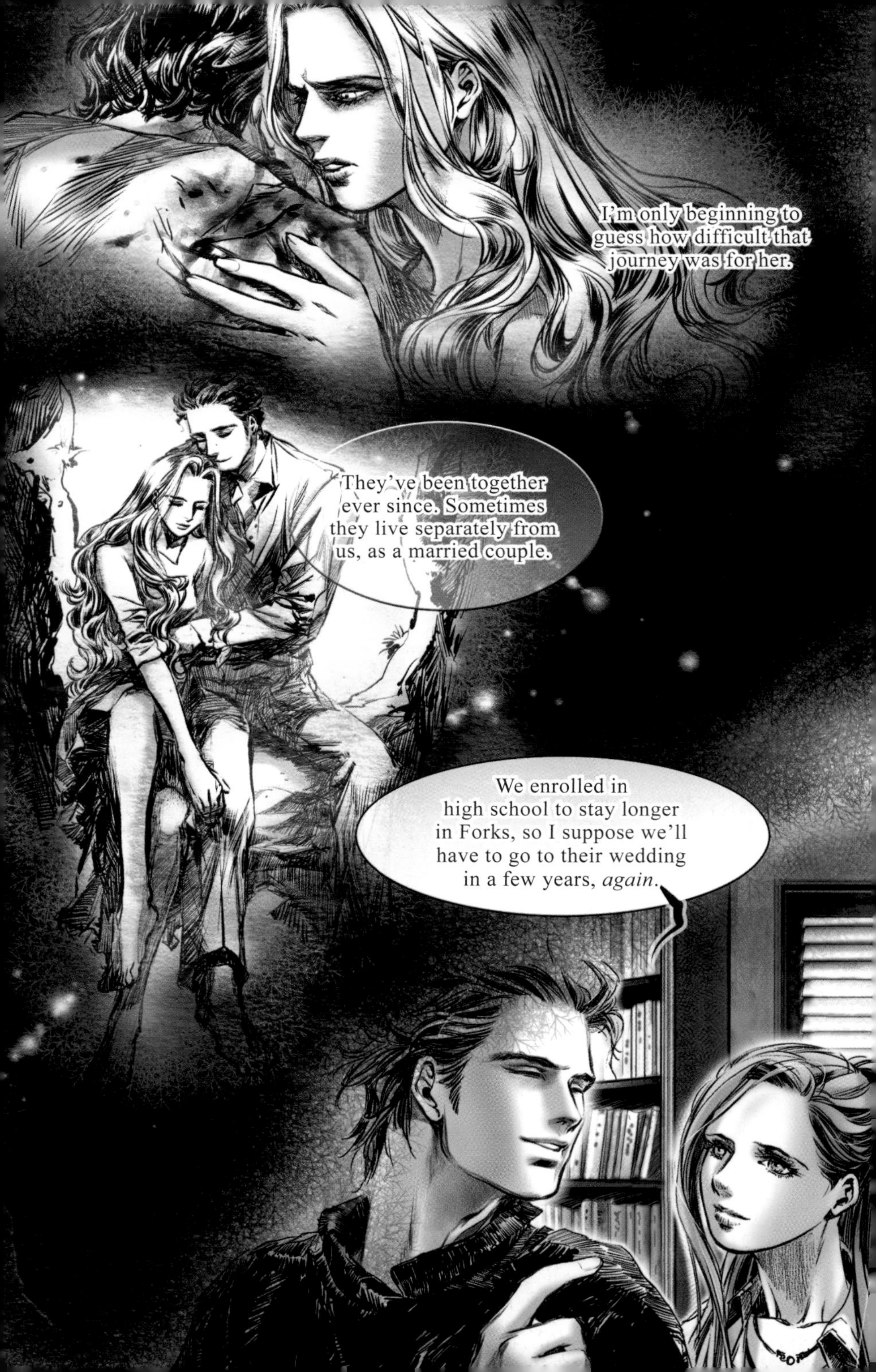
I'm only beginning to guess how difficult that journey was for her.
They've been together ever since. Sometimes they live separately from us, as a married couple.
We enrolled in high school to stay longer in Forks, so I suppose we'll have to go to their wedding in a few years, *again*.

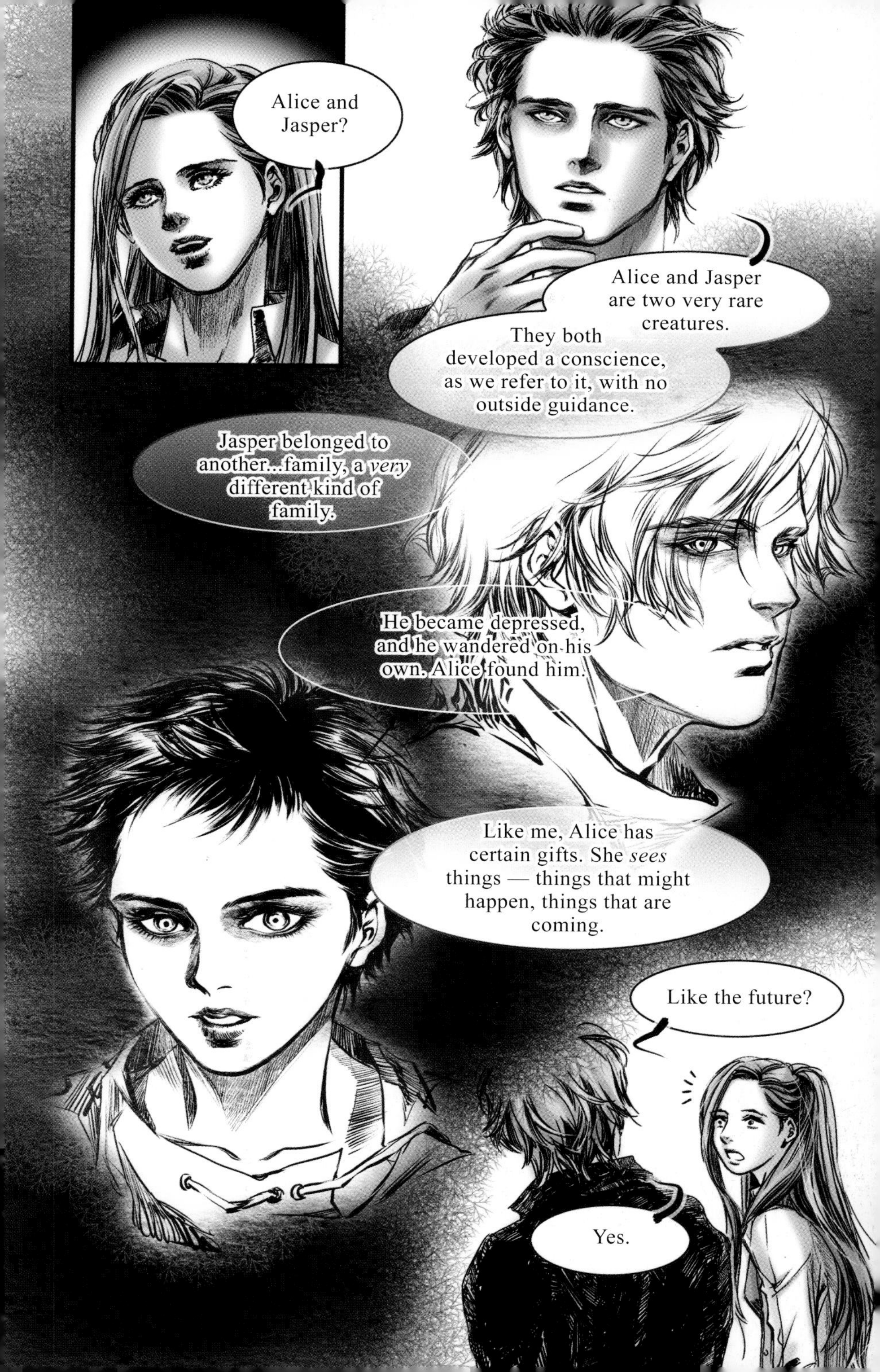
Alice and Jasper?
Alice and Jasper are two very rare creatures.
They both developed a conscience, as we refer to it, with no outside guidance.
Jasper belonged to another...family, a *very* different kind of family.
He became depressed, and he wandered on his own. Alice found him.
Like me, Alice has certain gifts. She *sees* things — things that might happen, things that are coming.
Like the future?
Yes.

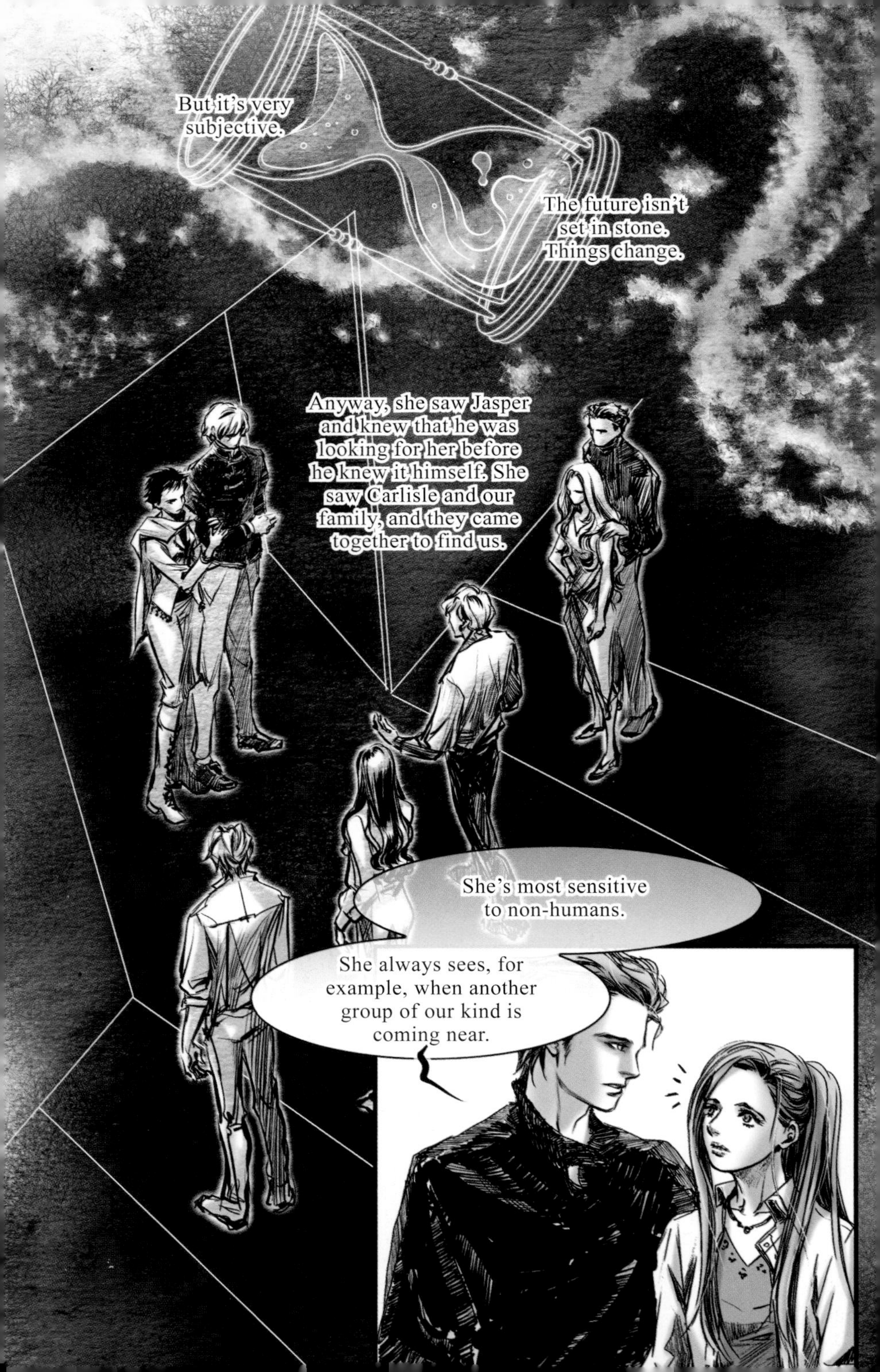

But it's very subjective.
The future isn't set in stone. Things change.
Anyway, she saw Jasper and knew that he was looking for her before he knew it himself. She saw Carlisle and our family, and they came together to find us.
She's most sensitive to non-humans.
She always sees, for example, when another group of our kind is coming near.

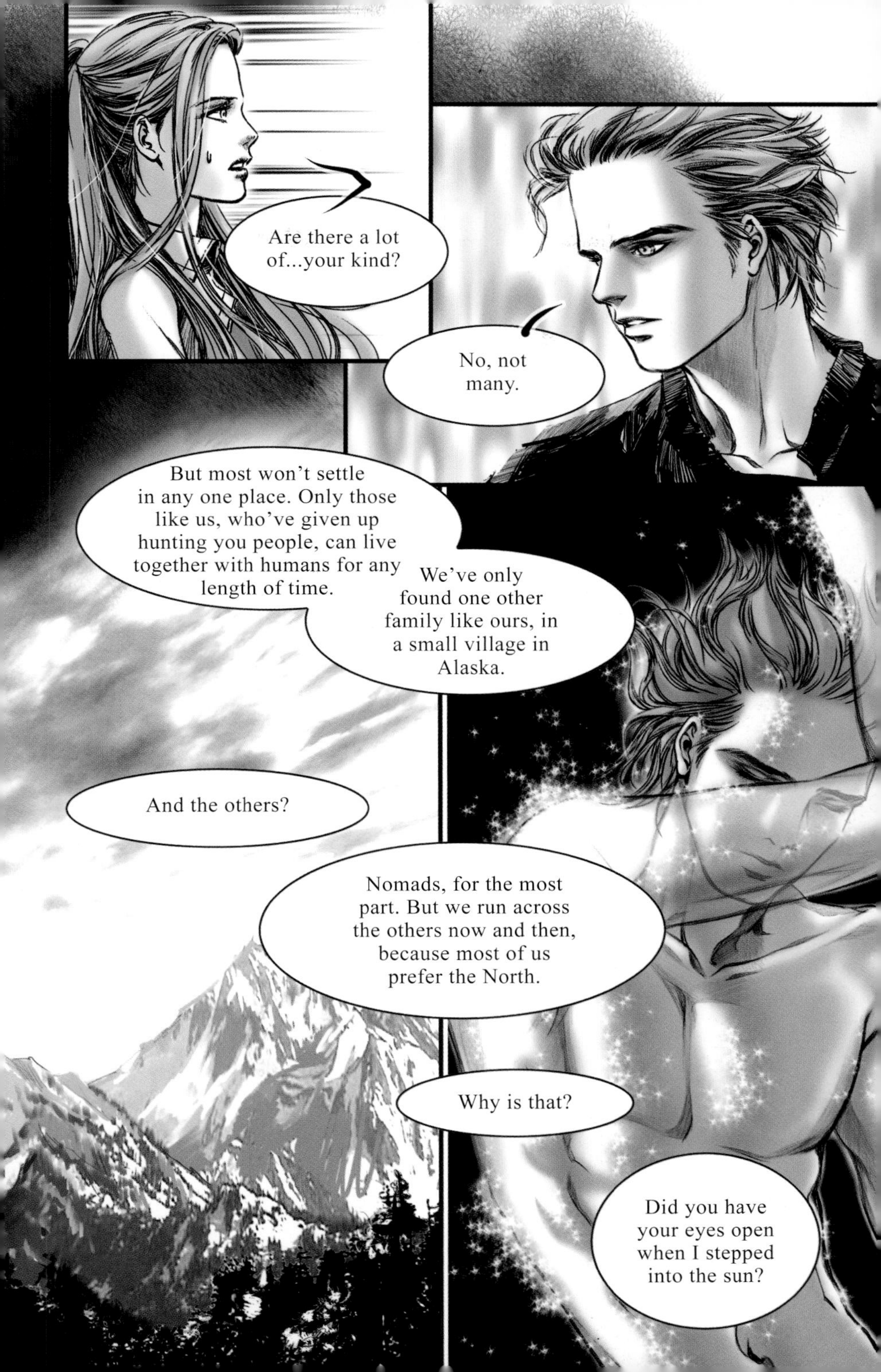
Are there a lot of...your kind?
No, not many.
But most won't settle in any one place. Only those like us, who've given up hunting you people, can live together with humans for any length of time.
We've only found one other family like ours, in a small village in Alaska.
And the others?
Nomads, for the most part. But we run across the others now and then, because most of us prefer the North.
Why is that?
Did you have your eyes open when I stepped into the sun?

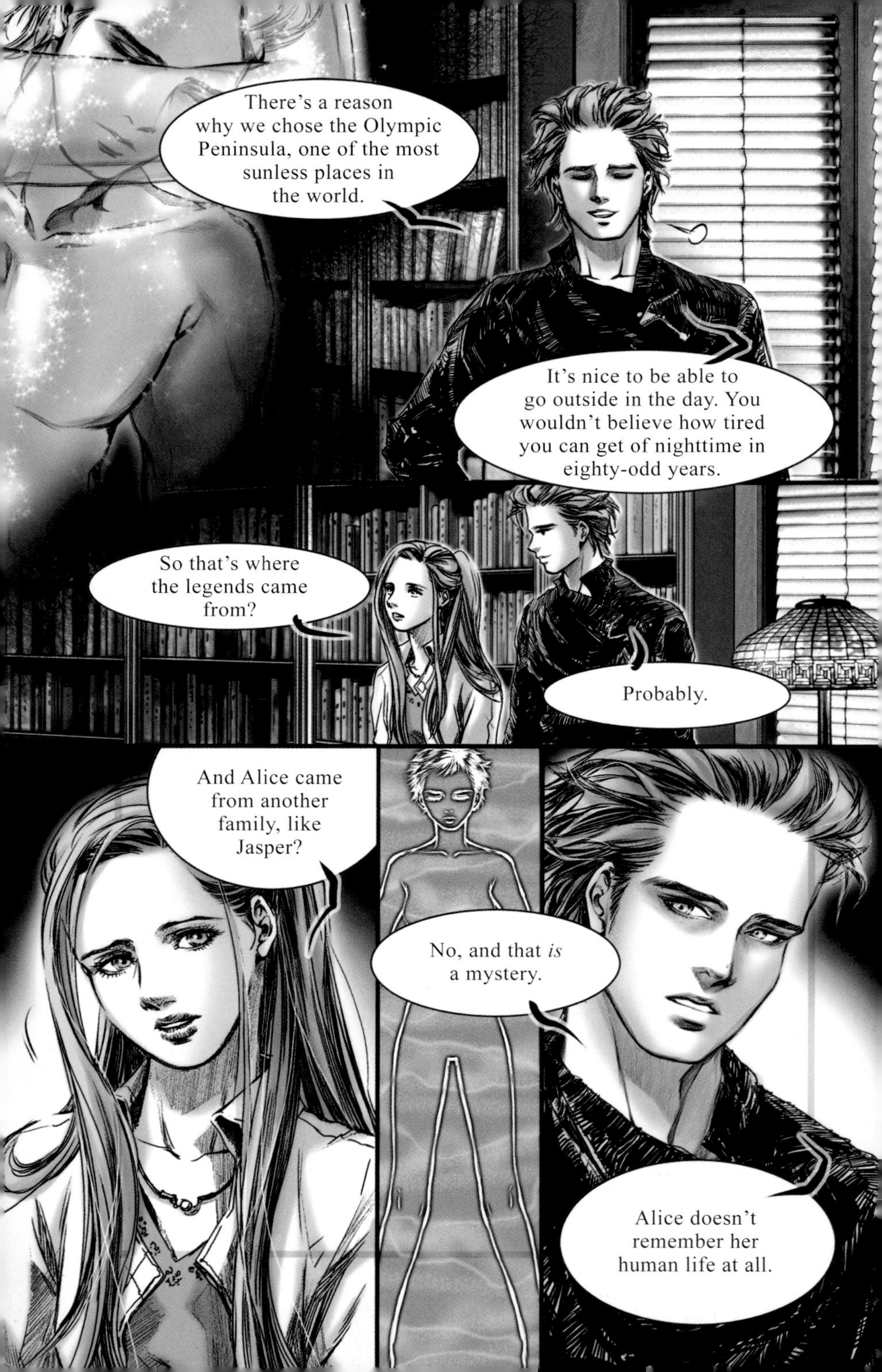
There's a reason why we chose the Olympic Peninsula, one of the most sunless places in the world.
It's nice to be able to go outside in the day. You wouldn't believe how tired you can get of nighttime in eighty-odd years.
So that's where the legends came from?
Probably.
And Alice came from another family, like Jasper?
No, and that *is* a mystery.
Alice doesn't remember her human life at all.

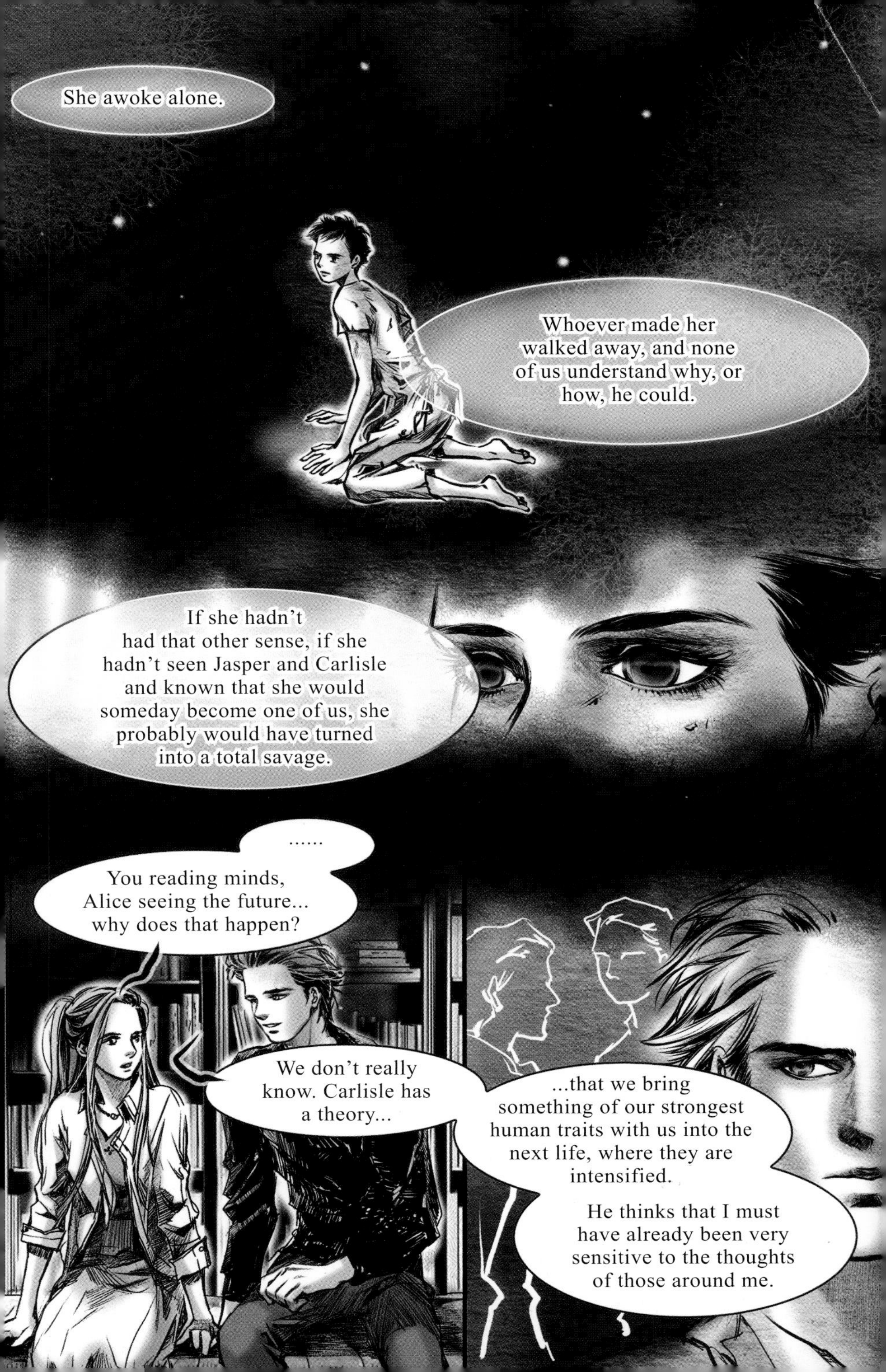

She awoke alone.
Whoever made her walked away, and none of us understand why, or how, he could.
If she hadn't had that other sense, if she hadn't seen Jasper and Carlisle and known that she would someday become one of us, she probably would have turned into a total savage.
......
You reading minds, Alice seeing the future... why does that happen?
We don't really know. Carlisle has a theory...
...that we bring something of our strongest human traits with us into the next life, where they are intensified.
He thinks that I must have already been very sensitive to the thoughts of those around me.

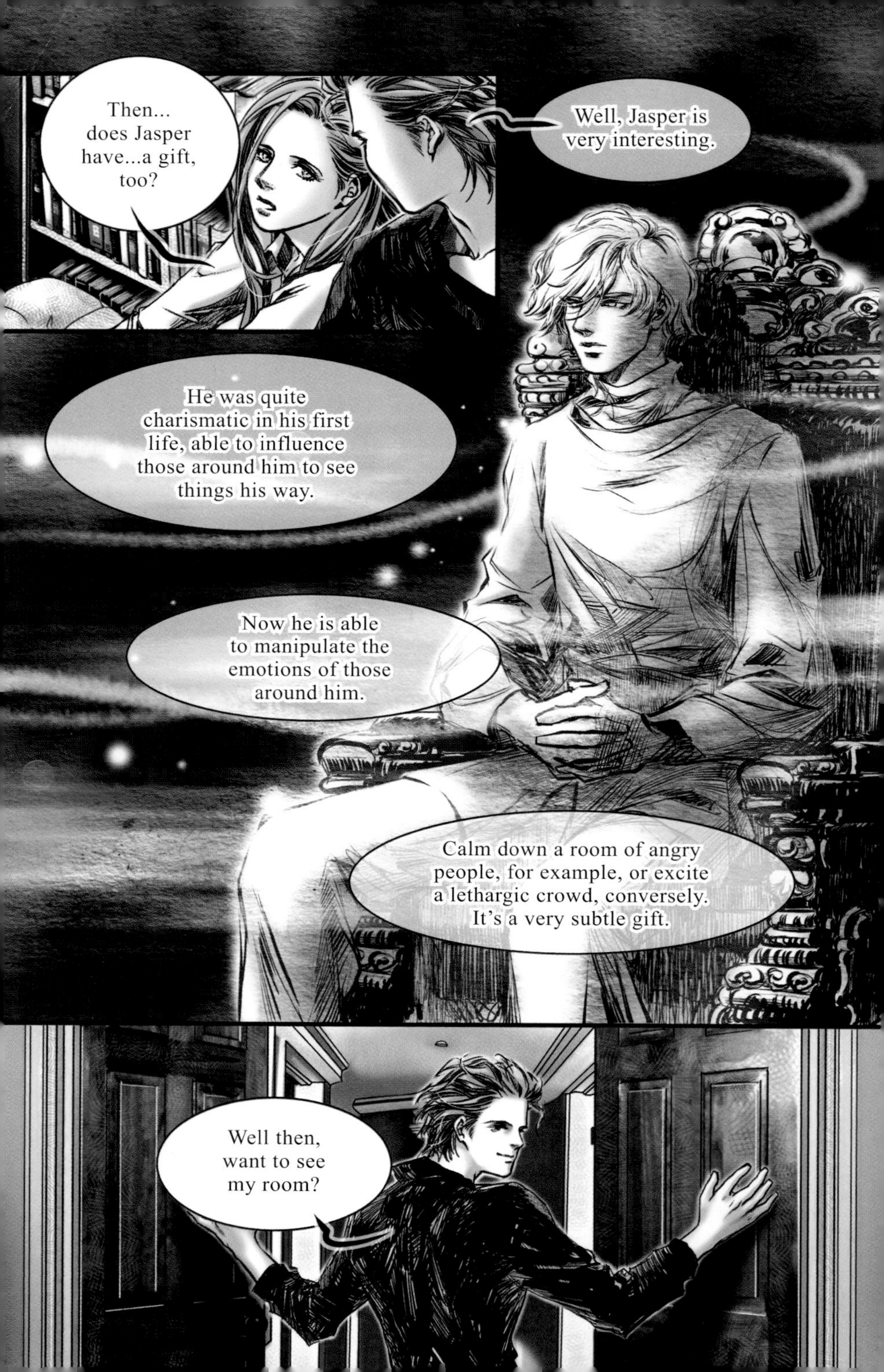
Then... does Jasper have...a gift, too?
Well, Jasper is very interesting.
He was quite charismatic in his first life, able to influence those around him to see things his way.
Now he is able to manipulate the emotions of those around him.
Calm down a room of angry people, for example, or excite a lethargic crowd, conversely. It's a very subtle gift.
Well then, want to see my room?

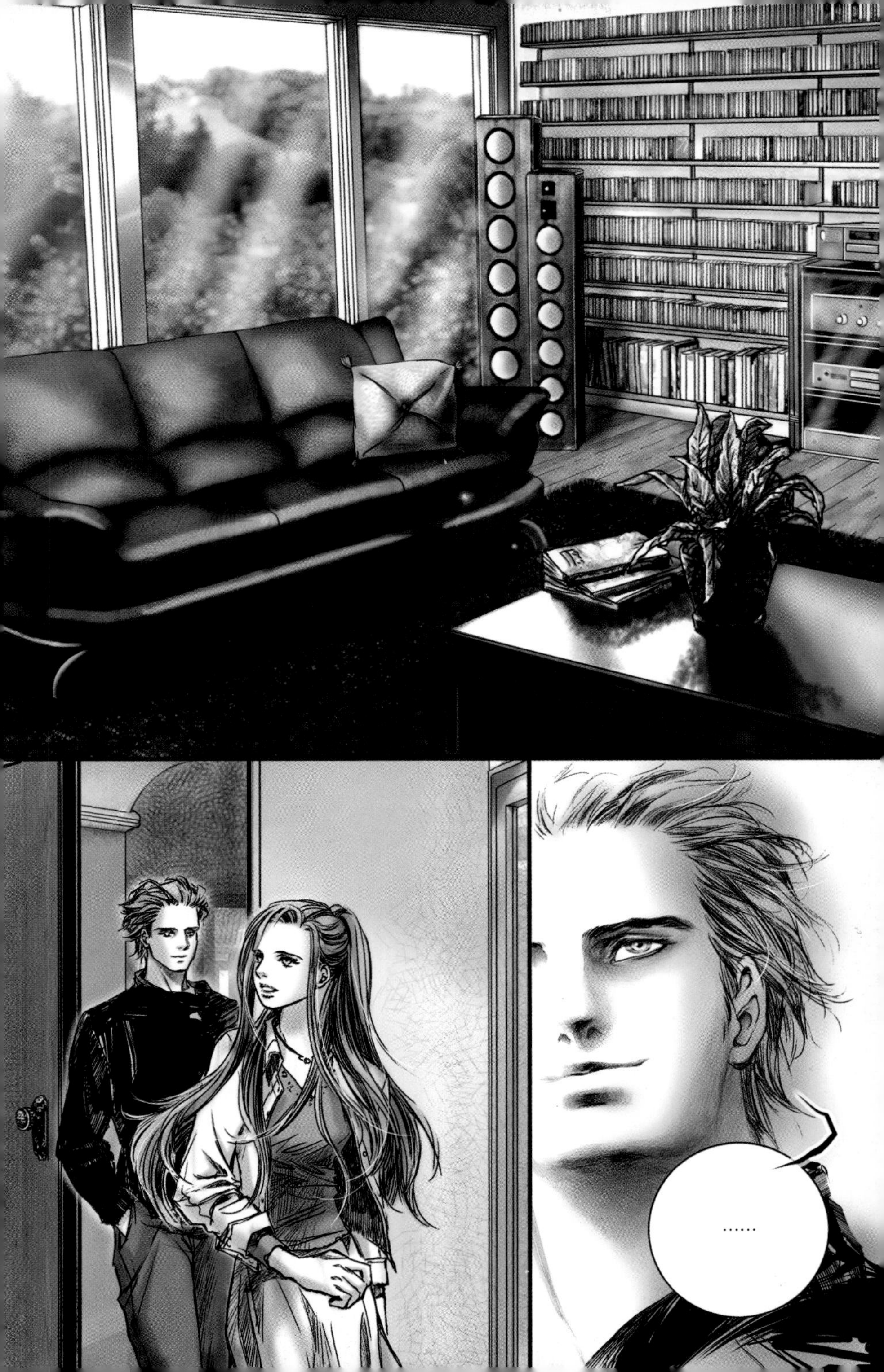
......

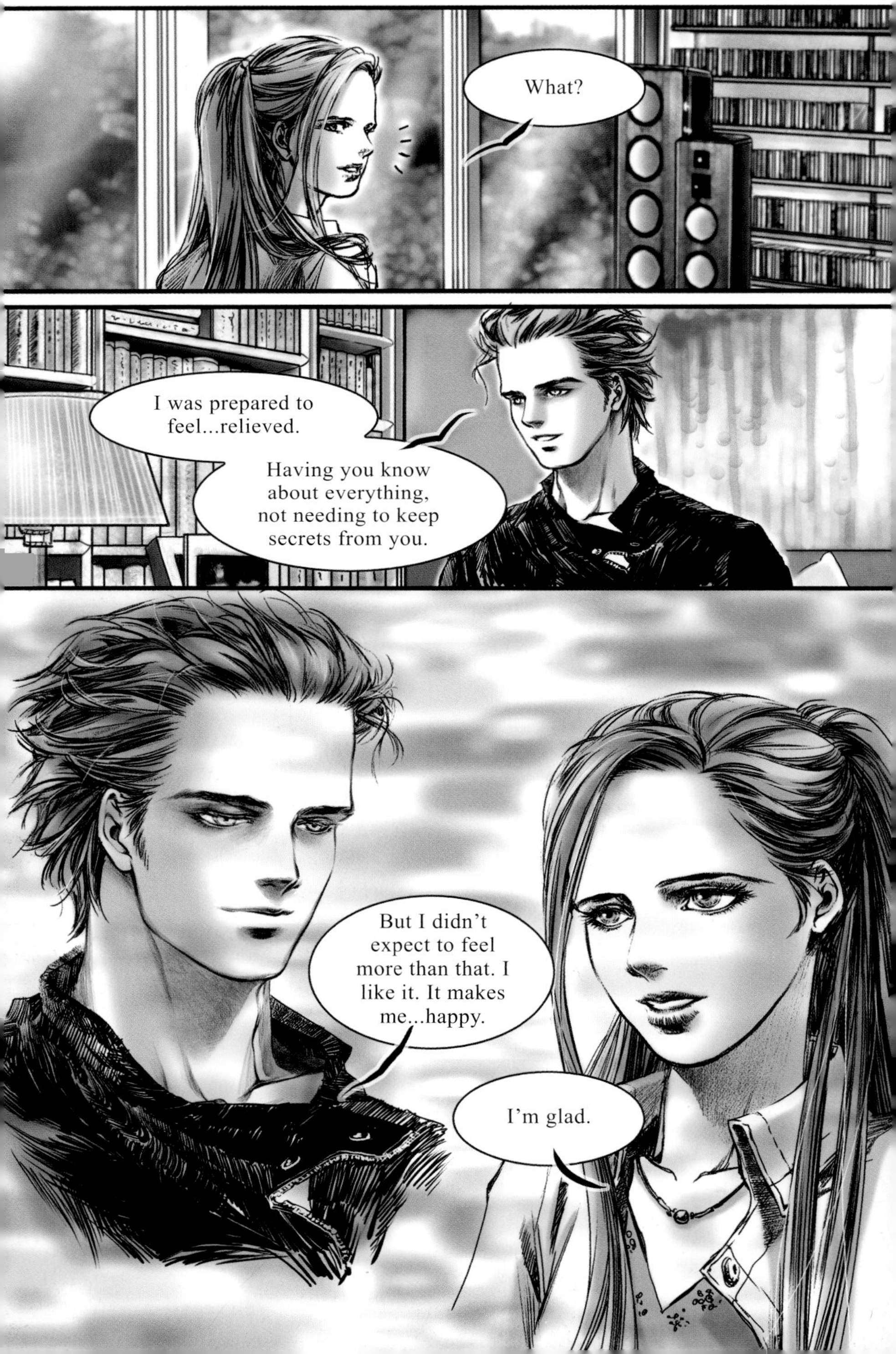
What?
I was prepared to feel...relieved.
Having you know about everything, not needing to keep secrets from you.
But I didn't expect to feel more than that. I like it. It makes me...happy.
I'm glad.

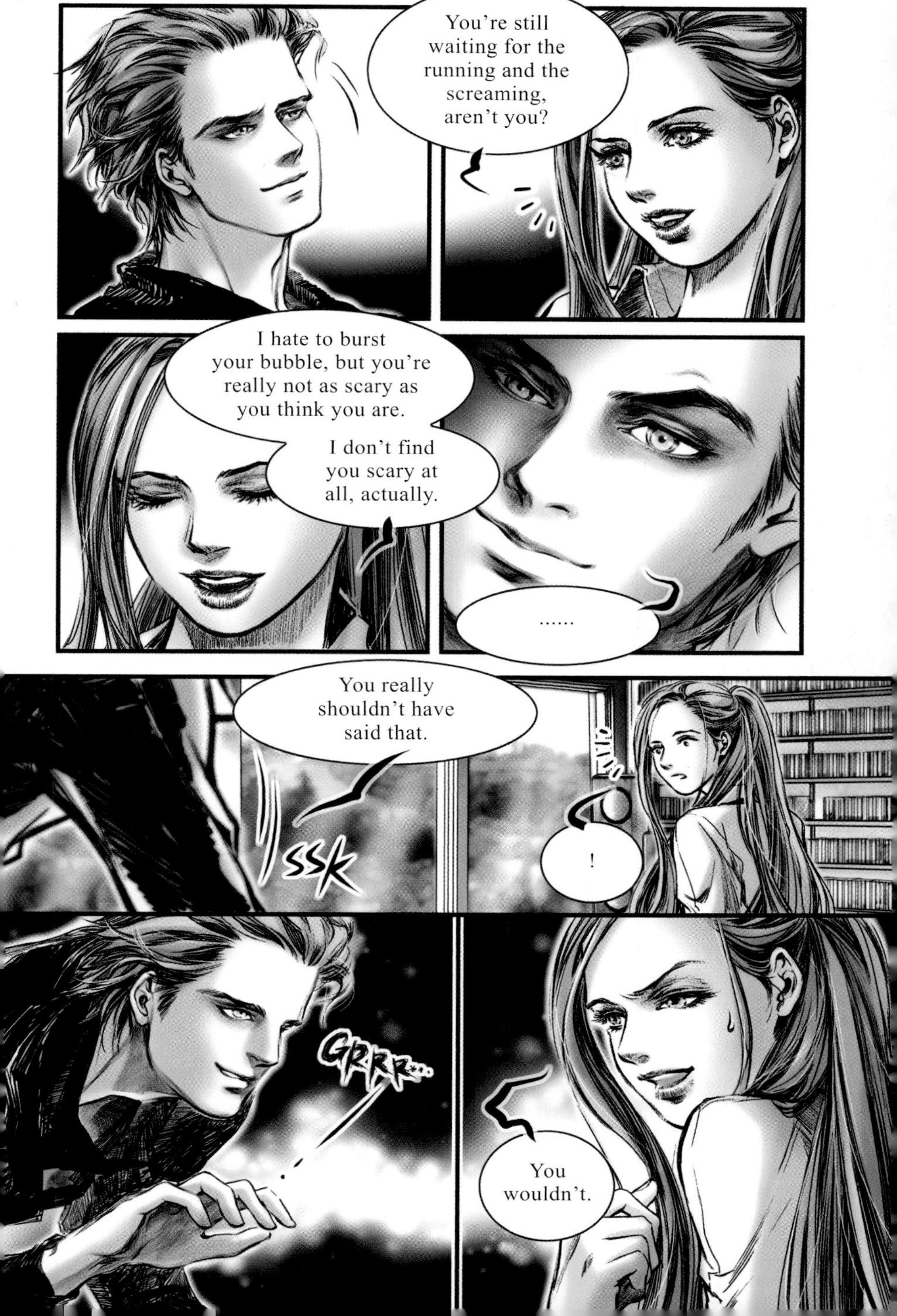
You're still waiting for the running and the screaming, aren't you?
I hate to burst your bubble, but you're really not as scary as you think you are.
I don't find you scary at all, actually.
......
You really shouldn't have said that.
SSK
!
GRRR...
You wouldn't.

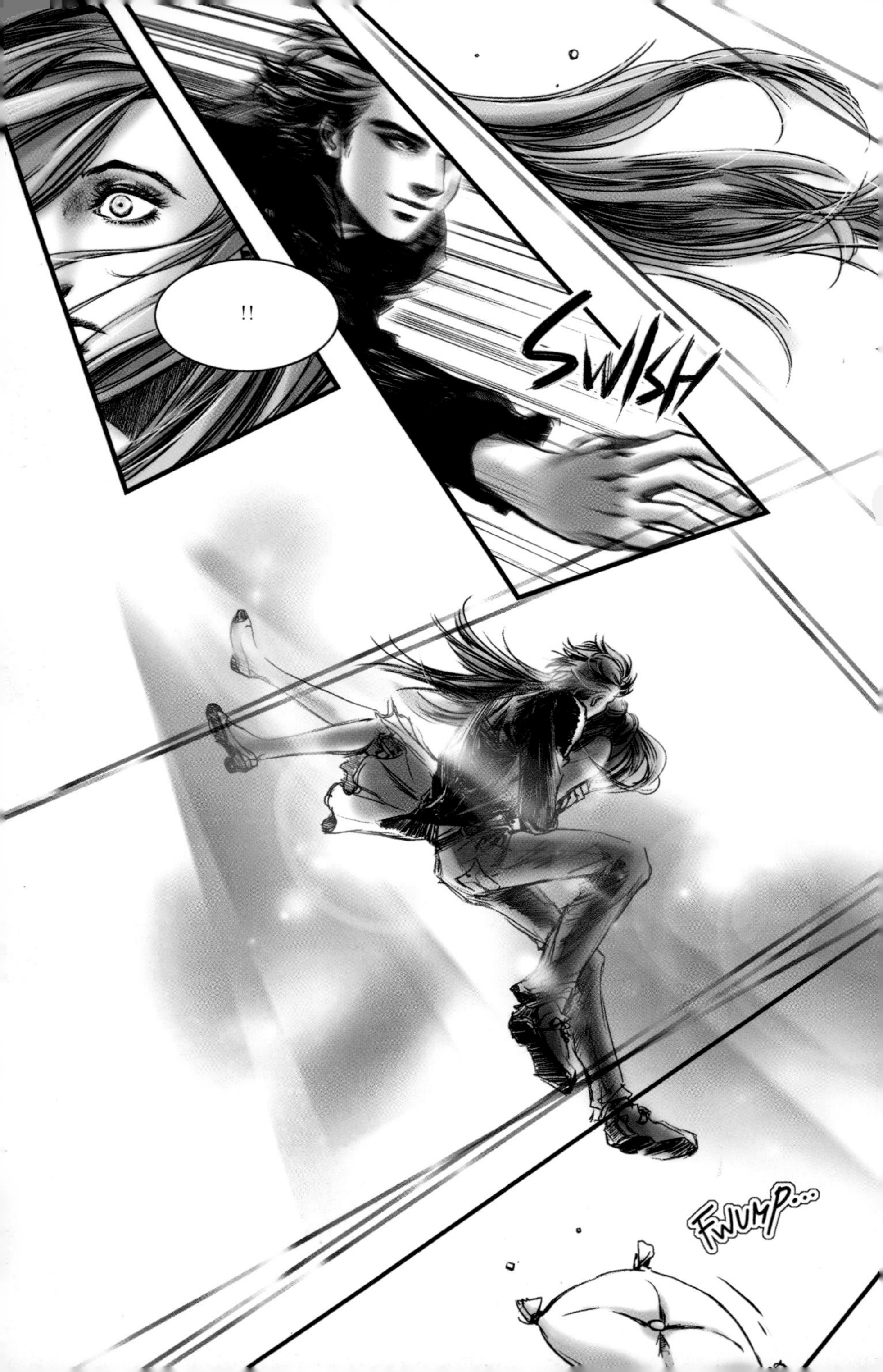
!!
SWISH
FWUMP...

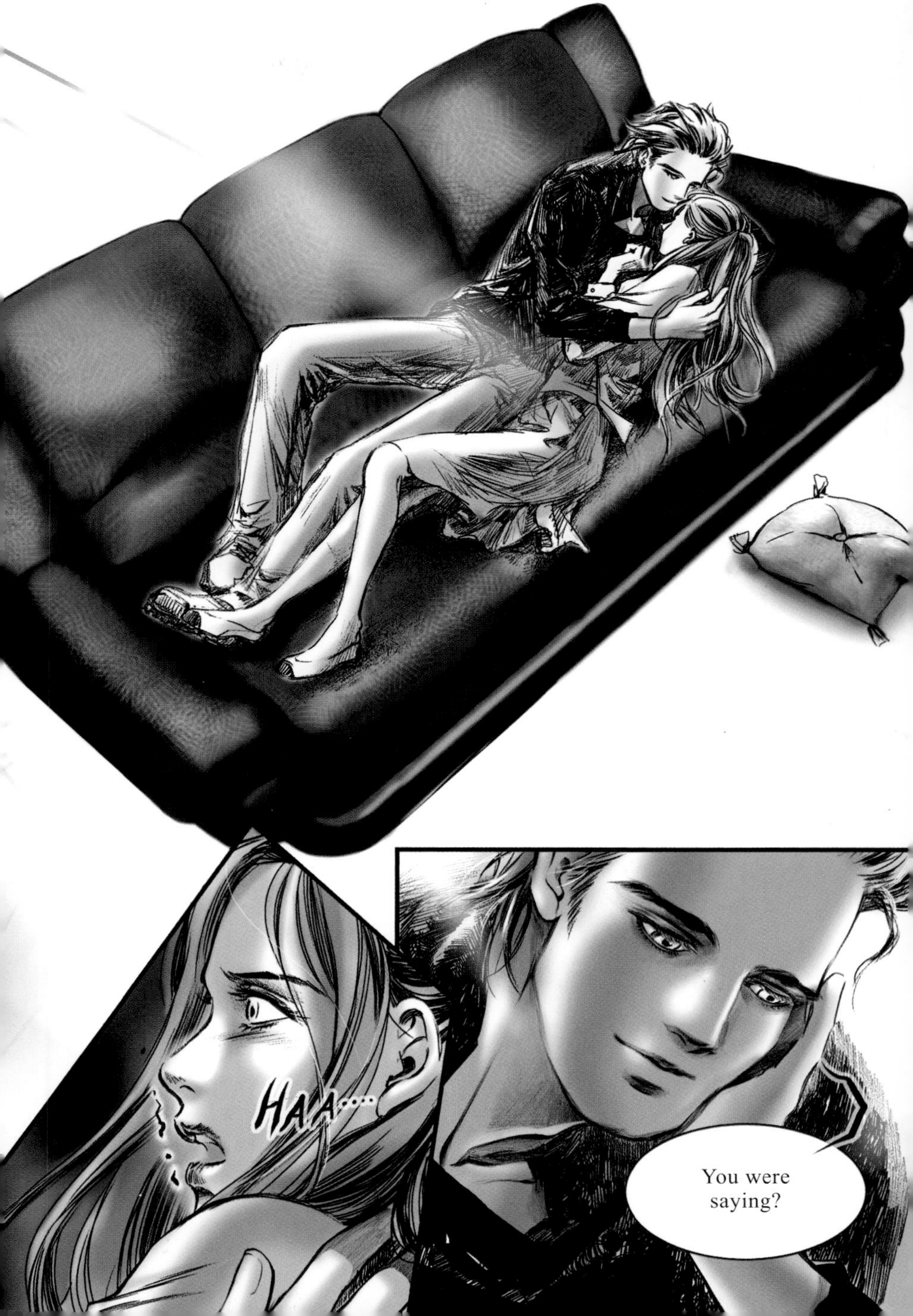
HAA....
You were saying?

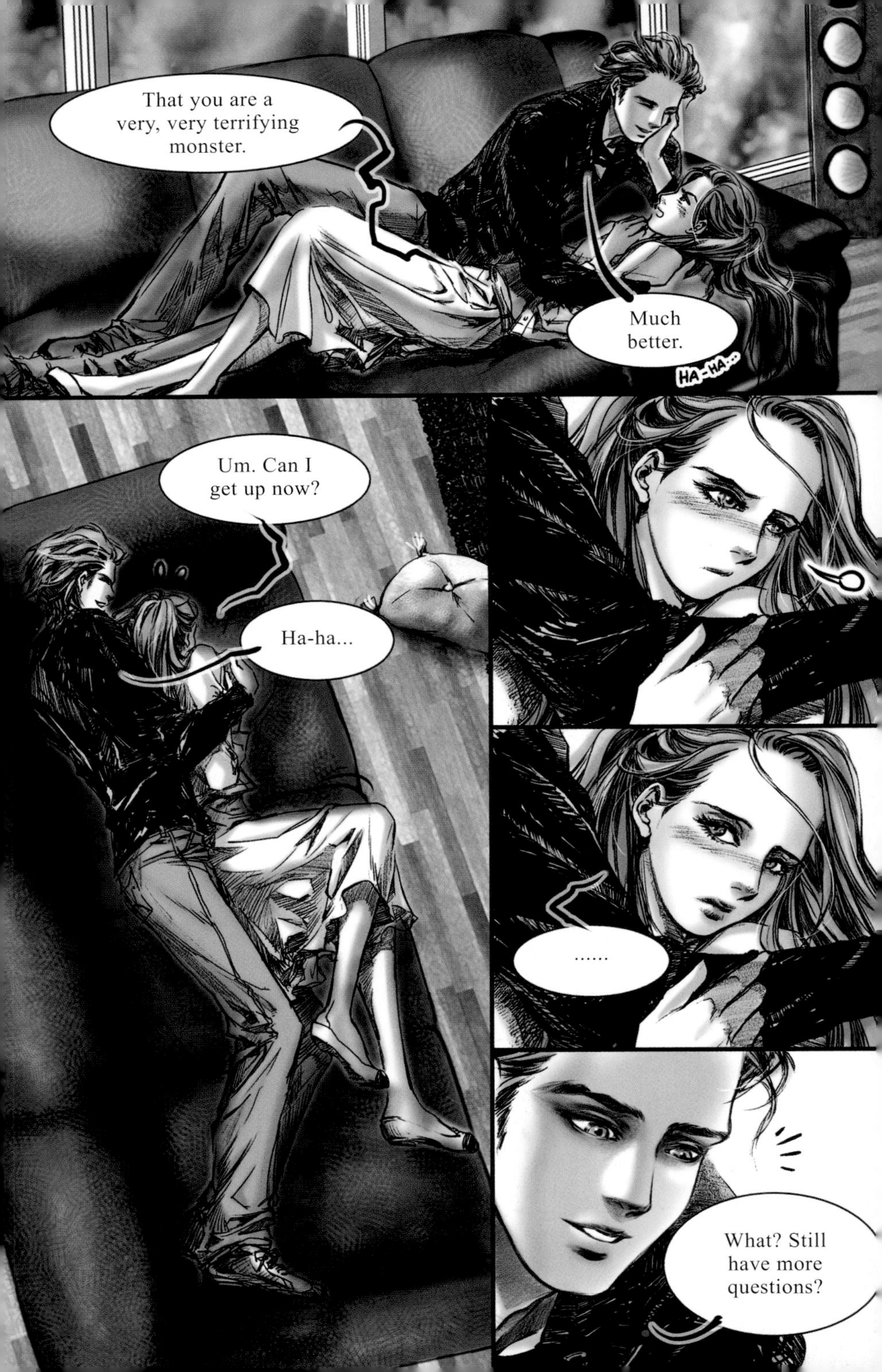
That you are a very, very terrifying monster.
Much better.
HA-HA...
Um. Can I get up now?
Ha-ha...
......
What? Still have more questions?

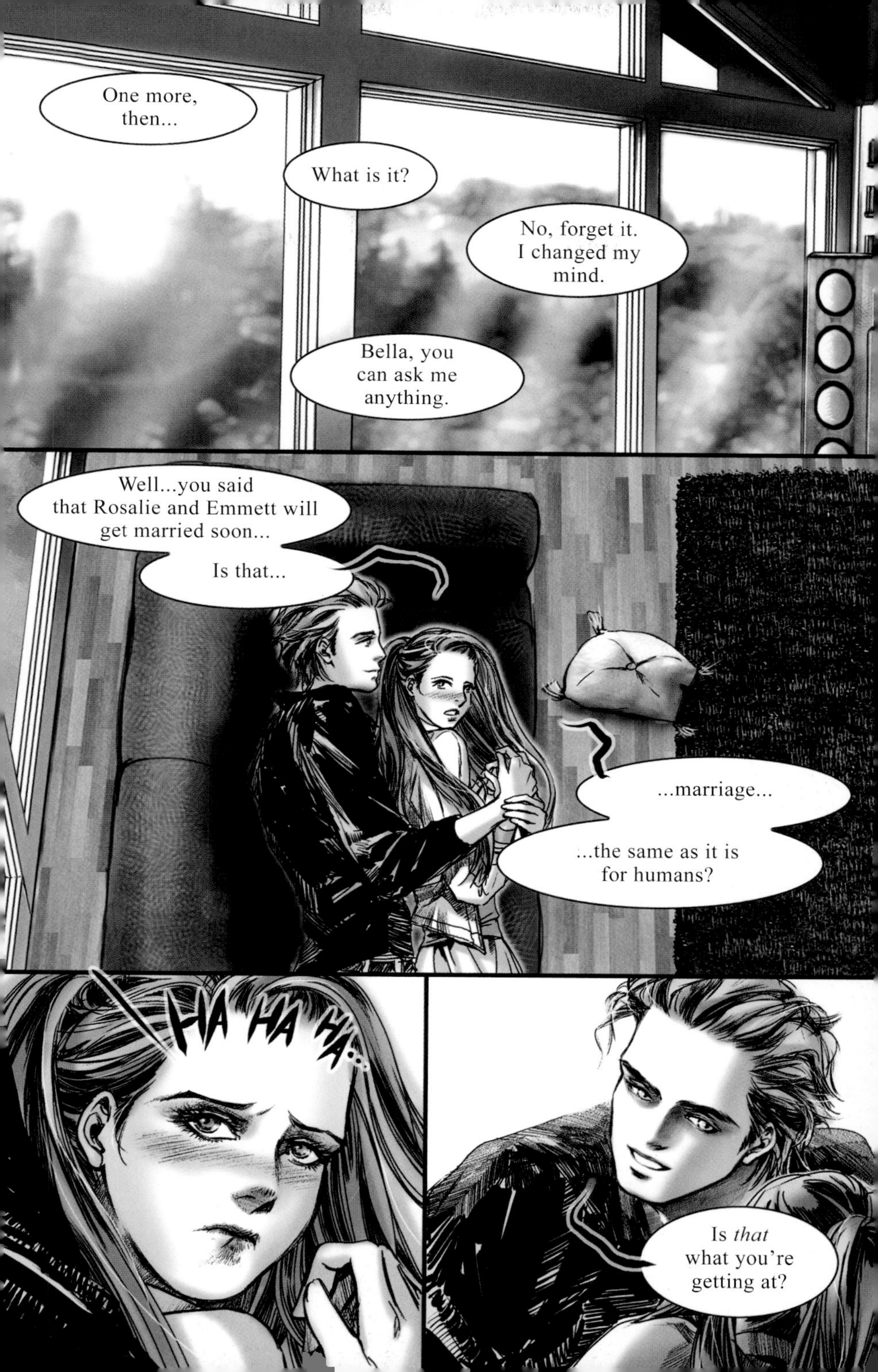
One more, then...
What is it?
No, forget it. I changed my mind.
Bella, you can ask me anything.
Well...you said that Rosalie and Emmett will get married soon...
Is that...
...marriage...
...the same as it is for humans?
HA HA HA...
Is *that* what you're getting at?

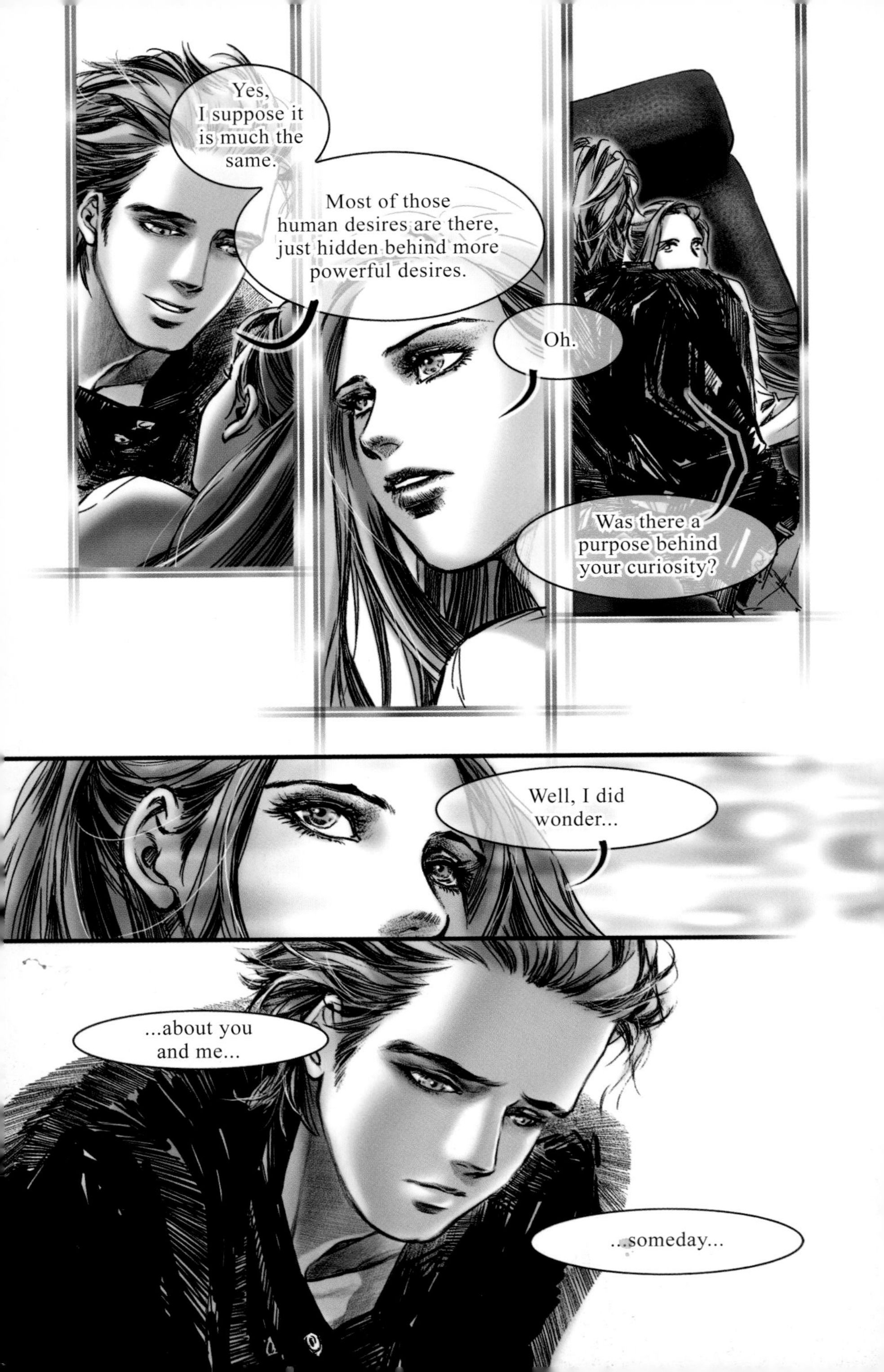
Yes, I suppose it is much the same.
Most of those human desires are there, just hidden behind more powerful desires.
Oh.
Was there a purpose behind your curiosity?
Well, I did wonder...
...about you and me...
...someday...

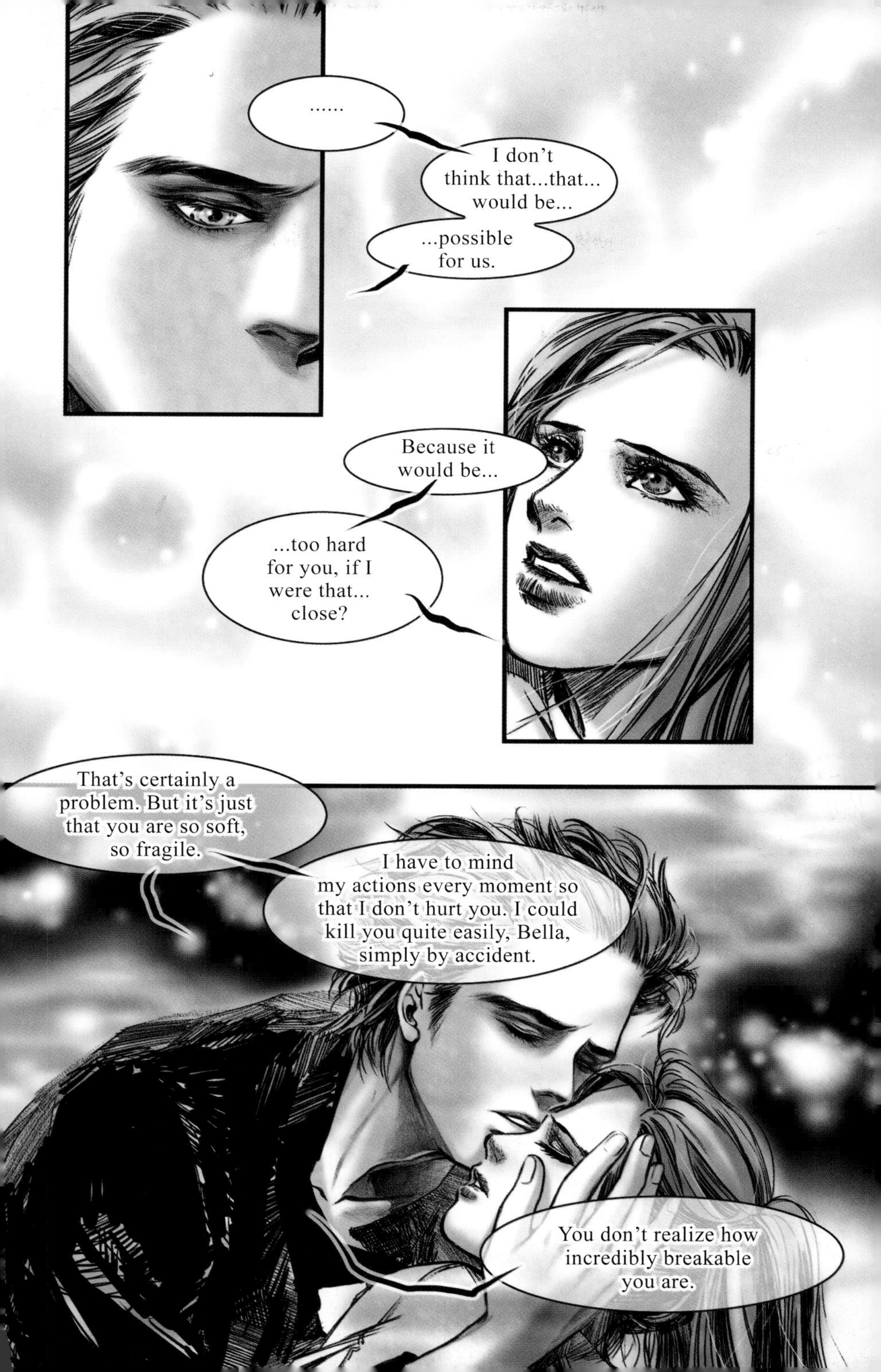
......
I don't think that...that... would be...
...possible for us.
Because it would be...
...too hard for you, if I were that... close?
That's certainly a problem. But it's just that you are so soft, so fragile.
I have to mind my actions every moment so that I don't hurt you. I could kill you quite easily, Bella, simply by accident.
You don't realize how incredibly breakable you are.

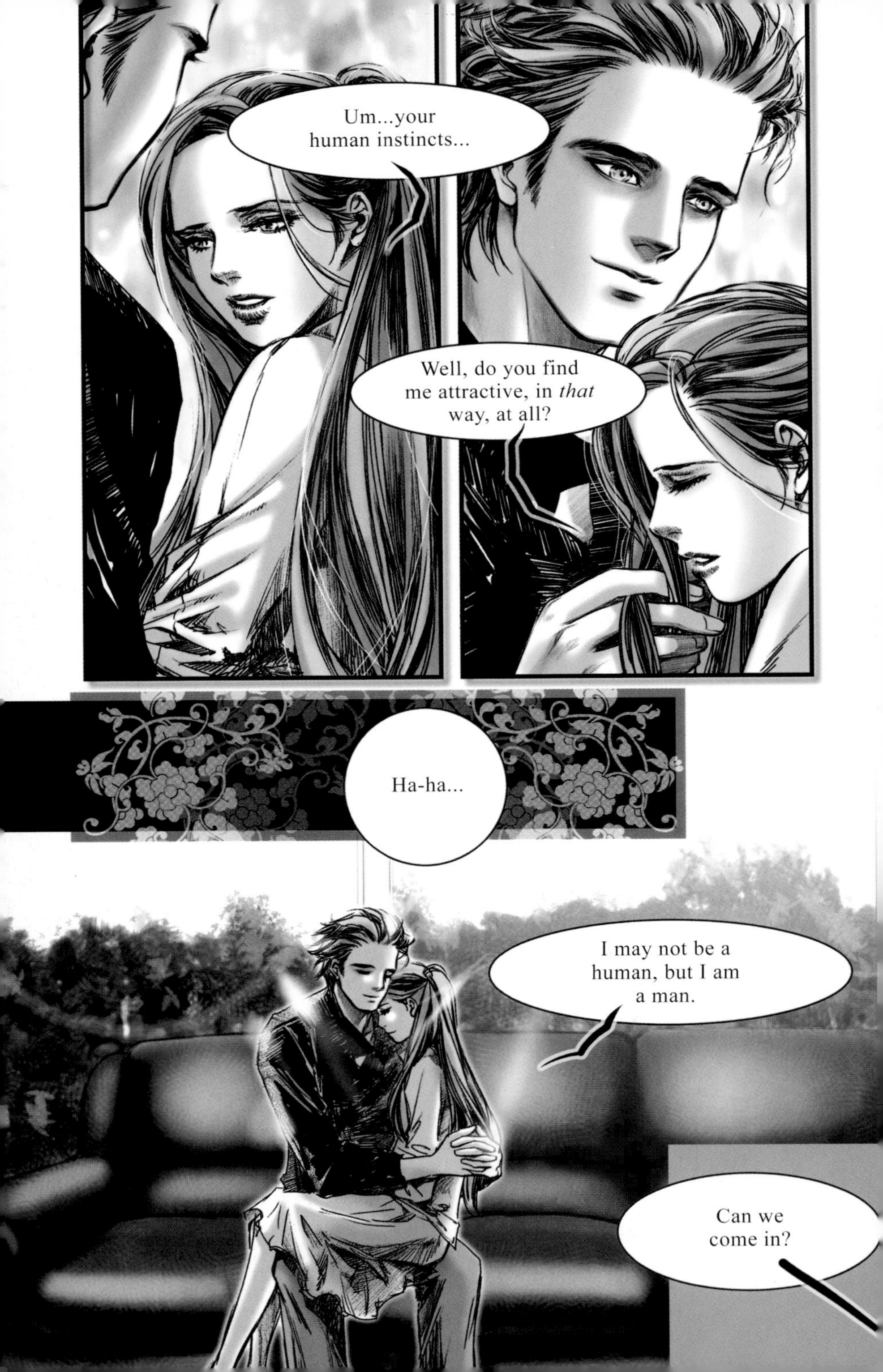
Um...your human instincts...
Well, do you find me attractive, in *that* way, at all?
Ha-ha...
I may not be a human, but I am a man.
Can we come in?

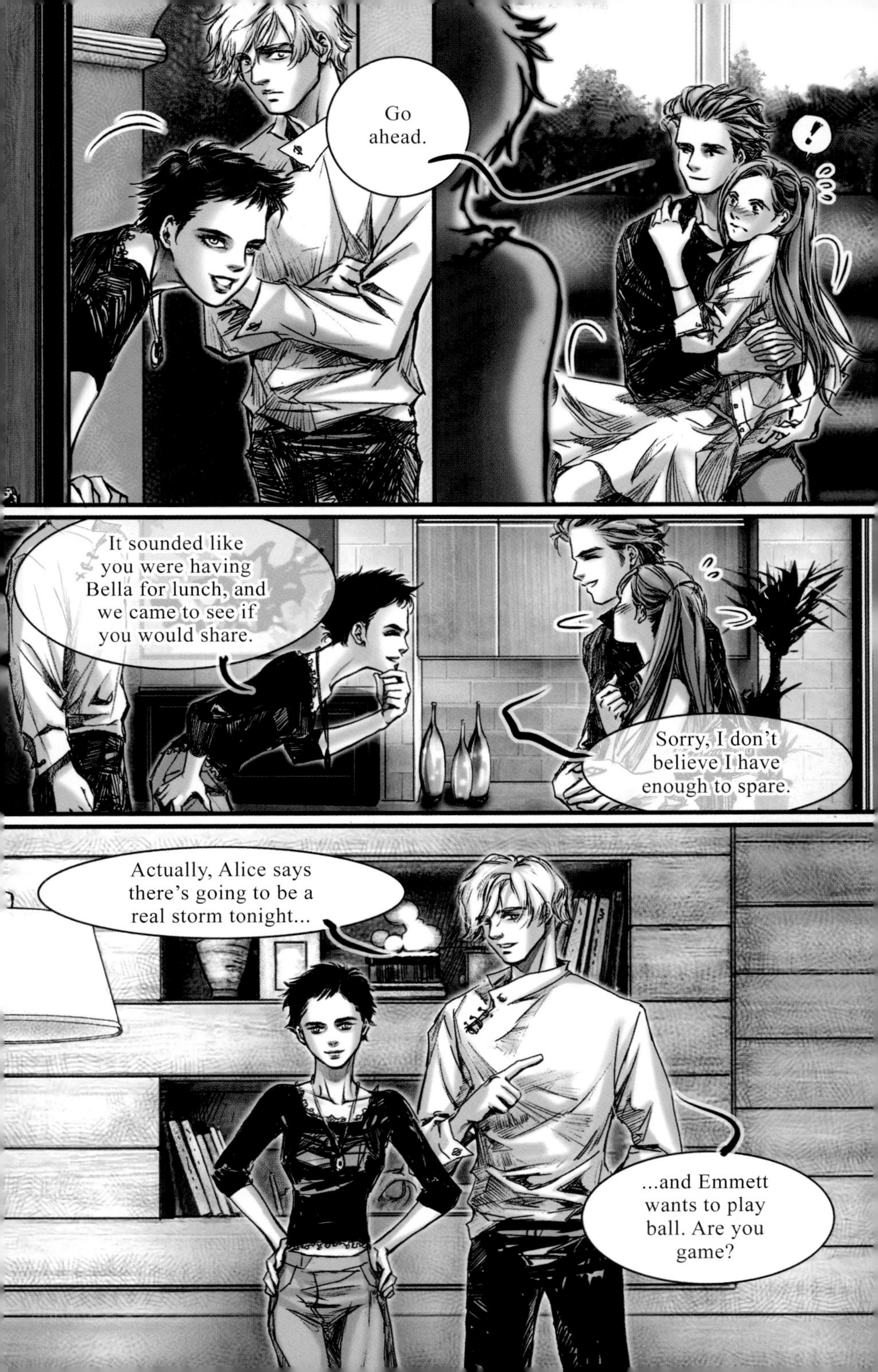
Go ahead.
It sounded like you were having Bella for lunch, and we came to see if you would share.
Sorry, I don't believe I have enough to spare.
Actually, Alice says there's going to be a real storm tonight...
...and Emmett wants to play ball. Are you game?

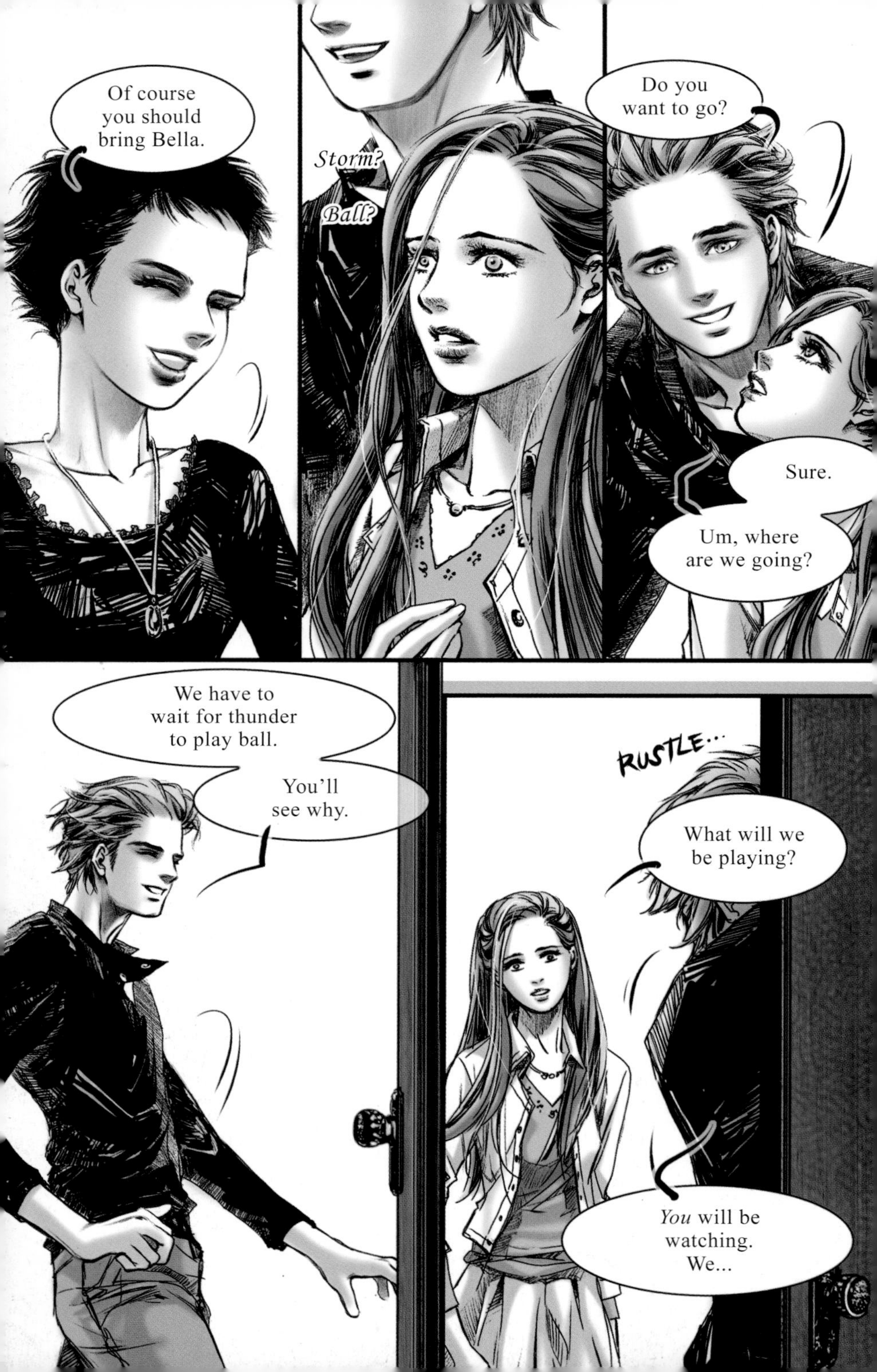
Of course you should bring Bella.
Storm?
Ball?
Do you want to go?
Sure.
Um, where are we going?
We have to wait for thunder to play ball.
You'll see why.
RUSTLE...
What will we be playing?
*You* will be watching. We...

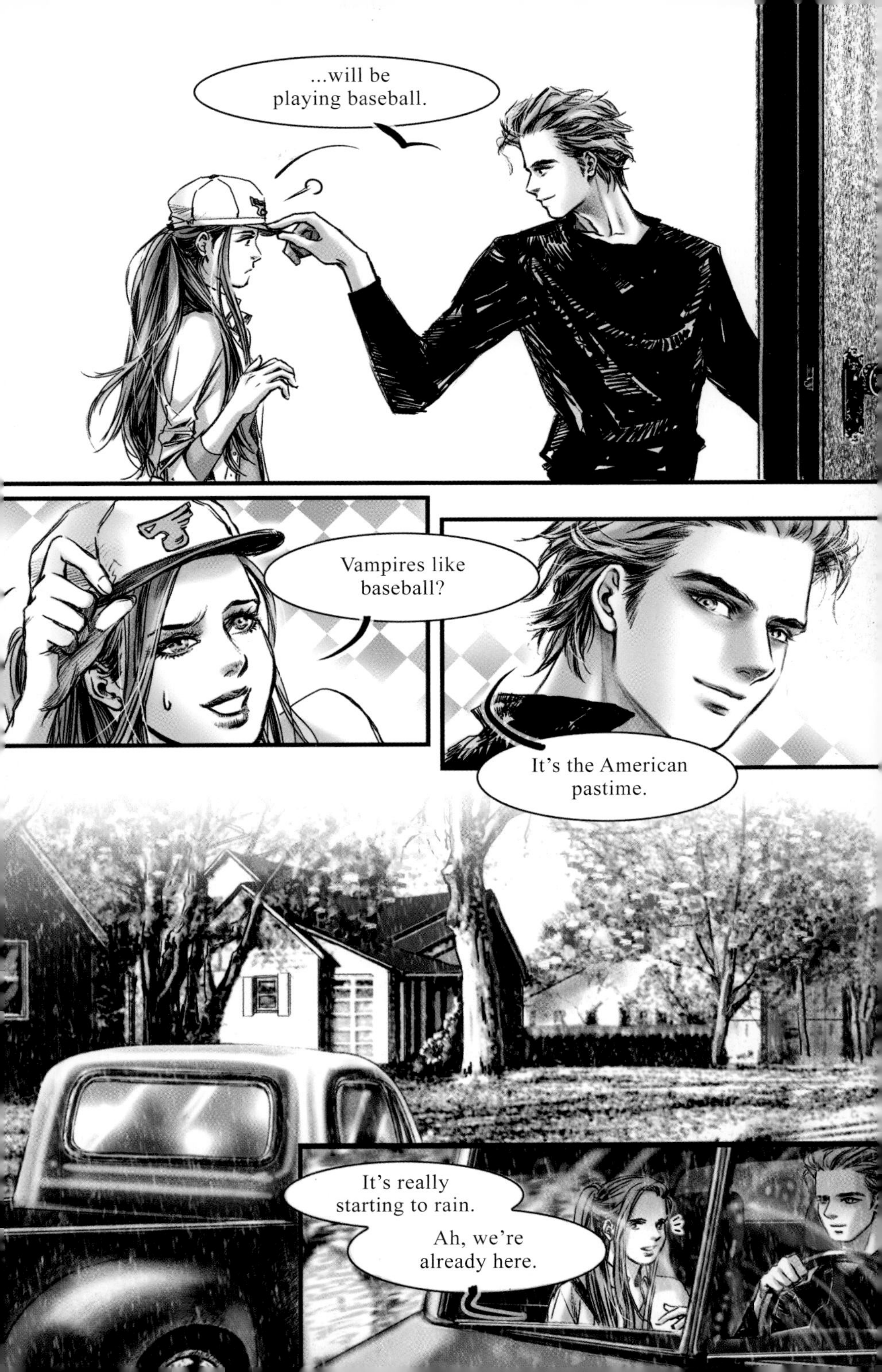
...will be playing baseball.
Vampires like baseball?
It's the American pastime.
It's really starting to rain.
Ah, we're already here.

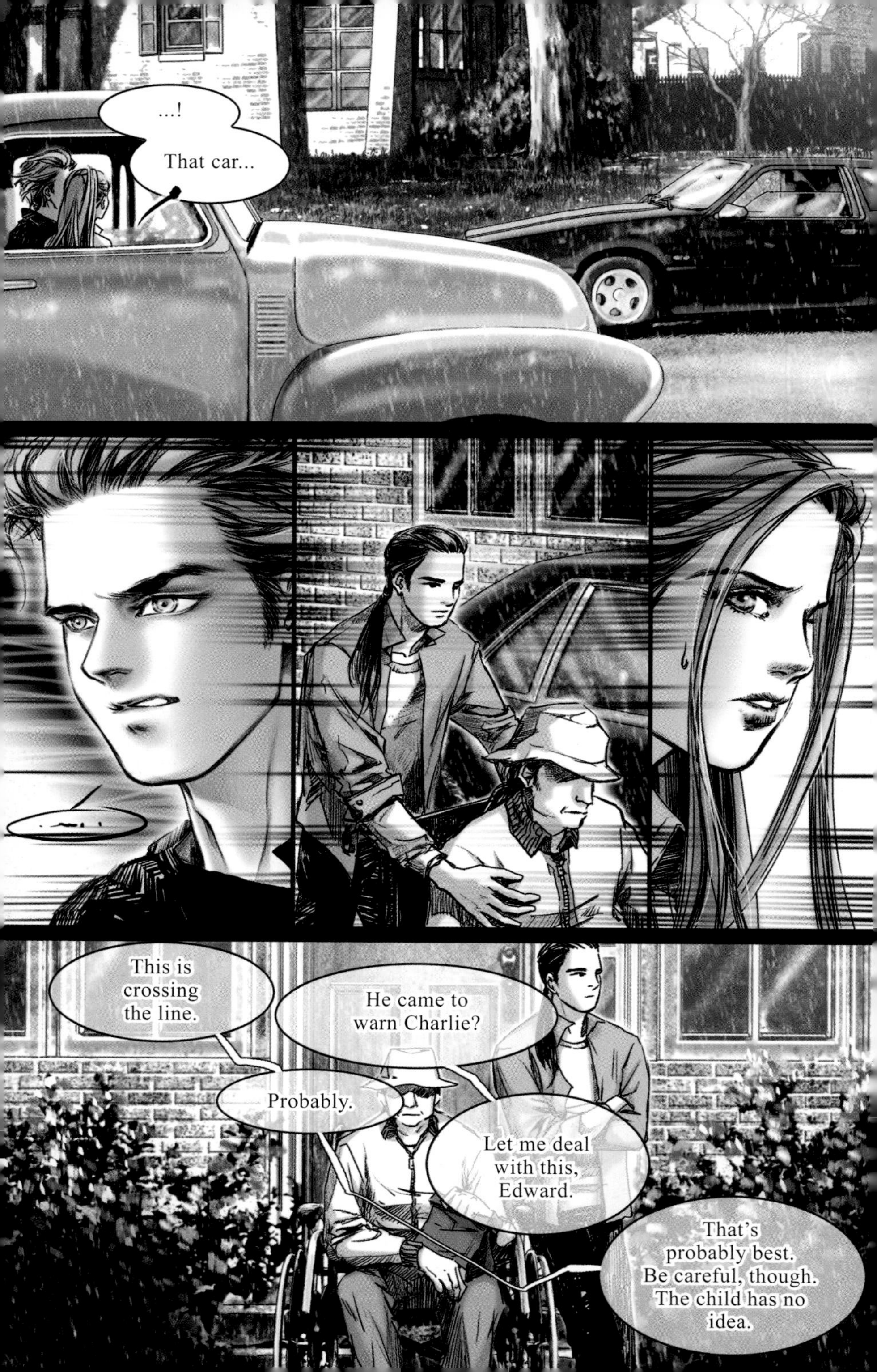
...!
That car...
This is crossing the line.
He came to warn Charlie?
Probably.
Let me deal with this, Edward.
That's probably best. Be careful, though. The child has no idea.

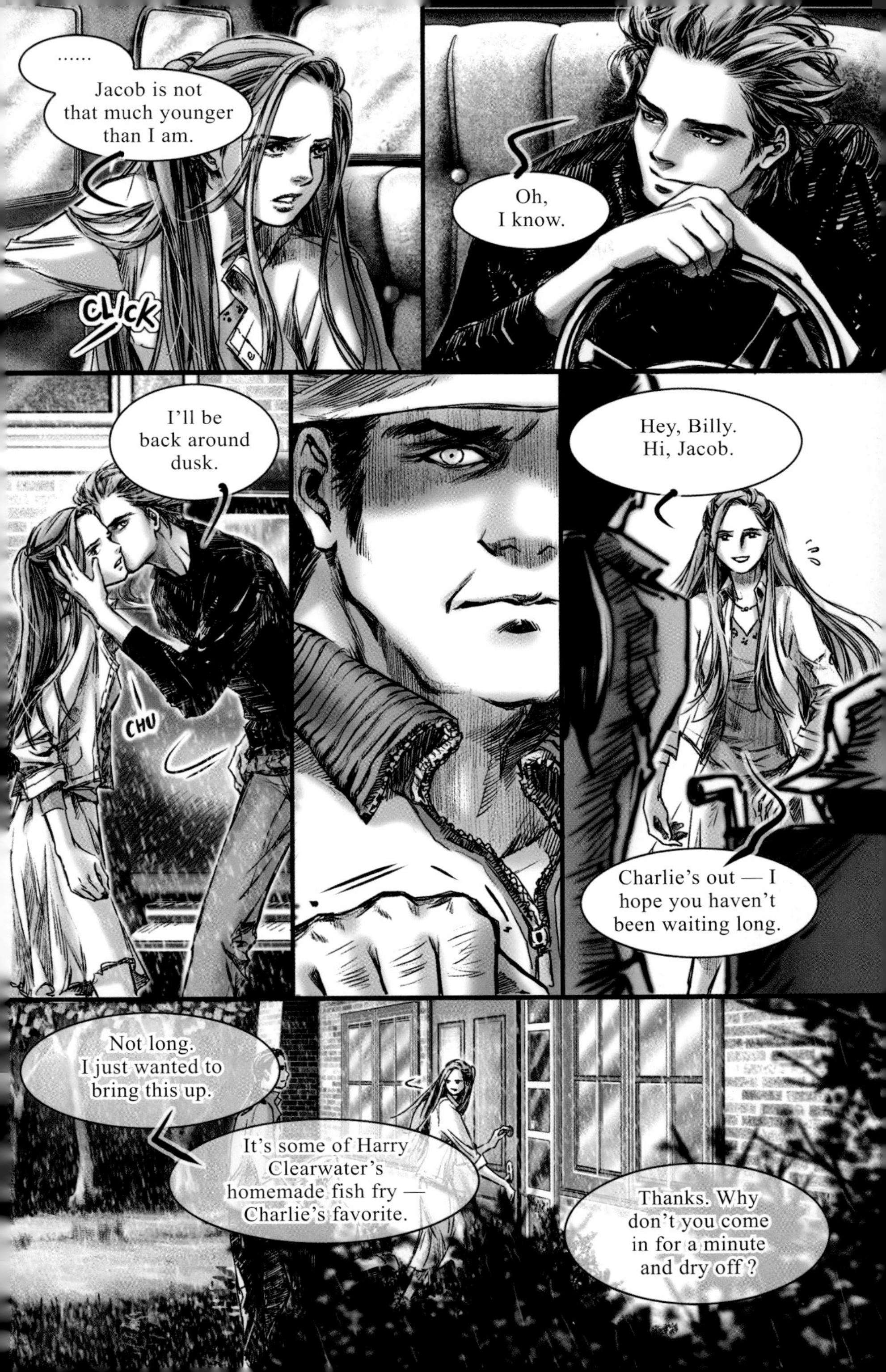

...... Jacob is not that much younger than I am.
CLICK
Oh, I know.
I'll be back around dusk.
CHU
Hey, Billy. Hi, Jacob.
Charlie's out — I hope you haven't been waiting long.
Not long. I just wanted to bring this up.
It's some of Harry Clearwater's homemade fish fry — Charlie's favorite.
Thanks. Why don't you come in for a minute and dry off ?

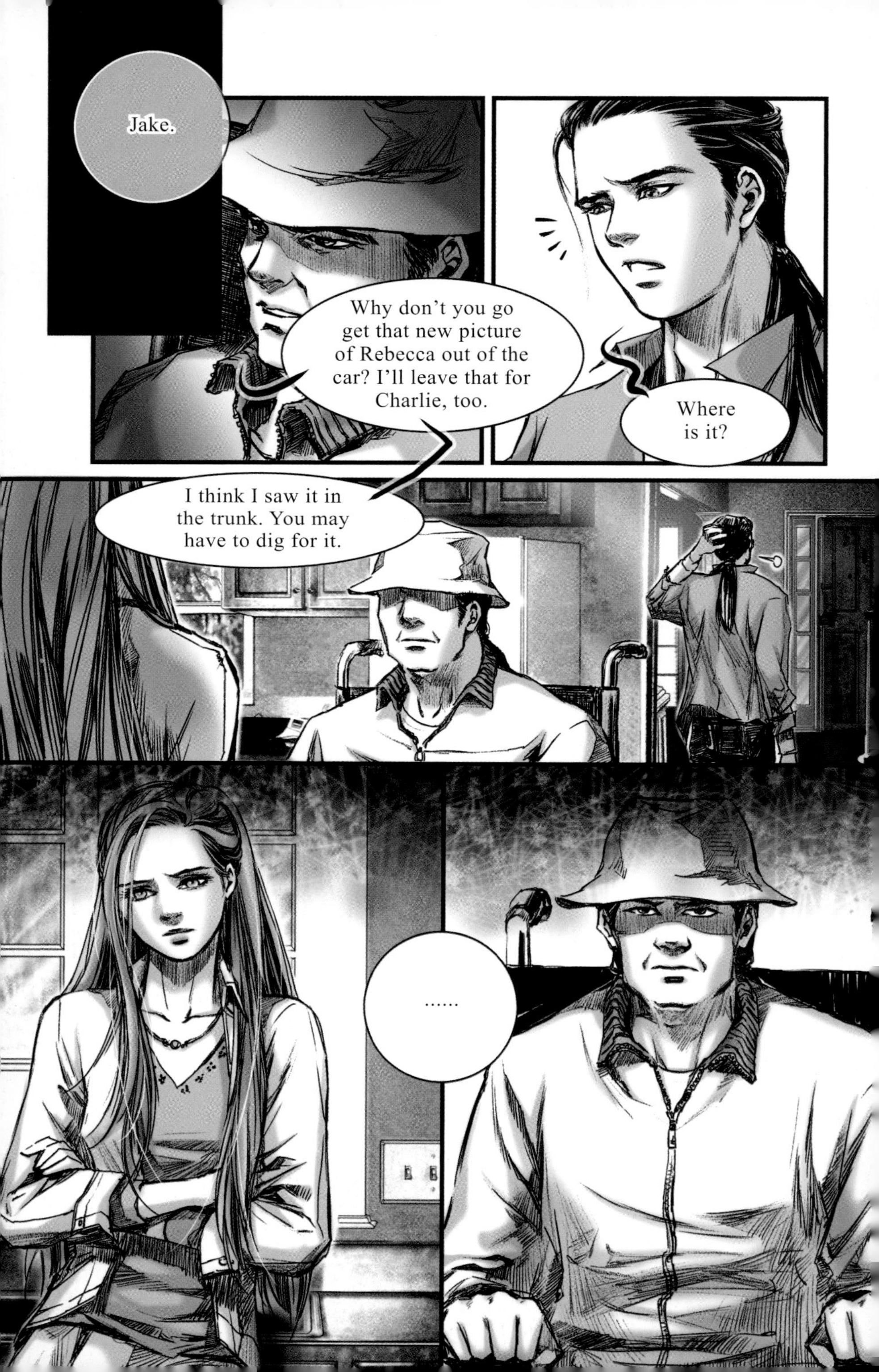
Jake.
Why don't you go get that new picture of Rebecca out of the car? I'll leave that for Charlie, too.
Where is it?
I think I saw it in the trunk. You may have to dig for it.
......

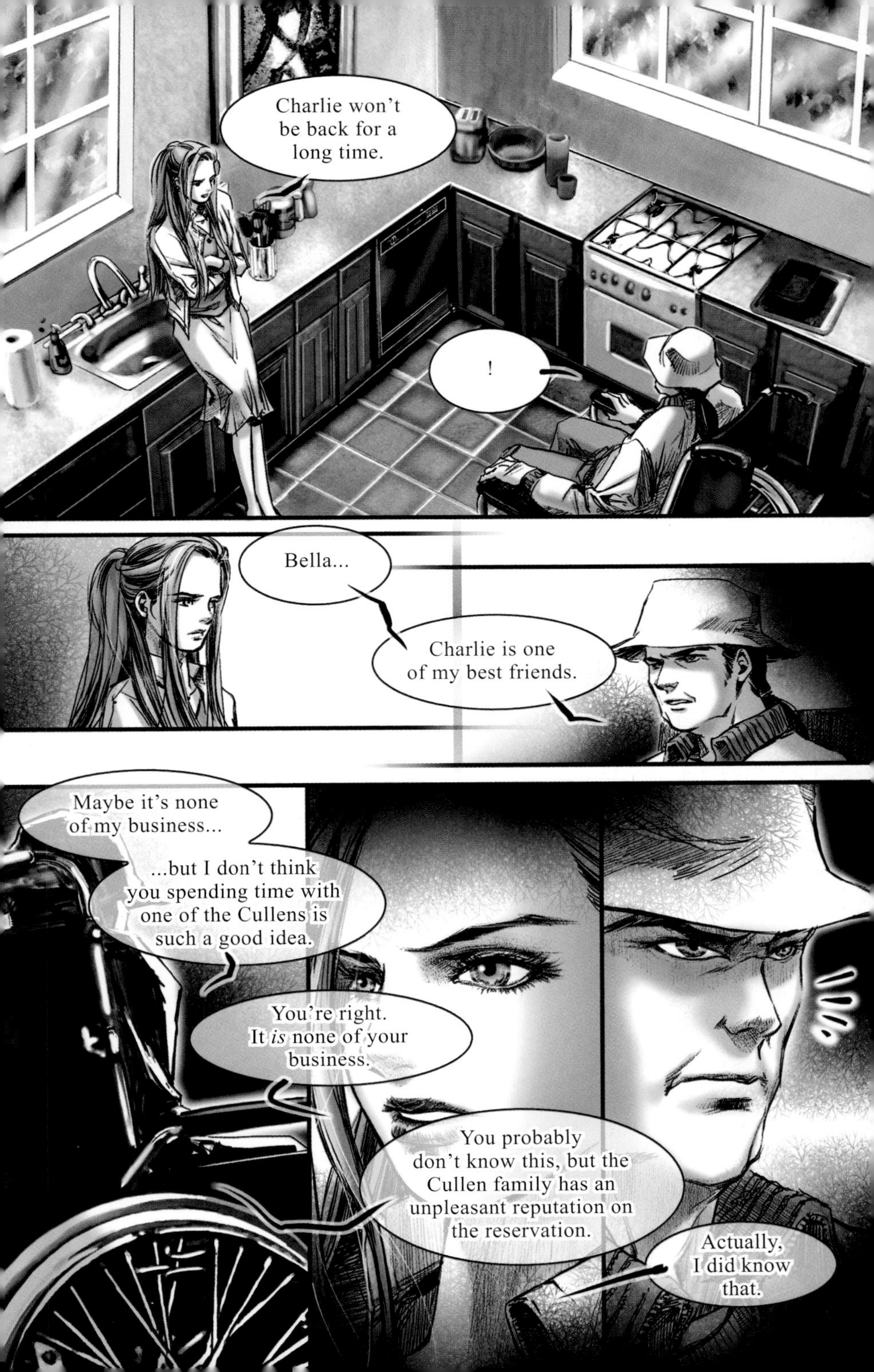
Charlie won't be back for a long time.
!
Bella...
Charlie is one of my best friends.
Maybe it's none of my business...
...but I don't think you spending time with one of the Cullens is such a good idea.
You're right. It *is* none of your business.
You probably don't know this, but the Cullen family has an unpleasant reputation on the reservation.
Actually, I did know that.

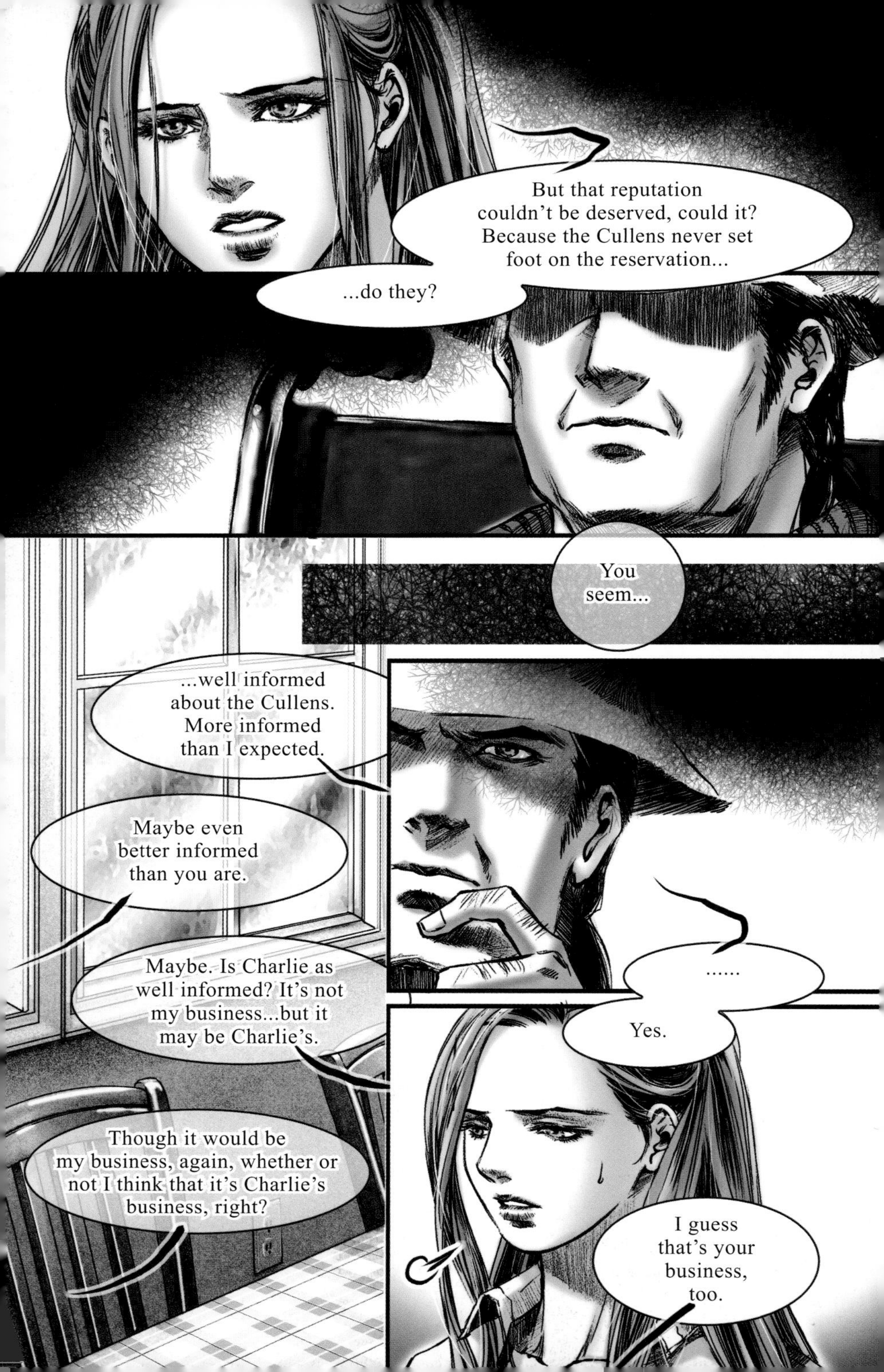
But that reputation couldn't be deserved, could it? Because the Cullens never set foot on the reservation...
...do they?
You seem...
...well informed about the Cullens. More informed than I expected.
Maybe even better informed than you are.
......
Maybe. Is Charlie as well informed? It's not my business...but it may be Charlie's.
Yes.
Though it would be my business, again, whether or not I think that it's Charlie's business, right?
I guess that's your business, too.

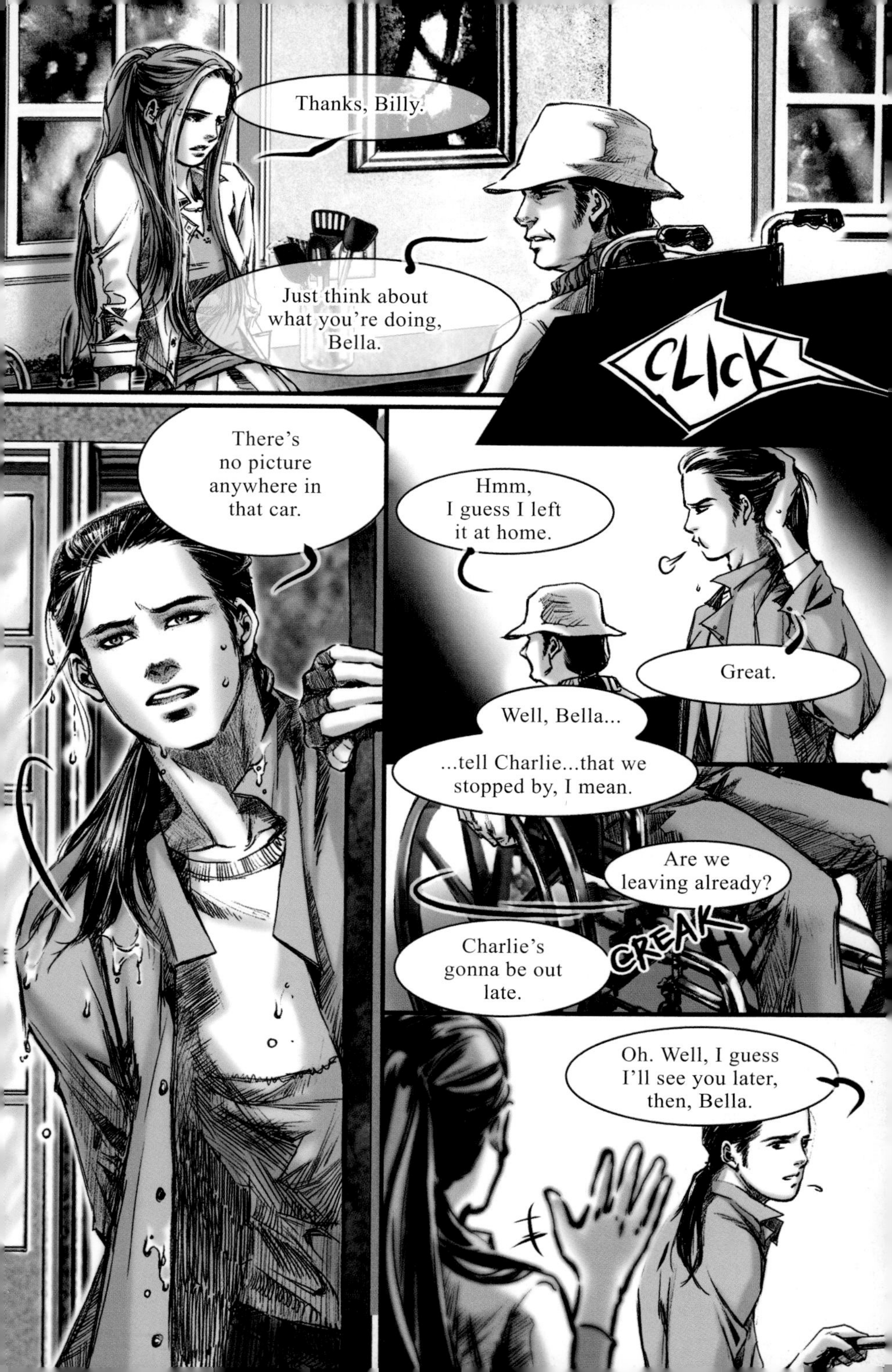
Thanks, Billy.
Just think about what you're doing, Bella.
CLICK
There's no picture anywhere in that car.
Hmm, I guess I left it at home.
Great.
Well, Bella...
...tell Charlie...that we stopped by, I mean.
Are we leaving already?
CREAK
Charlie's gonna be out late.
Oh. Well, I guess I'll see you later, then, Bella.

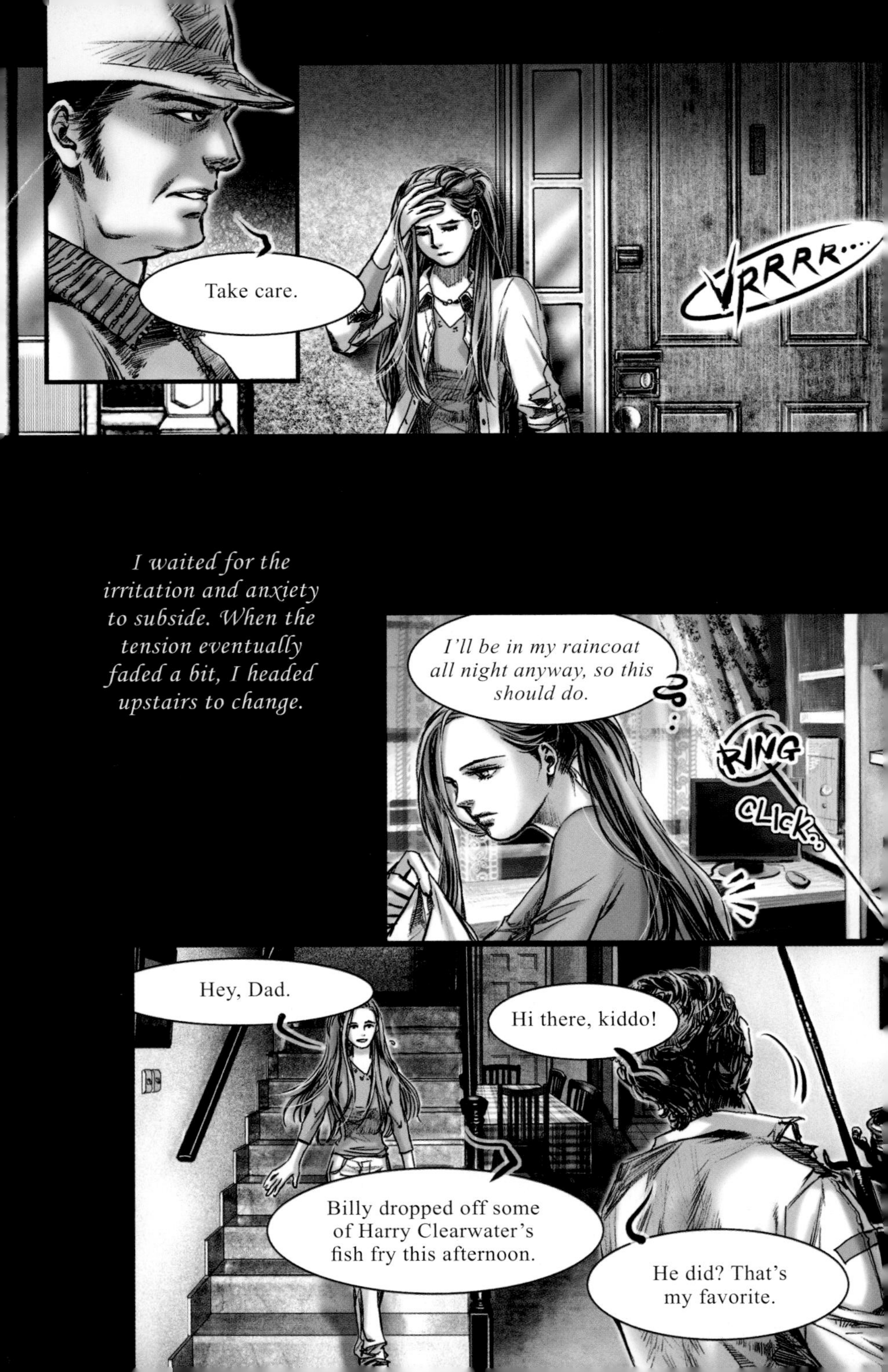

Take care.
VRRRR....
I waited for the irritation and anxiety to subside. When the tension eventually faded a bit, I headed upstairs to change.
I'll be in my raincoat all night anyway, so this should do.
RING
CLICK..
Hey, Dad.
Hi there, kiddo!
Billy dropped off some of Harry Clearwater's fish fry this afternoon.
He did? That's my favorite.

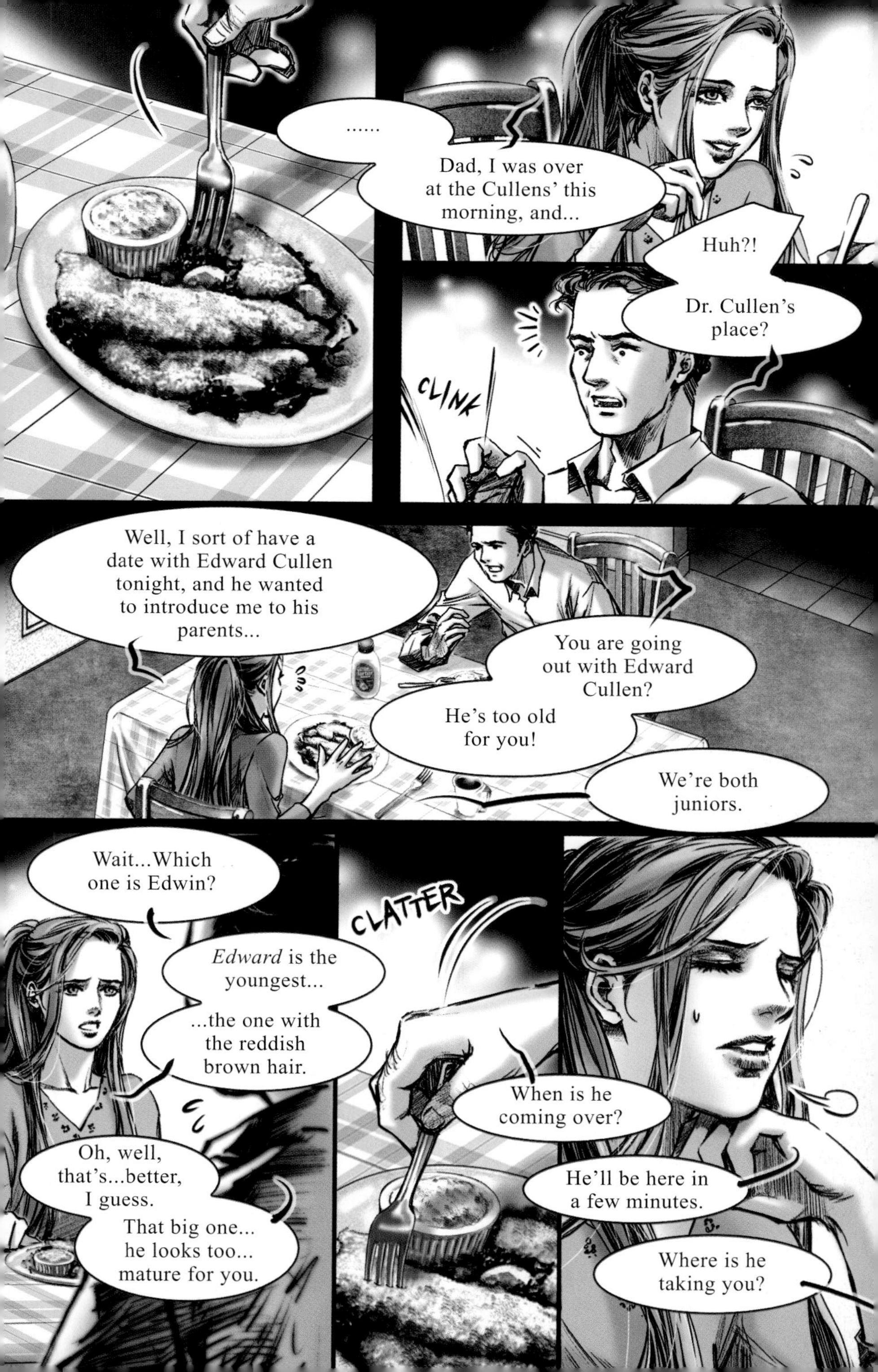
......
Dad, I was over at the Cullens' this morning, and...
Huh?!
Dr. Cullen's place?
CLINK
Well, I sort of have a date with Edward Cullen tonight, and he wanted to introduce me to his parents...
You are going out with Edward Cullen?
He's too old for you!
We're both juniors.
Wait...Which one is Edwin?
*Edward* is the youngest...
...the one with the reddish brown hair.
Oh, well, that's...better, I guess.
That big one... he looks too... mature for you.
CLATTER
When is he coming over?
He'll be here in a few minutes.
Where is he taking you?

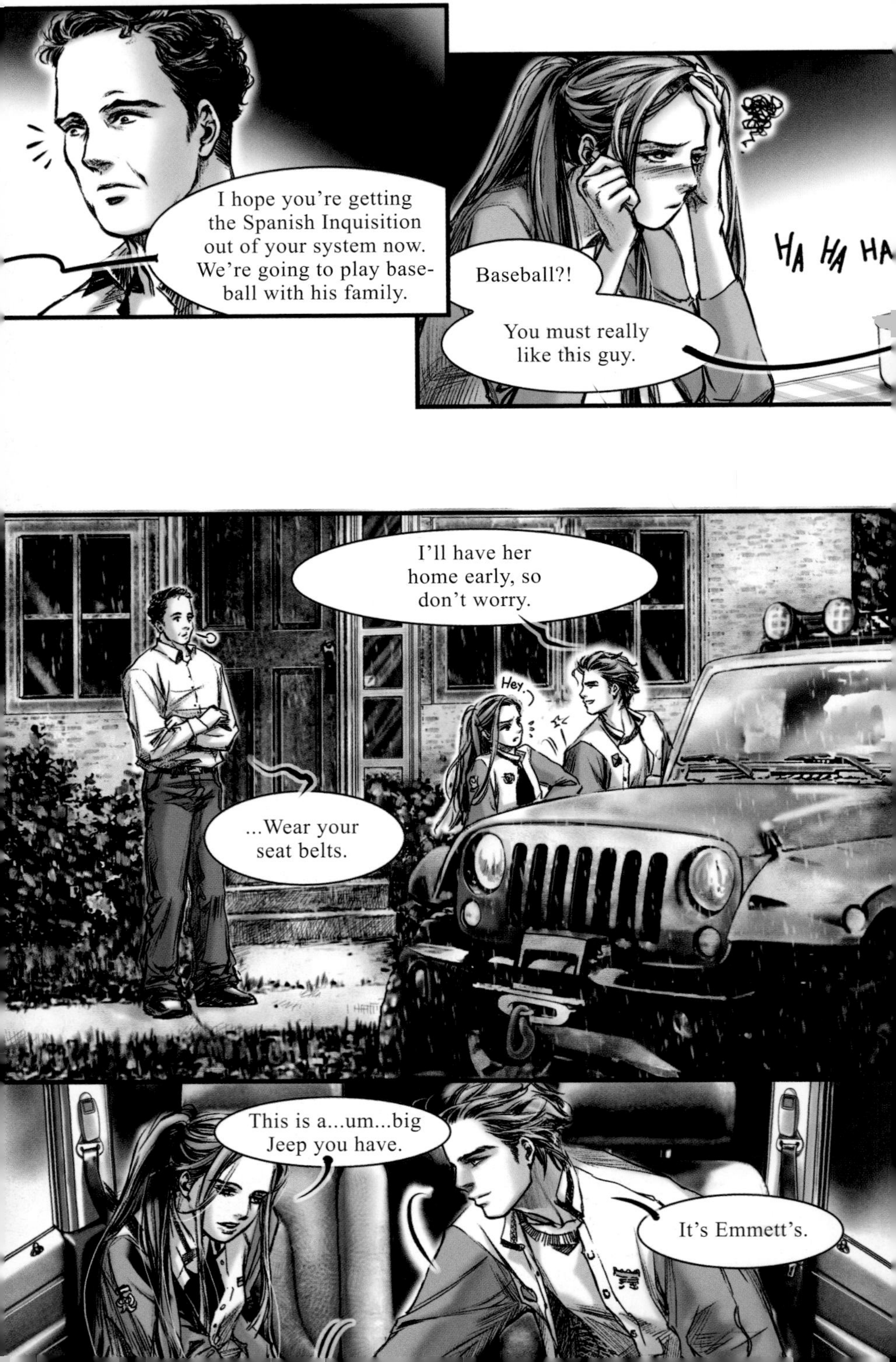
I hope you're getting the Spanish Inquisition out of your system now. We're going to play base-ball with his family.
Baseball?!
HA HA HA
You must really like this guy.
I'll have her home early, so don't worry.
Hey.
...Wear your seat belts.
This is a...um...big Jeep you have.
It's Emmett's.

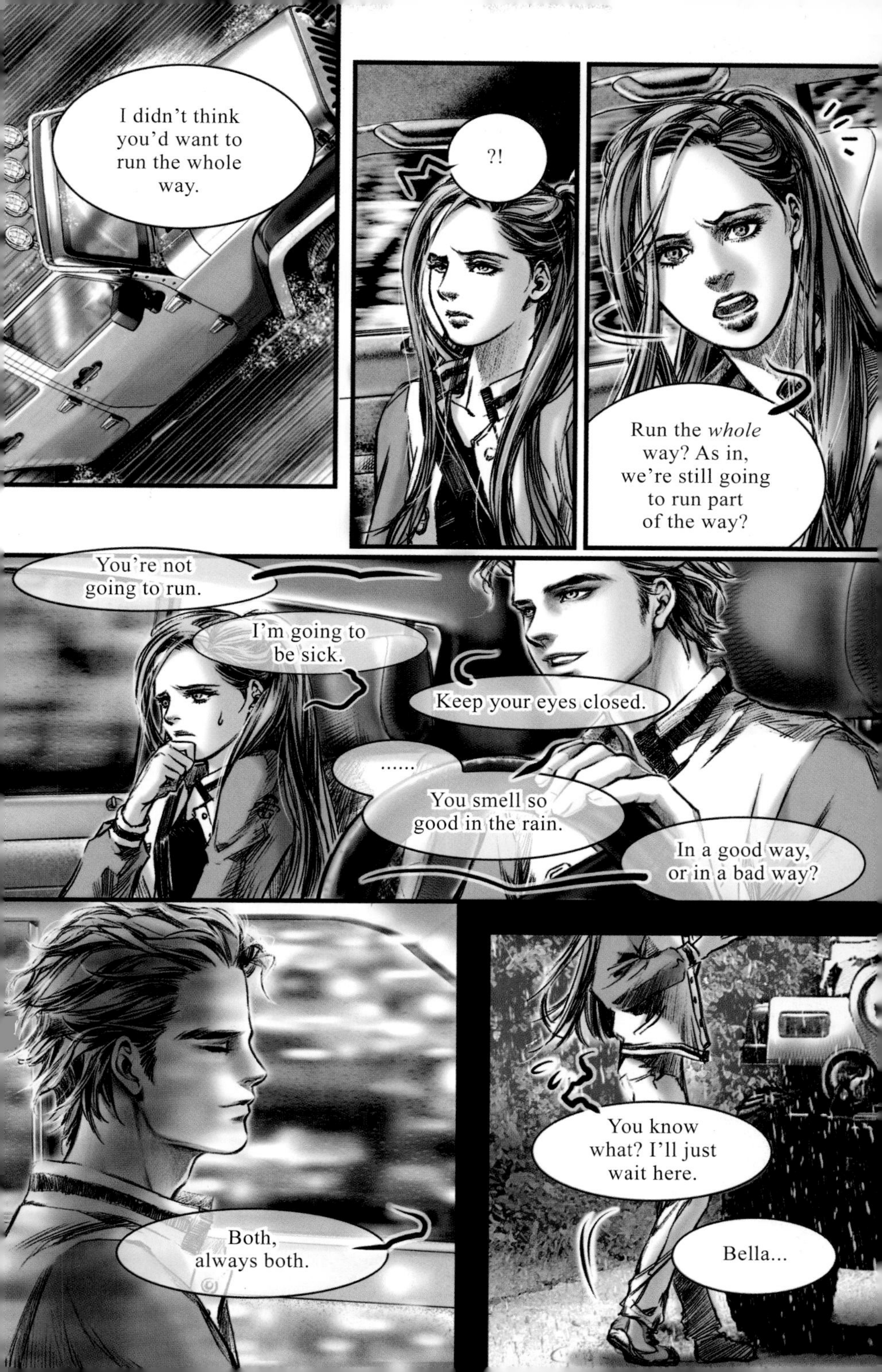
I didn't think you'd want to run the whole way.
?!
Run the *whole* way? As in, we're still going to run part of the way?
You're not going to run.
I'm going to be sick.
Keep your eyes closed.
......
You smell so good in the rain.
In a good way, or in a bad way?
Both, always both.
You know what? I'll just wait here.
Bella...

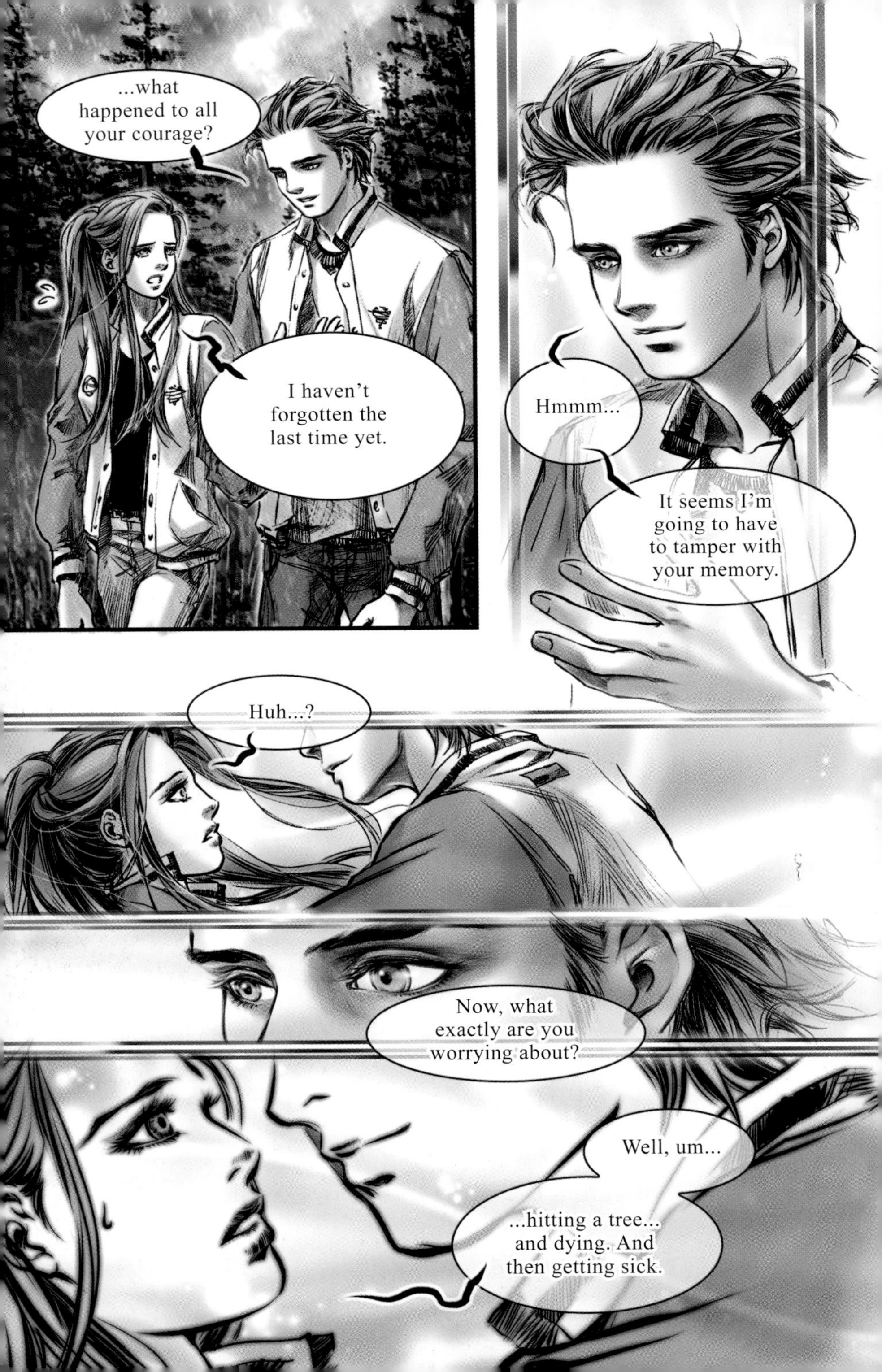
...what happened to all your courage?
I haven't forgotten the last time yet.
Hmmm...
It seems I'm going to have to tamper with your memory.
Huh...?
Now, what exactly are you worrying about?
Well, um...
...hitting a tree... and dying. And then getting sick.

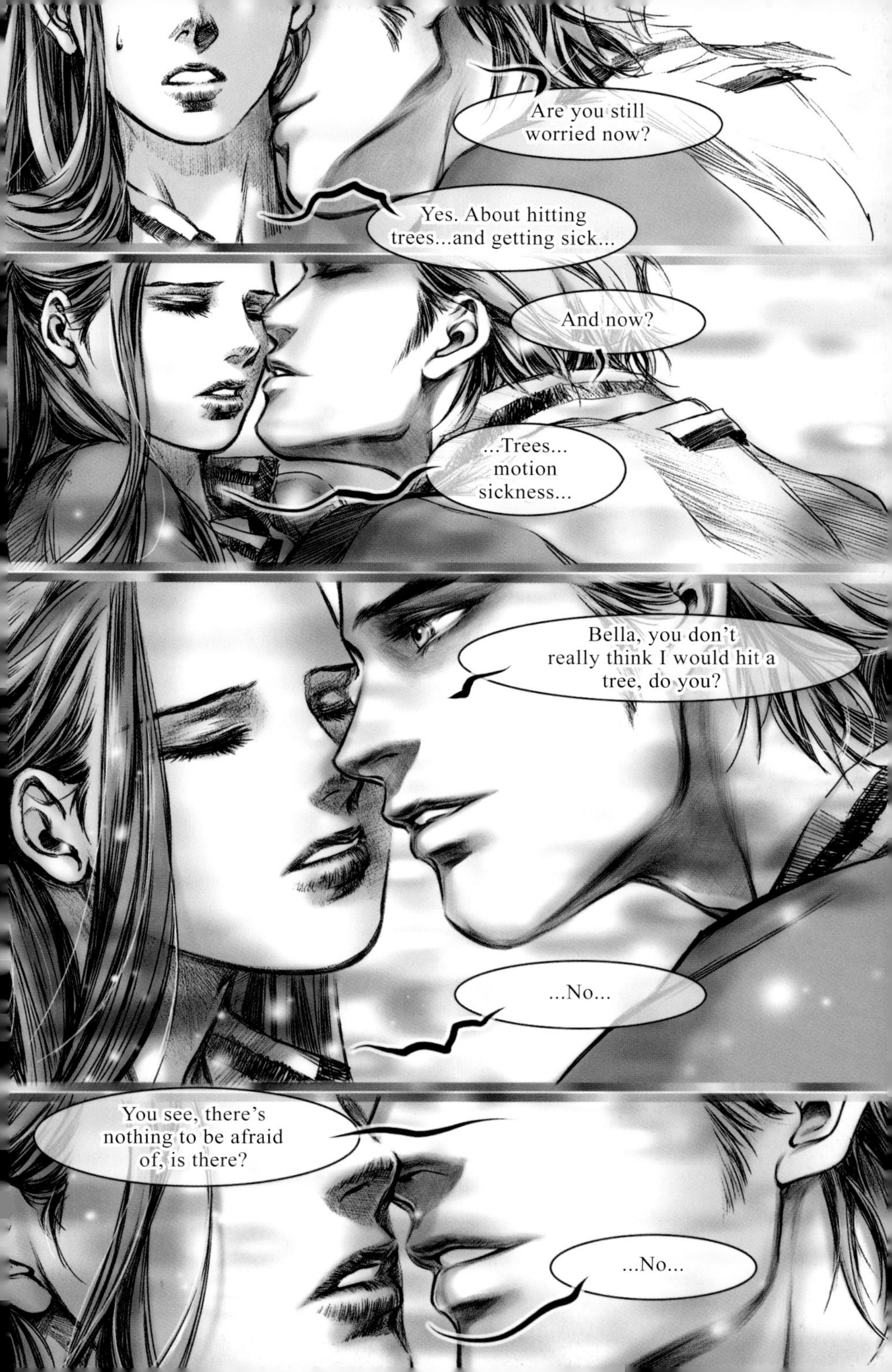
Are you still worried now?
Yes. About hitting trees...and getting sick...
And now?
...Trees... motion sickness...
Bella, you don't really think I would hit a tree, do you?
...No...
You see, there's nothing to be afraid of, is there?
...No...

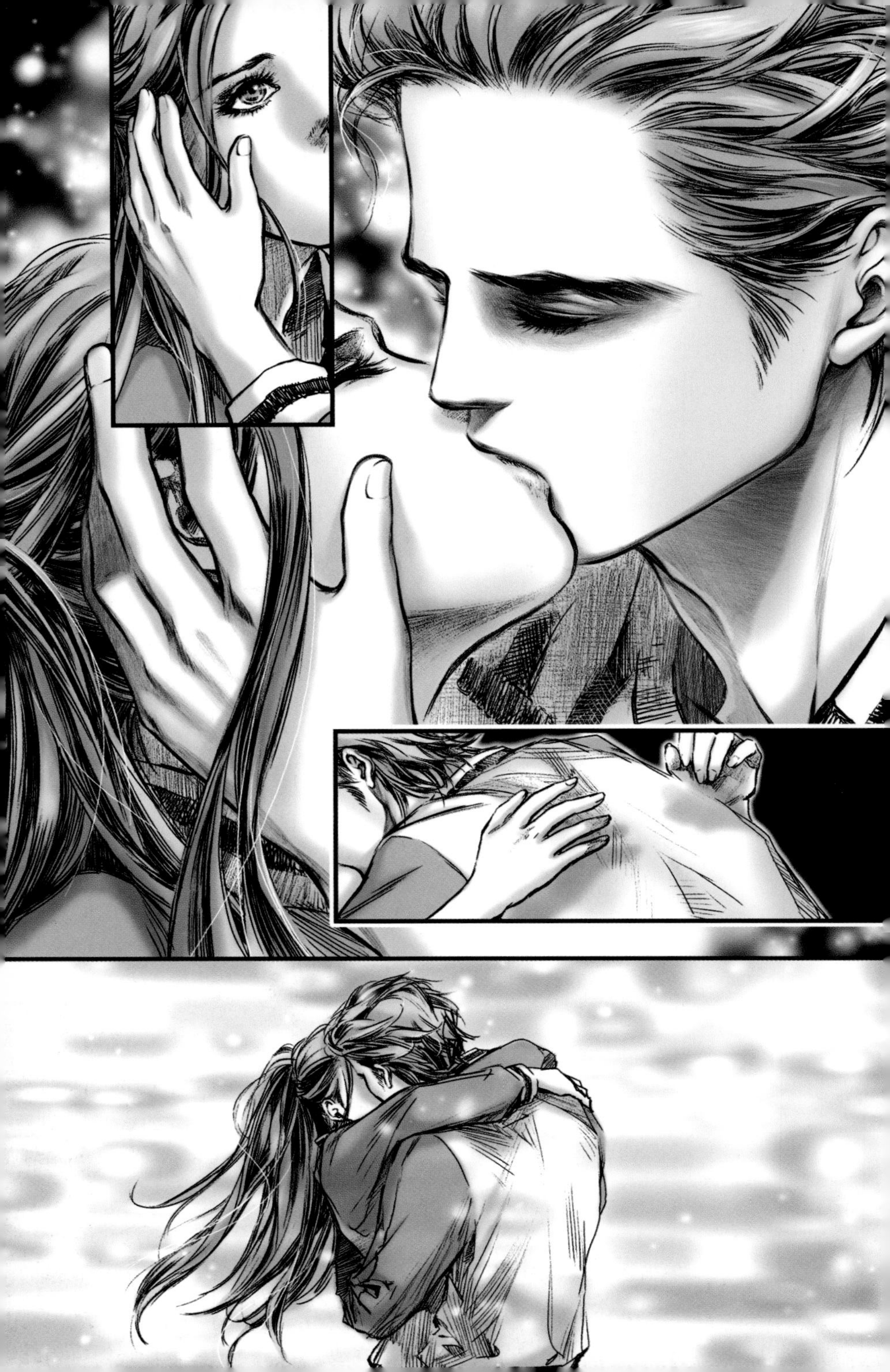

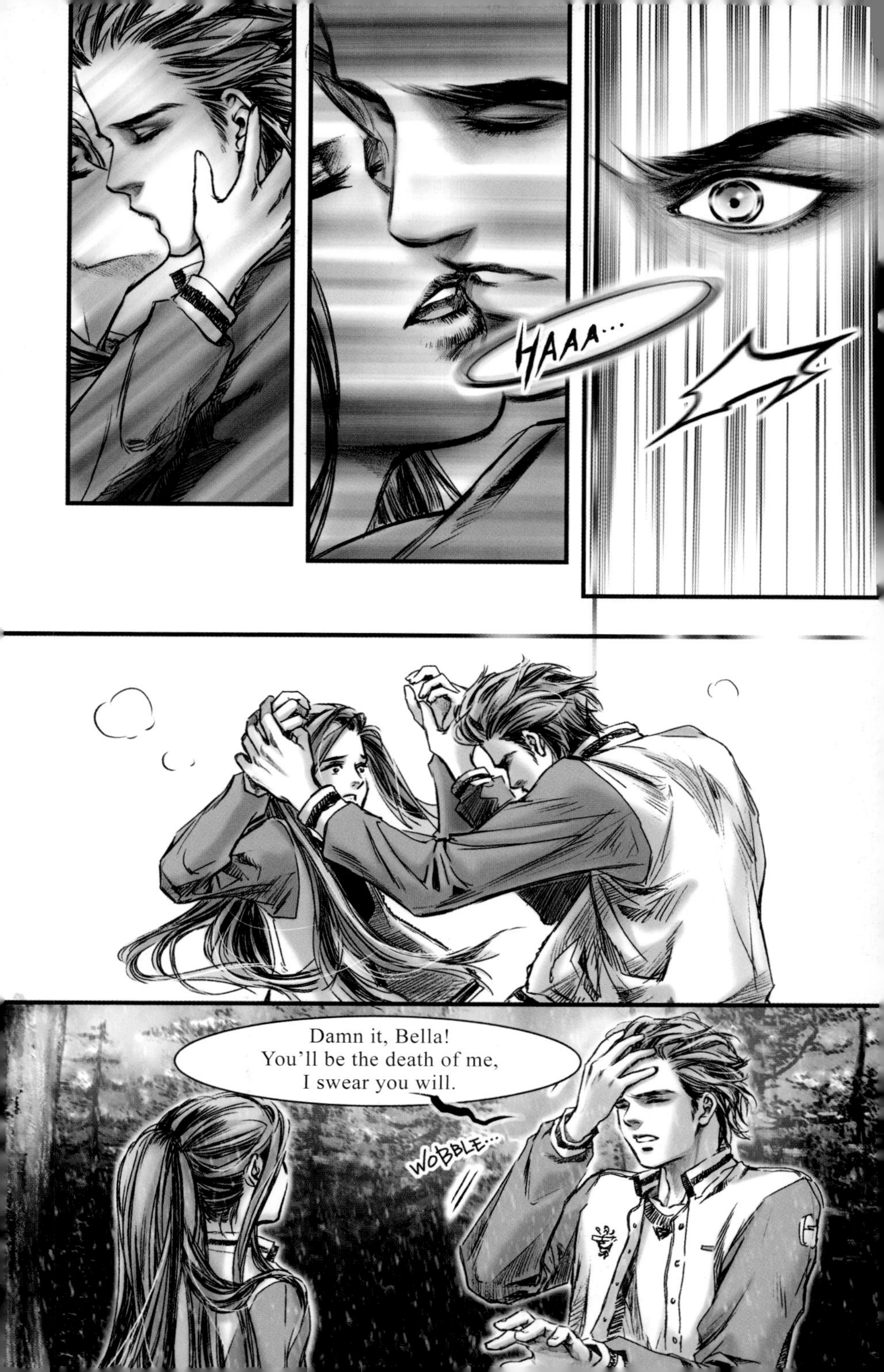
HAAA...
Damn it, Bella!
You'll be the death of me,
I swear you will.
WOBBLE...

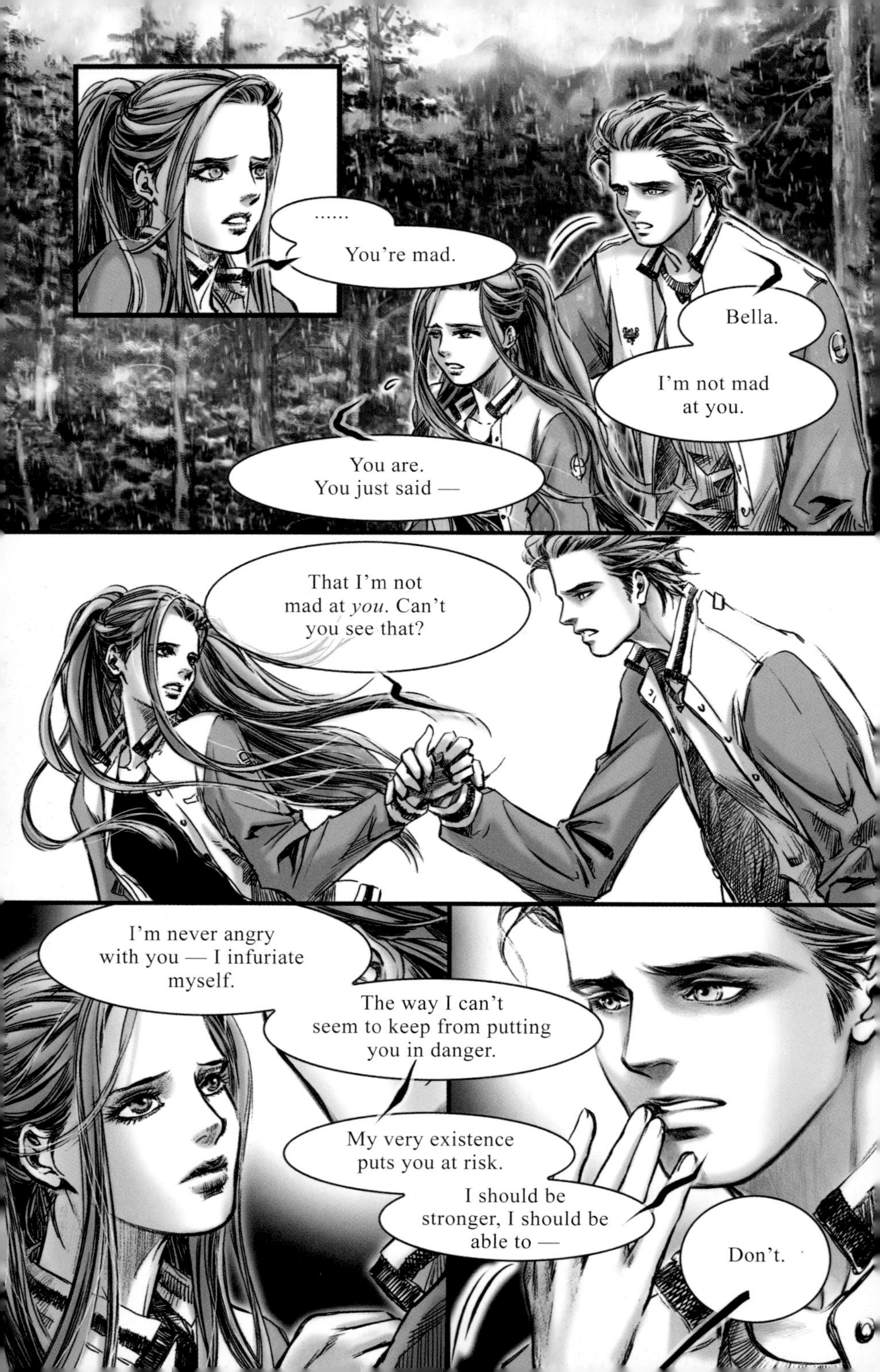
......
You're mad.
Bella.
I'm not mad at you.
You are. You just said —
That I'm not mad at *you*. Can't you see that?
I'm never angry with you — I infuriate myself.
The way I can't seem to keep from putting you in danger.
My very existence puts you at risk.
I should be stronger, I should be able to —
Don't.

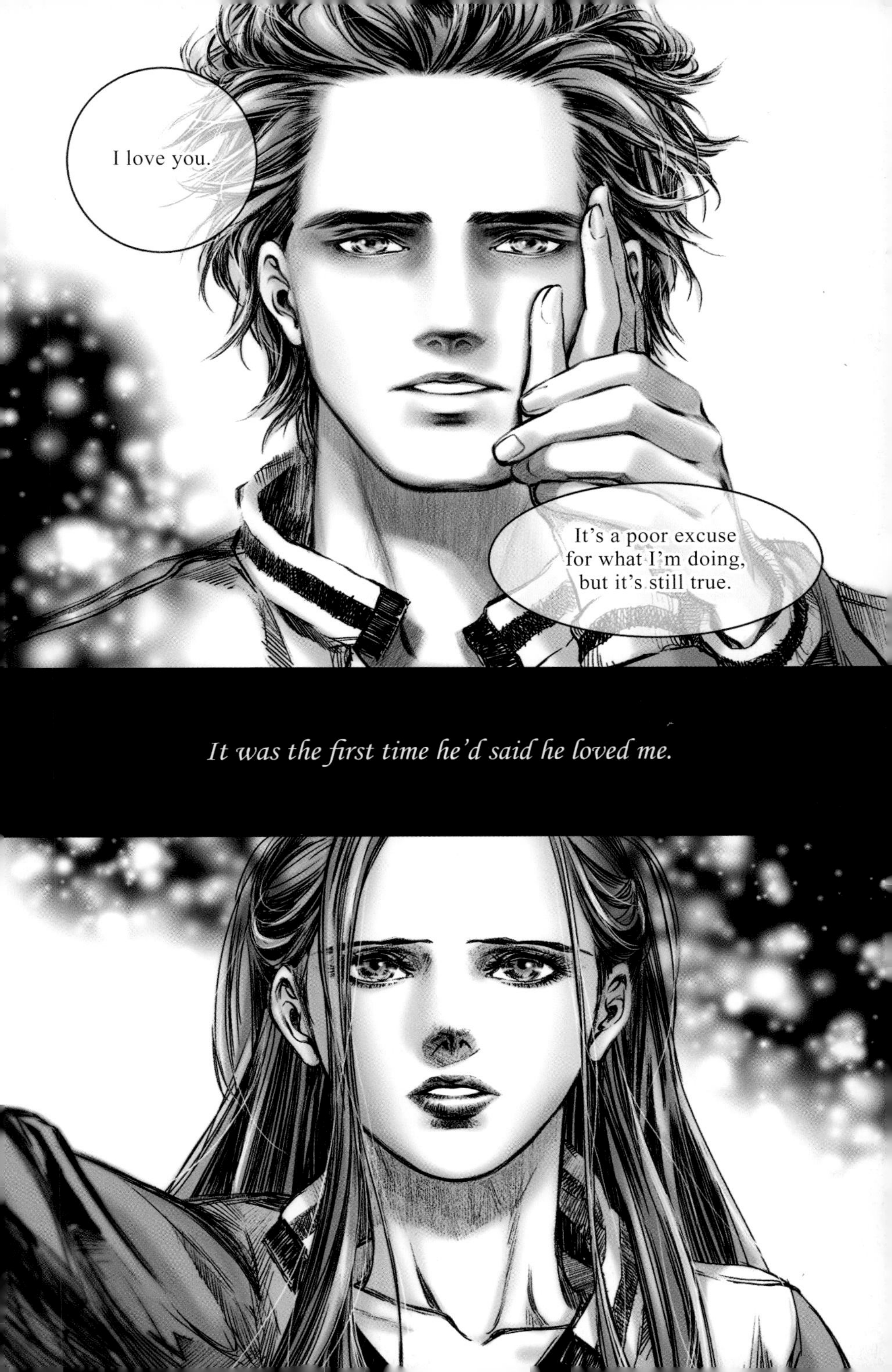
I love you.
It's a poor excuse for what I'm doing, but it's still true.
It was the first time he'd said he loved me.

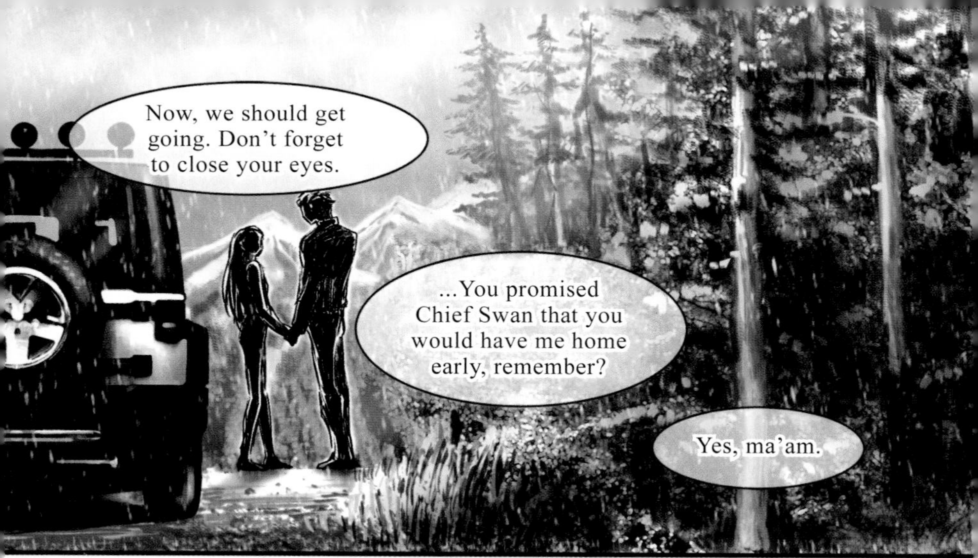
Now, we should get going. Don't forget to close your eyes.
...You promised Chief Swan that you would have me home early, remember?
Yes, ma'am.

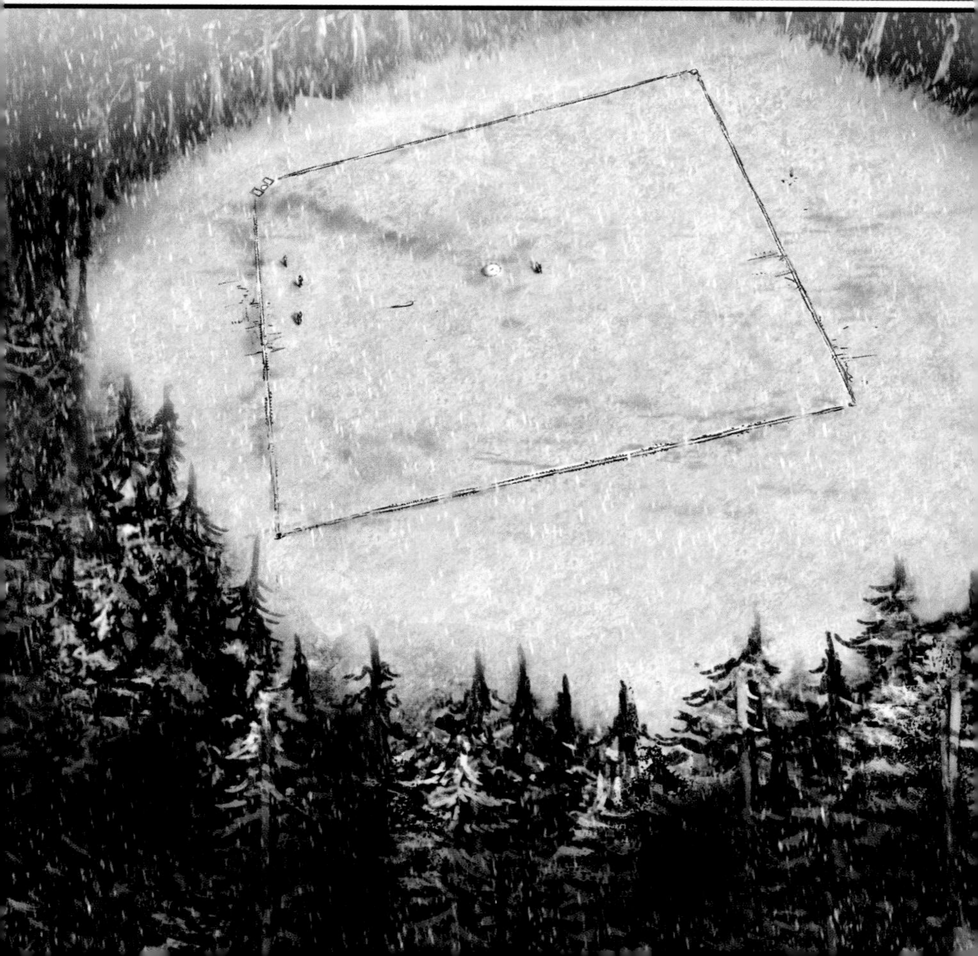

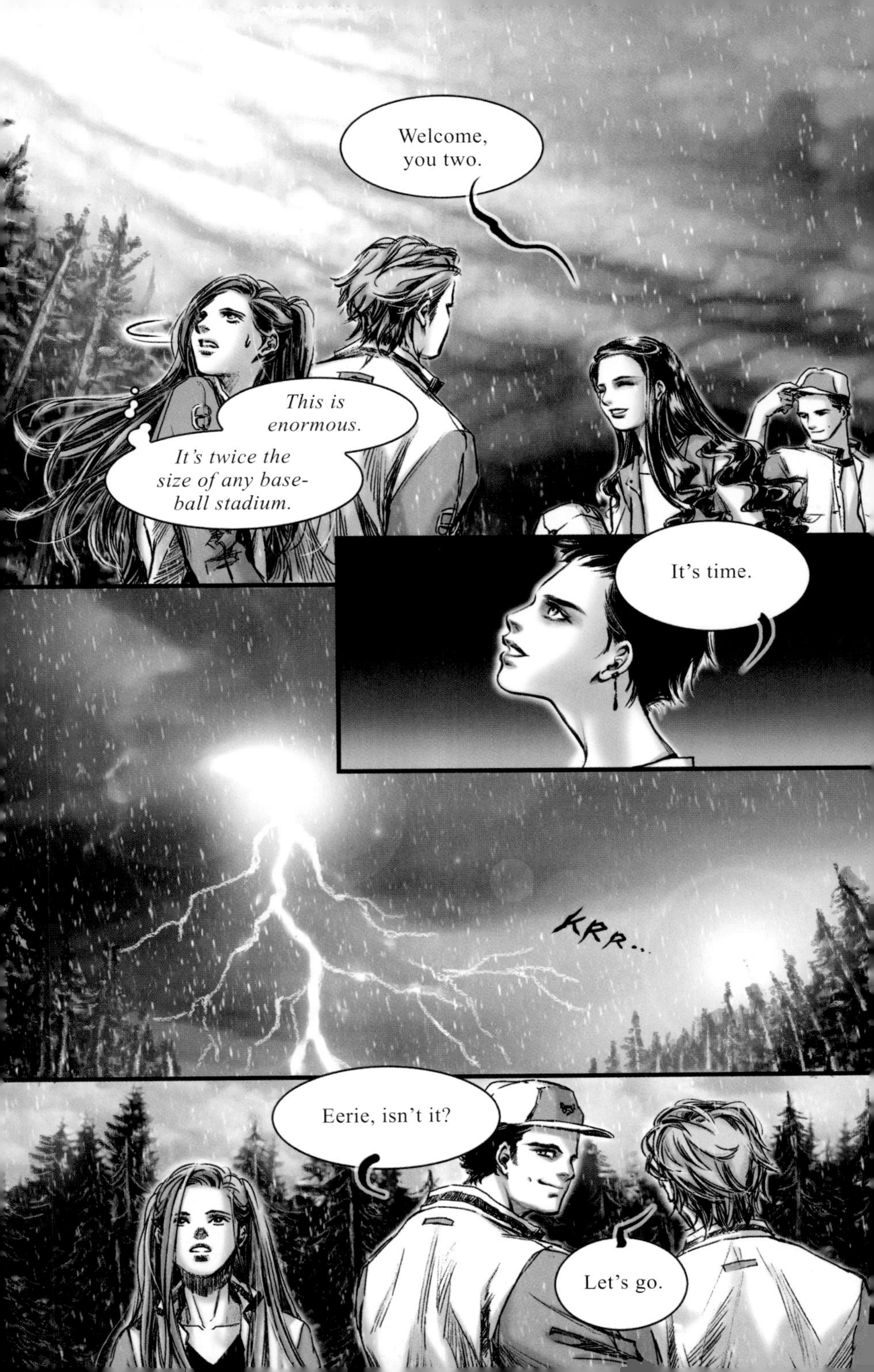
Welcome, you two.
*This is enormous.*
*It's twice the size of any base-ball stadium.*
It's time.
KRR...
Eerie, isn't it?
Let's go.

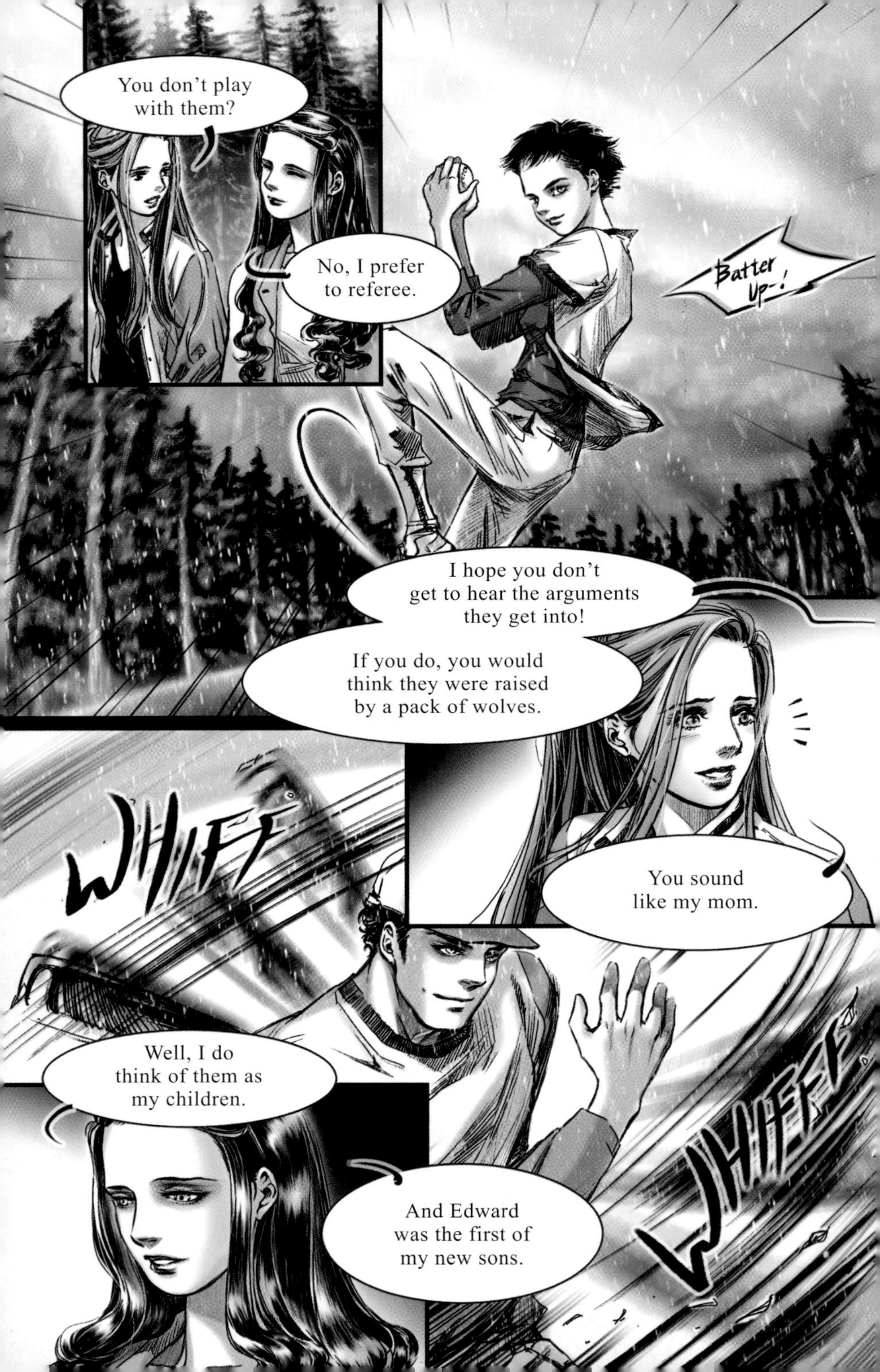
You don't play with them?
No, I prefer to referee.
Batter Up-!
I hope you don't get to hear the arguments they get into!
If you do, you would think they were raised by a pack of wolves.
You sound like my mom.
WHIFF
Well, I do think of them as my children.
And Edward was the first of my new sons.
WHIFF

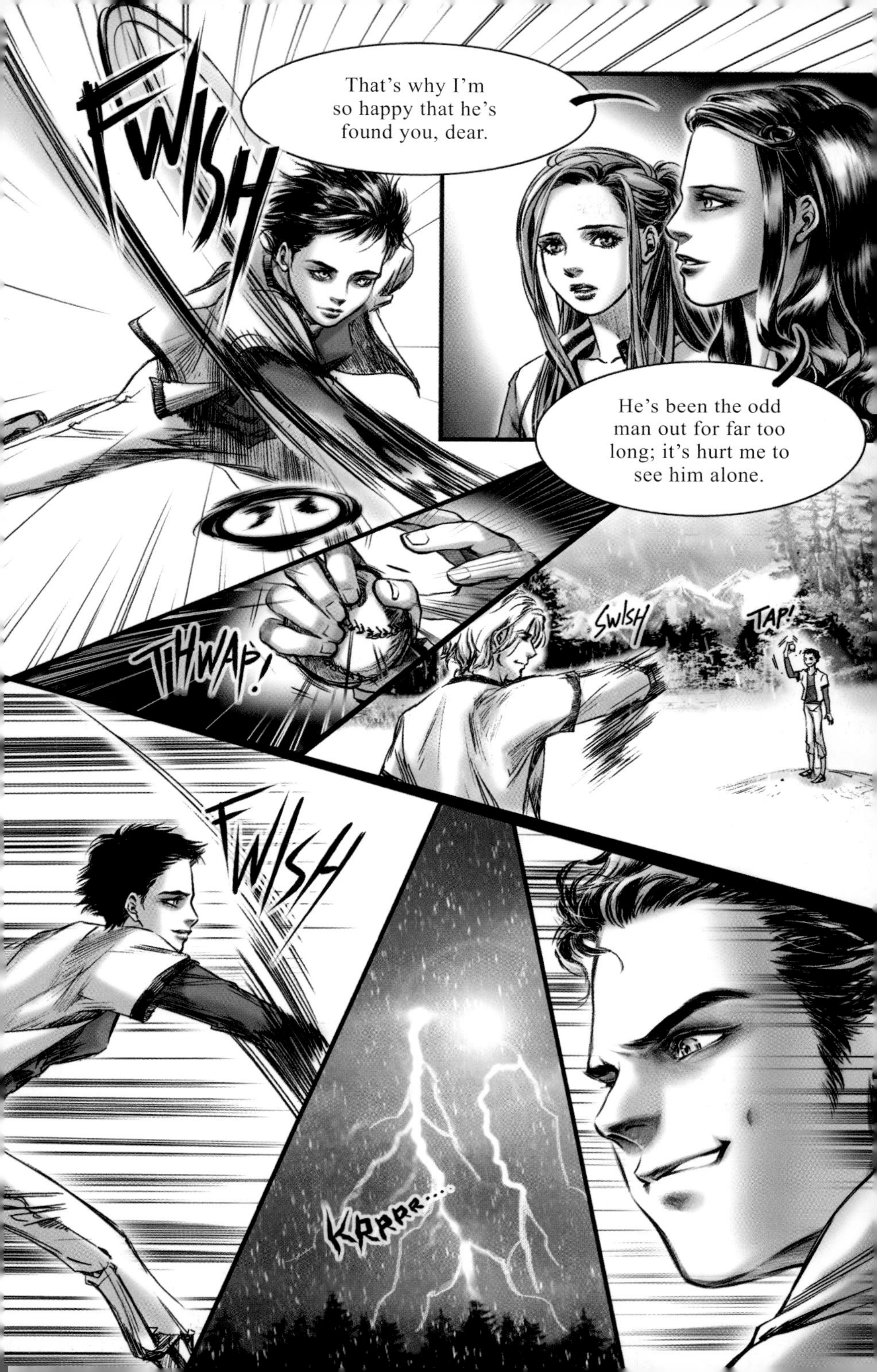
FWISH
That's why I'm so happy that he's found you, dear.
He's been the odd man out for far too long; it's hurt me to see him alone.
THWAP!
SWISH
TAP!
FWISH
KRRRR....

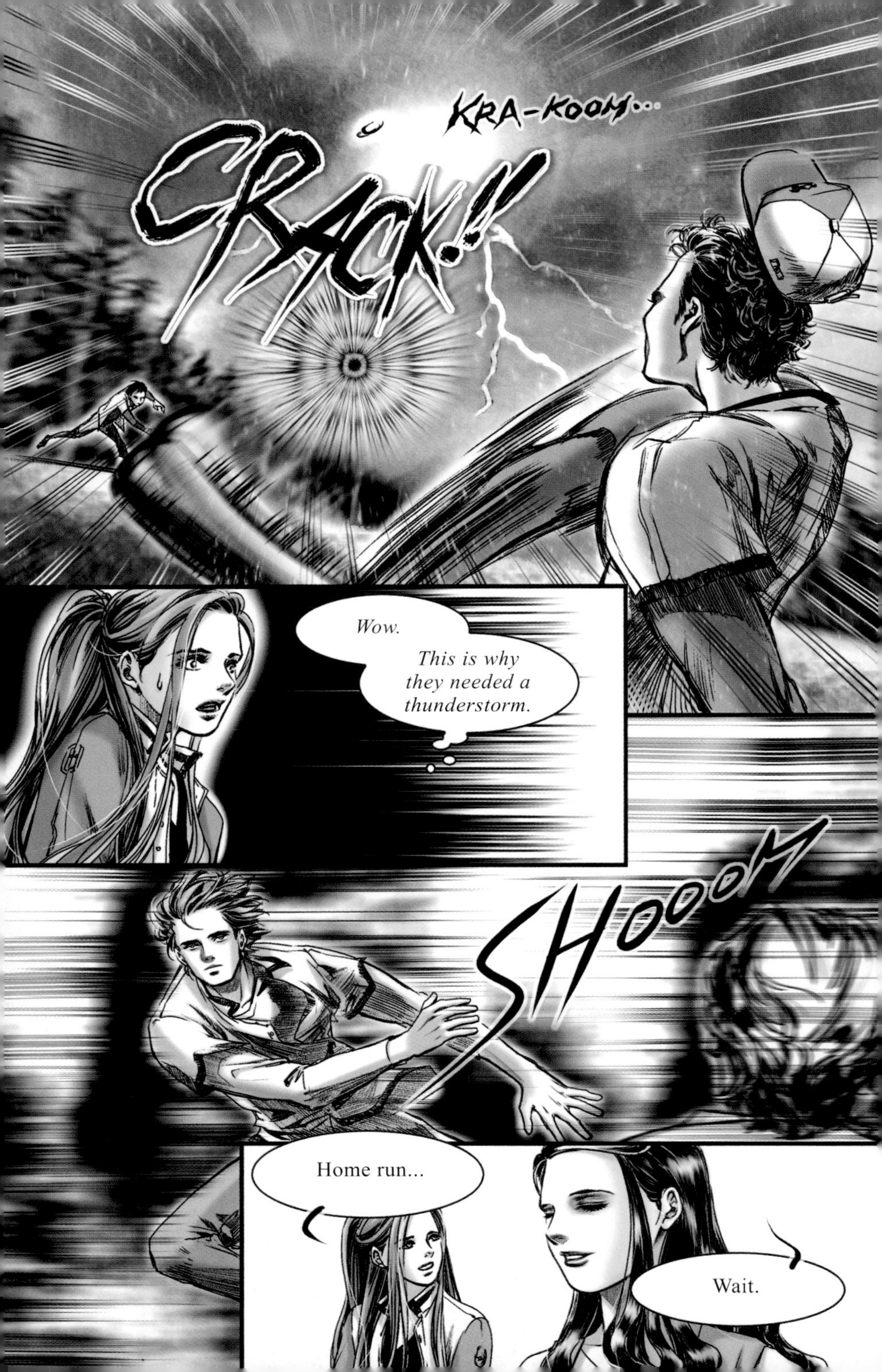
KRA-KOOM...
CRACK!!
Wow.
This is why they needed a thunderstorm.
SHOOOOM
Home run...
Wait.

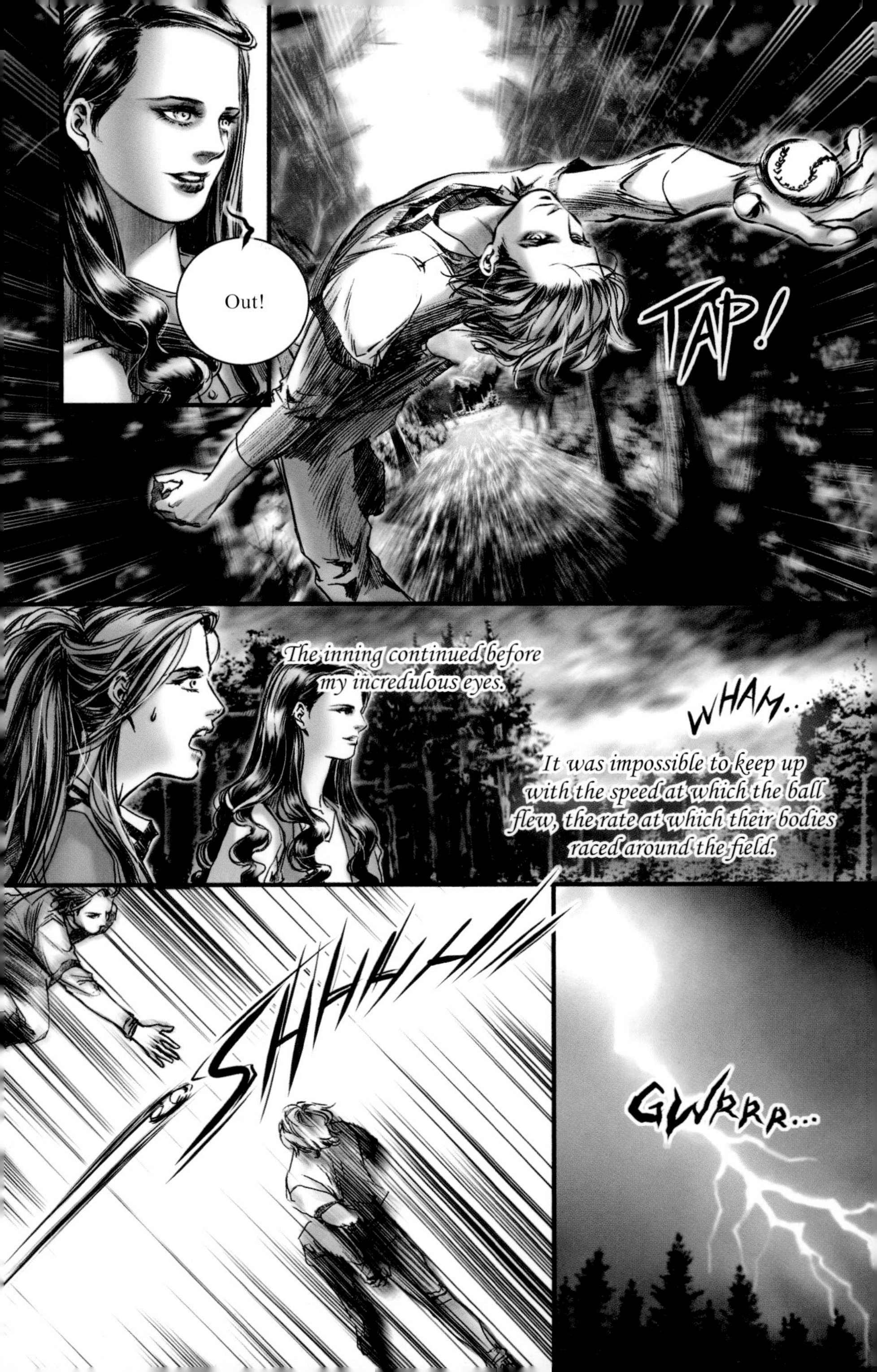

Out!
TAP!
The inning continued before my incredulous eyes.
WHAM...
It was impossible to keep up with the speed at which the ball flew, the rate at which their bodies raced around the field.
SHHHH!
GWRRR...

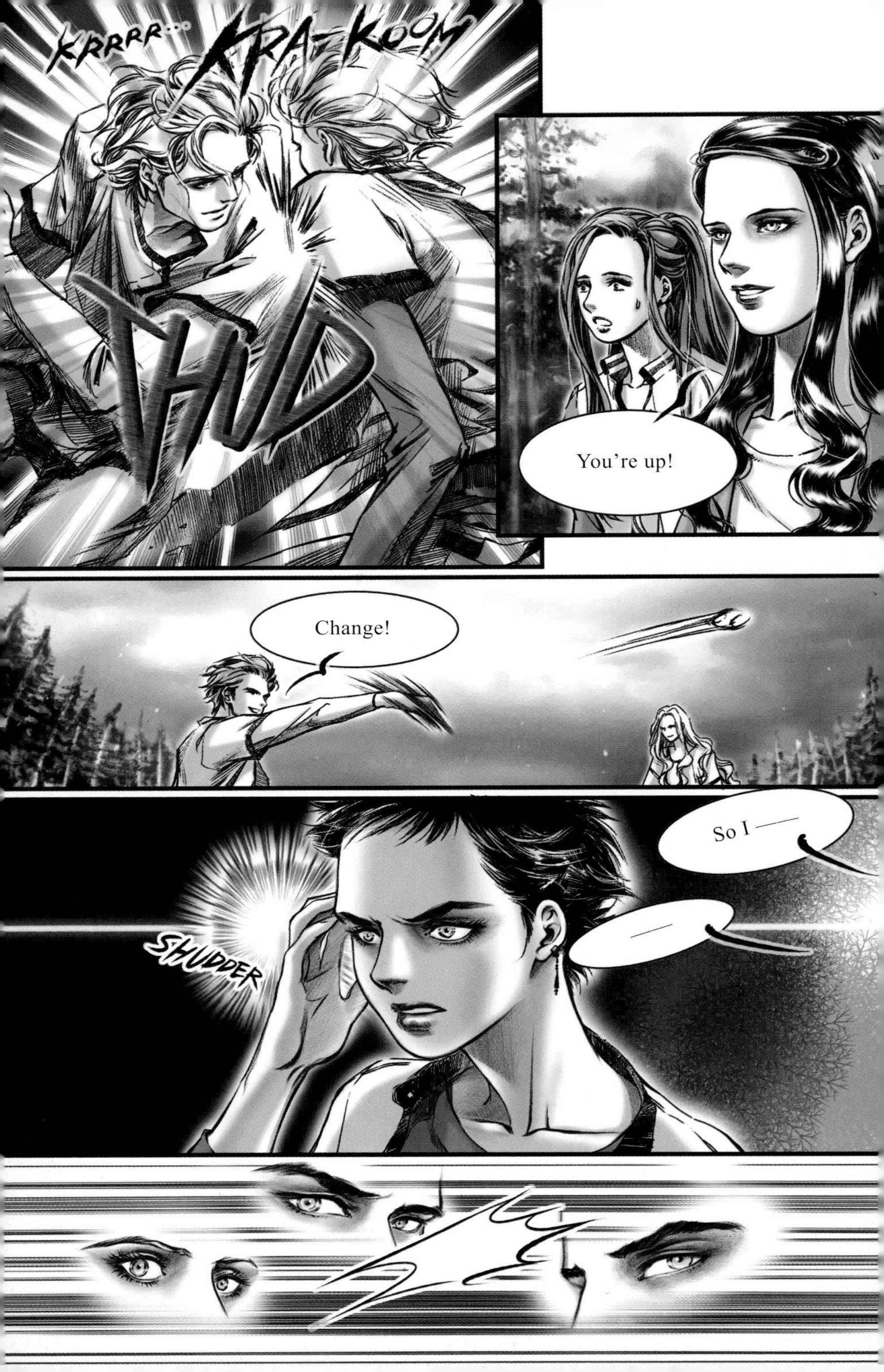
KRRRR...
KRA-KOOM
THUD
You're up!
Change!
SHUDDER
So I ——
——

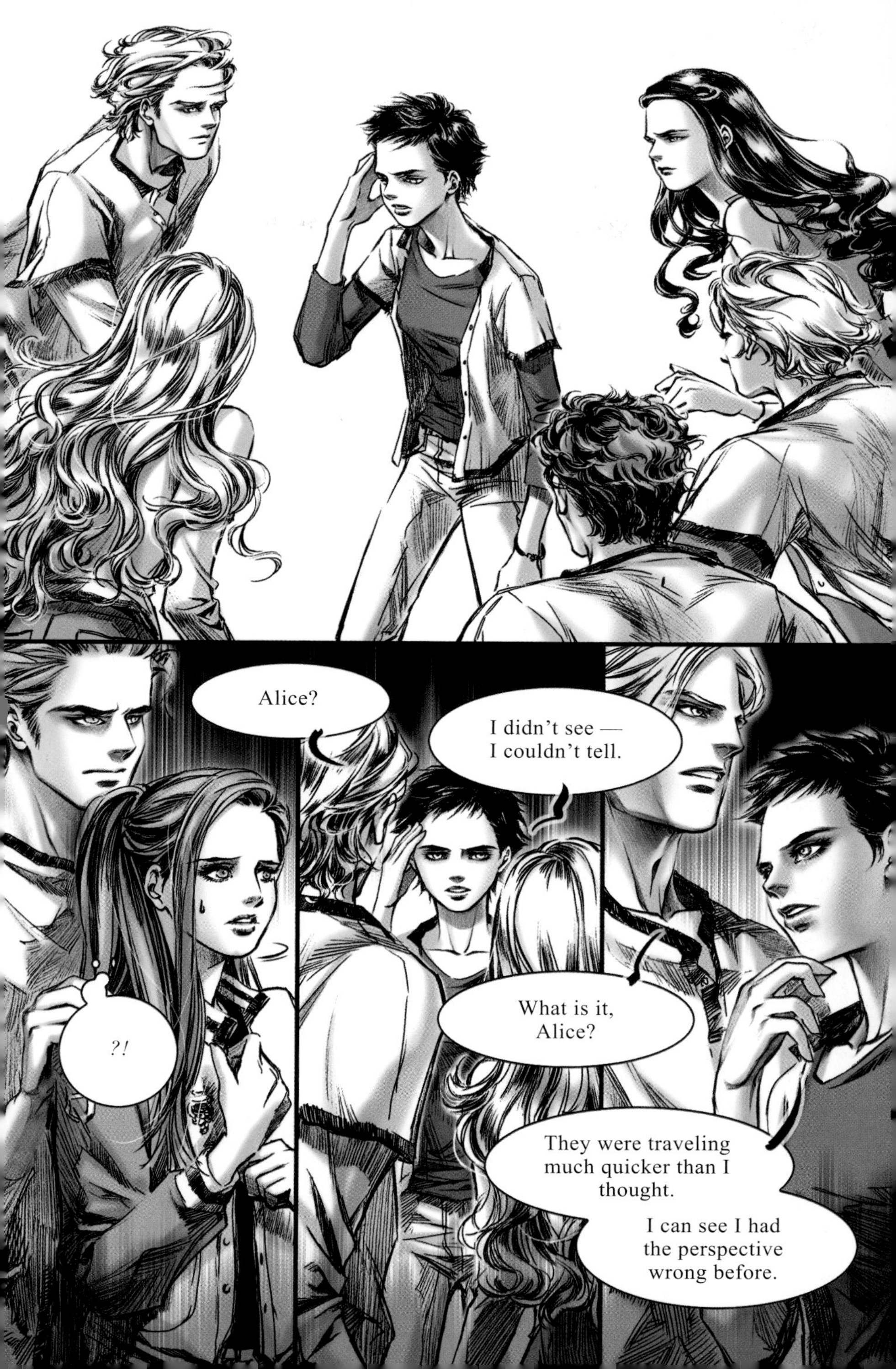
?!
Alice?
I didn't see — I couldn't tell.
What is it, Alice?
They were traveling much quicker than I thought.
I can see I had the perspective wrong before.

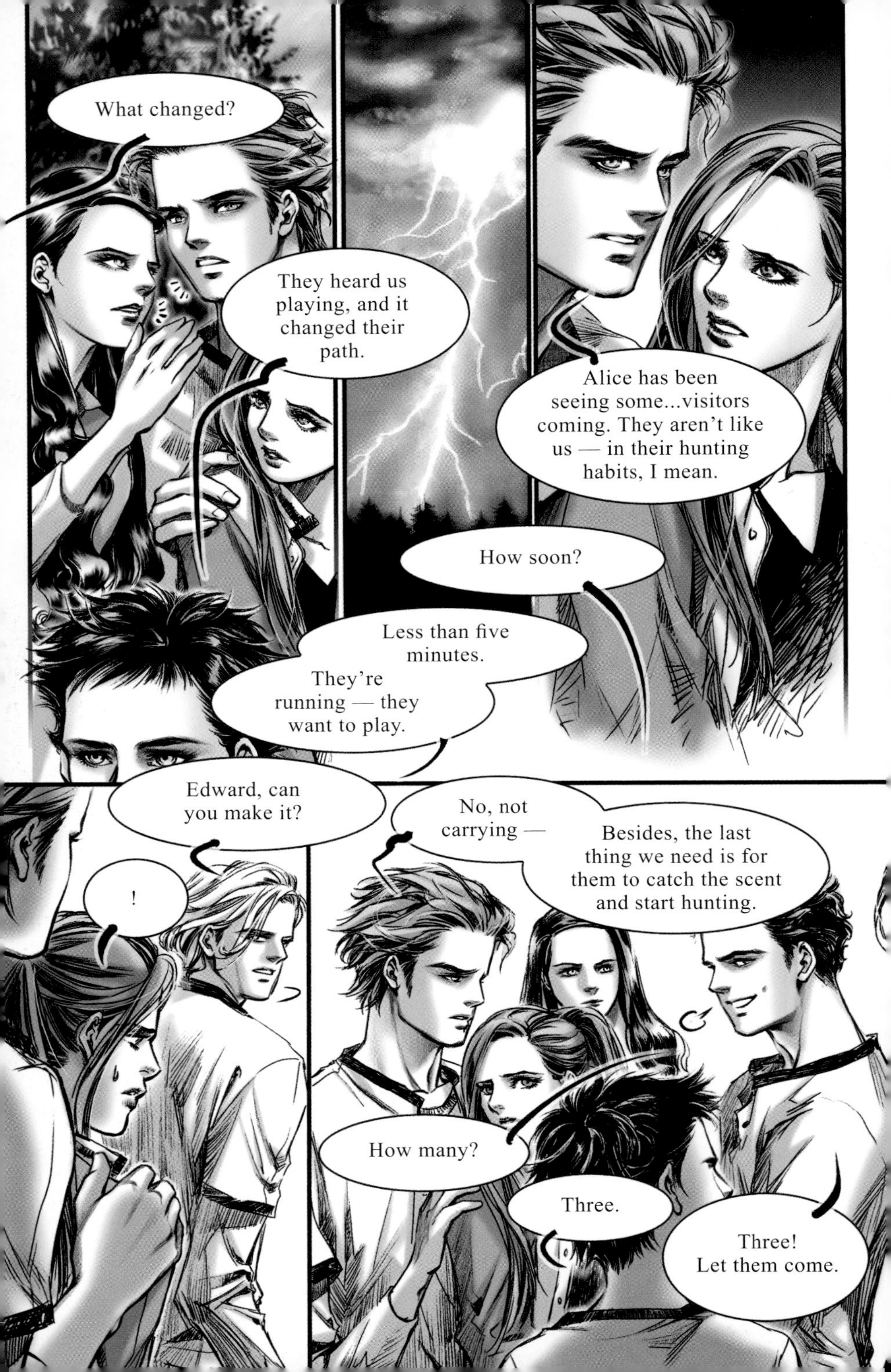
What changed?
They heard us playing, and it changed their path.
Alice has been seeing some...visitors coming. They aren't like us — in their hunting habits, I mean.
How soon?
Less than five minutes.
They're running — they want to play.
Edward, can you make it?
!
No, not carrying —
Besides, the last thing we need is for them to catch the scent and start hunting.
How many?
Three.
Three! Let them come.

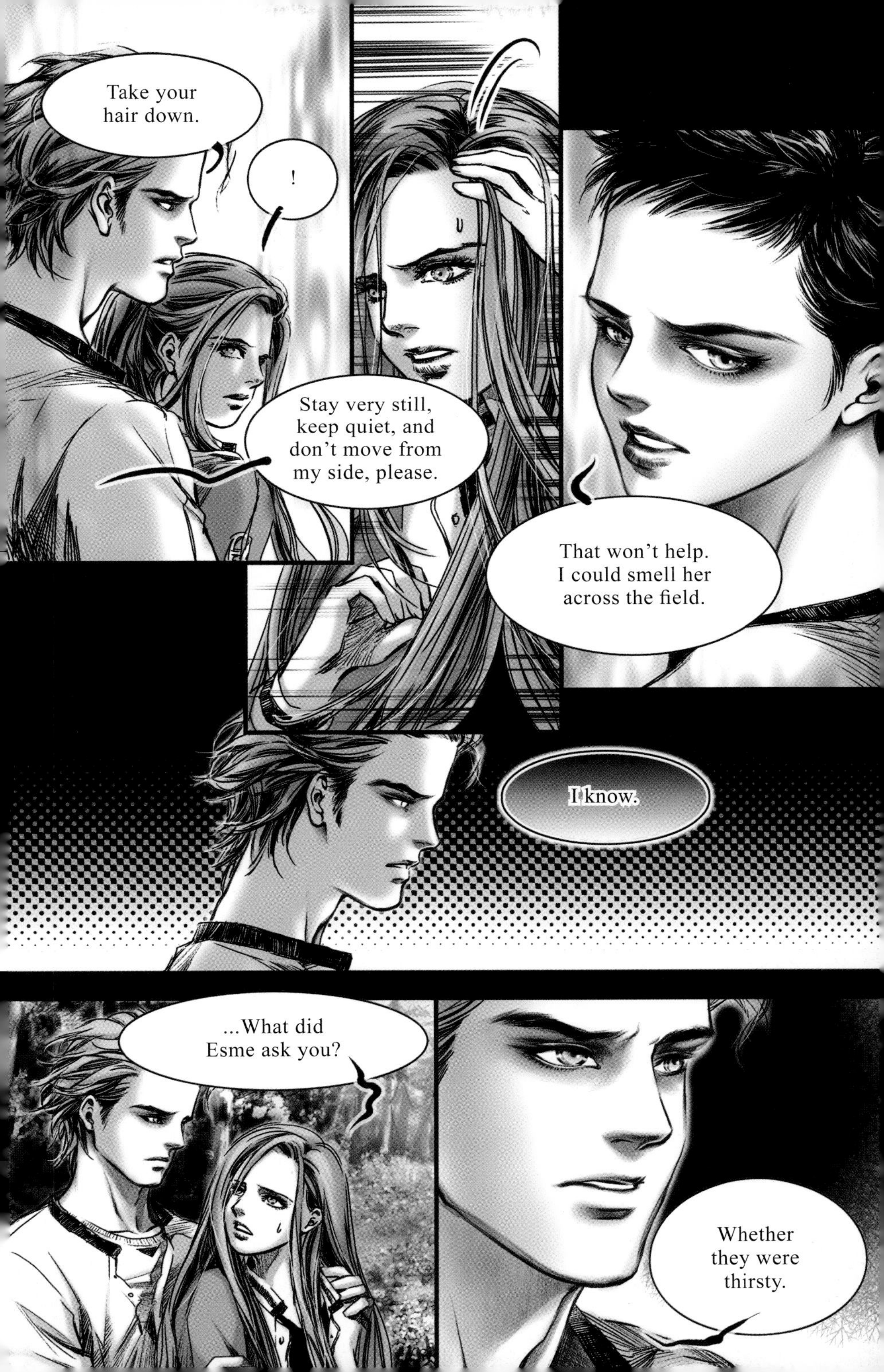

Take your hair down.
!
Stay very still, keep quiet, and don't move from my side, please.
That won't help. I could smell her across the field.
I know.
...What did Esme ask you?
Whether they were thirsty.

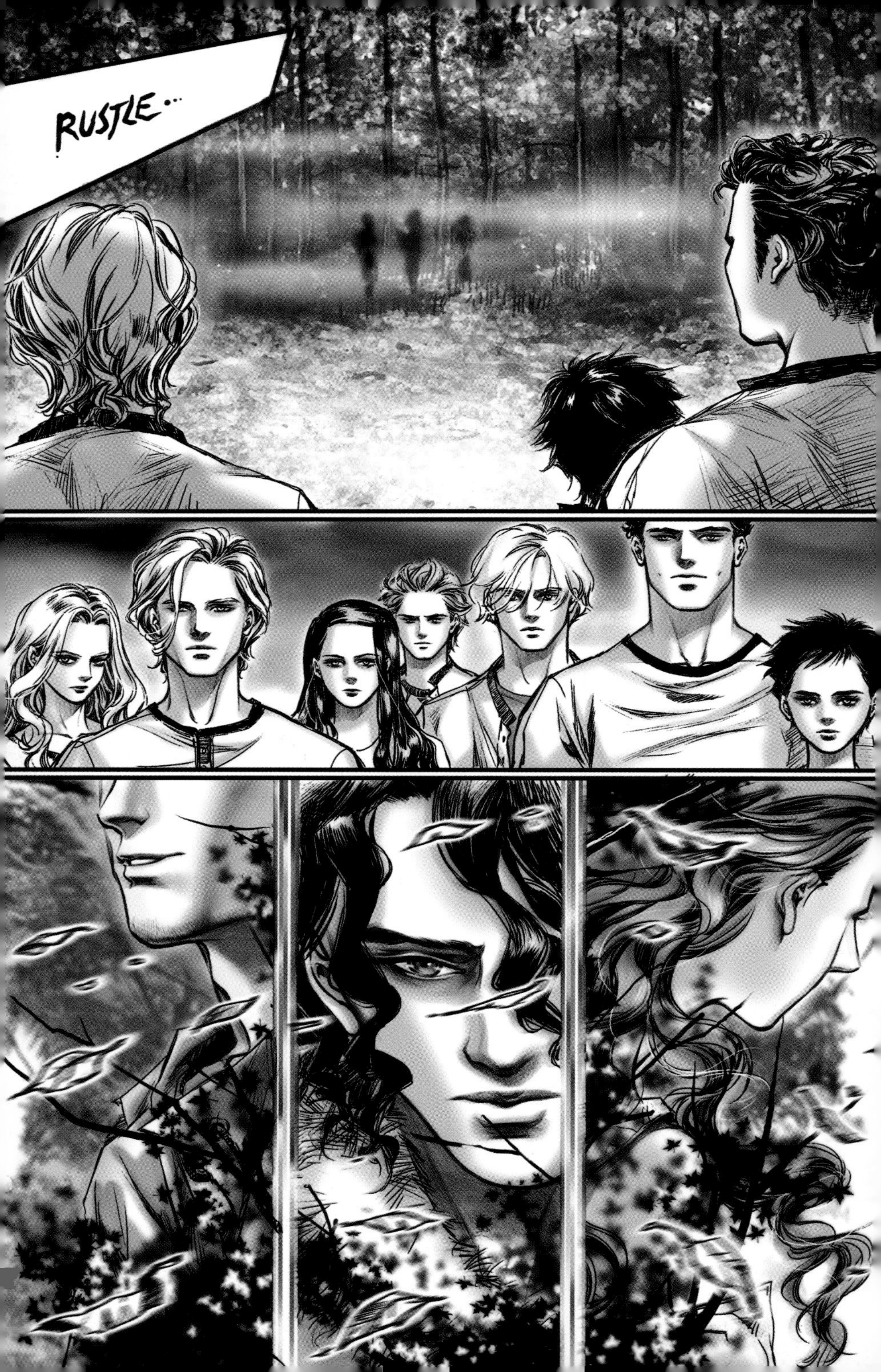
RUSTLE...

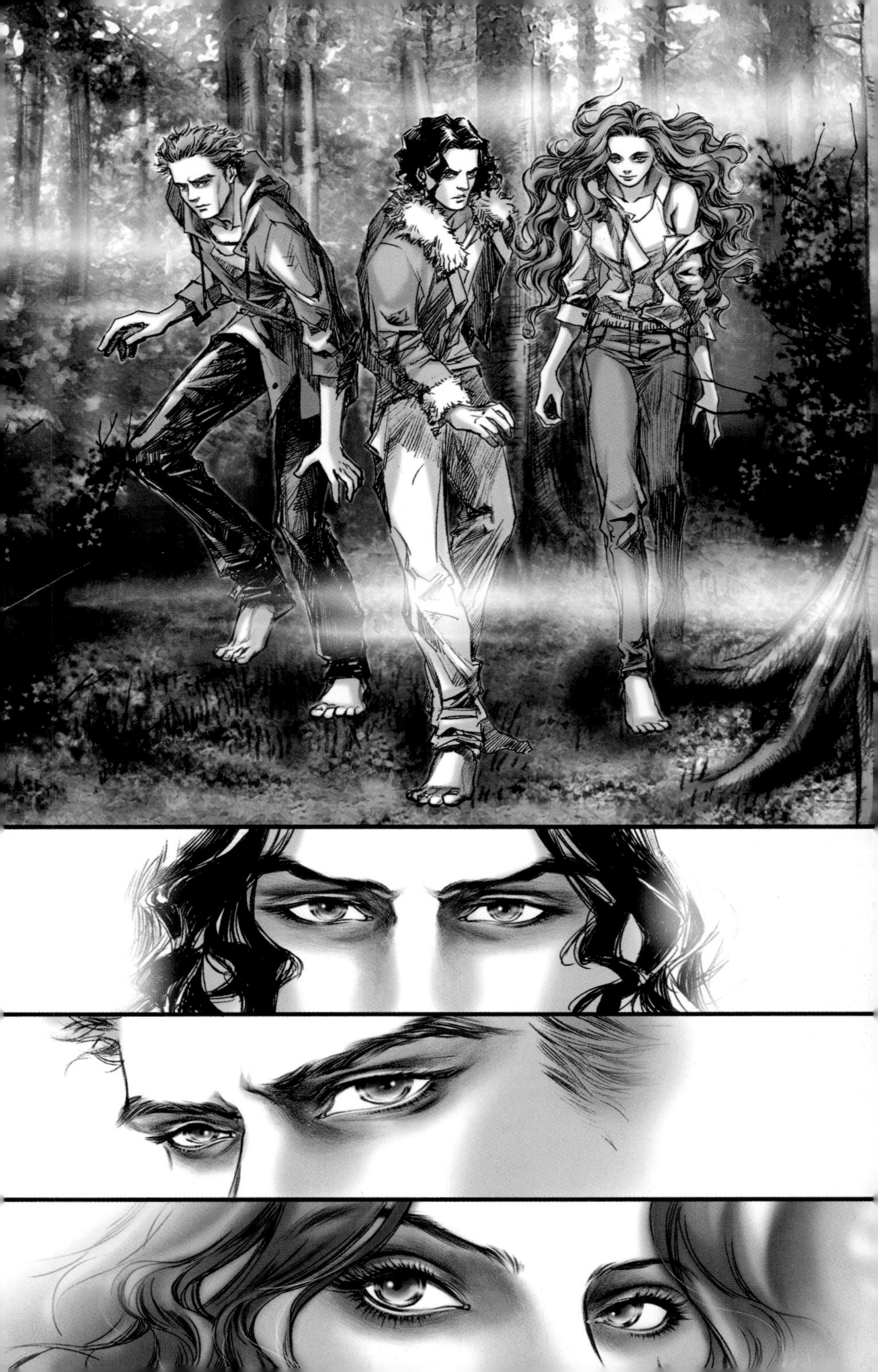

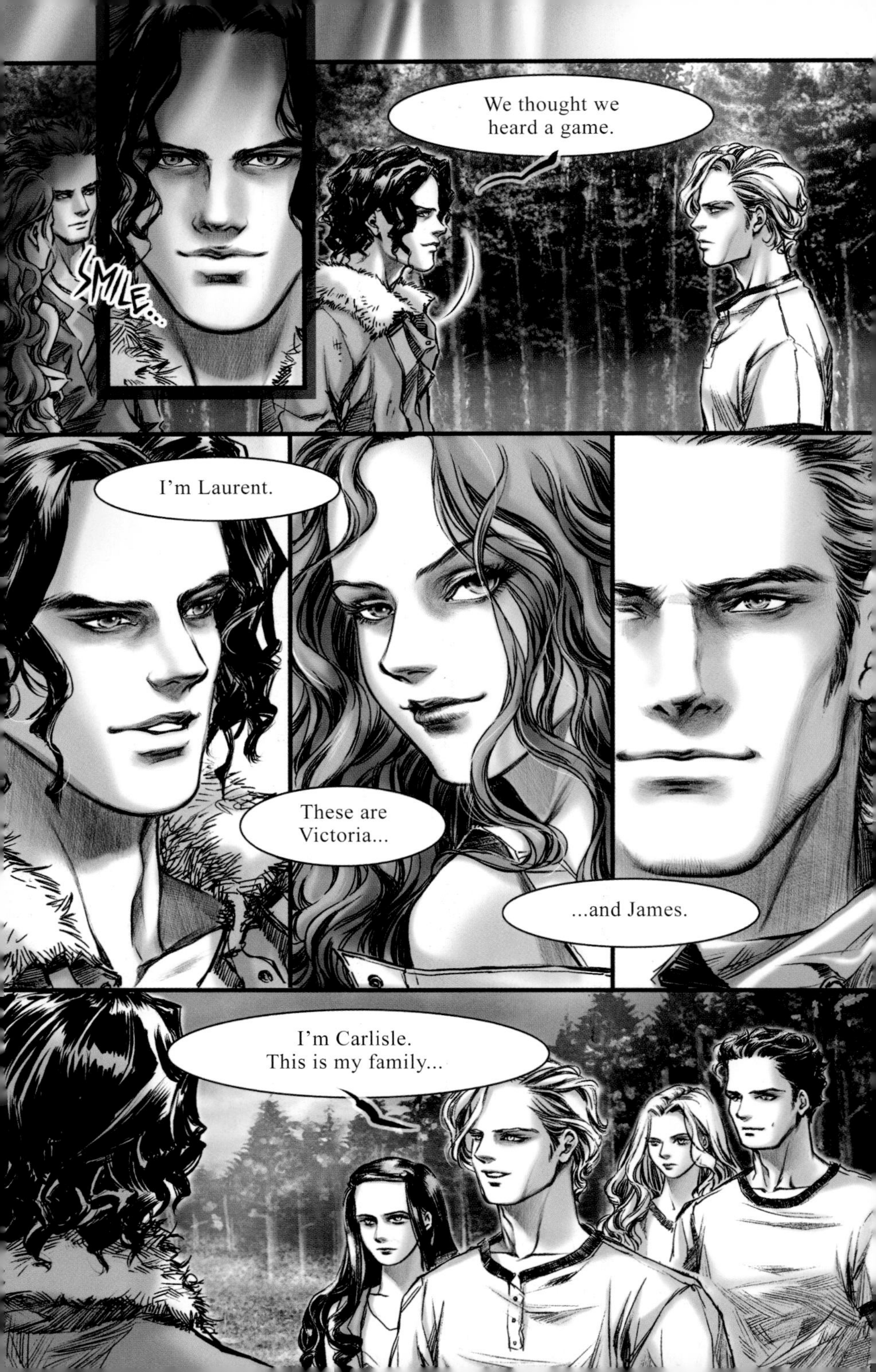
SMILE...
We thought we heard a game.
I'm Laurent.
These are Victoria...
...and James.
I'm Carlisle. This is my family...

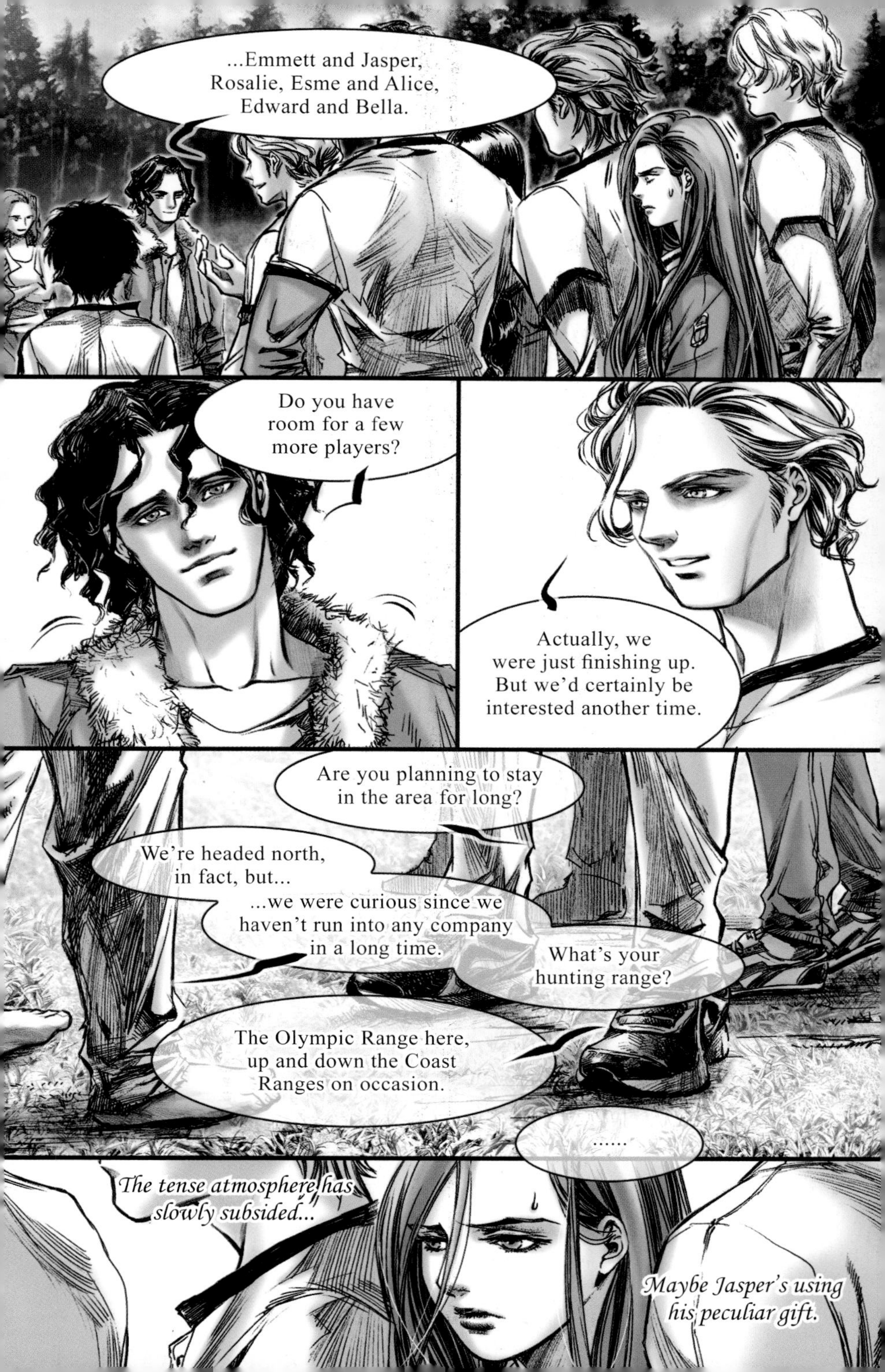
...Emmett and Jasper, Rosalie, Esme and Alice, Edward and Bella.
Do you have room for a few more players?
Actually, we were just finishing up. But we'd certainly be interested another time.
Are you planning to stay in the area for long?
We're headed north, in fact, but...
...we were curious since we haven't run into any company in a long time.
What's your hunting range?
The Olympic Range here, up and down the Coast Ranges on occasion.
......
*The tense atmosphere has slowly subsided...*
*Maybe Jasper's using his peculiar gift.*

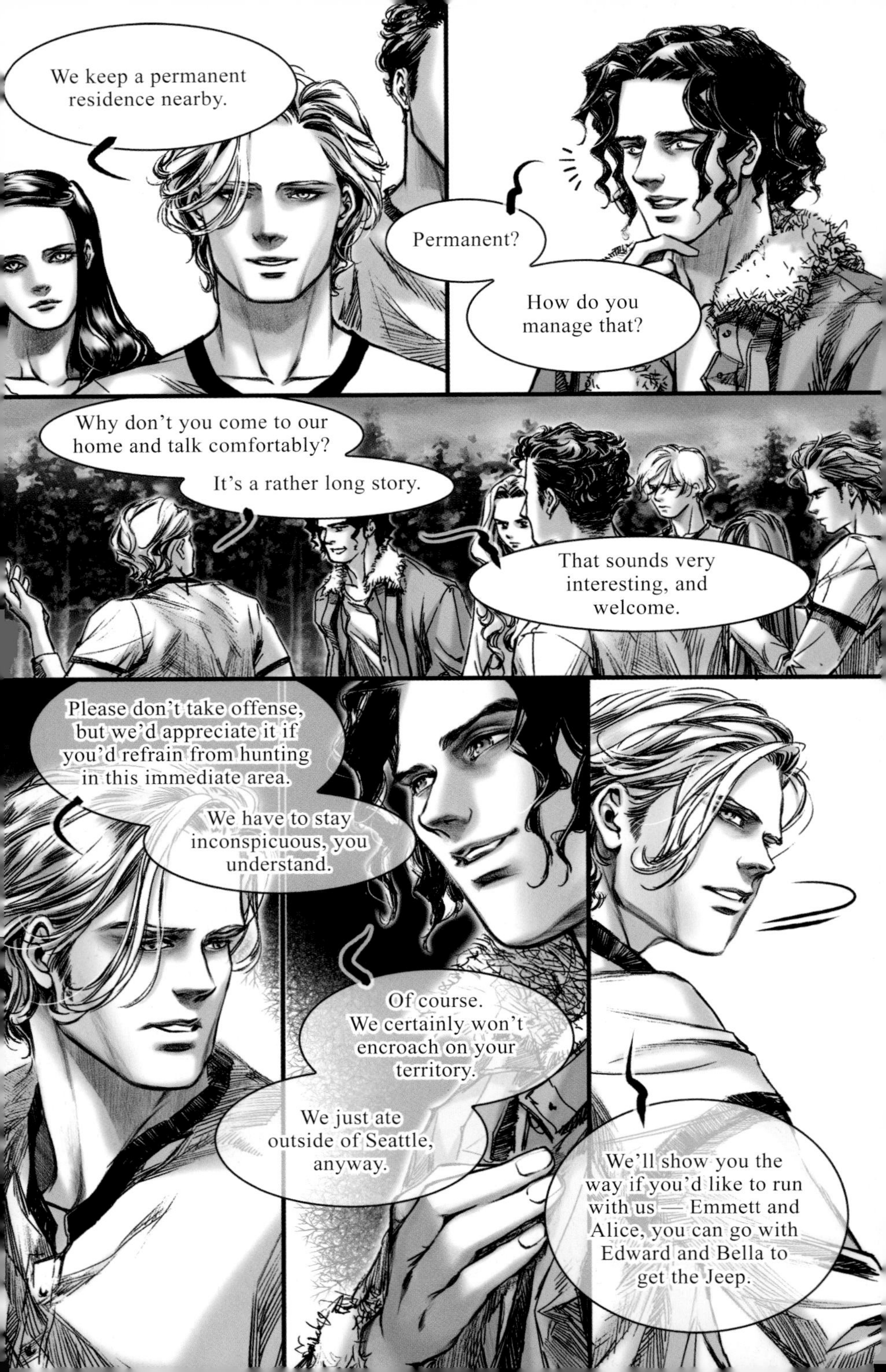
We keep a permanent residence nearby.
Permanent?
How do you manage that?
Why don't you come to our home and talk comfortably?
It's a rather long story.
That sounds very interesting, and welcome.
Please don't take offense, but we'd appreciate it if you'd refrain from hunting in this immediate area.
We have to stay inconspicuous, you understand.
Of course. We certainly won't encroach on your territory.
We just ate outside of Seattle, anyway.
We'll show you the way if you'd like to run with us — Emmett and Alice, you can go with Edward and Bella to get the Jeep.

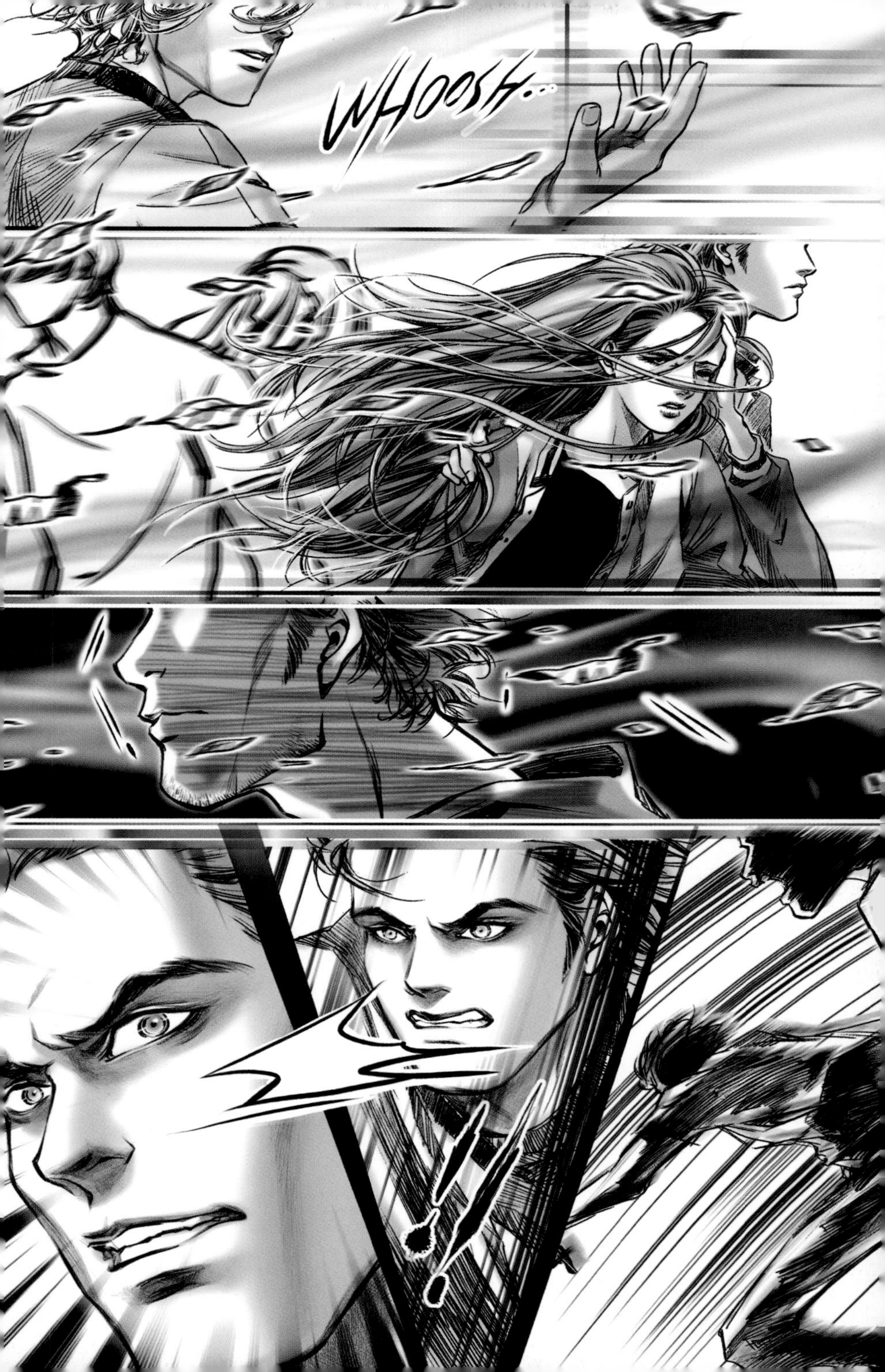
WHOOSH...

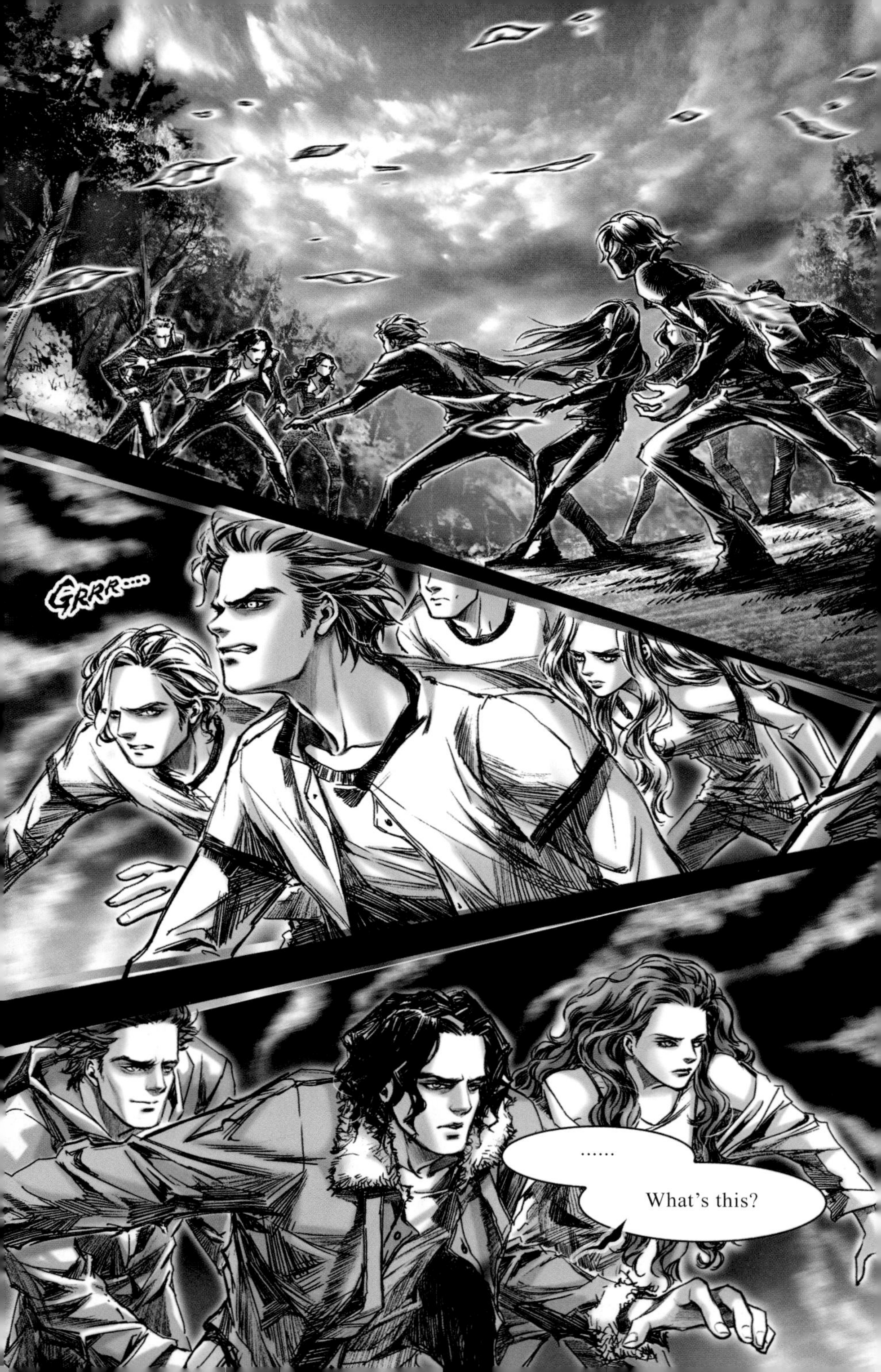
GRRR....
......
What's this?

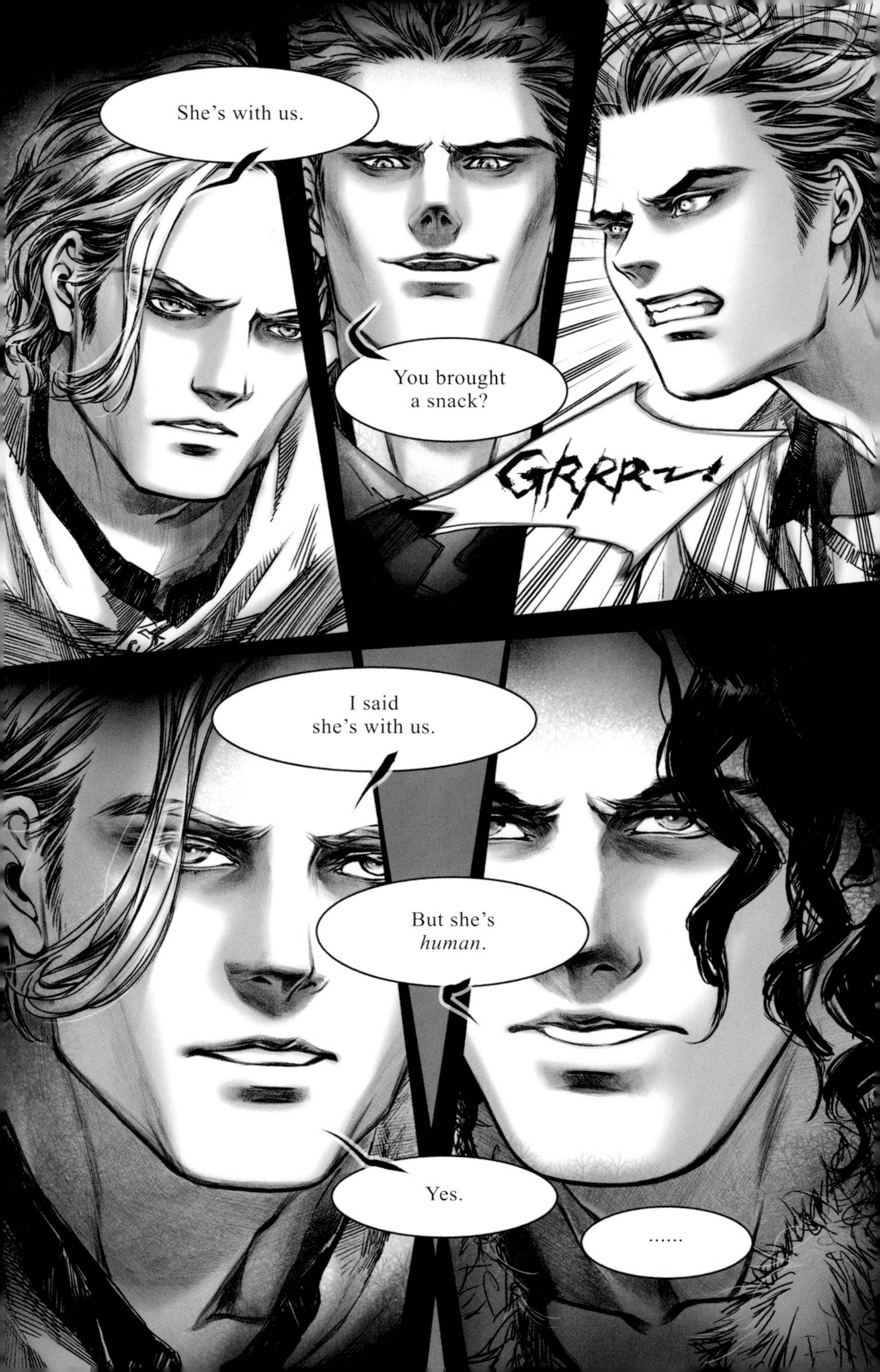

She's with us.
You brought a snack?
GRRR
I said she's with us.
But she's *human*.
Yes.
......

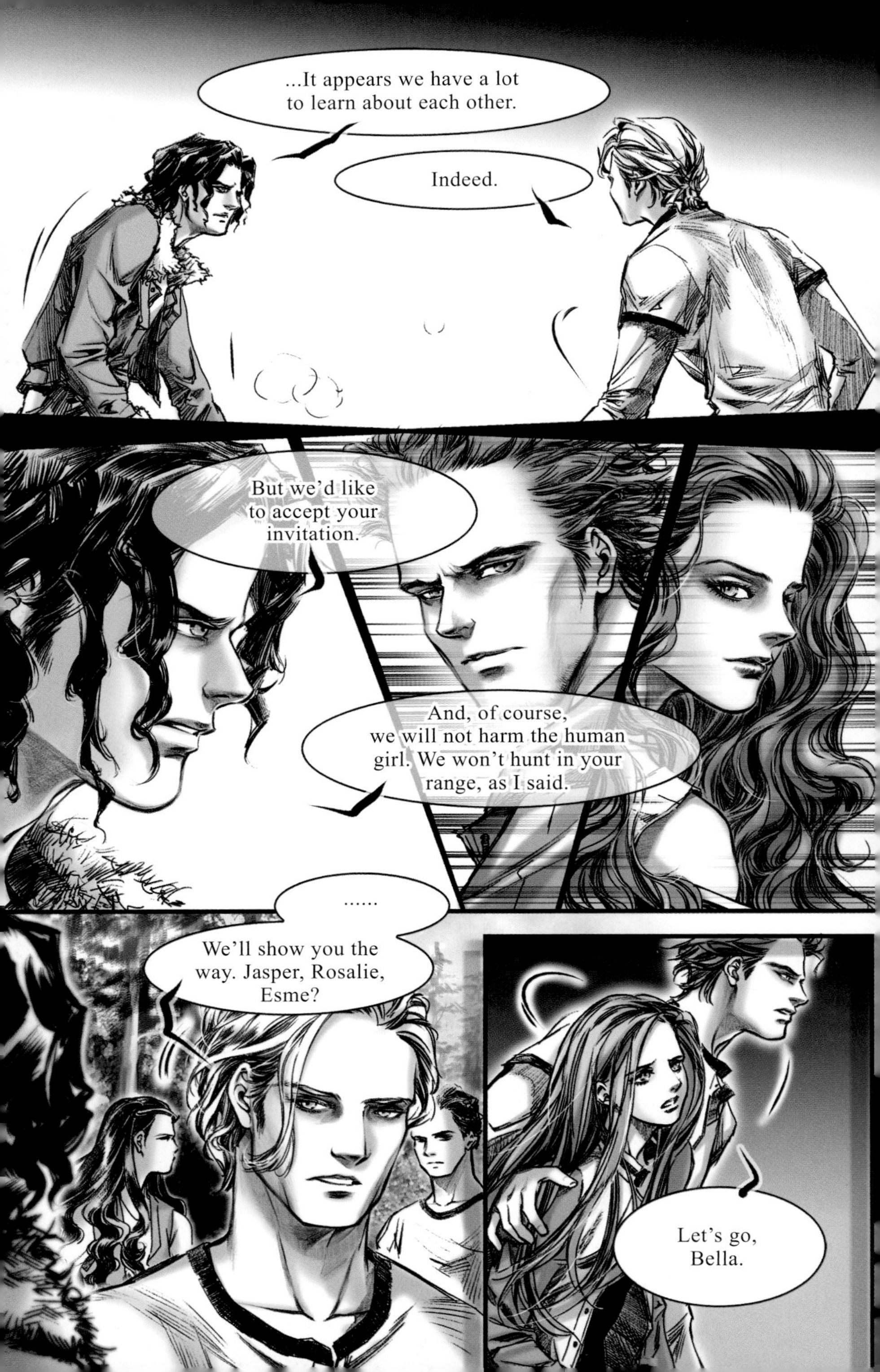
...It appears we have a lot to learn about each other.
Indeed.
But we'd like to accept your invitation.
And, of course, we will not harm the human girl. We won't hunt in your range, as I said.
......
We'll show you the way. Jasper, Rosalie, Esme?
Let's go, Bella.

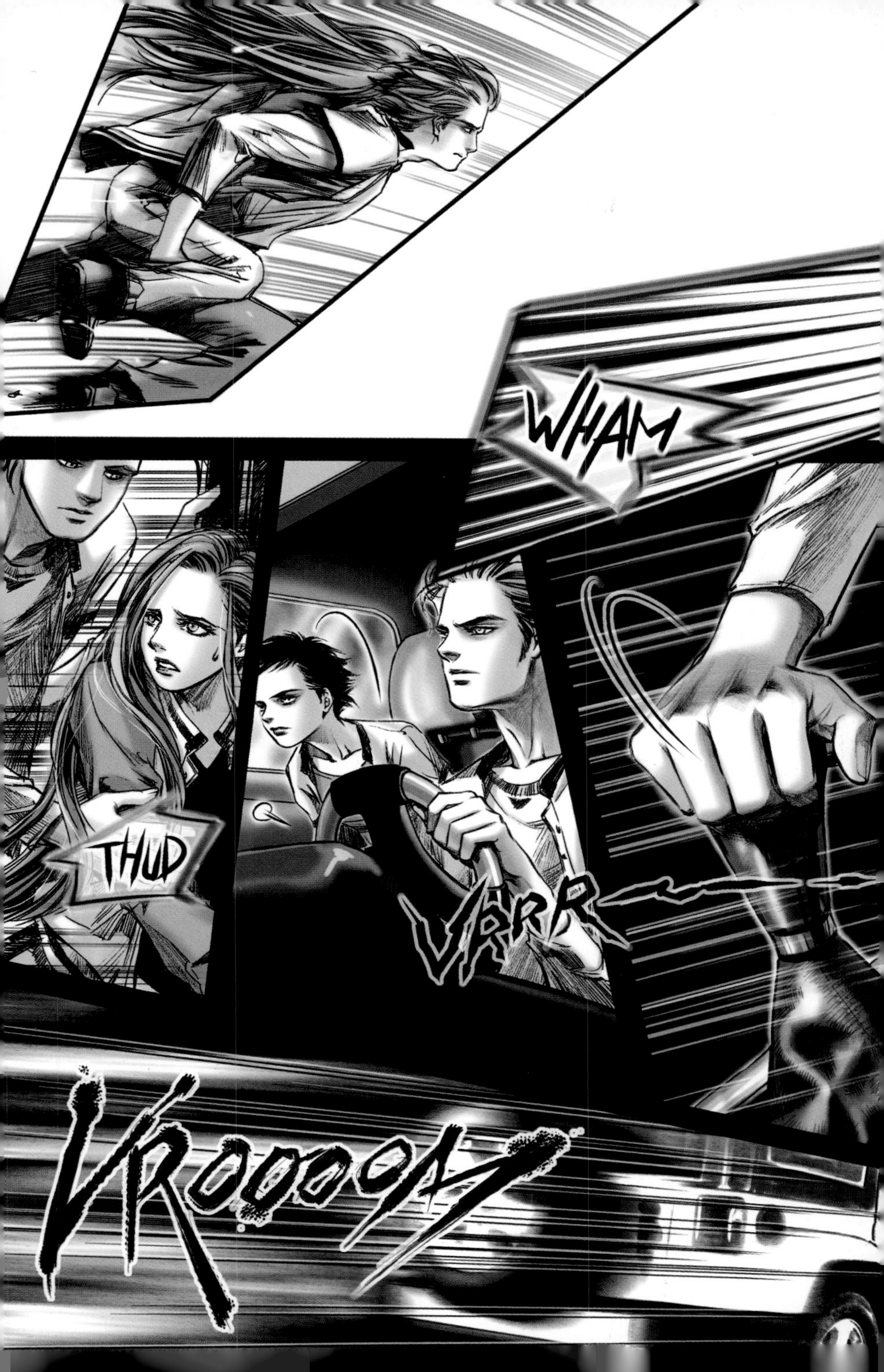
WHAM
THUD
VRRR
VROOOOM

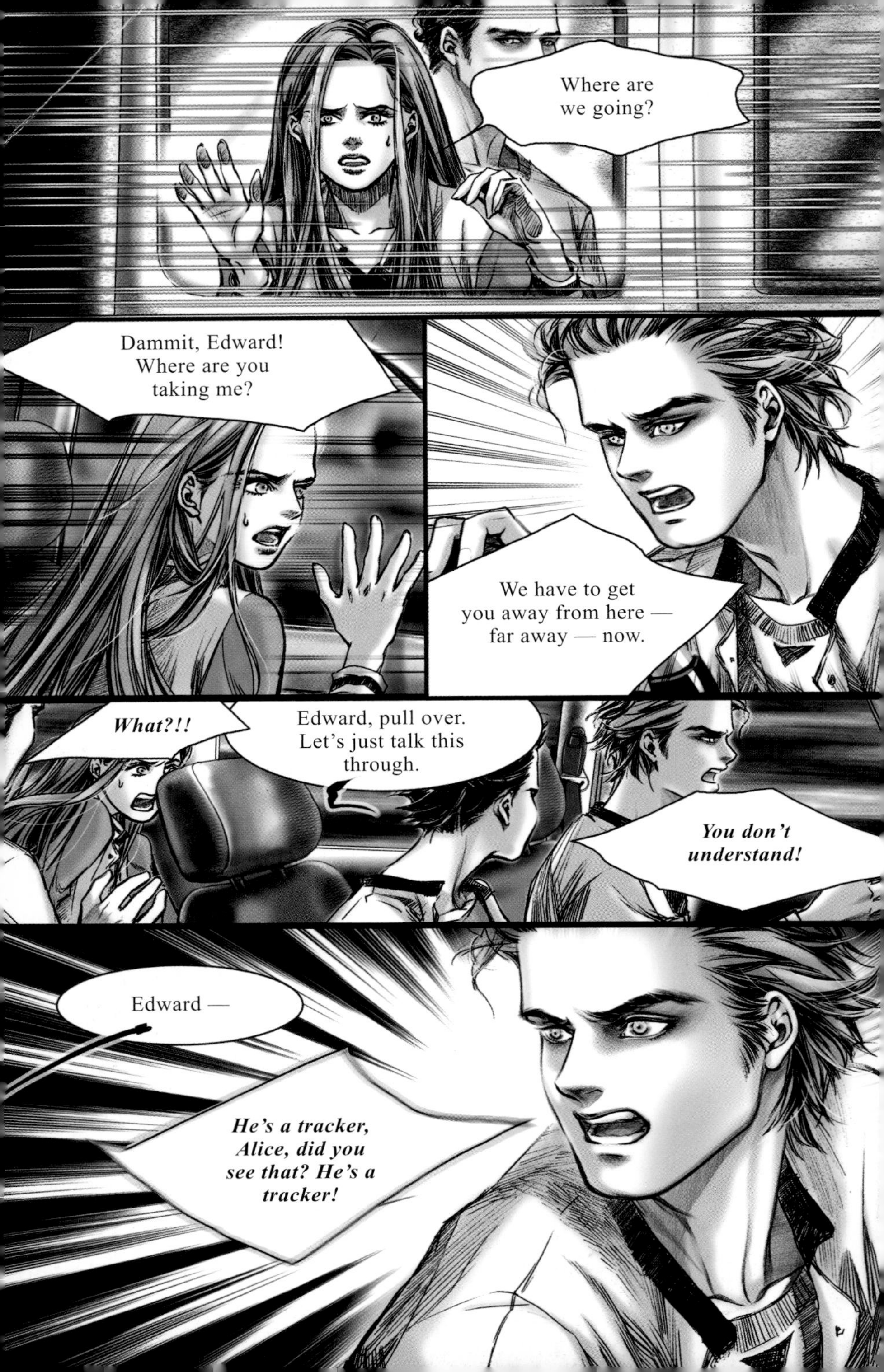
Where are we going?
Dammit, Edward! Where are you taking me?
We have to get you away from here — far away — now.
*What?!!*
Edward, pull over. Let's just talk this through.
*You don't understand!*
Edward —
*He's a tracker, Alice, did you see that? He's a tracker!*

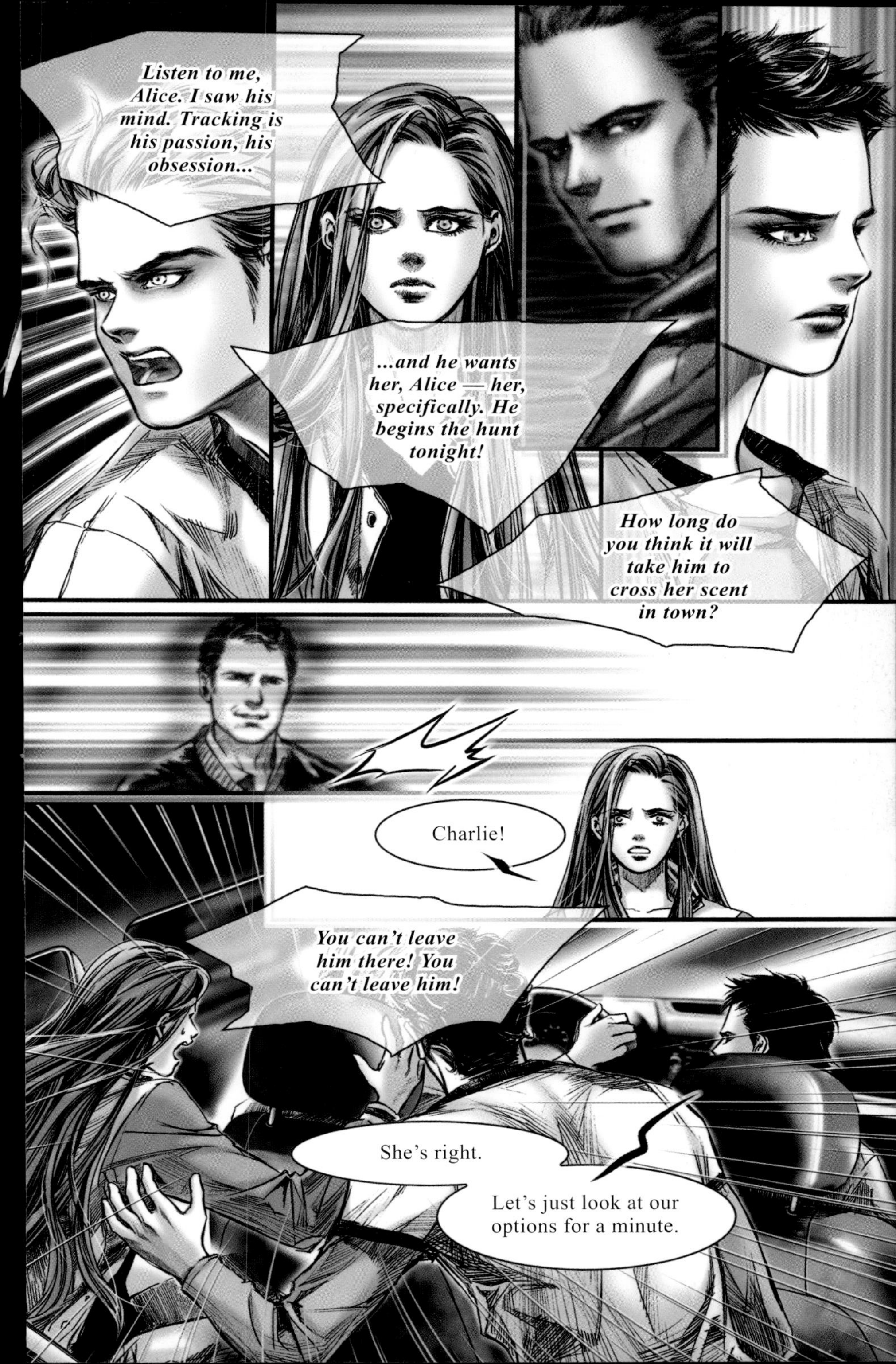
Listen to me, Alice. I saw his mind. Tracking is his passion, his obsession...
...and he wants her, Alice — her, specifically. He begins the hunt tonight!
How long do you think it will take him to cross her scent in town?
Charlie!
You can't leave him there! You can't leave him!
She's right.
Let's just look at our options for a minute.

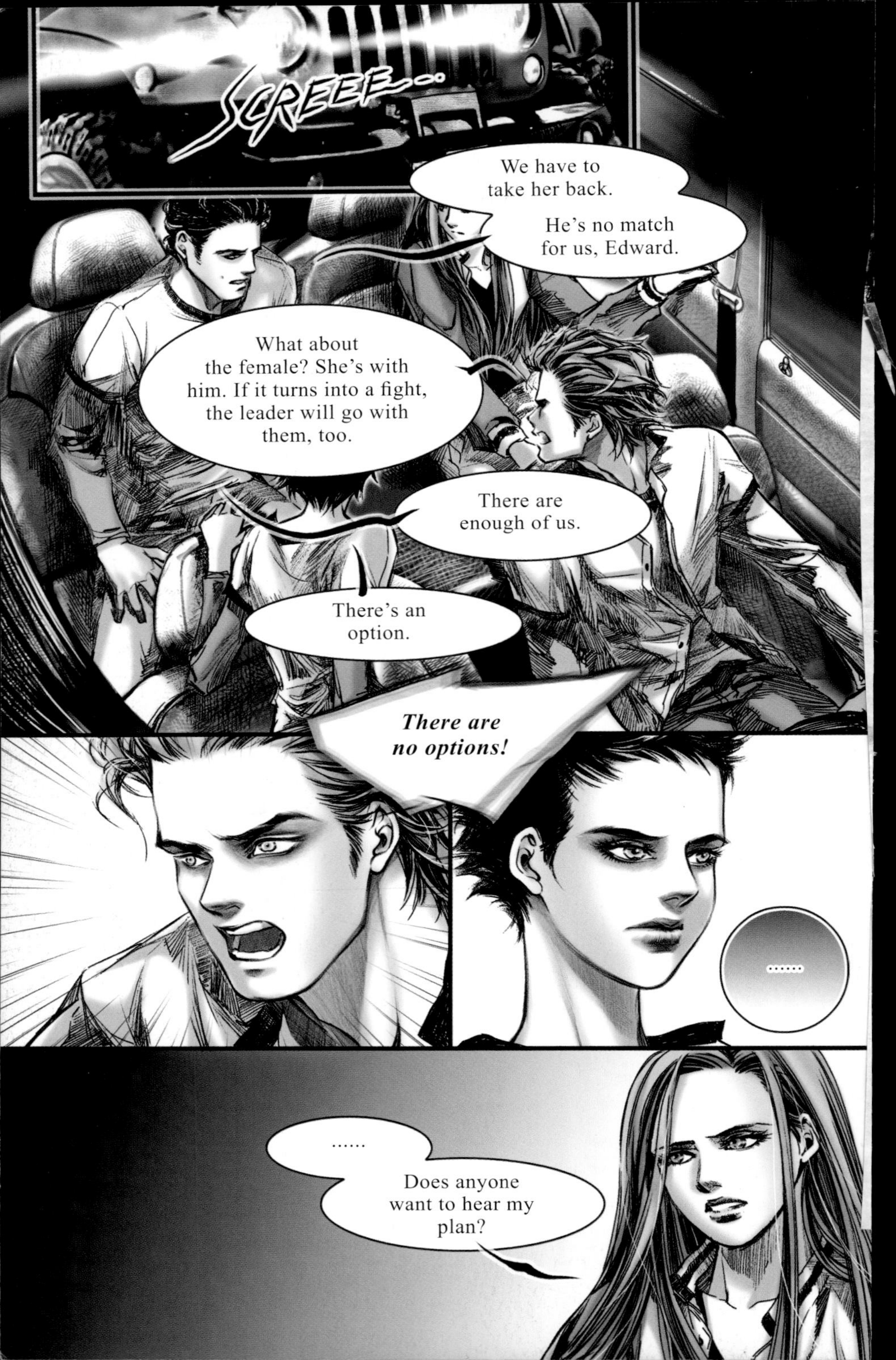
SCREEE...
We have to take her back.
He's no match for us, Edward.
What about the female? She's with him. If it turns into a fight, the leader will go with them, too.
There are enough of us.
There's an option.
***There are no options!***
......
......
Does anyone want to hear my plan?

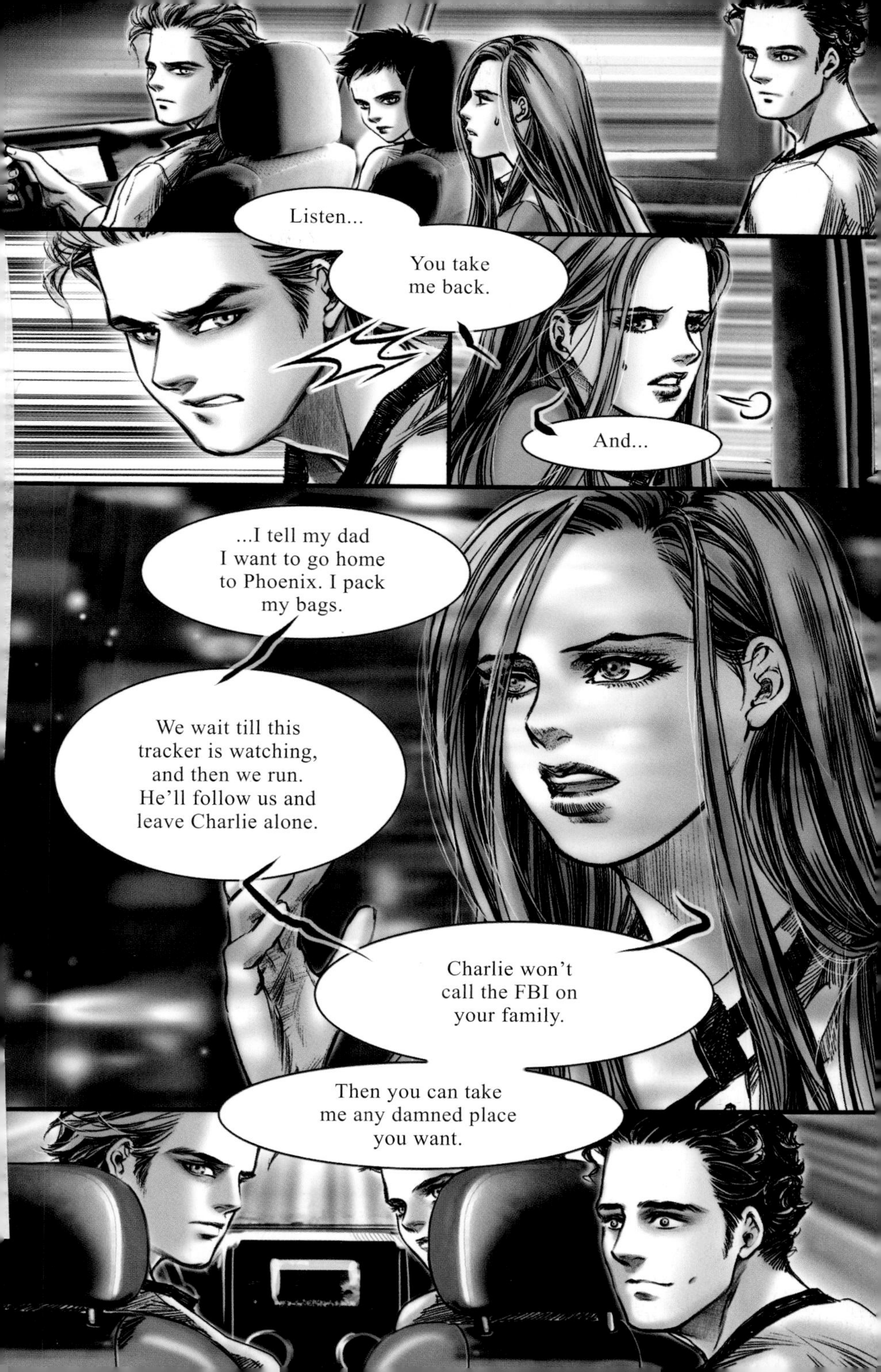
Listen...
You take me back.
And...
...I tell my dad I want to go home to Phoenix. I pack my bags.
We wait till this tracker is watching, and then we run. He'll follow us and leave Charlie alone.
Charlie won't call the FBI on your family.
Then you can take me any damned place you want.

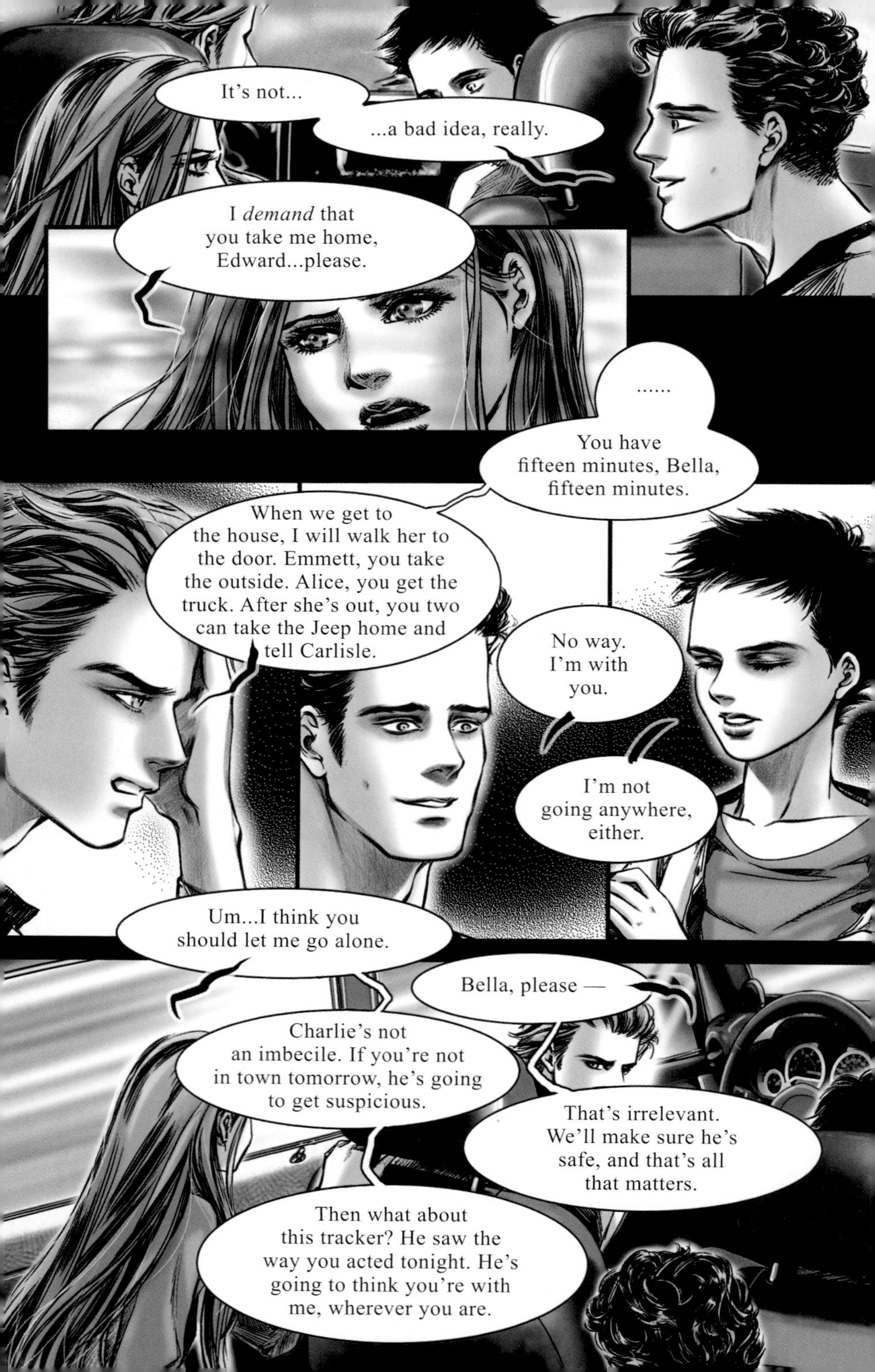
It's not...
...a bad idea, really.
I *demand* that you take me home, Edward...please.
......
You have fifteen minutes, Bella, fifteen minutes.
When we get to the house, I will walk her to the door. Emmett, you take the outside. Alice, you get the truck. After she's out, you two can take the Jeep home and tell Carlisle.
No way. I'm with you.
I'm not going anywhere, either.
Um...I think you should let me go alone.
Bella, please —
Charlie's not an imbecile. If you're not in town tomorrow, he's going to get suspicious.
That's irrelevant. We'll make sure he's safe, and that's all that matters.
Then what about this tracker? He saw the way you acted tonight. He's going to think you're with me, wherever you are.

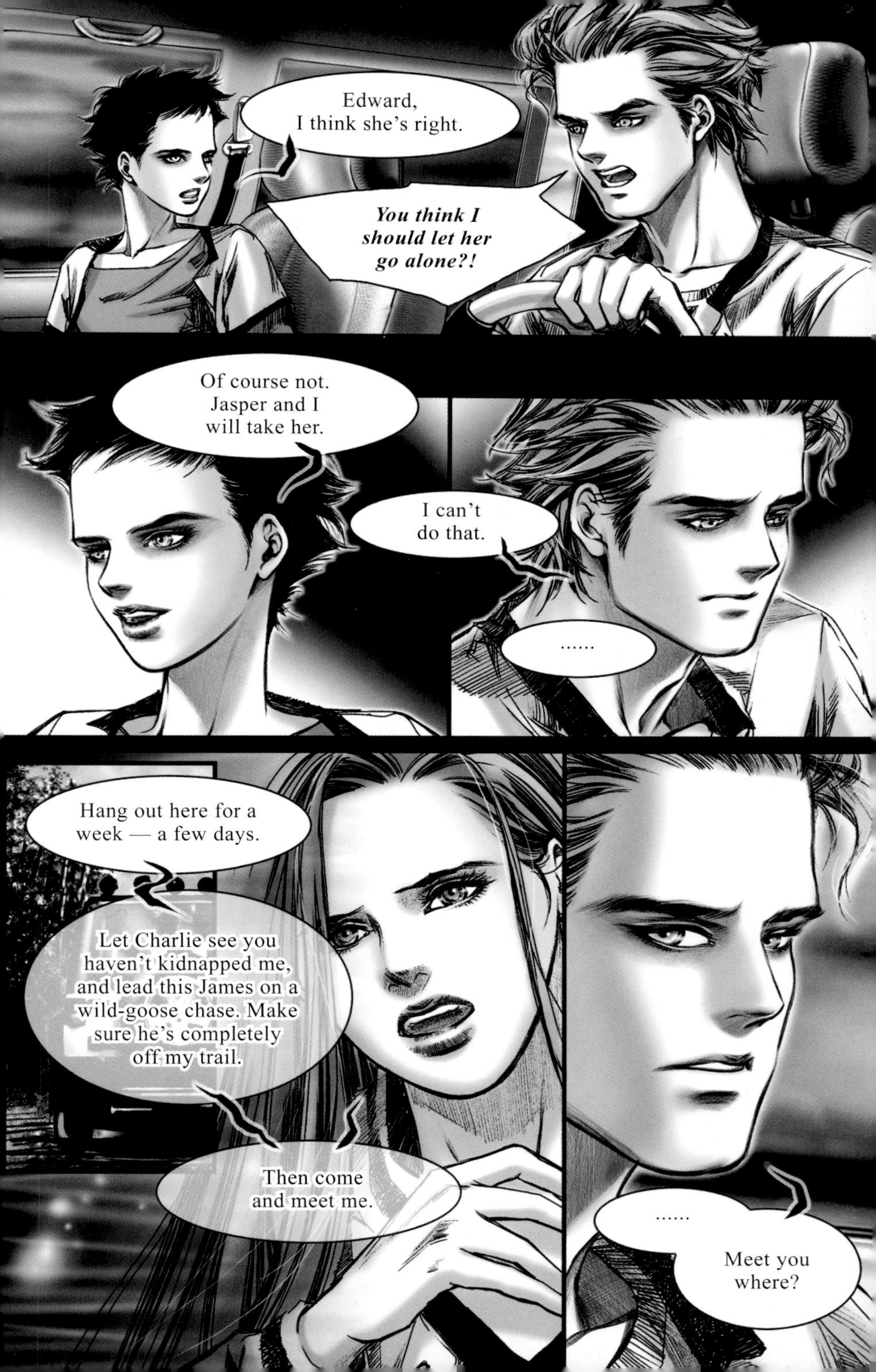

Edward, I think she's right.
*You think I should let her go alone?!*
Of course not. Jasper and I will take her.
I can't do that.
......
Hang out here for a week — a few days.
Let Charlie see you haven't kidnapped me, and lead this James on a wild-goose chase. Make sure he's completely off my trail.
Then come and meet me.
......
Meet you where?

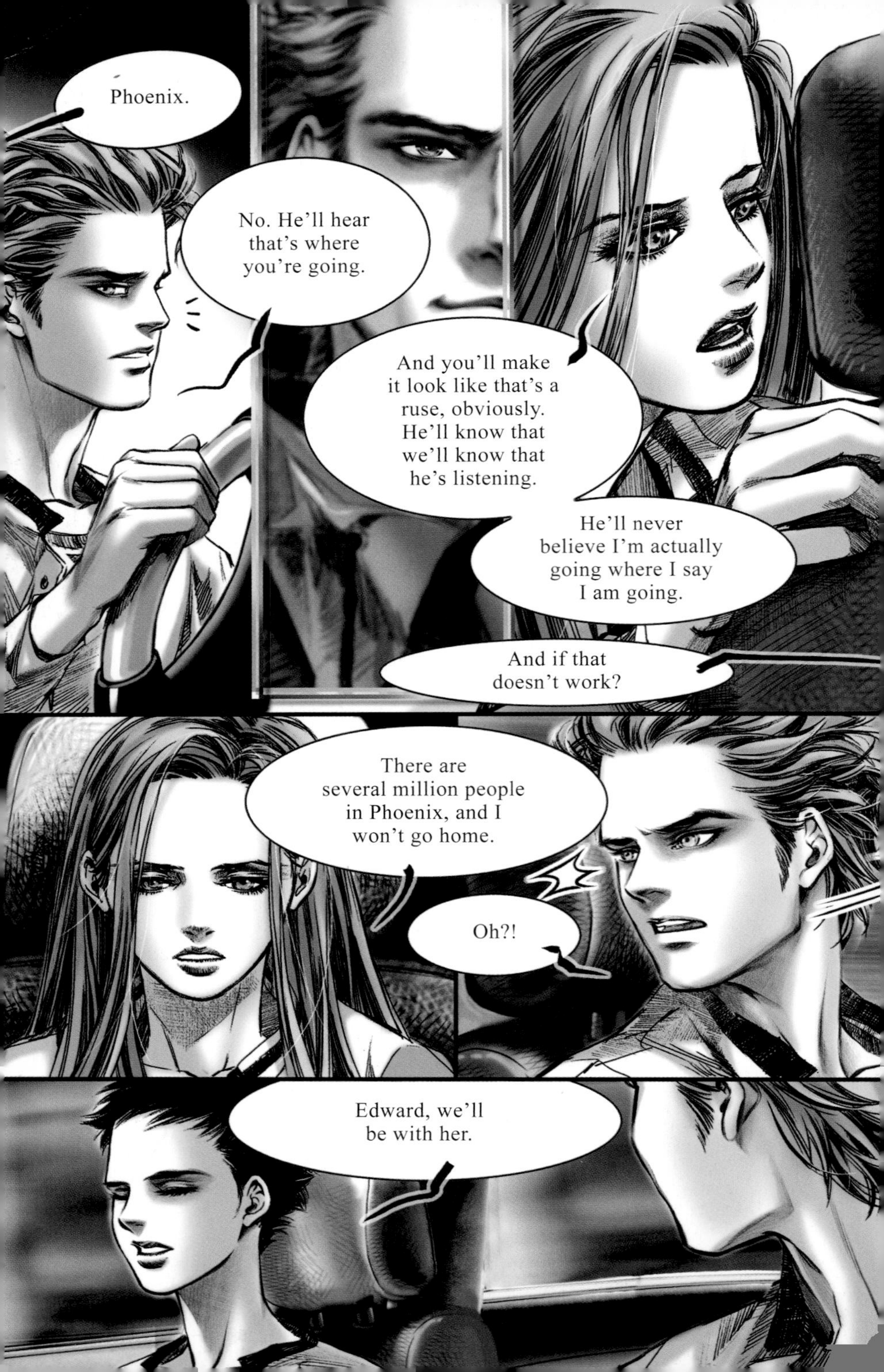
Phoenix.
No. He'll hear that's where you're going.
And you'll make it look like that's a ruse, obviously. He'll know that we'll know that he's listening.
He'll never believe I'm actually going where I say I am going.
And if that doesn't work?
There are several million people in Phoenix, and I won't go home.
Oh?!
Edward, we'll be with her.

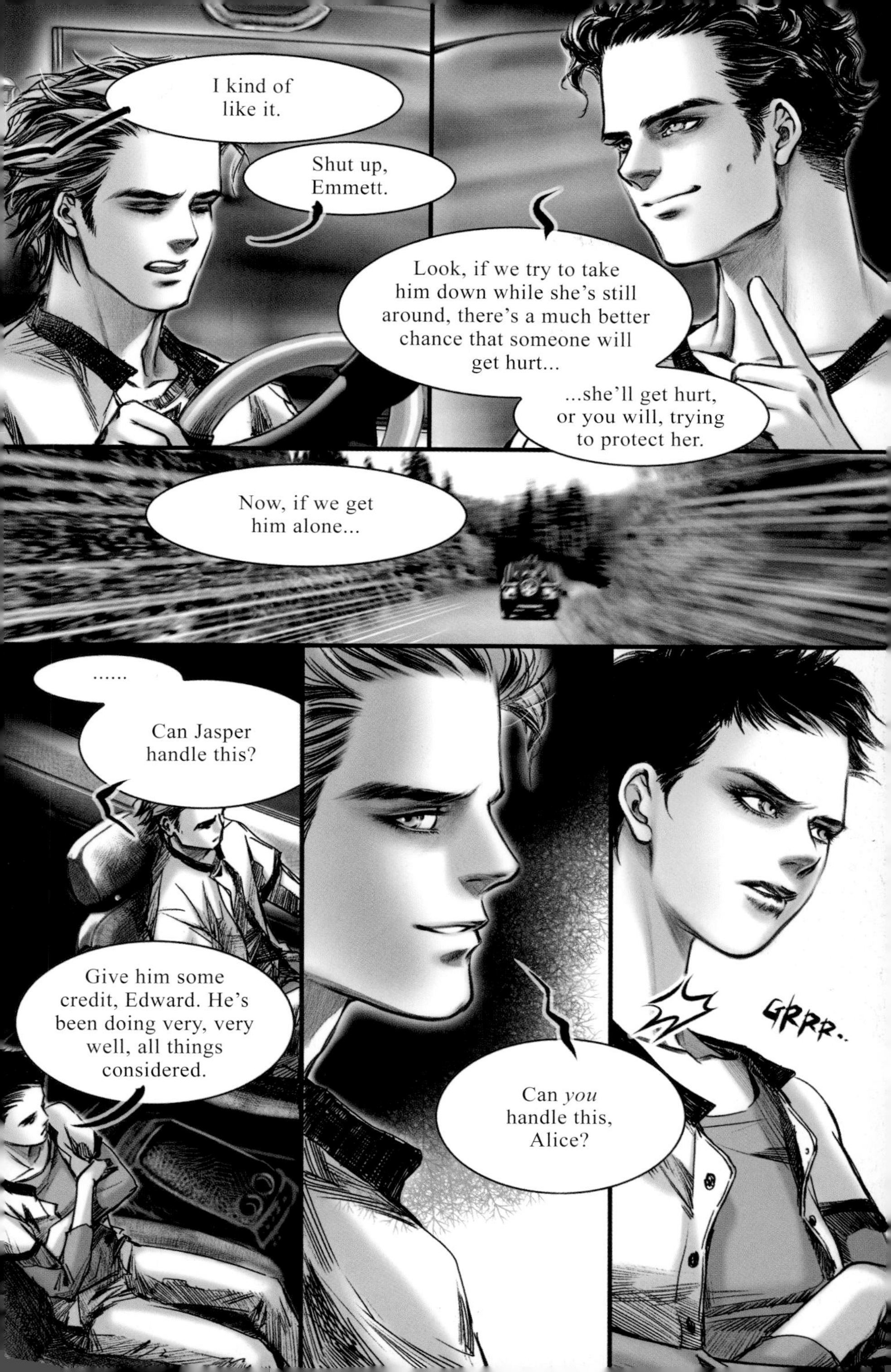
I kind of like it.
Shut up, Emmett.
Look, if we try to take him down while she's still around, there's a much better chance that someone will get hurt...
...she'll get hurt, or you will, trying to protect her.
Now, if we get him alone...
......
Can Jasper handle this?
Give him some credit, Edward. He's been doing very, very well, all things considered.
Can *you* handle this, Alice?
GRRR..

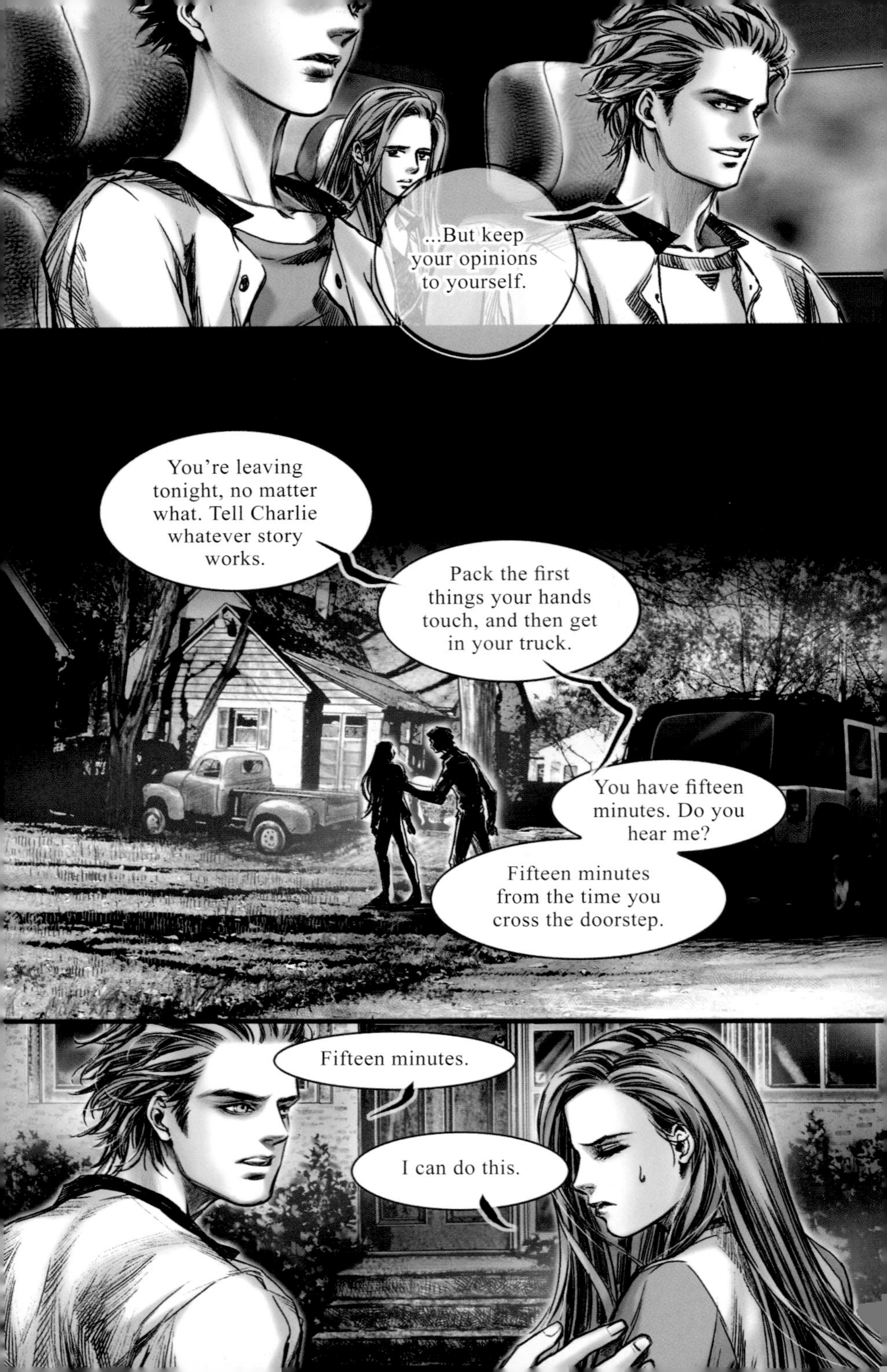
...But keep your opinions to yourself.
You're leaving tonight, no matter what. Tell Charlie whatever story works.
Pack the first things your hands touch, and then get in your truck.
You have fifteen minutes. Do you hear me?
Fifteen minutes from the time you cross the doorstep.
Fifteen minutes.
I can do this.

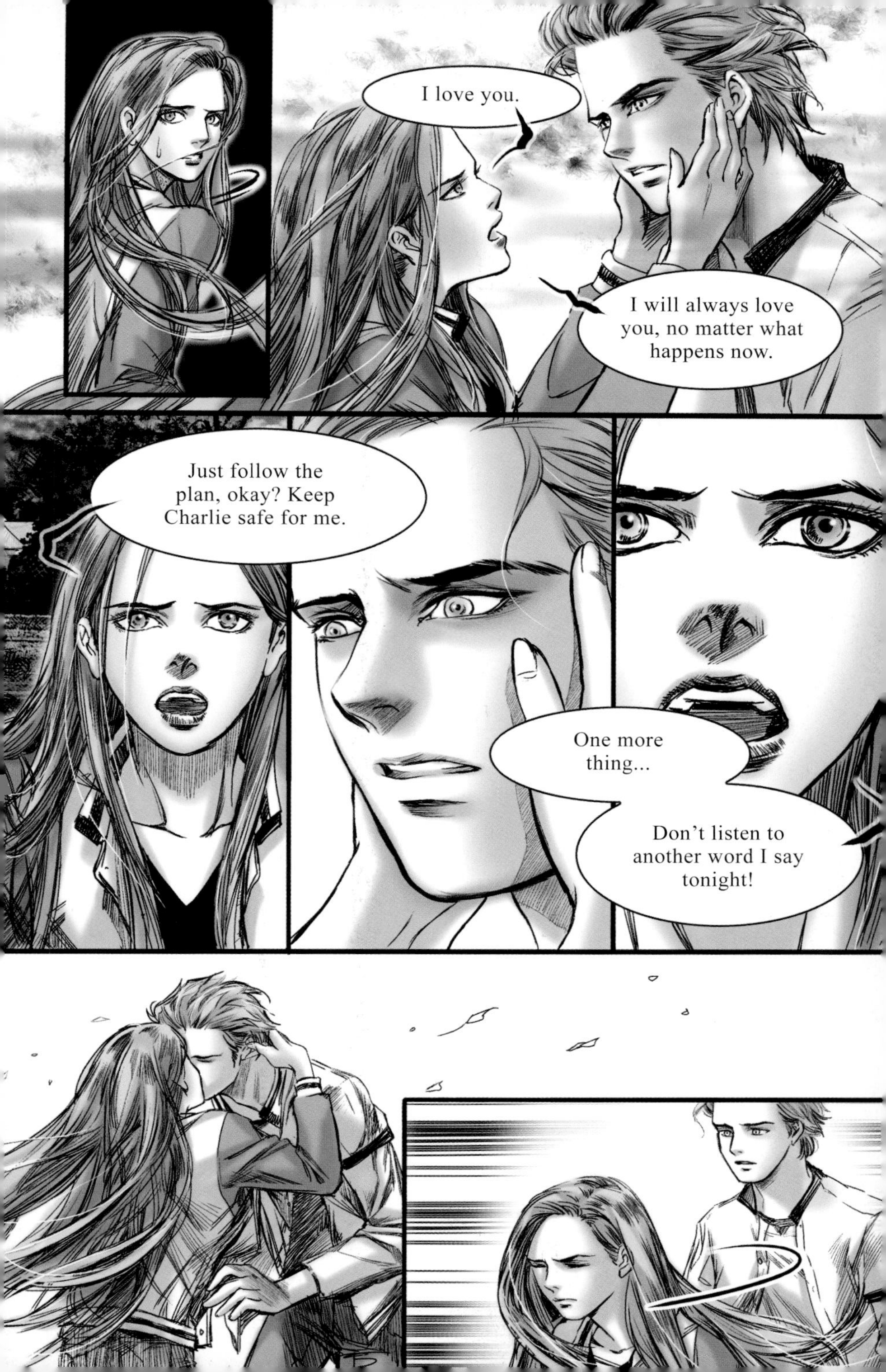
I love you.
I will always love you, no matter what happens now.
Just follow the plan, okay? Keep Charlie safe for me.
One more thing...
Don’t listen to another word I say tonight!

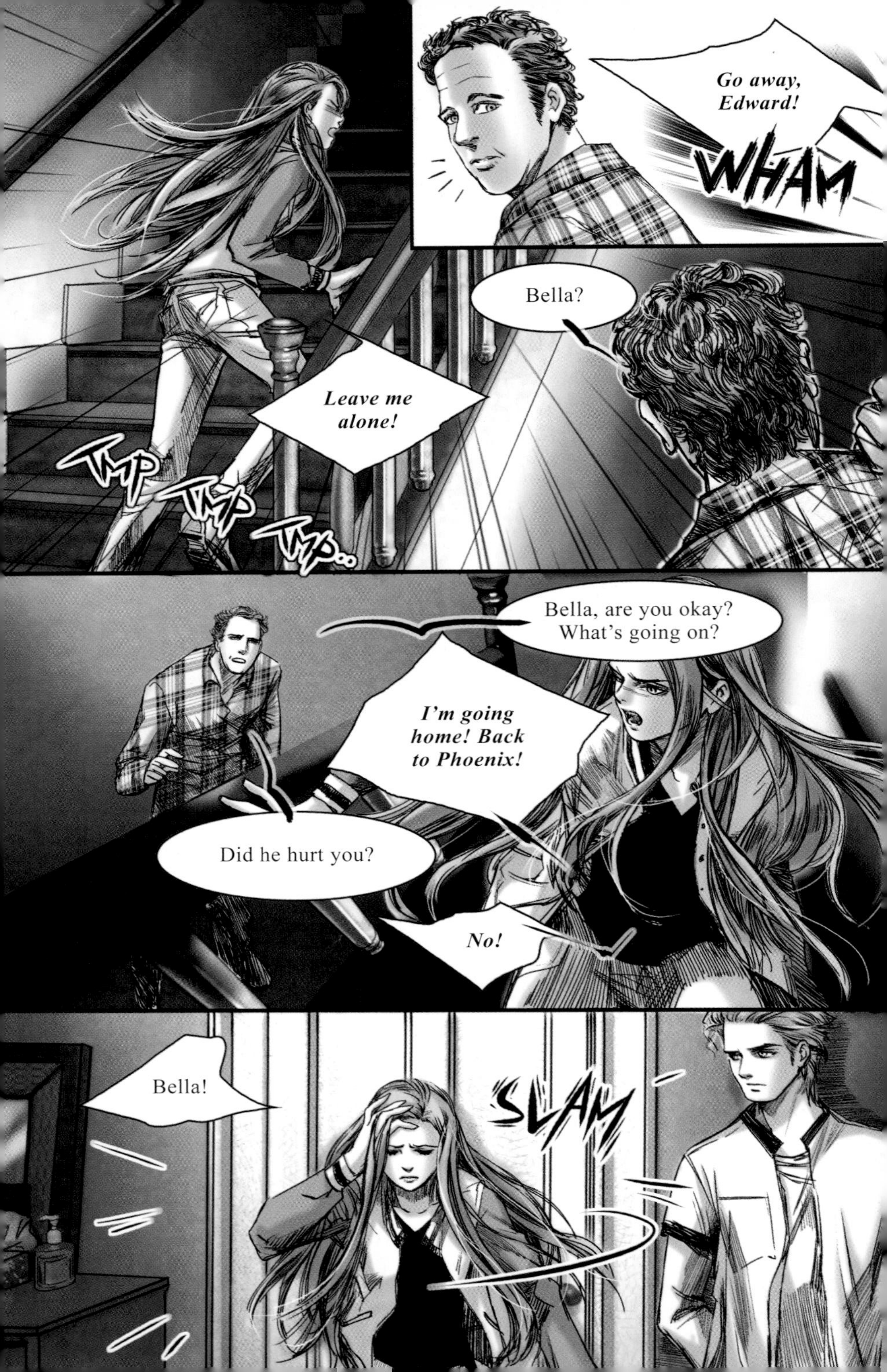

Go away, Edward!
WHAM
Bella?
Leave me alone!
TMP TMP TMP..
Bella, are you okay? What's going on?
I'm going home! Back to Phoenix!
Did he hurt you?
No!
Bella!
SLAM

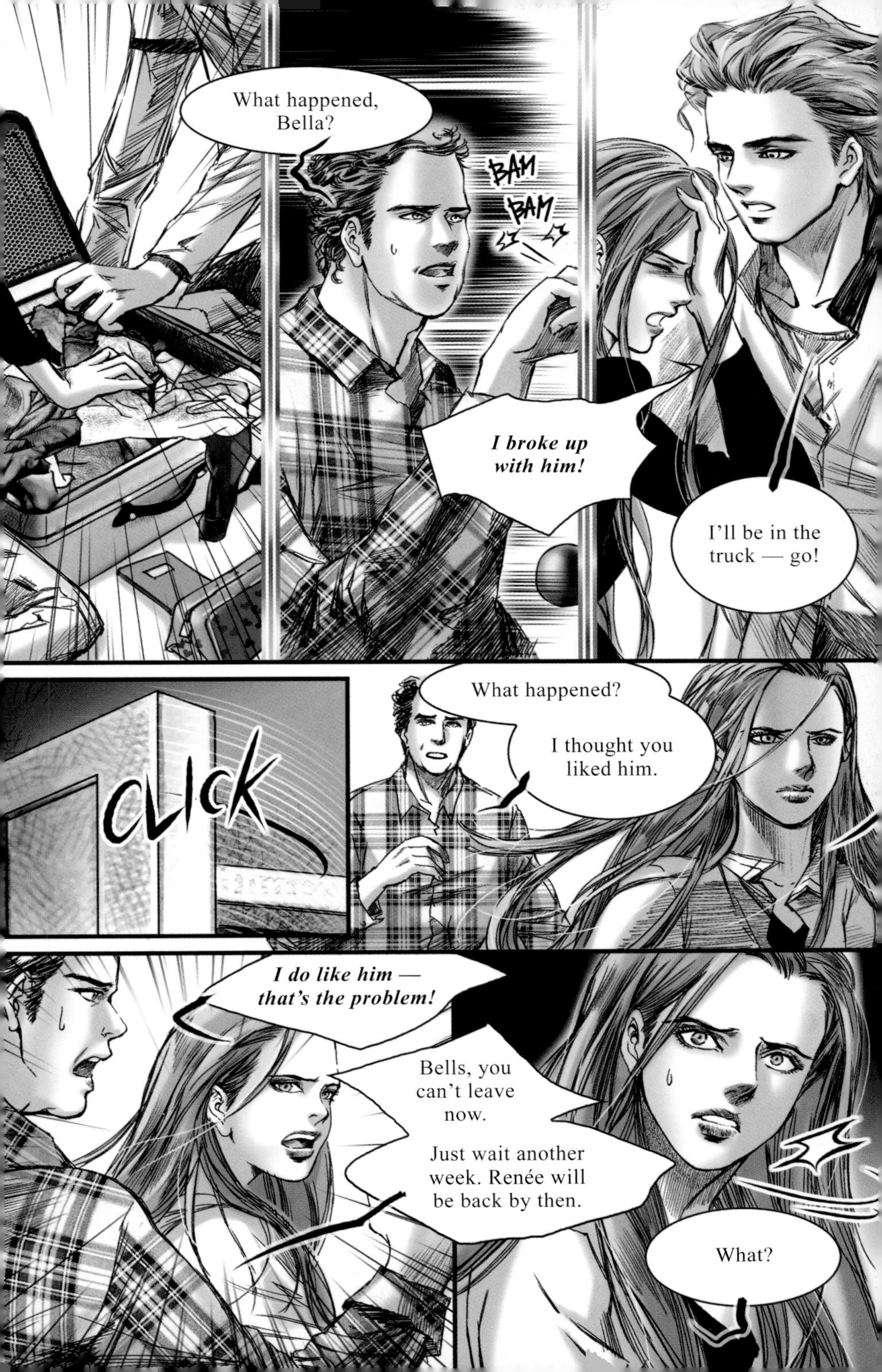
What happened, Bella?
BAM
BAM
I broke up with him!
I'll be in the truck — go!
CLICK
What happened?
I thought you liked him.
I do like him — that's the problem!
Bells, you can't leave now.
Just wait another week. Renée will be back by then.
What?

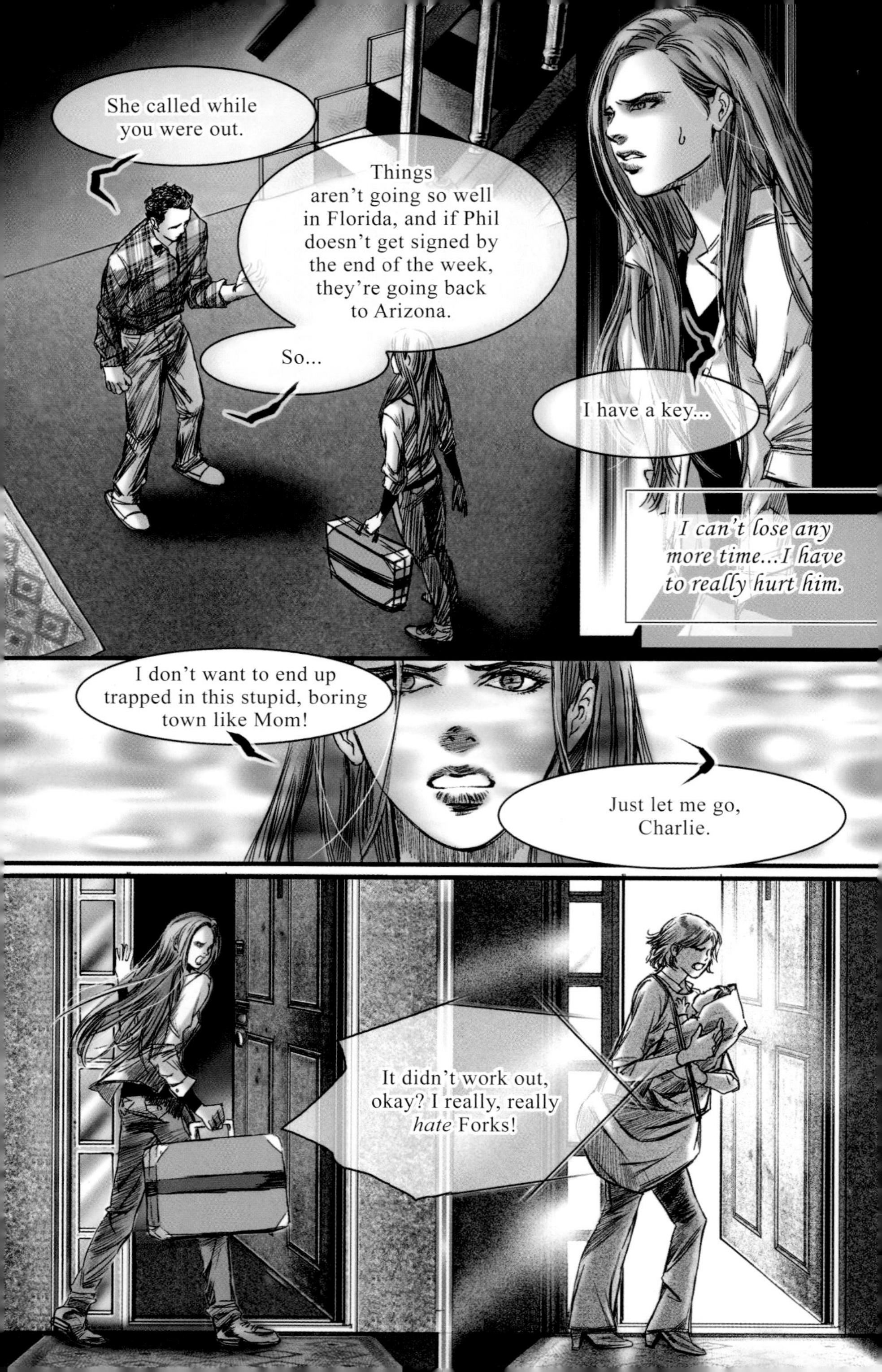
She called while you were out.
Things aren't going so well in Florida, and if Phil doesn't get signed by the end of the week, they're going back to Arizona.
So...
I have a key...
*I can't lose any more time...I have to really hurt him.*
I don't want to end up trapped in this stupid, boring town like Mom!
Just let me go, Charlie.
It didn't work out, okay? I really, really *hate* Forks!

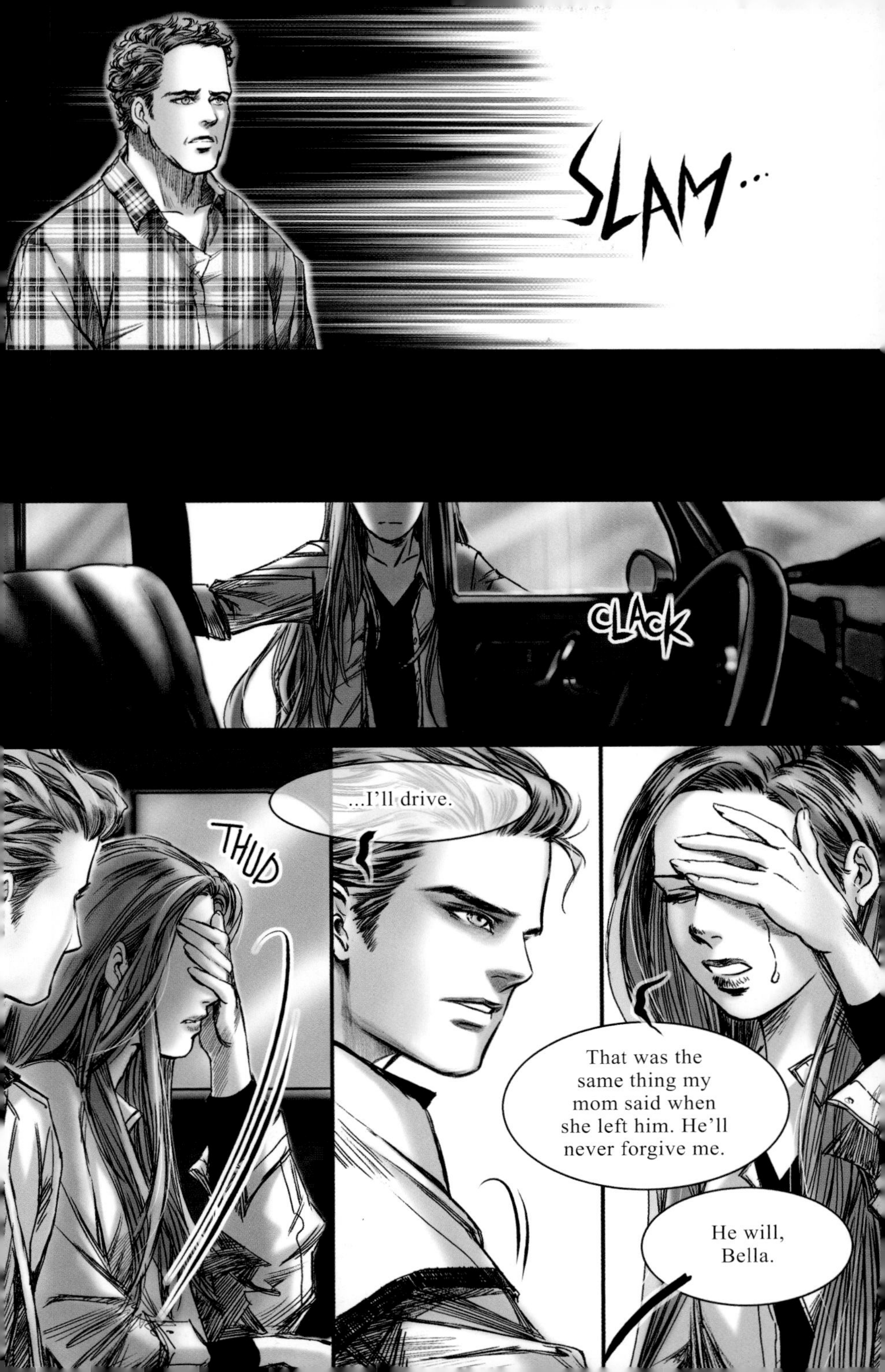
SLAM...
CLACK
THUD
...I'll drive.
That was the same thing my mom said when she left him. He'll never forgive me.
He will, Bella.

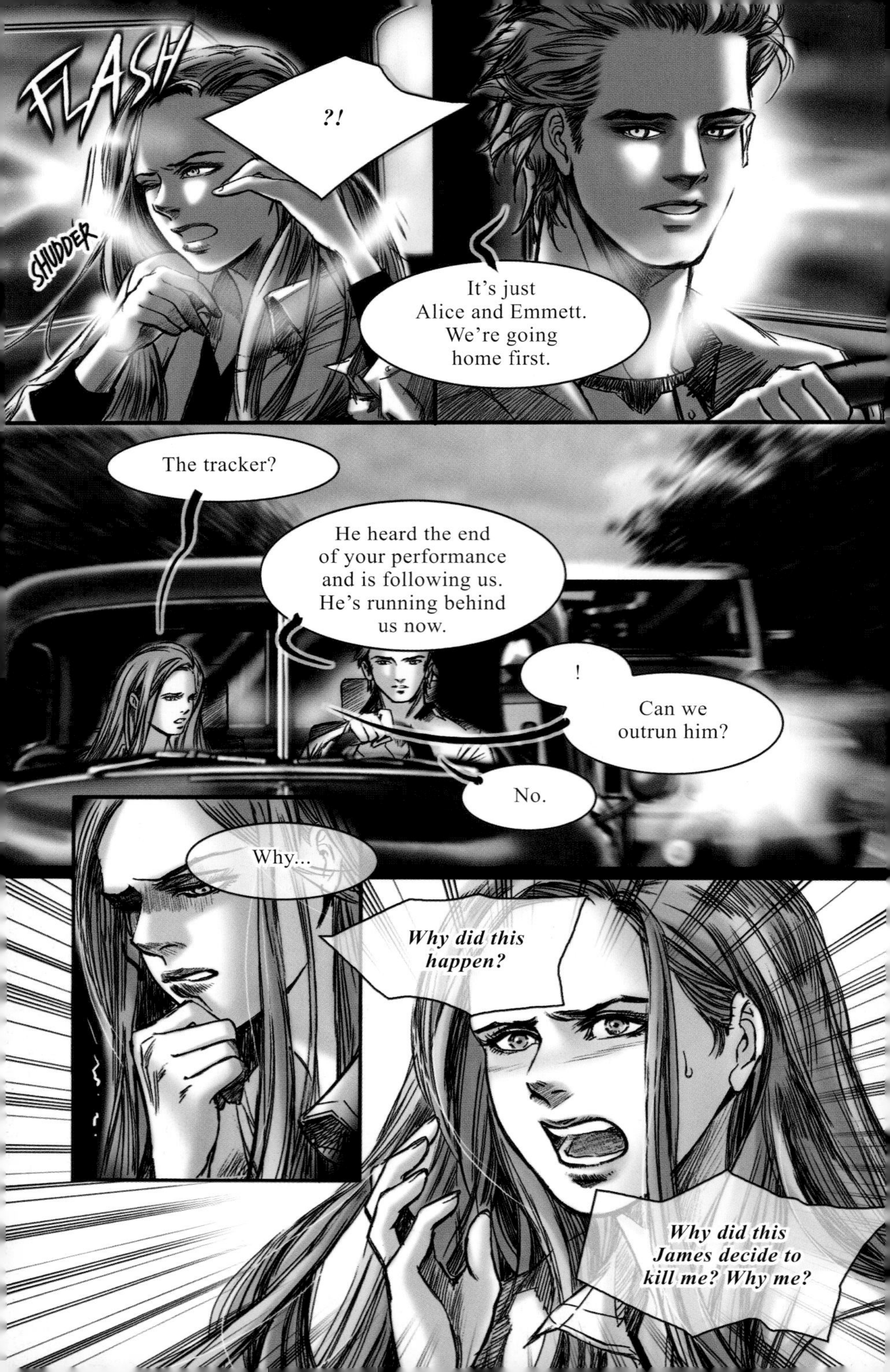
FLASH
SHUDDER
?!
It's just Alice and Emmett. We're going home first.
The tracker?
He heard the end of your performance and is following us. He's running behind us now.
!
Can we outrun him?
No.
Why...
Why did this happen?
Why did this James decide to kill me? Why me?

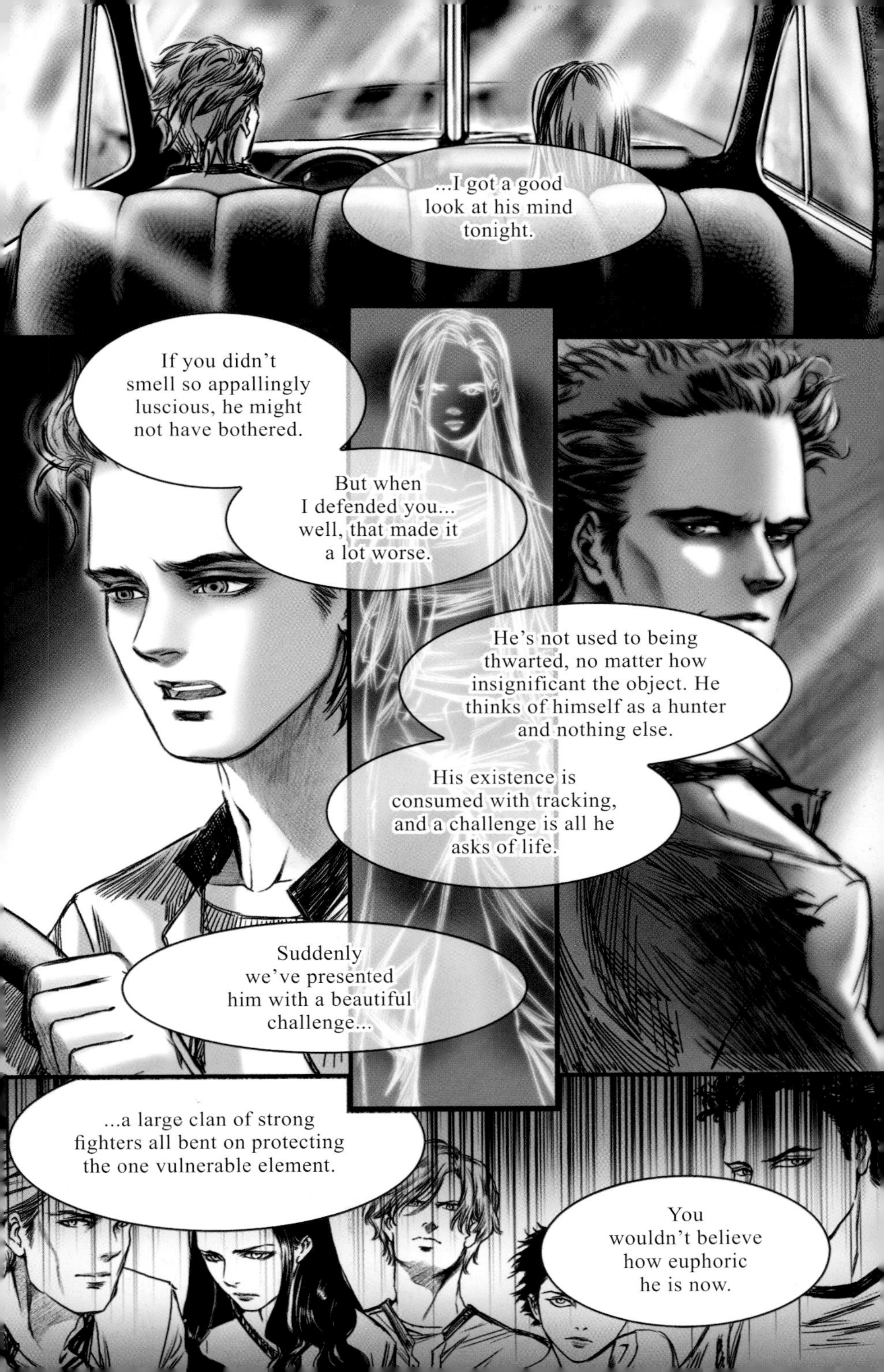
...I got a good look at his mind tonight.
If you didn't smell so appallingly luscious, he might not have bothered.
But when I defended you... well, that made it a lot worse.
He's not used to being thwarted, no matter how insignificant the object. He thinks of himself as a hunter and nothing else.
His existence is consumed with tracking, and a challenge is all he asks of life.
Suddenly we've presented him with a beautiful challenge...
...a large clan of strong fighters all bent on protecting the one vulnerable element.
You wouldn't believe how euphoric he is now.

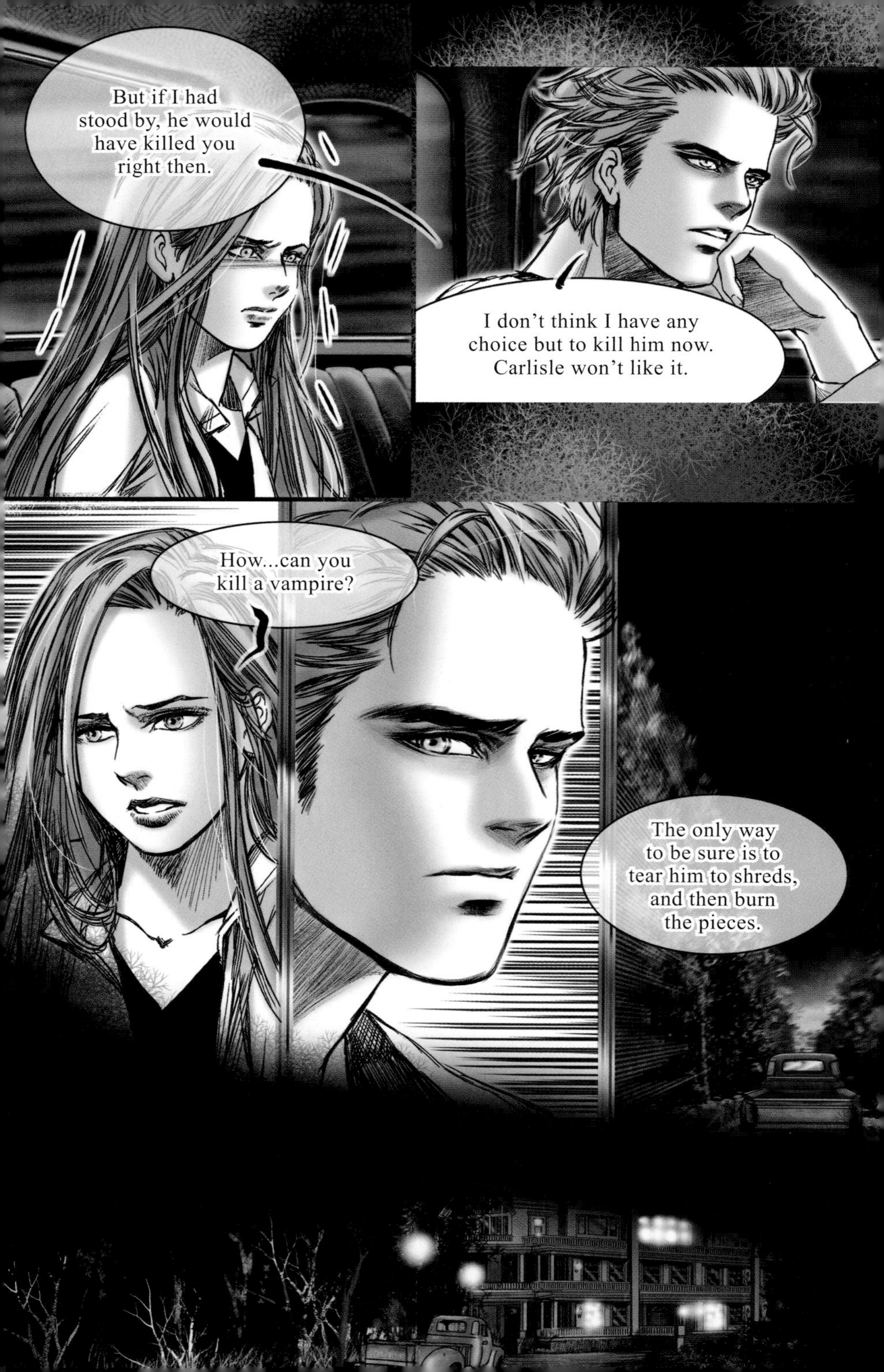
But if I had stood by, he would have killed you right then.
I don't think I have any choice but to kill him now. Carlisle won't like it.
How...can you kill a vampire?
The only way to be sure is to tear him to shreds, and then burn the pieces.

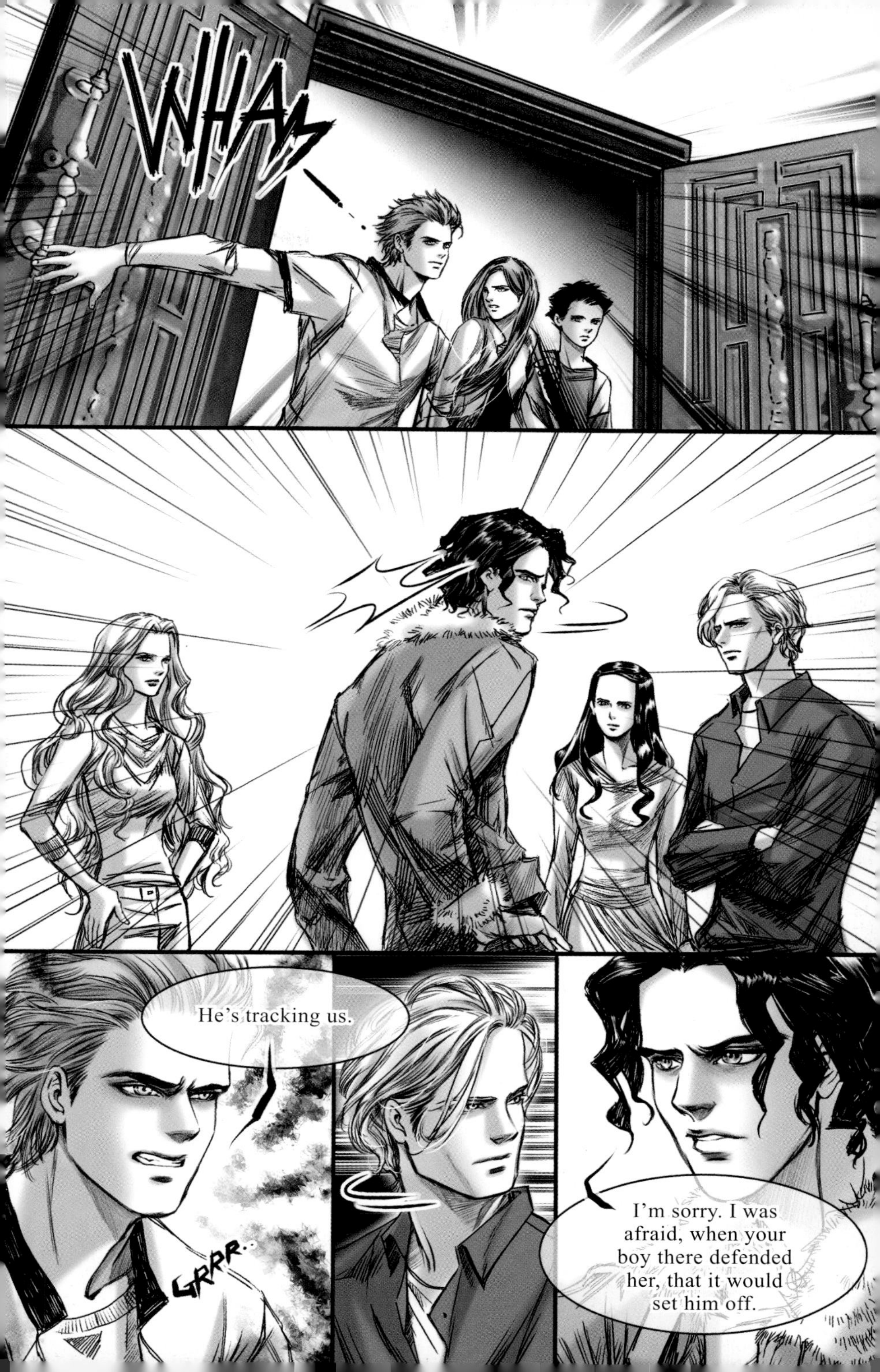
WHAM
He's tracking us.
GRRR..
I'm sorry. I was afraid, when your boy there defended her, that it would set him off.

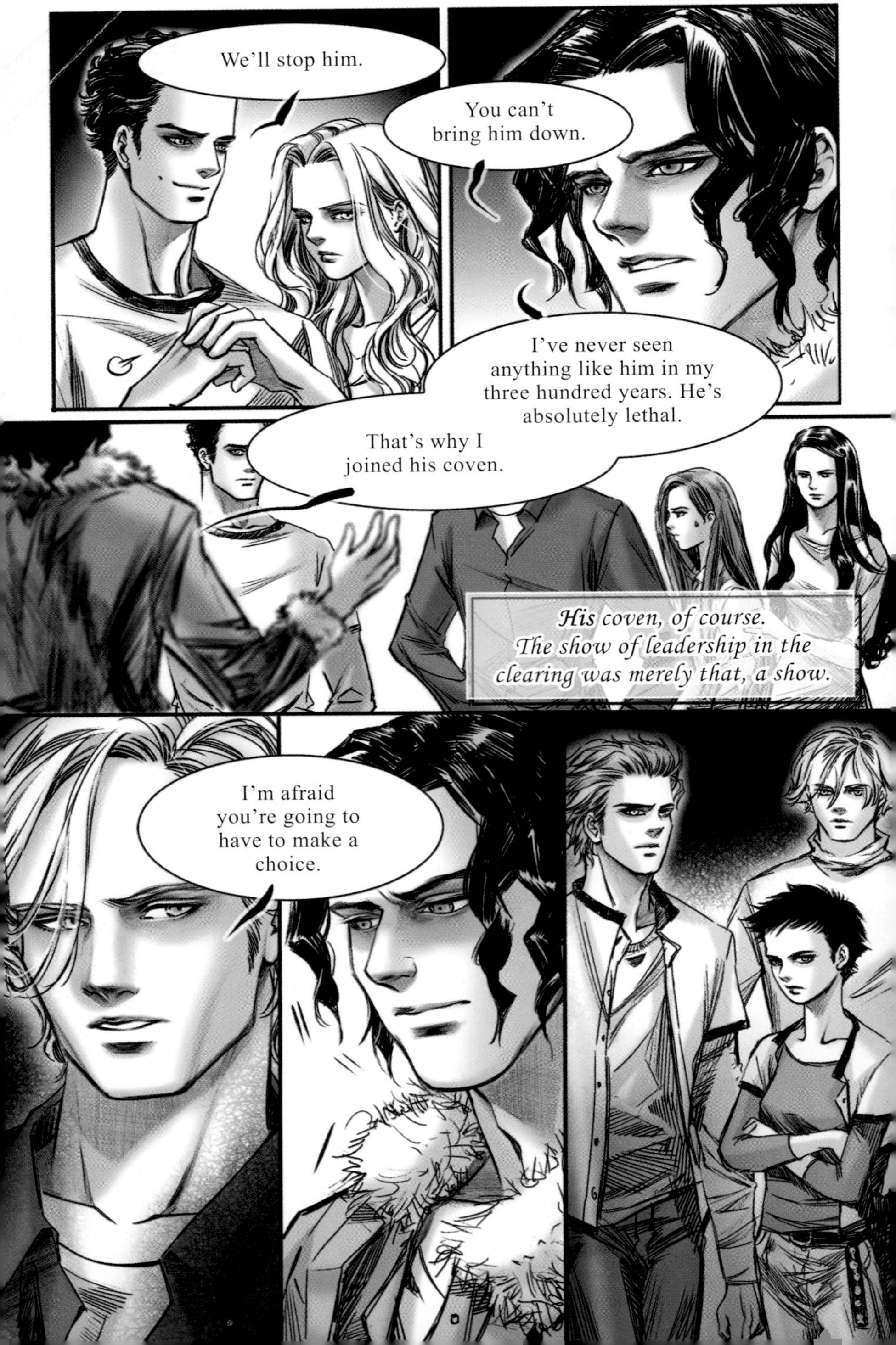
We'll stop him.
You can't bring him down.
I've never seen anything like him in my three hundred years. He's absolutely lethal.
That's why I joined his coven.
*His* coven, of course. The show of leadership in the clearing was merely that, a show.
I'm afraid you're going to have to make a choice.

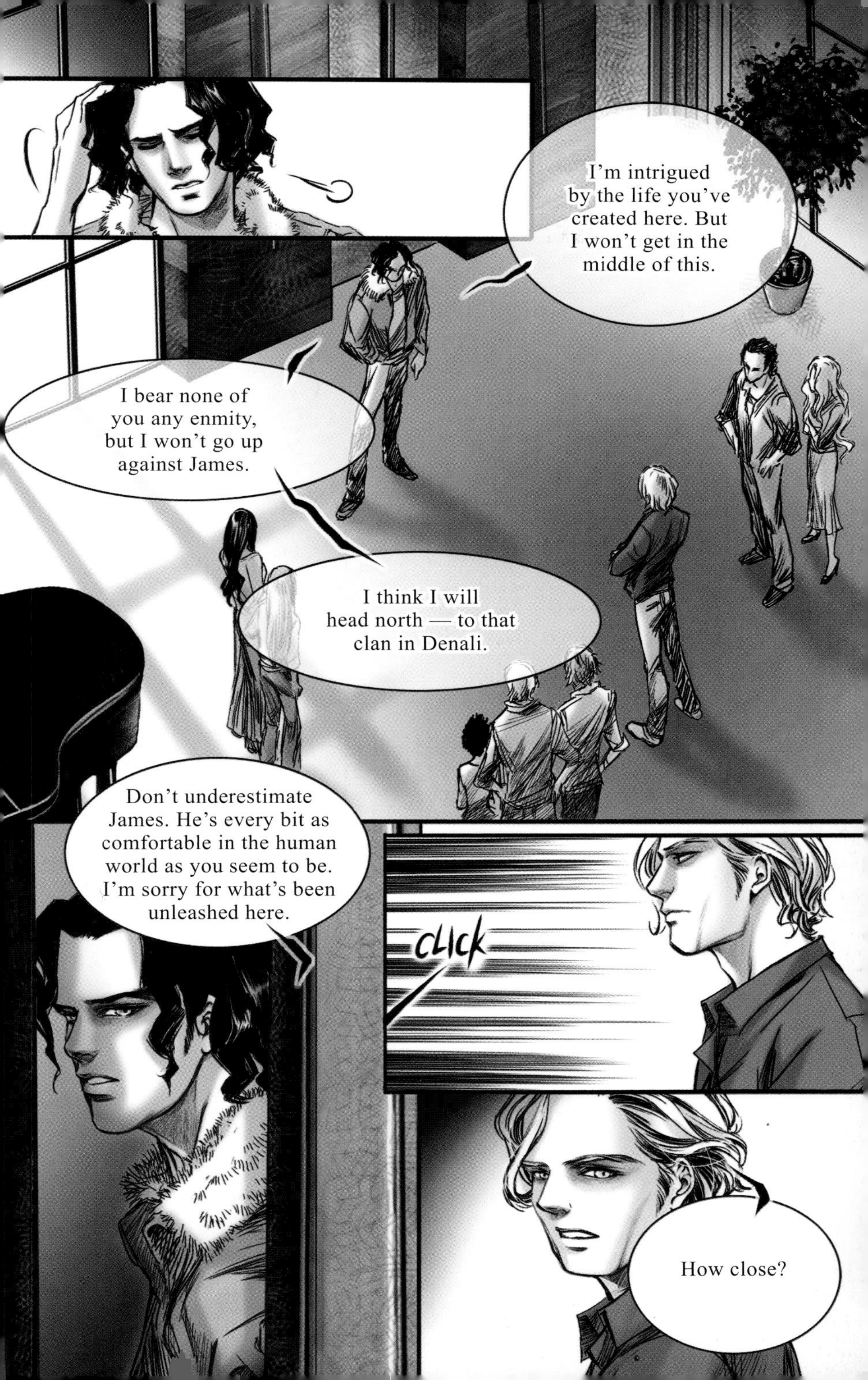
I'm intrigued by the life you've created here. But I won't get in the middle of this.
I bear none of you any enmity, but I won't go up against James.
I think I will head north — to that clan in Denali.
Don't underestimate James. He's every bit as comfortable in the human world as you seem to be. I'm sorry for what's been unleashed here.
CLICK
How close?

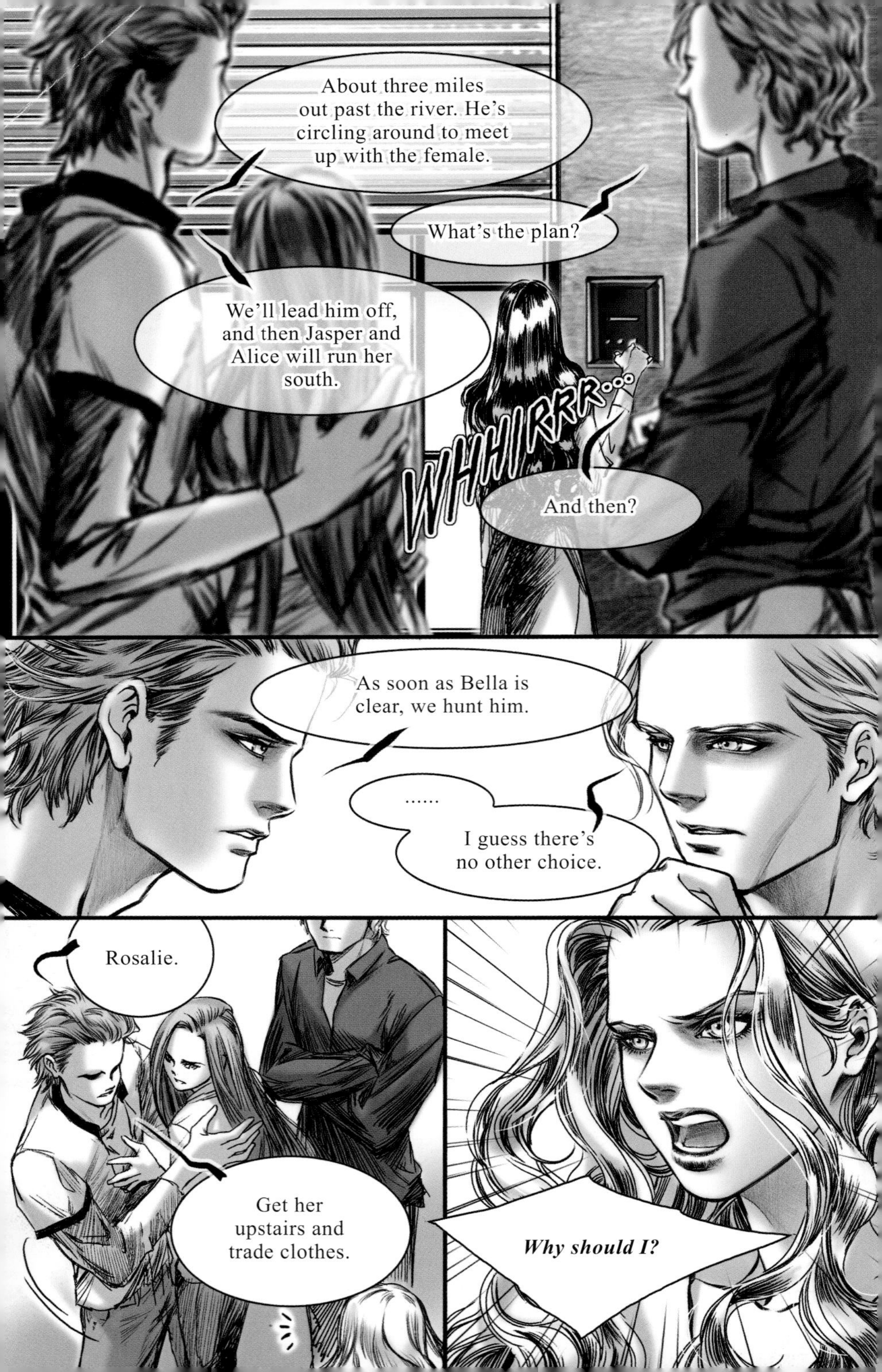
About three miles out past the river. He's circling around to meet up with the female.
What's the plan?
We'll lead him off, and then Jasper and Alice will run her south.
WHHIRRR...
And then?
As soon as Bella is clear, we hunt him.
......
I guess there's no other choice.
Rosalie.
Get her upstairs and trade clothes.
*Why should I?*

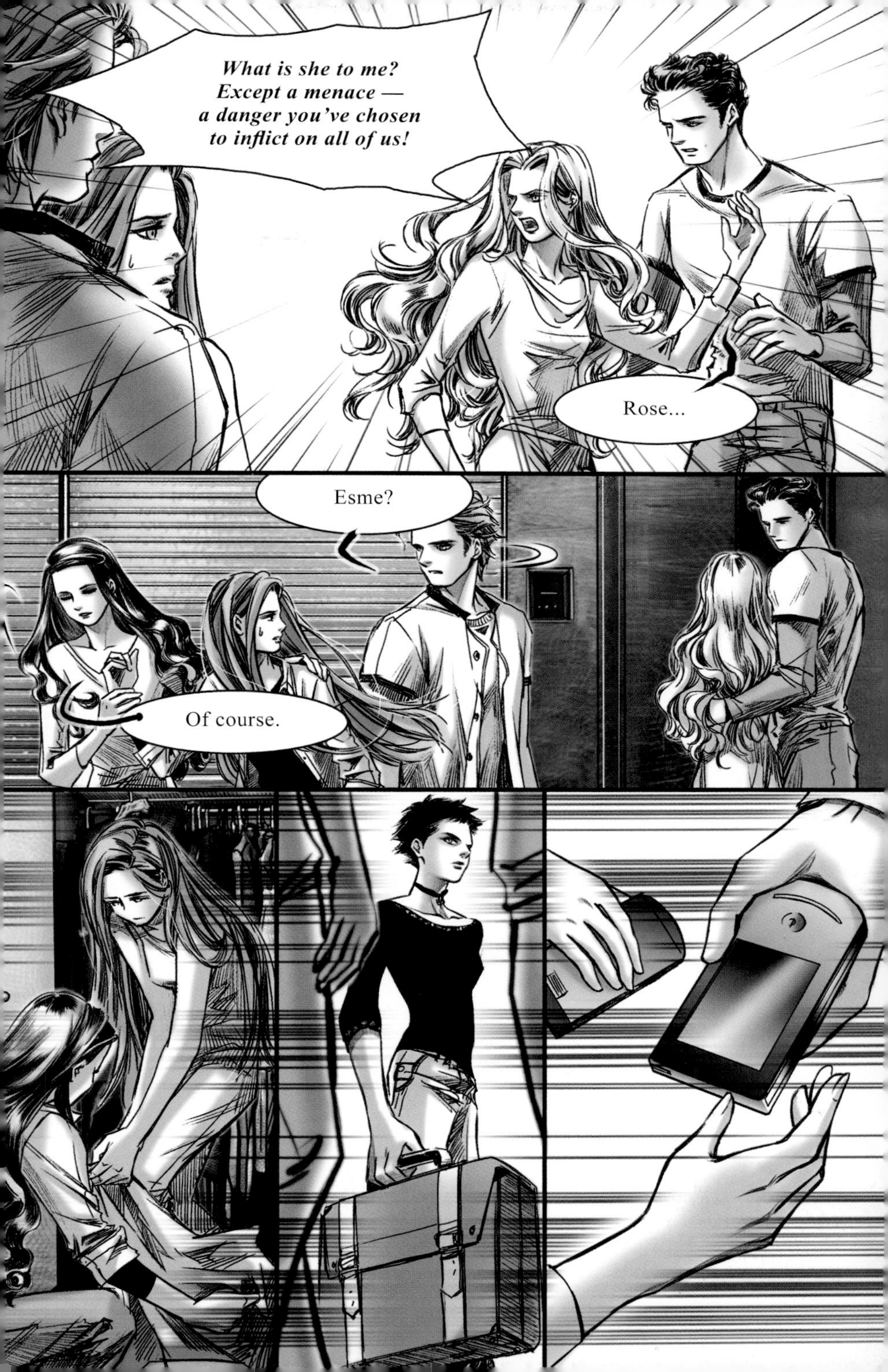
*What is she to me? Except a menace — a danger you've chosen to inflict on all of us!*
Rose...
Esme?
Of course.

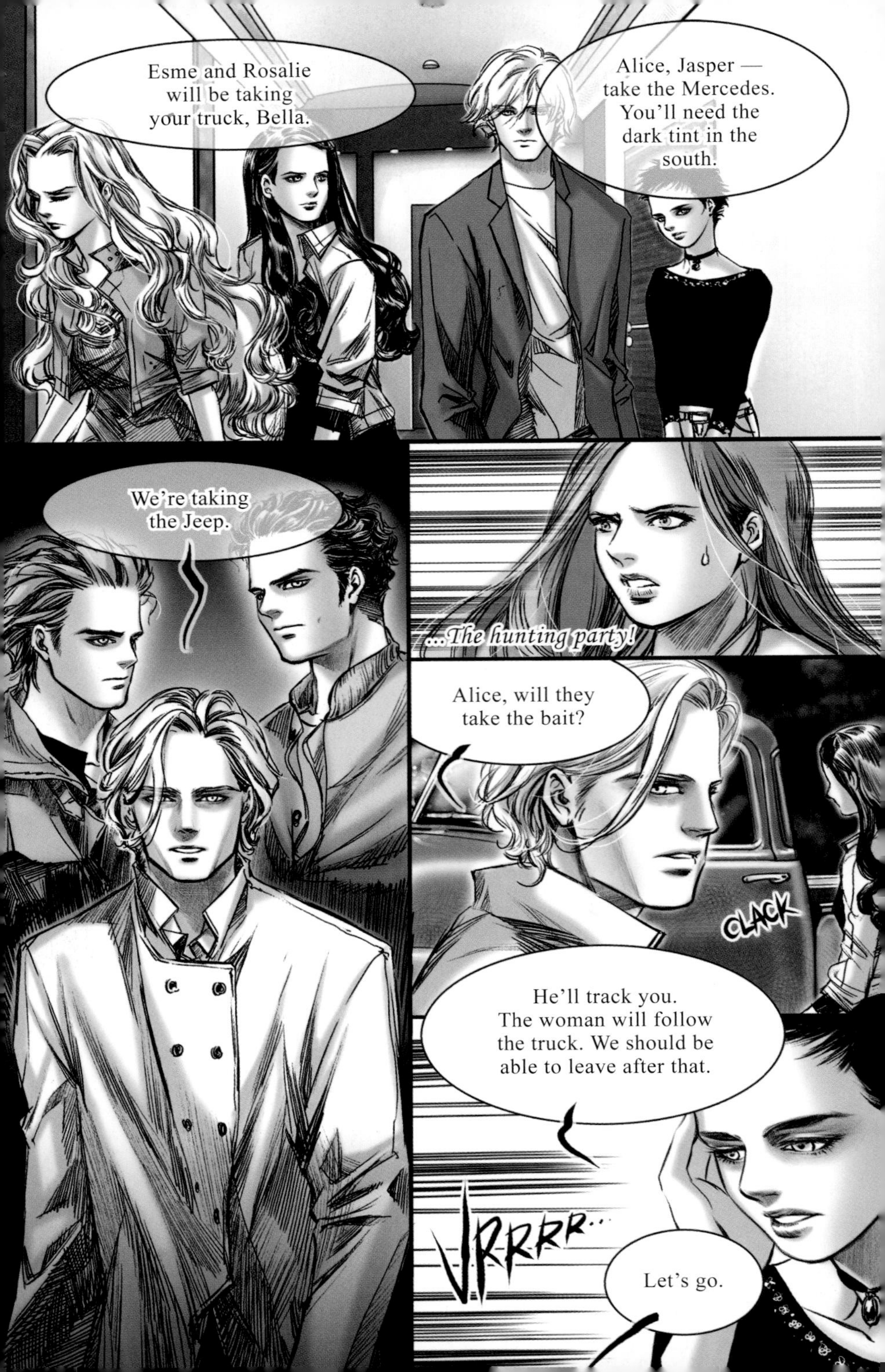
Esme and Rosalie will be taking your truck, Bella.
Alice, Jasper — take the Mercedes. You'll need the dark tint in the south.
We're taking the Jeep.
...The hunting party!
Alice, will they take the bait?
CLACK
He'll track you. The woman will follow the truck. We should be able to leave after that.
VRRRR...
Let's go.

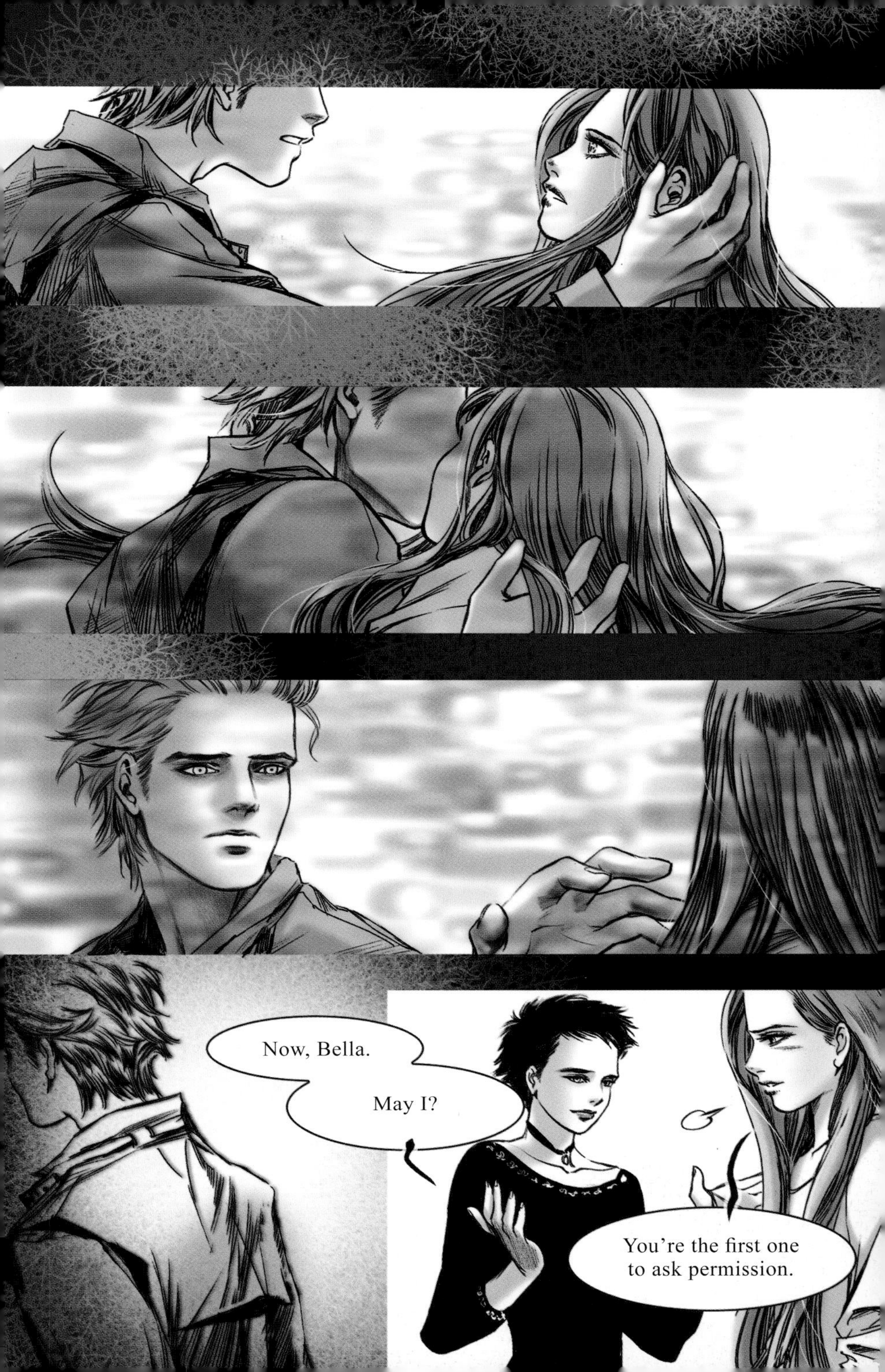
Now, Bella.
May I?
You're the first one to ask permission.

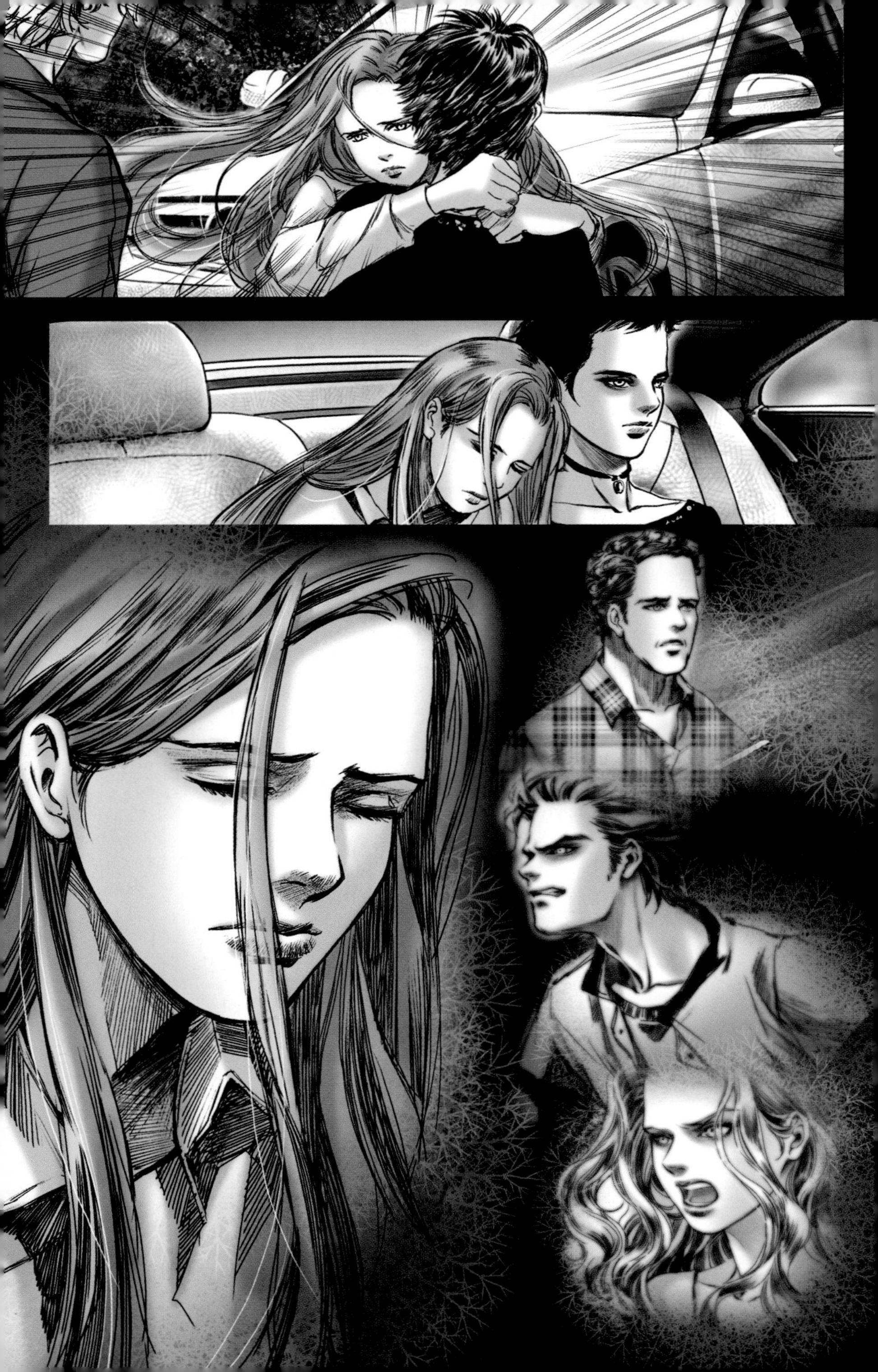

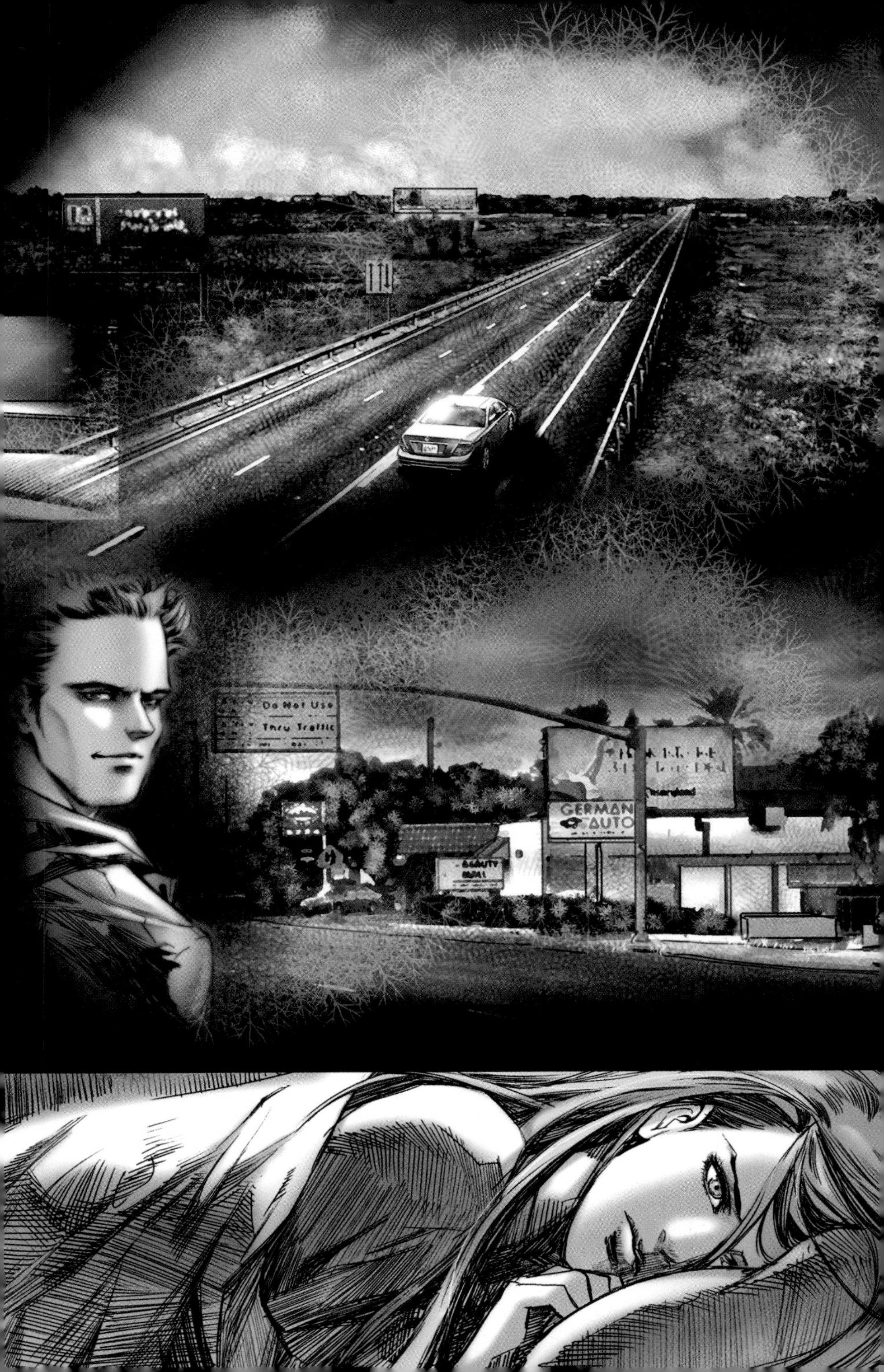
Do Not Use
Thru Traffic
GERMAN AUTO

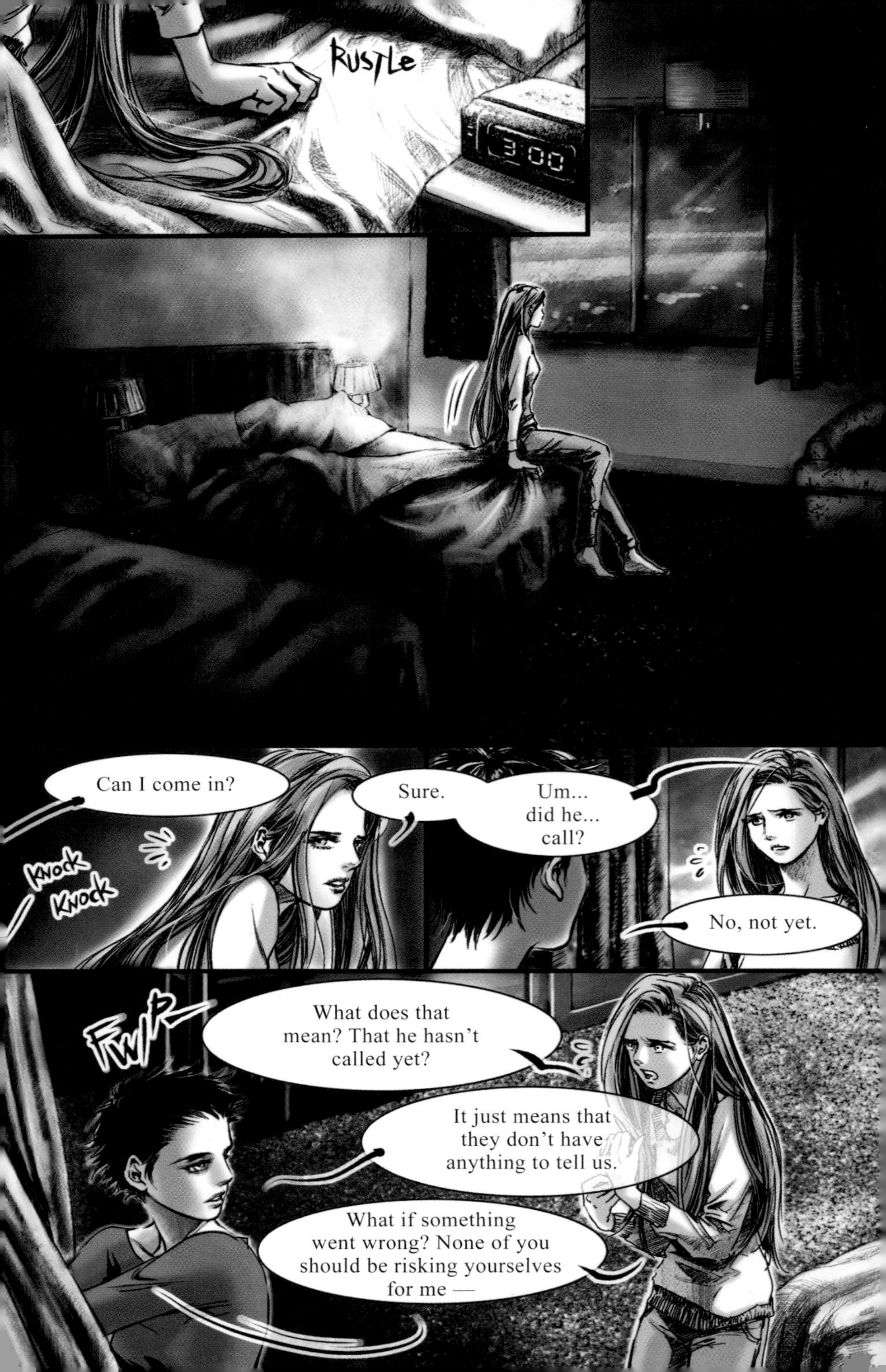
RUSTLE
3:00
KNOCK KNOCK
Can I come in?
Sure.
Um... did he... call?
No, not yet.
FWIP
What does that mean? That he hasn't called yet?
It just means that they don't have anything to tell us.
What if something went wrong? None of you should be risking yourselves for me —

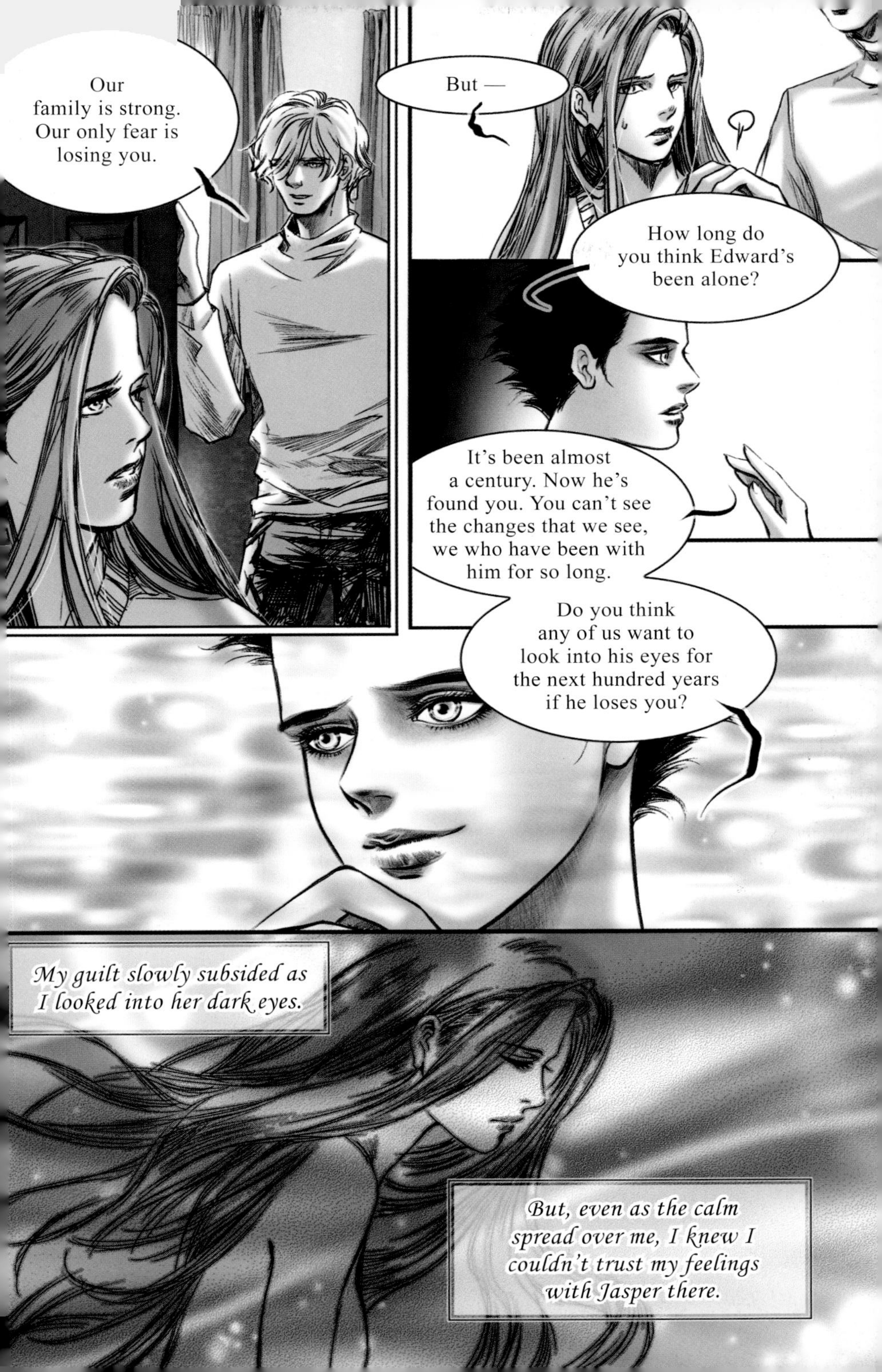
Our family is strong. Our only fear is losing you.
But —
How long do you think Edward's been alone?
It's been almost a century. Now he's found you. You can't see the changes that we see, we who have been with him for so long.
Do you think any of us want to look into his eyes for the next hundred years if he loses you?
My guilt slowly subsided as I looked into her dark eyes.
But, even as the calm spread over me, I knew I couldn't trust my feelings with Jasper there.

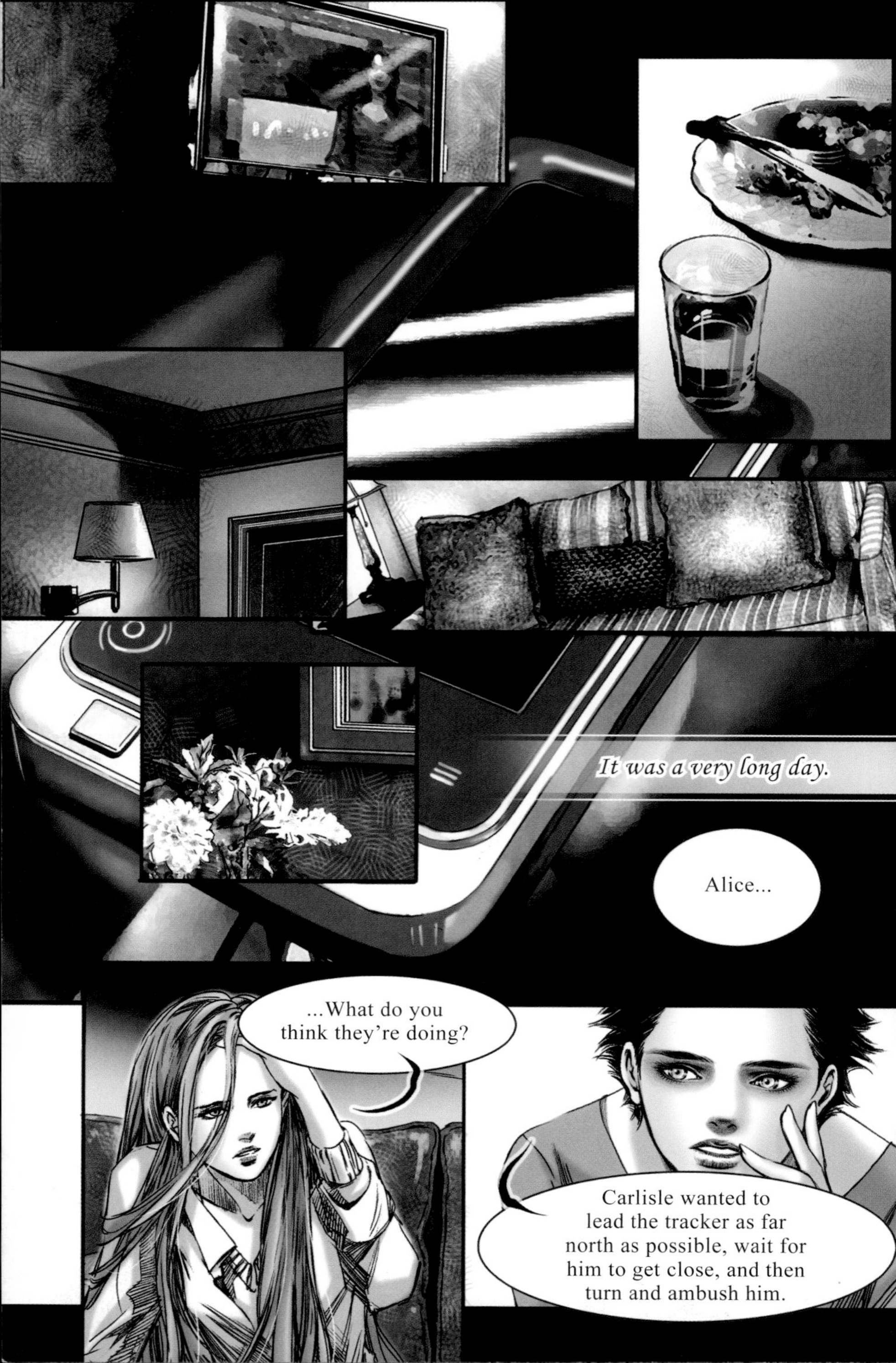
It was a very long day.
Alice...
...What do you think they're doing?
Carlisle wanted to lead the tracker as far north as possible, wait for him to get close, and then turn and ambush him.

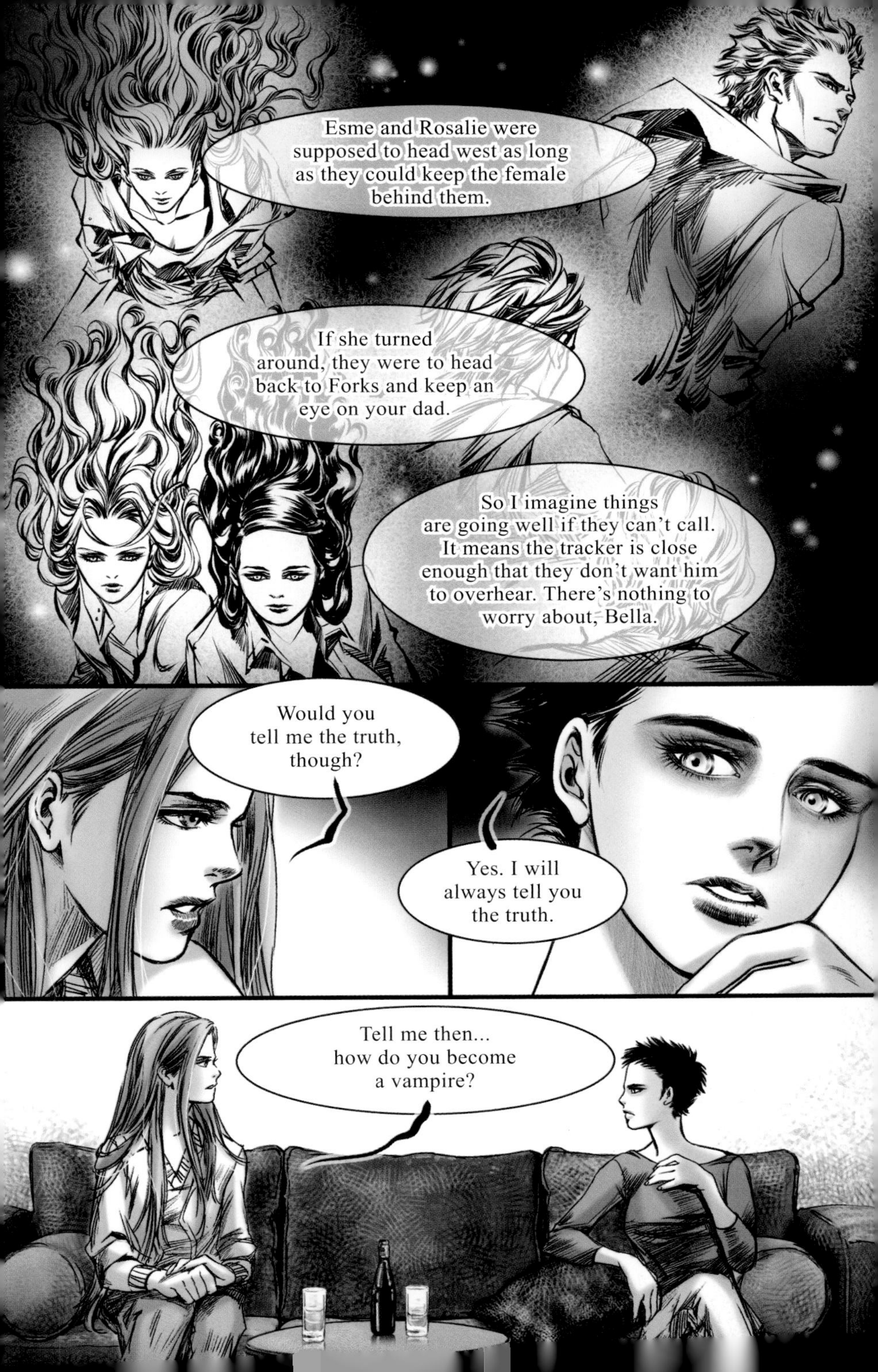

Esme and Rosalie were supposed to head west as long as they could keep the female behind them.
If she turned around, they were to head back to Forks and keep an eye on your dad.
So I imagine things are going well if they can't call. It means the tracker is close enough that they don't want him to overhear. There's nothing to worry about, Bella.
Would you tell me the truth, though?
Yes. I will always tell you the truth.
Tell me then... how do you become a vampire?

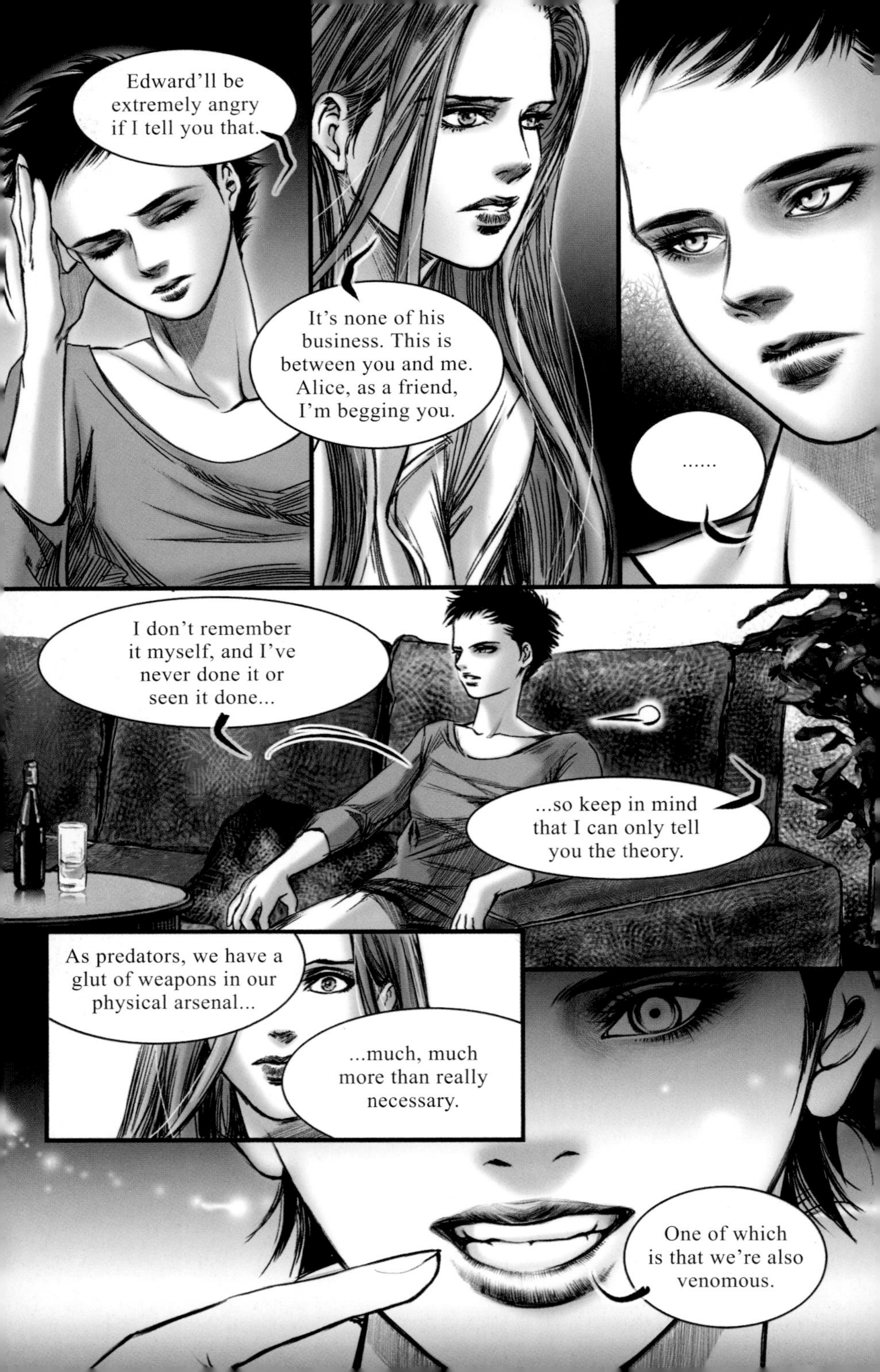
Edward'll be extremely angry if I tell you that.
It's none of his business. This is between you and me. Alice, as a friend, I'm begging you.
......
I don't remember it myself, and I've never done it or seen it done...
...so keep in mind that I can only tell you the theory.
As predators, we have a glut of weapons in our physical arsenal...
...much, much more than really necessary.
One of which is that we're also venomous.

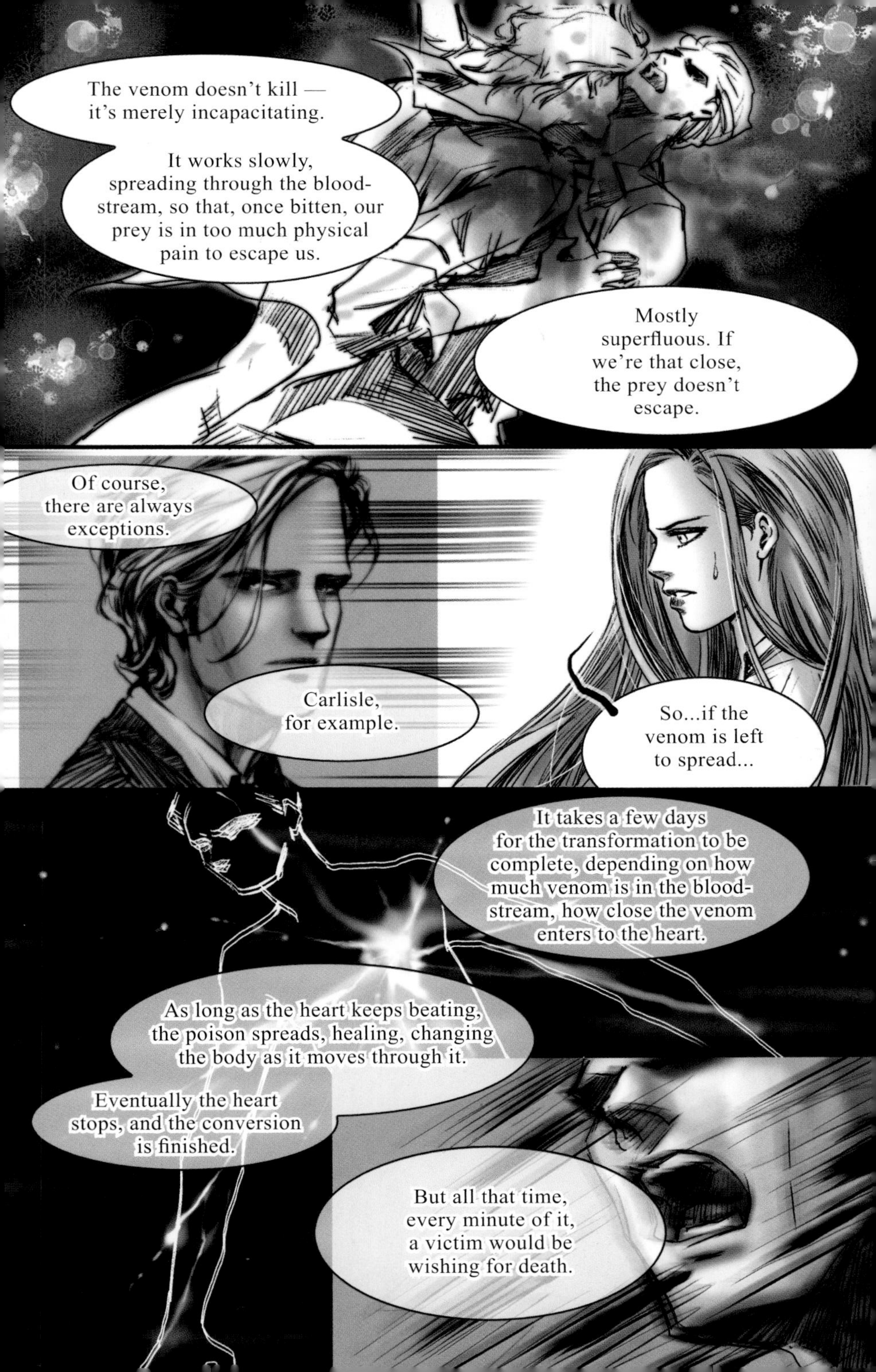
The venom doesn't kill — it's merely incapacitating.
It works slowly, spreading through the blood-stream, so that, once bitten, our prey is in too much physical pain to escape us.
Mostly superfluous. If we're that close, the prey doesn't escape.
Of course, there are always exceptions.
Carlisle, for example.
So...if the venom is left to spread...
It takes a few days for the transformation to be complete, depending on how much venom is in the blood-stream, how close the venom enters to the heart.
As long as the heart keeps beating, the poison spreads, healing, changing the body as it moves through it.
Eventually the heart stops, and the conversion is finished.
But all that time, every minute of it, a victim would be wishing for death.

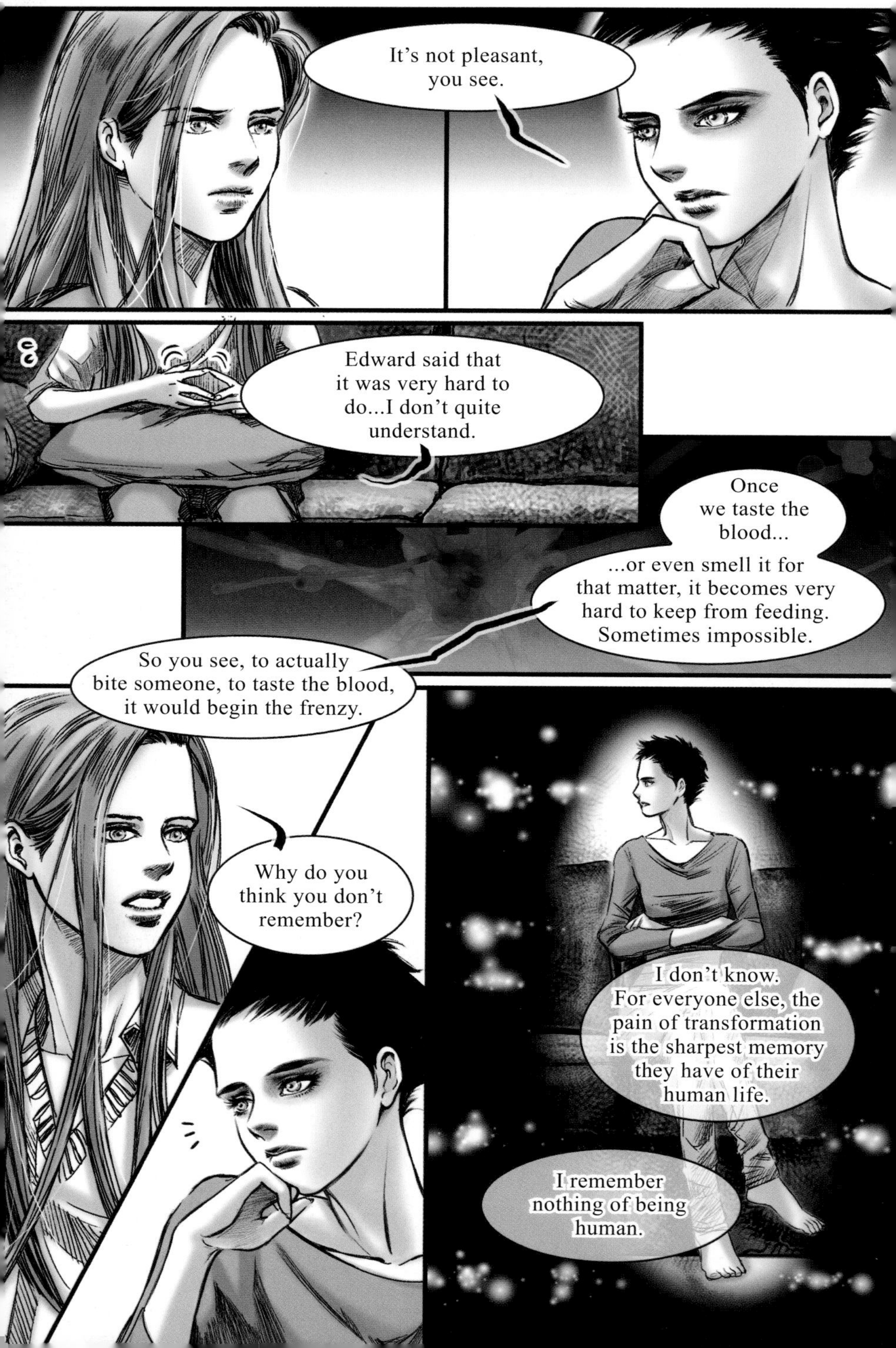
It's not pleasant, you see.
Edward said that it was very hard to do...I don't quite understand.
Once we taste the blood...
...or even smell it for that matter, it becomes very hard to keep from feeding. Sometimes impossible.
So you see, to actually bite someone, to taste the blood, it would begin the frenzy.
Why do you think you don't remember?
I don't know. For everyone else, the pain of transformation is the sharpest memory they have of their human life.
I remember nothing of being human.

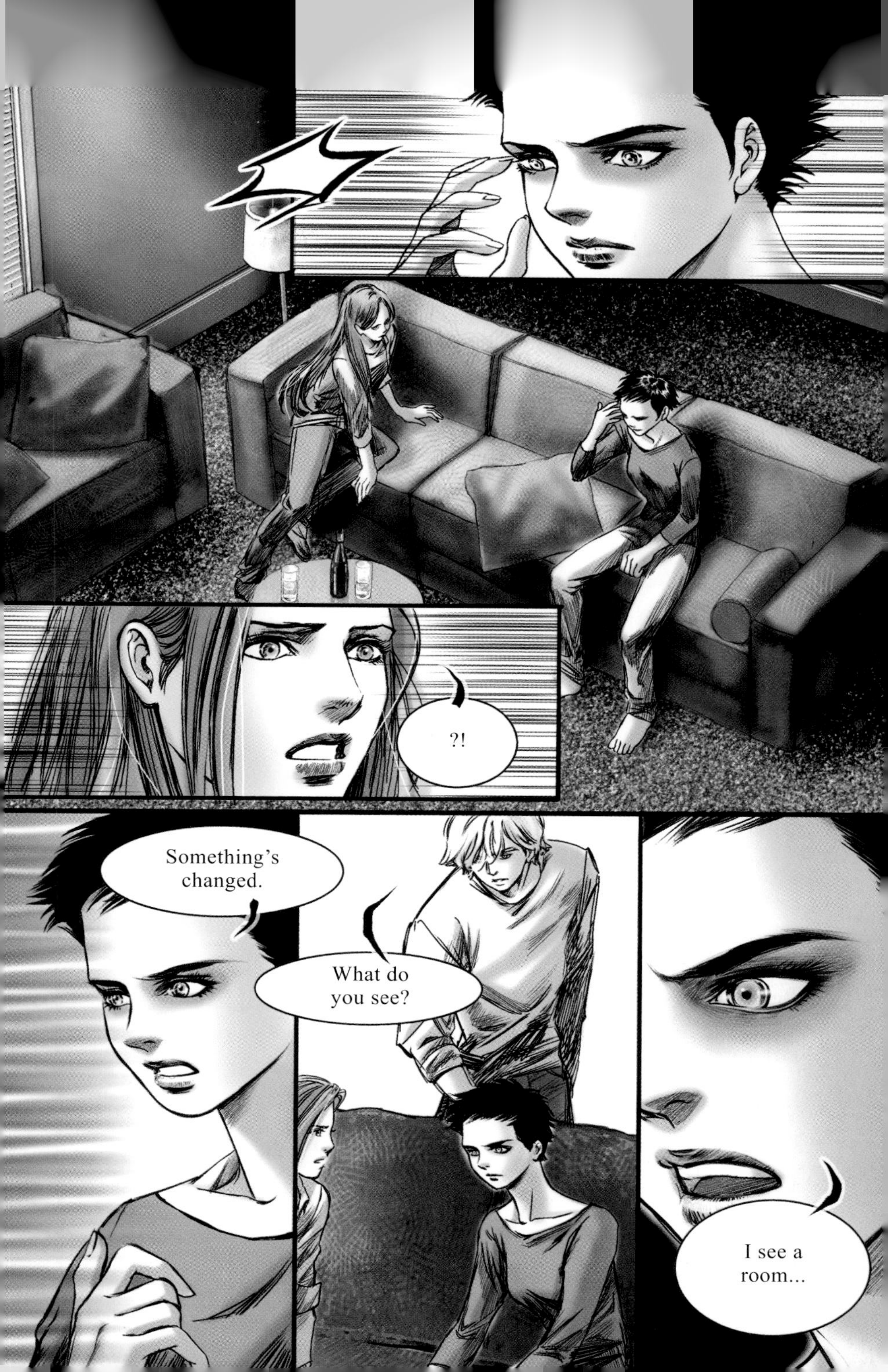
?!
Something's changed.
What do you see?
I see a room...

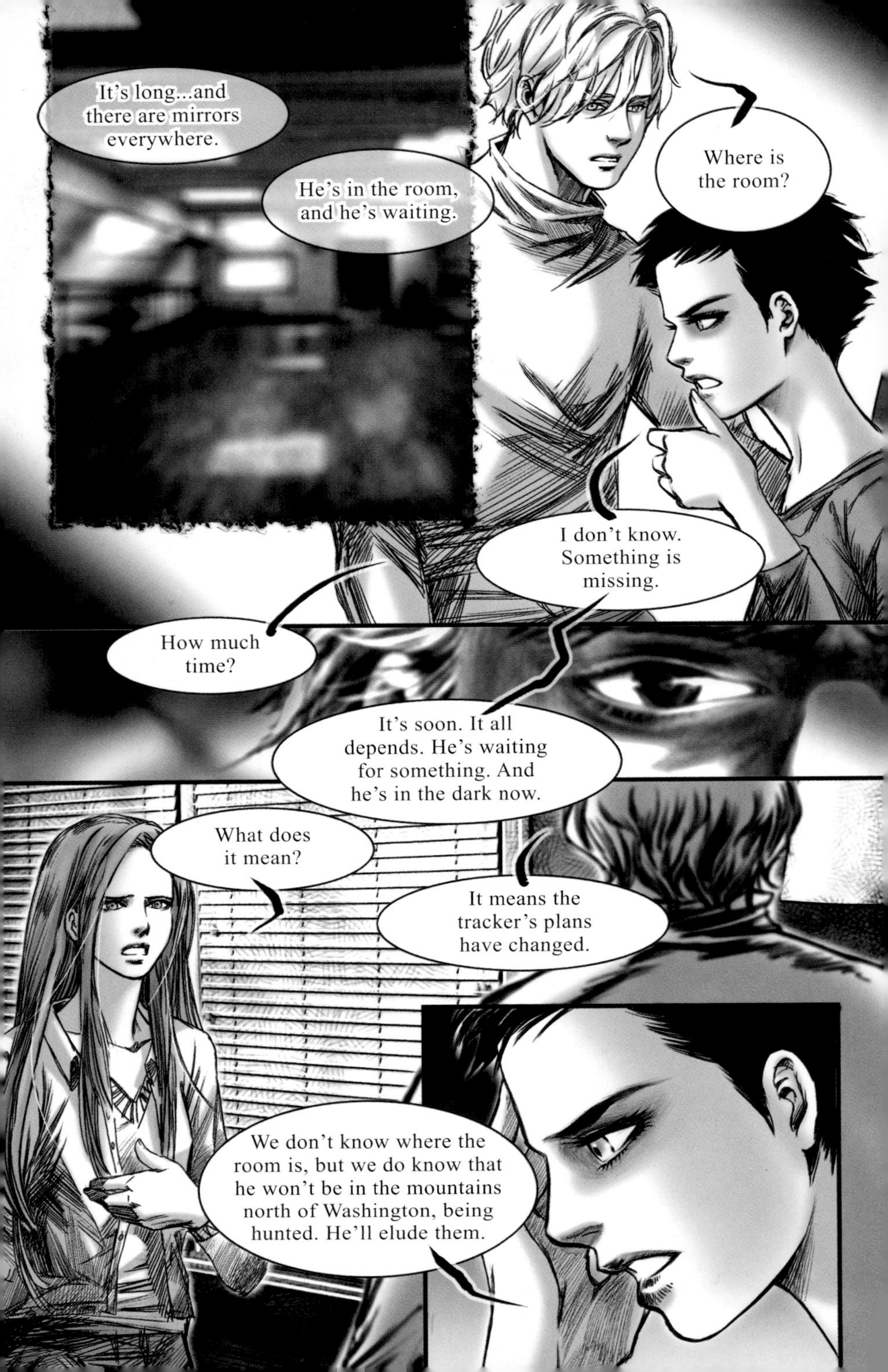
It's long...and there are mirrors everywhere.
He's in the room, and he's waiting.
Where is the room?
I don't know. Something is missing.
How much time?
It's soon. It all depends. He's waiting for something. And he's in the dark now.
What does it mean?
It means the tracker's plans have changed.
We don't know where the room is, but we do know that he won't be in the mountains north of Washington, being hunted. He'll elude them.

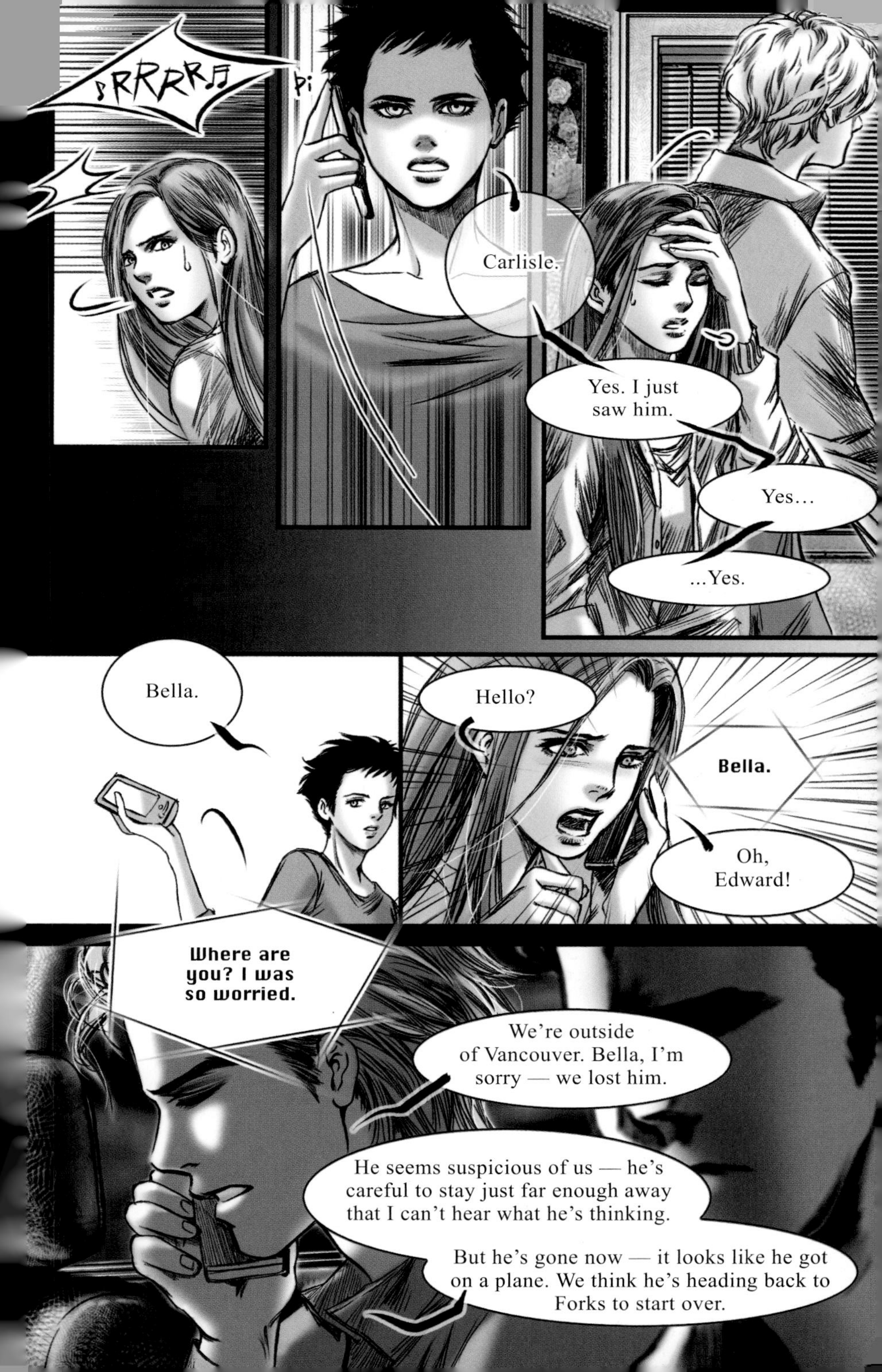

♪RRRR♫
pi
Carlisle.
Yes. I just saw him.
Yes…
...Yes.
Bella.
Hello?
Bella.
Oh, Edward!
Where are you? I was so worried.
We're outside of Vancouver. Bella, I'm sorry — we lost him.
He seems suspicious of us — he's careful to stay just far enough away that I can't hear what he's thinking.
But he's gone now — it looks like he got on a plane. We think he's heading back to Forks to start over.

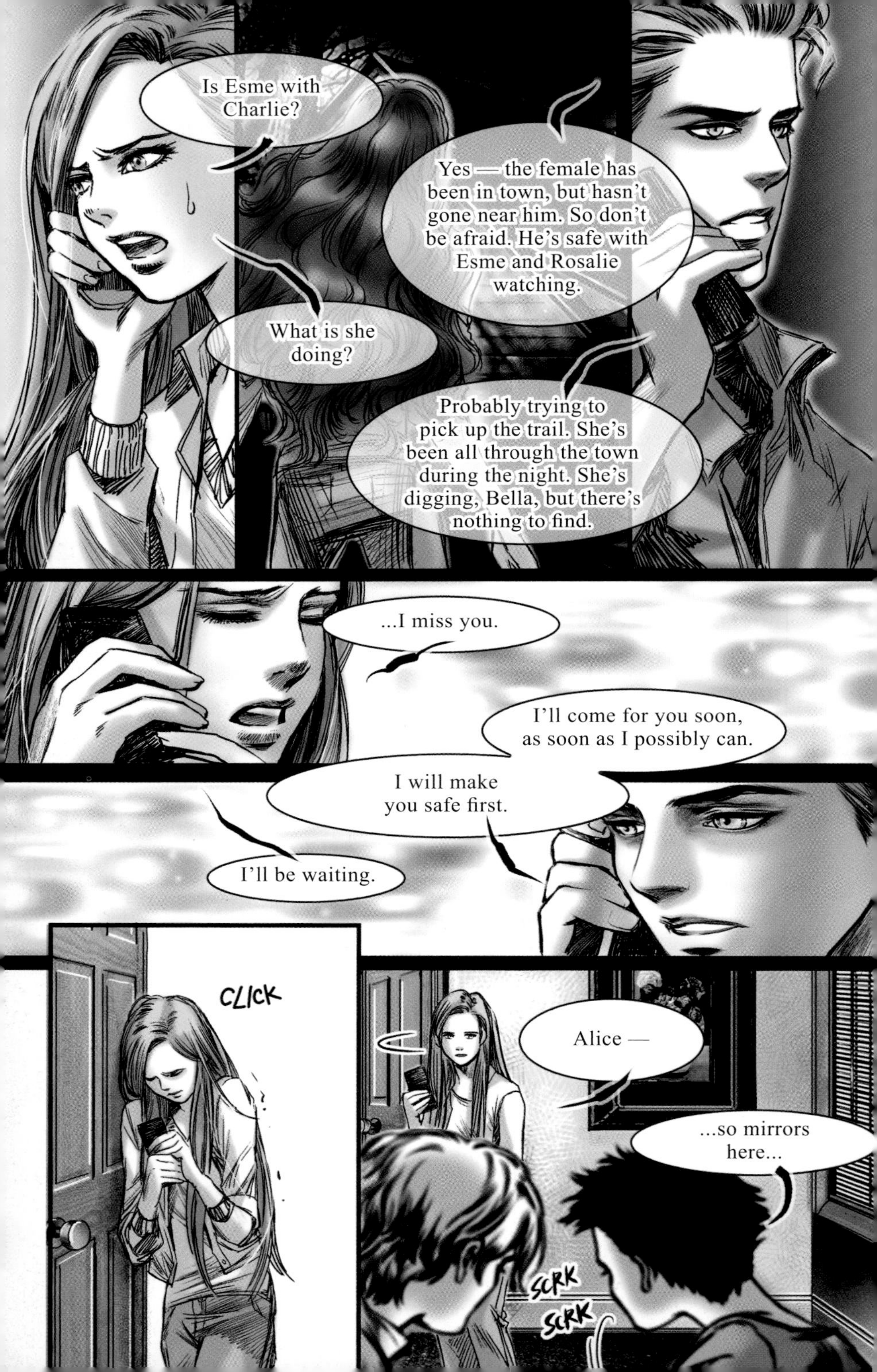
Is Esme with Charlie?
Yes — the female has been in town, but hasn't gone near him. So don't be afraid. He's safe with Esme and Rosalie watching.
What is she doing?
Probably trying to pick up the trail. She's been all through the town during the night. She's digging, Bella, but there's nothing to find.
...I miss you.
I'll come for you soon, as soon as I possibly can.
I will make you safe first.
I'll be waiting.
CLICK
Alice —
...so mirrors here...
SCRK
SCRK

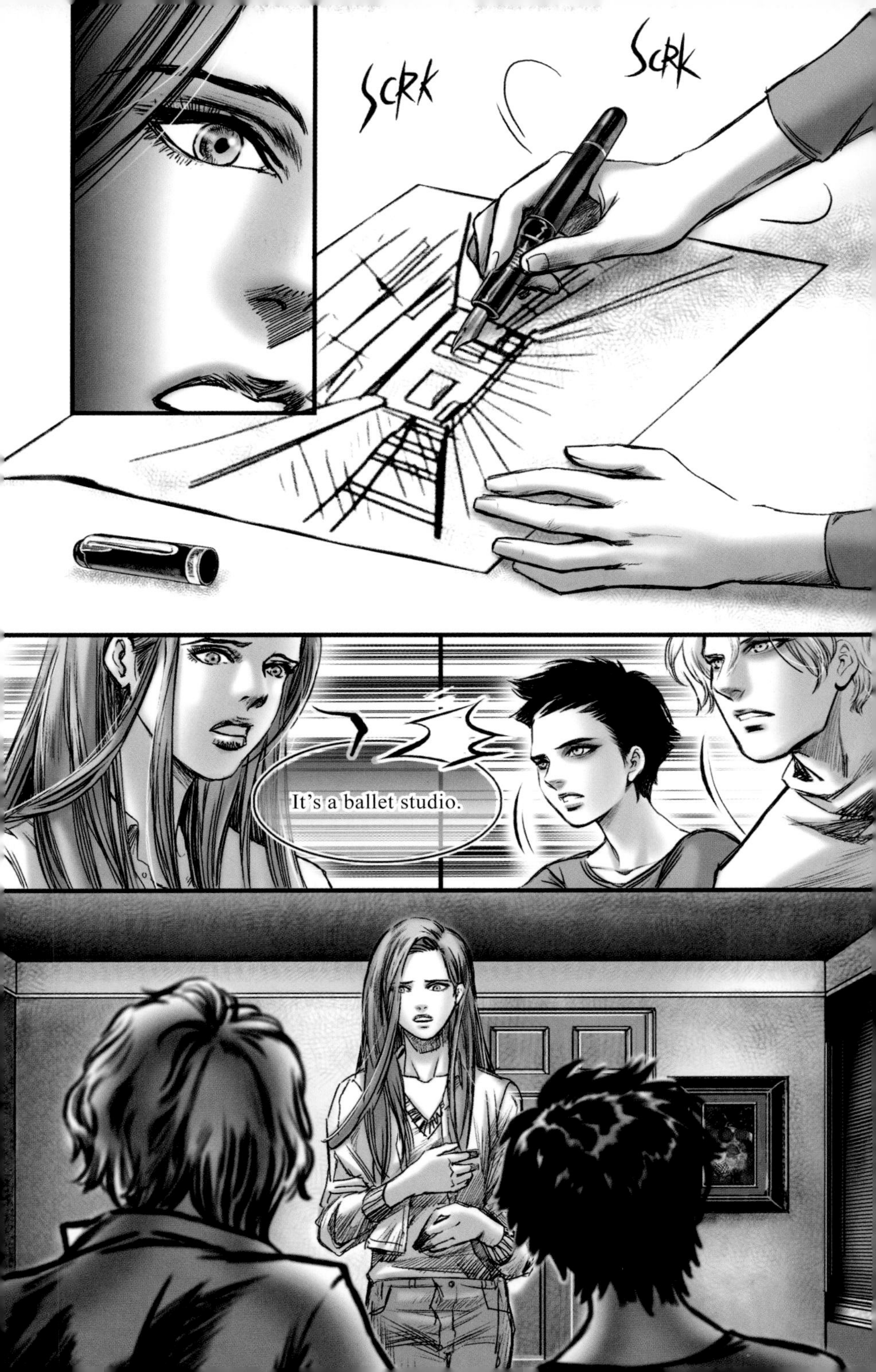
SCRK
SCRK
It's a ballet studio.

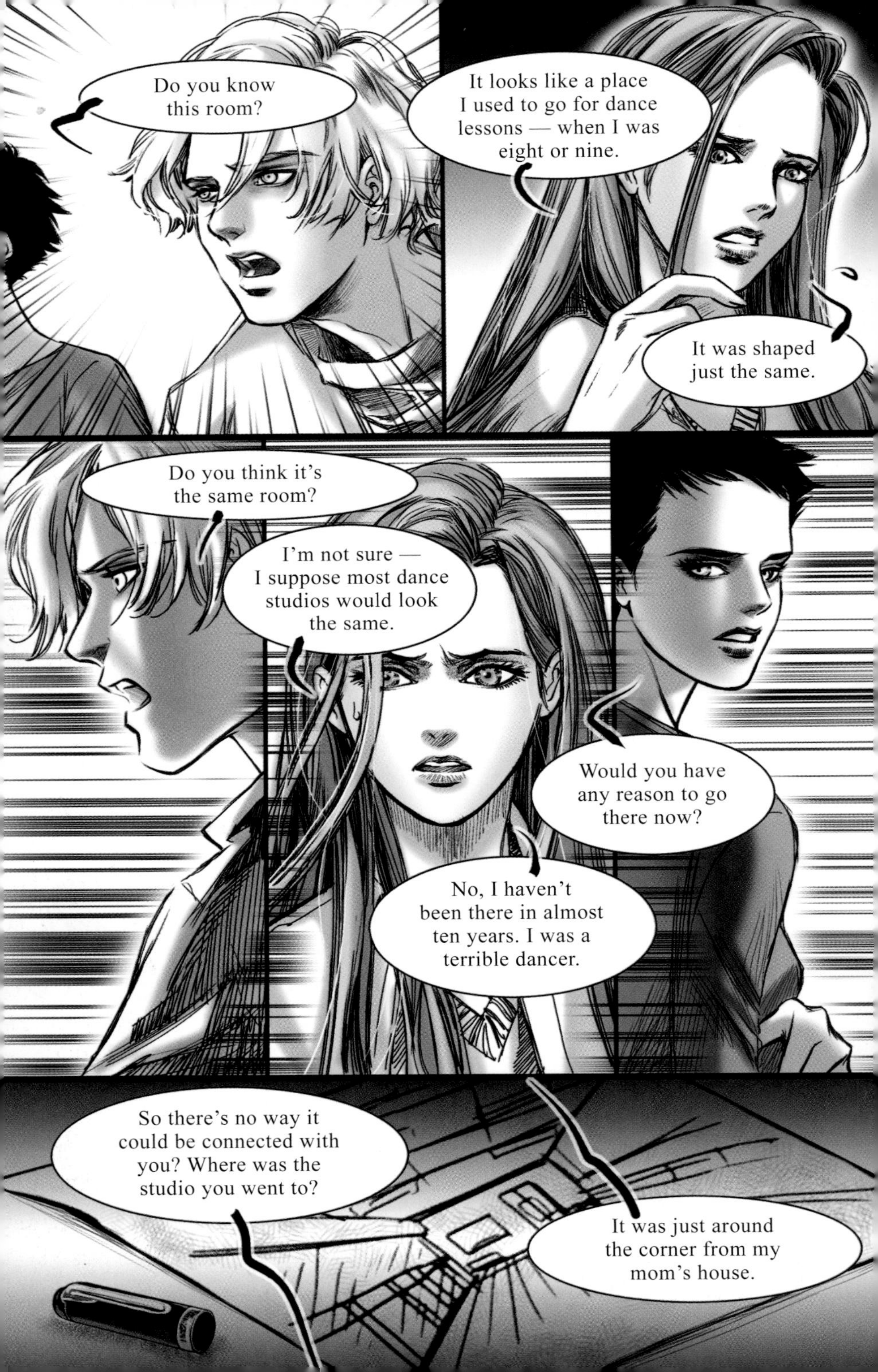
Do you know this room?
It looks like a place I used to go for dance lessons — when I was eight or nine.
It was shaped just the same.
Do you think it's the same room?
I'm not sure — I suppose most dance studios would look the same.
Would you have any reason to go there now?
No, I haven't been there in almost ten years. I was a terrible dancer.
So there's no way it could be connected with you? Where was the studio you went to?
It was just around the corner from my mom's house.

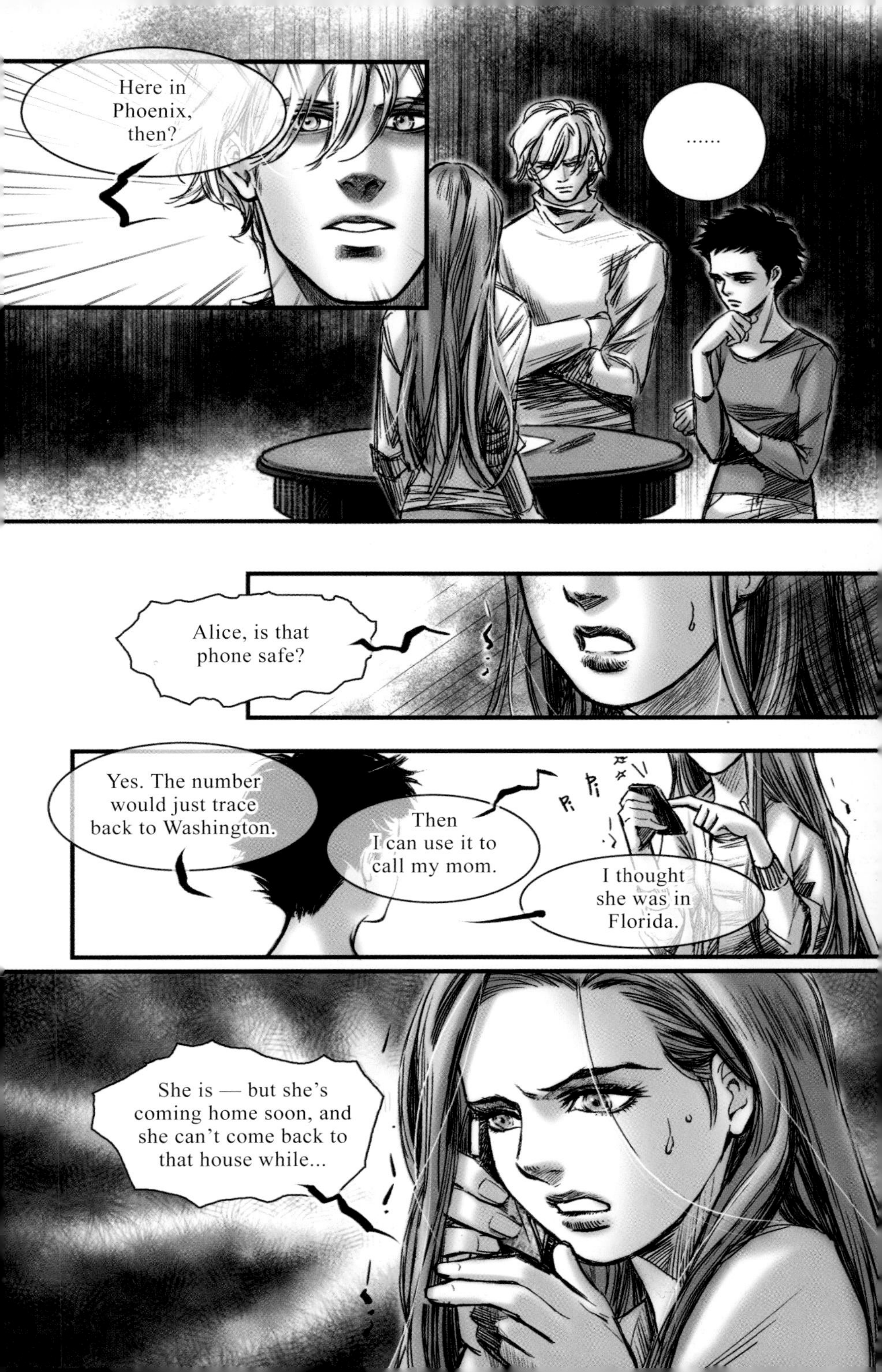
Here in Phoenix, then?
......
Alice, is that phone safe?
Yes. The number would just trace back to Washington.
Then I can use it to call my mom.
Pi Pi
I thought she was in Florida.
She is — but she's coming home soon, and she can't come back to that house while...

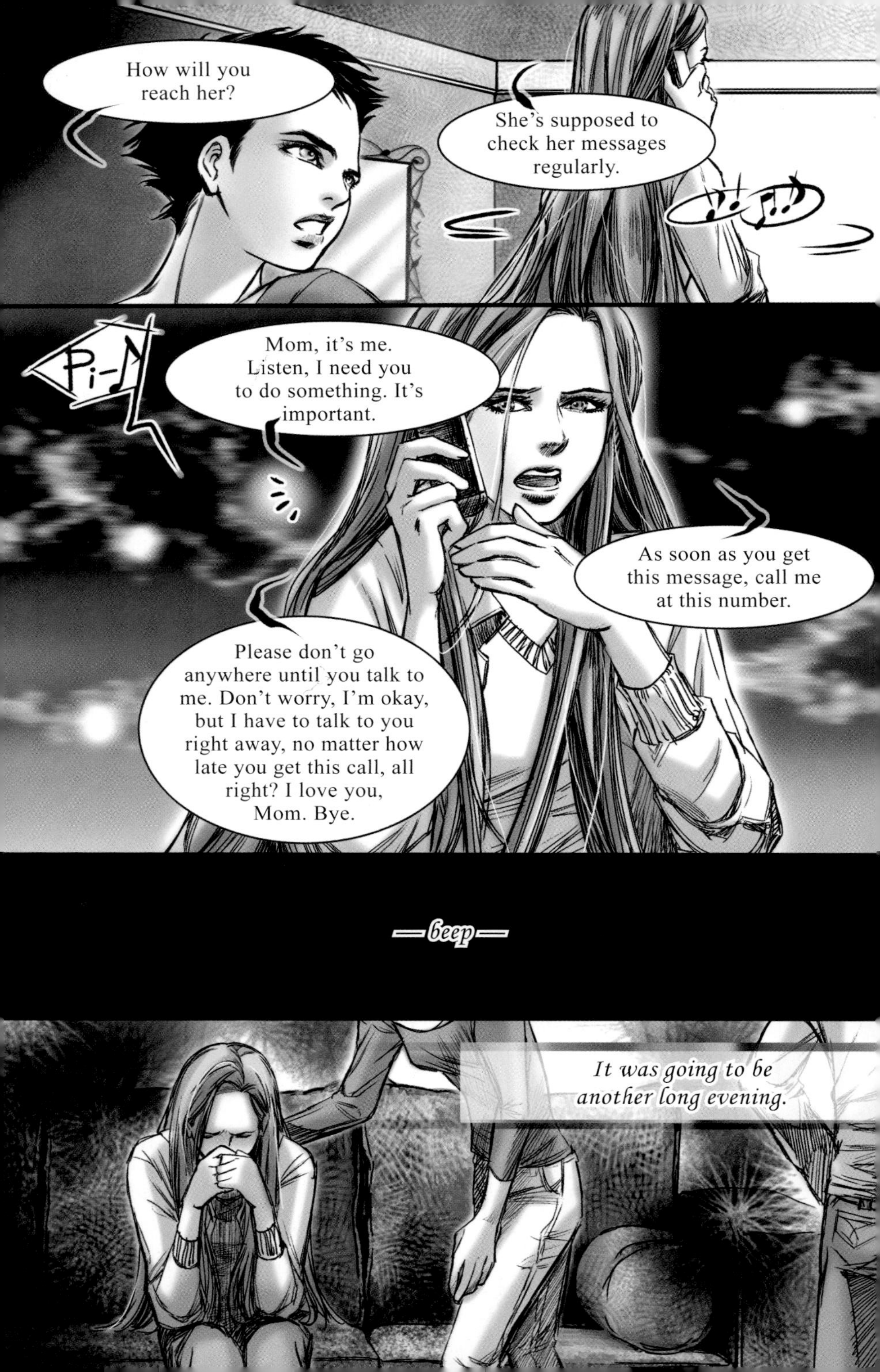
How will you reach her?
She's supposed to check her messages regularly.
Pi-
Mom, it's me. Listen, I need you to do something. It's important.
As soon as you get this message, call me at this number.
Please don't go anywhere until you talk to me. Don't worry, I'm okay, but I have to talk to you right away, no matter how late you get this call, all right? I love you, Mom. Bye.
—beep—
It was going to be another long evening.

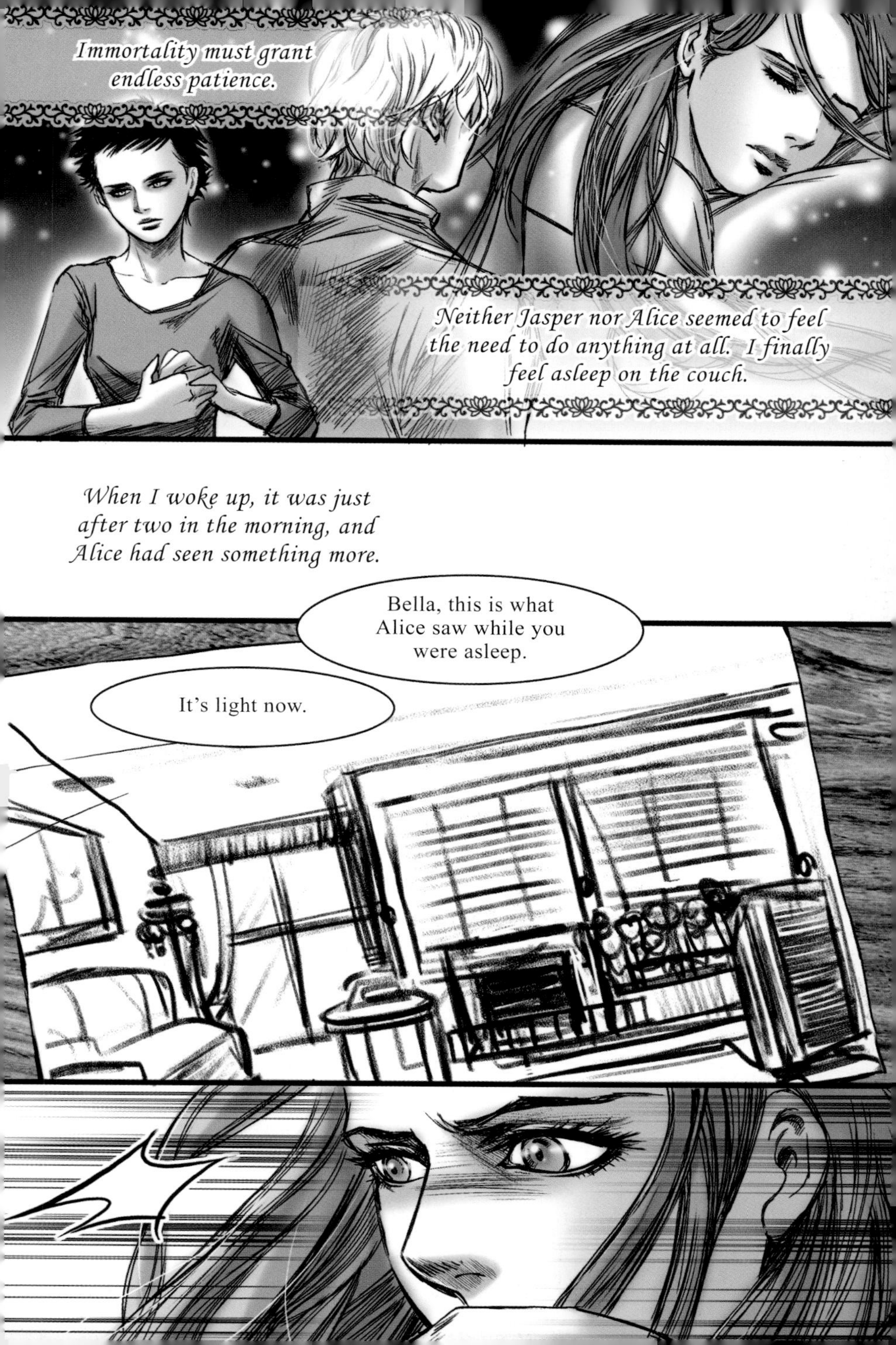
Immortality must grant endless patience.
Neither Jasper nor Alice seemed to feel the need to do anything at all. I finally feel asleep on the couch.
When I woke up, it was just after two in the morning, and Alice had seen something more.
Bella, this is what Alice saw while you were asleep.
It's light now.

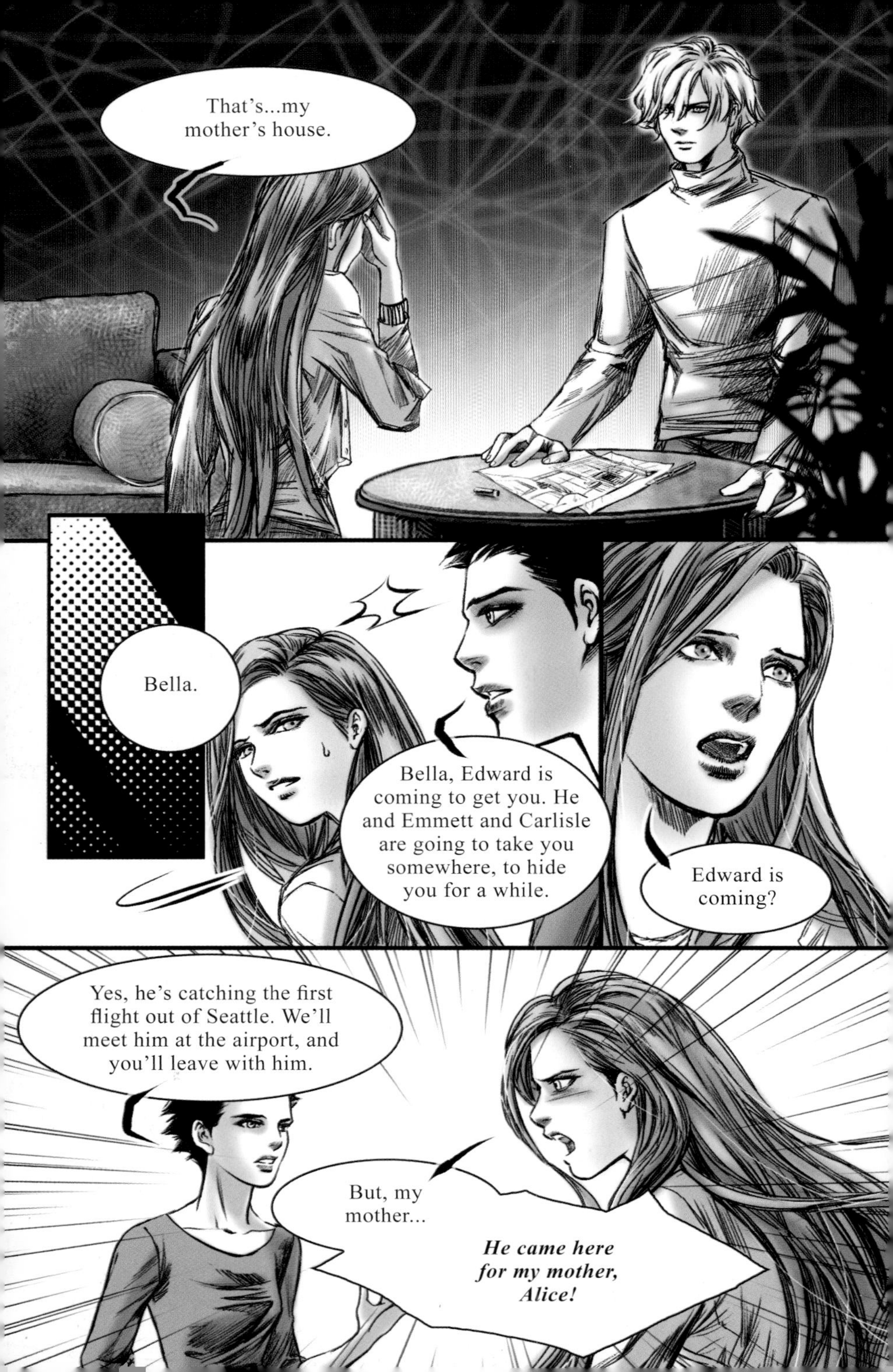
That's...my mother's house.
Bella.
Bella, Edward is coming to get you. He and Emmett and Carlisle are going to take you somewhere, to hide you for a while.
Edward is coming?
Yes, he's catching the first flight out of Seattle. We'll meet him at the airport, and you'll leave with him.
But, my mother...
***He came here for my mother, Alice!***

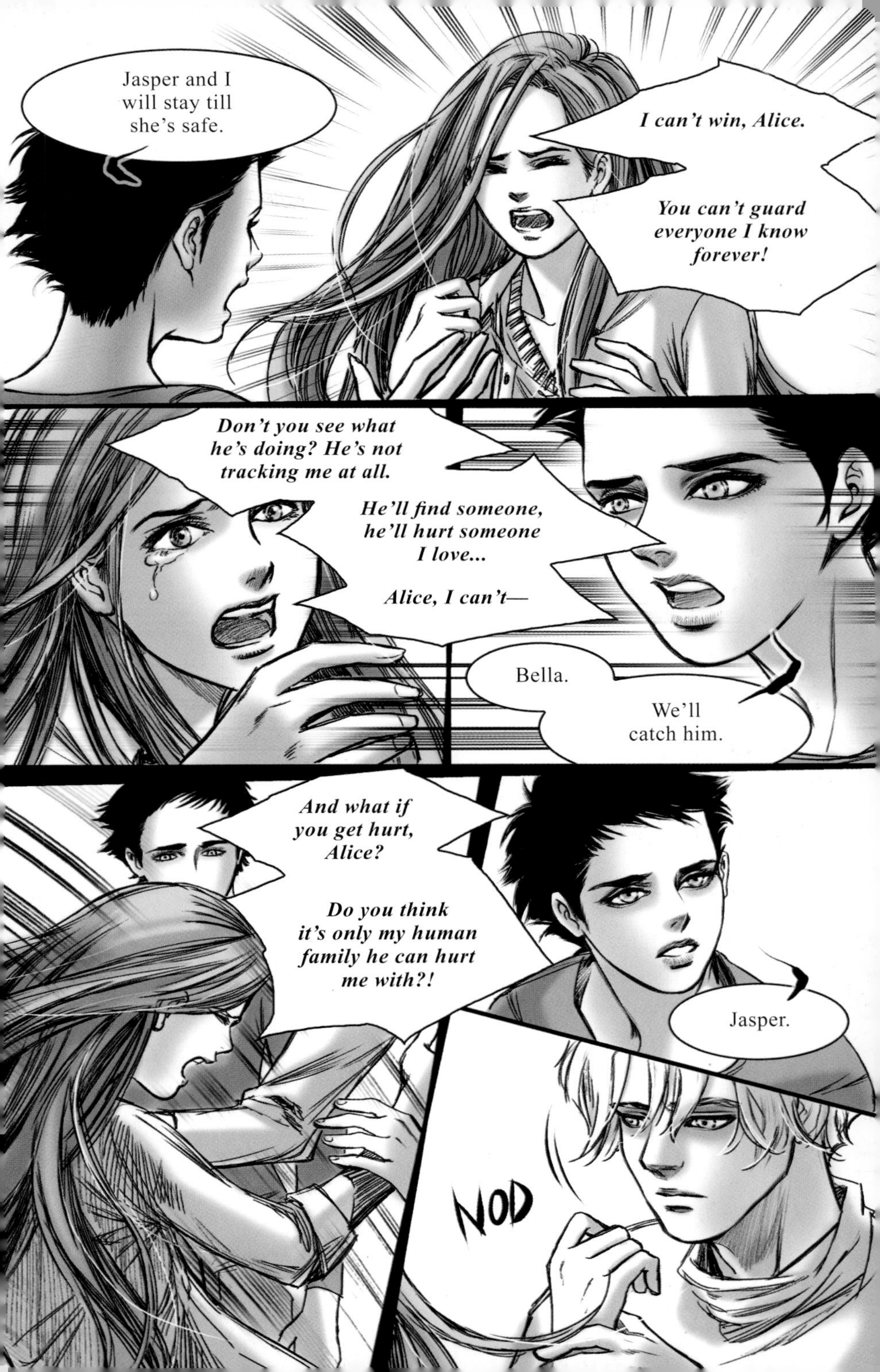
Jasper and I will stay till she's safe.
I can't win, Alice.
You can't guard everyone I know forever!
Don't you see what he's doing? He's not tracking me at all.
He'll find someone, he'll hurt someone I love...
Alice, I can't—
Bella.
We'll catch him.
And what if you get hurt, Alice?
Do you think it's only my human family he can hurt me with?!
Jasper.
NOD

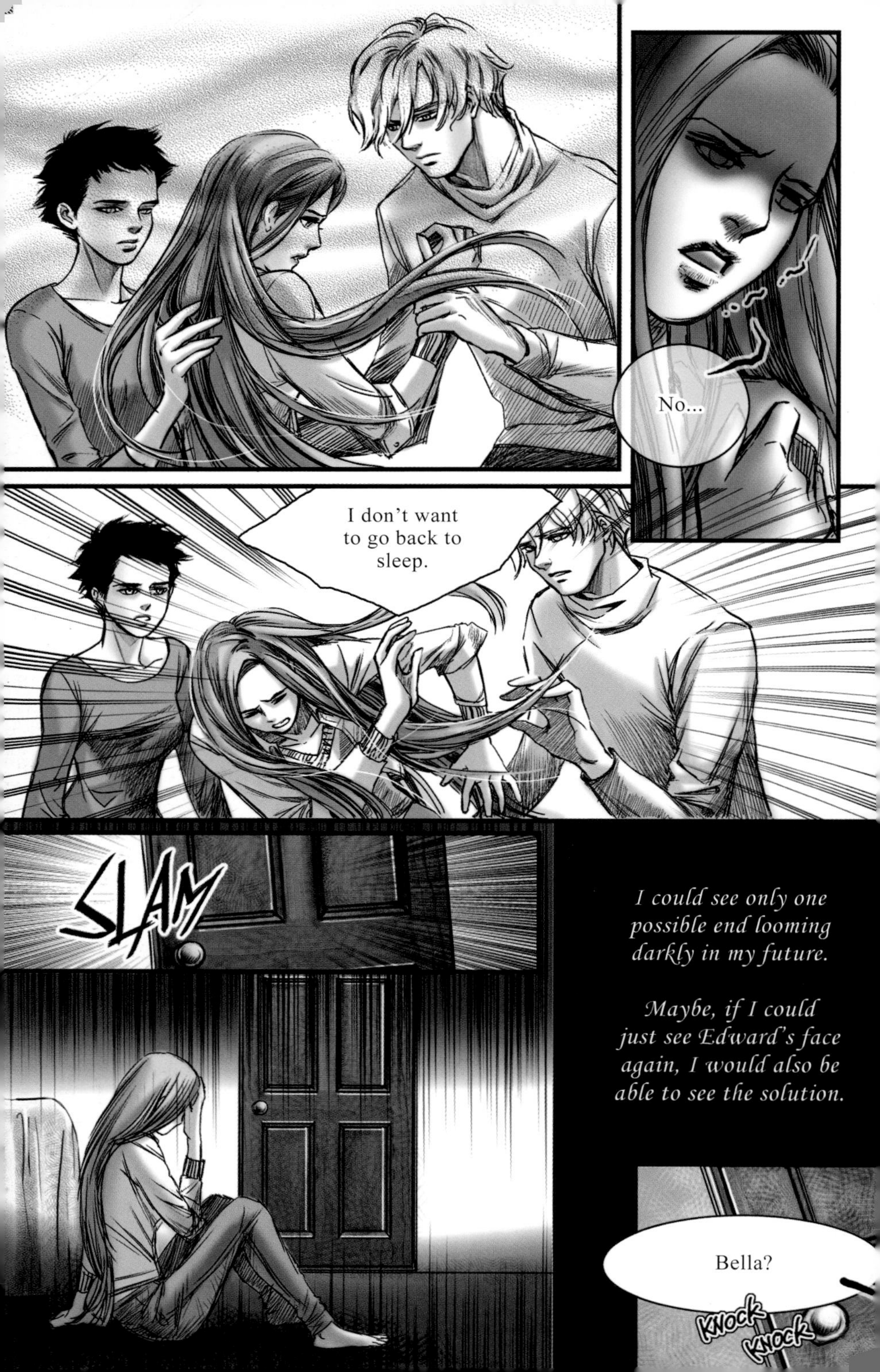

No...
I don't want to go back to sleep.
SLAM
I could see only one possible end looming darkly in my future.
Maybe, if I could just see Edward's face again, I would also be able to see the solution.
Bella?
KNOCK KNOCK

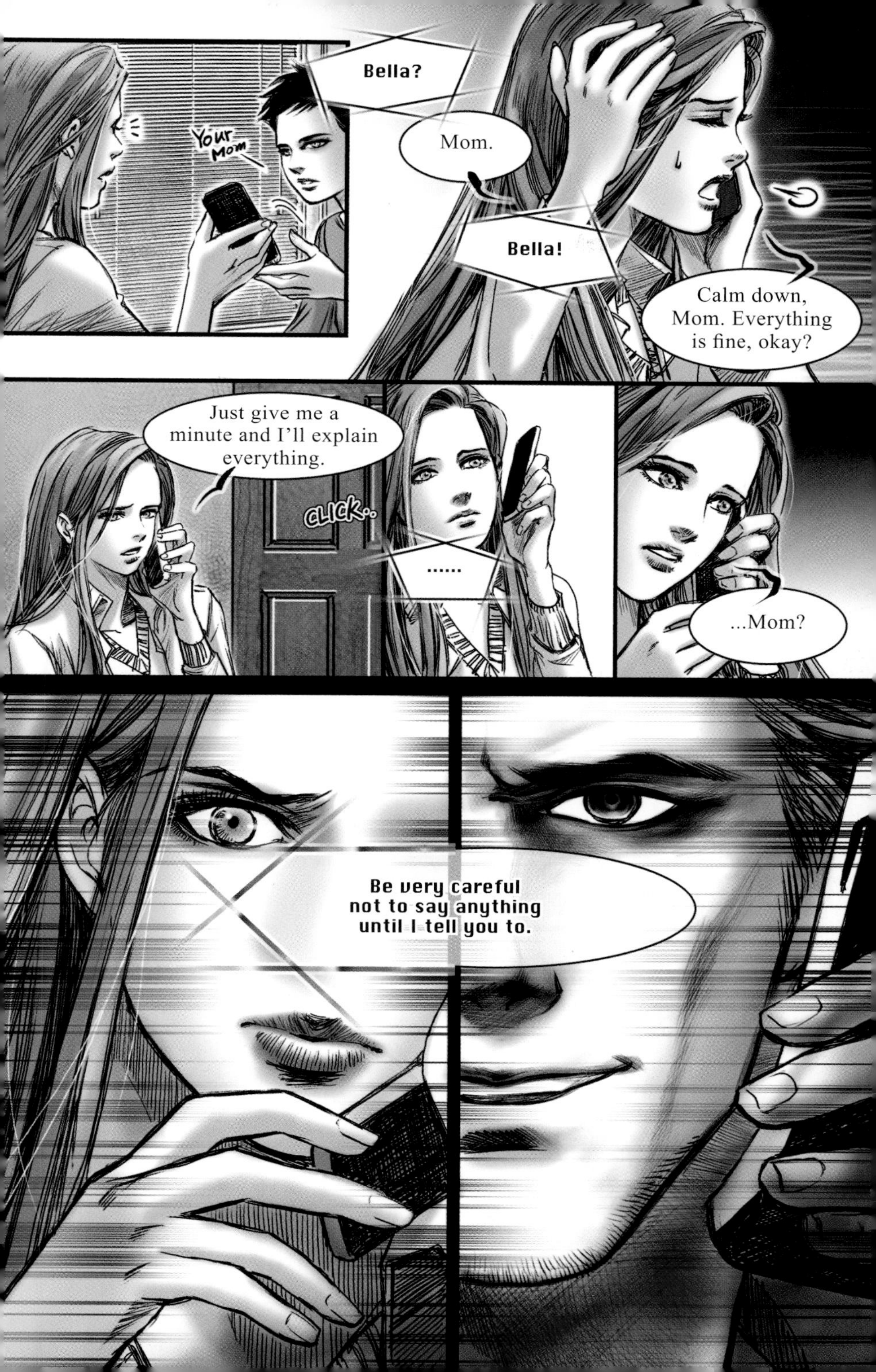
Your Mom
Bella?
Mom.
Bella!
Calm down, Mom. Everything is fine, okay?
Just give me a minute and I'll explain everything.
CLICK..
......
...Mom?
Be very careful not to say anything until I tell you to.

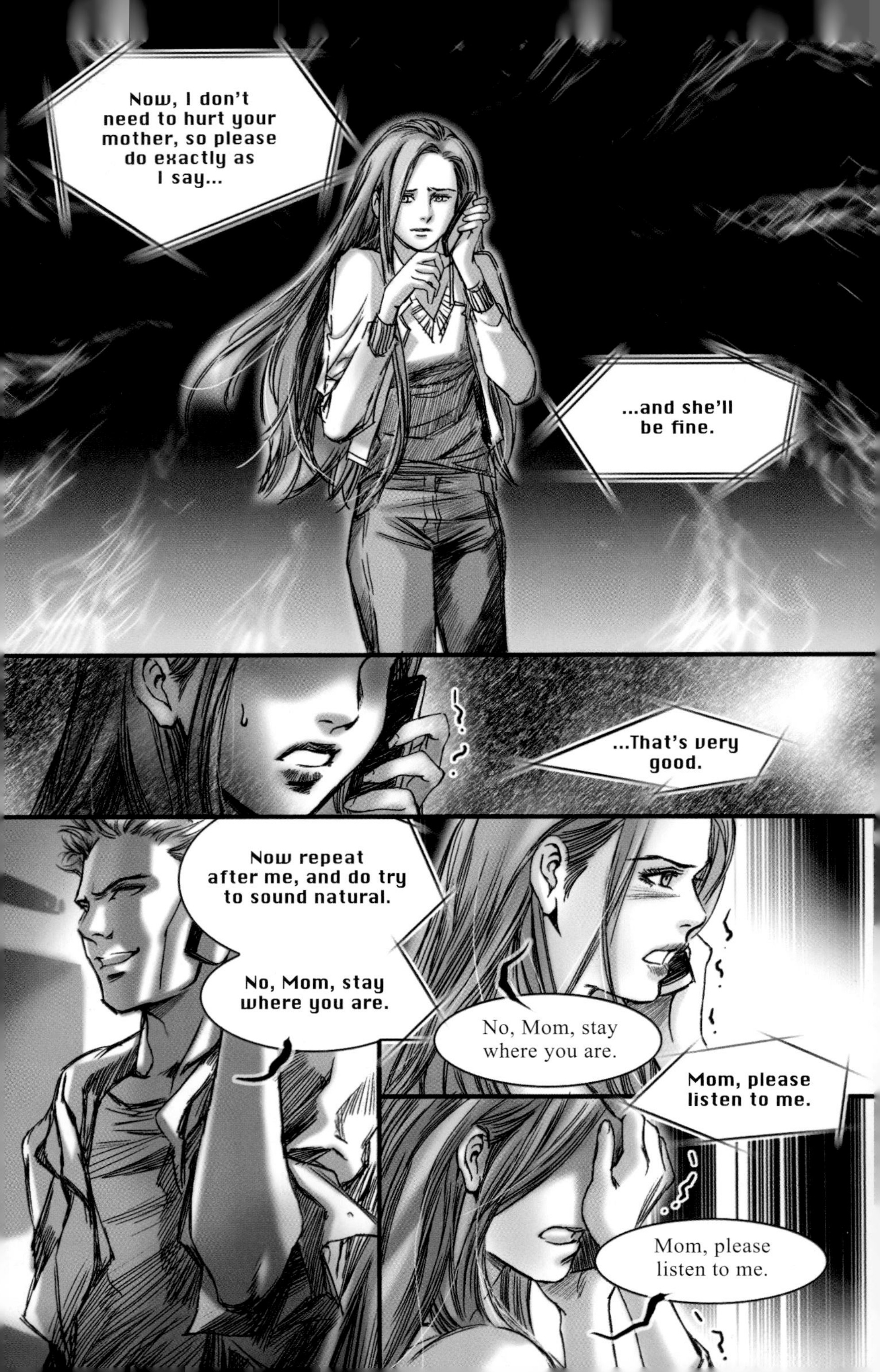

Now, I don't need to hurt your mother, so please do exactly as I say...
...and she'll be fine.
...That's very good.
Now repeat after me, and do try to sound natural.
No, Mom, stay where you are.
No, Mom, stay where you are.
Mom, please listen to me.
Mom, please listen to me.

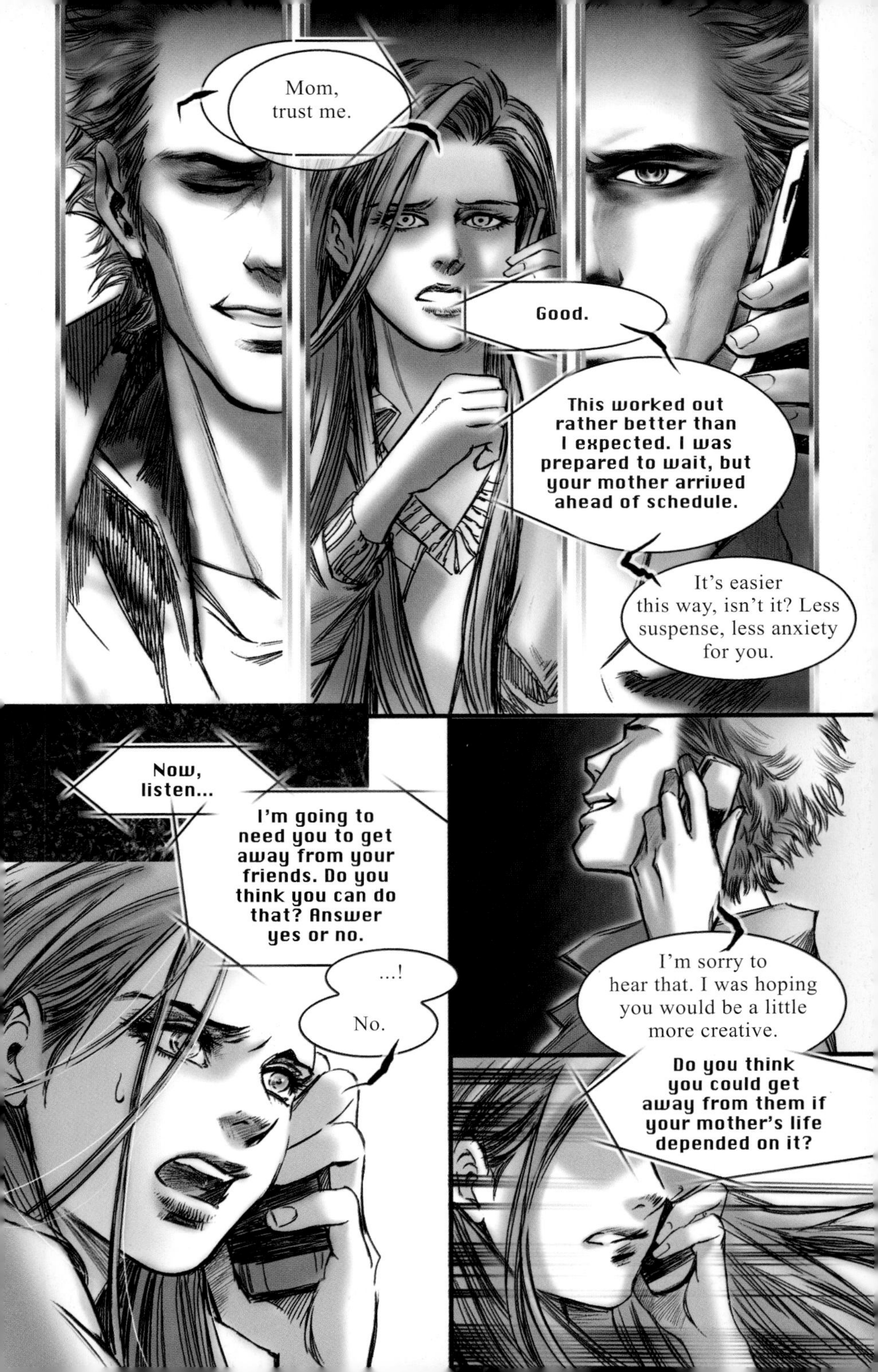
Mom, trust me.
Good.
This worked out rather better than I expected. I was prepared to wait, but your mother arrived ahead of schedule.
It's easier this way, isn't it? Less suspense, less anxiety for you.
Now, listen...
I'm going to need you to get away from your friends. Do you think you can do that? Answer yes or no.
...!
No.
I'm sorry to hear that. I was hoping you would be a little more creative.
Do you think you could get away from them if your mother's life depended on it?

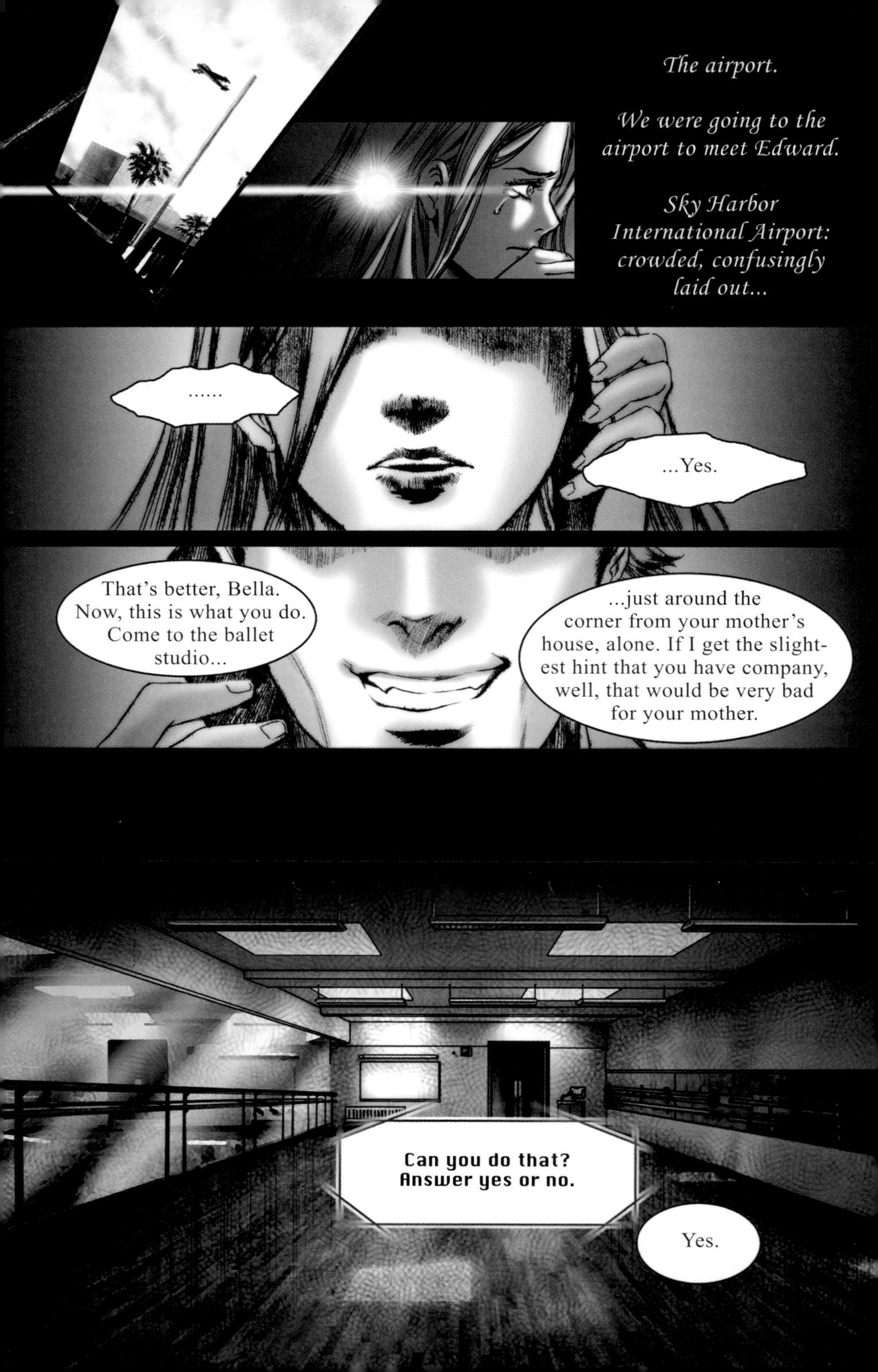
The airport.
We were going to the airport to meet Edward.
Sky Harbor International Airport: crowded, confusingly laid out...
......
...Yes.
That's better, Bella. Now, this is what you do. Come to the ballet studio...
...just around the corner from your mother's house, alone. If I get the slightest hint that you have company, well, that would be very bad for your mother.
Can you do that? Answer yes or no.
Yes.

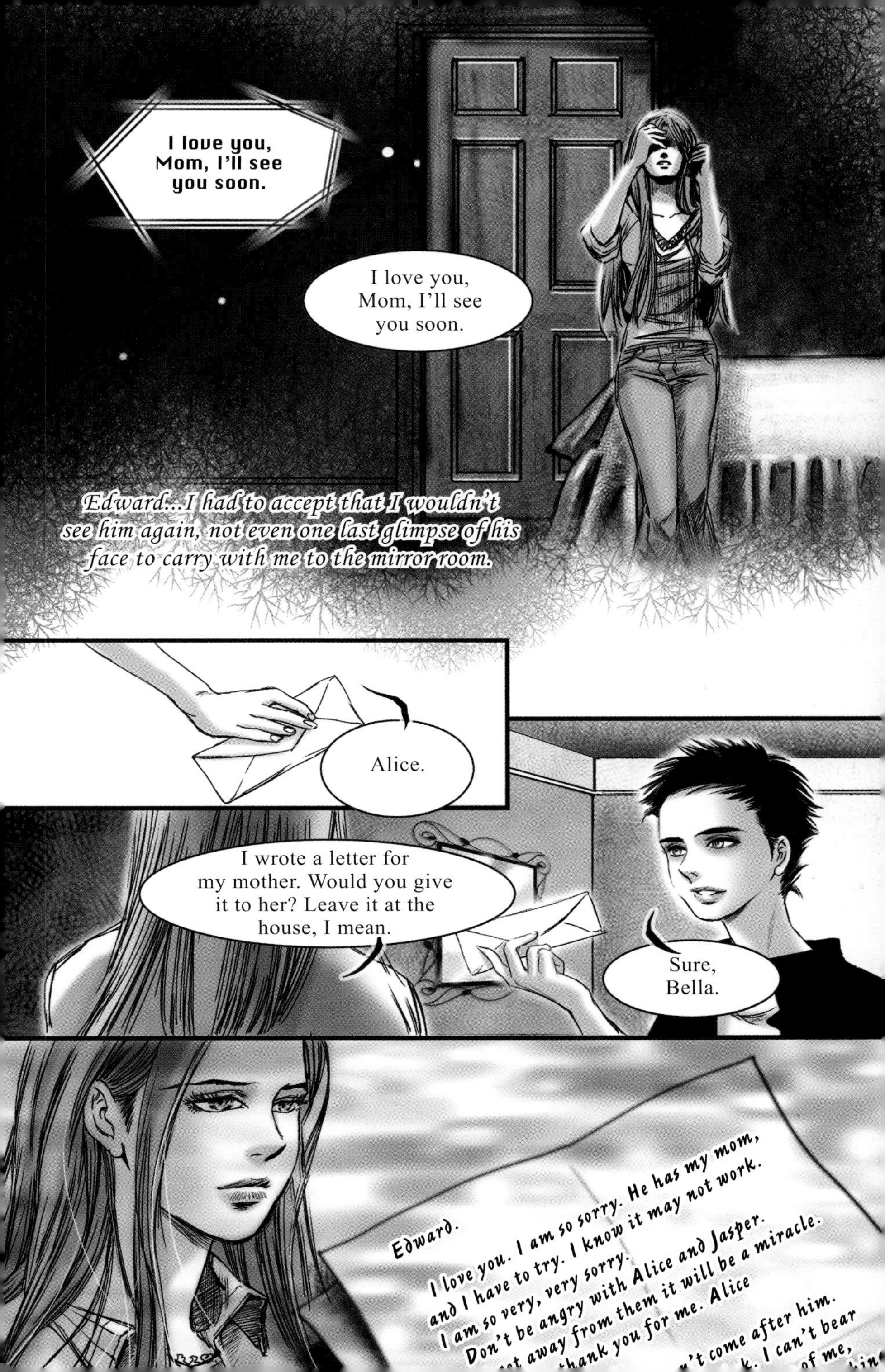

I love you, Mom, I'll see you soon.
I love you, Mom, I'll see you soon.
Edward...I had to accept that I wouldn't see him again, not even one last glimpse of his face to carry with me to the mirror room.
Alice.
I wrote a letter for my mother. Would you give it to her? Leave it at the house, I mean.
Sure, Bella.
Edward.
I love you. I am so sorry. He has my mom,
and I have to try. I know it may not work.
I am so very, very sorry.
Don't be angry with Alice and Jasper.
away from them it will be a miracle.
thank you for me. Alice
come after him.
I can't bear
of me,

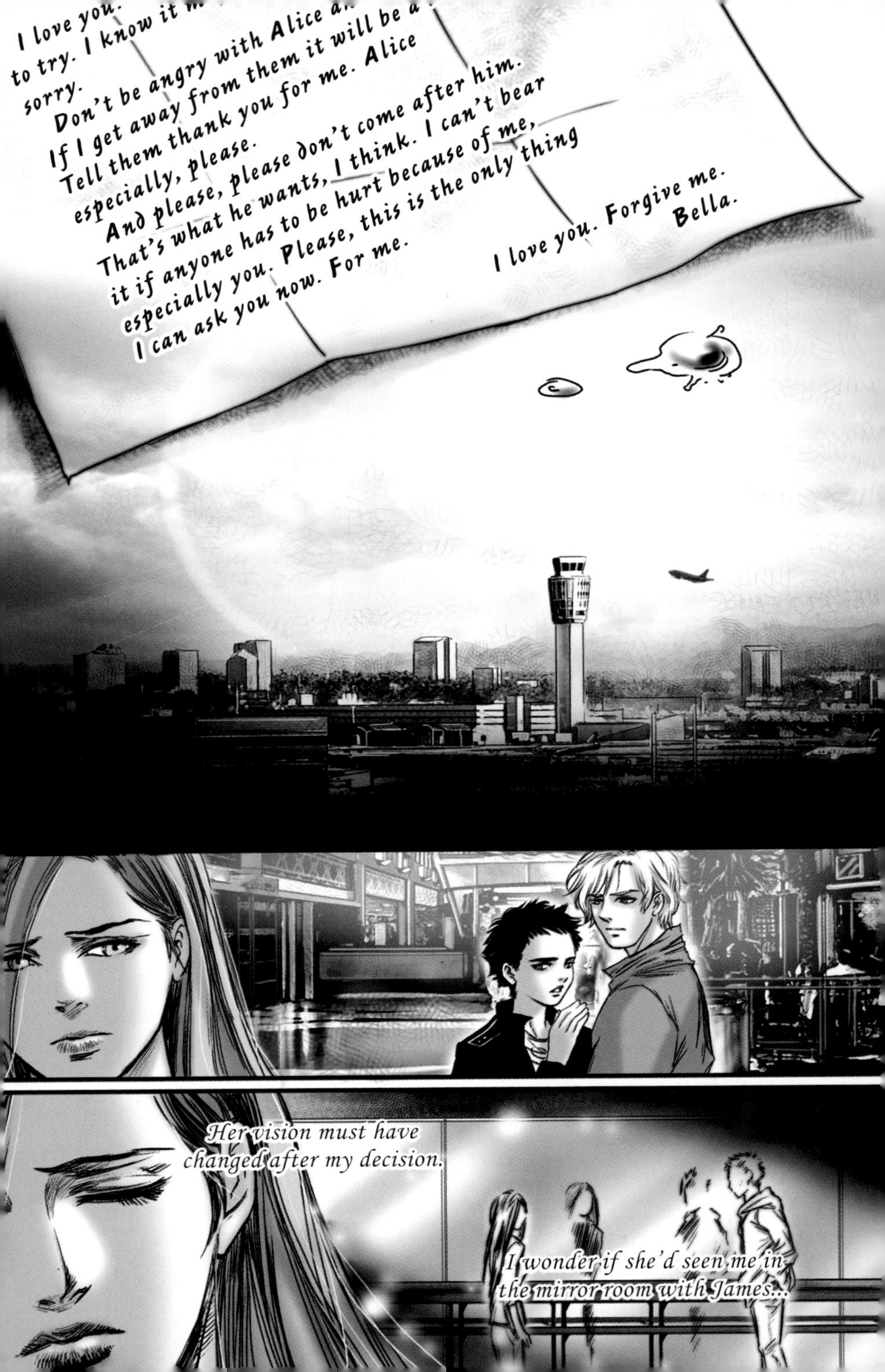
I love you.
to try. I know it
sorry.
Don't be angry with Alice
If I get away from them it will be a
Tell them thank you for me. Alice
especially, please.
And please, please don't come after him.
That's what he wants, I think. I can't bear
it if anyone has to be hurt because of me,
especially you. Please, this is the only thing
I can ask you now. For me.
I love you. Forgive me.
Bella.
Her vision must have changed after my decision.
I wonder if she'd seen me in the mirror room with James...

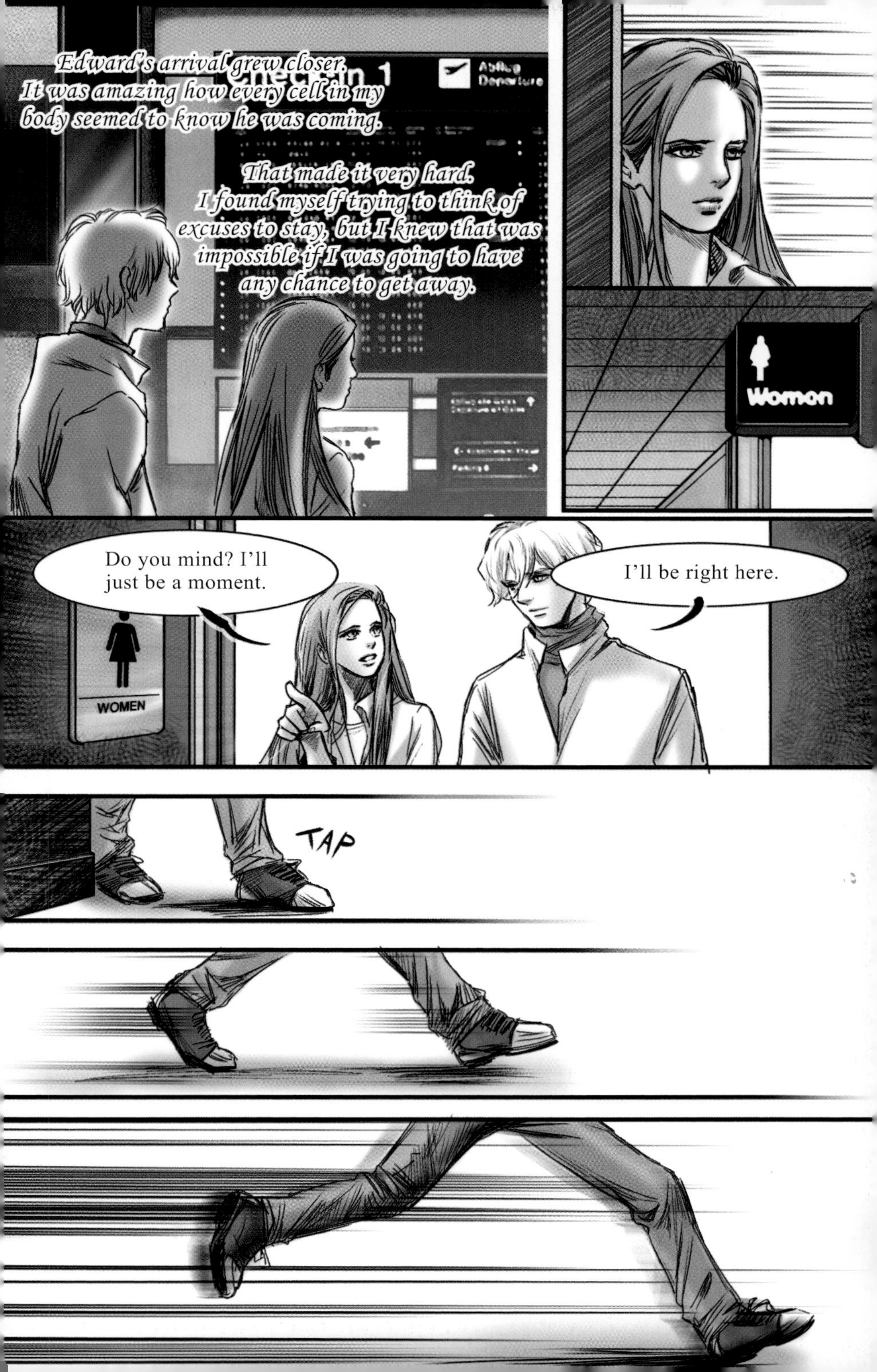
Edward's arrival grew closer. It was amazing how every cell in my body seemed to know he was coming.
That made it very hard. I found myself trying to think of excuses to stay, but I knew that was impossible if I was going to have any chance to get away.
Woman
WOMEN
Do you mind? I'll just be a moment.
I'll be right here.
TAP

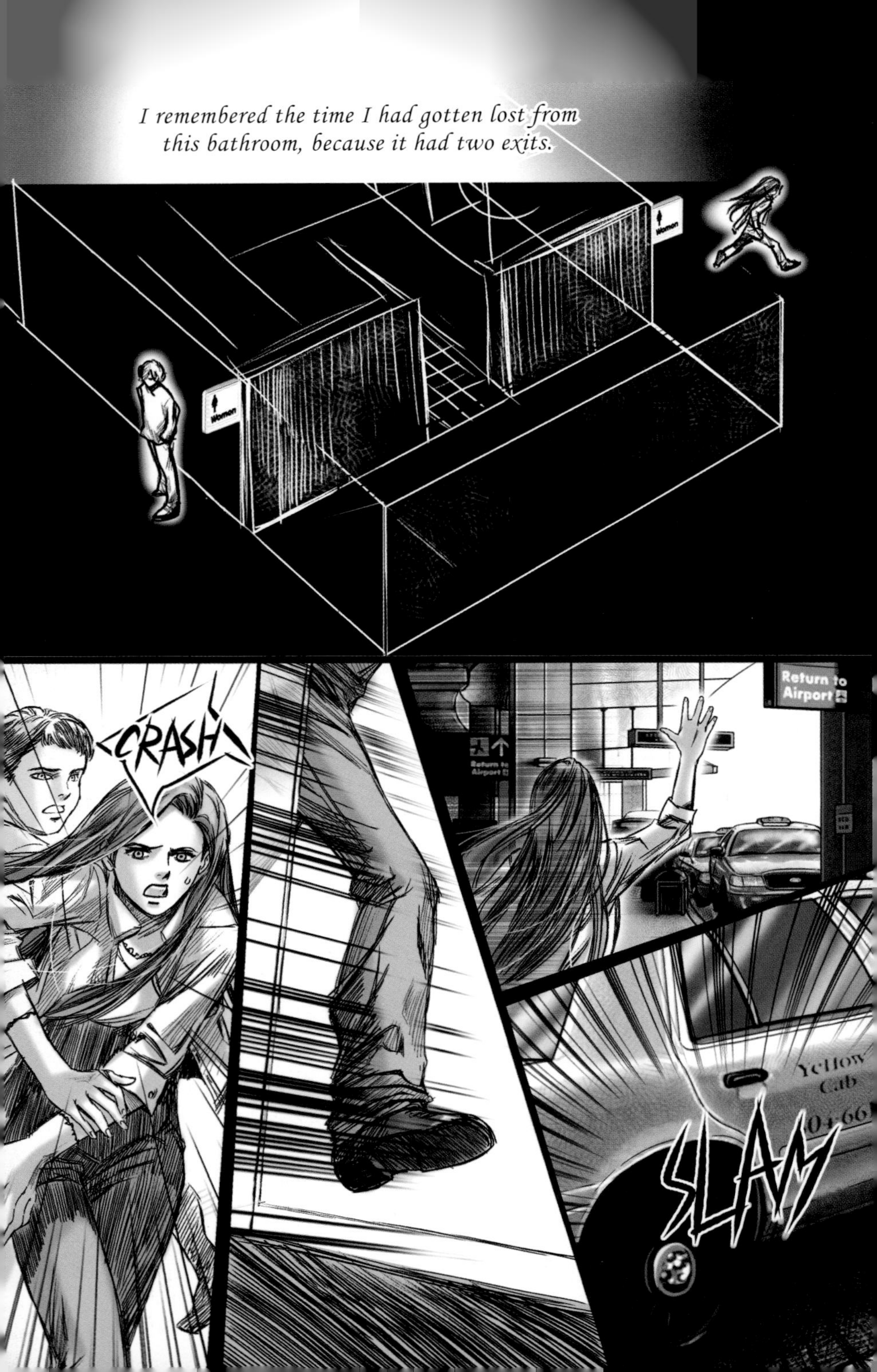
I remembered the time I had gotten lost from this bathroom, because it had two exits.
Women
Women
CRASH
Return to Airport
Return to Airport
Yellow Cab
SLAM

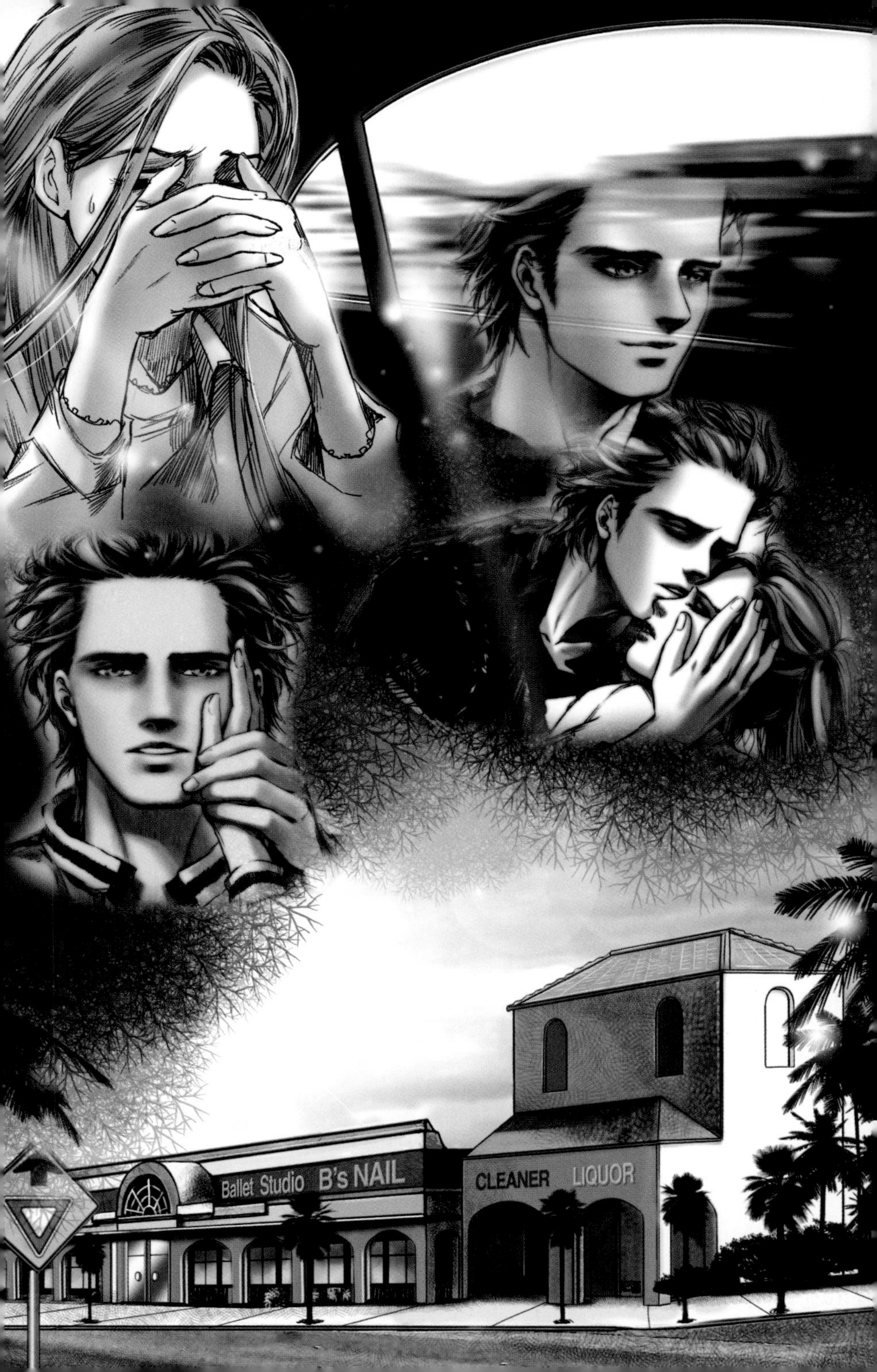
Ballet Studio
B's NAIL
CLEANER
LIQUOR

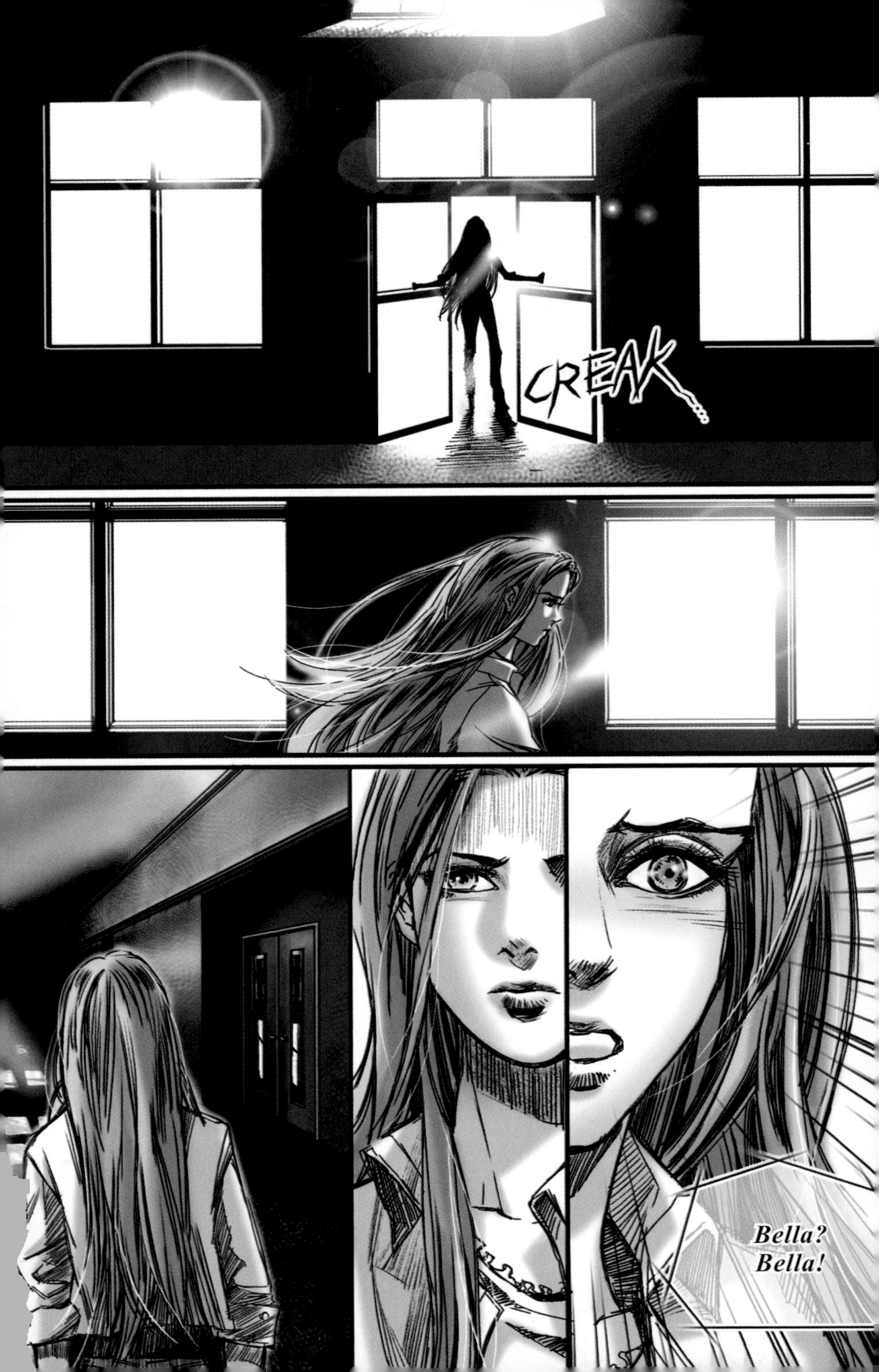
CREAK
Bella?
Bella!

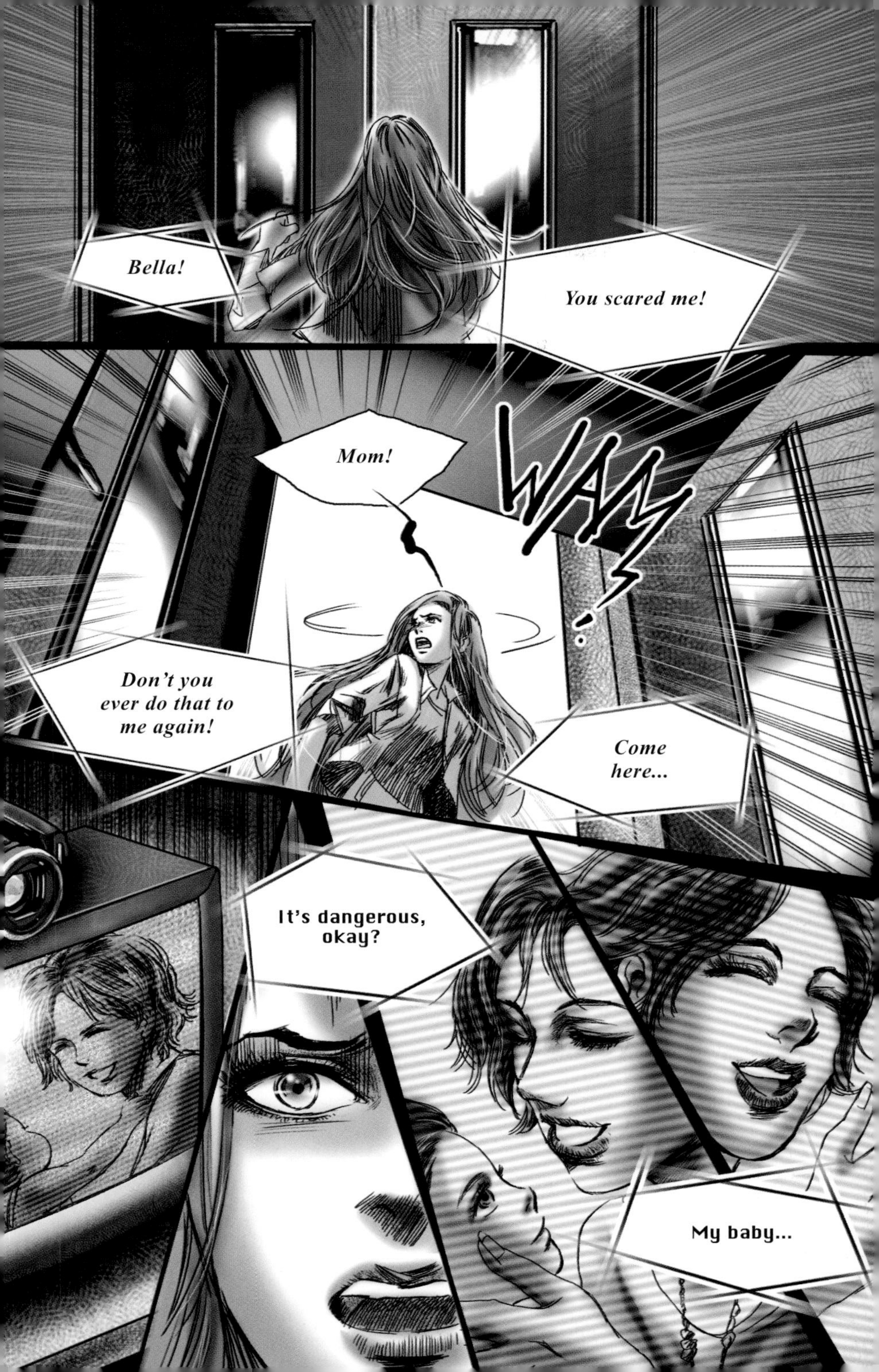
Bella!
You scared me!
Mom!
WAM!
Don't you ever do that to me again!
Come here...
It's dangerous, okay?
My baby...

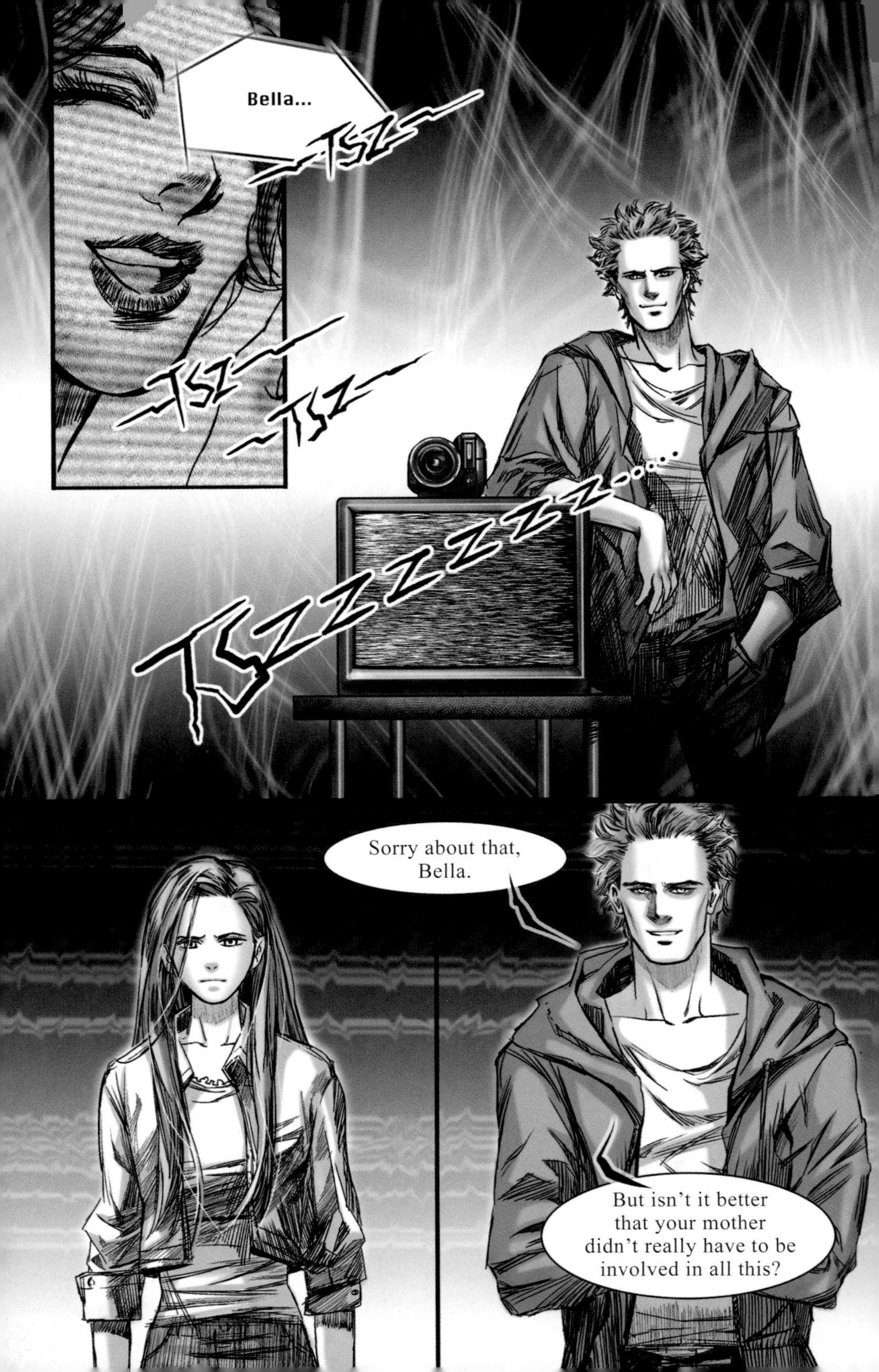
Bella...
TSZ
TSZ
TSZ
TSZZZZZZZ....
Sorry about that, Bella.
But isn't it better that your mother didn't really have to be involved in all this?

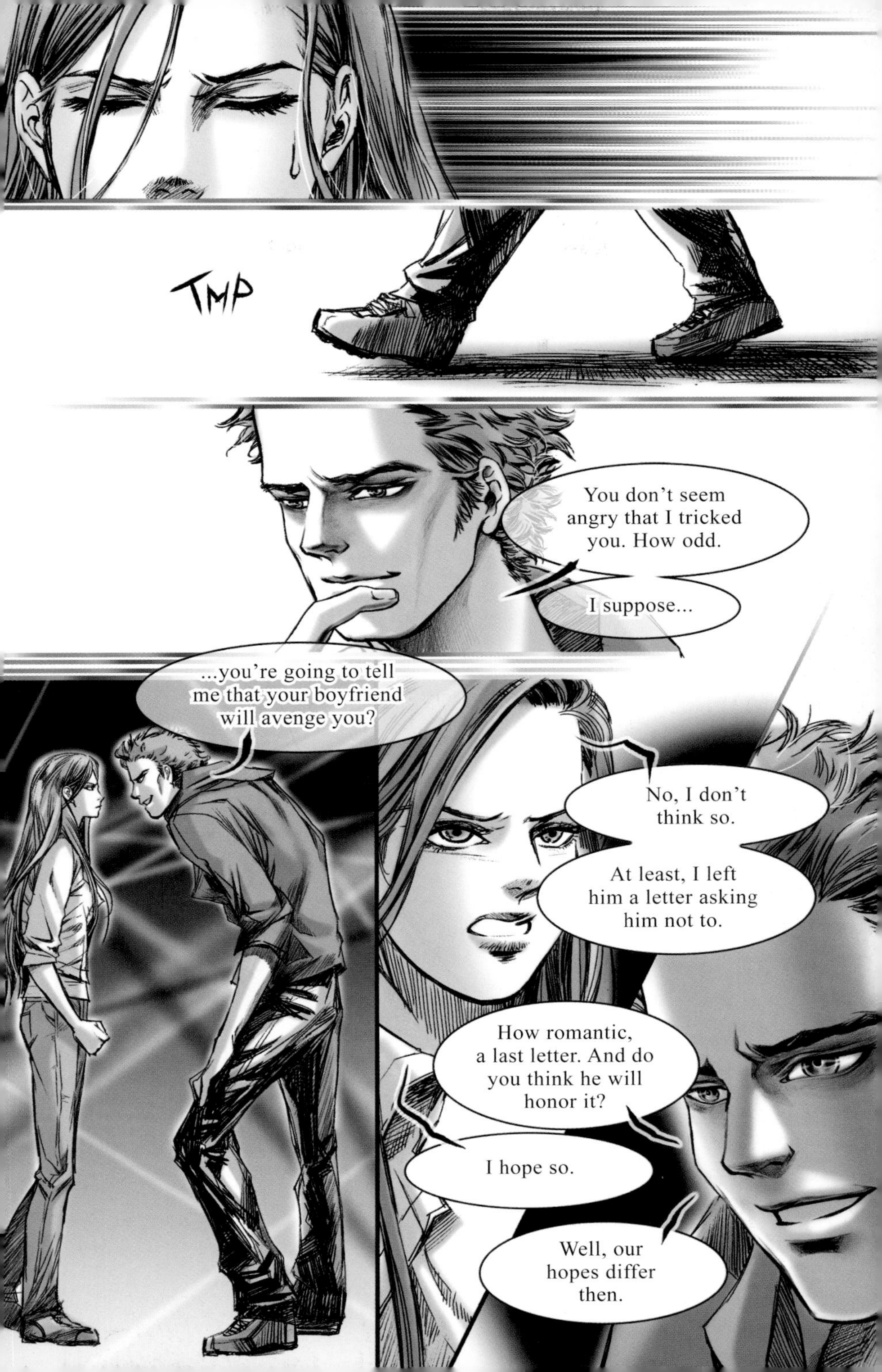
TMP
You don't seem angry that I tricked you. How odd.
I suppose...
...you're going to tell me that your boyfriend will avenge you?
No, I don't think so.
At least, I left him a letter asking him not to.
How romantic, a last letter. And do you think he will honor it?
I hope so.
Well, our hopes differ then.

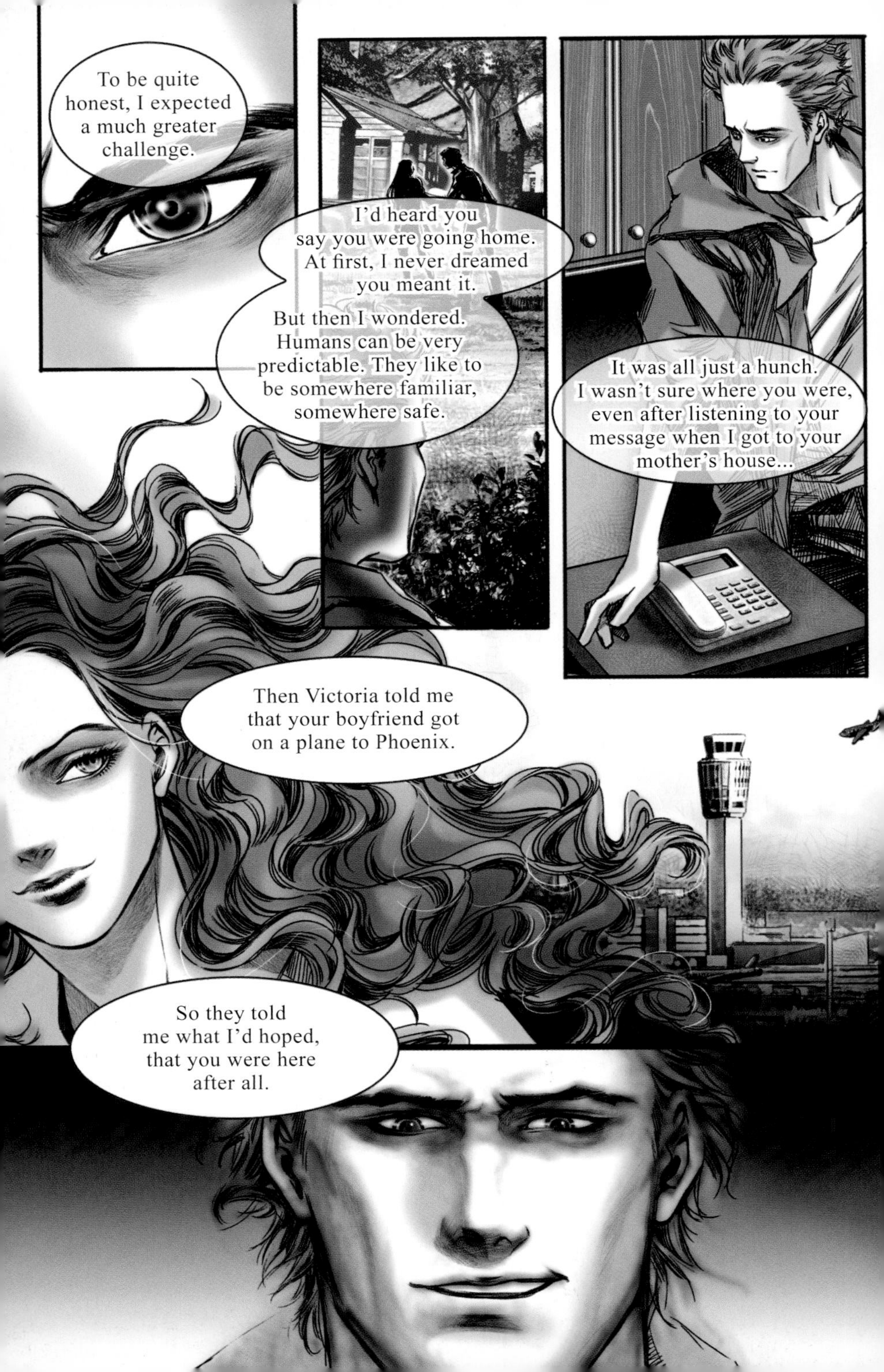
To be quite honest, I expected a much greater challenge.
I'd heard you say you were going home. At first, I never dreamed you meant it.
But then I wondered. Humans can be very predictable. They like to be somewhere familiar, somewhere safe.
It was all just a hunch. I wasn't sure where you were, even after listening to your message when I got to your mother's house...
Then Victoria told me that your boyfriend got on a plane to Phoenix.
So they told me what I'd hoped, that you were here after all.

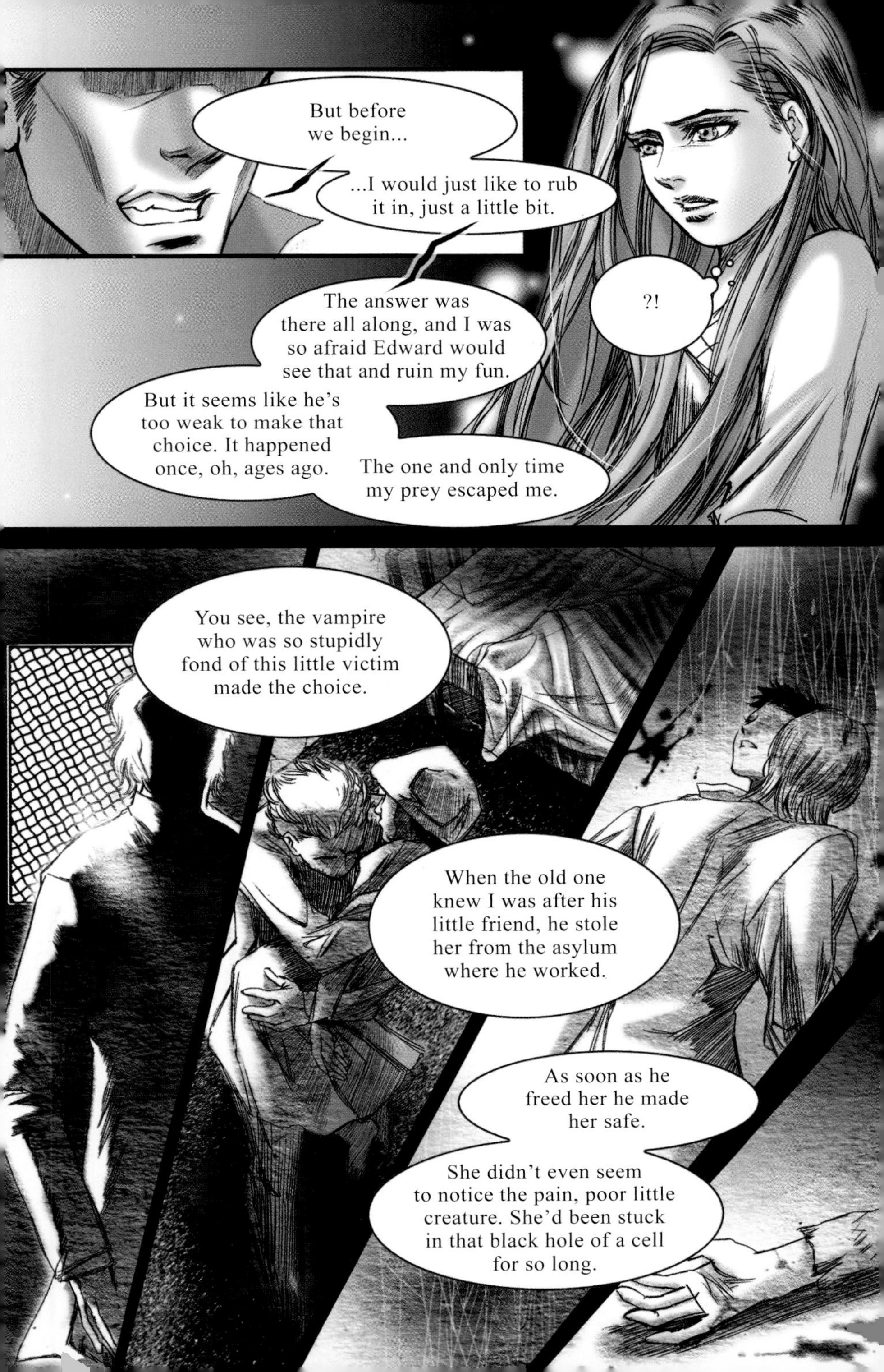
But before we begin...
...I would just like to rub it in, just a little bit.
?!
The answer was there all along, and I was so afraid Edward would see that and ruin my fun.
But it seems like he's too weak to make that choice. It happened once, oh, ages ago.
The one and only time my prey escaped me.
You see, the vampire who was so stupidly fond of this little victim made the choice.
When the old one knew I was after his little friend, he stole her from the asylum where he worked.
As soon as he freed her he made her safe.
She didn't even seem to notice the pain, poor little creature. She'd been stuck in that black hole of a cell for so long.

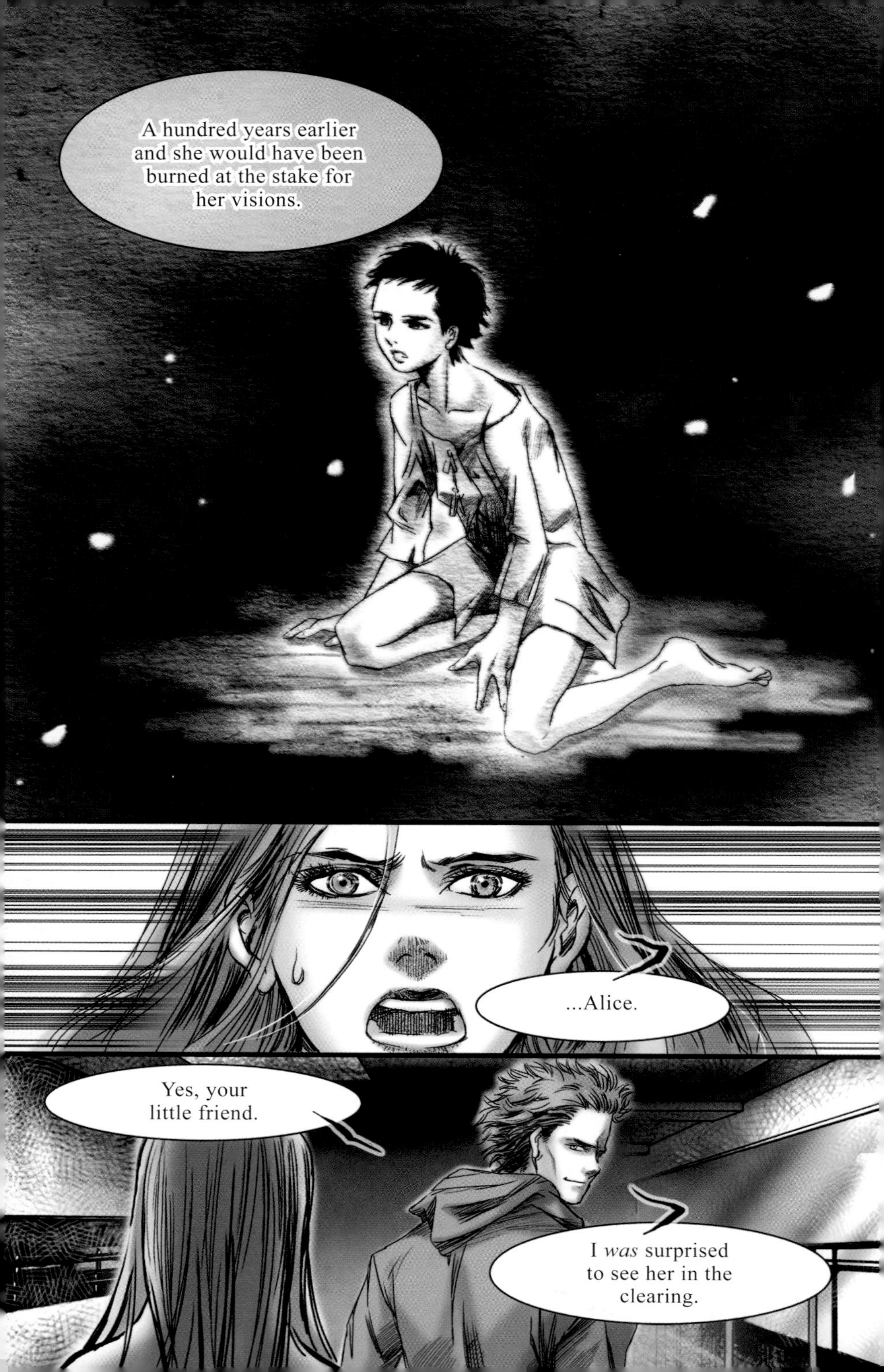
A hundred years earlier and she would have been burned at the stake for her visions.
...Alice.
Yes, your little friend.
I *was* surprised to see her in the clearing.

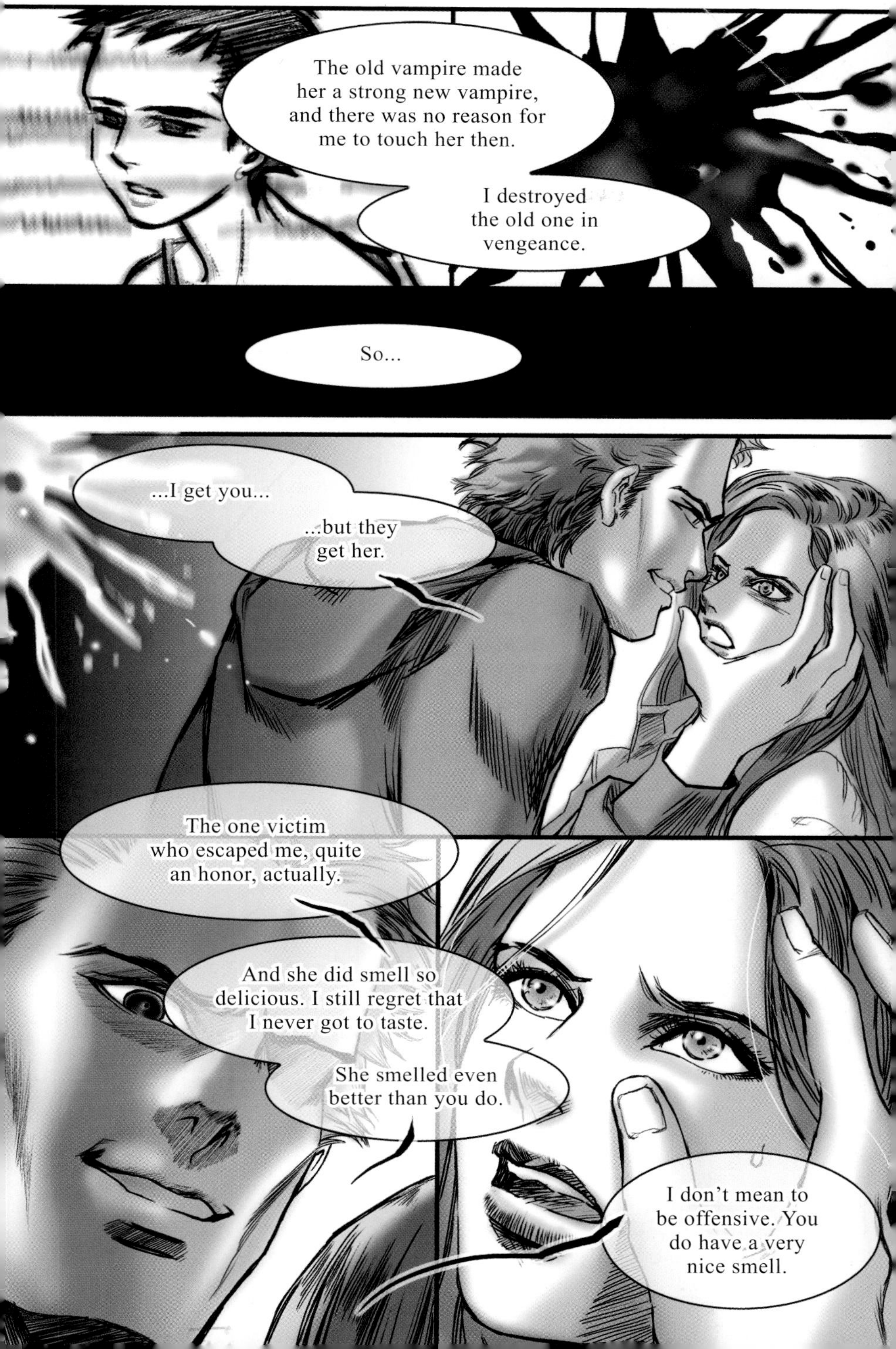
The old vampire made her a strong new vampire, and there was no reason for me to touch her then.
I destroyed the old one in vengeance.
So...
...I get you...
...but they get her.
The one victim who escaped me, quite an honor, actually.
And she did smell so delicious. I still regret that I never got to taste.
She smelled even better than you do.
I don't mean to be offensive. You do have a very nice smell.

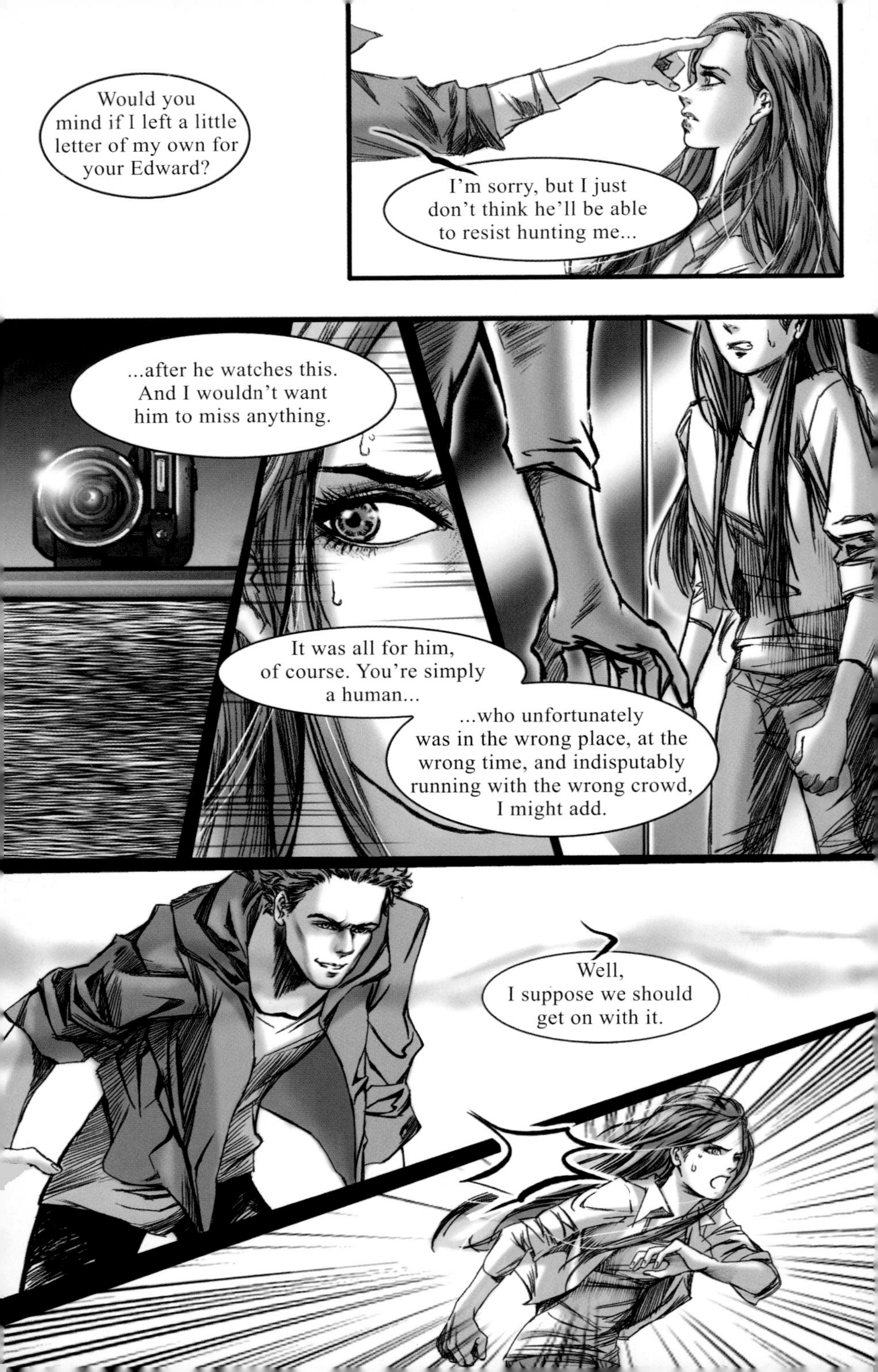
Would you mind if I left a little letter of my own for your Edward?
I'm sorry, but I just don't think he'll be able to resist hunting me...
...after he watches this. And I wouldn't want him to miss anything.
It was all for him, of course. You're simply a human...
...who unfortunately was in the wrong place, at the wrong time, and indisputably running with the wrong crowd, I might add.
Well, I suppose we should get on with it.

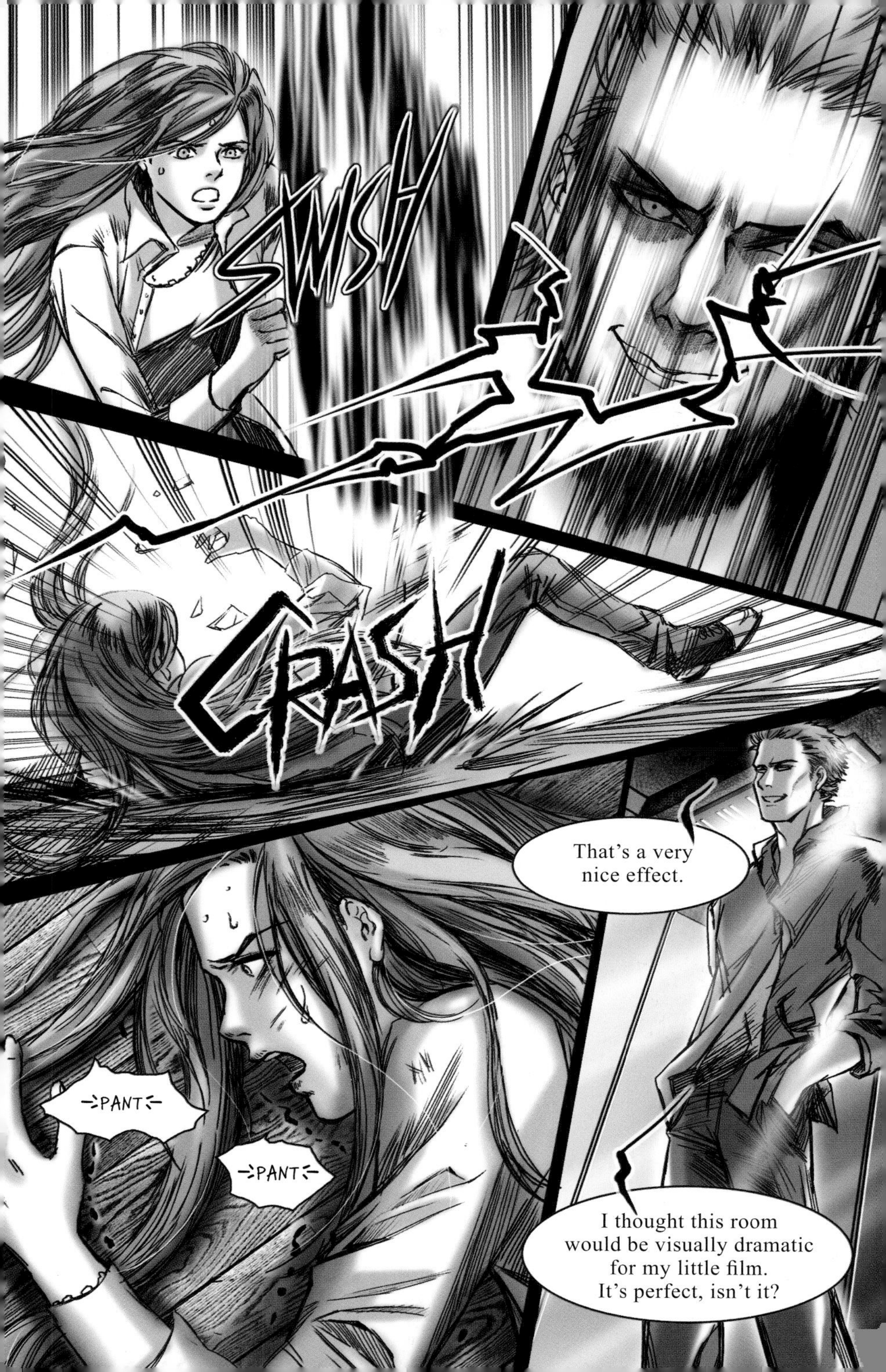
SWISH
CRASH
That's a very nice effect.
-PANT-
-PANT-
I thought this room would be visually dramatic for my little film. It's perfect, isn't it?

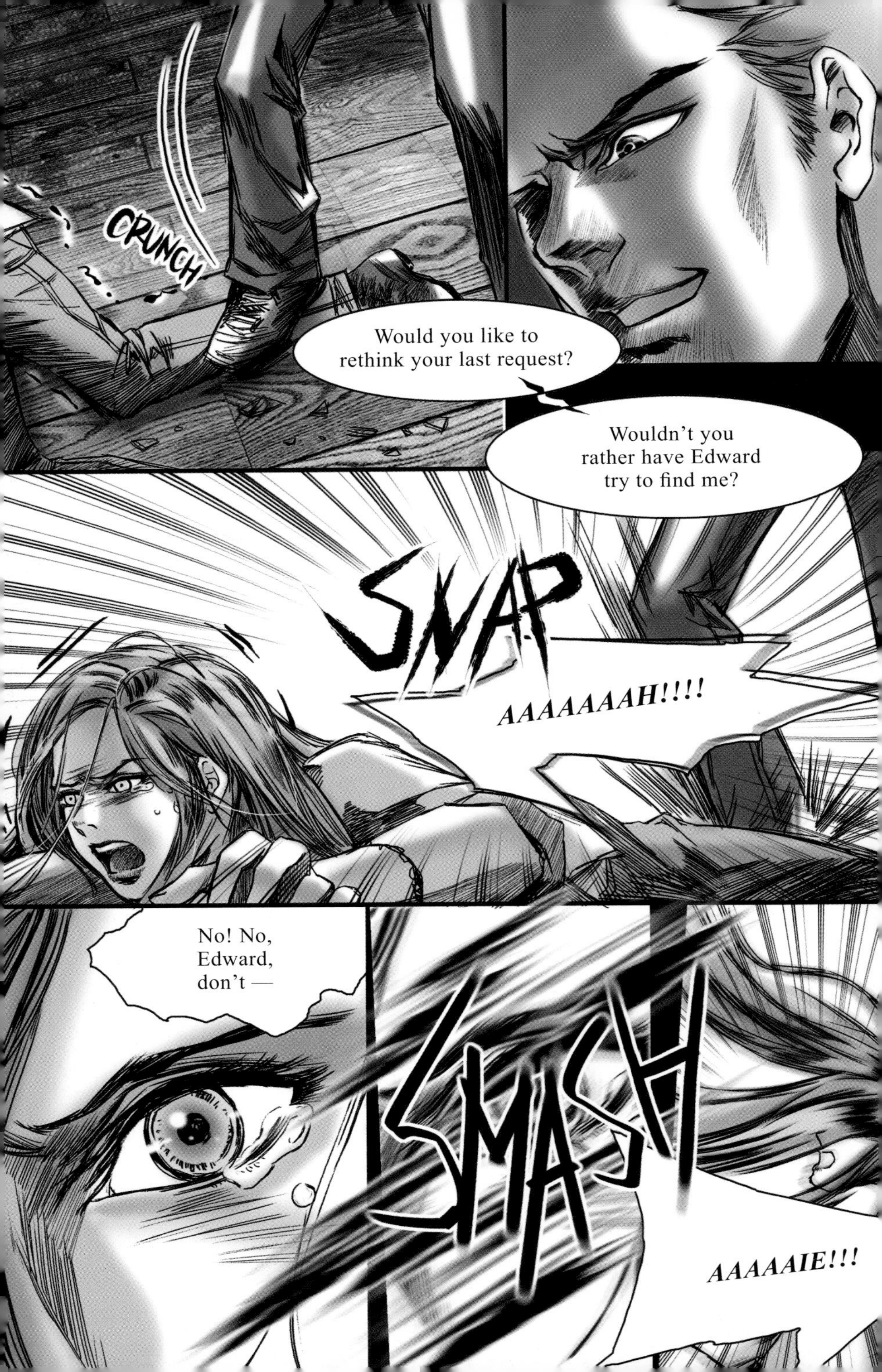
CRUNCH
Would you like to rethink your last request?
Wouldn't you rather have Edward try to find me?
SNAP
AAAAAAAH!!!!
No! No, Edward, don't —
SMASH
AAAAAIE!!!

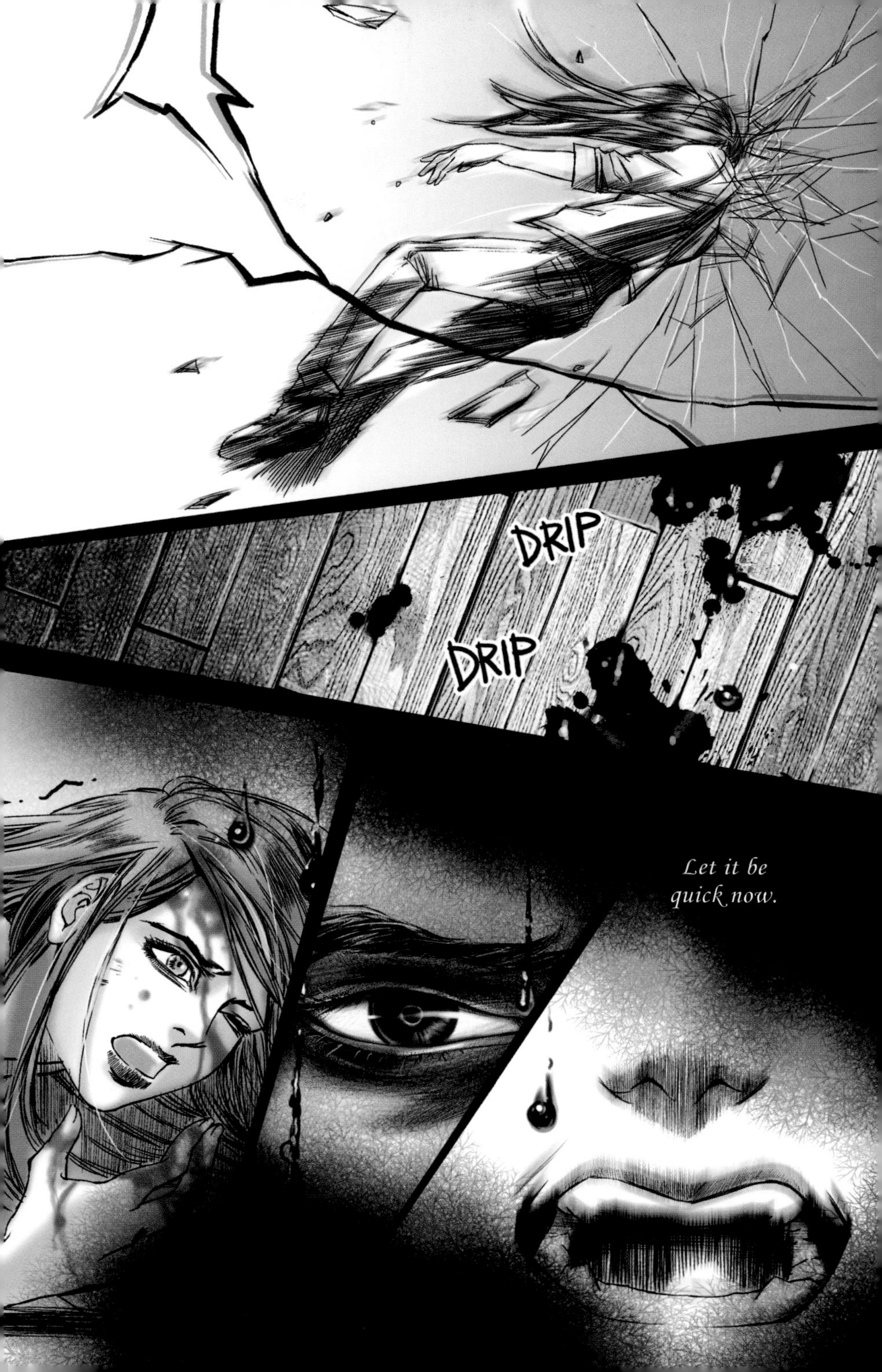
DRIP
DRIP
Let it be quick now.

*Bella, no!*

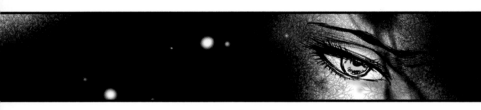

*Am I dead?*

*I can hear the sound
of an angel calling me to
the only heaven I want.*

*Bella, please!
Bella, listen
to me, please,
please, Bella,
please!*

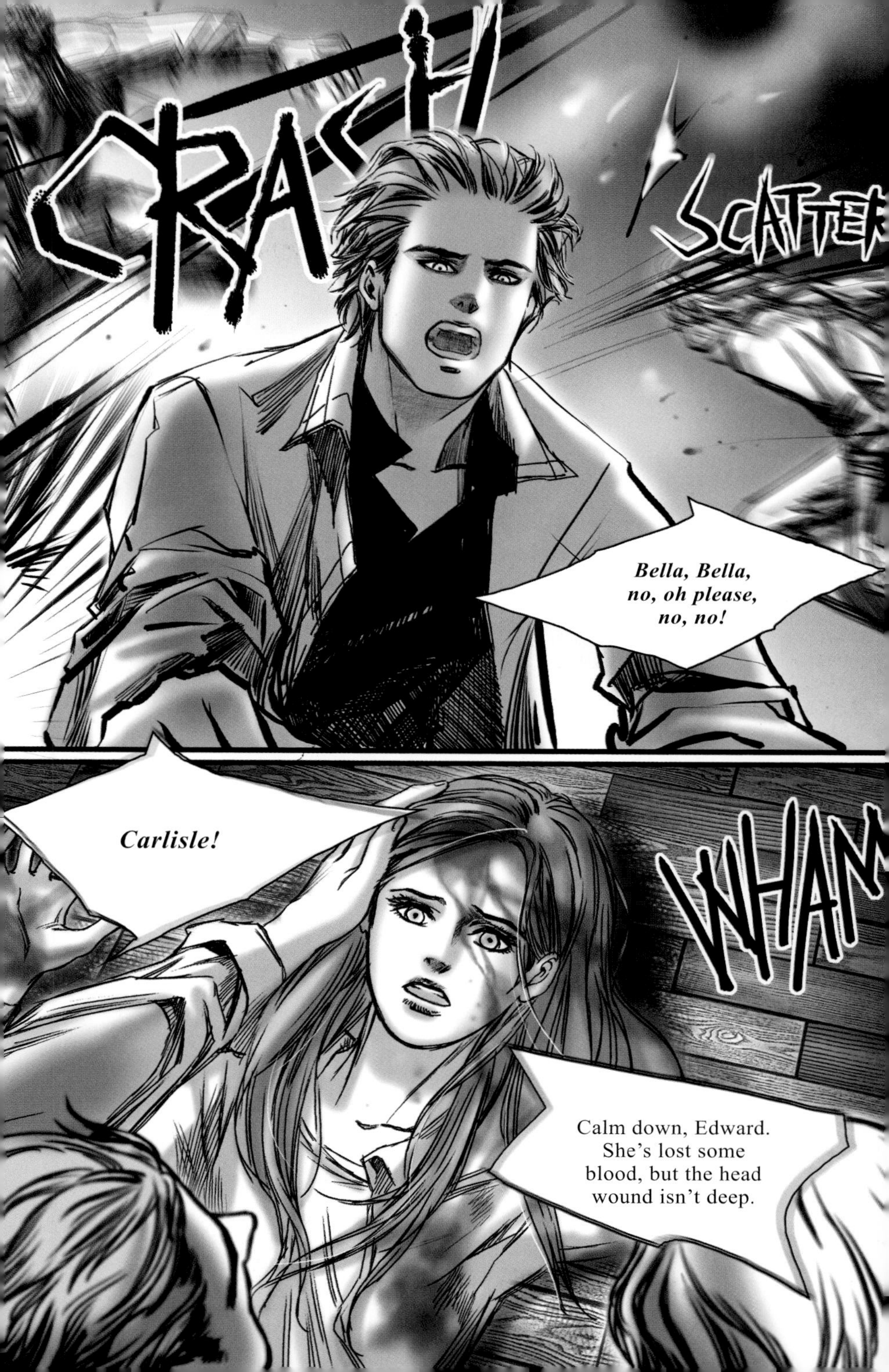
CRASH
SCATTER
Bella, Bella, no, oh please, no, no!
Carlisle!
WHAM
Calm down, Edward. She's lost some blood, but the head wound isn't deep.

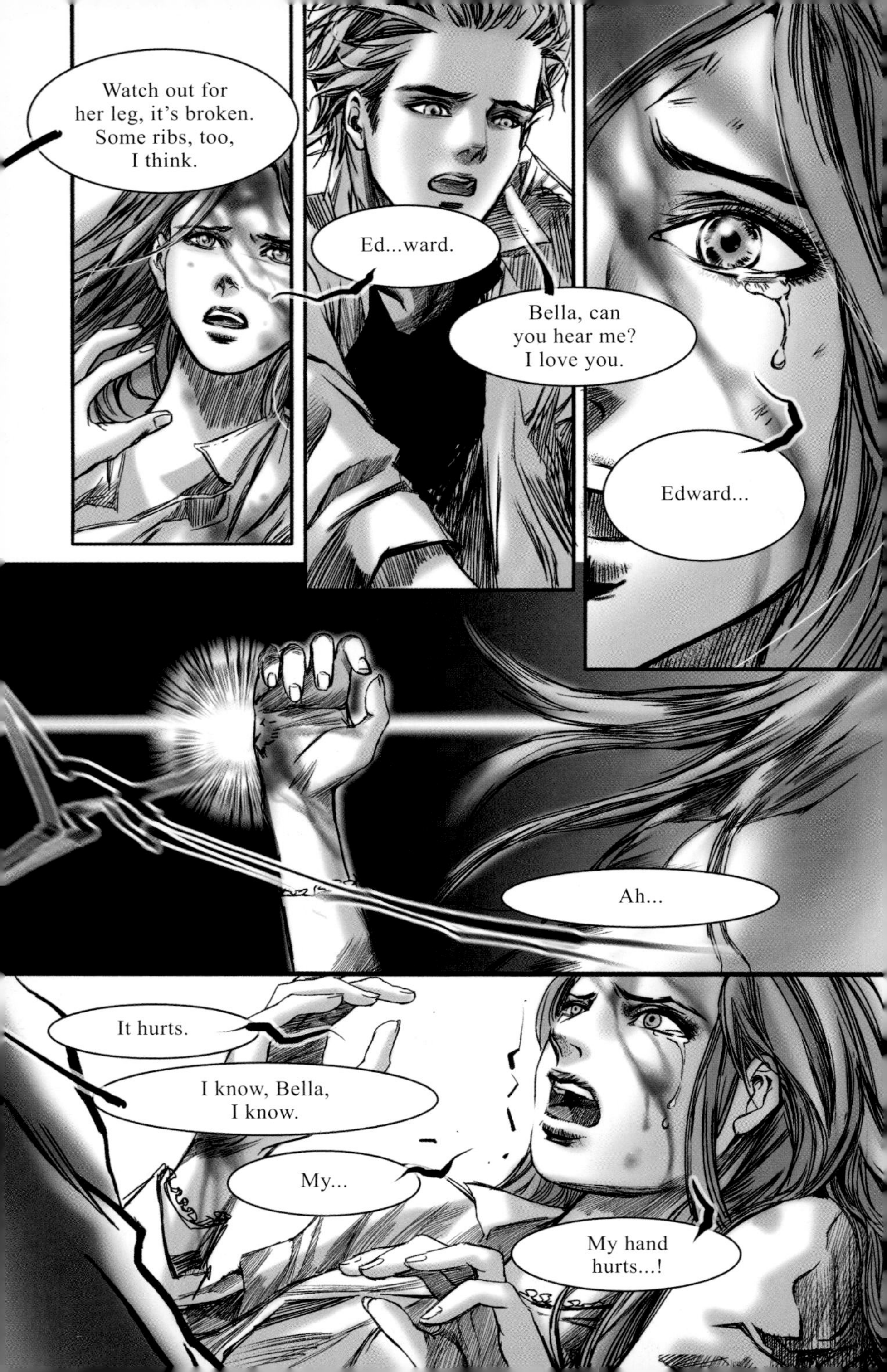
Watch out for her leg, it's broken. Some ribs, too, I think.
Ed...ward.
Bella, can you hear me? I love you.
Edward...
Ah...
It hurts.
I know, Bella, I know.
My...
My hand hurts...!

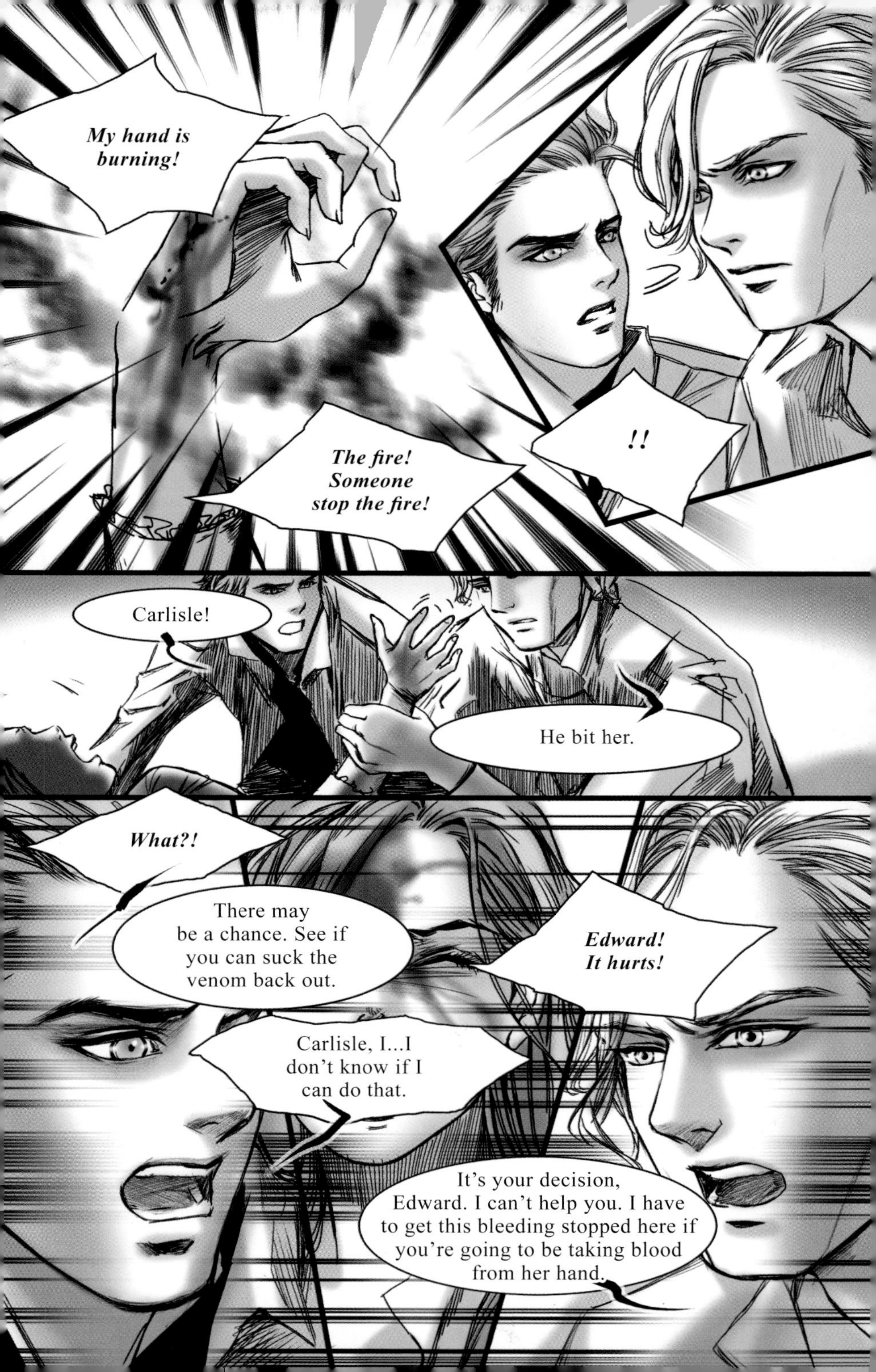
My hand is burning!
!!
The fire! Someone stop the fire!
Carlisle!
He bit her.
What?!
There may be a chance. See if you can suck the venom back out.
Edward! It hurts!
Carlisle, I...I don't know if I can do that.
It's your decision, Edward. I can't help you. I have to get this bleeding stopped here if you're going to be taking blood from her hand.

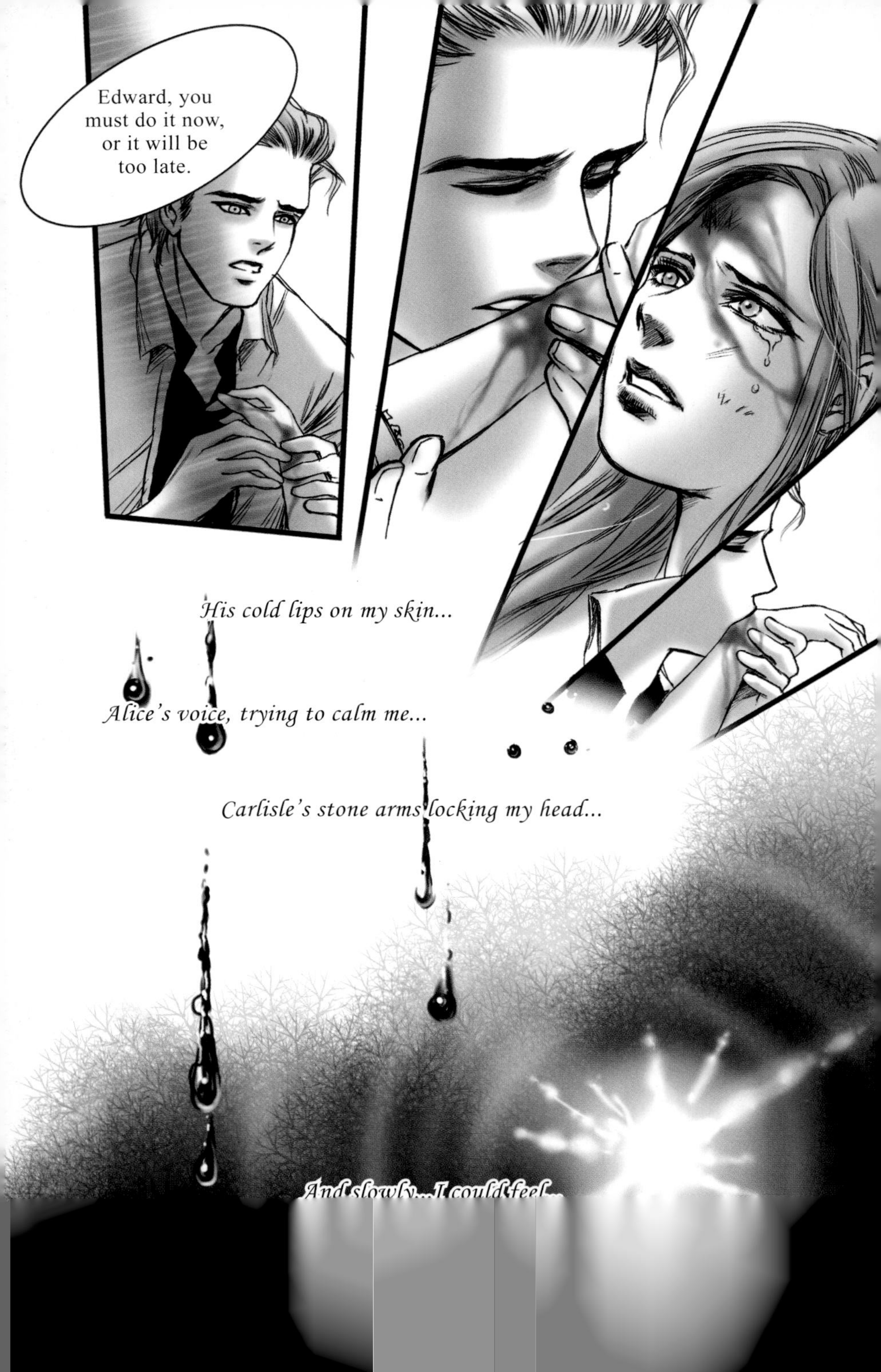

Edward, you must do it now, or it will be too late.
His cold lips on my skin...
Alice's voice, trying to calm me...
Carlisle's stone arms locking my head...
And slowly...I could feel...

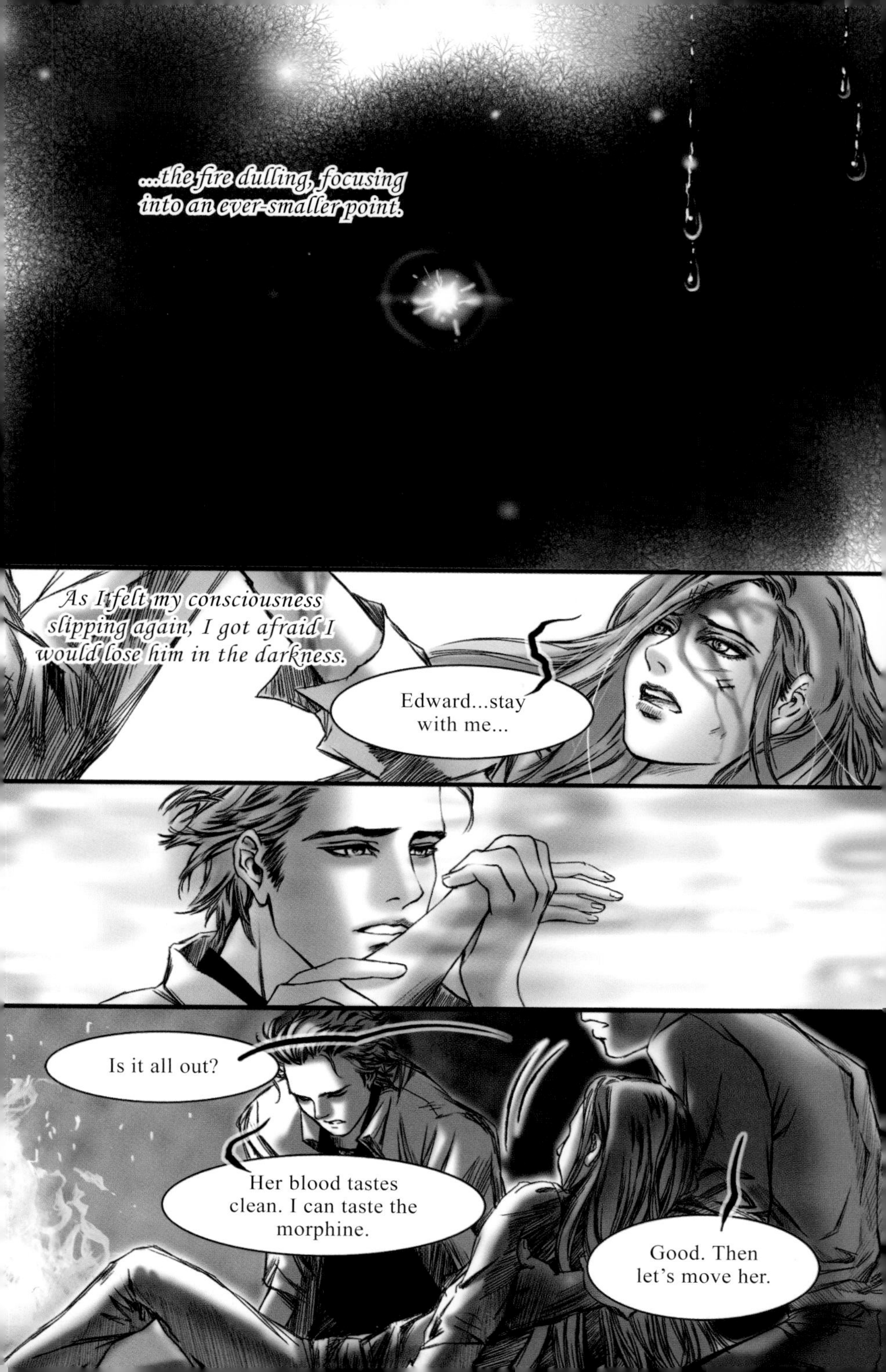
...the fire dulling, focusing into an ever-smaller point.
As I felt my consciousness slipping again, I got afraid I would lose him in the darkness.
Edward...stay with me...
Is it all out?
Her blood tastes clean. I can taste the morphine.
Good. Then let's move her.

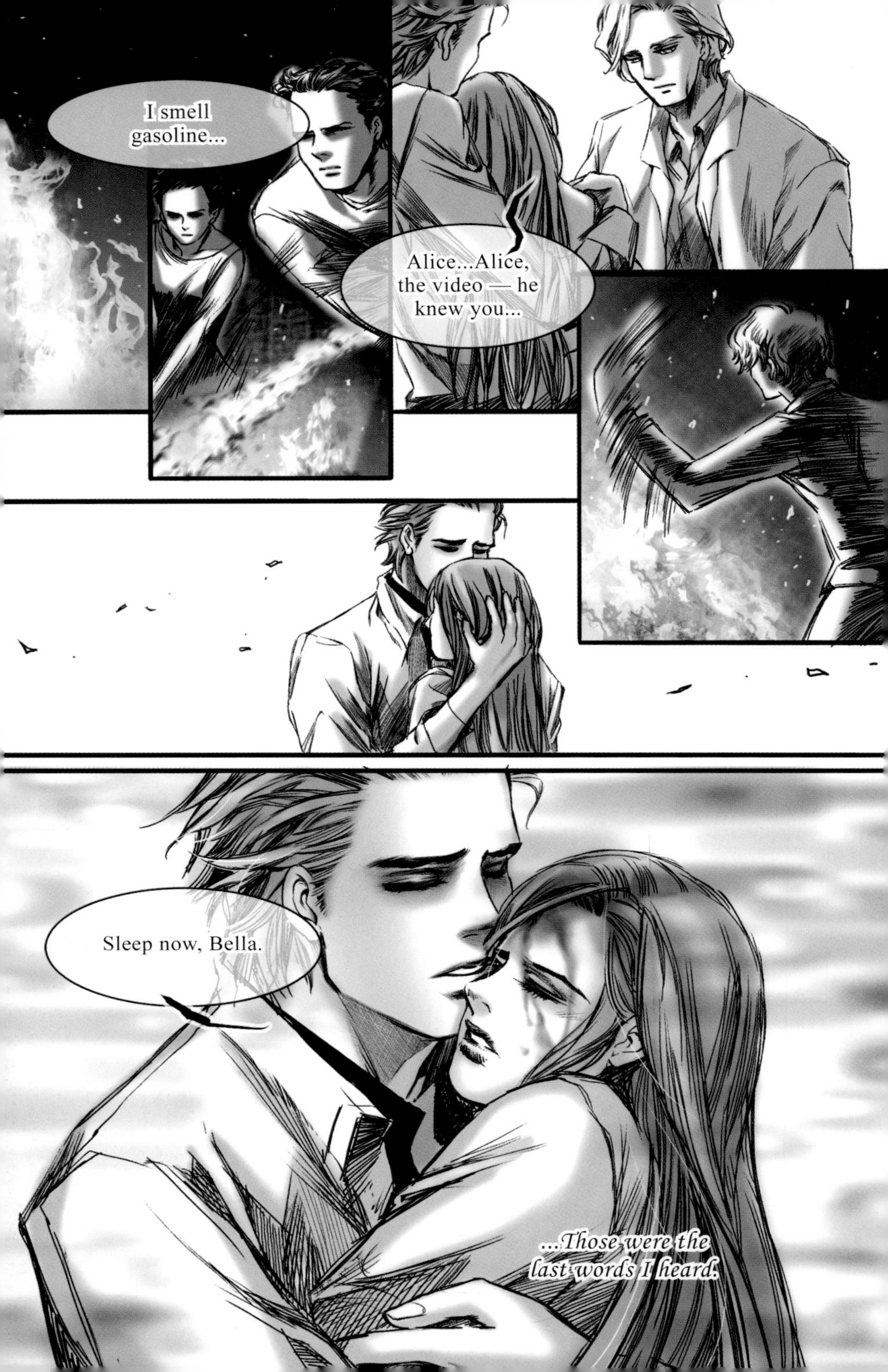
I smell gasoline...
Alice...Alice, the video — he knew you...
Sleep now, Bella.
...Those were the last words I heard.

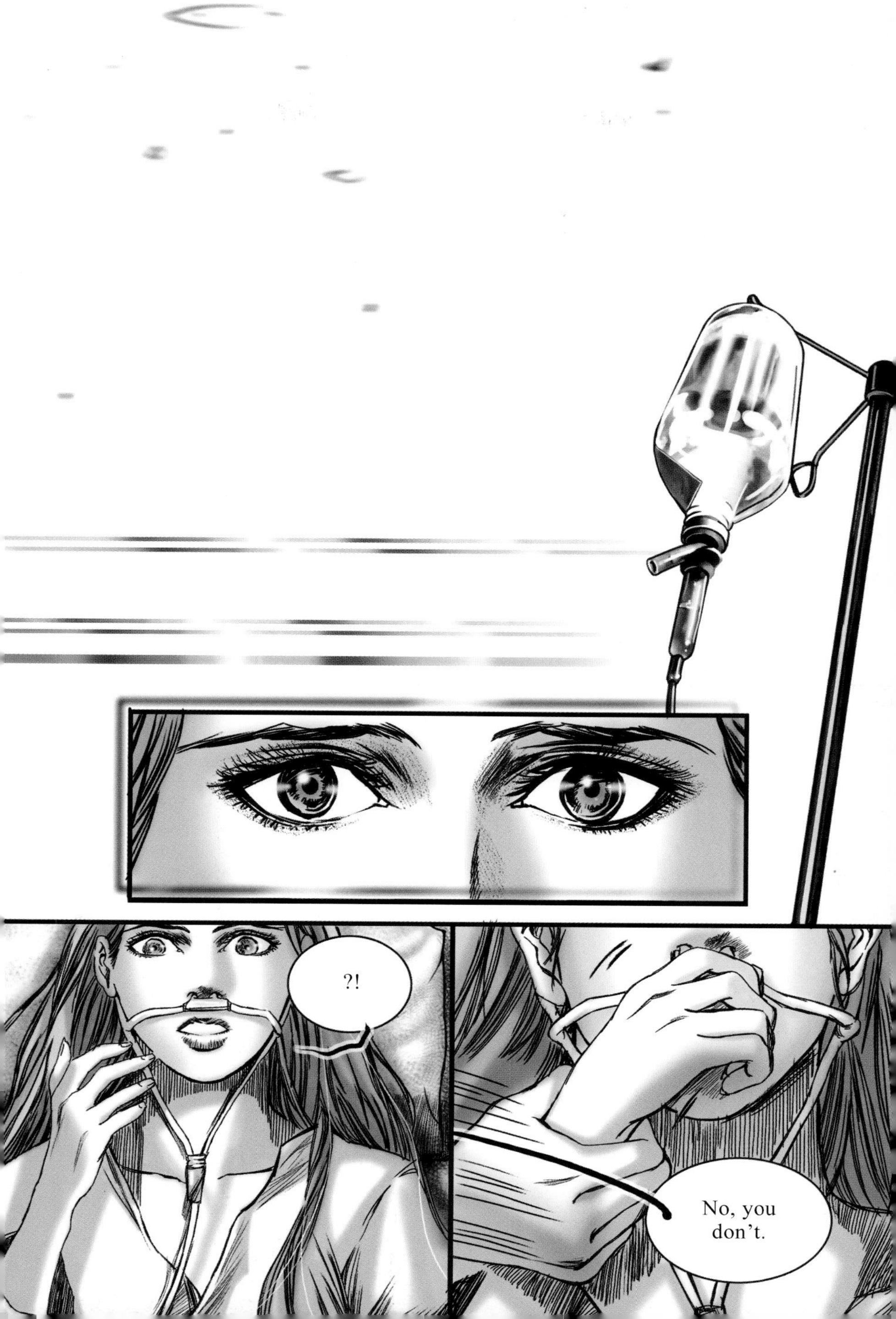
?!
No, you don't.

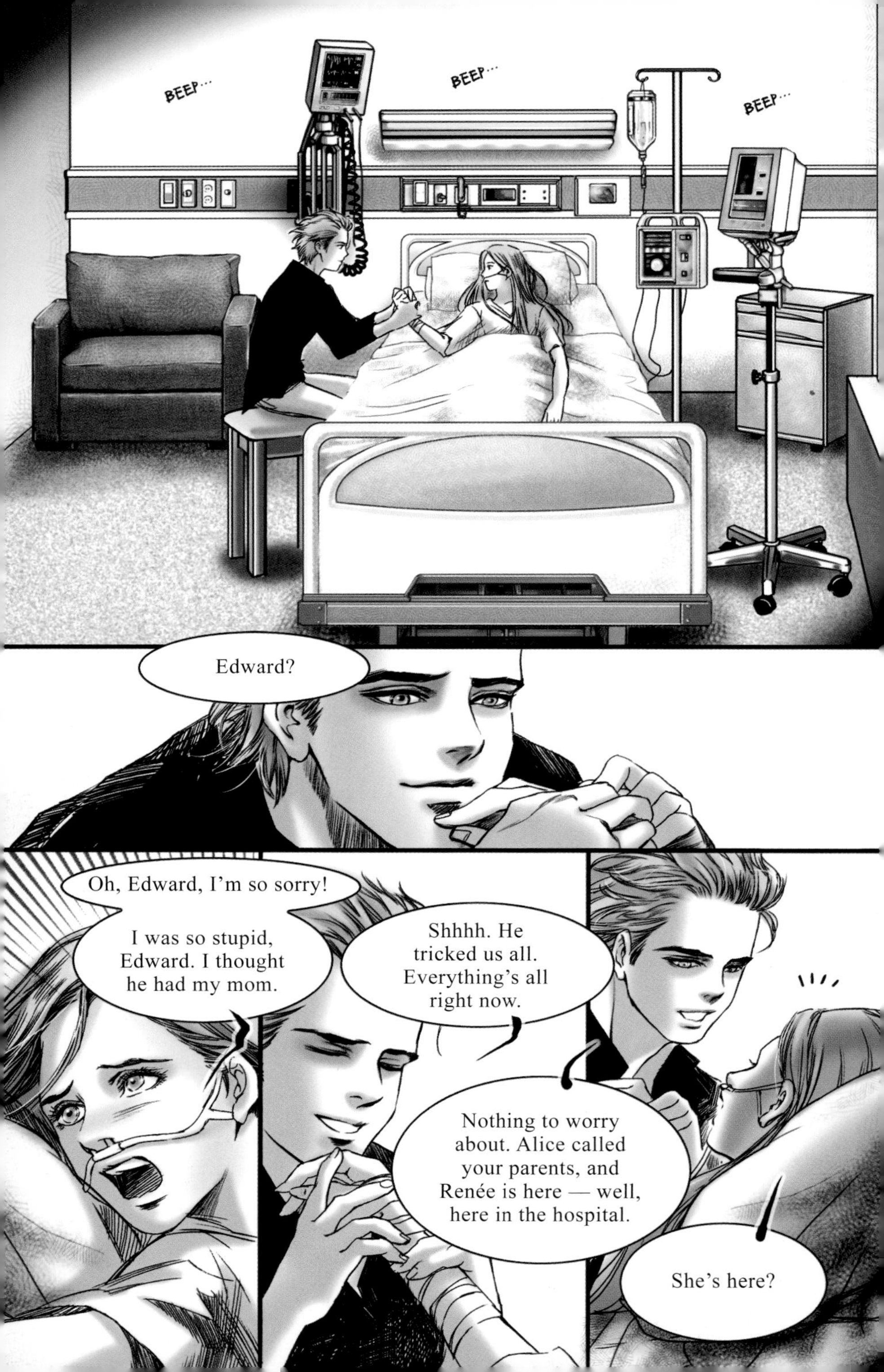
BEEP...
BEEP...
BEEP...
Edward?
Oh, Edward, I'm so sorry!
I was so stupid, Edward. I thought he had my mom.
Shhhh. He tricked us all. Everything's all right now.
Nothing to worry about. Alice called your parents, and Renée is here — well, here in the hospital.
She's here?

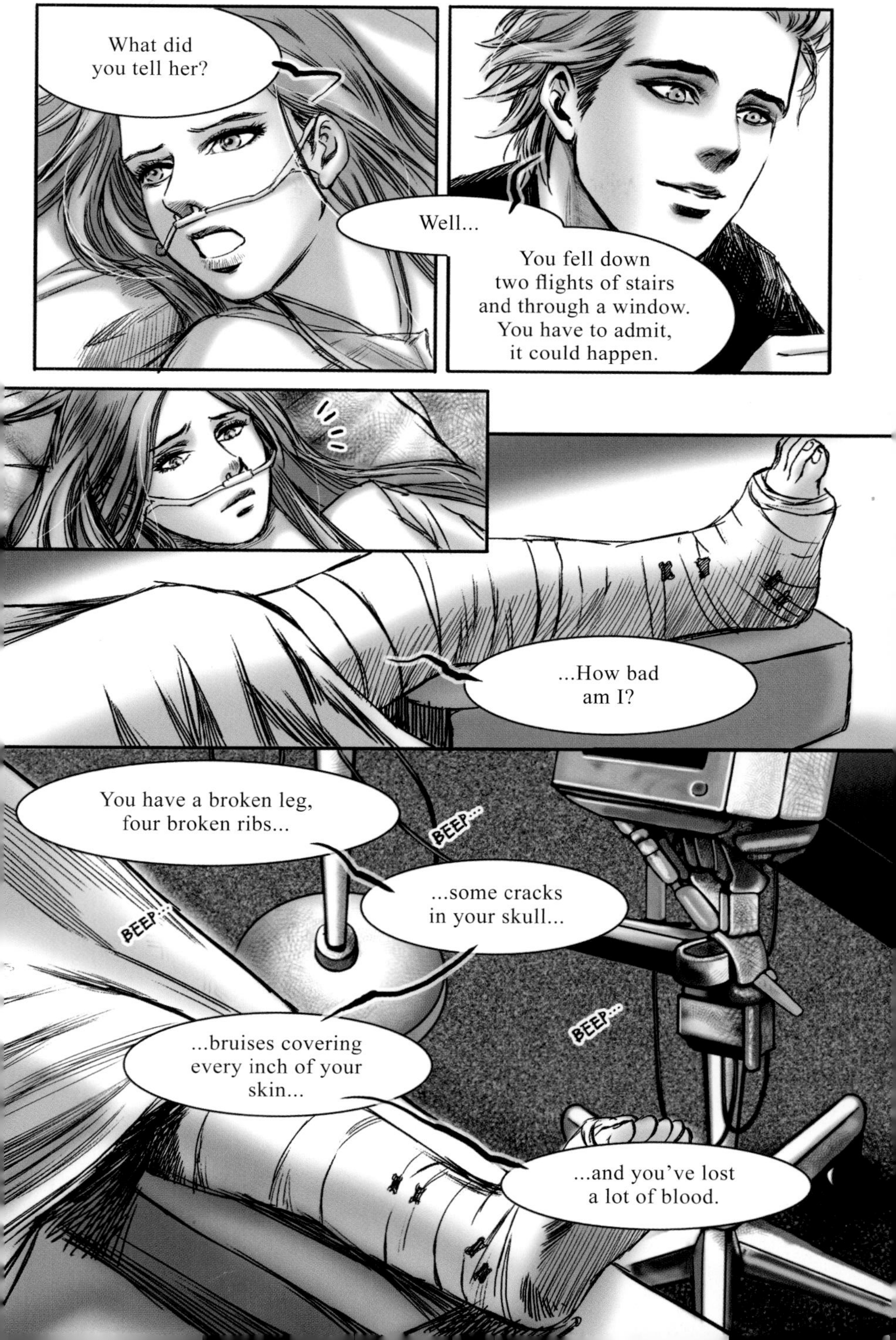
What did you tell her?
Well...
You fell down two flights of stairs and through a window. You have to admit, it could happen.
...How bad am I?
You have a broken leg, four broken ribs...
BEEP...
...some cracks in your skull...
BEEP...
...bruises covering every inch of your skin...
BEEP...
...and you've lost a lot of blood.

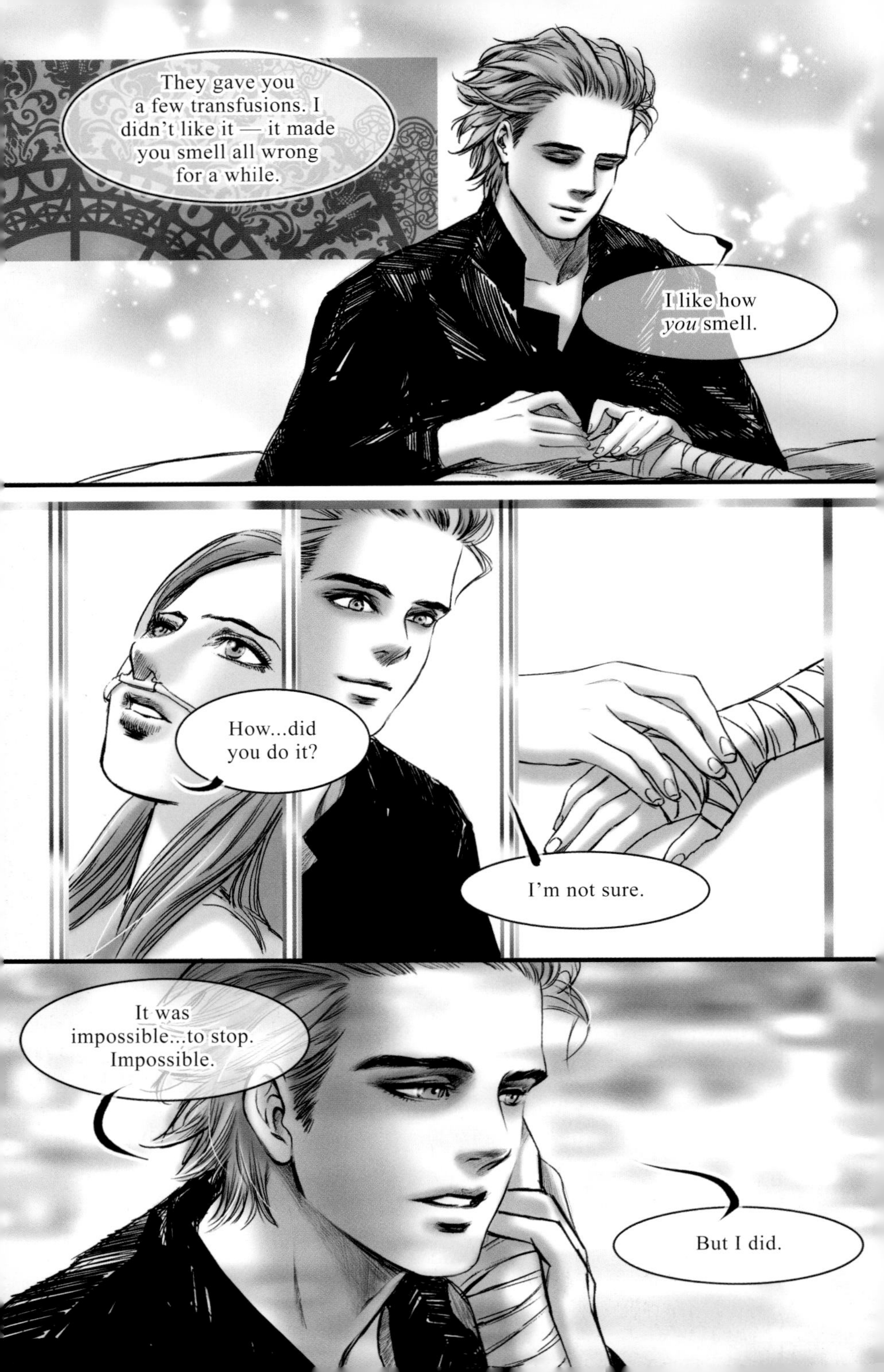
They gave you a few transfusions. I didn't like it — it made you smell all wrong for a while.
I like how *you* smell.
How...did you do it?
I'm not sure.
It was impossible...to stop. Impossible.
But I did.

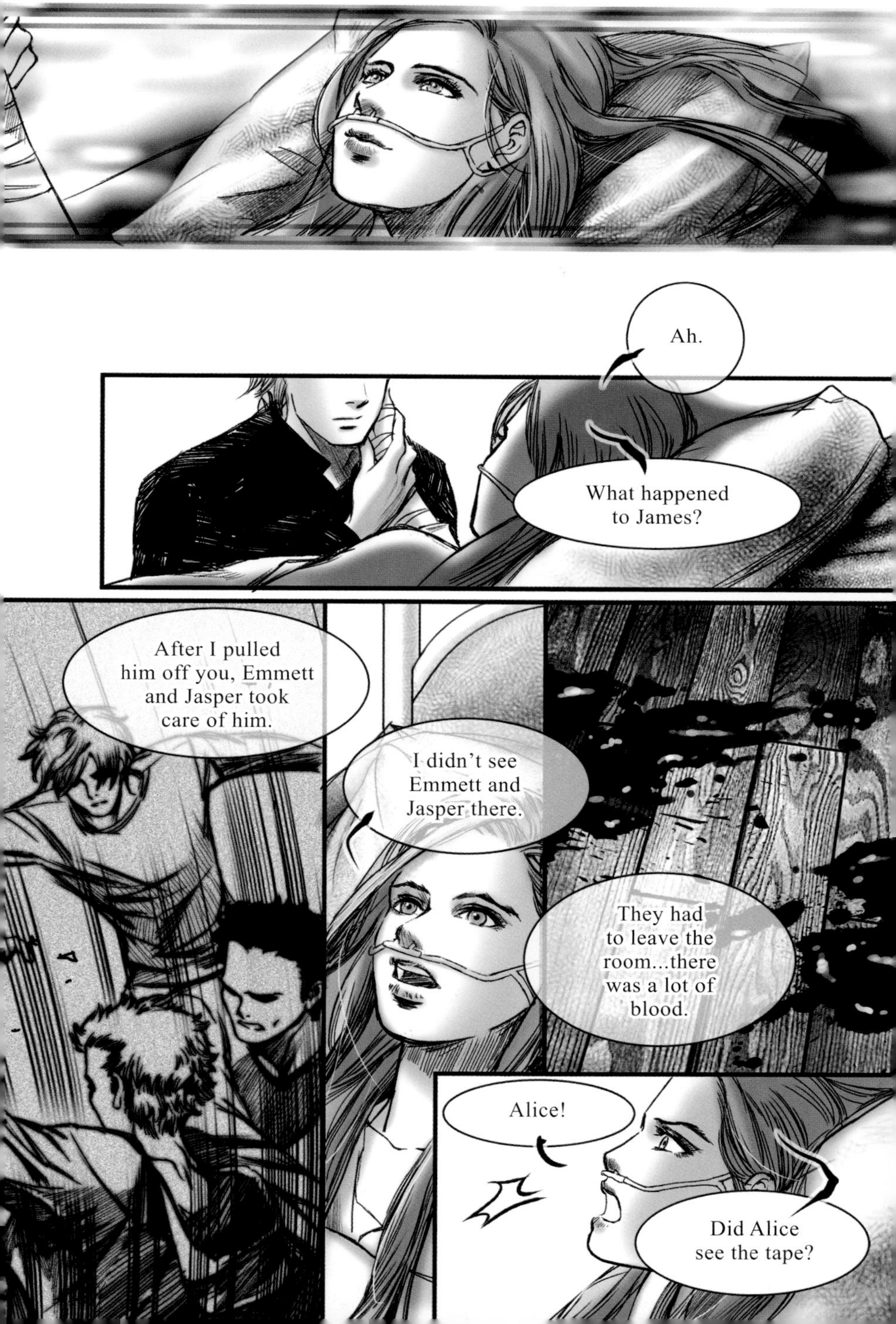
Ah.
What happened to James?
After I pulled him off you, Emmett and Jasper took care of him.
I didn't see Emmett and Jasper there.
They had to leave the room...there was a lot of blood.
Alice!
Did Alice see the tape?

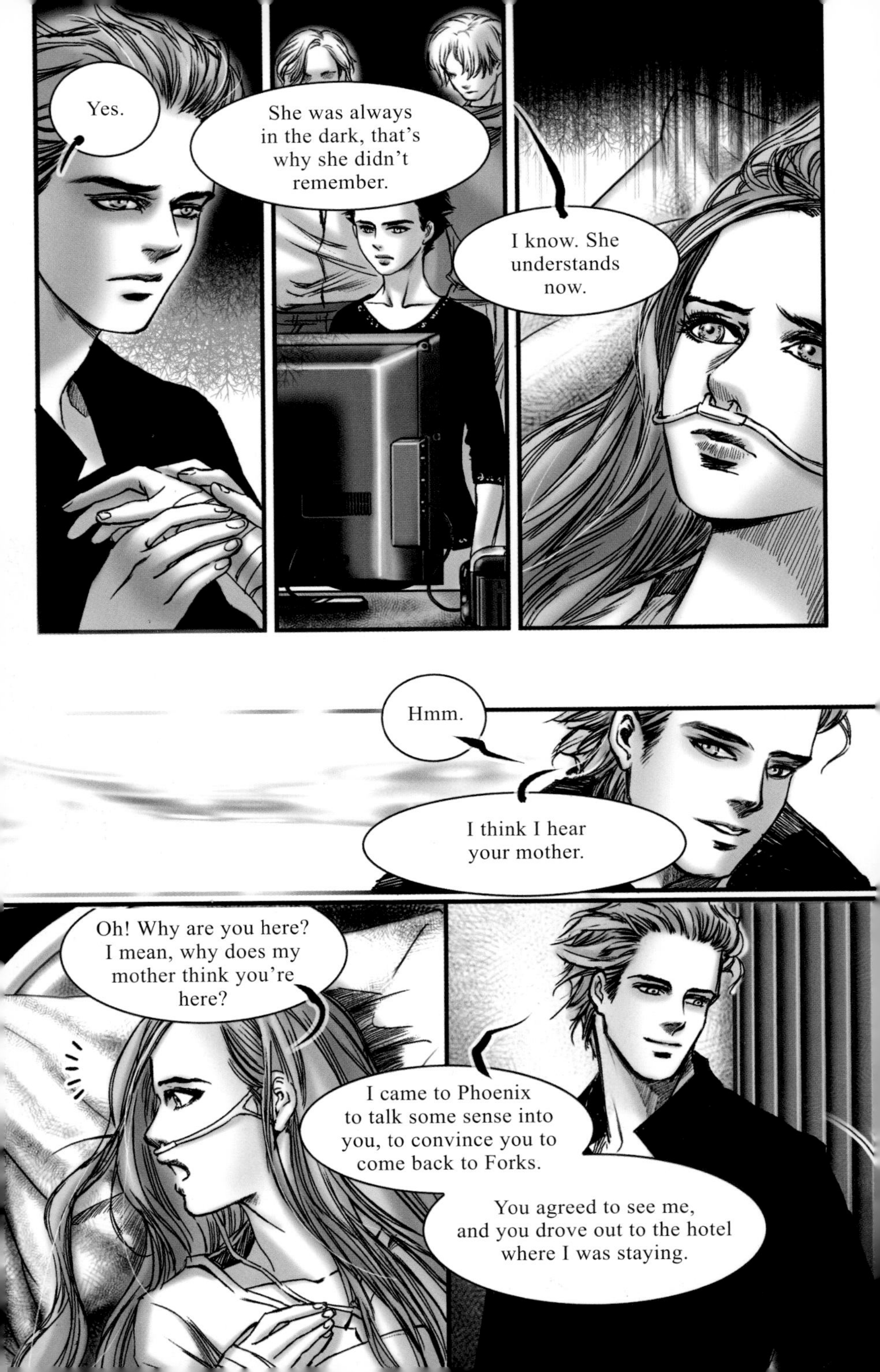
Yes.
She was always in the dark, that's why she didn't remember.
I know. She understands now.
Hmm.
I think I hear your mother.
Oh! Why are you here? I mean, why does my mother think you're here?
I came to Phoenix to talk some sense into you, to convince you to come back to Forks.
You agreed to see me, and you drove out to the hotel where I was staying.

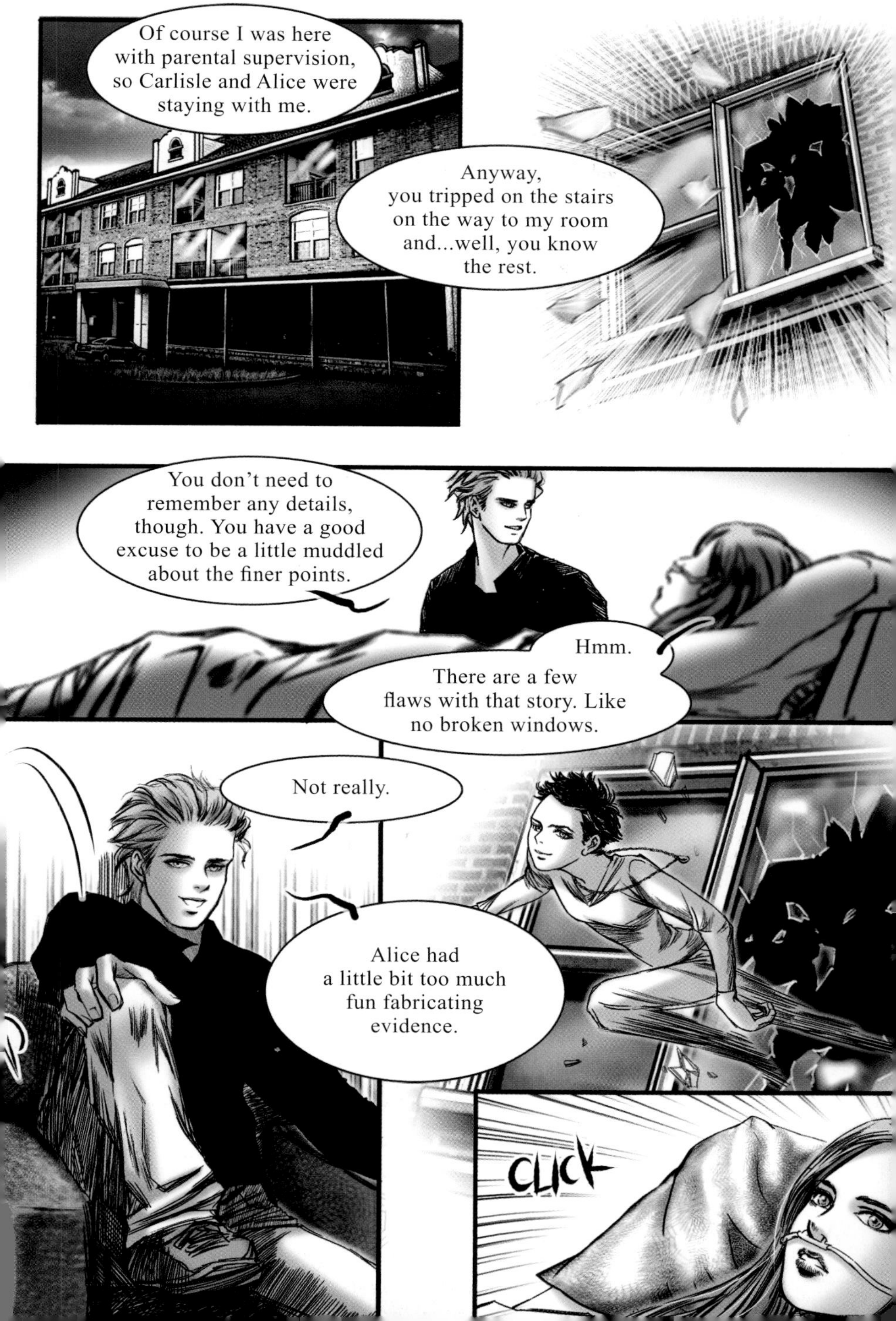
Of course I was here with parental supervision, so Carlisle and Alice were staying with me.
Anyway, you tripped on the stairs on the way to my room and...well, you know the rest.
You don't need to remember any details, though. You have a good excuse to be a little muddled about the finer points.
Hmm. There are a few flaws with that story. Like no broken windows.
Not really.
Alice had a little bit too much fun fabricating evidence.
CLICK

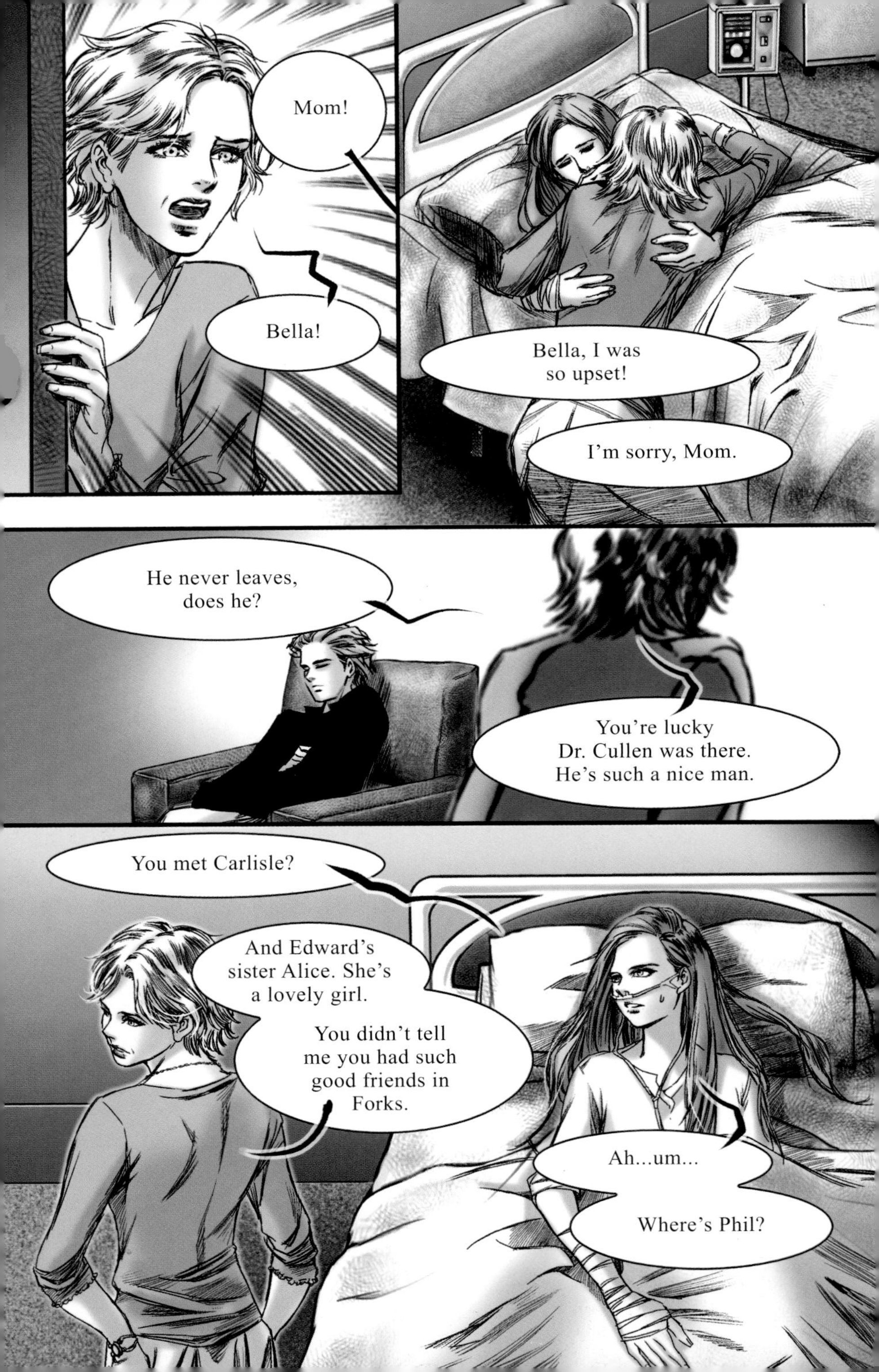
Mom!
Bella!
Bella, I was so upset!
I'm sorry, Mom.
He never leaves, does he?
You're lucky Dr. Cullen was there. He's such a nice man.
You met Carlisle?
And Edward's sister Alice. She's a lovely girl.
You didn't tell me you had such good friends in Forks.
Ah...um...
Where's Phil?

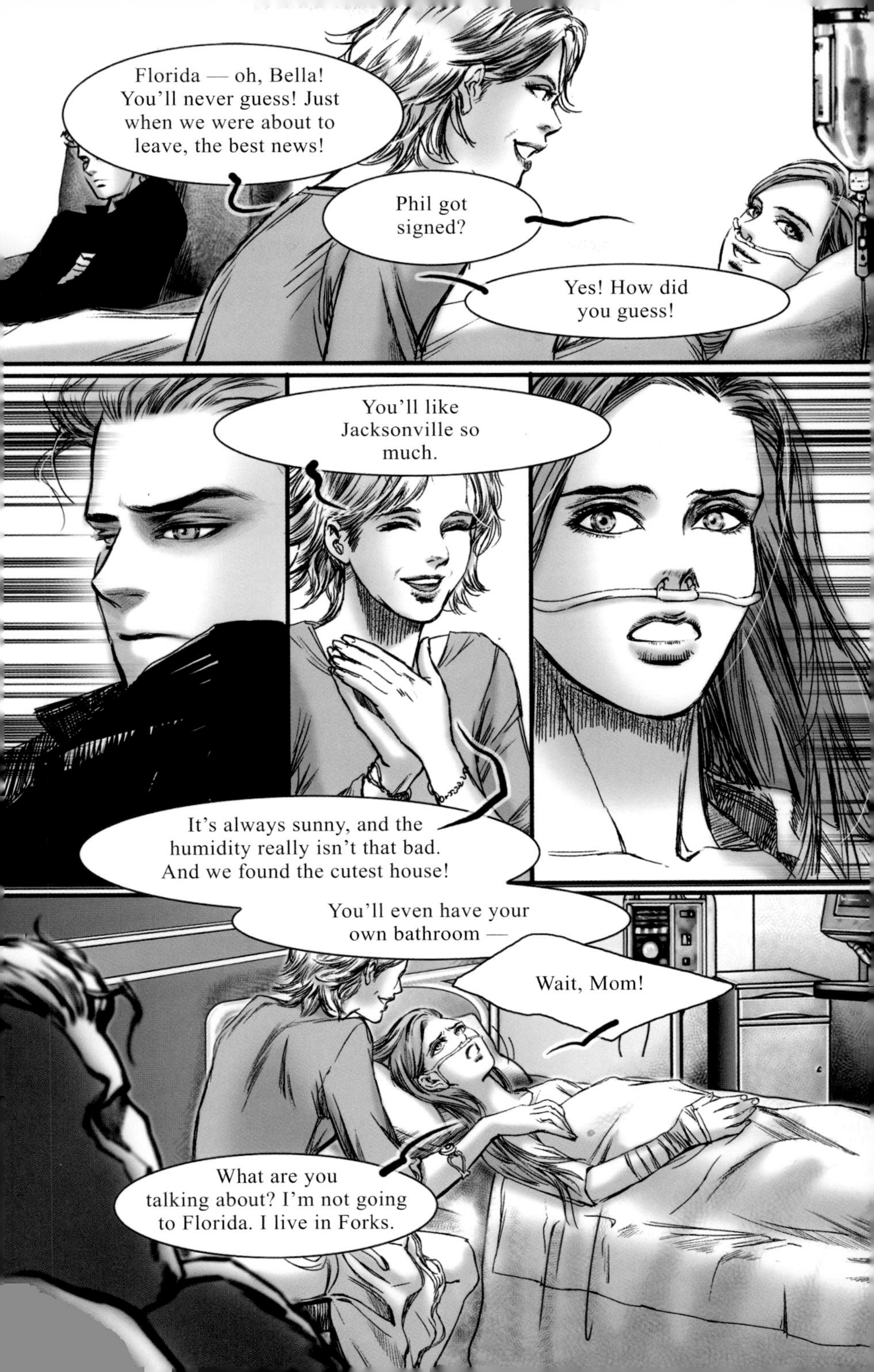
Florida — oh, Bella! You'll never guess! Just when we were about to leave, the best news!
Phil got signed?
Yes! How did you guess!
You'll like Jacksonville so much.
It's always sunny, and the humidity really isn't that bad. And we found the cutest house!
You'll even have your own bathroom —
Wait, Mom!
What are you talking about? I'm not going to Florida. I live in Forks.

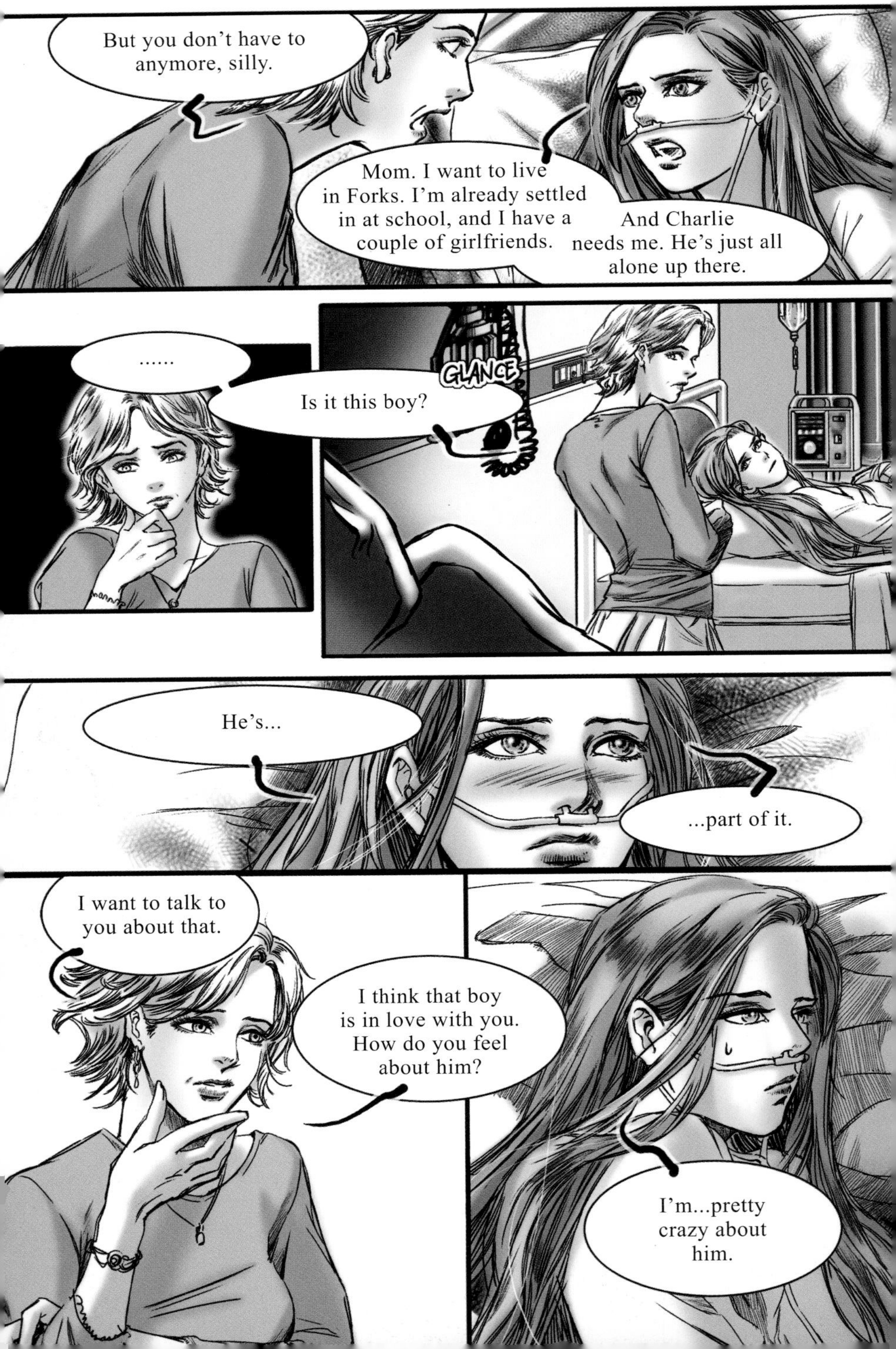
But you don't have to anymore, silly.
Mom. I want to live in Forks. I'm already settled in at school, and I have a couple of girlfriends.
And Charlie needs me. He's just all alone up there.
......
Is it this boy?
GLANCE
He's...
...part of it.
I want to talk to you about that.
I think that boy is in love with you. How do you feel about him?
I'm...pretty crazy about him.

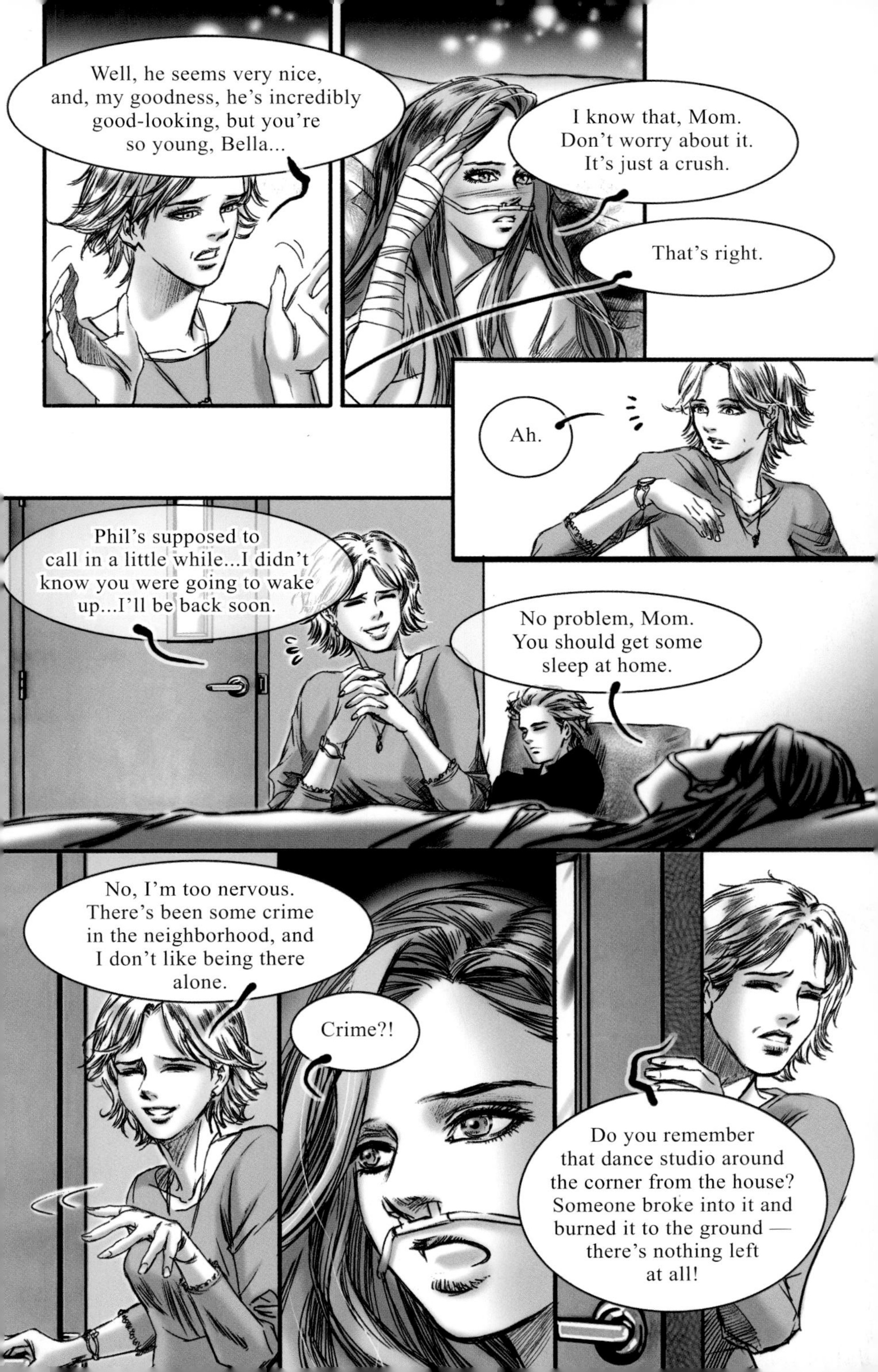
Well, he seems very nice, and, my goodness, he's incredibly good-looking, but you're so young, Bella...
I know that, Mom. Don't worry about it. It's just a crush.
That's right.
Ah.
Phil's supposed to call in a little while...I didn't know you were going to wake up...I'll be back soon.
No problem, Mom. You should get some sleep at home.
No, I'm too nervous. There's been some crime in the neighborhood, and I don't like being there alone.
Crime?!
Do you remember that dance studio around the corner from the house? Someone broke into it and burned it to the ground — there's nothing left at all!

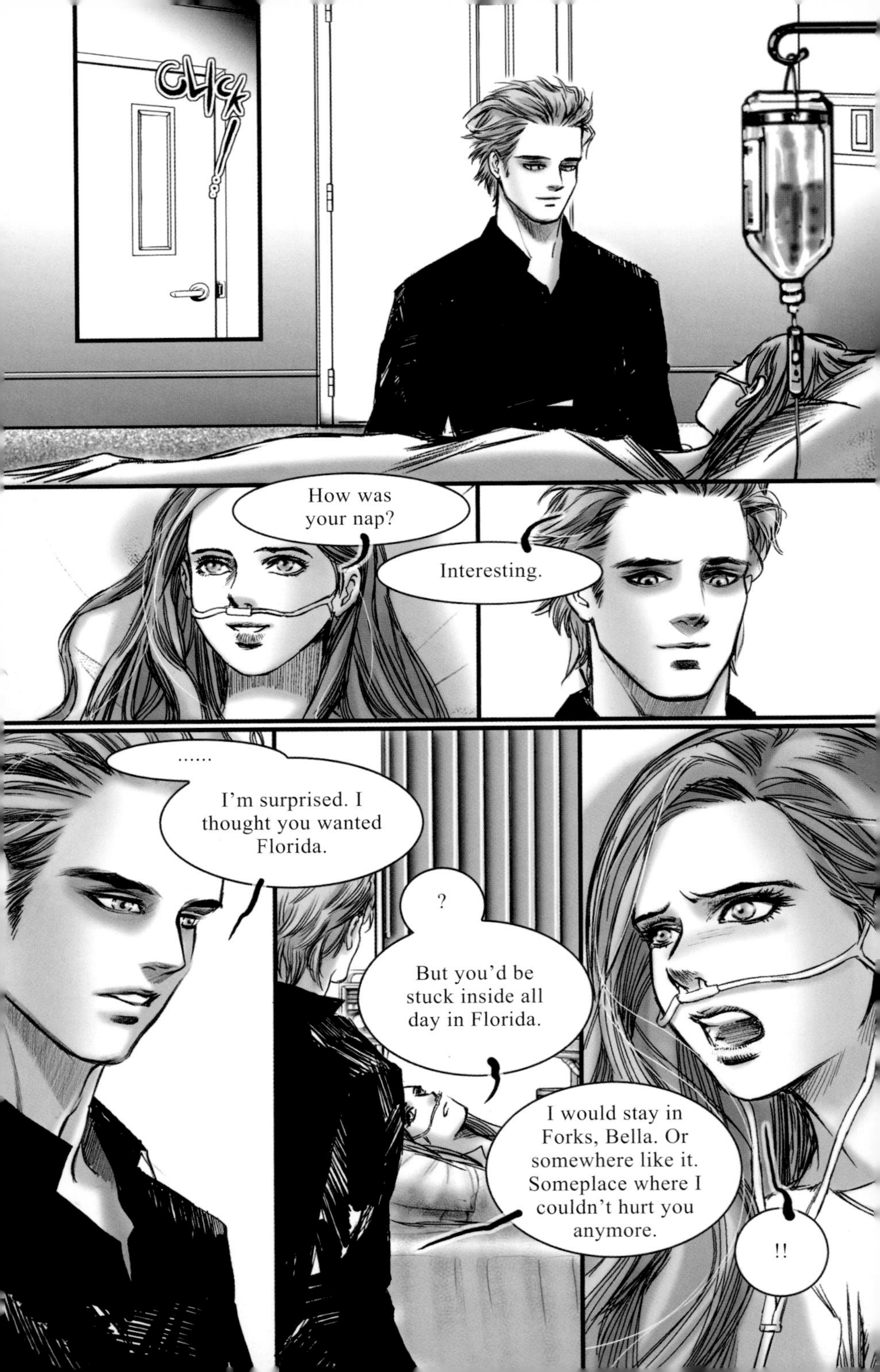
CLICK
How was your nap?
Interesting.
......
I'm surprised. I thought you wanted Florida.
?
But you'd be stuck inside all day in Florida.
I would stay in Forks, Bella. Or somewhere like it. Someplace where I couldn't hurt you anymore.
!!

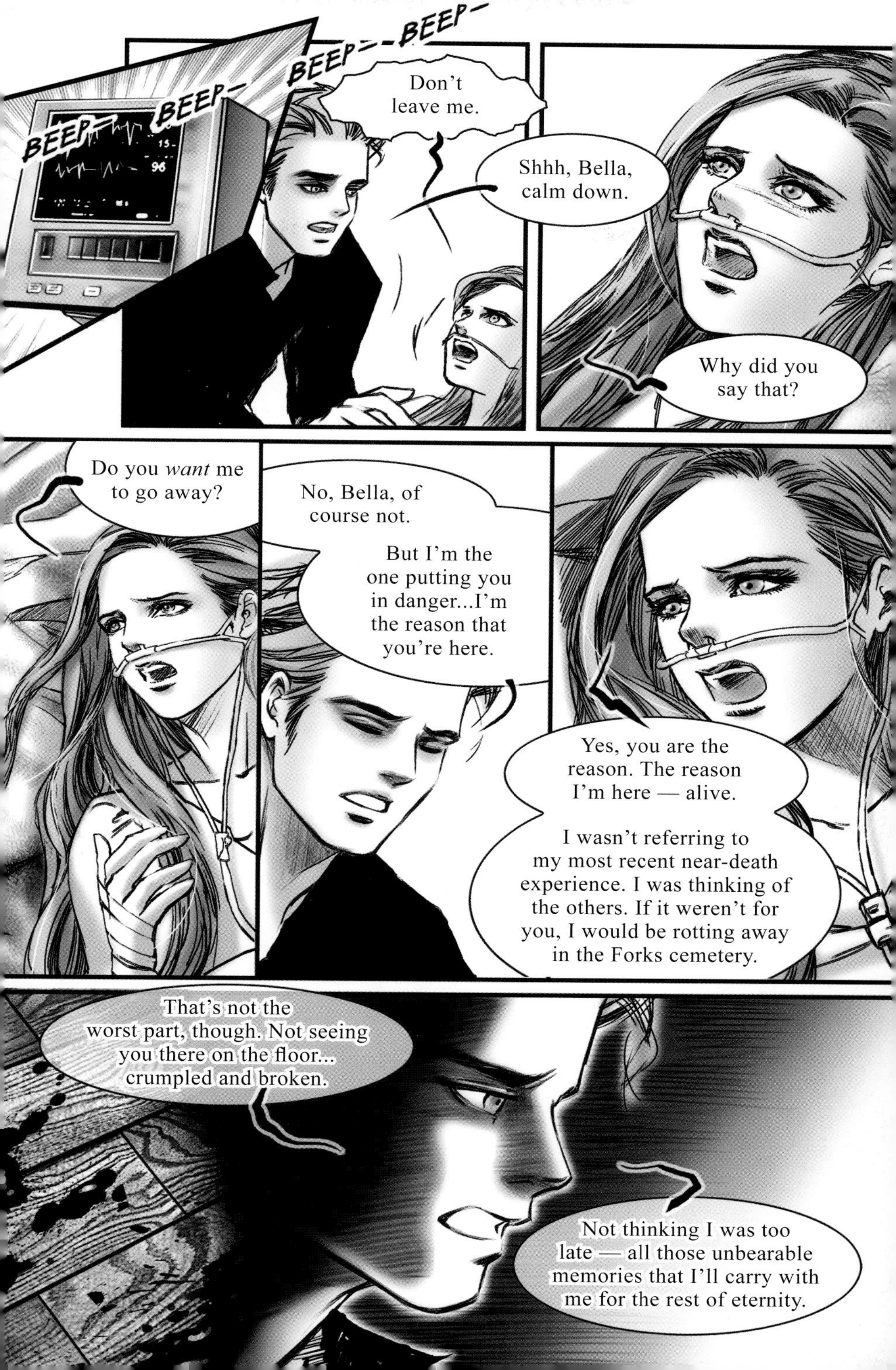
BEEP— BEEP— BEEP—— BEEP—
Don't leave me.
Shhh, Bella, calm down.
Why did you say that?
Do you *want* me to go away?
No, Bella, of course not.
But I'm the one putting you in danger...I'm the reason that you're here.
Yes, you are the reason. The reason I'm here — alive.
I wasn't referring to my most recent near-death experience. I was thinking of the others. If it weren't for you, I would be rotting away in the Forks cemetery.
That's not the worst part, though. Not seeing you there on the floor... crumpled and broken.
Not thinking I was too late — all those unbearable memories that I'll carry with me for the rest of eternity.

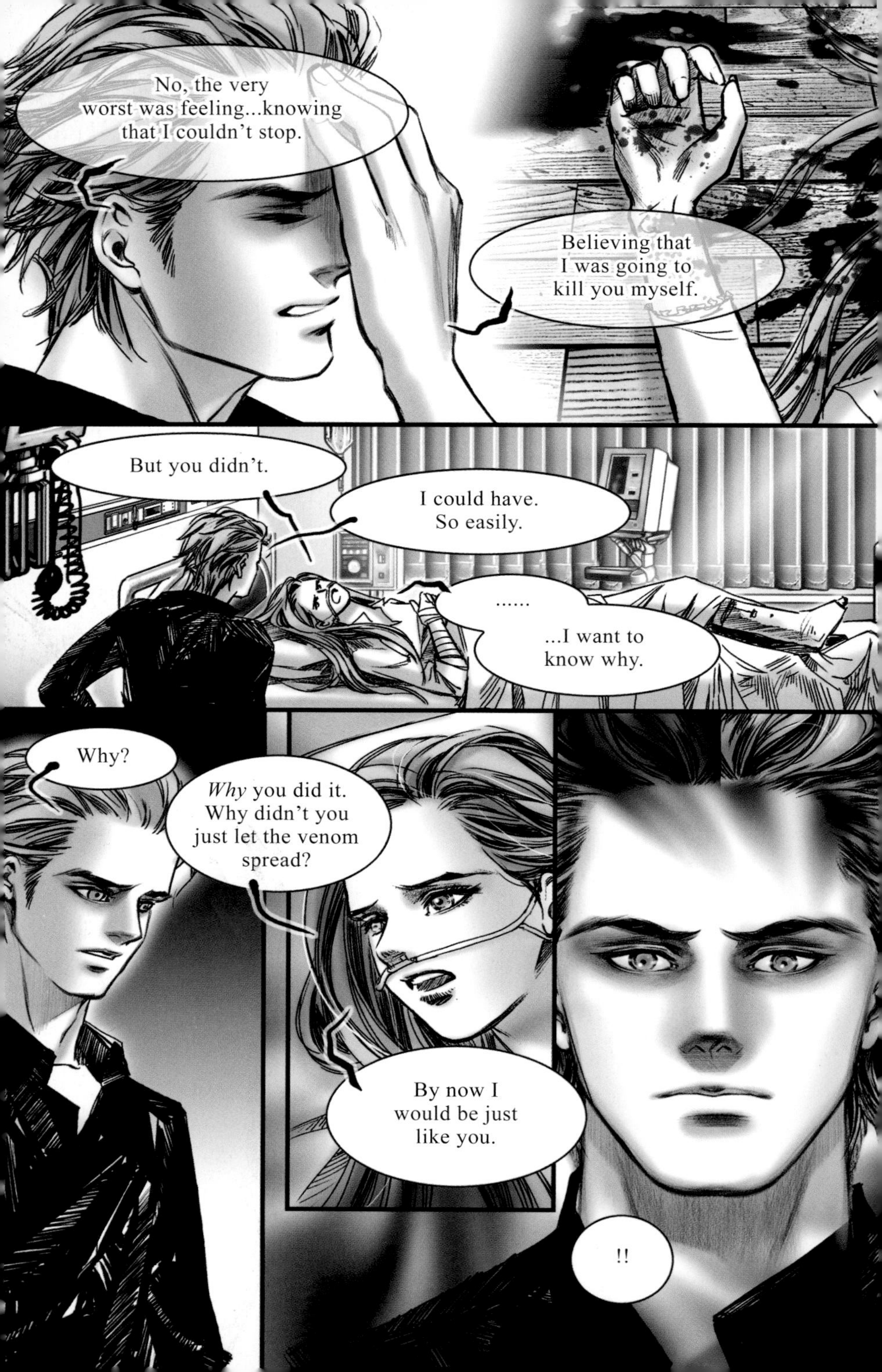
No, the very worst was feeling...knowing that I couldn't stop.
Believing that I was going to kill you myself.
But you didn't.
I could have. So easily.
......
...I want to know why.
Why?
*Why* you did it. Why didn't you just let the venom spread?
By now I would be just like you.
!!

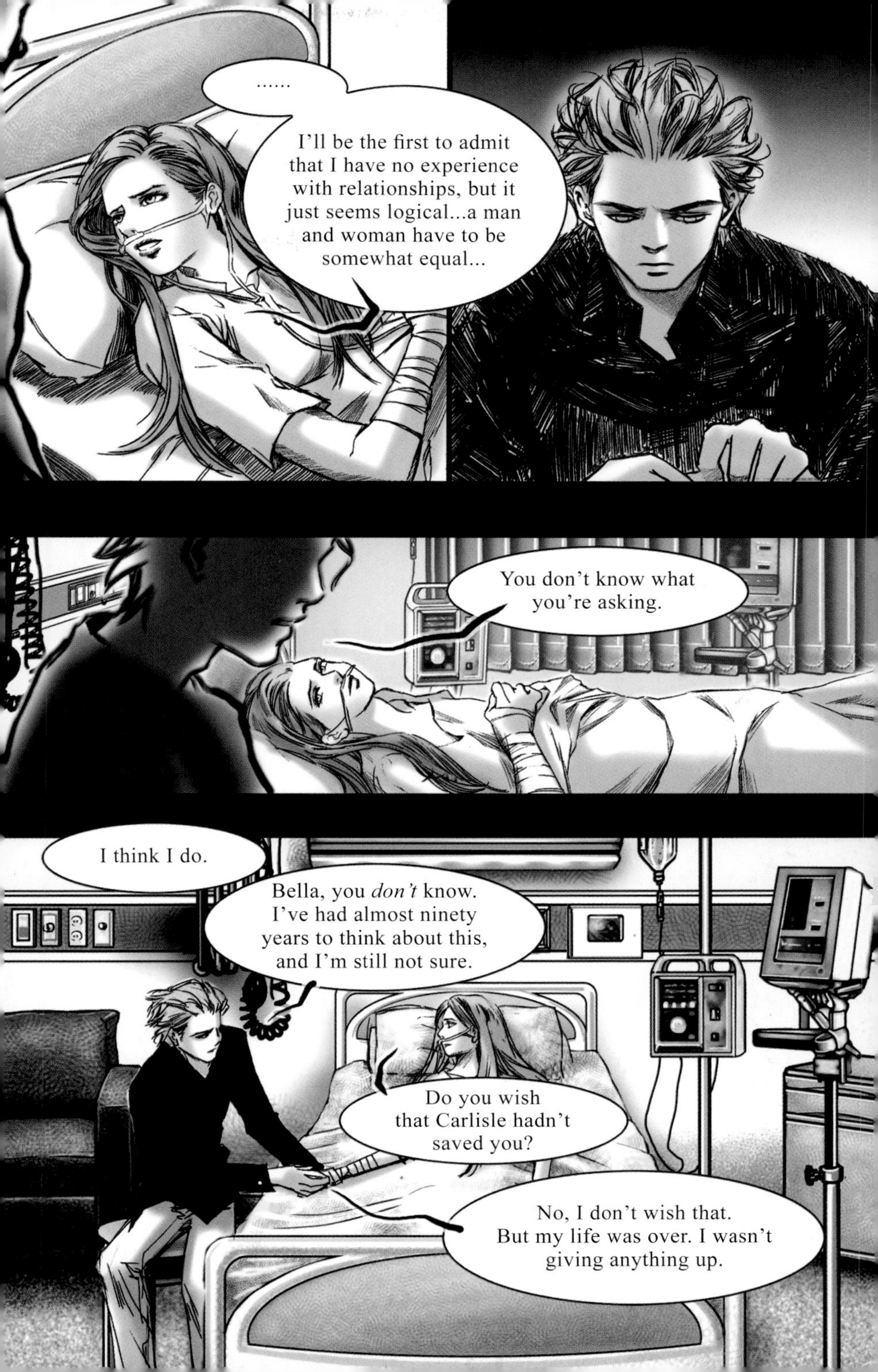
......
I'll be the first to admit that I have no experience with relationships, but it just seems logical...a man and woman have to be somewhat equal...
You don't know what you're asking.
I think I do.
Bella, you *don't* know. I've had almost ninety years to think about this, and I'm still not sure.
Do you wish that Carlisle hadn't saved you?
No, I don't wish that. But my life was over. I wasn't giving anything up.

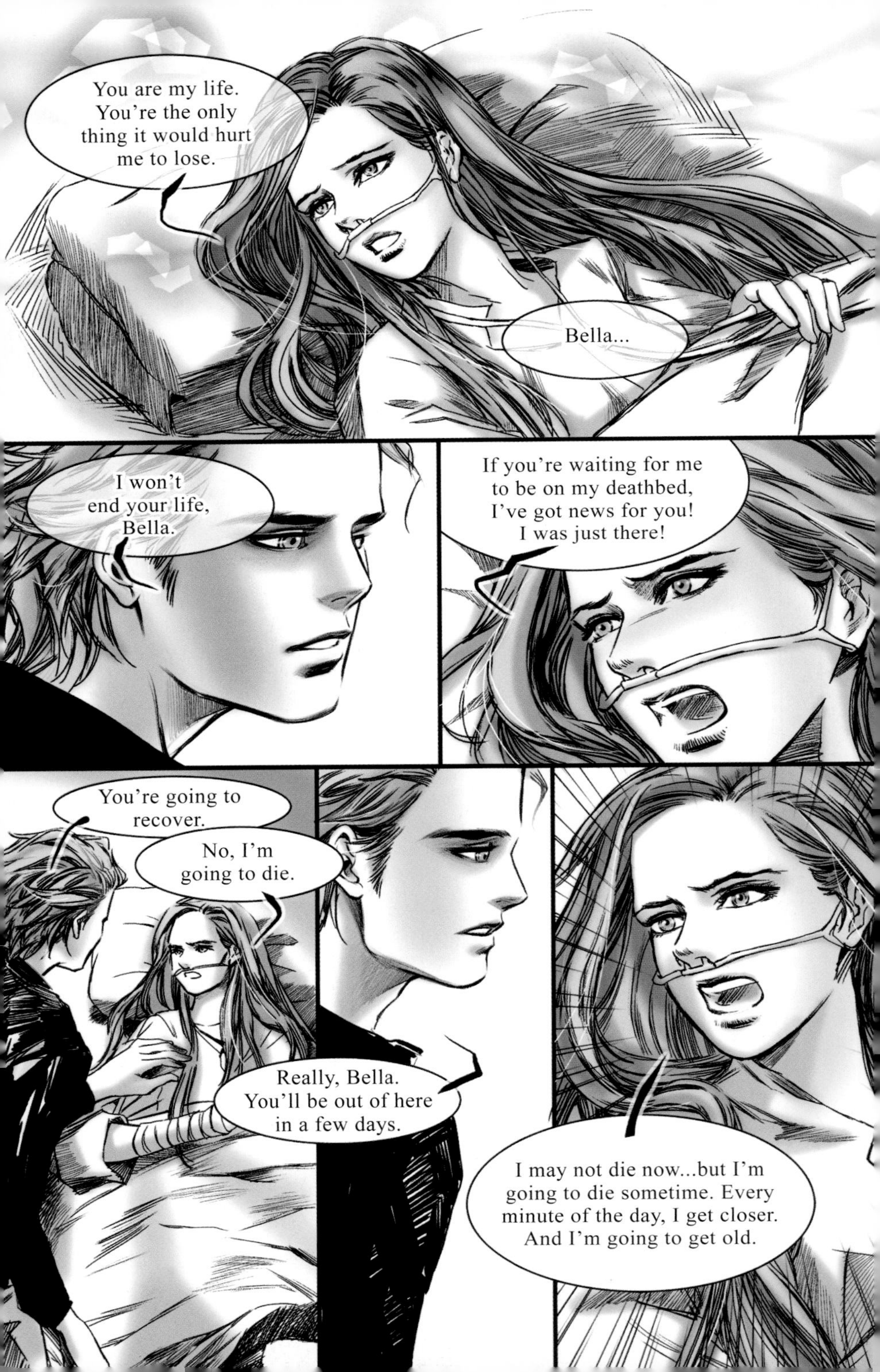
You are my life. You're the only thing it would hurt me to lose.
Bella...
I won't end your life, Bella.
If you're waiting for me to be on my deathbed, I've got news for you! I was just there!
You're going to recover.
No, I'm going to die.
Really, Bella. You'll be out of here in a few days.
I may not die now...but I'm going to die sometime. Every minute of the day, I get closer. And I'm going to get old.

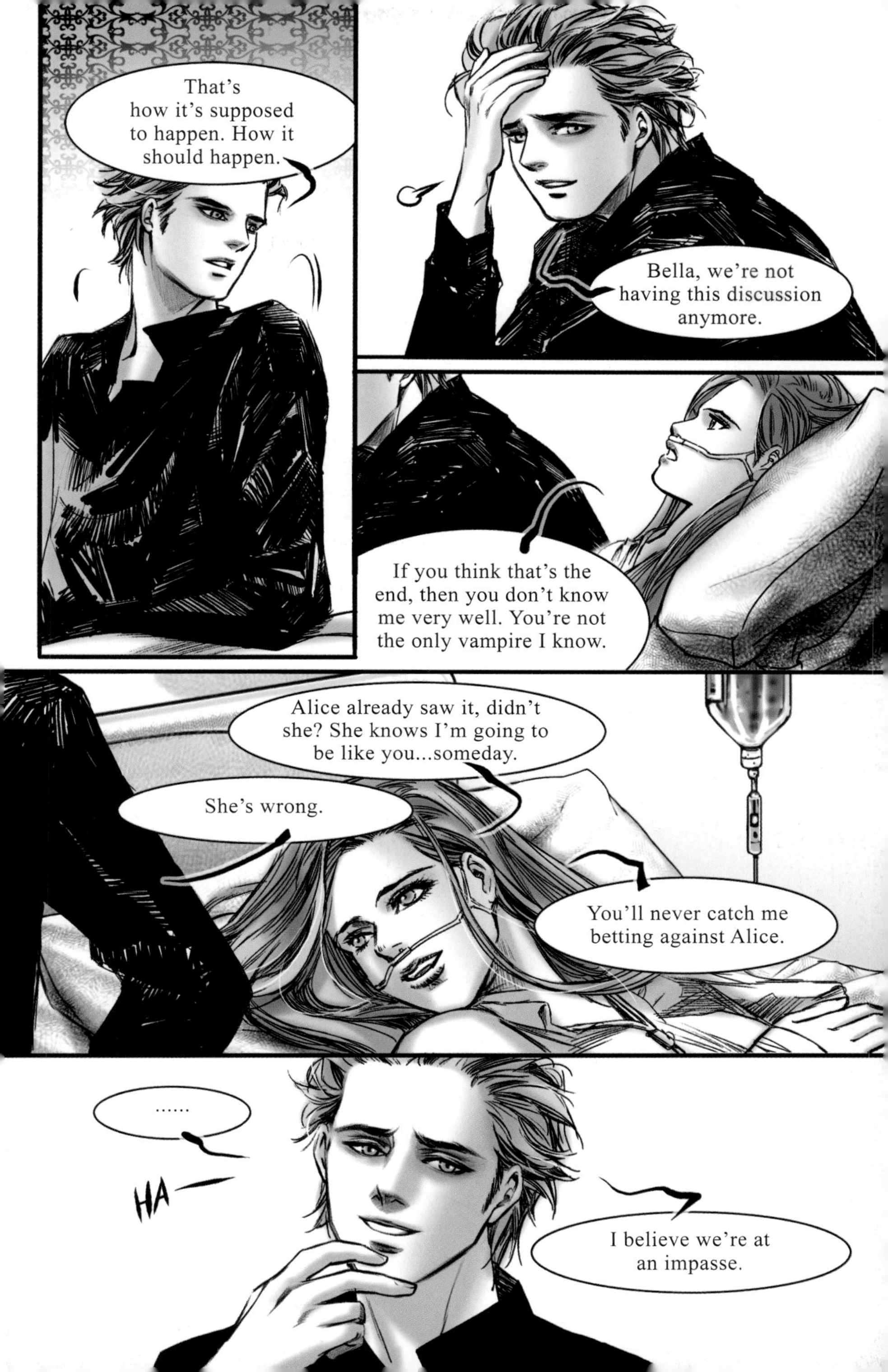
That's how it's supposed to happen. How it should happen.
Bella, we're not having this discussion anymore.
If you think that's the end, then you don't know me very well. You're not the only vampire I know.
Alice already saw it, didn't she? She knows I'm going to be like you...someday.
She's wrong.
You'll never catch me betting against Alice.
......
HA
I believe we're at an impasse.

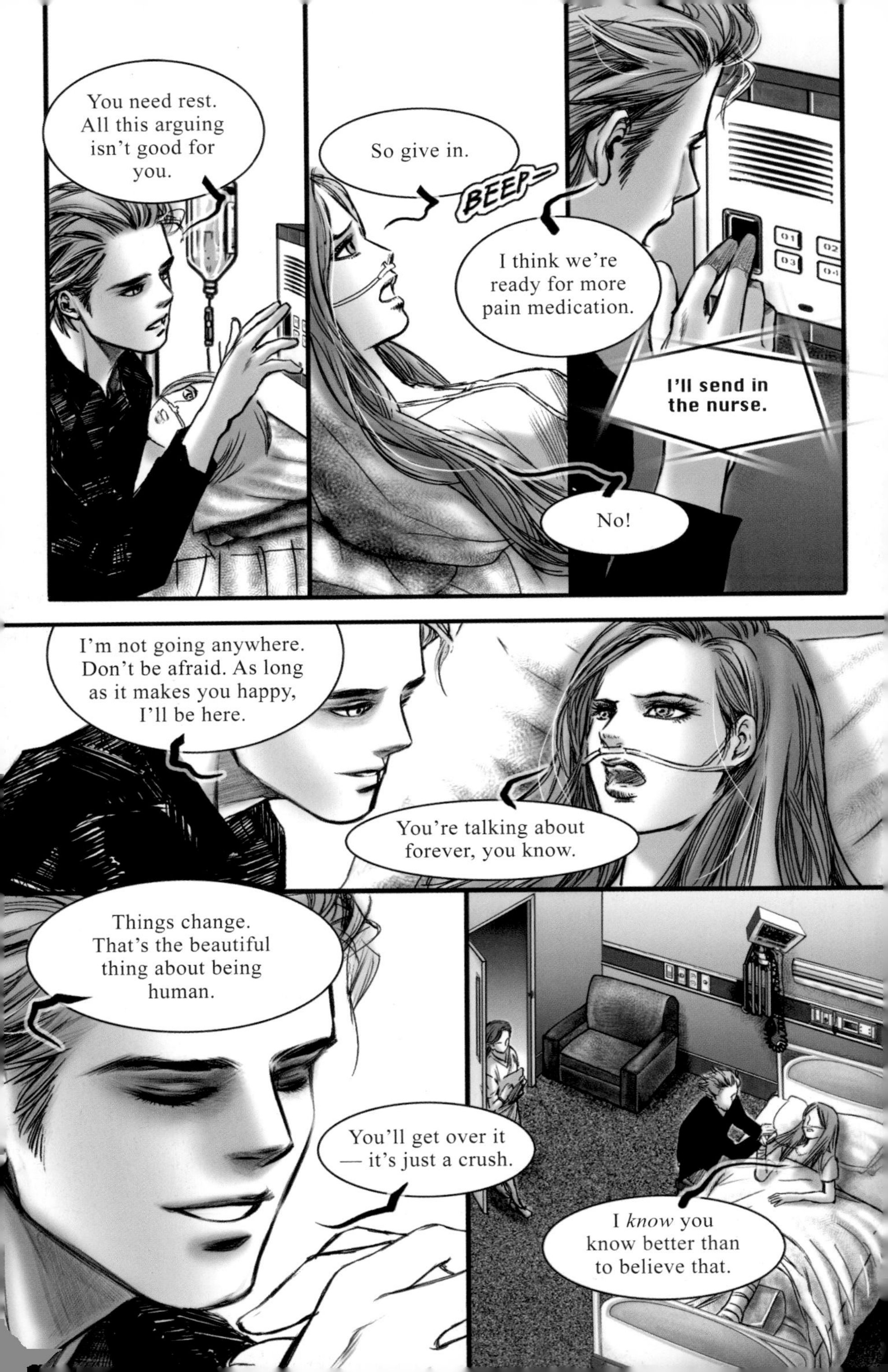
You need rest. All this arguing isn't good for you.
So give in.
BEEP—
I think we're ready for more pain medication.
I'll send in the nurse.
No!
I'm not going anywhere. Don't be afraid. As long as it makes you happy, I'll be here.
You're talking about forever, you know.
Things change. That's the beautiful thing about being human.
You'll get over it — it's just a crush.
I *know* you know better than to believe that.

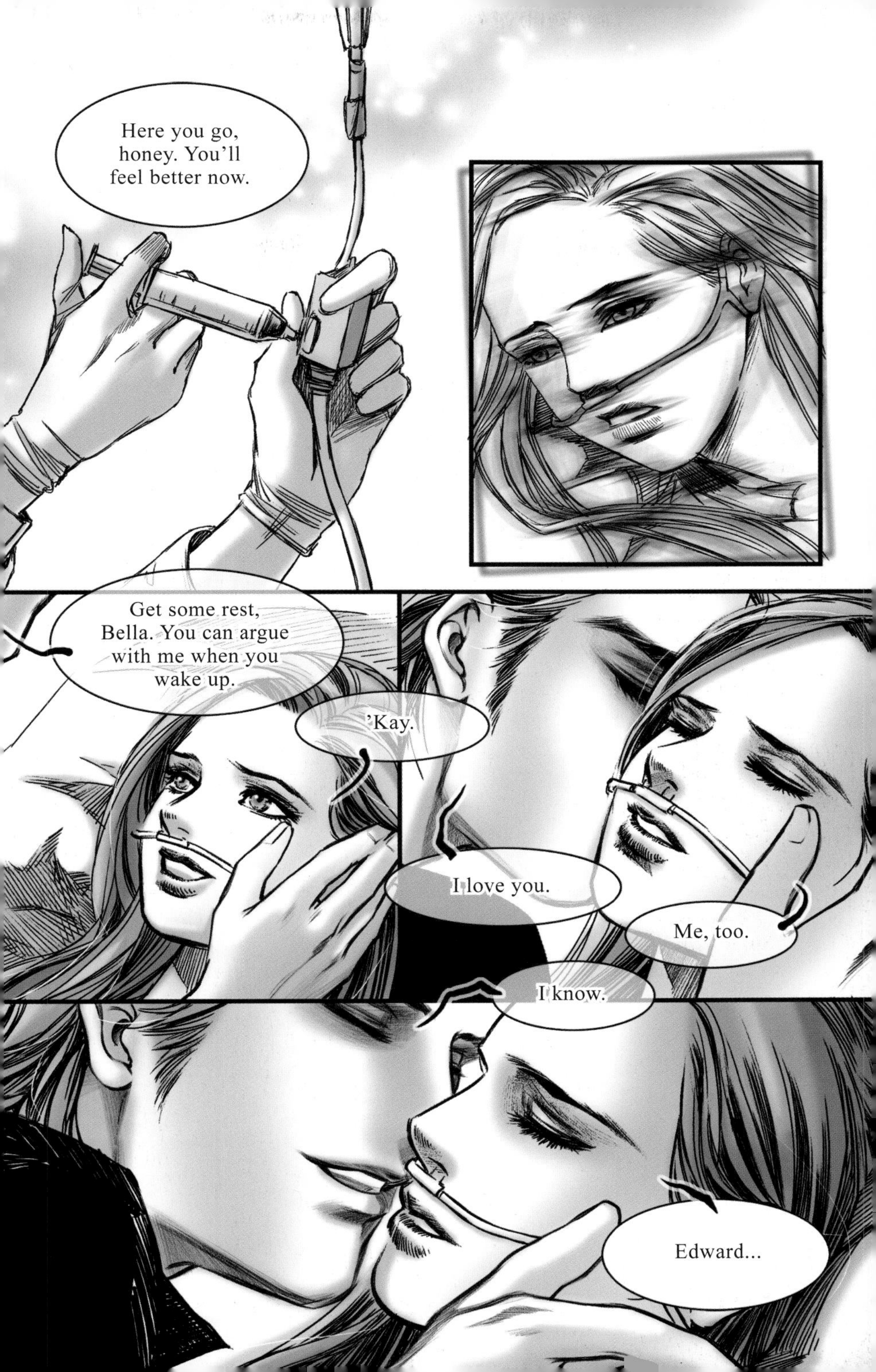
Here you go, honey. You'll feel better now.
Get some rest, Bella. You can argue with me when you wake up.
'Kay.
I love you.
Me, too.
I know.
Edward...

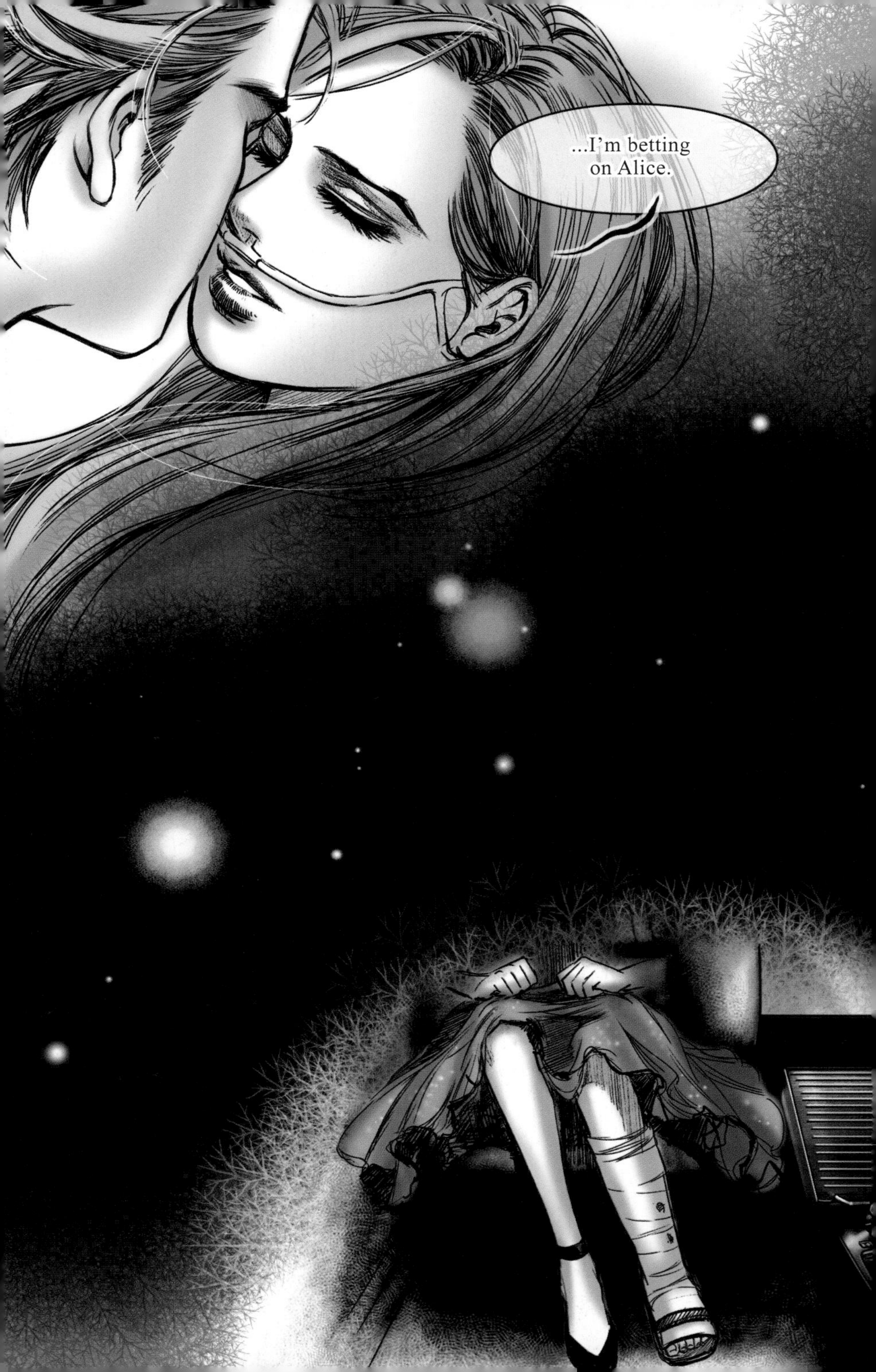
...I'm betting on Alice.

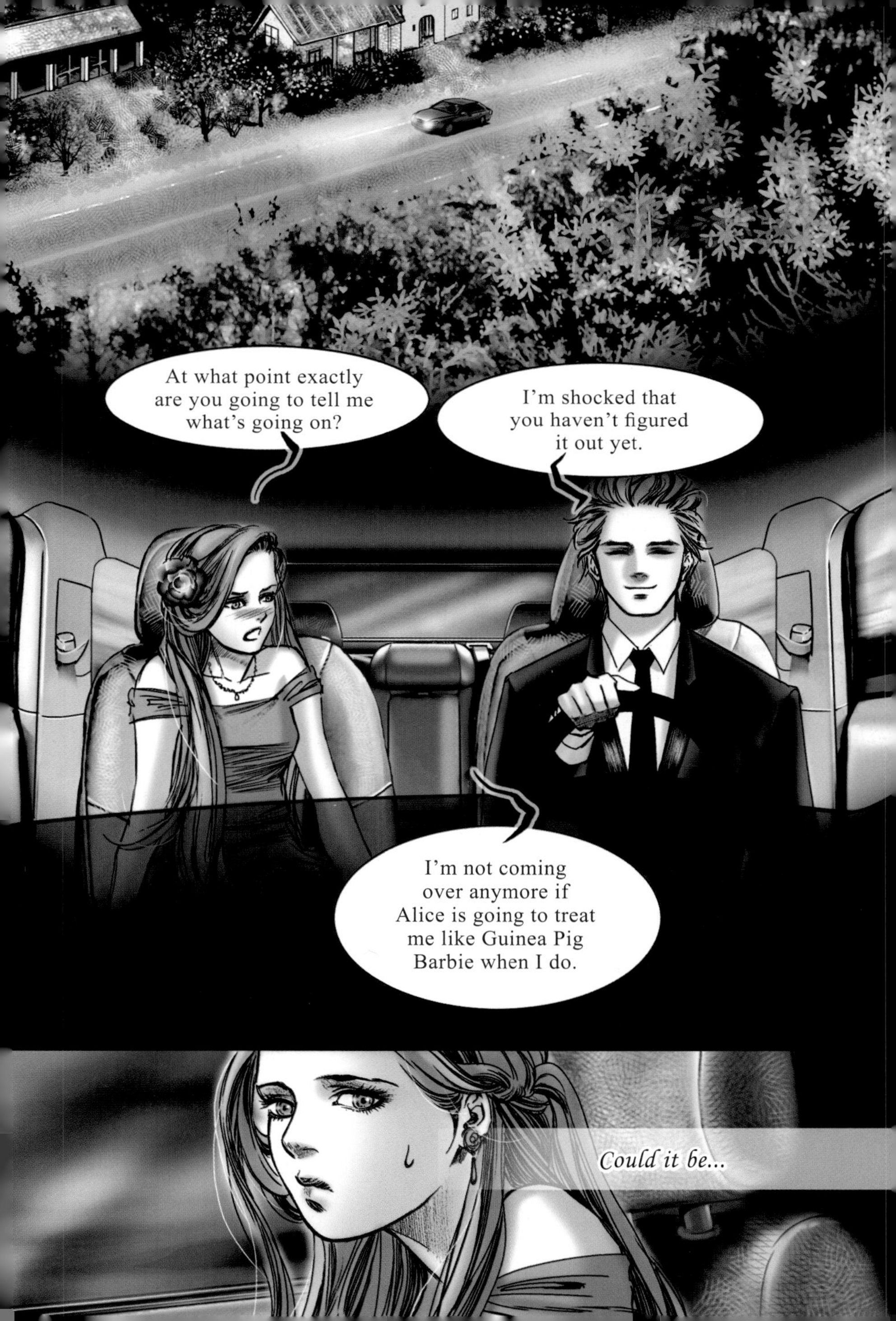
At what point exactly are you going to tell me what's going on?
I'm shocked that you haven't figured it out yet.
I'm not coming over anymore if Alice is going to treat me like Guinea Pig Barbie when I do.
Could it be...

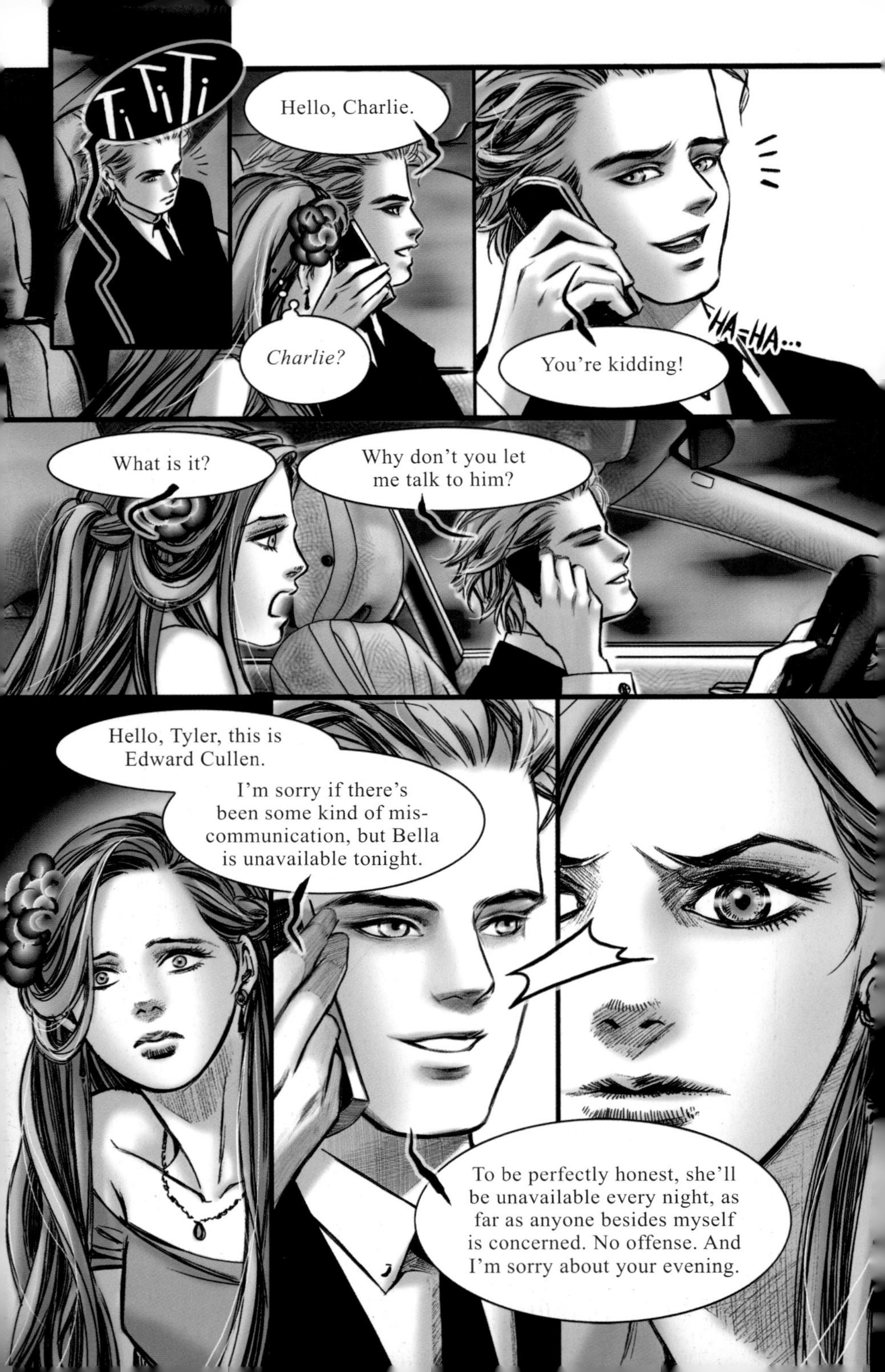
TiTiTi
Hello, Charlie.
*Charlie?*
You're kidding!
HA-HA...
What is it?
Why don't you let me talk to him?
Hello, Tyler, this is Edward Cullen.
I'm sorry if there's been some kind of miscommunication, but Bella is unavailable tonight.
To be perfectly honest, she'll be unavailable every night, as far as anyone besides myself is concerned. No offense. And I'm sorry about your evening.

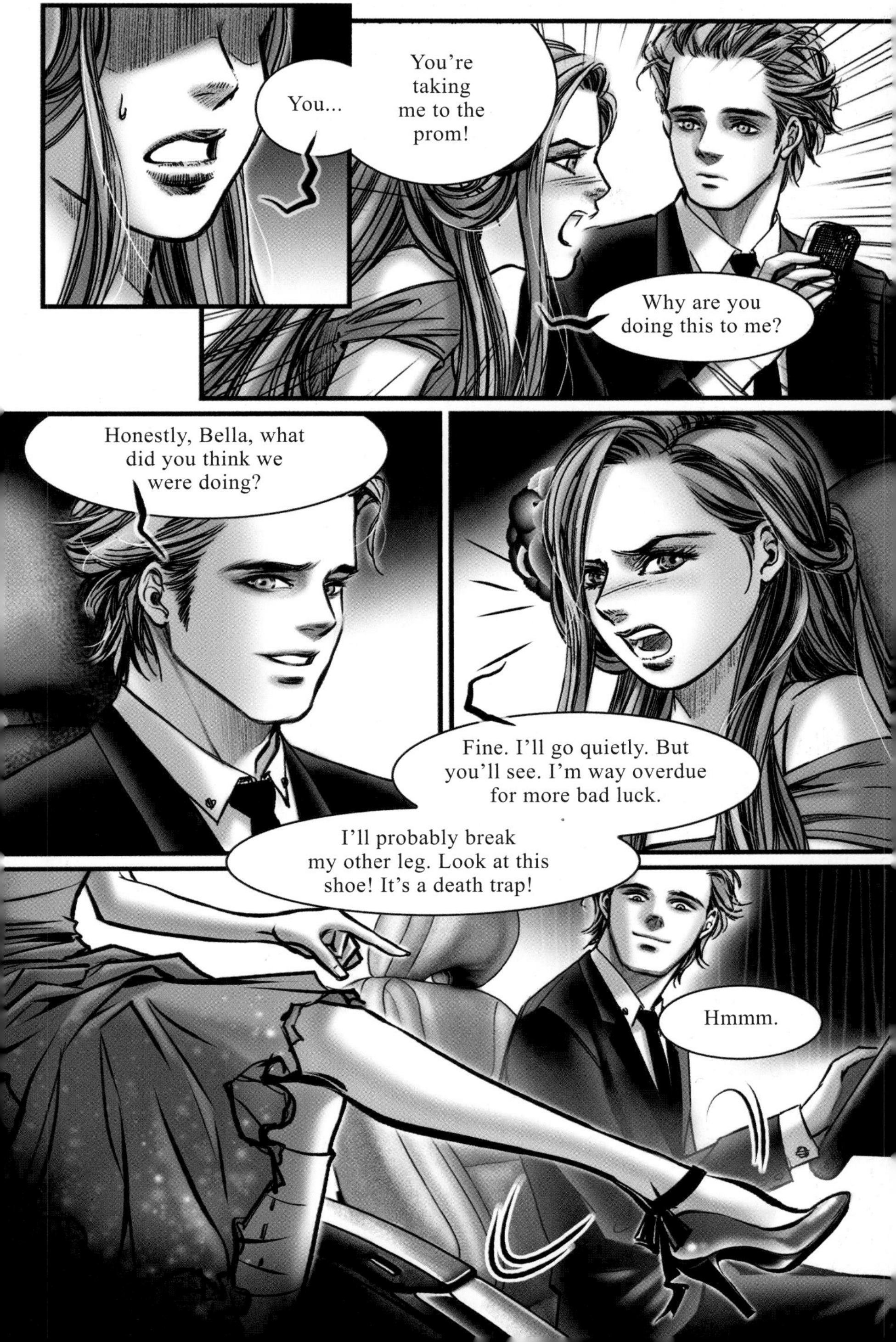
You...
You're taking me to the prom!
Why are you doing this to me?
Honestly, Bella, what did you think we were doing?
Fine. I'll go quietly. But you'll see. I'm way overdue for more bad luck.
I'll probably break my other leg. Look at this shoe! It's a death trap!
Hmmm.

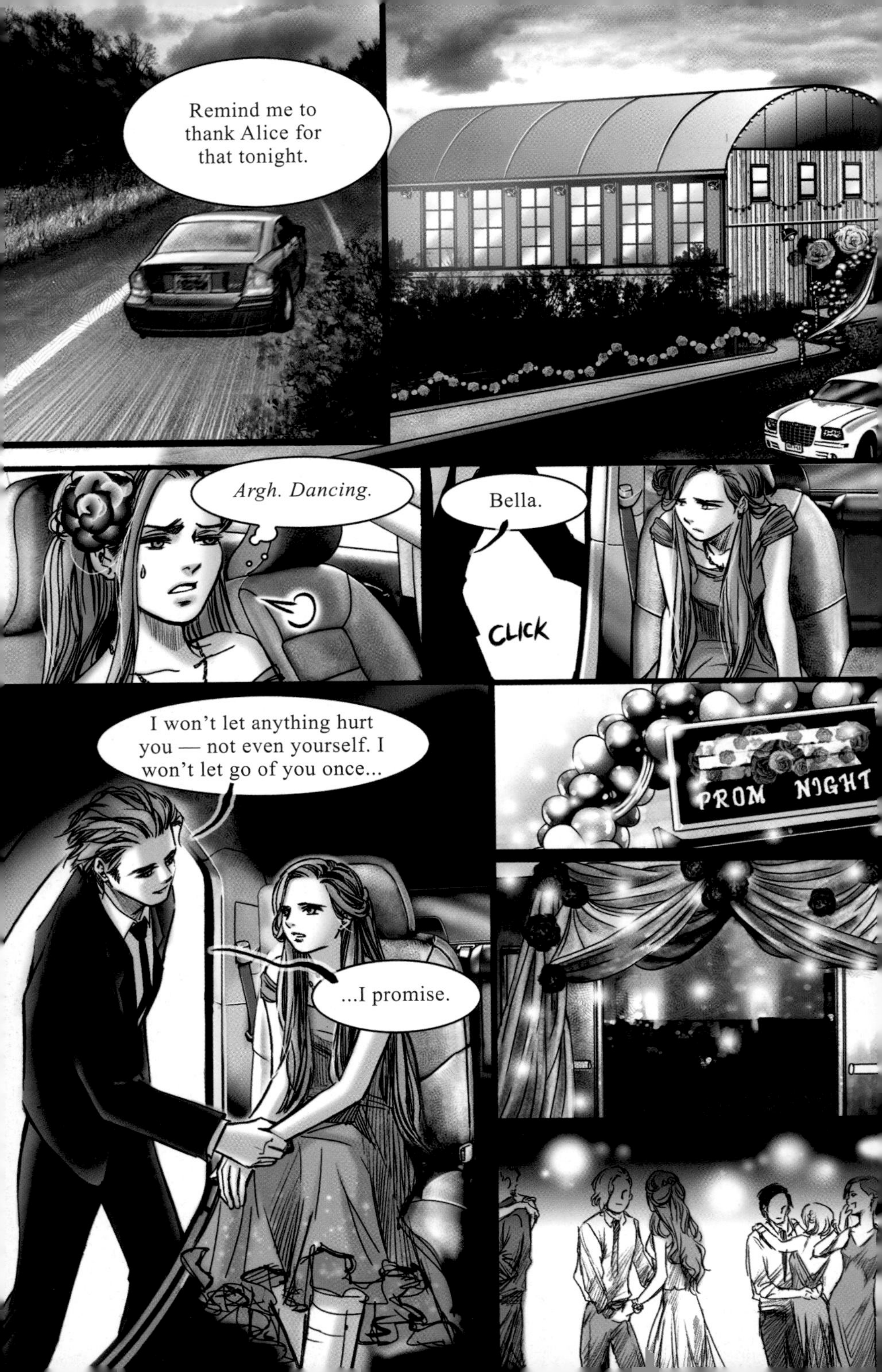
Remind me to thank Alice for that tonight.
Argh. Dancing.
Bella.
CLICK
I won't let anything hurt you — not even yourself. I won't let go of you once...
...I promise.
PROM NIGHT

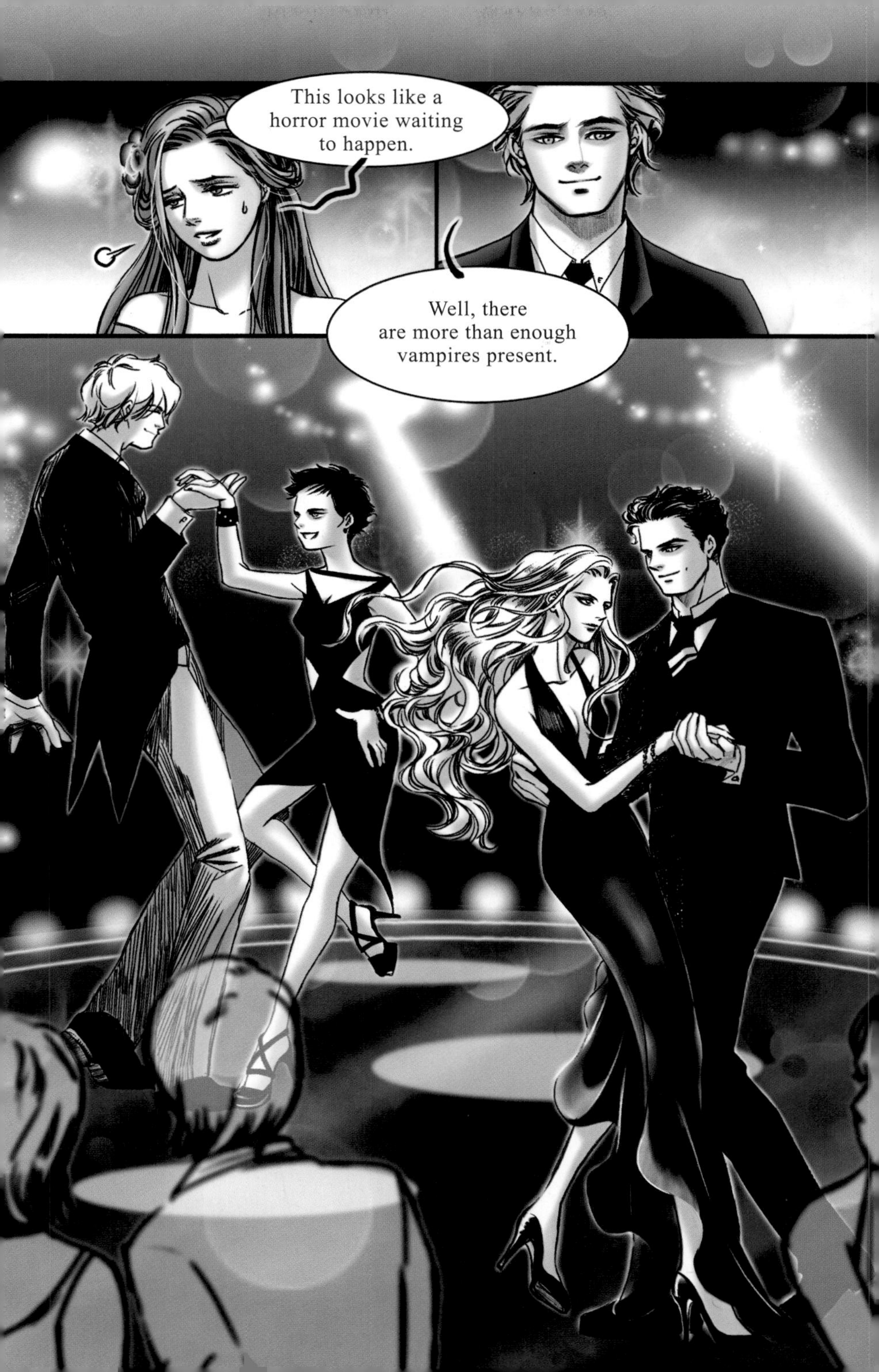
This looks like a horror movie waiting to happen.
Well, there are more than enough vampires present.

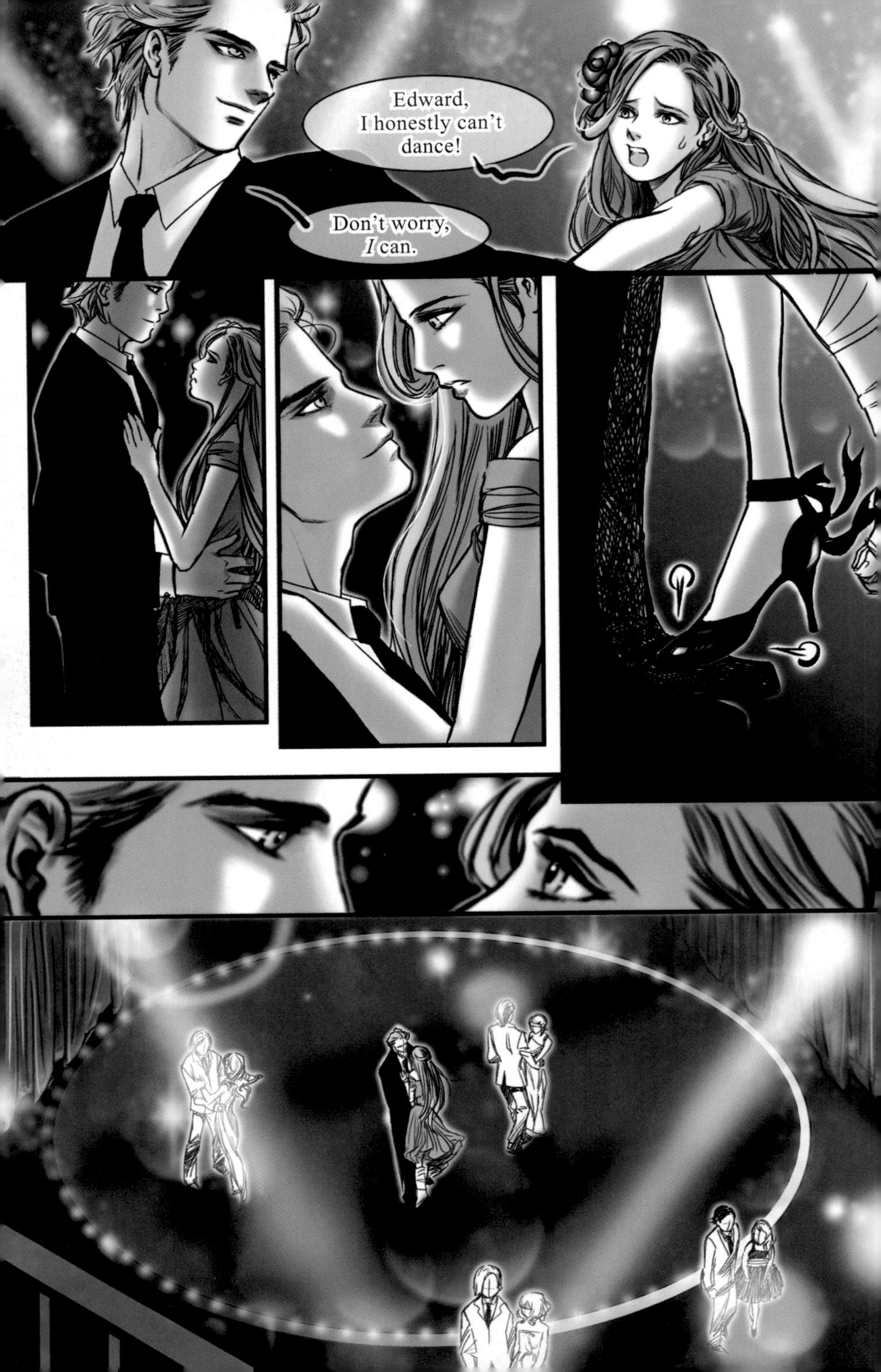

Edward,
I honestly can't
dance!
Don't worry,
*I* can.

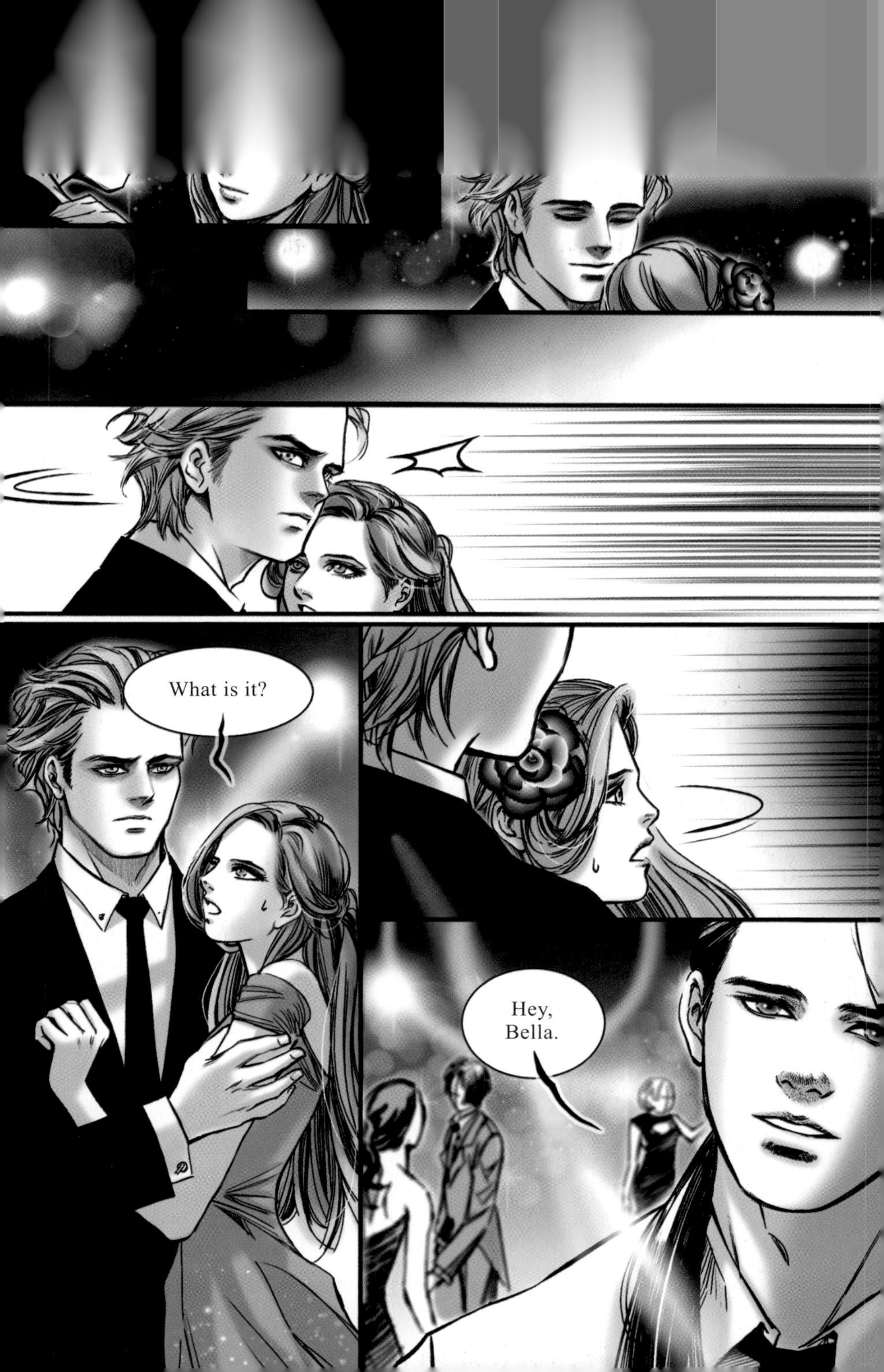
What is it?
Hey, Bella.

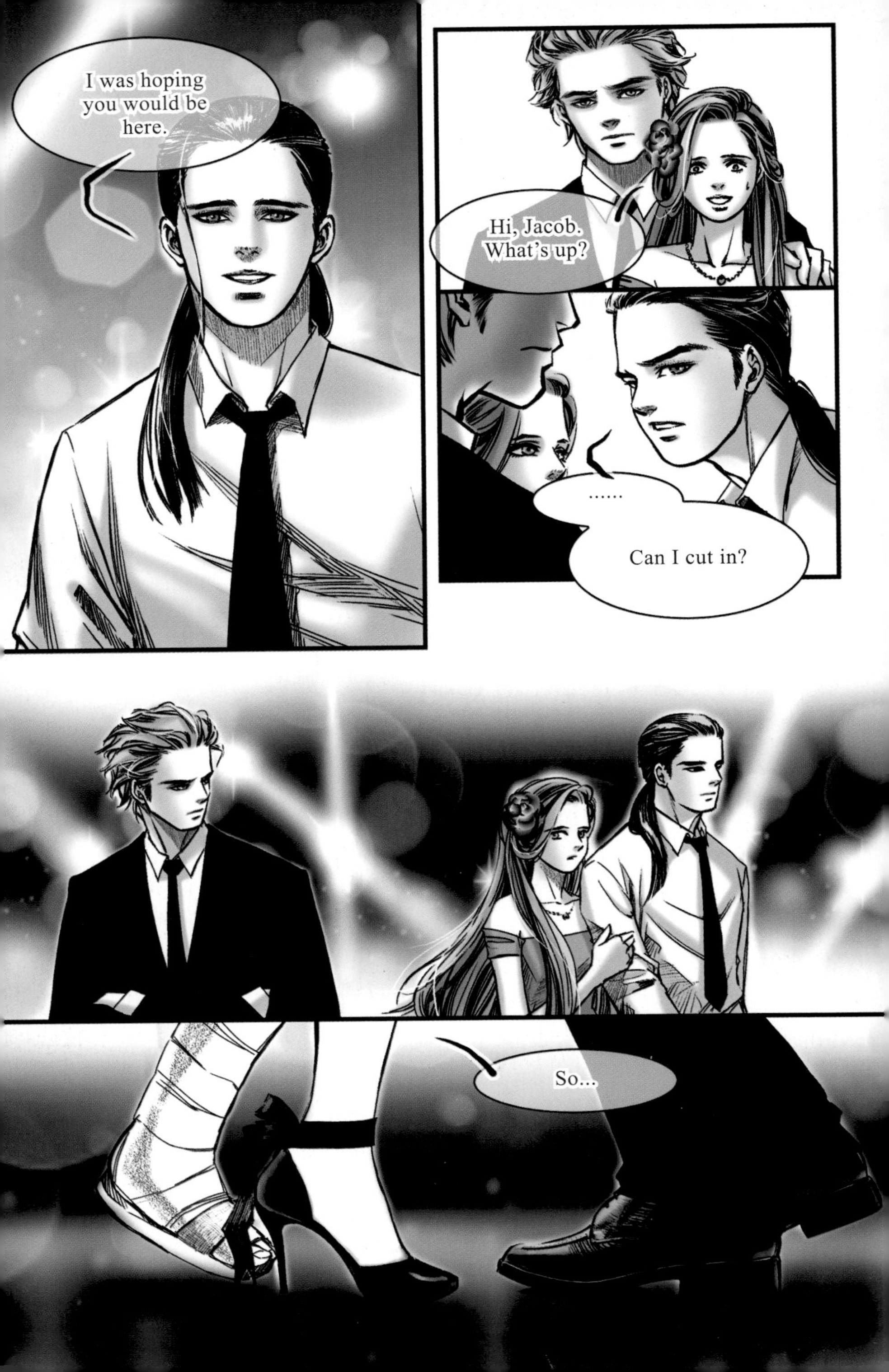
I was hoping you would be here.
Hi, Jacob. What's up?
......
Can I cut in?
So...

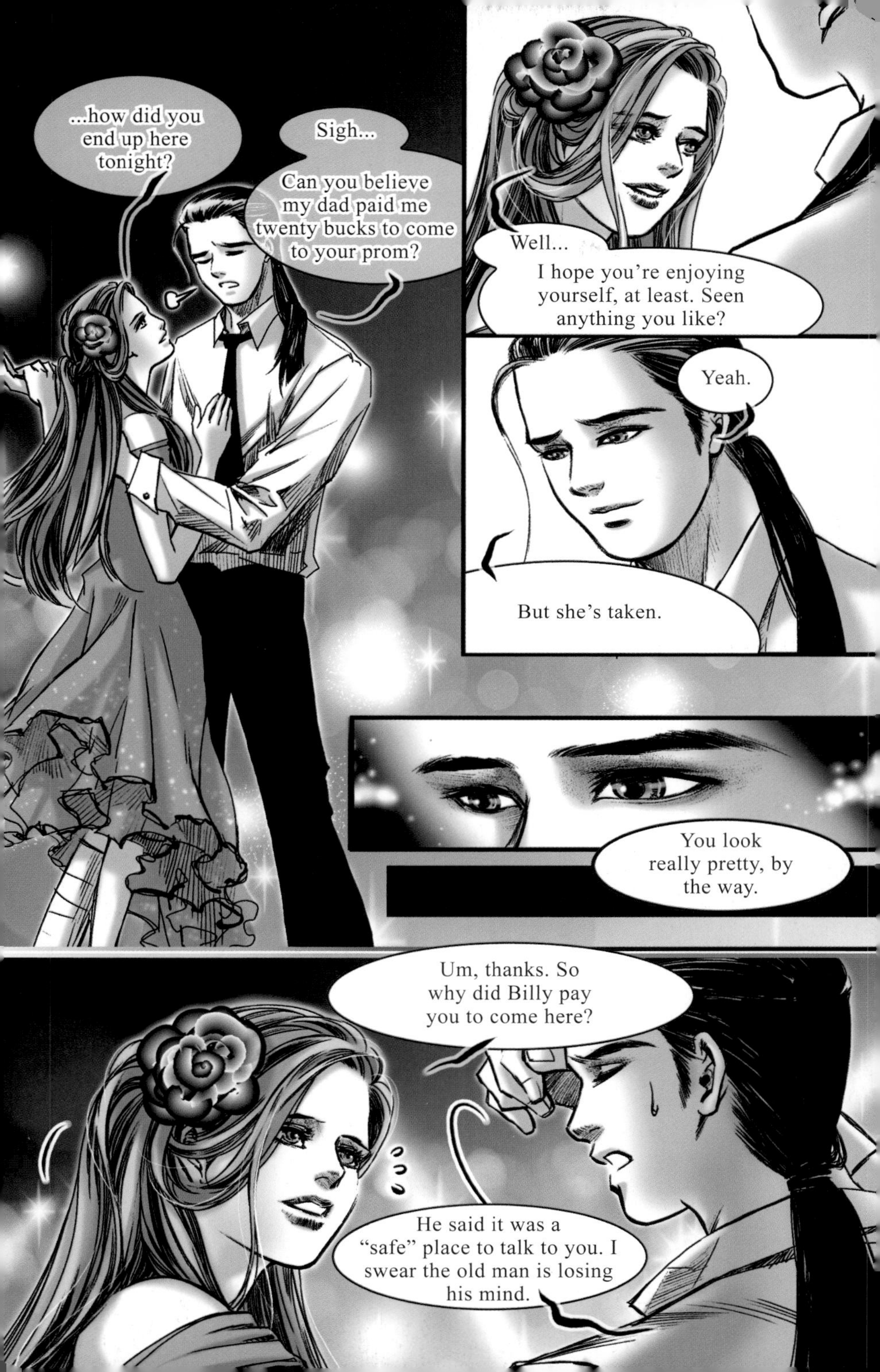
...how did you end up here tonight?
Sigh...
Can you believe my dad paid me twenty bucks to come to your prom?
Well...
I hope you're enjoying yourself, at least. Seen anything you like?
Yeah.
But she's taken.
You look really pretty, by the way.
Um, thanks. So why did Billy pay you to come here?
He said it was a "safe" place to talk to you. I swear the old man is losing his mind.

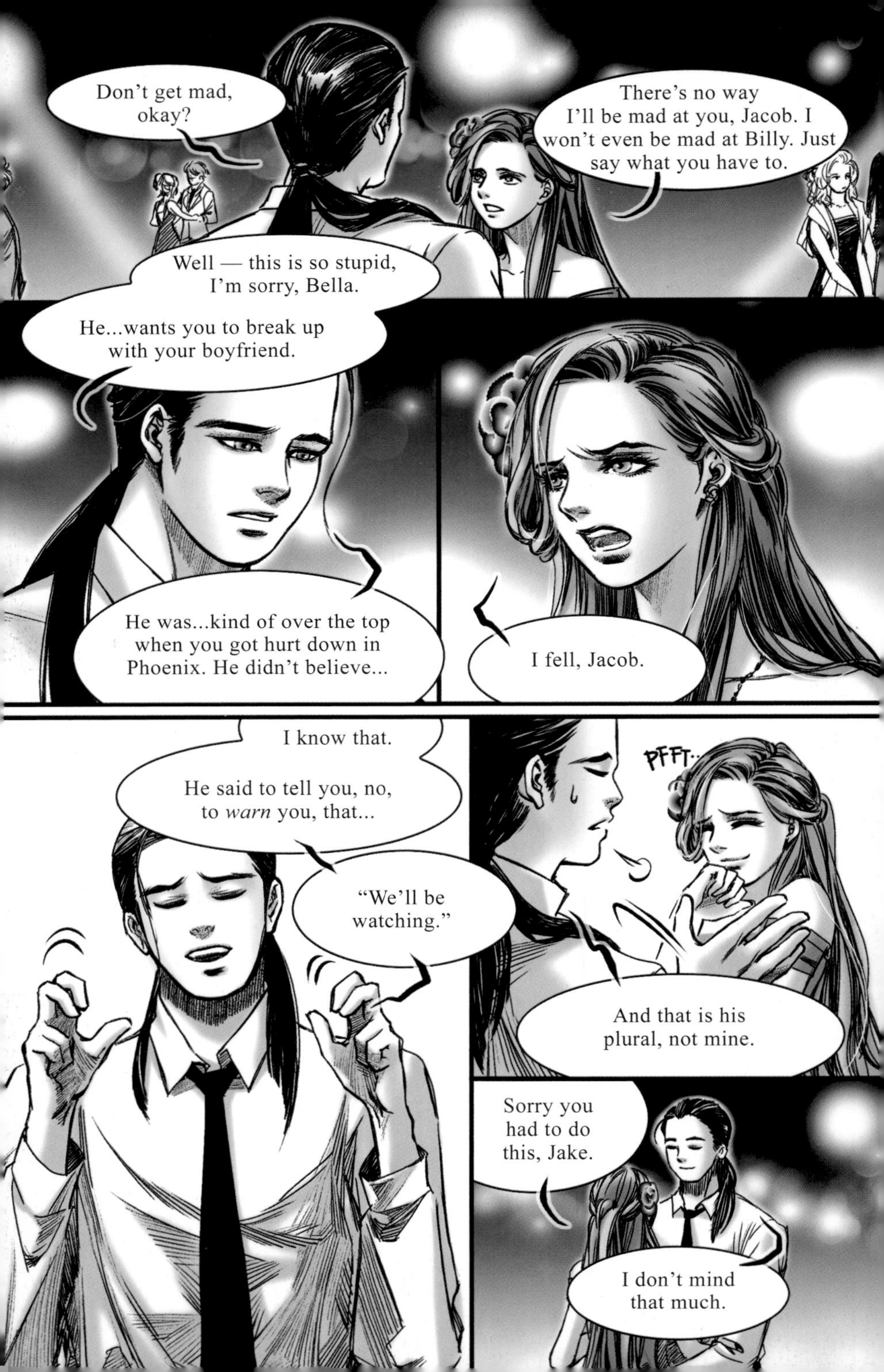
Don't get mad, okay?
There's no way I'll be mad at you, Jacob. I won't even be mad at Billy. Just say what you have to.
Well — this is so stupid, I'm sorry, Bella.
He...wants you to break up with your boyfriend.
He was...kind of over the top when you got hurt down in Phoenix. He didn't believe...
I fell, Jacob.
I know that.
He said to tell you, no, to *warn* you, that...
"We'll be watching."
PFFT...
And that is his plural, not mine.
Sorry you had to do this, Jake.
I don't mind that much.

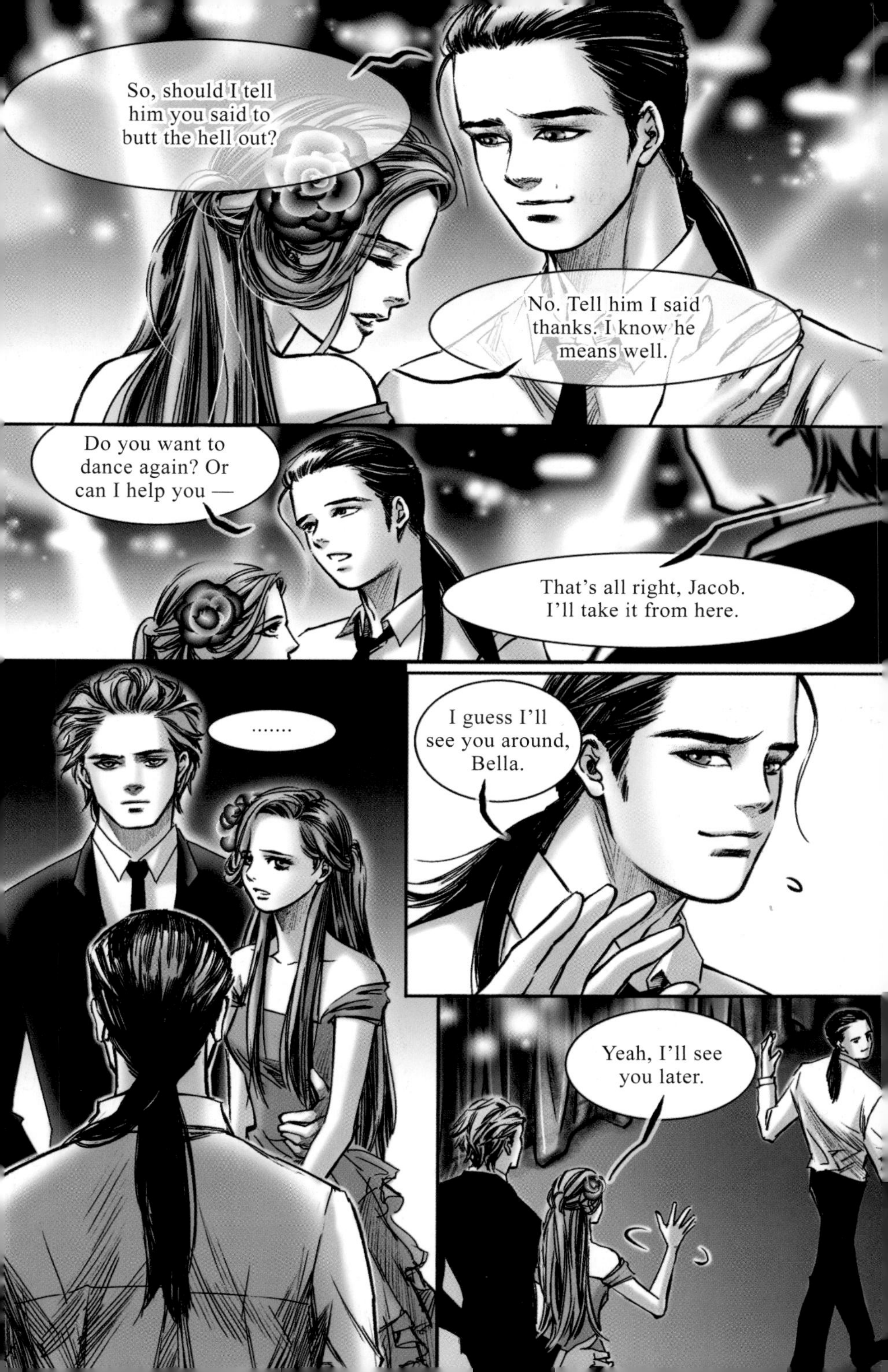
So, should I tell him you said to butt the hell out?
No. Tell him I said thanks. I know he means well.
Do you want to dance again? Or can I help you —
That's all right, Jacob. I'll take it from here.
.......
I guess I'll see you around, Bella.
Yeah, I'll see you later.

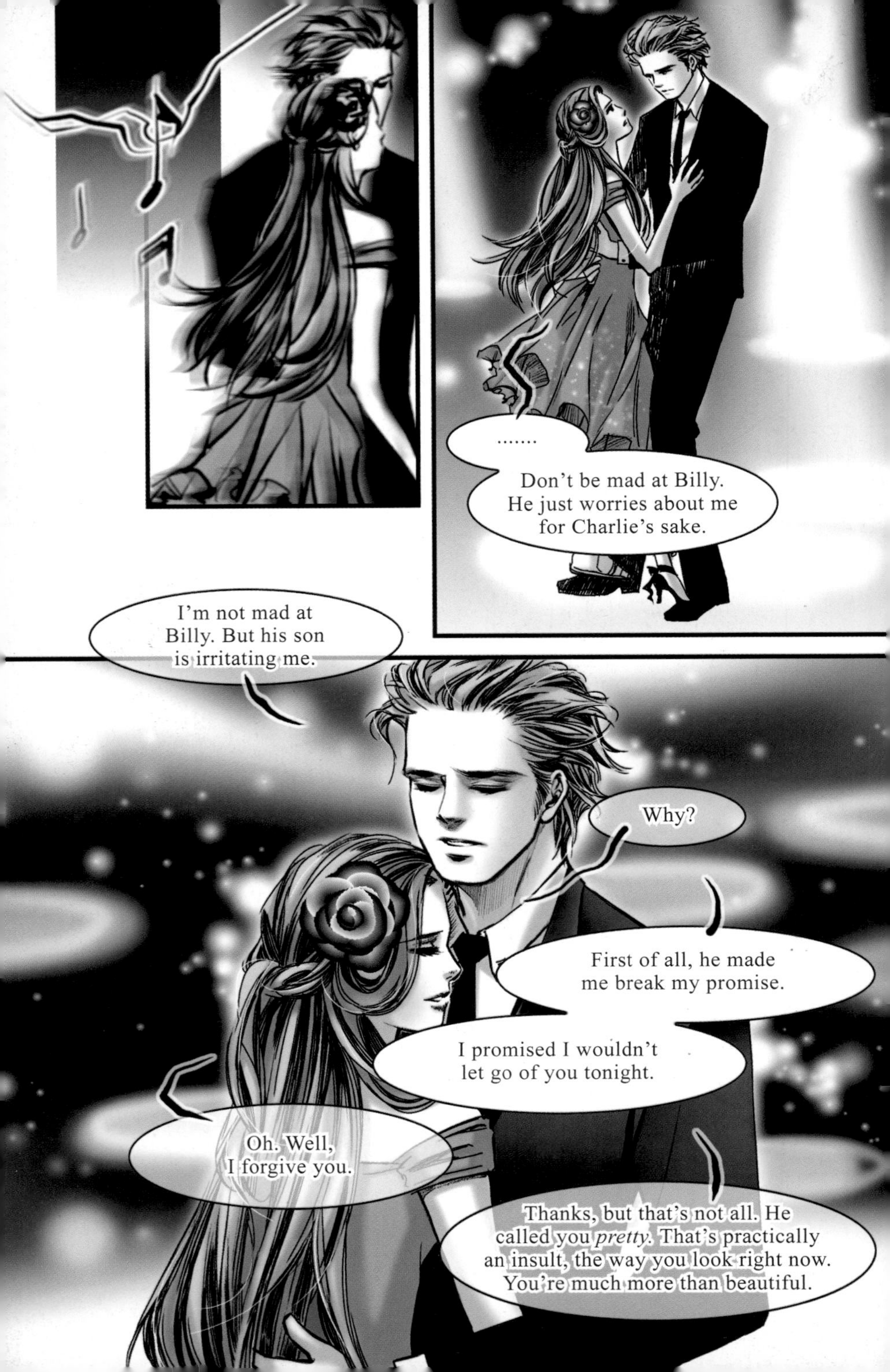
.......
Don't be mad at Billy. He just worries about me for Charlie's sake.
I'm not mad at Billy. But his son is irritating me.
Why?
First of all, he made me break my promise.
I promised I wouldn't let go of you tonight.
Oh. Well, I forgive you.
Thanks, but that's not all. He called you *pretty*. That's practically an insult, the way you look right now. You're much more than beautiful.

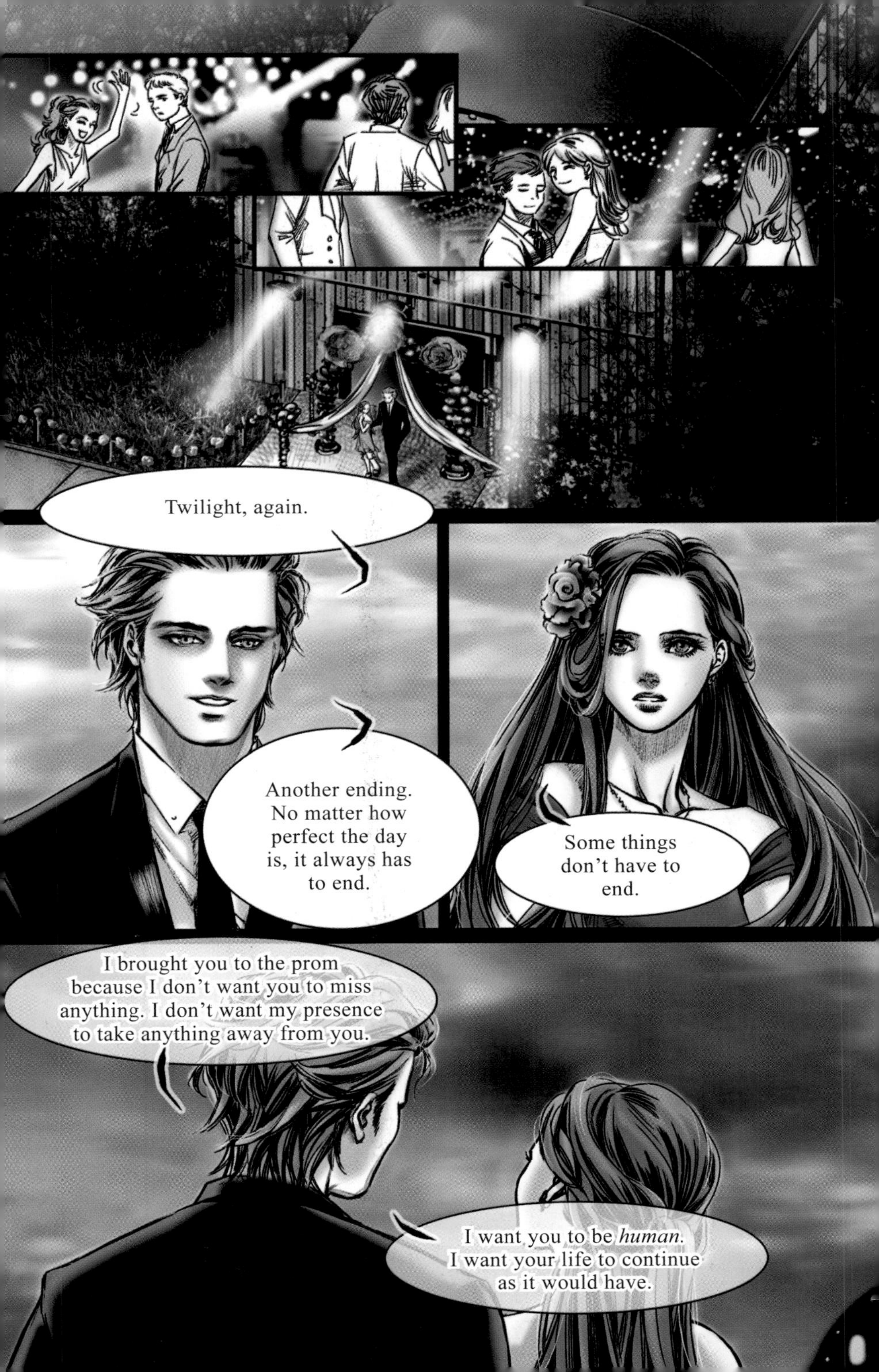
Twilight, again.
Another ending. No matter how perfect the day is, it always has to end.
Some things don't have to end.
I brought you to the prom because I don't want you to miss anything. I don't want my presence to take anything away from you.
I want you to be *human*. I want your life to continue as it would have.

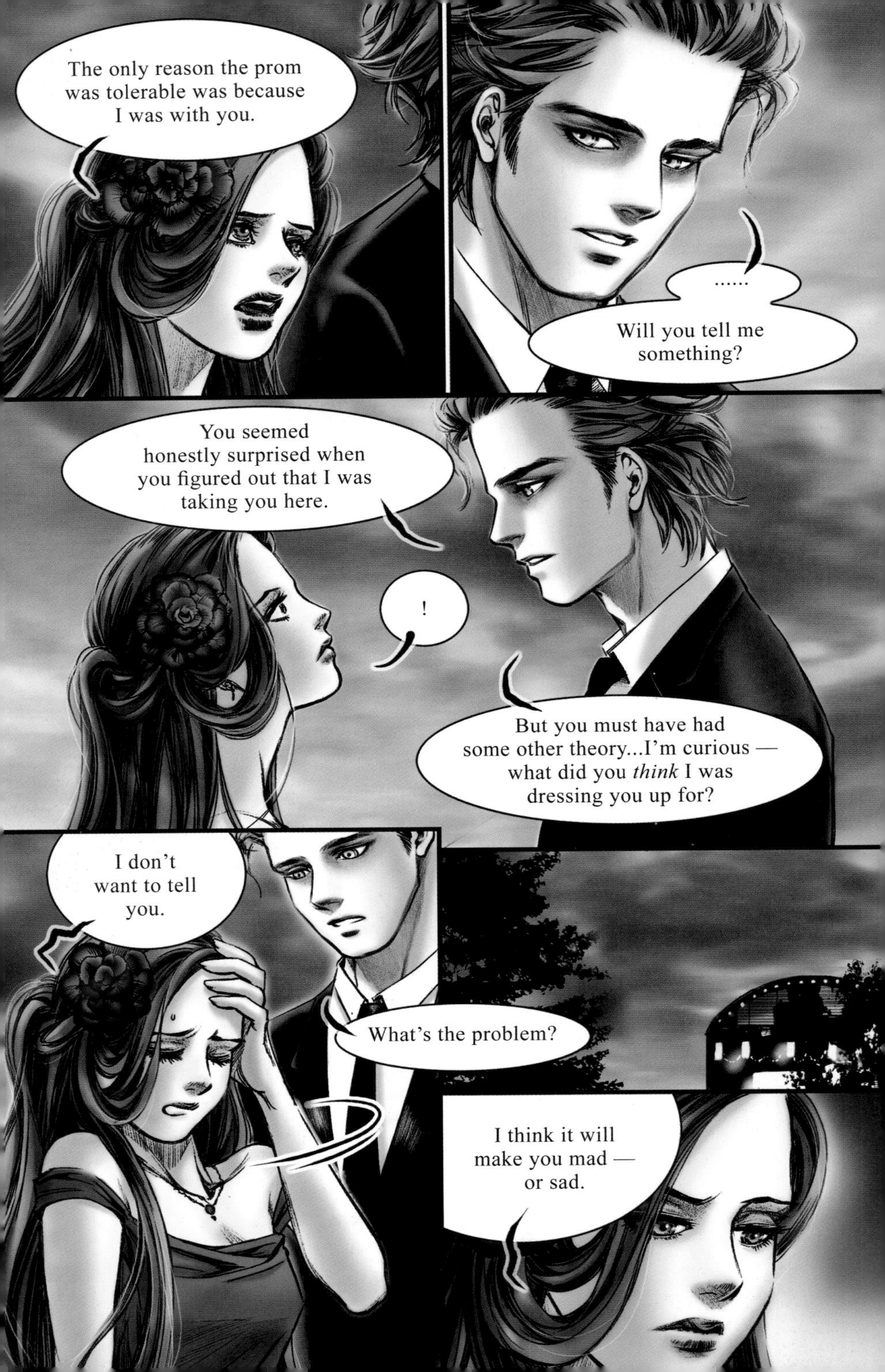
The only reason the prom was tolerable was because I was with you.
......
Will you tell me something?
You seemed honestly surprised when you figured out that I was taking you here.
!
But you must have had some other theory...I'm curious — what did you *think* I was dressing you up for?
I don't want to tell you.
What's the problem?
I think it will make you mad — or sad.

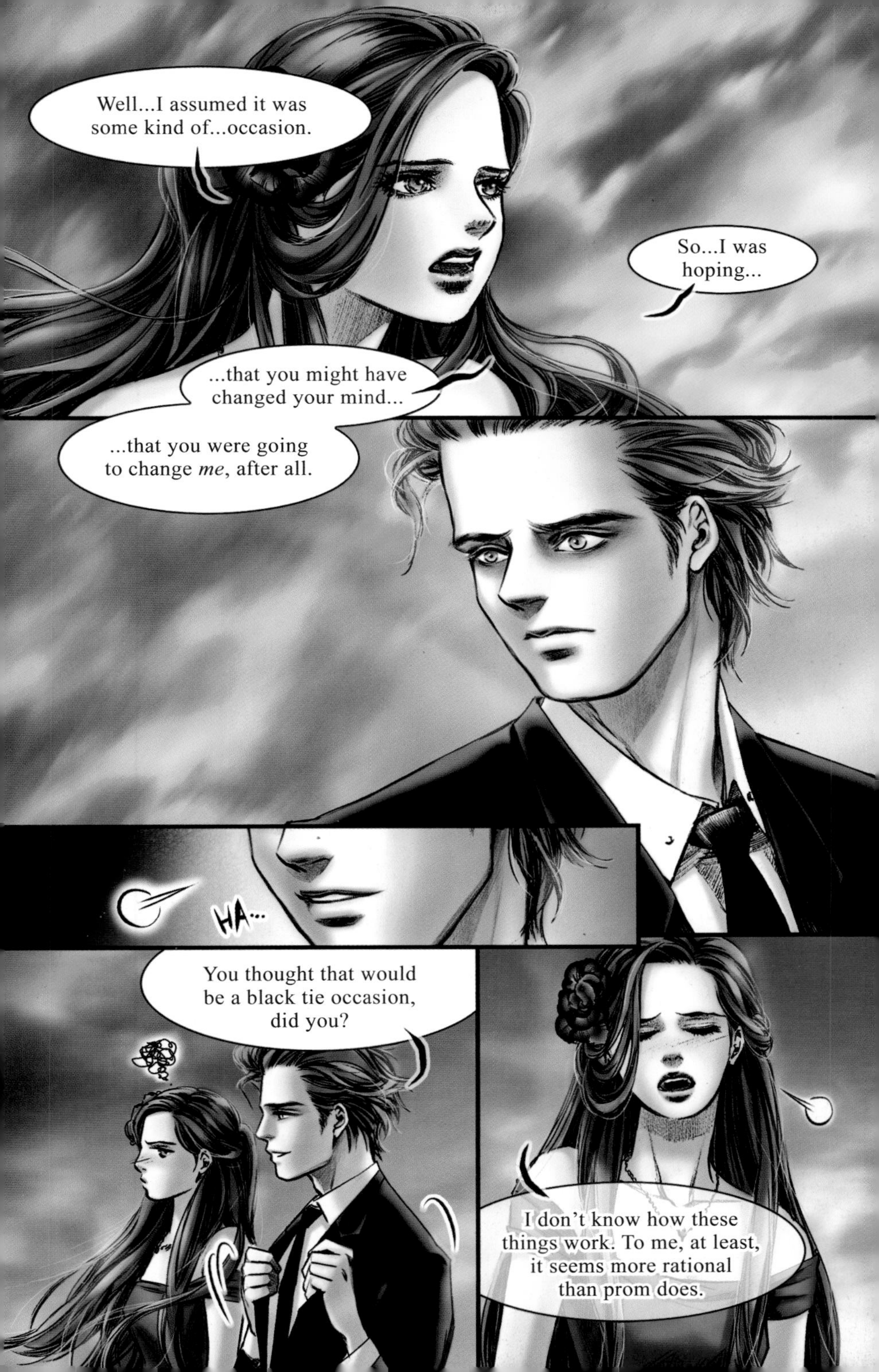
Well...I assumed it was some kind of...occasion.
So...I was hoping...
...that you might have changed your mind...
...that you were going to change *me*, after all.
HA...
You thought that would be a black tie occasion, did you?
I don't know how these things work. To me, at least, it seems more rational than prom does.

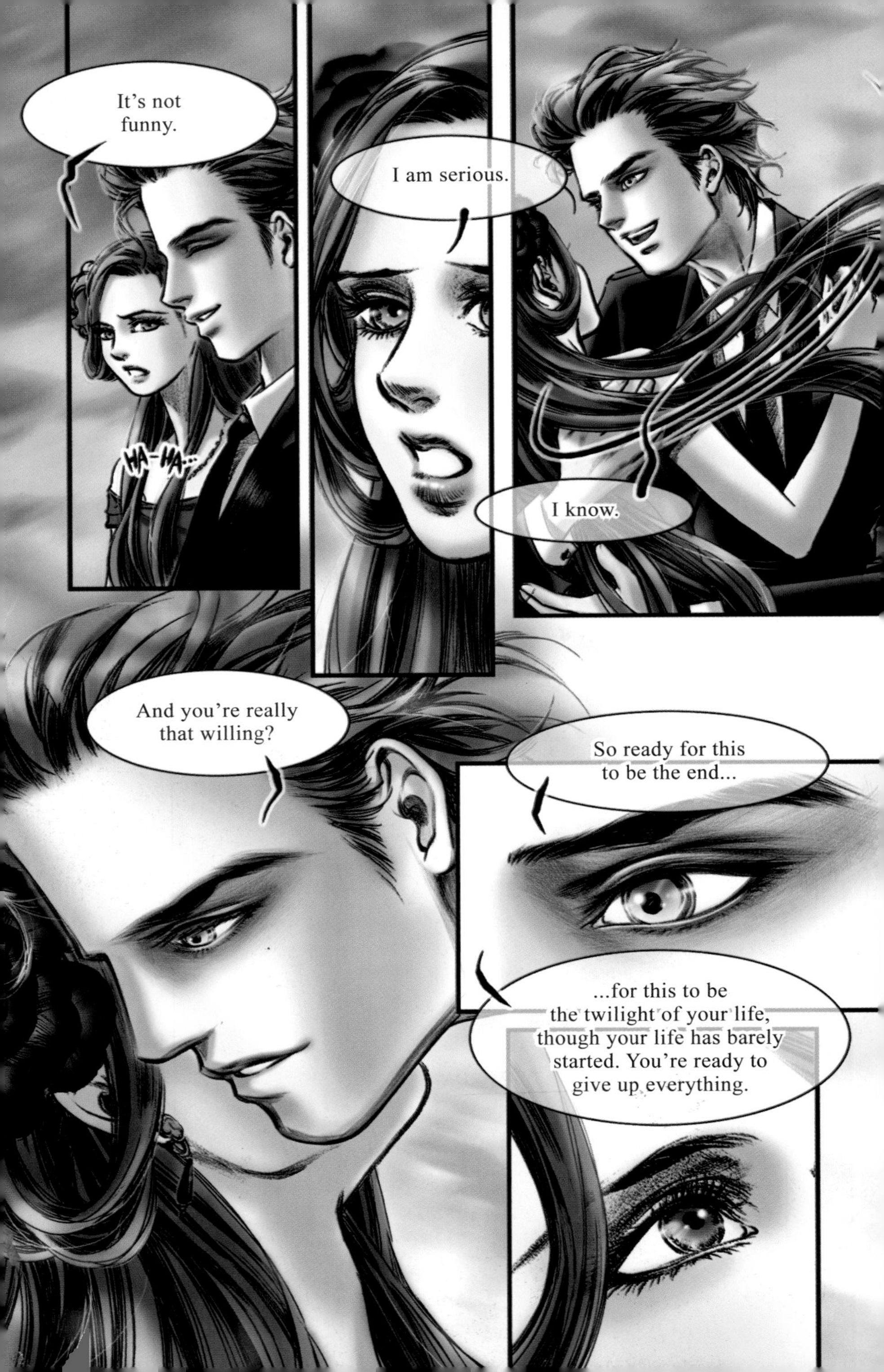
It's not funny.
HA-HA...
I am serious.
I know.
And you're really that willing?
So ready for this to be the end...
...for this to be the twilight of your life, though your life has barely started. You're ready to give up everything.

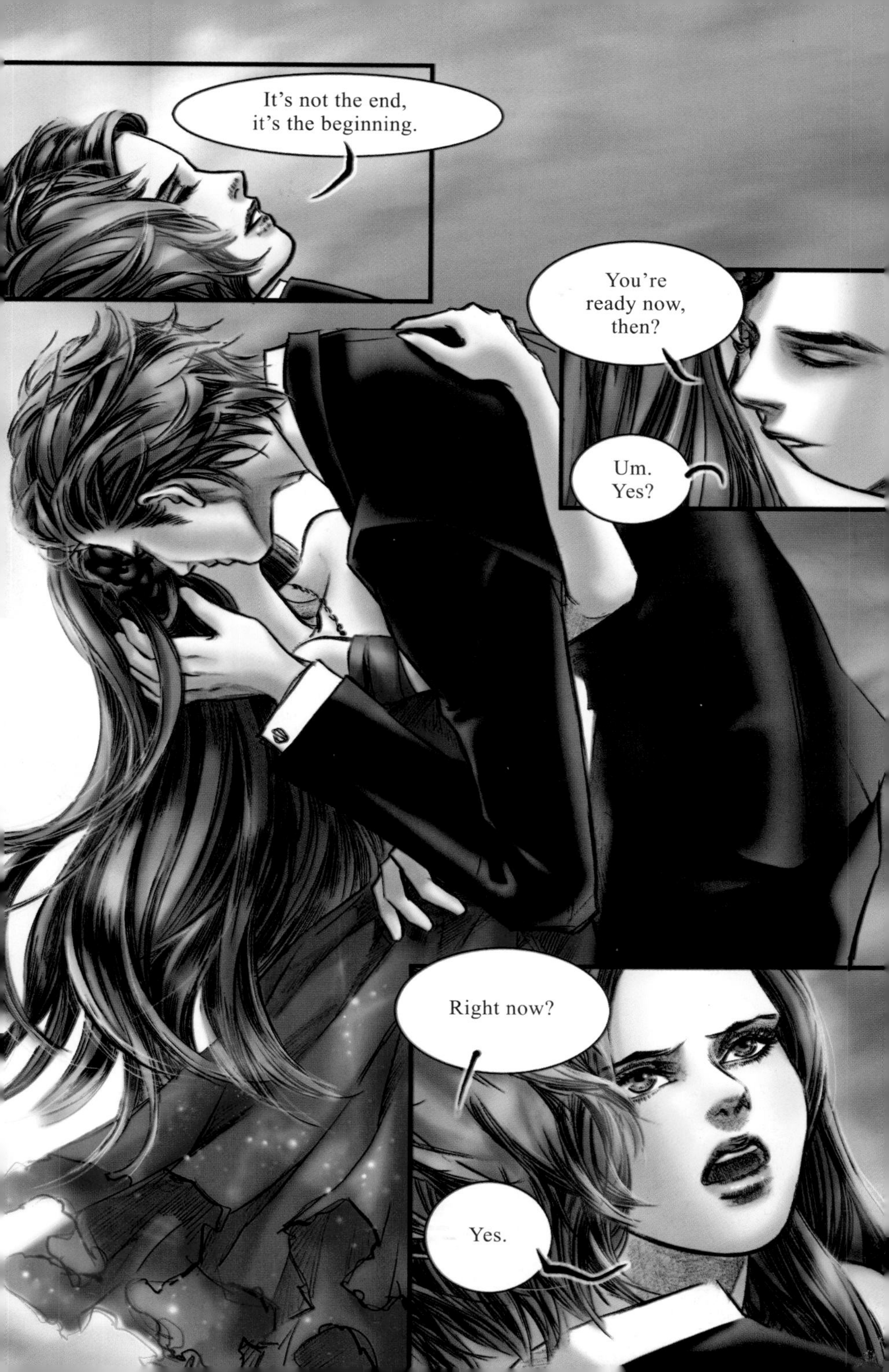
It's not the end,
it's the beginning.
You're
ready now,
then?
Um.
Yes?
Right now?
Yes.

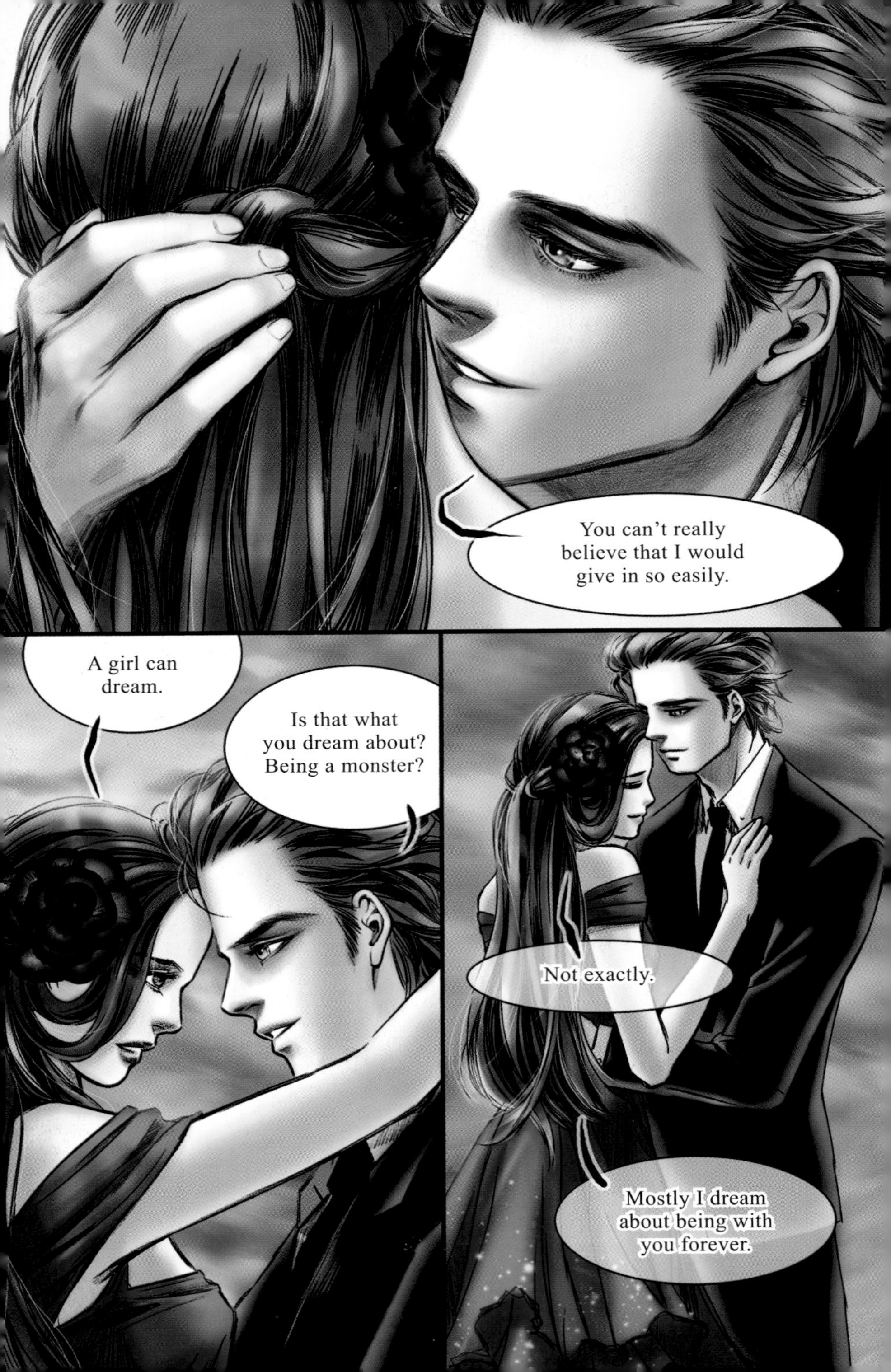
You can't really believe that I would give in so easily.
A girl can dream.
Is that what you dream about? Being a monster?
Not exactly.
Mostly I dream about being with you forever.

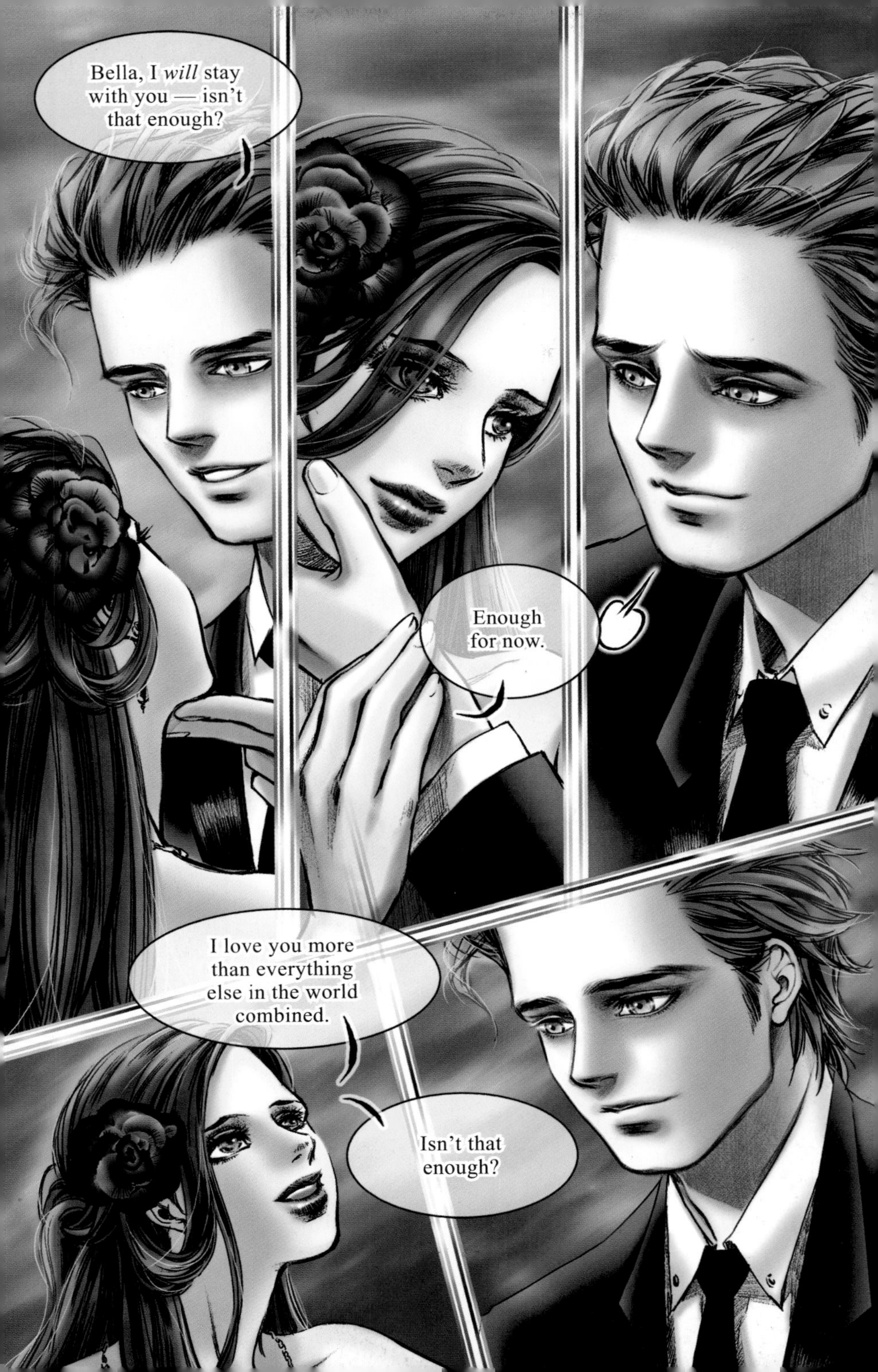

Bella, I *will* stay with you — isn't that enough?
Enough for now.
I love you more than everything else in the world combined.
Isn't that enough?

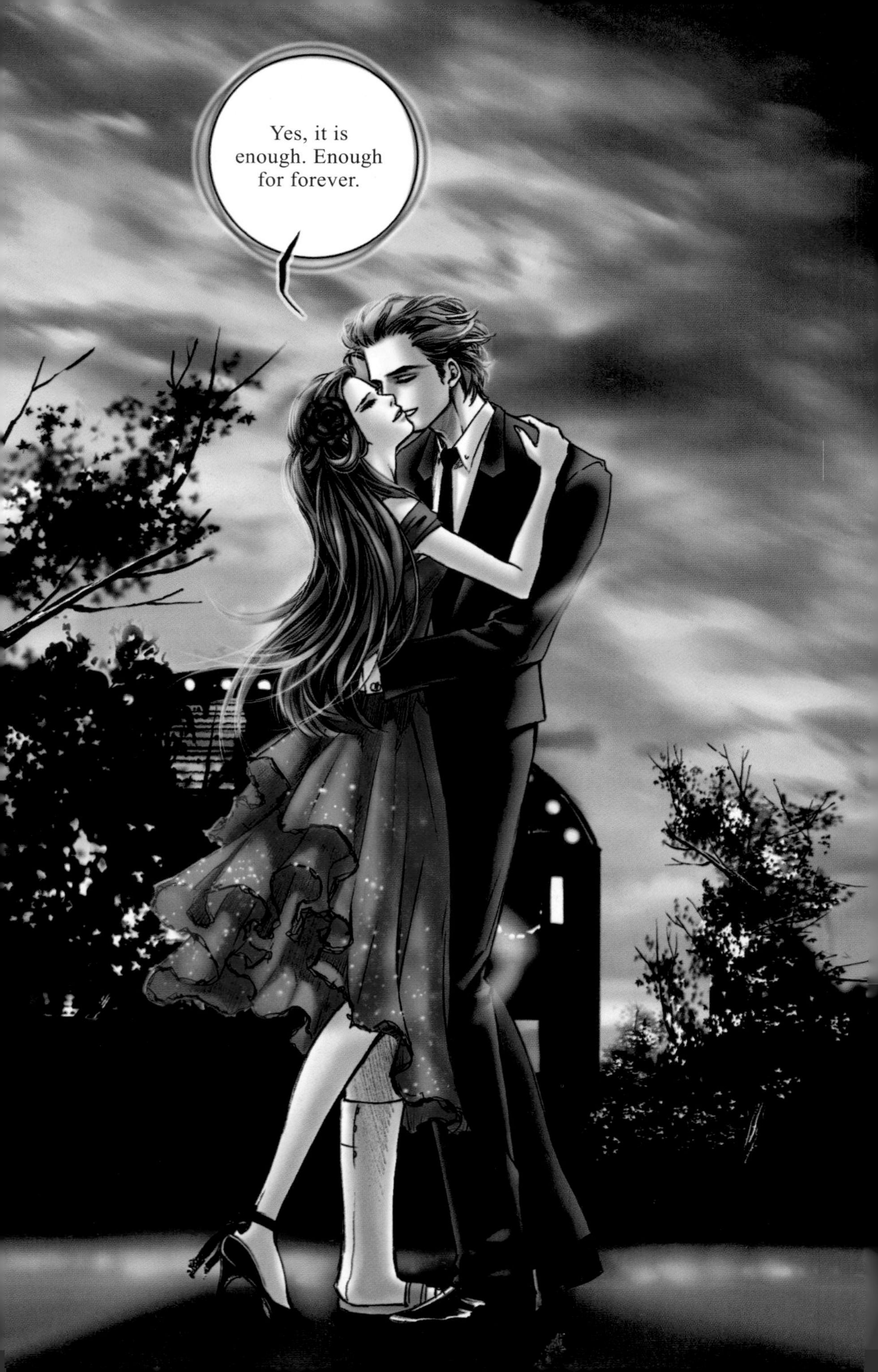
Yes, it is enough. Enough for forever.

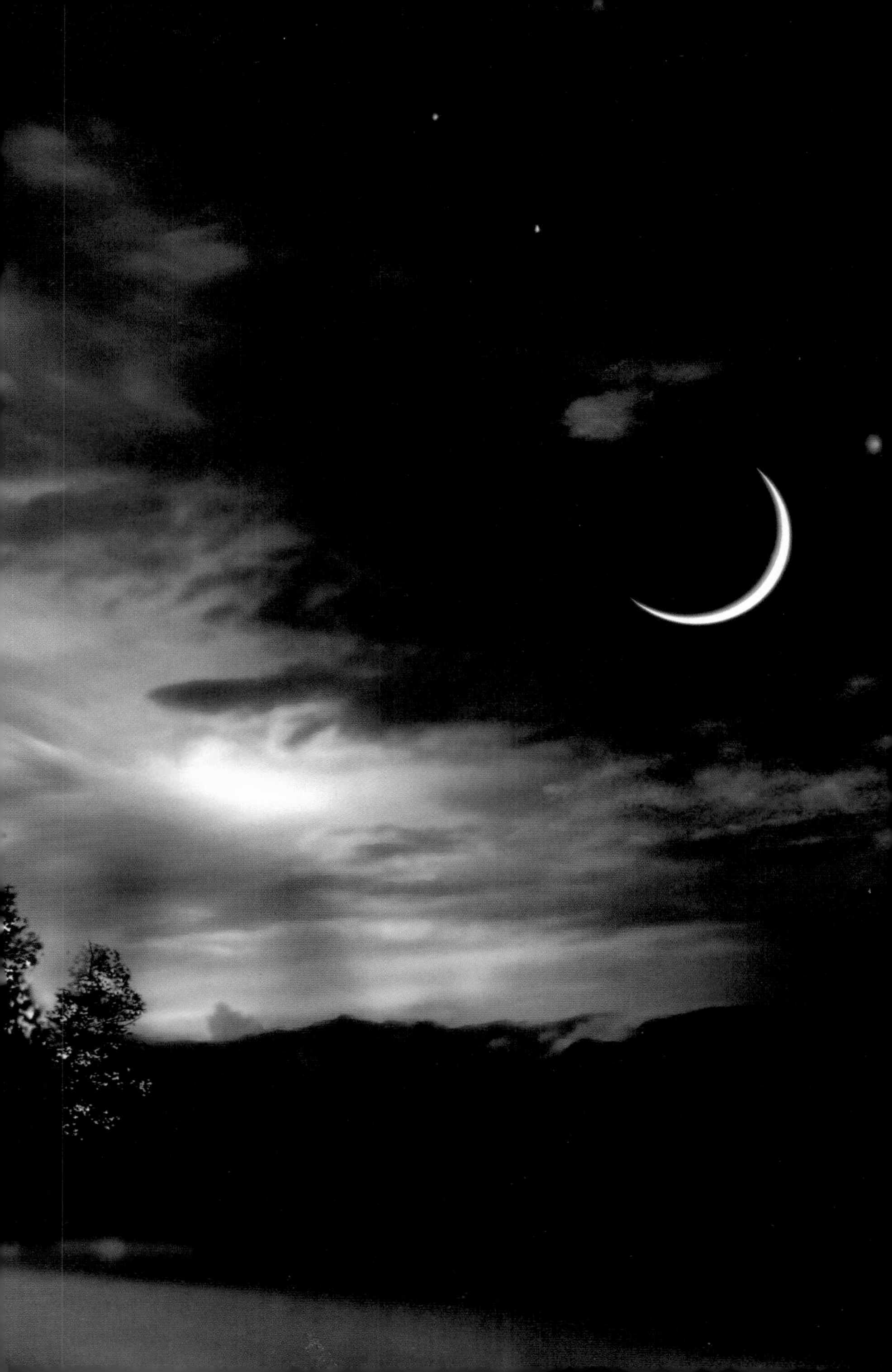